Walt Disney's

UNCLE $CROOGE

by Carl Barks

Publisher: GARY GROTH
Senior Editor: J. MICHAEL CATRON
Color Editor: JUSTIN ALLAN-SPENCER
Colorists: GARY LEACH, SUSAN DAIGLE-LEACH, ERIK ROSENGARTEN, DIGIKORE STUDIOS
Series Design: JACOB COVEY
Volume Design: JUSTIN ALLAN-SPENCER
Production: PAUL BARESH and CHRISTINA HWANG
Associate Publisher: ERIC REYNOLDS

Fantagraphics Books, Inc.
7563 Lake City Way NE
Seattle WA 98115
(800) 657-1100

Visit us at fantagraphics.com. Follow us on Twitter at @fantagraphics and on Facebook at facebook.com/fantagraphics.

Special thanks to Thomas Jensen and Kim Weston.

Second printing: July 2022
ISBN 978-1-68396-291-5
Library of Congress Control Number: 2019945359
Printed in China

Now available in this series:

Walt Disney's Donald Duck: "Christmas on Bear Mountain" (Vol. 5)
Walt Disney's Donald Duck: "The Old Castle's Secret" (Vol. 6)
Walt Disney's Donald Duck: "Lost in the Andes" (Vol. 7)
Walt Disney's Donald Duck: "Trail of the Unicorn" (Vol. 8)
Walt Disney's Donald Duck: "The Pixilated Parrot" (Vol. 9)
Walt Disney's Donald Duck: "Terror of the Beagle Boys" (Vol. 10)
Walt Disney's Donald Duck: "A Christmas for Shacktown" (Vol. 11)
Walt Disney's Uncle Scrooge: "Only a Poor Old Man" (Vol. 12)
Walt Disney's Donald Duck: "Trick or Treat" (Vol. 13)
Walt Disney's Uncle Scrooge: "The Seven Cities of Gold" (Vol. 14)
Walt Disney's Donald Duck: "The Ghost Sheriff of Last Gasp" (Vol. 15)
Walt Disney's Uncle Scrooge: "The Lost Crown of Genghis Khan" (Vol. 16)
Walt Disney's Donald Duck: "Secret of Hondorica" (Vol. 17)
Walt Disney's Donald Duck: "The Lost Peg Leg Mine" (Vol. 18)
Walt Disney's Donald Duck: "The Black Pearls of Tabu Yama" (Vol. 19)
Walt Disney's Uncle Scrooge: "The Mines of King Solomon" (Vol. 20)
Walt Disney's Donald Duck: "Christmas in Duckburg" (Vol. 21)
Walt Disney's Uncle Scrooge: "The Twenty-four Carat Moon" (Vol. 22)
Walt Disney's Donald Duck: "Under the Polar Ice" (Vol. 23)
Walt Disney's Uncle Scrooge: "Island in the Sky" (Vol. 24)
Walt Disney's Donald Duck: "Balloonatics" (Vol. 25)
Walt Disney's Uncle Scrooge: "The Golden Nugget Boat" (Vol. 26)

Walt Disney's

UNCLE $CROOGE

"The Twenty-four Carat Moon"

by Carl Barks

FANTAGRAPHICS BOOKS SEATTLE

Contents

All comics stories written and drawn by Carl Barks.

This title includes negative depictions and mistreatment of people or cultures. These stereotypes were wrong then and are wrong now. Rather than remove this content, we want to acknowledge its harmful impact, learn from it, and spark conversation to create a more inclusive future together. Disney is committed to creating stories with inspirational and aspirational themes that reflect the rich diversity of the human experience around the globe. To learn more about how stories have impacted society, please visit www.disney.com/StoriesMatter.

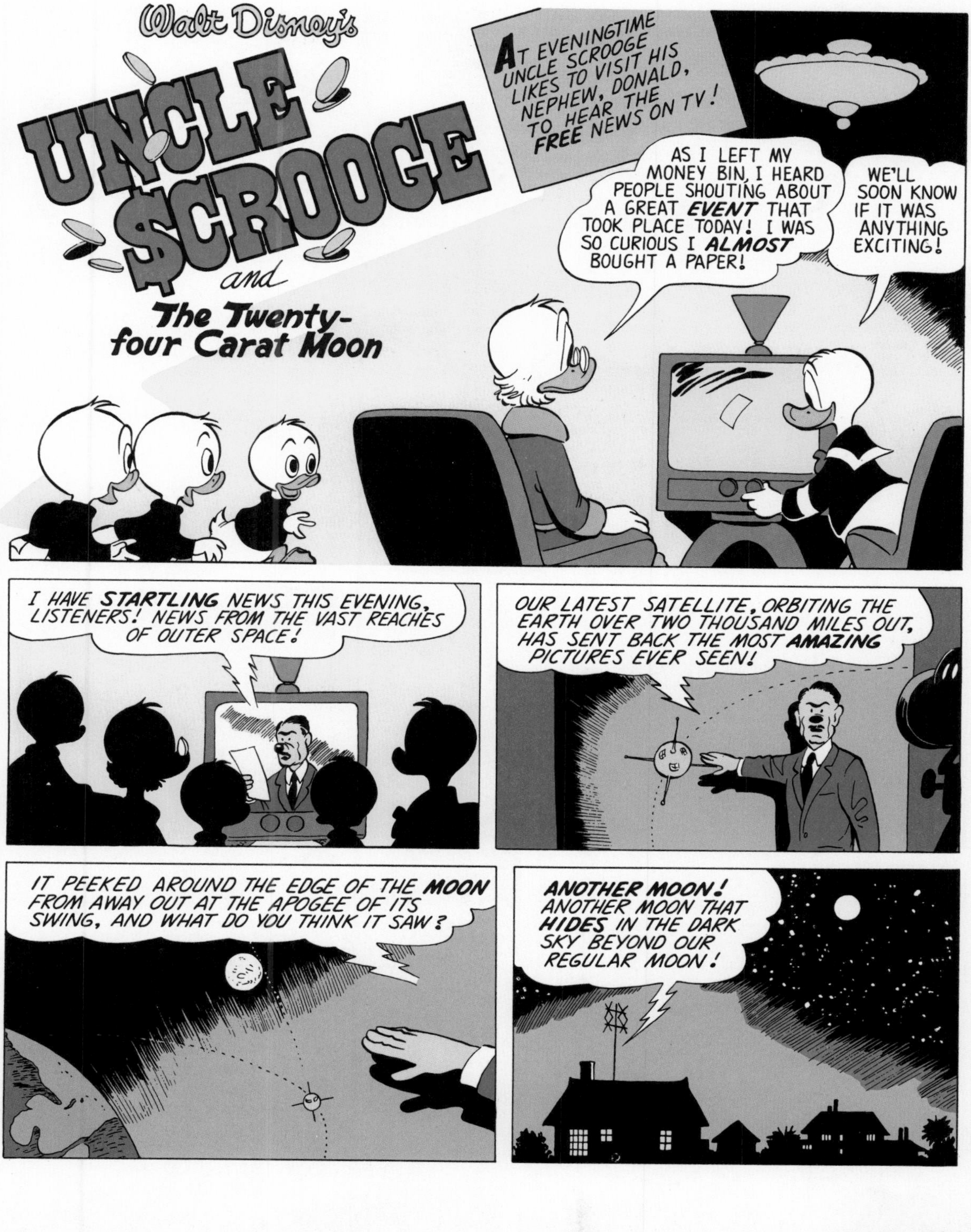
Walt Disney's
UNCLE $CROOGE
and
The Twenty-four Carat Moon
AT EVENINGTIME UNCLE SCROOGE LIKES TO VISIT HIS NEPHEW, DONALD, TO HEAR THE FREE NEWS ON TV!
AS I LEFT MY MONEY BIN, I HEARD PEOPLE SHOUTING ABOUT A GREAT EVENT THAT TOOK PLACE TODAY! I WAS SO CURIOUS I ALMOST BOUGHT A PAPER!
WE'LL SOON KNOW IF IT WAS ANYTHING EXCITING!
I HAVE STARTLING NEWS THIS EVENING, LISTENERS! NEWS FROM THE VAST REACHES OF OUTER SPACE!
OUR LATEST SATELLITE, ORBITING THE EARTH OVER TWO THOUSAND MILES OUT, HAS SENT BACK THE MOST AMAZING PICTURES EVER SEEN!
IT PEEKED AROUND THE EDGE OF THE MOON FROM AWAY OUT AT THE APOGEE OF ITS SWING, AND WHAT DO YOU THINK IT SAW?
ANOTHER MOON! ANOTHER MOON THAT HIDES IN THE DARK SKY BEYOND OUR REGULAR MOON!

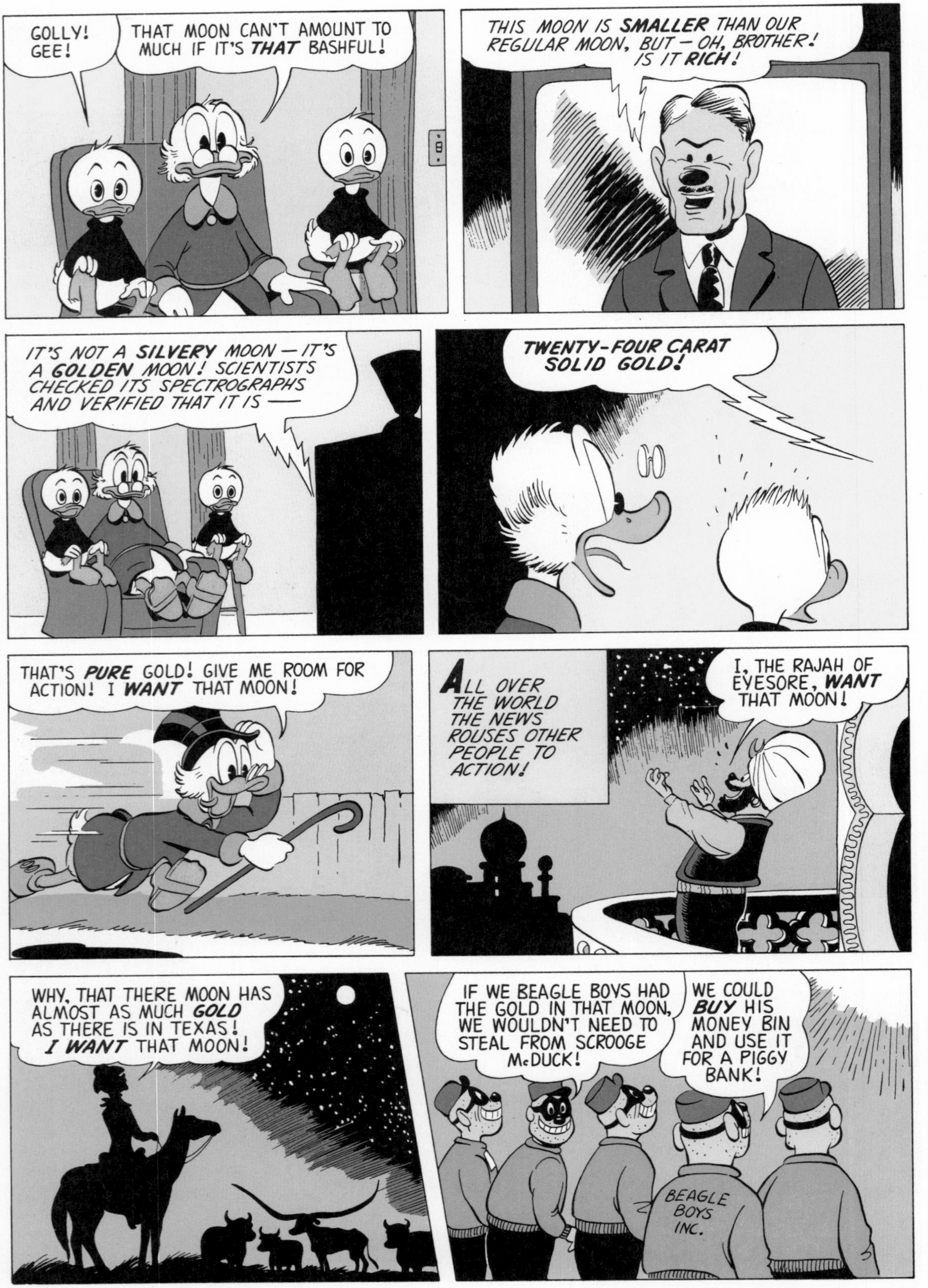
GOLLY! GEE!
THAT MOON CAN'T AMOUNT TO MUCH IF IT'S THAT BASHFUL!
THIS MOON IS SMALLER THAN OUR REGULAR MOON, BUT — OH, BROTHER! IS IT RICH!
IT'S NOT A SILVERY MOON — IT'S A GOLDEN MOON! SCIENTISTS CHECKED ITS SPECTROGRAPHS AND VERIFIED THAT IT IS —
TWENTY-FOUR CARAT SOLID GOLD!
THAT'S PURE GOLD! GIVE ME ROOM FOR ACTION! I WANT THAT MOON!
ALL OVER THE WORLD THE NEWS ROUSES OTHER PEOPLE TO ACTION!
I, THE RAJAH OF EYESORE, WANT THAT MOON!
WHY, THAT THERE MOON HAS ALMOST AS MUCH GOLD AS THERE IS IN TEXAS! I WANT THAT MOON!
IF WE BEAGLE BOYS HAD THE GOLD IN THAT MOON, WE WOULDN'T NEED TO STEAL FROM SCROOGE McDUCK!
WE COULD BUY HIS MONEY BIN AND USE IT FOR A PIGGY BANK!
BEAGLE BOYS INC.

SOON MANY ROCKETS ARE BEING BUILT!

I WANT A ROCKET THAT WILL NOT ONLY FLY TO THAT NEW MOON BUT WILL CARRY BACK FIVE *TONS* OF GOLD EACH TRIP!

YES, SIR! IT'LL COST YOU A *LOT* OF MONEY, SIR!

PHOOEY ON THE COST! I AIM TO BE *FIRST* TO STAKE MY CLAIM TO THAT MOON!

IF I CAN BE *FIRST* TO REACH THAT GOLDEN MOON, WHAT MATTER IF THE ROCKET COSTS MY WEIGHT IN *DIAMONDS*!

WHIP UP A ROCKET *FAST*! I WANT TO BE THE FIRST BEEF KING TO *GOLD PLATE* HIS STEERS!

ALAMO ROCKET WORKS

YOU GUYS MAKE THE ROCKET! WE BEAGLE BOYS WILL GET IT TO THAT MOON *AHEAD* OF EVERYBODY!

ROCKET PLANS PROPERTY OF BUGLESS AIRCRAFT CORP. TOP SECRET

ROCKET PL... PROPERTY OF BOW WING...

TOP SECRET PROPERTY OF LACKHEED AIRCRAF...

AND IF WE *DON'T*, WE'LL *TAKE* THE MOON, ANYWAY!

THERE WON'T BE ANY *COPS* IN OUTER SPACE!

SKEEK!

176-116

176-671 BEAGLE BOYS INC.

THE MOST FANTASTIC GOLD RUSH OF ALL TIME IS SHAPING UP! THE RACE OF GOLD-HUNGRY EARTHMEN TO SEIZE THE TWENTY-FOUR CARAT MOON!

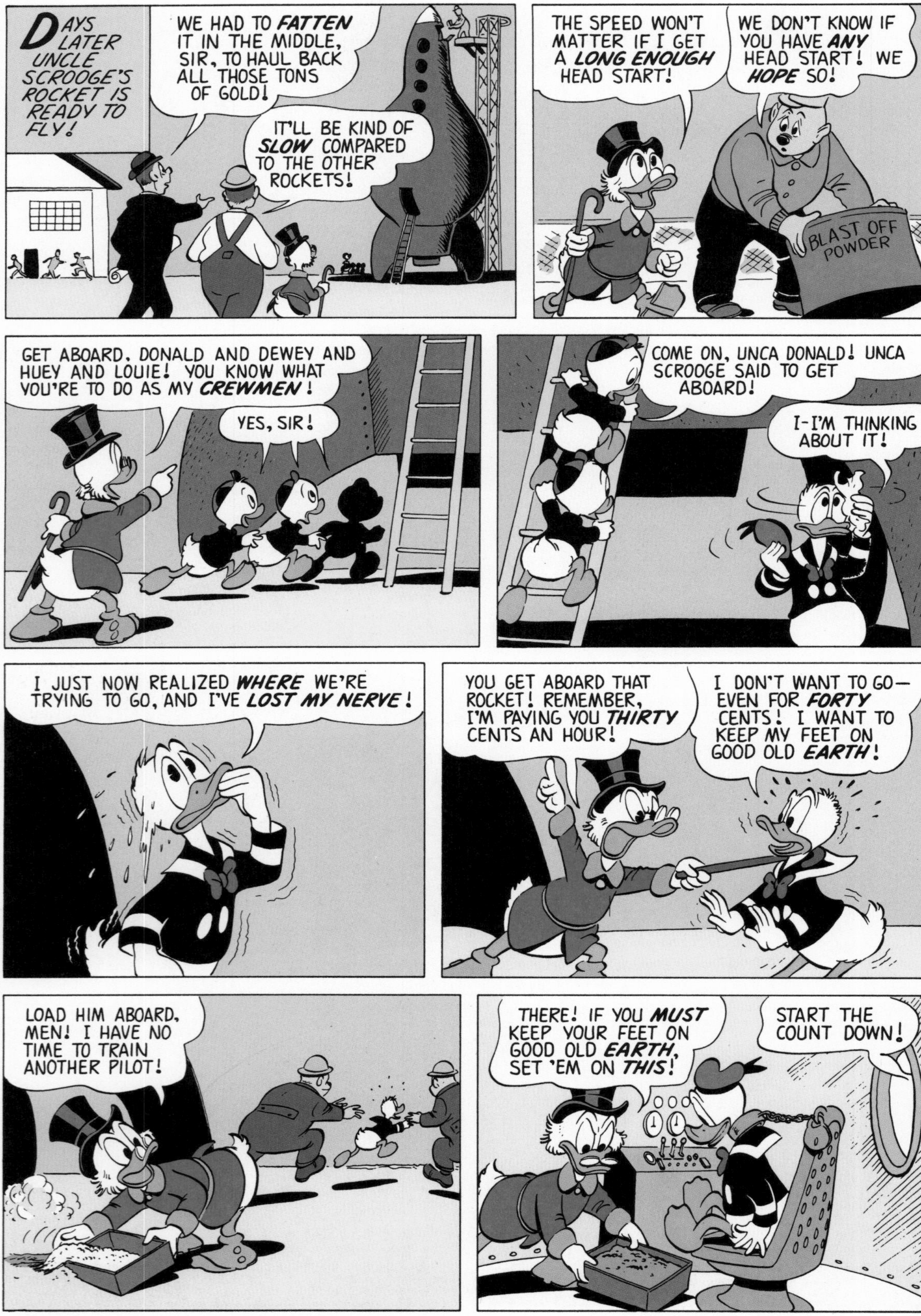
DAYS LATER UNCLE SCROOGE'S ROCKET IS READY TO FLY!
WE HAD TO FATTEN IT IN THE MIDDLE, SIR, TO HAUL BACK ALL THOSE TONS OF GOLD!
IT'LL BE KIND OF SLOW COMPARED TO THE OTHER ROCKETS!
THE SPEED WON'T MATTER IF I GET A LONG ENOUGH HEAD START!
WE DON'T KNOW IF YOU HAVE ANY HEAD START! WE HOPE SO!
BLAST OFF POWDER
GET ABOARD, DONALD AND DEWEY AND HUEY AND LOUIE! YOU KNOW WHAT YOU'RE TO DO AS MY CREWMEN!
YES, SIR!
COME ON, UNCA DONALD! UNCA SCROOGE SAID TO GET ABOARD!
I-I'M THINKING ABOUT IT!
I JUST NOW REALIZED WHERE WE'RE TRYING TO GO, AND I'VE LOST MY NERVE!
YOU GET ABOARD THAT ROCKET! REMEMBER, I'M PAYING YOU THIRTY CENTS AN HOUR!
I DON'T WANT TO GO— EVEN FOR FORTY CENTS! I WANT TO KEEP MY FEET ON GOOD OLD EARTH!
LOAD HIM ABOARD, MEN! I HAVE NO TIME TO TRAIN ANOTHER PILOT!
THERE! IF YOU MUST KEEP YOUR FEET ON GOOD OLD EARTH, SET 'EM ON THIS!
START THE COUNT DOWN!

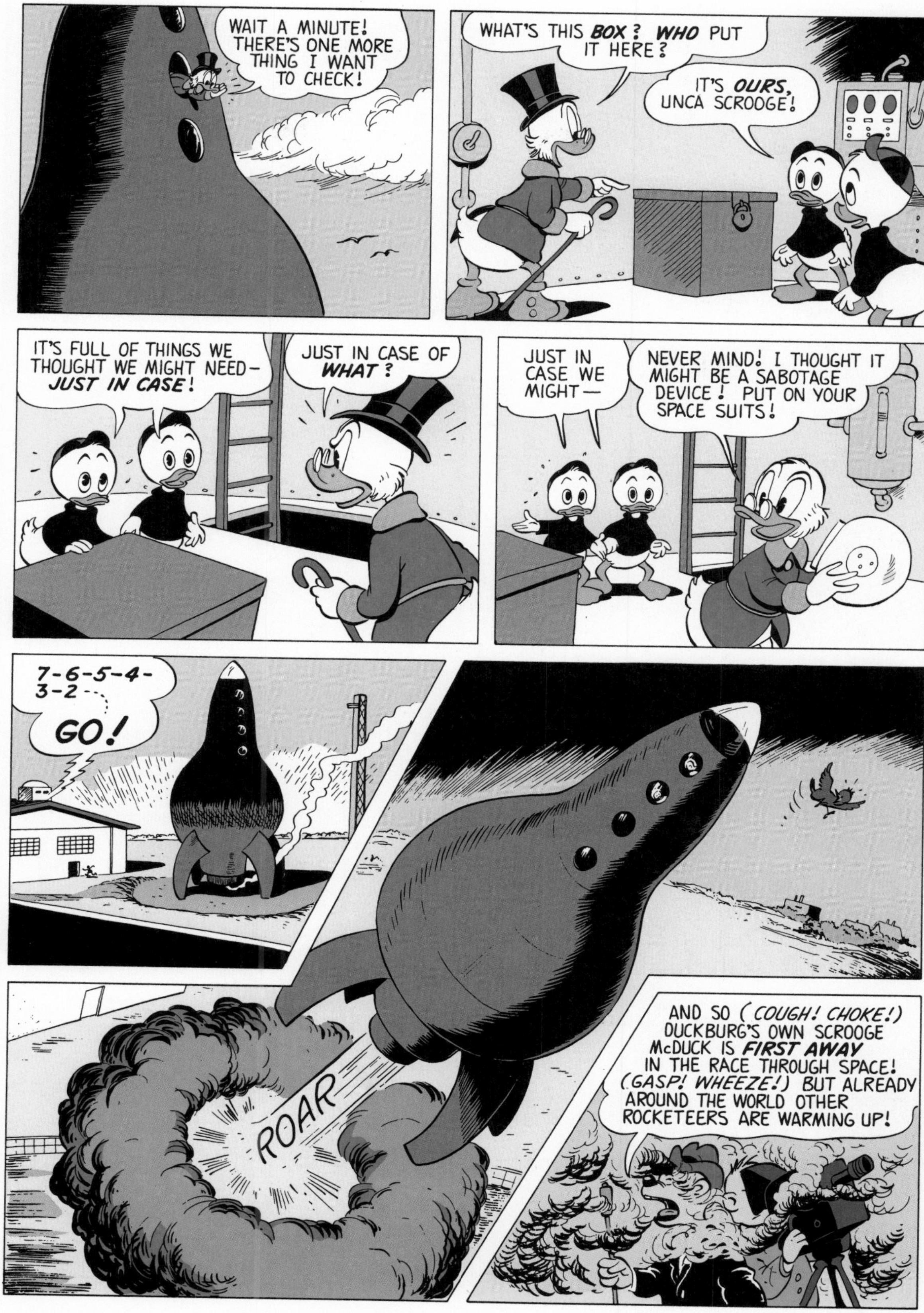
WAIT A MINUTE! THERE'S ONE MORE THING I WANT TO CHECK!
WHAT'S THIS **BOX**? **WHO** PUT IT HERE?
IT'S **OURS**, UNCA SCROOGE!
IT'S FULL OF THINGS WE THOUGHT WE MIGHT NEED— **JUST IN CASE**!
JUST IN CASE OF **WHAT**?
JUST IN CASE WE MIGHT—
NEVER MIND! I THOUGHT IT MIGHT BE A SABOTAGE DEVICE! PUT ON YOUR SPACE SUITS!
7-6-5-4-3-2
GO!
ROAR
AND SO (*COUGH! CHOKE!*) DUCKBURG'S OWN SCROOGE McDUCK IS **FIRST AWAY** IN THE RACE THROUGH SPACE! (*GASP! WHEEZE!*) BUT ALREADY AROUND THE WORLD OTHER ROCKETEERS ARE WARMING UP!

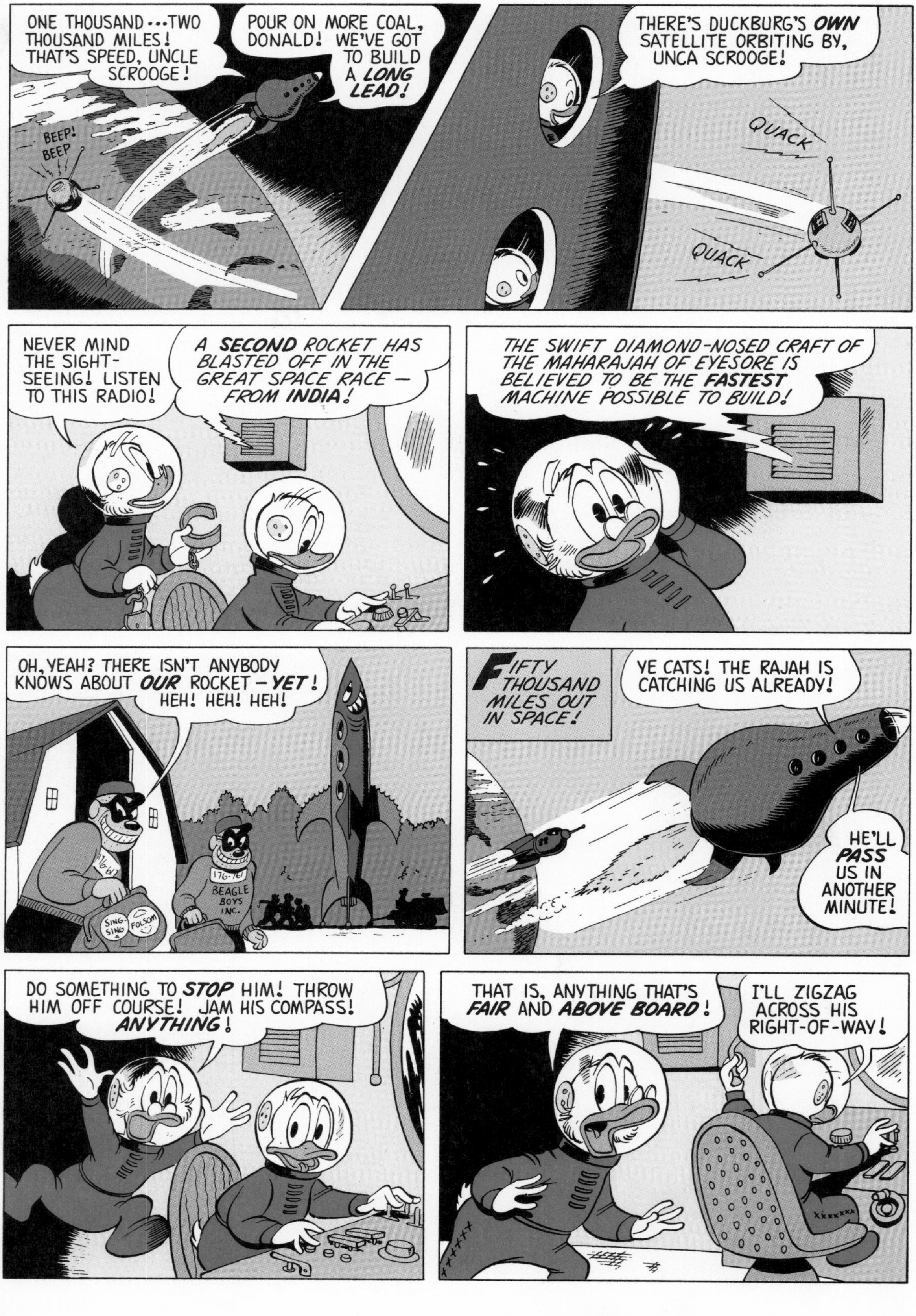
ONE THOUSAND ... TWO THOUSAND MILES! THAT'S SPEED, UNCLE SCROOGE!
POUR ON MORE COAL, DONALD! WE'VE GOT TO BUILD A LONG LEAD!
BEEP! BEEP
THERE'S DUCKBURG'S OWN SATELLITE ORBITING BY, UNCA SCROOGE!
QUACK
QUACK
NEVER MIND THE SIGHT-SEEING! LISTEN TO THIS RADIO!
A SECOND ROCKET HAS BLASTED OFF IN THE GREAT SPACE RACE — FROM INDIA!
THE SWIFT DIAMOND-NOSED CRAFT OF THE MAHARAJAH OF EYESORE IS BELIEVED TO BE THE FASTEST MACHINE POSSIBLE TO BUILD!
OH, YEAH? THERE ISN'T ANYBODY KNOWS ABOUT OUR ROCKET — YET! HEH! HEH! HEH!
176-167
176-761
BEAGLE BOYS INC.
SING-SING
FOLSOM
FIFTY THOUSAND MILES OUT IN SPACE!
YE CATS! THE RAJAH IS CATCHING US ALREADY!
HE'LL PASS US IN ANOTHER MINUTE!
DO SOMETHING TO STOP HIM! THROW HIM OFF COURSE! JAM HIS COMPASS! ANYTHING!
THAT IS, ANYTHING THAT'S FAIR AND ABOVE BOARD!
I'LL ZIGZAG ACROSS HIS RIGHT-OF-WAY!

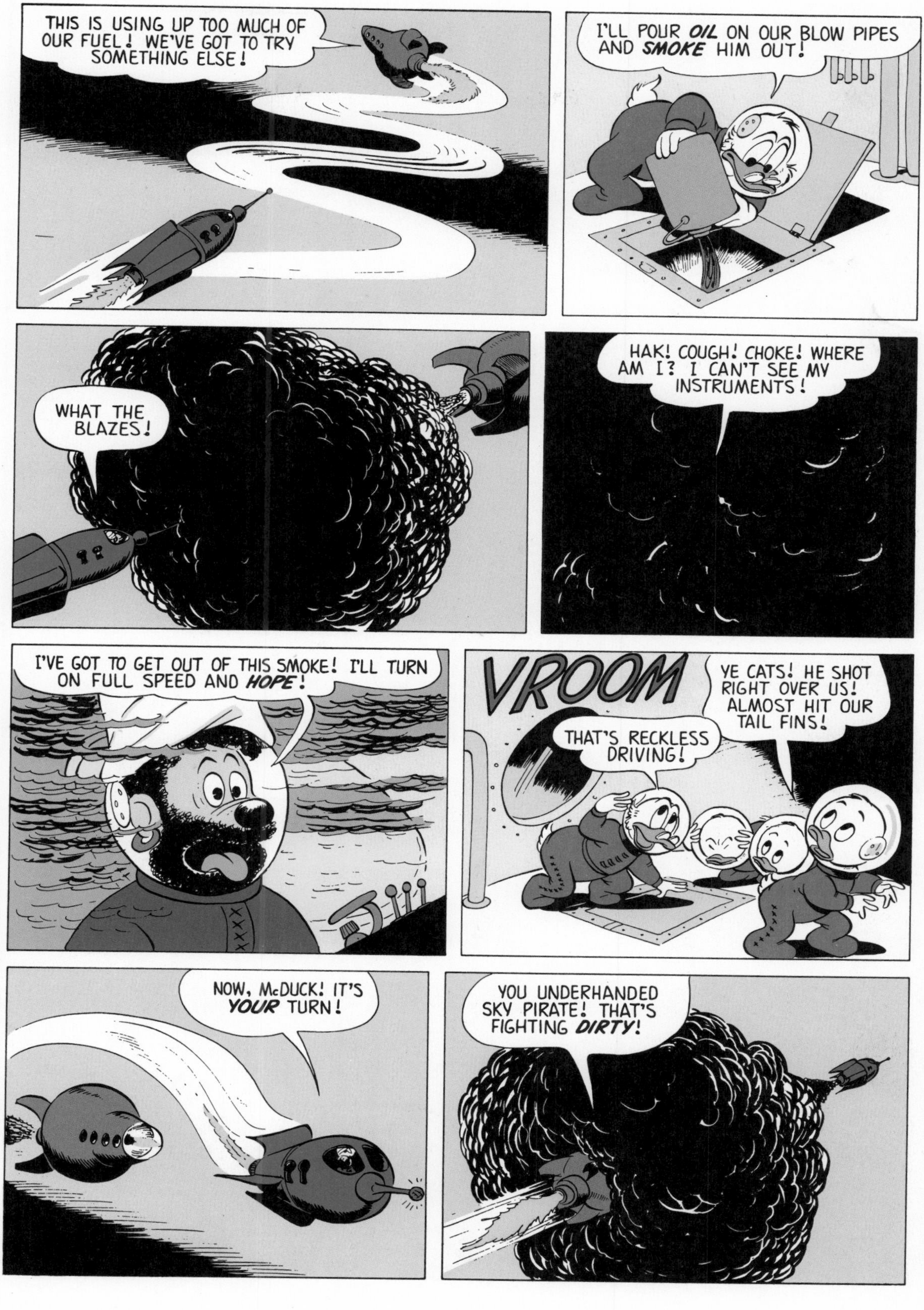

THIS IS USING UP TOO MUCH OF OUR FUEL! WE'VE GOT TO TRY SOMETHING ELSE!
I'LL POUR **OIL** ON OUR BLOW PIPES AND **SMOKE** HIM OUT!
WHAT THE BLAZES!
HAK! COUGH! CHOKE! WHERE AM I? I CAN'T SEE MY INSTRUMENTS!
I'VE GOT TO GET OUT OF THIS SMOKE! I'LL TURN ON FULL SPEED AND **HOPE**!
VROOM
YE CATS! HE SHOT RIGHT OVER US! ALMOST HIT OUR TAIL FINS!
THAT'S RECKLESS DRIVING!
NOW, McDUCK! IT'S **YOUR** TURN!
YOU UNDERHANDED SKY PIRATE! THAT'S FIGHTING **DIRTY**!

HEY! A SECOND ROCKET IS PASSING US!

WHO'S THAT?

VROOM

NOT THE FABULOUS CATTLE KING! HE HASN'T TAKEN OFF YET!

A *MYSTERY* SHIP!

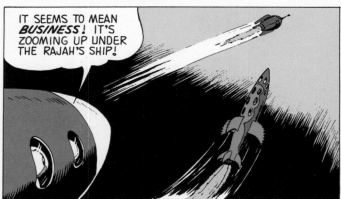

IT SEEMS TO MEAN *BUSINESS*! IT'S ZOOMING UP UNDER THE RAJAH'S SHIP!

GREAT VISHNU! THAT ROCKET IS TRYING TO *RAM* ME!

ROAR

DOGFIGHT! ROCKET BATTLE IN THE SKY!

THAT MYSTERY SHIP — I CAN MAKE OUT A *NAME* ON ITS SIDE!

THE *BEAGLE BOYS*! THE *TERRIBLE* BEAGLE BOYS!

GET *AHEAD* OF THEM, UNCA DONALD, WHILE THEY'RE HASSLING WITH THE RAJAH!

WHAT DO YOU THINK I'M DOING — TROMPING THE BRAKE?

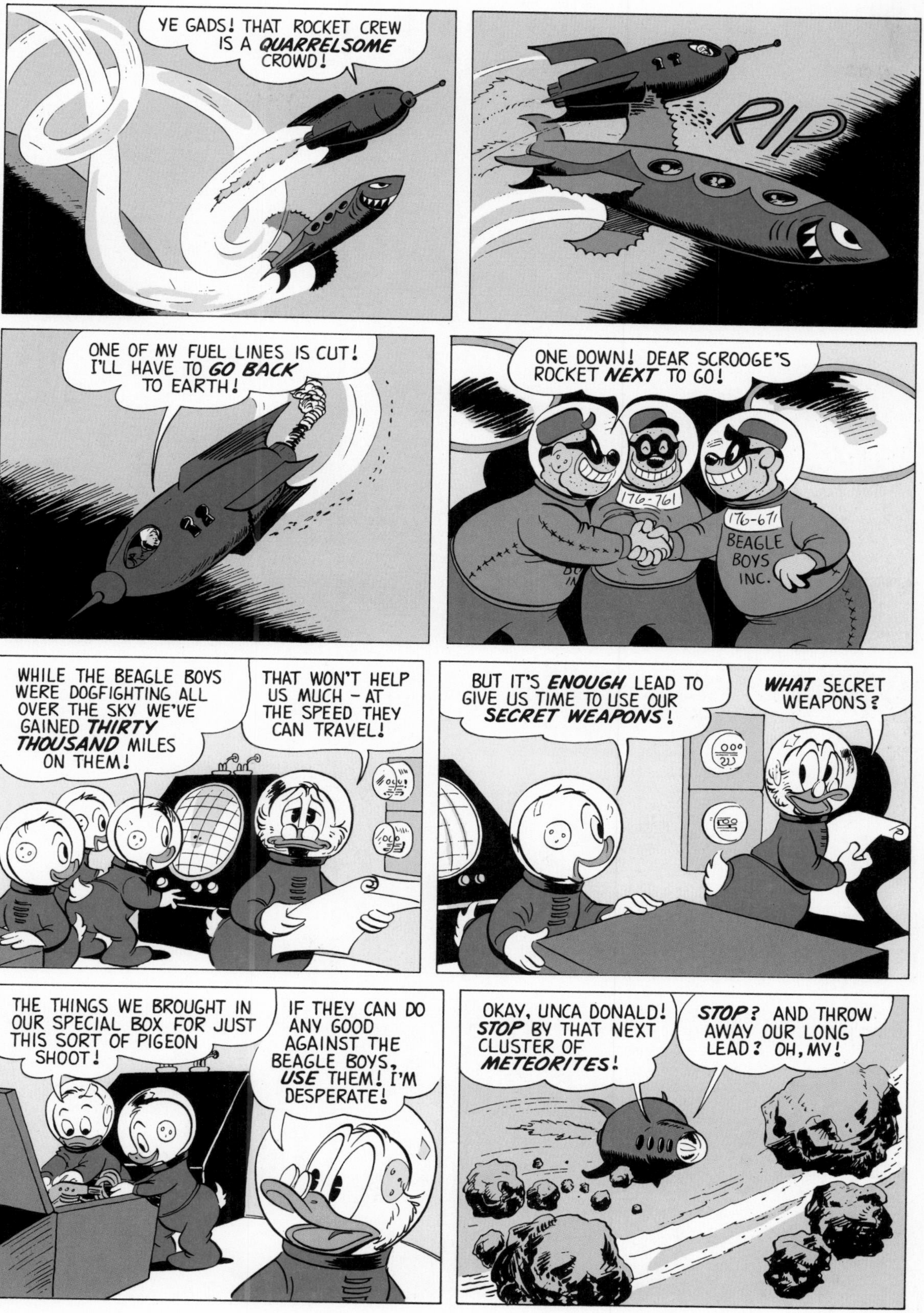
YE GADS! THAT ROCKET CREW IS A QUARRELSOME CROWD!
RIP
ONE OF MY FUEL LINES IS CUT! I'LL HAVE TO GO BACK TO EARTH!
ONE DOWN! DEAR SCROOGE'S ROCKET NEXT TO GO!
176-761
176-671
BEAGLE BOYS INC.
WHILE THE BEAGLE BOYS WERE DOGFIGHTING ALL OVER THE SKY WE'VE GAINED THIRTY THOUSAND MILES ON THEM!
THAT WON'T HELP US MUCH - AT THE SPEED THEY CAN TRAVEL!
BUT IT'S ENOUGH LEAD TO GIVE US TIME TO USE OUR SECRET WEAPONS!
WHAT SECRET WEAPONS?
THE THINGS WE BROUGHT IN OUR SPECIAL BOX FOR JUST THIS SORT OF PIGEON SHOOT!
IF THEY CAN DO ANY GOOD AGAINST THE BEAGLE BOYS, USE THEM! I'M DESPERATE!
OKAY, UNCA DONALD! STOP BY THAT NEXT CLUSTER OF METEORITES!
STOP? AND THROW AWAY OUR LONG LEAD? OH, MY!

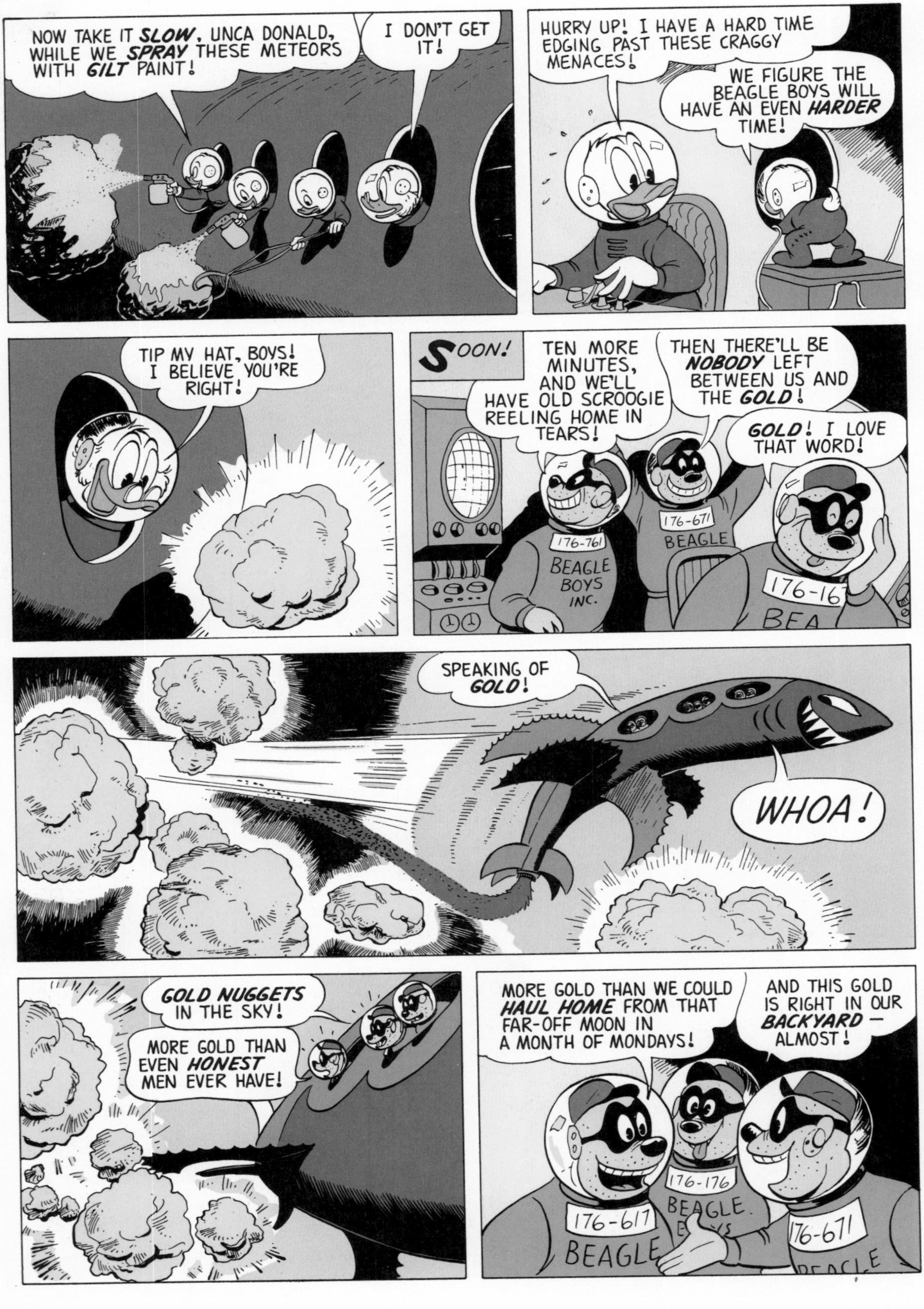
NOW TAKE IT SLOW, UNCA DONALD, WHILE WE SPRAY THESE METEORS WITH GILT PAINT!
I DON'T GET IT!
HURRY UP! I HAVE A HARD TIME EDGING PAST THESE CRAGGY MENACES!
WE FIGURE THE BEAGLE BOYS WILL HAVE AN EVEN HARDER TIME!
TIP MY HAT, BOYS! I BELIEVE YOU'RE RIGHT!
SOON!
TEN MORE MINUTES, AND WE'LL HAVE OLD SCROOGIE REELING HOME IN TEARS!
THEN THERE'LL BE NOBODY LEFT BETWEEN US AND THE GOLD!
GOLD! I LOVE THAT WORD!
176-761
BEAGLE BOYS INC.
176-671
BEAGLE
176-16
BEA
SPEAKING OF GOLD!
WHOA!
GOLD NUGGETS IN THE SKY!
MORE GOLD THAN EVEN HONEST MEN EVER HAVE!
MORE GOLD THAN WE COULD HAUL HOME FROM THAT FAR-OFF MOON IN A MONTH OF MONDAYS!
AND THIS GOLD IS RIGHT IN OUR BACKYARD — ALMOST!
176-176
176-617
BEAGLE
176-671

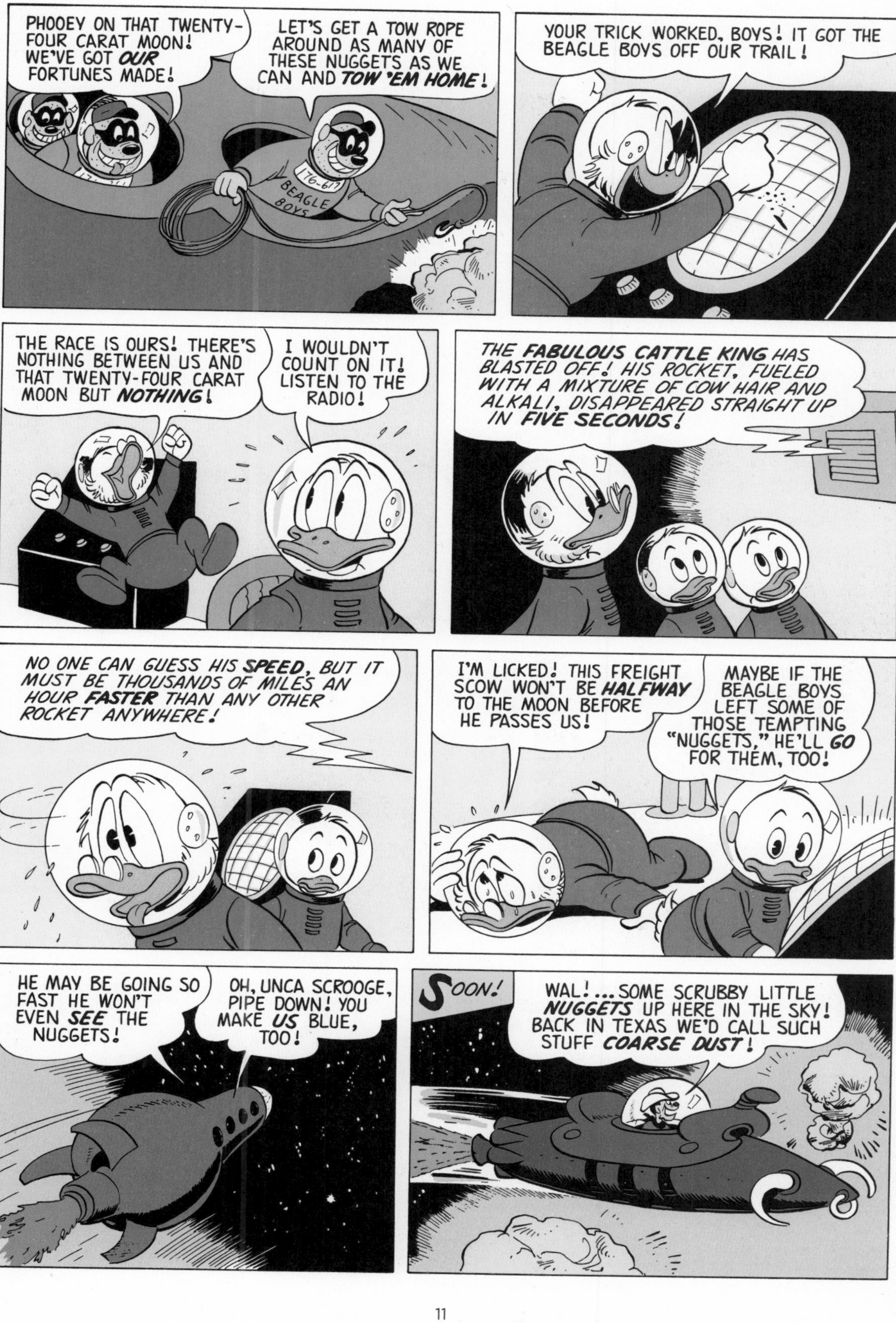
PHOOEY ON THAT TWENTY-FOUR CARAT MOON! WE'VE GOT OUR FORTUNES MADE!
LET'S GET A TOW ROPE AROUND AS MANY OF THESE NUGGETS AS WE CAN AND TOW 'EM HOME!
176-617
BEAGLE BOYS
YOUR TRICK WORKED, BOYS! IT GOT THE BEAGLE BOYS OFF OUR TRAIL!
THE RACE IS OURS! THERE'S NOTHING BETWEEN US AND THAT TWENTY-FOUR CARAT MOON BUT NOTHING!
I WOULDN'T COUNT ON IT! LISTEN TO THE RADIO!
THE FABULOUS CATTLE KING HAS BLASTED OFF! HIS ROCKET, FUELED WITH A MIXTURE OF COW HAIR AND ALKALI, DISAPPEARED STRAIGHT UP IN FIVE SECONDS!
NO ONE CAN GUESS HIS SPEED, BUT IT MUST BE THOUSANDS OF MILES AN HOUR FASTER THAN ANY OTHER ROCKET ANYWHERE!
I'M LICKED! THIS FREIGHT SCOW WON'T BE HALFWAY TO THE MOON BEFORE HE PASSES US!
MAYBE IF THE BEAGLE BOYS LEFT SOME OF THOSE TEMPTING "NUGGETS," HE'LL GO FOR THEM, TOO!
HE MAY BE GOING SO FAST HE WON'T EVEN SEE THE NUGGETS!
OH, UNCA SCROOGE, PIPE DOWN! YOU MAKE US BLUE, TOO!
SOON!
WAL! ... SOME SCRUBBY LITTLE NUGGETS UP HERE IN THE SKY! BACK IN TEXAS WE'D CALL SUCH STUFF COARSE DUST!

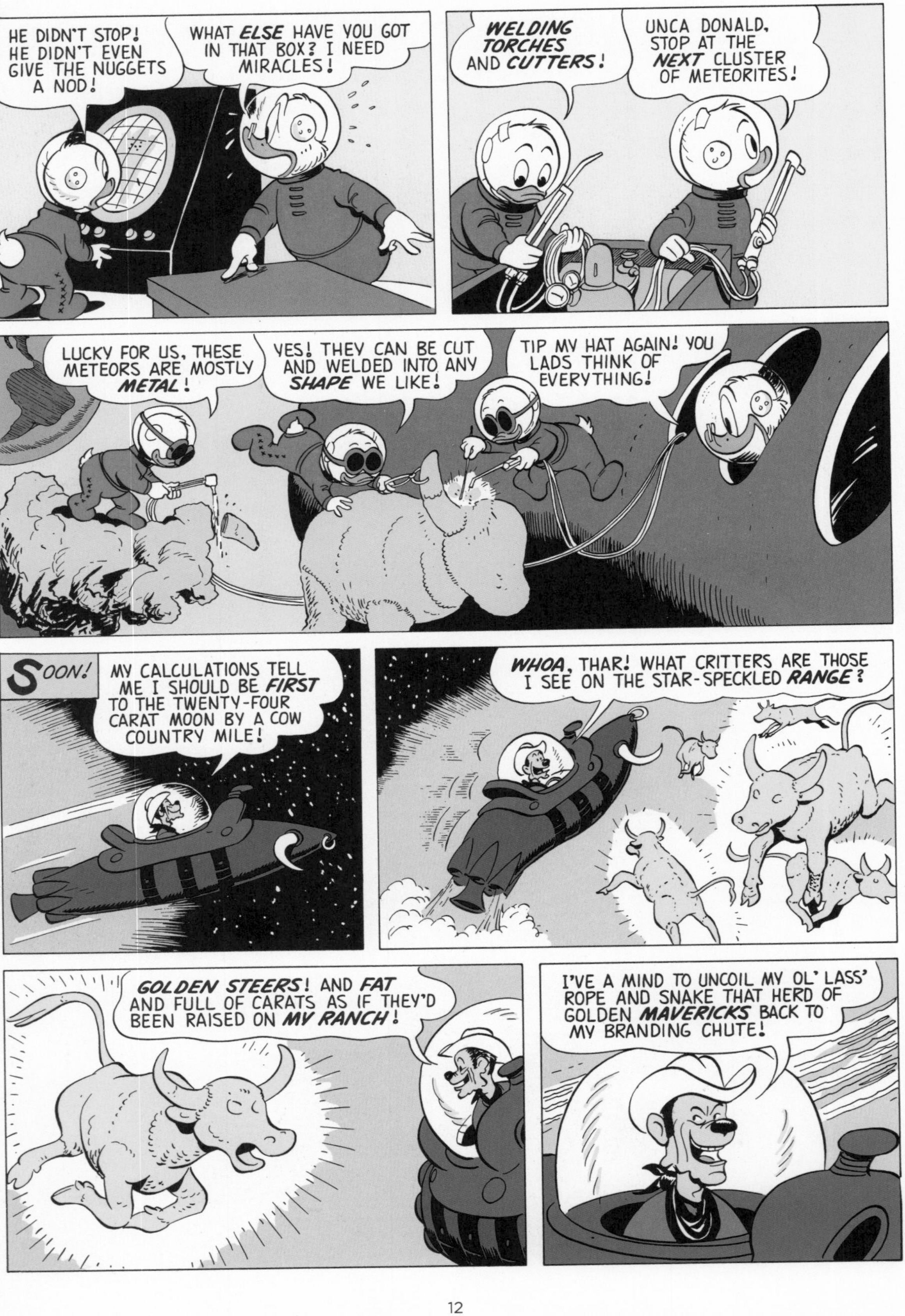
HE DIDN'T STOP! HE DIDN'T EVEN GIVE THE NUGGETS A NOD!
WHAT ELSE HAVE YOU GOT IN THAT BOX? I NEED MIRACLES!
WELDING TORCHES AND CUTTERS!
UNCA DONALD, STOP AT THE NEXT CLUSTER OF METEORITES!
LUCKY FOR US, THESE METEORS ARE MOSTLY METAL!
YES! THEY CAN BE CUT AND WELDED INTO ANY SHAPE WE LIKE!
TIP MY HAT AGAIN! YOU LADS THINK OF EVERYTHING!
SOON!
MY CALCULATIONS TELL ME I SHOULD BE FIRST TO THE TWENTY-FOUR CARAT MOON BY A COW COUNTRY MILE!
WHOA, THAR! WHAT CRITTERS ARE THOSE I SEE ON THE STAR-SPECKLED RANGE?
GOLDEN STEERS! AND FAT AND FULL OF CARATS AS IF THEY'D BEEN RAISED ON MY RANCH!
I'VE A MIND TO UNCOIL MY OL' LASS' ROPE AND SNAKE THAT HERD OF GOLDEN MAVERICKS BACK TO MY BRANDING CHUTE!

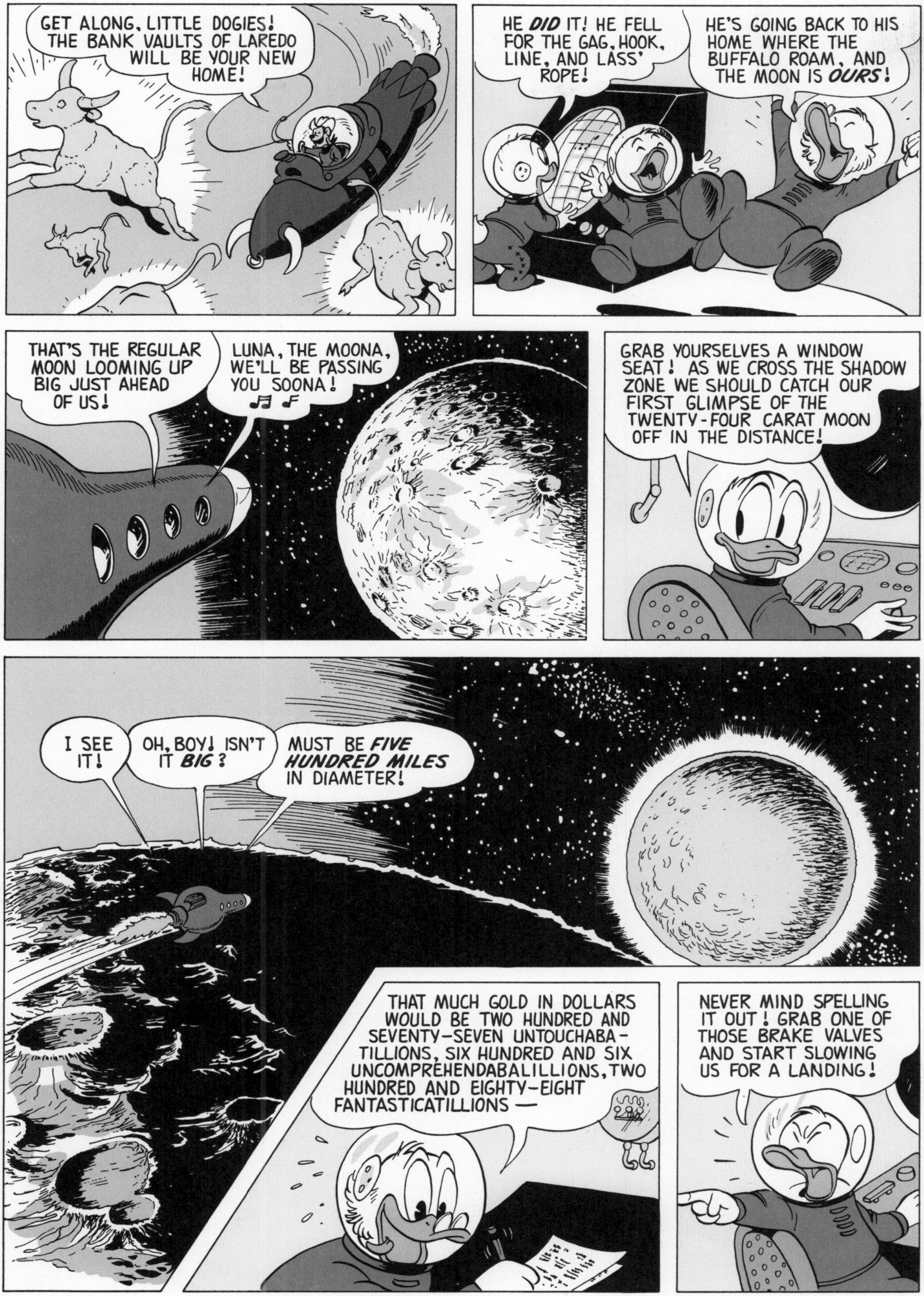
GET ALONG, LITTLE DOGIES! THE BANK VAULTS OF LAREDO WILL BE YOUR NEW HOME!
HE *DID* IT! HE FELL FOR THE GAG, HOOK, LINE, AND LASS' ROPE!
HE'S GOING BACK TO HIS HOME WHERE THE BUFFALO ROAM, AND THE MOON IS *OURS*!
THAT'S THE REGULAR MOON LOOMING UP BIG JUST AHEAD OF US!
LUNA, THE MOONA, WE'LL BE PASSING YOU SOONA!
GRAB YOURSELVES A WINDOW SEAT! AS WE CROSS THE SHADOW ZONE WE SHOULD CATCH OUR FIRST GLIMPSE OF THE TWENTY-FOUR CARAT MOON OFF IN THE DISTANCE!
I SEE IT!
OH, BOY! ISN'T IT *BIG*?
MUST BE *FIVE HUNDRED MILES* IN DIAMETER!
THAT MUCH GOLD IN DOLLARS WOULD BE TWO HUNDRED AND SEVENTY-SEVEN UNTOUCHABA-TILLIONS, SIX HUNDRED AND SIX UNCOMPREHENDABALILLIONS, TWO HUNDRED AND EIGHTY-EIGHT FANTASTICATILLIONS —
NEVER MIND SPELLING IT OUT! GRAB ONE OF THOSE BRAKE VALVES AND START SLOWING US FOR A LANDING!

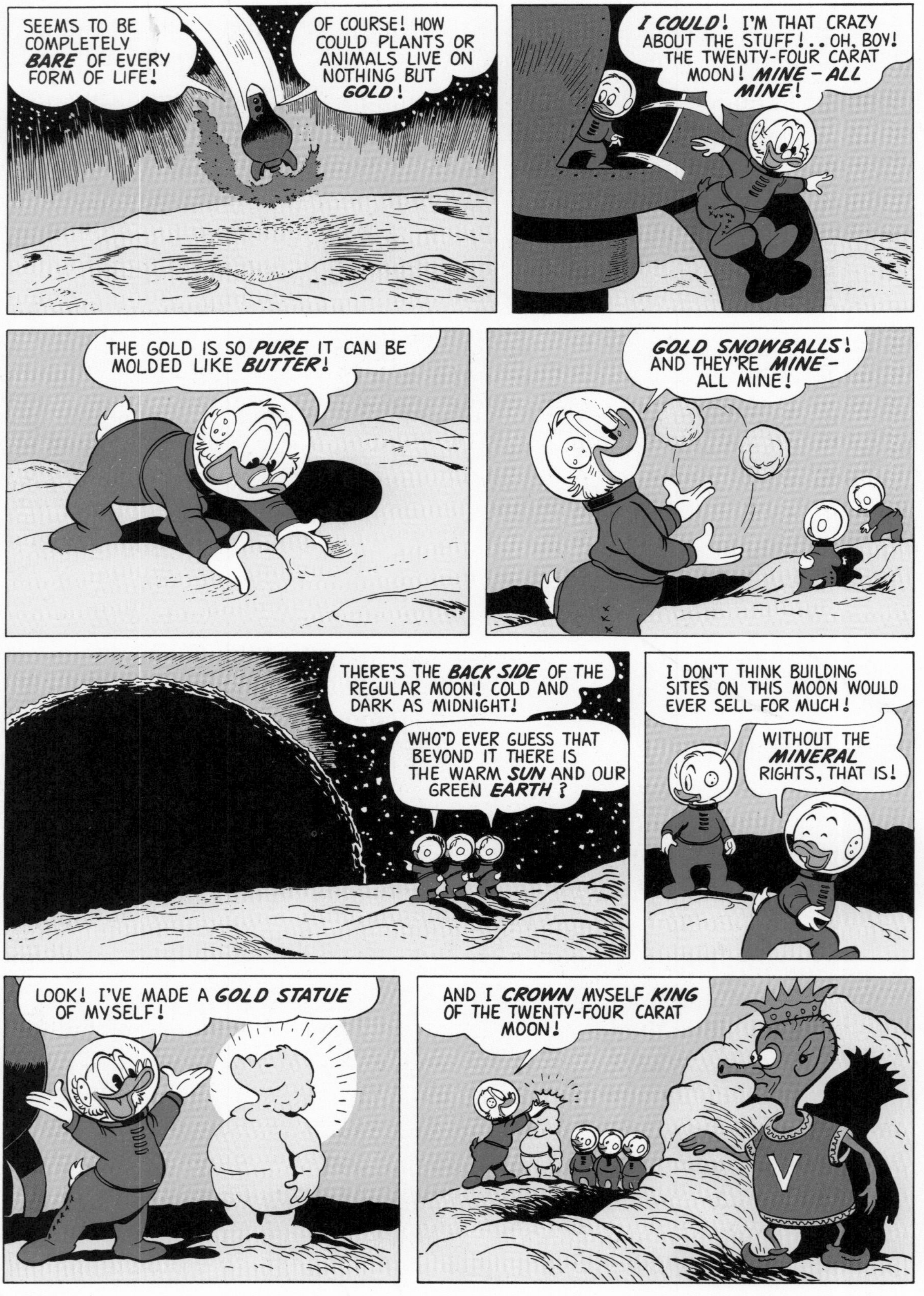
SEEMS TO BE COMPLETELY BARE OF EVERY FORM OF LIFE!
OF COURSE! HOW COULD PLANTS OR ANIMALS LIVE ON NOTHING BUT GOLD!
I COULD! I'M THAT CRAZY ABOUT THE STUFF!.. OH, BOY! THE TWENTY-FOUR CARAT MOON! MINE—ALL MINE!
THE GOLD IS SO PURE IT CAN BE MOLDED LIKE BUTTER!
GOLD SNOWBALLS! AND THEY'RE MINE—ALL MINE!
THERE'S THE BACK SIDE OF THE REGULAR MOON! COLD AND DARK AS MIDNIGHT!
WHO'D EVER GUESS THAT BEYOND IT THERE IS THE WARM SUN AND OUR GREEN EARTH?
I DON'T THINK BUILDING SITES ON THIS MOON WOULD EVER SELL FOR MUCH!
WITHOUT THE MINERAL RIGHTS, THAT IS!
LOOK! I'VE MADE A GOLD STATUE OF MYSELF!
AND I CROWN MYSELF KING OF THE TWENTY-FOUR CARAT MOON!
V

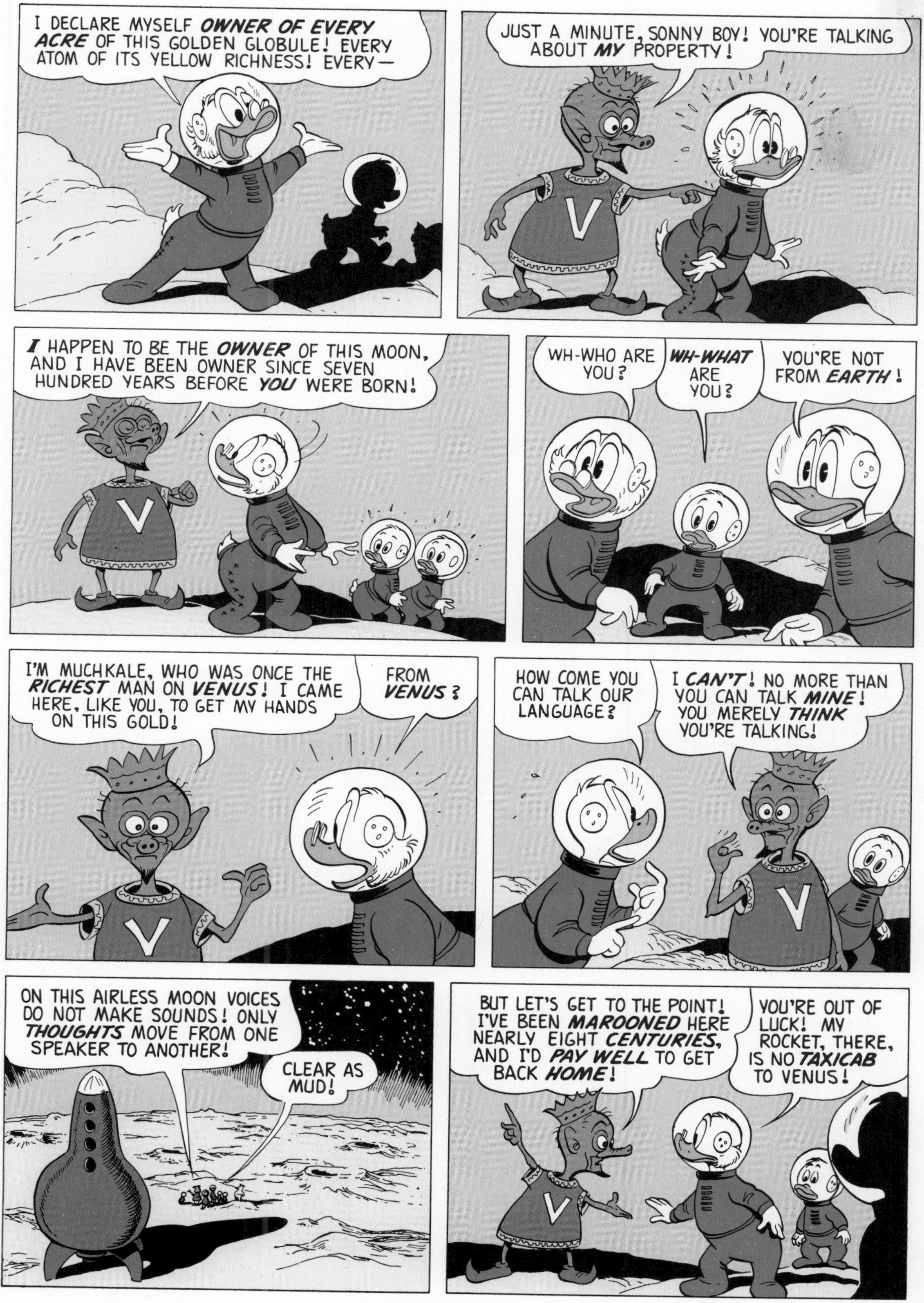

I DECLARE MYSELF OWNER OF EVERY ACRE OF THIS GOLDEN GLOBULE! EVERY ATOM OF ITS YELLOW RICHNESS! EVERY—
JUST A MINUTE, SONNY BOY! YOU'RE TALKING ABOUT MY PROPERTY!
I HAPPEN TO BE THE OWNER OF THIS MOON, AND I HAVE BEEN OWNER SINCE SEVEN HUNDRED YEARS BEFORE YOU WERE BORN!
WH-WHO ARE YOU?
WH-WHAT ARE YOU?
YOU'RE NOT FROM EARTH!
I'M MUCHKALE, WHO WAS ONCE THE RICHEST MAN ON VENUS! I CAME HERE, LIKE YOU, TO GET MY HANDS ON THIS GOLD!
FROM VENUS?
HOW COME YOU CAN TALK OUR LANGUAGE?
I CAN'T! NO MORE THAN YOU CAN TALK MINE! YOU MERELY THINK YOU'RE TALKING!
ON THIS AIRLESS MOON VOICES DO NOT MAKE SOUNDS! ONLY THOUGHTS MOVE FROM ONE SPEAKER TO ANOTHER!
CLEAR AS MUD!
BUT LET'S GET TO THE POINT! I'VE BEEN MAROONED HERE NEARLY EIGHT CENTURIES, AND I'D PAY WELL TO GET BACK HOME!
YOU'RE OUT OF LUCK! MY ROCKET, THERE, IS NO TAXICAB TO VENUS!

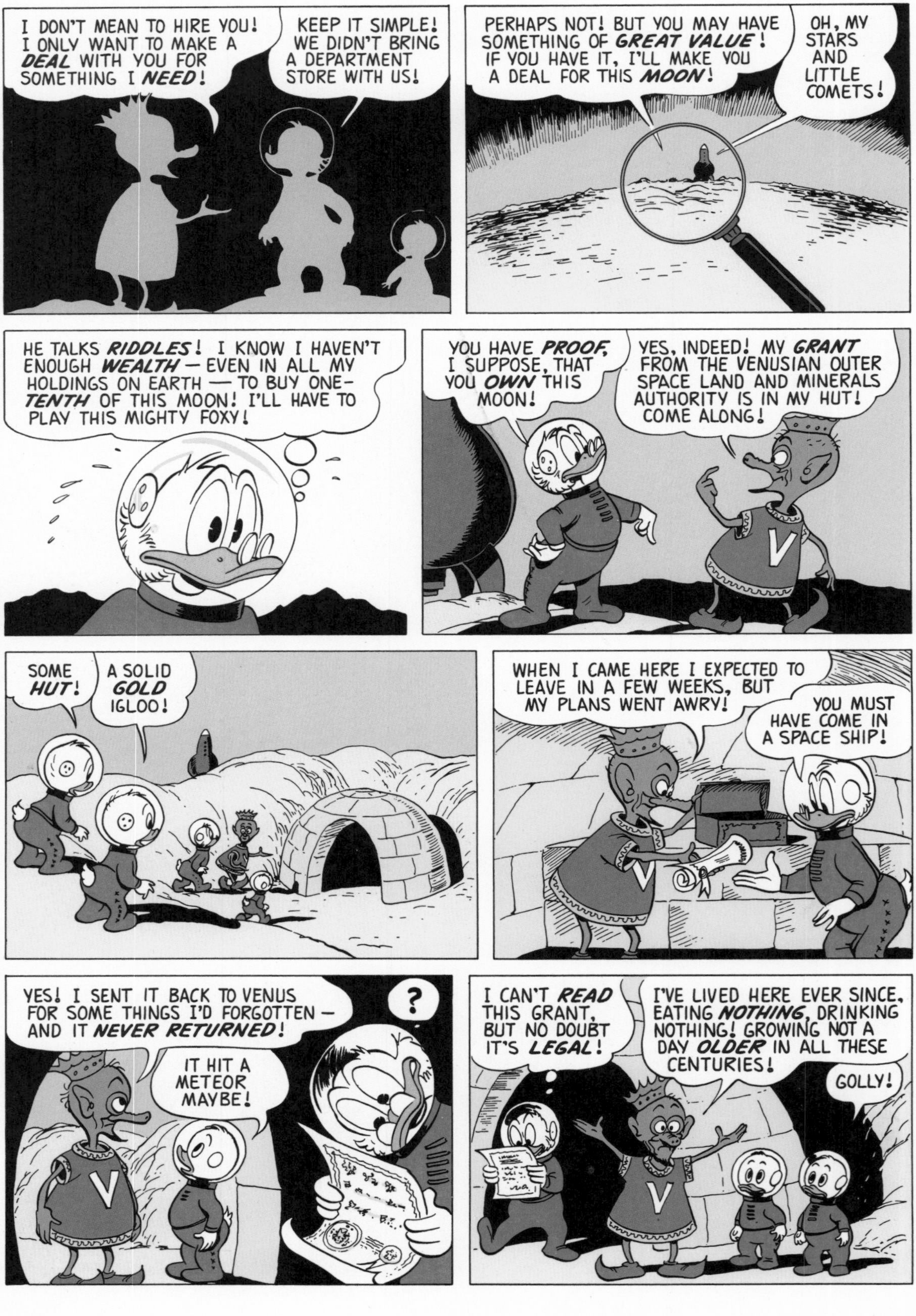

I DON'T MEAN TO HIRE YOU! I ONLY WANT TO MAKE A DEAL WITH YOU FOR SOMETHING I NEED!
KEEP IT SIMPLE! WE DIDN'T BRING A DEPARTMENT STORE WITH US!
PERHAPS NOT! BUT YOU MAY HAVE SOMETHING OF GREAT VALUE! IF YOU HAVE IT, I'LL MAKE YOU A DEAL FOR THIS MOON!
OH, MY STARS AND LITTLE COMETS!
HE TALKS RIDDLES! I KNOW I HAVEN'T ENOUGH WEALTH — EVEN IN ALL MY HOLDINGS ON EARTH — TO BUY ONE-TENTH OF THIS MOON! I'LL HAVE TO PLAY THIS MIGHTY FOXY!
YOU HAVE PROOF, I SUPPOSE, THAT YOU OWN THIS MOON!
YES, INDEED! MY GRANT FROM THE VENUSIAN OUTER SPACE LAND AND MINERALS AUTHORITY IS IN MY HUT! COME ALONG!
SOME HUT!
A SOLID GOLD IGLOO!
WHEN I CAME HERE I EXPECTED TO LEAVE IN A FEW WEEKS, BUT MY PLANS WENT AWRY!
YOU MUST HAVE COME IN A SPACE SHIP!
YES! I SENT IT BACK TO VENUS FOR SOME THINGS I'D FORGOTTEN — AND IT NEVER RETURNED!
IT HIT A METEOR MAYBE!
?
I CAN'T READ THIS GRANT, BUT NO DOUBT IT'S LEGAL!
I'VE LIVED HERE EVER SINCE, EATING NOTHING, DRINKING NOTHING! GROWING NOT A DAY OLDER IN ALL THESE CENTURIES!
GOLLY!

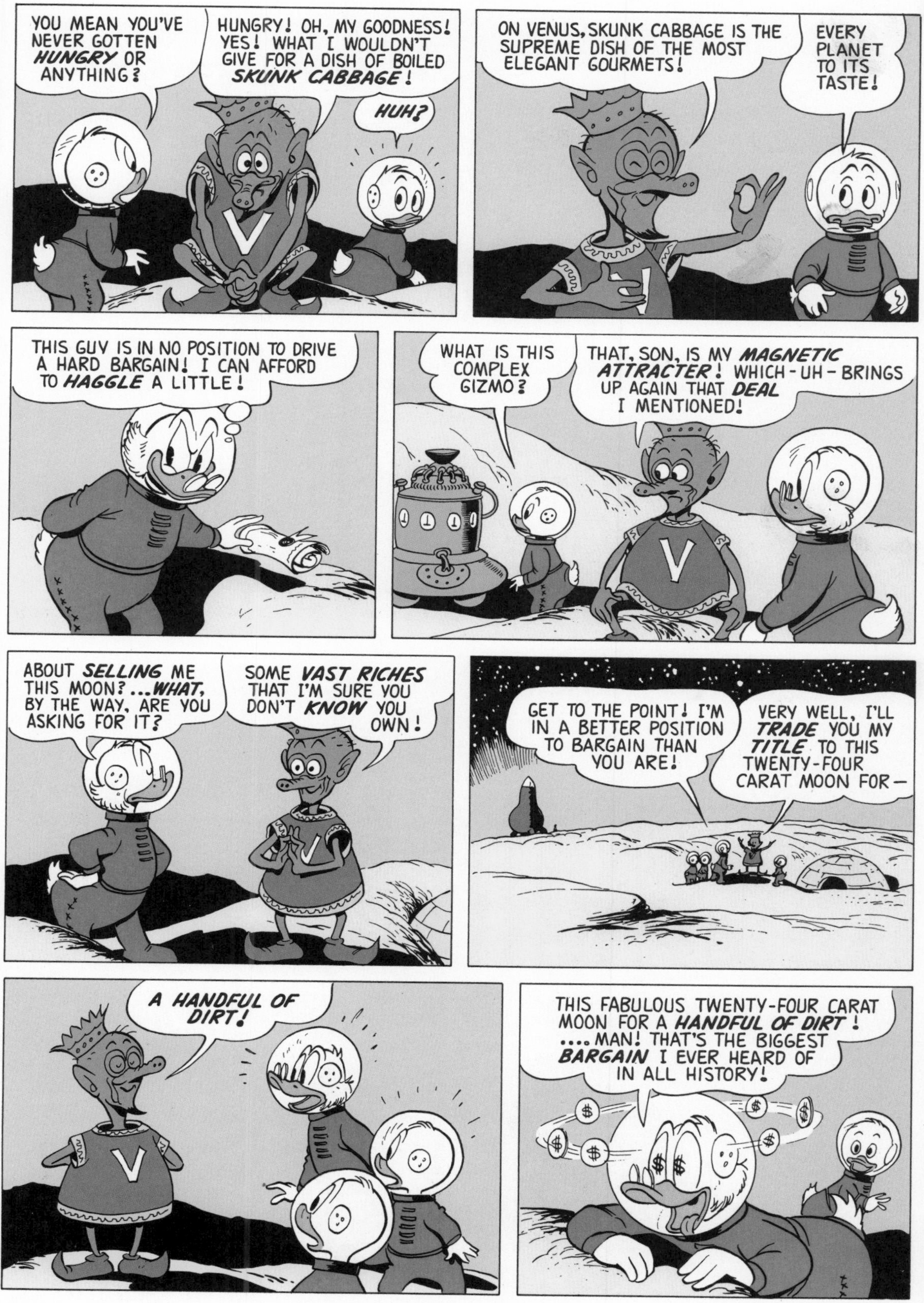

YOU MEAN YOU'VE NEVER GOTTEN HUNGRY OR ANYTHING?
HUNGRY! OH, MY GOODNESS! YES! WHAT I WOULDN'T GIVE FOR A DISH OF BOILED SKUNK CABBAGE!
HUH?
ON VENUS, SKUNK CABBAGE IS THE SUPREME DISH OF THE MOST ELEGANT GOURMETS!
EVERY PLANET TO ITS TASTE!
THIS GUY IS IN NO POSITION TO DRIVE A HARD BARGAIN! I CAN AFFORD TO HAGGLE A LITTLE!
WHAT IS THIS COMPLEX GIZMO?
THAT, SON, IS MY MAGNETIC ATTRACTER! WHICH-UH-BRINGS UP AGAIN THAT DEAL I MENTIONED!
ABOUT SELLING ME THIS MOON? ...WHAT, BY THE WAY, ARE YOU ASKING FOR IT?
SOME VAST RICHES THAT I'M SURE YOU DON'T KNOW YOU OWN!
GET TO THE POINT! I'M IN A BETTER POSITION TO BARGAIN THAN YOU ARE!
VERY WELL, I'LL TRADE YOU MY TITLE TO THIS TWENTY-FOUR CARAT MOON FOR—
A HANDFUL OF DIRT!
THIS FABULOUS TWENTY-FOUR CARAT MOON FOR A HANDFUL OF DIRT! ....MAN! THAT'S THE BIGGEST BARGAIN I EVER HEARD OF IN ALL HISTORY!

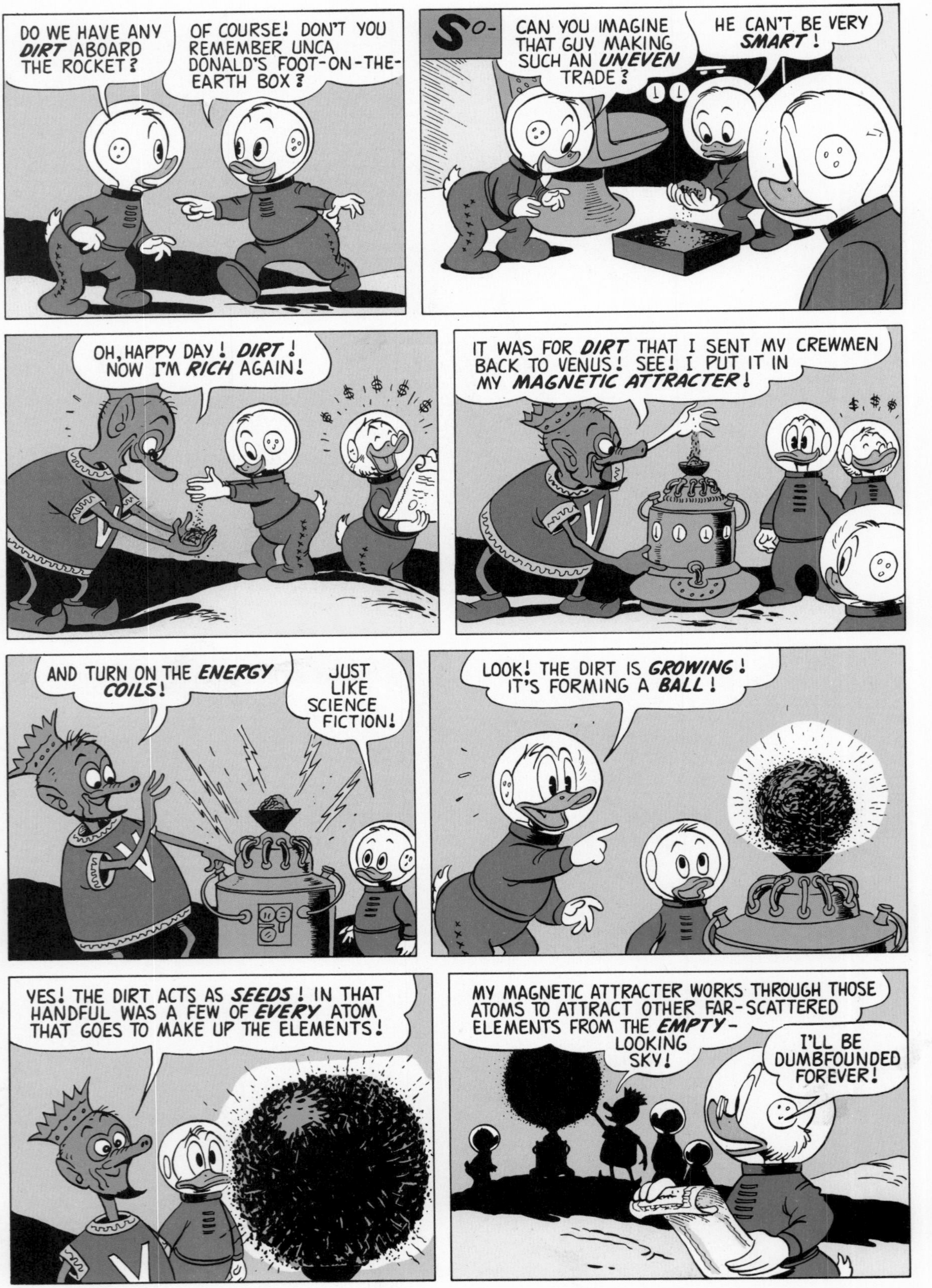
DO WE HAVE ANY DIRT ABOARD THE ROCKET?
OF COURSE! DON'T YOU REMEMBER UNCA DONALD'S FOOT-ON-THE-EARTH BOX?
SO-
CAN YOU IMAGINE THAT GUY MAKING SUCH AN UNEVEN TRADE?
HE CAN'T BE VERY SMART!
OH, HAPPY DAY! DIRT! NOW I'M RICH AGAIN!
IT WAS FOR DIRT THAT I SENT MY CREWMEN BACK TO VENUS! SEE! I PUT IT IN MY MAGNETIC ATTRACTER!
AND TURN ON THE ENERGY COILS!
JUST LIKE SCIENCE FICTION!
LOOK! THE DIRT IS GROWING! IT'S FORMING A BALL!
YES! THE DIRT ACTS AS SEEDS! IN THAT HANDFUL WAS A FEW OF EVERY ATOM THAT GOES TO MAKE UP THE ELEMENTS!
MY MAGNETIC ATTRACTER WORKS THROUGH THOSE ATOMS TO ATTRACT OTHER FAR-SCATTERED ELEMENTS FROM THE EMPTY-LOOKING SKY!
I'LL BE DUMBFOUNDED FOREVER!

SEE! THE ELEMENTS ARE FORMING INTO COMMON THINGS LIKE IRON, CARBON, SALT— EVEN *GOLD*!

AND *WATER*! YOU'RE GROWING A LITTLE *WORLD*!

YES, INDEED! WITH A *CLIMATE*, EVEN! LOOK AT THE *RAINSTORM* IN THE NORTHERN HEMISPHERE!

I'M AFRAID TO OPEN MY MOUTH! MY BRAINS MIGHT FALL OUT!

SEAS ARE FORMING!

AND *VEGETABLE* LIFE IS BEGINNING TO APPEAR!

SKUNK CABBAGE! I *LIVE* AGAIN!

WHAT ARE YOU GOING TO DO WITH YOUR LITTLE WORLD — GROW GREEN STUFF?

MORE THAN THAT!

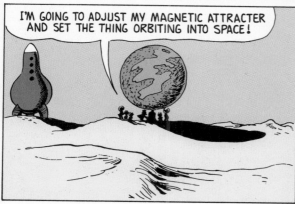

I'M GOING TO ADJUST MY MAGNETIC ATTRACTER AND SET THE THING ORBITING INTO SPACE!

YESSIR! I WAS QUITE *IMPOVERISHED* HERE, WITH ONLY ATOMS OF *GOLD* TO WORK WITH!

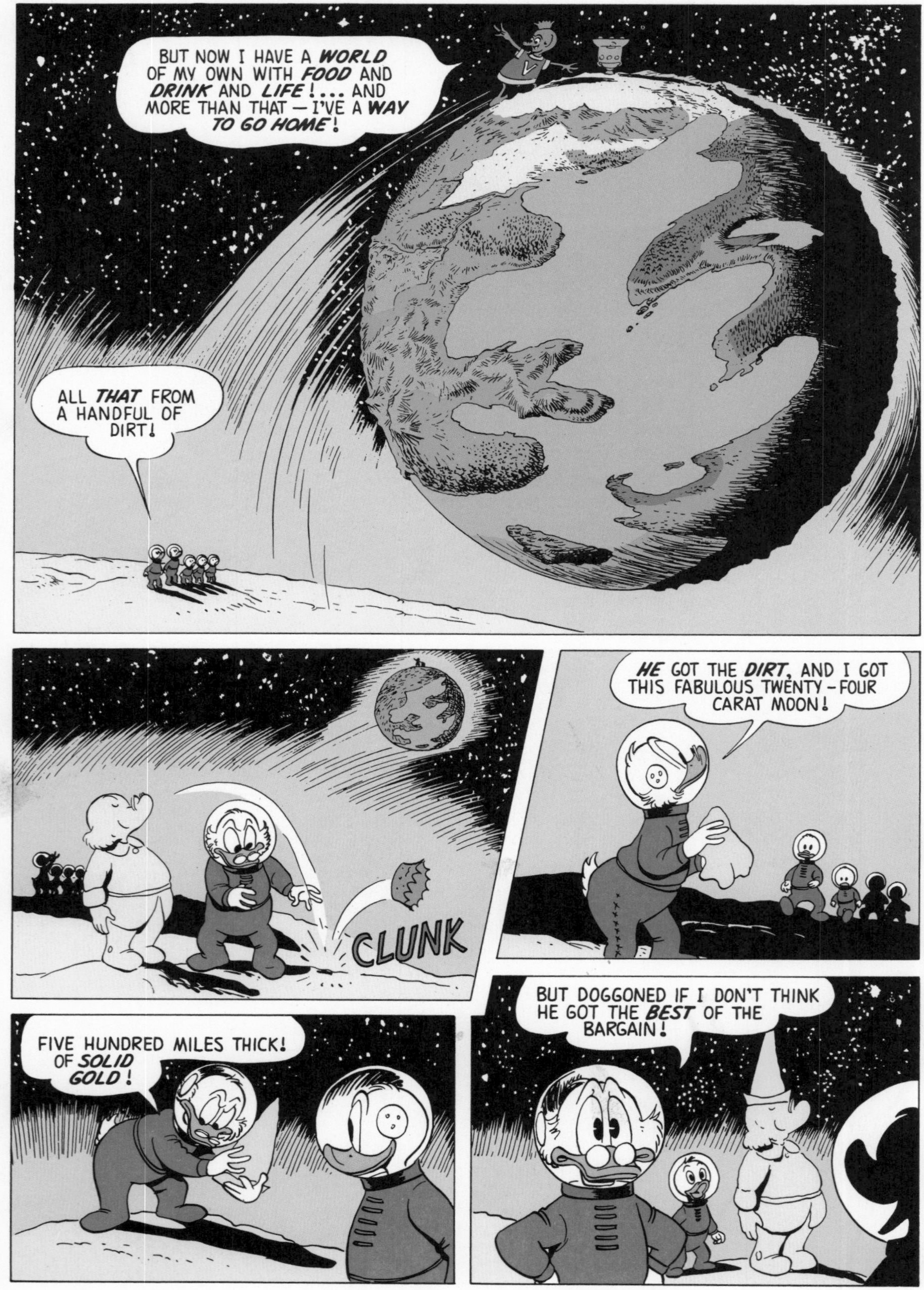
BUT NOW I HAVE A WORLD OF MY OWN WITH FOOD AND DRINK AND LIFE!... AND MORE THAN THAT — I'VE A WAY TO GO HOME!
ALL THAT FROM A HANDFUL OF DIRT!
HE GOT THE DIRT, AND I GOT THIS FABULOUS TWENTY-FOUR CARAT MOON!
CLUNK
FIVE HUNDRED MILES THICK! OF SOLID GOLD!
BUT DOGGONED IF I DON'T THINK HE GOT THE BEST OF THE BARGAIN!

Walt Disney's
UNCLE
$CROOGE

THERE GOES RICH OLD SCROOGE McDUCK! HE HAS A ROLL THAT WOULD CHOKE A HORSE!

YOU WOULDN'T THINK IT, BUT THAT DUMPY OLD DUCK HAS A ROLL THAT WOULD CHOKE A HORSE!

YES, HORSIE! I HAVE AN APPLE FOR YOU IN MY POCKET!

UH, OH! WRONG POCKET!

SEE WHAT I TOLD YOU?

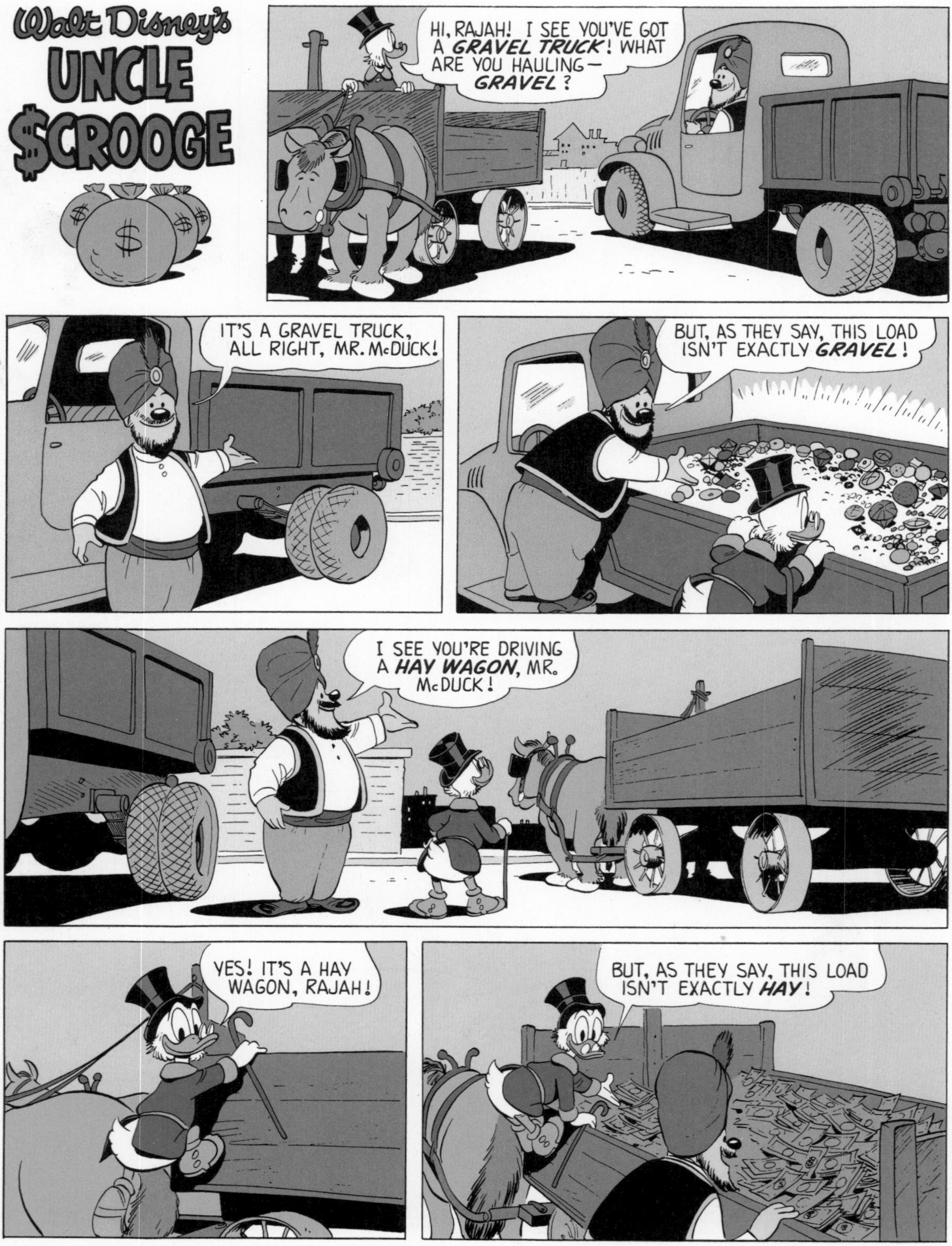
Walt Disney's
UNCLE $CROOGE
HI, RAJAH! I SEE YOU'VE GOT A GRAVEL TRUCK! WHAT ARE YOU HAULING— GRAVEL?
IT'S A GRAVEL TRUCK, ALL RIGHT, MR. McDUCK!
BUT, AS THEY SAY, THIS LOAD ISN'T EXACTLY GRAVEL!
I SEE YOU'RE DRIVING A HAY WAGON, MR. McDUCK!
YES! IT'S A HAY WAGON, RAJAH!
BUT, AS THEY SAY, THIS LOAD ISN'T EXACTLY HAY!

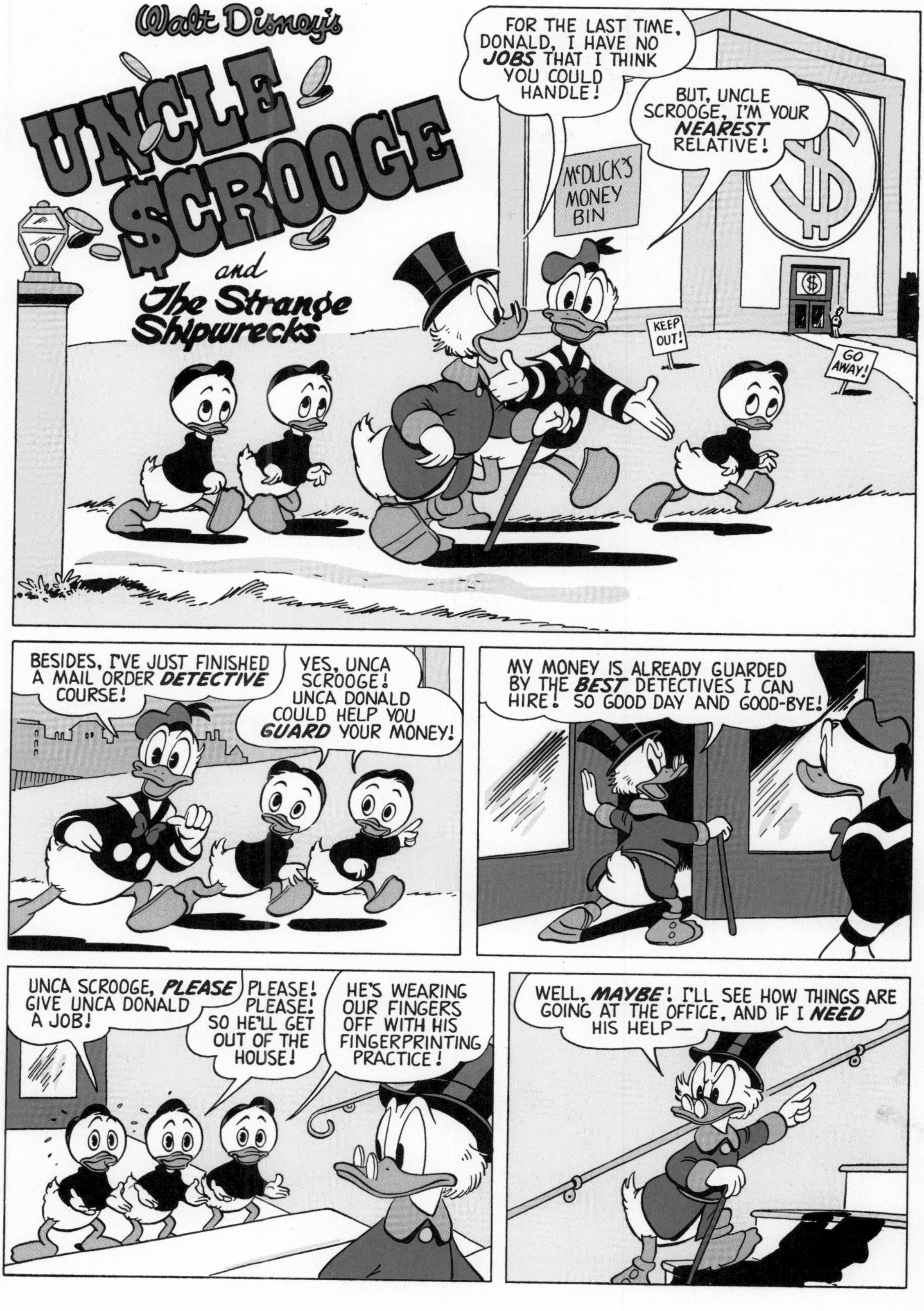
Walt Disney's
UNCLE $CROOGE
and
The Strange Shipwrecks
FOR THE LAST TIME, DONALD, I HAVE NO JOBS THAT I THINK YOU COULD HANDLE!
BUT, UNCLE SCROOGE, I'M YOUR NEAREST RELATIVE!
McDUCK'S MONEY BIN
KEEP OUT!
GO AWAY!
BESIDES, I'VE JUST FINISHED A MAIL ORDER DETECTIVE COURSE!
YES, UNCA SCROOGE! UNCA DONALD COULD HELP YOU GUARD YOUR MONEY!
MY MONEY IS ALREADY GUARDED BY THE BEST DETECTIVES I CAN HIRE! SO GOOD DAY AND GOOD-BYE!
UNCA SCROOGE, PLEASE GIVE UNCA DONALD A JOB!
PLEASE! PLEASE! SO HE'LL GET OUT OF THE HOUSE!
HE'S WEARING OUR FINGERS OFF WITH HIS FINGERPRINTING PRACTICE!
WELL, MAYBE! I'LL SEE HOW THINGS ARE GOING AT THE OFFICE, AND IF I NEED HIS HELP—

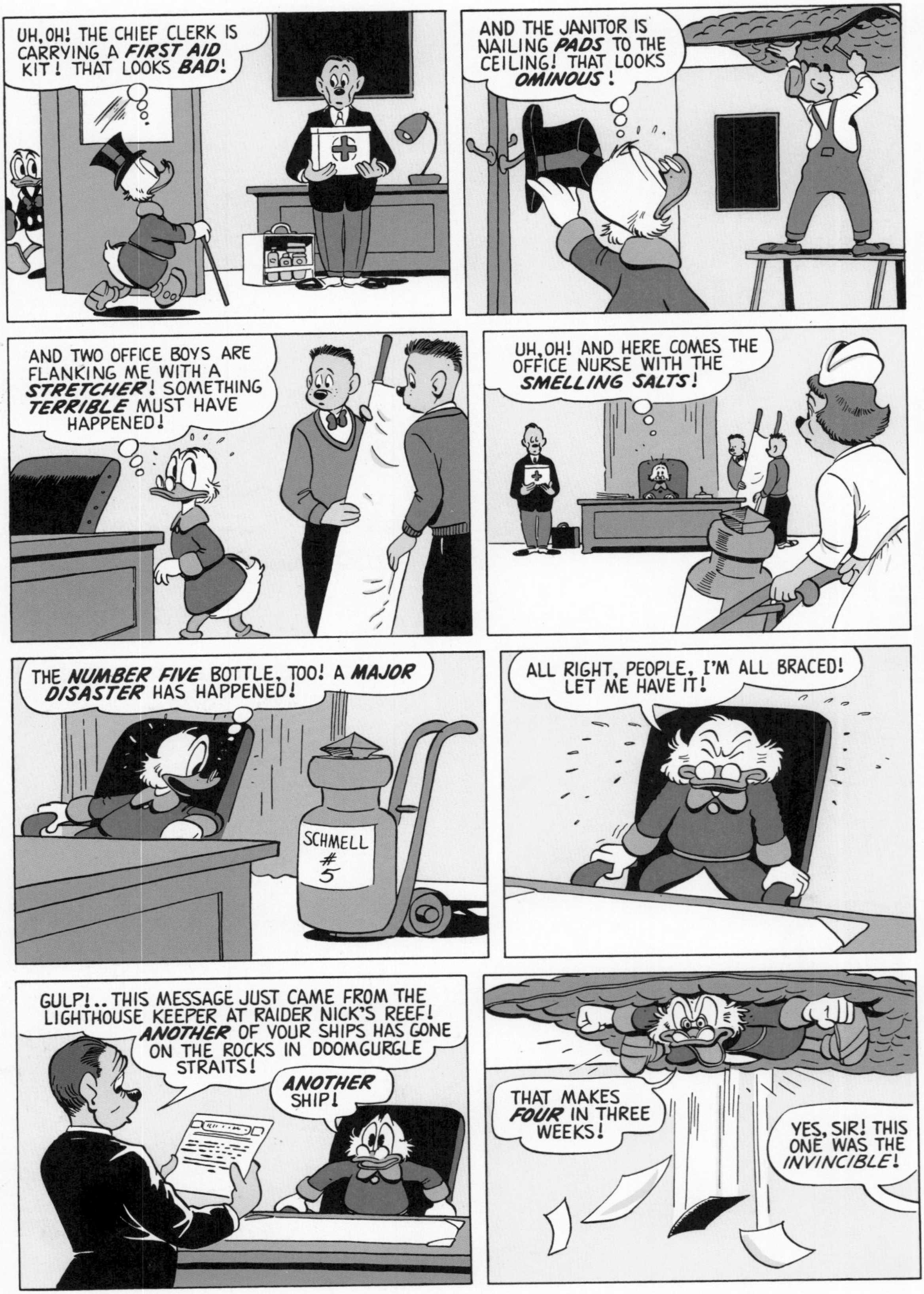
UH, OH! THE CHIEF CLERK IS CARRYING A FIRST AID KIT! THAT LOOKS BAD!
AND THE JANITOR IS NAILING PADS TO THE CEILING! THAT LOOKS OMINOUS!
AND TWO OFFICE BOYS ARE FLANKING ME WITH A STRETCHER! SOMETHING TERRIBLE MUST HAVE HAPPENED!
UH, OH! AND HERE COMES THE OFFICE NURSE WITH THE SMELLING SALTS!
THE NUMBER FIVE BOTTLE, TOO! A MAJOR DISASTER HAS HAPPENED!
SCHMELL # 5
ALL RIGHT, PEOPLE, I'M ALL BRACED! LET ME HAVE IT!
GULP!.. THIS MESSAGE JUST CAME FROM THE LIGHTHOUSE KEEPER AT RAIDER NICK'S REEF! ANOTHER OF YOUR SHIPS HAS GONE ON THE ROCKS IN DOOMGURGLE STRAITS!
ANOTHER SHIP!
THAT MAKES FOUR IN THREE WEEKS!
YES, SIR! THIS ONE WAS THE INVINCIBLE!

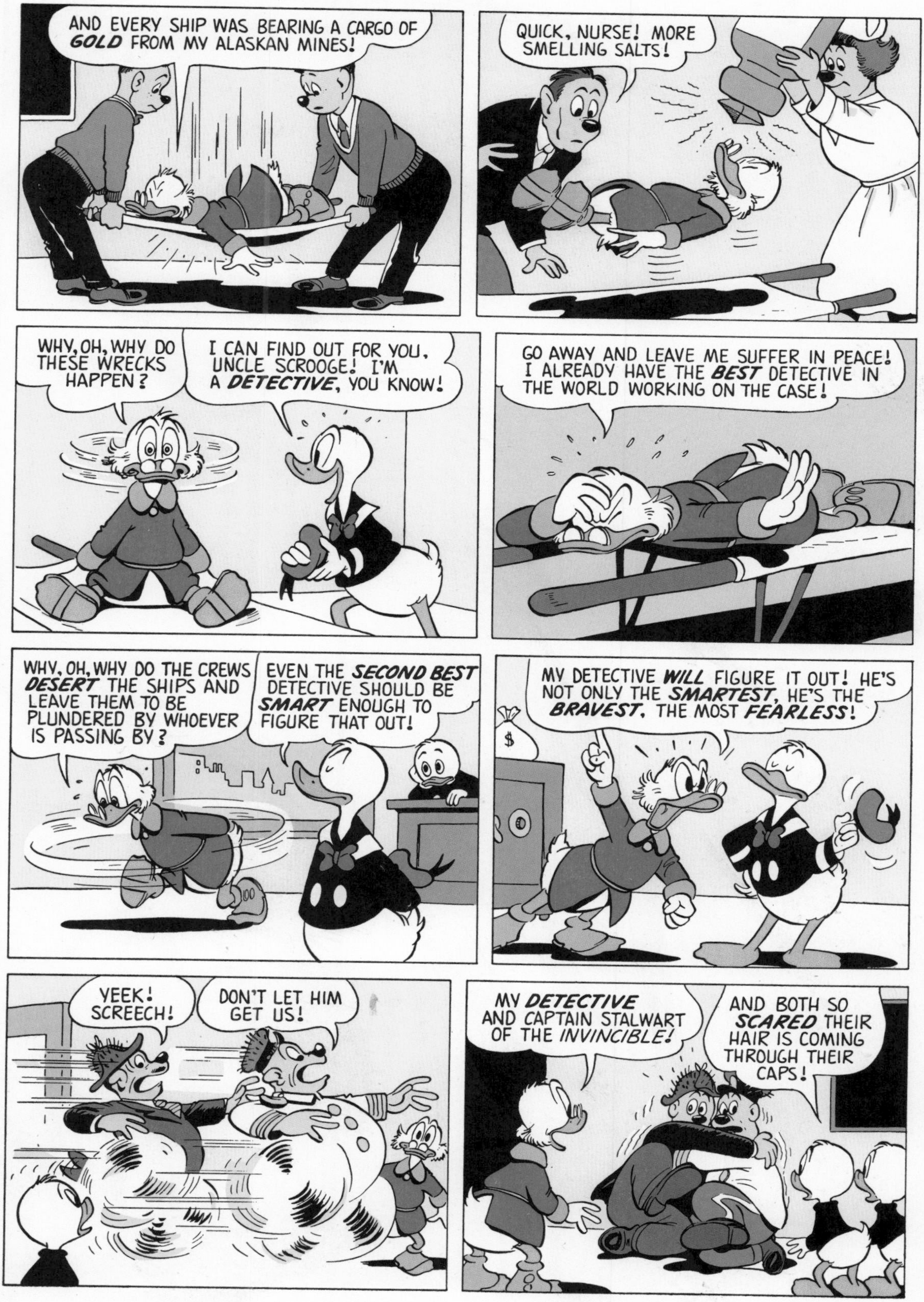
AND EVERY SHIP WAS BEARING A CARGO OF GOLD FROM MY ALASKAN MINES!
QUICK, NURSE! MORE SMELLING SALTS!
WHY, OH, WHY DO THESE WRECKS HAPPEN?
I CAN FIND OUT FOR YOU, UNCLE SCROOGE! I'M A DETECTIVE, YOU KNOW!
GO AWAY AND LEAVE ME SUFFER IN PEACE! I ALREADY HAVE THE BEST DETECTIVE IN THE WORLD WORKING ON THE CASE!
WHY, OH, WHY DO THE CREWS DESERT THE SHIPS AND LEAVE THEM TO BE PLUNDERED BY WHOEVER IS PASSING BY?
EVEN THE SECOND BEST DETECTIVE SHOULD BE SMART ENOUGH TO FIGURE THAT OUT!
MY DETECTIVE WILL FIGURE IT OUT! HE'S NOT ONLY THE SMARTEST, HE'S THE BRAVEST, THE MOST FEARLESS!
YEEK! SCREECH!
DON'T LET HIM GET US!
MY DETECTIVE AND CAPTAIN STALWART OF THE INVINCIBLE!
AND BOTH SO SCARED THEIR HAIR IS COMING THROUGH THEIR CAPS!

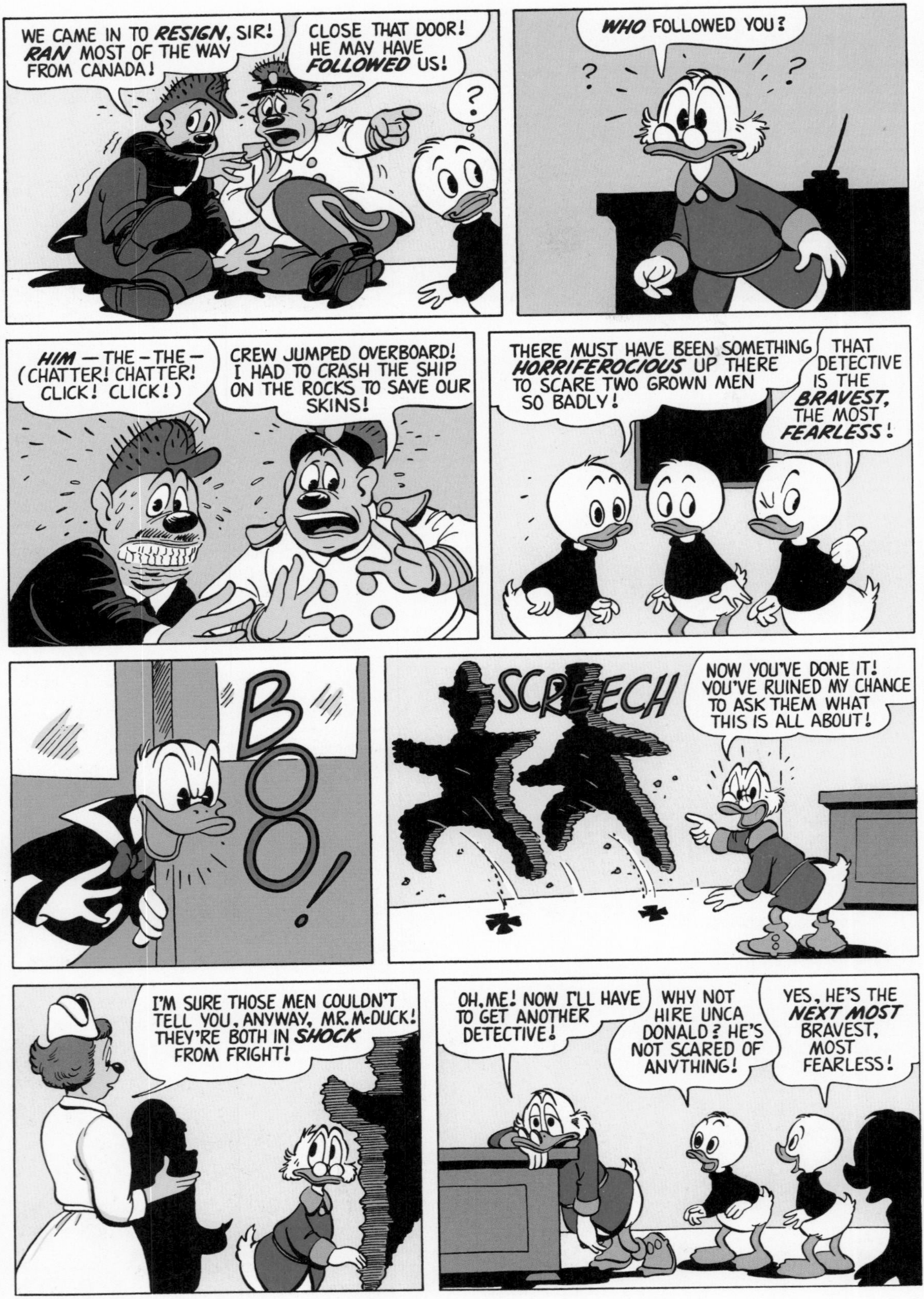

WE CAME IN TO RESIGN, SIR! RAN MOST OF THE WAY FROM CANADA!
CLOSE THAT DOOR! HE MAY HAVE FOLLOWED US!
?
WHO FOLLOWED YOU?
? ?
HIM — THE – THE – (CHATTER! CHATTER! CLICK! CLICK!)
CREW JUMPED OVERBOARD! I HAD TO CRASH THE SHIP ON THE ROCKS TO SAVE OUR SKINS!
THERE MUST HAVE BEEN SOMETHING HORRIFEROCIOUS UP THERE TO SCARE TWO GROWN MEN SO BADLY!
THAT DETECTIVE IS THE BRAVEST, THE MOST FEARLESS!
BOO!
SCREECH
NOW YOU'VE DONE IT! YOU'VE RUINED MY CHANCE TO ASK THEM WHAT THIS IS ALL ABOUT!
I'M SURE THOSE MEN COULDN'T TELL YOU, ANYWAY, MR. McDUCK! THEY'RE BOTH IN SHOCK FROM FRIGHT!
OH, ME! NOW I'LL HAVE TO GET ANOTHER DETECTIVE!
WHY NOT HIRE UNCA DONALD? HE'S NOT SCARED OF ANYTHING!
YES, HE'S THE NEXT MOST BRAVEST, MOST FEARLESS!

ALL RIGHT, BY THUNDER! I'M DESPERATE ENOUGH TO HIRE EVEN DONALD! THAT MYSTERY *MUST* BE SOLVED!

COME HERE, UNCA DONALD!

YES! COME HERE! I'M OFFERING YOU A *JOB*!

YOU'LL HAVE TO CATCH ME FIRST! *THAT* JOB LOOKS TOO *SCARY* FOR ME!

COME BACK HERE YOU INGRATE! REMEMBER I'M YOUR *NEAREST* RELATIVE!

SO— IT'S ALL ARRANGED, THEN, THAT YOU, DONALD, WITH HUEY AND DEWEY, WILL FLY NORTH AND BOARD MY NEXT GOLD SHIP AT SITKA!

YESSIR! I'LL CHECK FOR ANY SUSPICIOUS ACTIONS BY THE CREW!

ACE DETECTIVE KIT

HAVE THE CAPTAIN *AVOID* THE DOOMGURGLE STRAITS UNLESS I WIRE YOU *OTHER* ORDERS!

YESSIR!

I WILL TAKE LOUIE AND FLY TO THE SCENE OF THE WRECKS AND DO A LITTLE INVESTIGATING ON MY OWN!

*N*EXT DAY!

THERE'S RAIDER NICK'S REEF LIGHTHOUSE, LOUIE!

PEACEFUL-LOOKING PLACE! NOTHING *HAIR-RAISING* IN SIGHT!

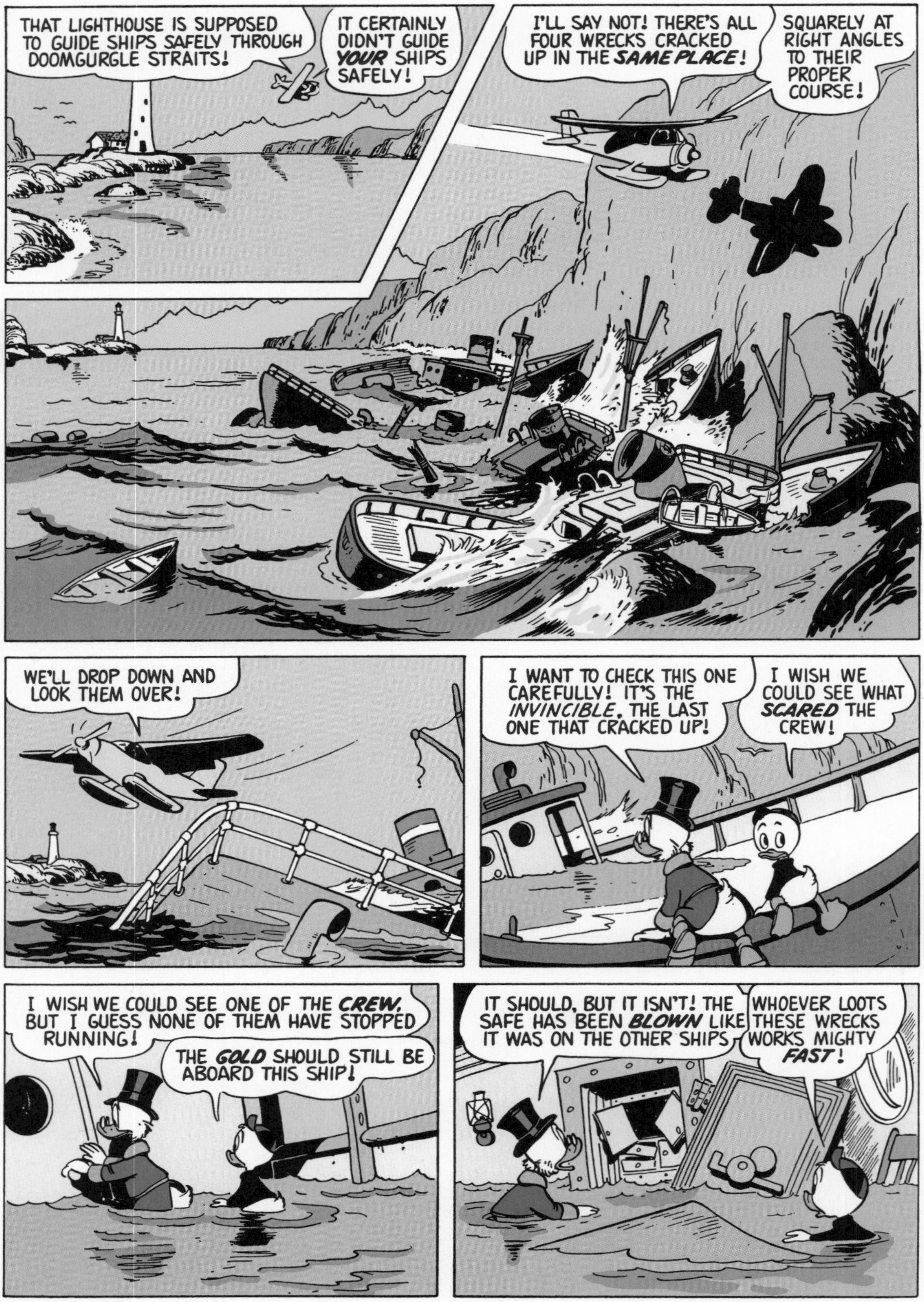
THAT LIGHTHOUSE IS SUPPOSED TO GUIDE SHIPS SAFELY THROUGH DOOMGURGLE STRAITS!
IT CERTAINLY DIDN'T GUIDE YOUR SHIPS SAFELY!
I'LL SAY NOT! THERE'S ALL FOUR WRECKS CRACKED UP IN THE SAME PLACE!
SQUARELY AT RIGHT ANGLES TO THEIR PROPER COURSE!
WE'LL DROP DOWN AND LOOK THEM OVER!
I WANT TO CHECK THIS ONE CAREFULLY! IT'S THE INVINCIBLE, THE LAST ONE THAT CRACKED UP!
I WISH WE COULD SEE WHAT SCARED THE CREW!
I WISH WE COULD SEE ONE OF THE CREW, BUT I GUESS NONE OF THEM HAVE STOPPED RUNNING!
THE GOLD SHOULD STILL BE ABOARD THIS SHIP!
IT SHOULD, BUT IT ISN'T! THE SAFE HAS BEEN BLOWN LIKE IT WAS ON THE OTHER SHIPS
WHOEVER LOOTS THESE WRECKS WORKS MIGHTY FAST!

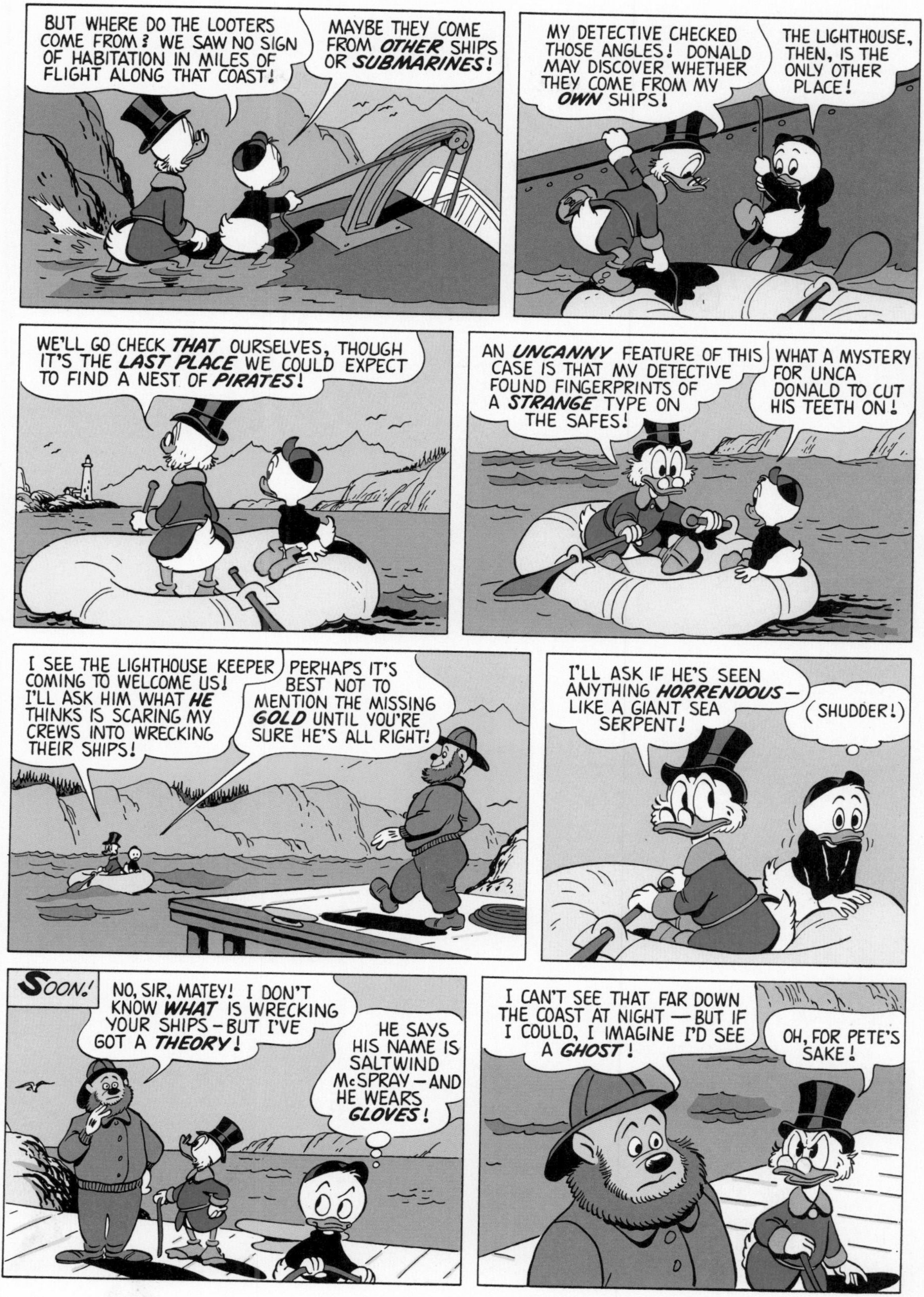
BUT WHERE DO THE LOOTERS COME FROM? WE SAW NO SIGN OF HABITATION IN MILES OF FLIGHT ALONG THAT COAST!
MAYBE THEY COME FROM OTHER SHIPS OR SUBMARINES!
MY DETECTIVE CHECKED THOSE ANGLES! DONALD MAY DISCOVER WHETHER THEY COME FROM MY OWN SHIPS!
THE LIGHTHOUSE, THEN, IS THE ONLY OTHER PLACE!
WE'LL GO CHECK THAT OURSELVES, THOUGH IT'S THE LAST PLACE WE COULD EXPECT TO FIND A NEST OF PIRATES!
AN UNCANNY FEATURE OF THIS CASE IS THAT MY DETECTIVE FOUND FINGERPRINTS OF A STRANGE TYPE ON THE SAFES!
WHAT A MYSTERY FOR UNCA DONALD TO CUT HIS TEETH ON!
I SEE THE LIGHTHOUSE KEEPER COMING TO WELCOME US! I'LL ASK HIM WHAT HE THINKS IS SCARING MY CREWS INTO WRECKING THEIR SHIPS!
PERHAPS IT'S BEST NOT TO MENTION THE MISSING GOLD UNTIL YOU'RE SURE HE'S ALL RIGHT!
I'LL ASK IF HE'S SEEN ANYTHING HORRENDOUS — LIKE A GIANT SEA SERPENT!
(SHUDDER!)
SOON!
NO, SIR, MATEY! I DON'T KNOW WHAT IS WRECKING YOUR SHIPS — BUT I'VE GOT A THEORY!
HE SAYS HIS NAME IS SALTWIND McSPRAY — AND HE WEARS GLOVES!
I CAN'T SEE THAT FAR DOWN THE COAST AT NIGHT — BUT IF I COULD, I IMAGINE I'D SEE A GHOST!
OH, FOR PETE'S SAKE!

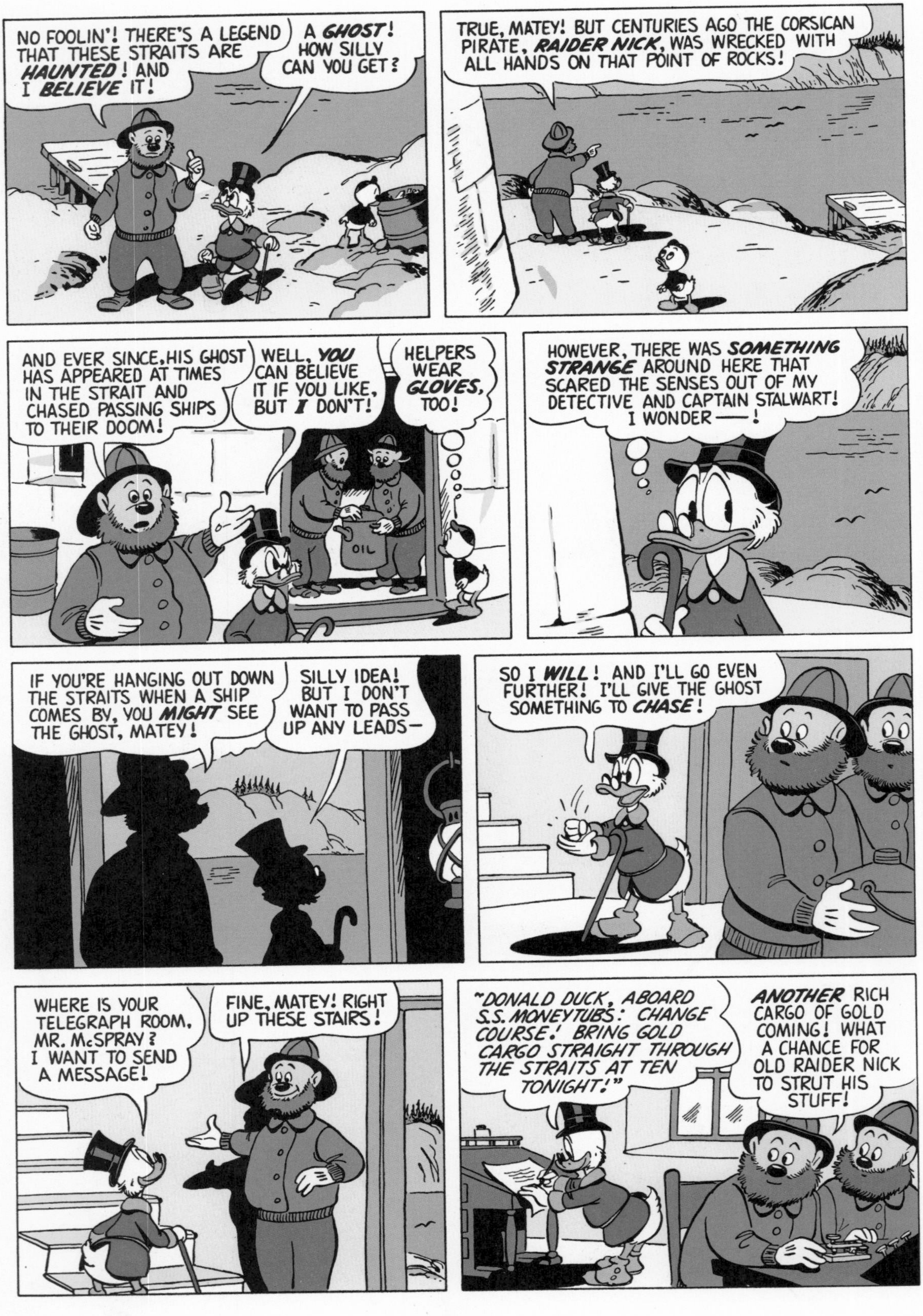
NO FOOLIN'! THERE'S A LEGEND THAT THESE STRAITS ARE HAUNTED! AND I BELIEVE IT!
A GHOST! HOW SILLY CAN YOU GET?
TRUE, MATEY! BUT CENTURIES AGO THE CORSICAN PIRATE, RAIDER NICK, WAS WRECKED WITH ALL HANDS ON THAT POINT OF ROCKS!
AND EVER SINCE, HIS GHOST HAS APPEARED AT TIMES IN THE STRAIT AND CHASED PASSING SHIPS TO THEIR DOOM!
WELL, YOU CAN BELIEVE IT IF YOU LIKE, BUT I DON'T!
HELPERS WEAR GLOVES, TOO!
OIL
HOWEVER, THERE WAS SOMETHING STRANGE AROUND HERE THAT SCARED THE SENSES OUT OF MY DETECTIVE AND CAPTAIN STALWART! I WONDER —!
IF YOU'RE HANGING OUT DOWN THE STRAITS WHEN A SHIP COMES BY, YOU MIGHT SEE THE GHOST, MATEY!
SILLY IDEA! BUT I DON'T WANT TO PASS UP ANY LEADS—
SO I WILL! AND I'LL GO EVEN FURTHER! I'LL GIVE THE GHOST SOMETHING TO CHASE!
WHERE IS YOUR TELEGRAPH ROOM, MR. McSPRAY? I WANT TO SEND A MESSAGE!
FINE, MATEY! RIGHT UP THESE STAIRS!
"DONALD DUCK, ABOARD S.S. MONEYTUBS: CHANGE COURSE! BRING GOLD CARGO STRAIGHT THROUGH THE STRAITS AT TEN TONIGHT!"
ANOTHER RICH CARGO OF GOLD COMING! WHAT A CHANCE FOR OLD RAIDER NICK TO STRUT HIS STUFF!

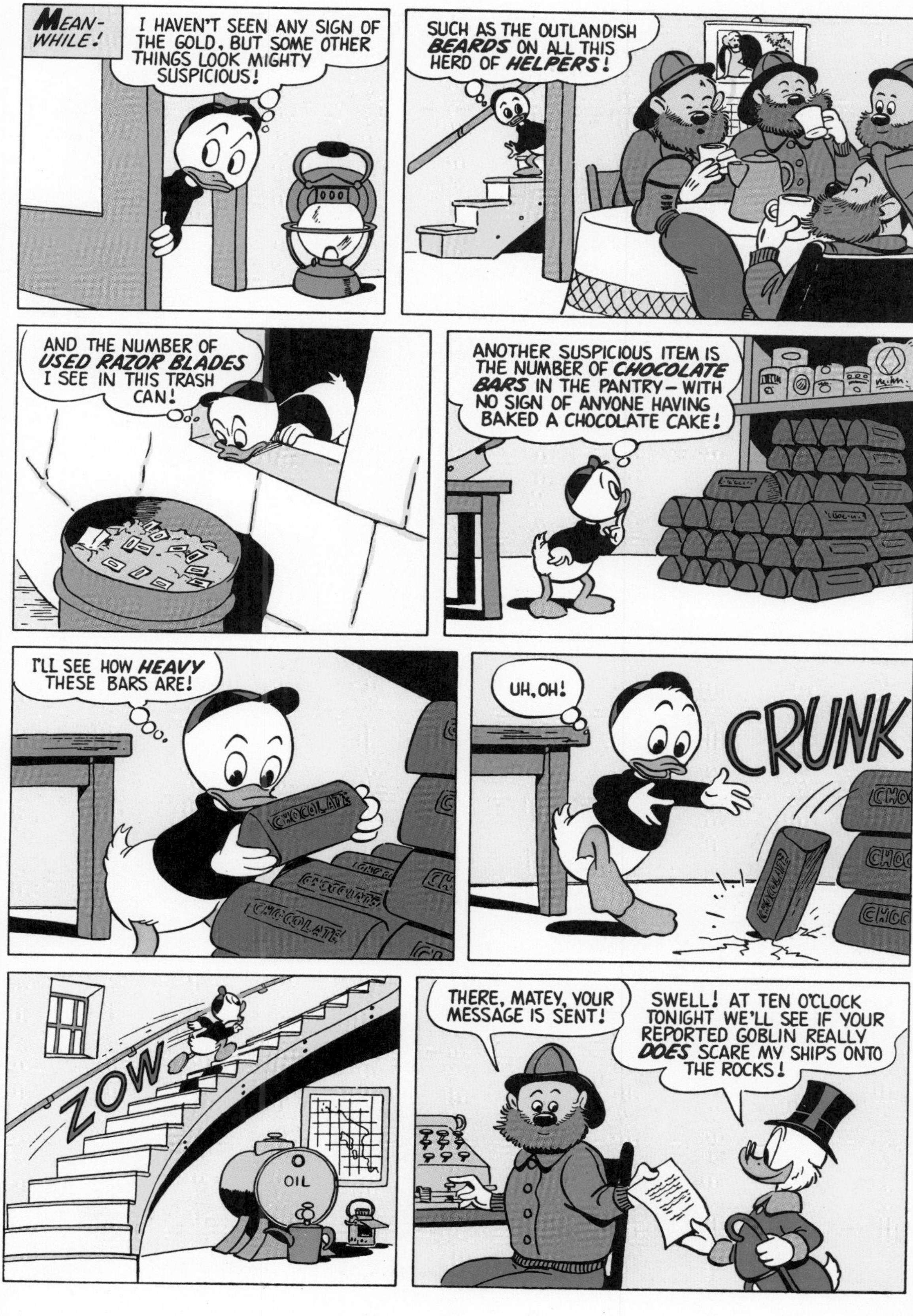
MEAN-WHILE!
I HAVEN'T SEEN ANY SIGN OF THE GOLD, BUT SOME OTHER THINGS LOOK MIGHTY SUSPICIOUS!
SUCH AS THE OUTLANDISH BEARDS ON ALL THIS HERD OF HELPERS!
AND THE NUMBER OF USED RAZOR BLADES I SEE IN THIS TRASH CAN!
ANOTHER SUSPICIOUS ITEM IS THE NUMBER OF CHOCOLATE BARS IN THE PANTRY—WITH NO SIGN OF ANYONE HAVING BAKED A CHOCOLATE CAKE!
I'LL SEE HOW HEAVY THESE BARS ARE!
CHOCOLATE
UH, OH!
CRUNK
CHOCOLATE
ZOW
OIL
THERE, MATEY, YOUR MESSAGE IS SENT!
SWELL! AT TEN O'CLOCK TONIGHT WE'LL SEE IF YOUR REPORTED GOBLIN REALLY DOES SCARE MY SHIPS ONTO THE ROCKS!

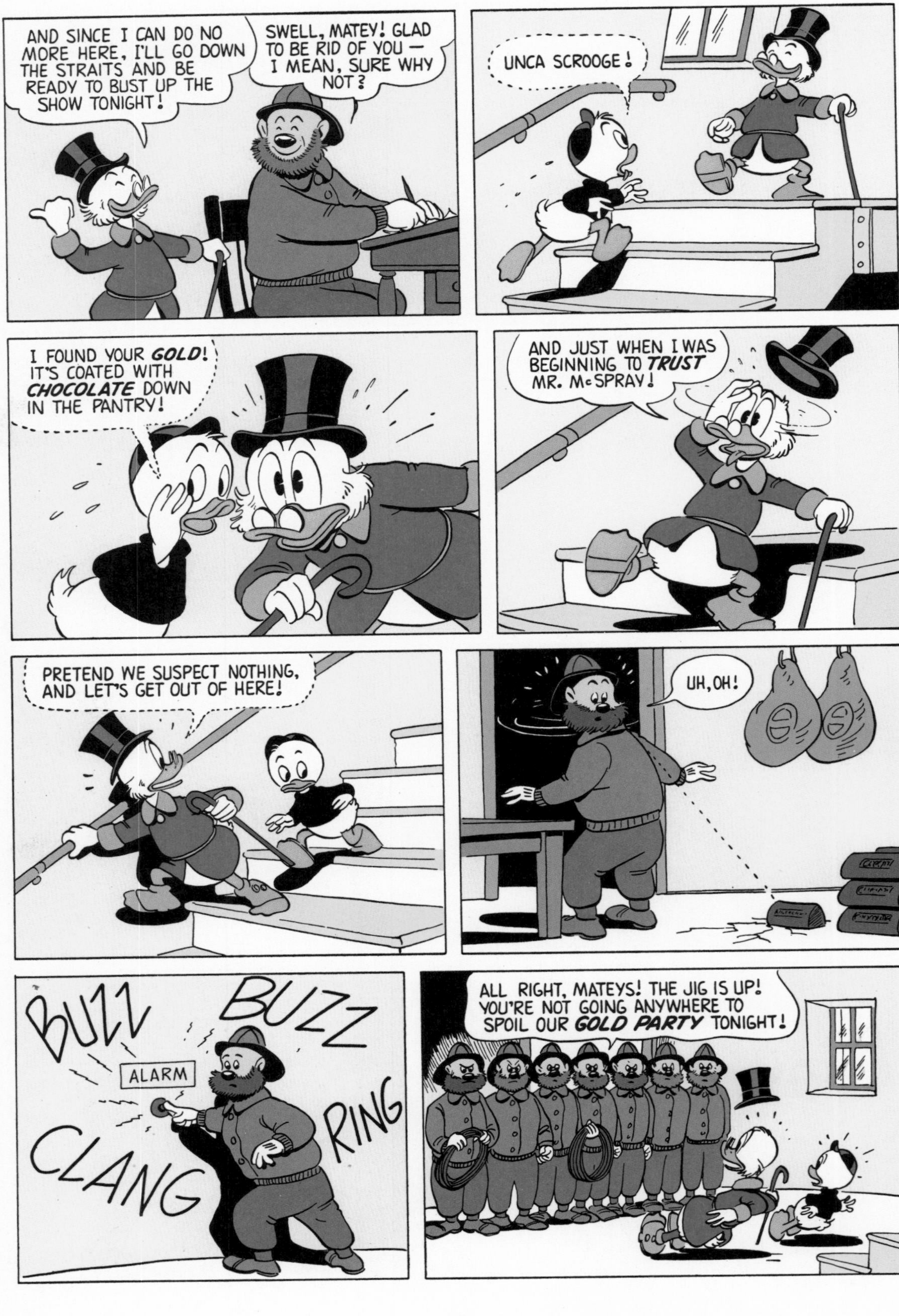
AND SINCE I CAN DO NO MORE HERE, I'LL GO DOWN THE STRAITS AND BE READY TO BUST UP THE SHOW TONIGHT!
SWELL, MATEY! GLAD TO BE RID OF YOU — I MEAN, SURE WHY NOT?
UNCA SCROOGE!
I FOUND YOUR GOLD! IT'S COATED WITH CHOCOLATE DOWN IN THE PANTRY!
AND JUST WHEN I WAS BEGINNING TO TRUST MR. McSPRAY!
PRETEND WE SUSPECT NOTHING, AND LET'S GET OUT OF HERE!
UH, OH!
BUZZ BUZZ
ALARM
RING
CLANG
ALL RIGHT, MATEYS! THE JIG IS UP! YOU'RE NOT GOING ANYWHERE TO SPOIL OUR GOLD PARTY TONIGHT!

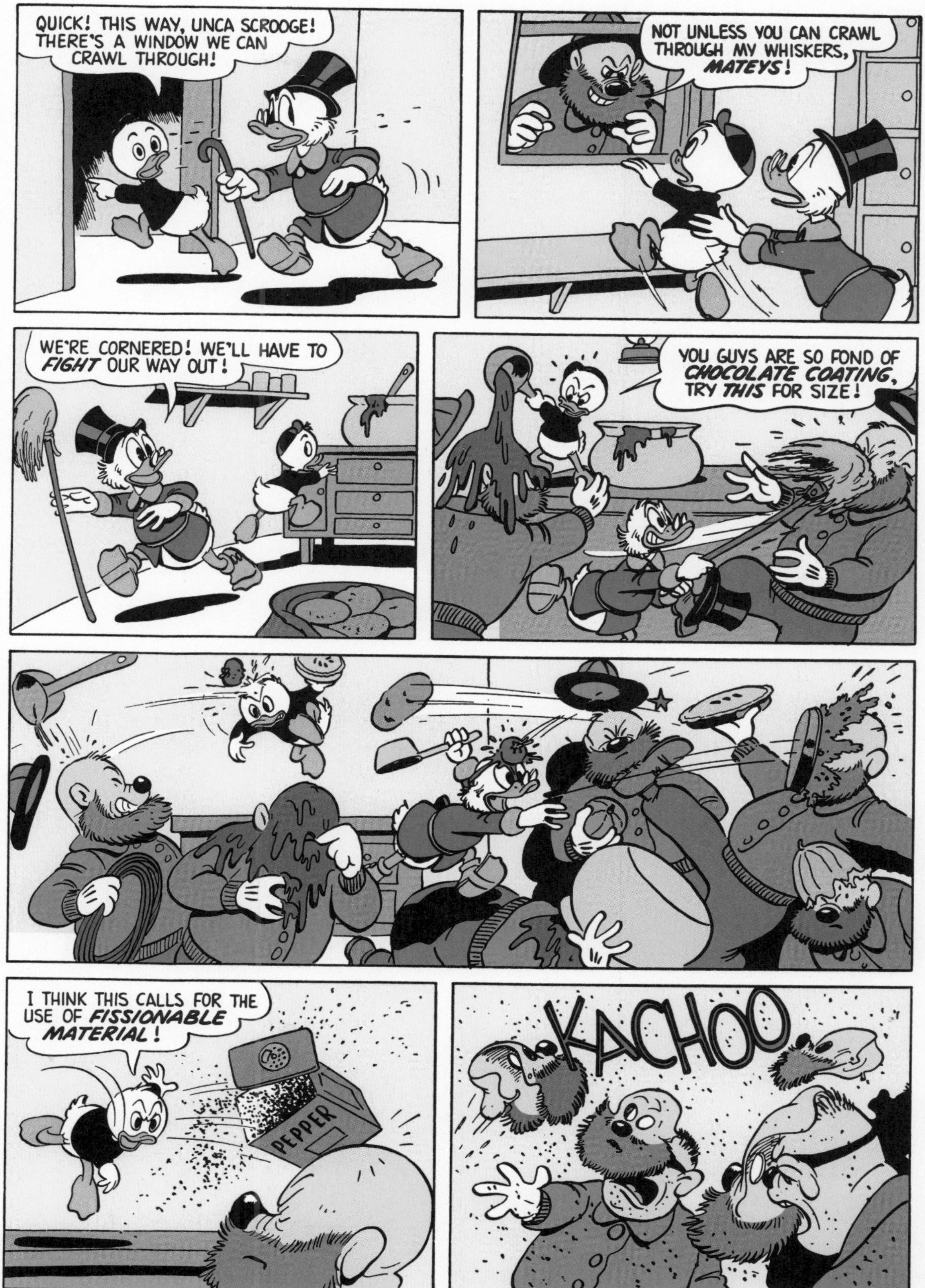
QUICK! THIS WAY, UNCA SCROOGE! THERE'S A WINDOW WE CAN CRAWL THROUGH!
NOT UNLESS YOU CAN CRAWL THROUGH MY WHISKERS, MATEYS!
WE'RE CORNERED! WE'LL HAVE TO FIGHT OUR WAY OUT!
YOU GUYS ARE SO FOND OF CHOCOLATE COATING, TRY THIS FOR SIZE!
I THINK THIS CALLS FOR THE USE OF FISSIONABLE MATERIAL!
PEPPER
KACHOO

THAT GOT THEM OUT OF THE *BUSHES*! NOW WE CAN SEE WHO WE'RE DEALING WITH!

THE BEAGLE BOYS! THE *TERRIBLE* BEAGLE BOYS!

BEAGLE BOYS INC.

BEAGLE BOYS INC.

So—

HOW DID YOU AWFUL HIGHBINDERS GET IN CHARGE OF THIS LIGHTHOUSE?

BEAGLE BOYS

BEAGLE BOYS INC.

WELL IT WASN'T *EASY*!

BUT WE MANAGED IT!

FIRST *LEGAL* JOB WE EVER HAD!

BEAGLE BOYS INC.

BEAGLE BOYS INC.

BEAGLE BOYS INC.

YESSIR! AND WE'RE JUST ABOUT TO MAKE IT *PAY*!

TONIGHT'S HAUL SHOULD PUT US IN THE *BLACK*!

BOYS INC.

BEAGLE BOYS INC.

YOU MEAN YOU PIRATES HAVEN'T BEEN MAKING A *PROFIT*?

WELL, NOT *YET*! THIS SET-UP WE'VE GOT COST A *LOT OF MONEY*!

BEAGLE BOYS INC.

A LOT OF MONEY, AND A LOT OF *TIME*!

AND *WORK*! MAN, WE'VE SPENT *TWO YEARS* ON THIS COLD ROCK *WORKING* EVERY MINUTE!

BEAGLE

SO THAT *GOLD* SHIPMENT OF YOURS TONIGHT BETTER BE *RICH*, OR WE'RE GOING TO HAVE TO *HOLD YOU* HERE TILL WE PLUNDER YOUR *WHOLE FLEET*!

YES! AND, MAN! WE'LL BE MEANER THAN BOX-ANKLED HOUNDS!

BEAG

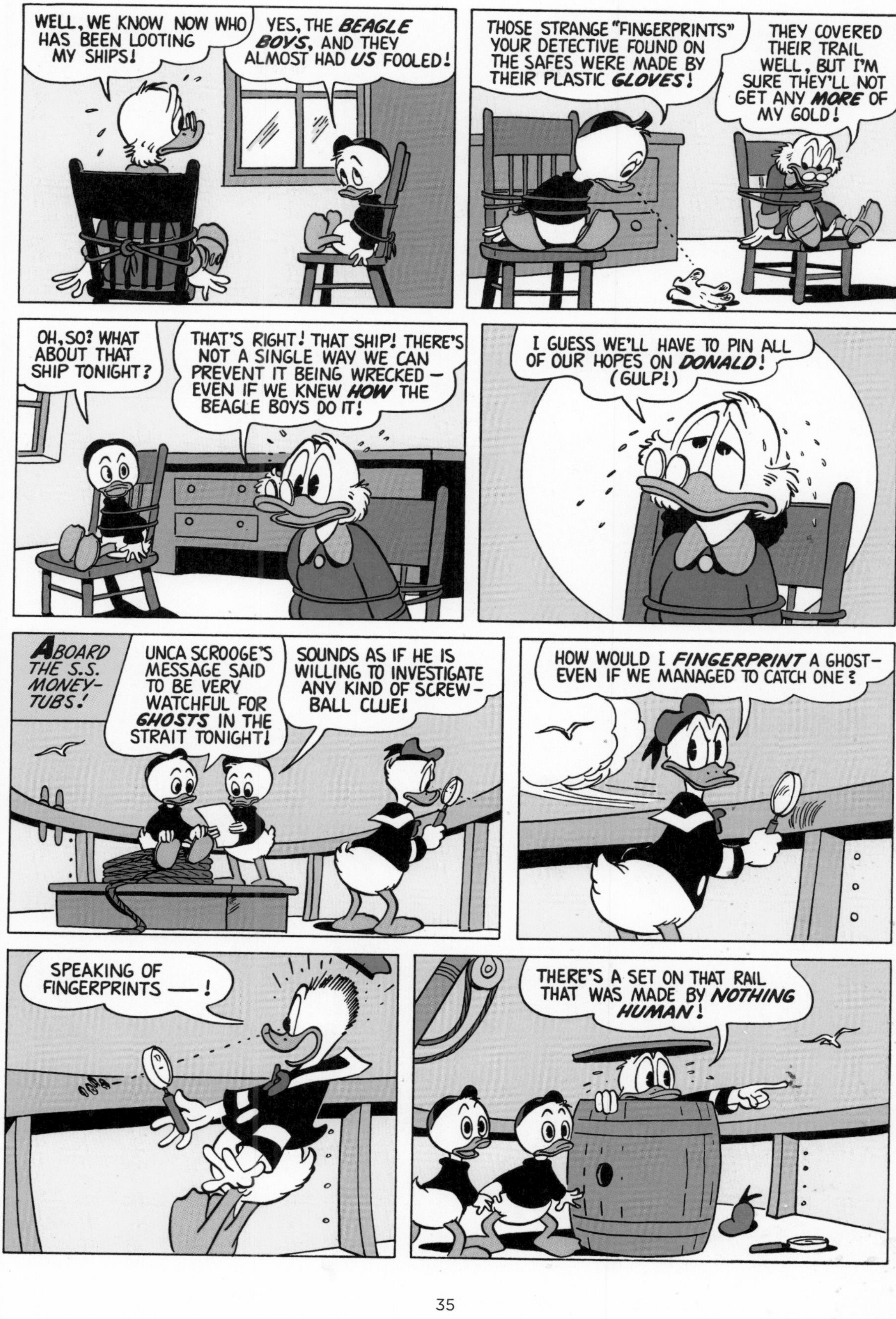
WELL, WE KNOW NOW WHO HAS BEEN LOOTING MY SHIPS!
YES, THE BEAGLE BOYS, AND THEY ALMOST HAD US FOOLED!
THOSE STRANGE "FINGERPRINTS" YOUR DETECTIVE FOUND ON THE SAFES WERE MADE BY THEIR PLASTIC GLOVES!
THEY COVERED THEIR TRAIL WELL, BUT I'M SURE THEY'LL NOT GET ANY MORE OF MY GOLD!
OH, SO? WHAT ABOUT THAT SHIP TONIGHT?
THAT'S RIGHT! THAT SHIP! THERE'S NOT A SINGLE WAY WE CAN PREVENT IT BEING WRECKED — EVEN IF WE KNEW HOW THE BEAGLE BOYS DO IT!
I GUESS WE'LL HAVE TO PIN ALL OF OUR HOPES ON DONALD! (GULP!)
ABOARD THE S.S. MONEY-TUBS!
UNCA SCROOGE'S MESSAGE SAID TO BE VERY WATCHFUL FOR GHOSTS IN THE STRAIT TONIGHT!
SOUNDS AS IF HE IS WILLING TO INVESTIGATE ANY KIND OF SCREW-BALL CLUE!
HOW WOULD I FINGERPRINT A GHOST— EVEN IF WE MANAGED TO CATCH ONE?
SPEAKING OF FINGERPRINTS —!
THERE'S A SET ON THAT RAIL THAT WAS MADE BY NOTHING HUMAN!

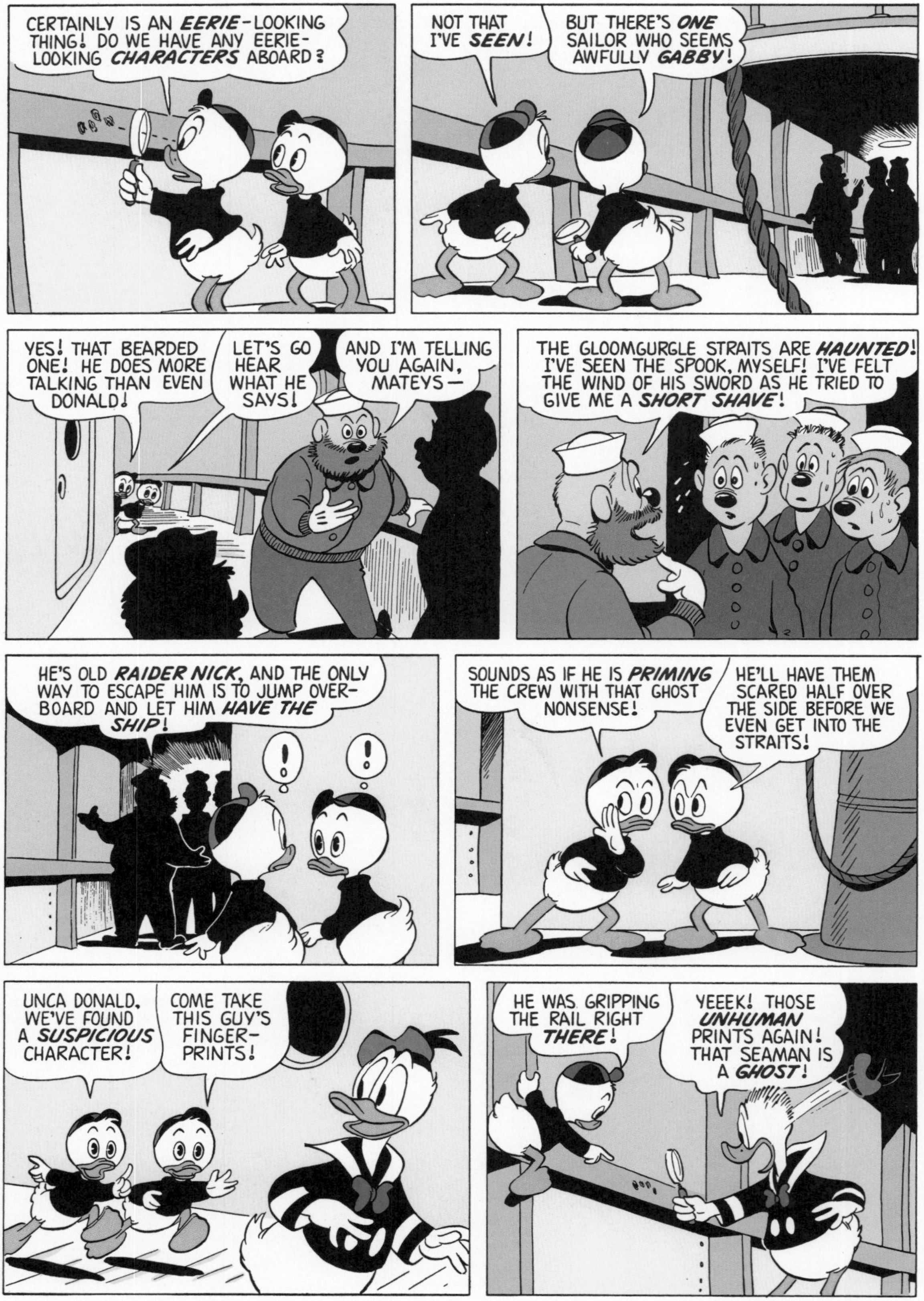
CERTAINLY IS AN EERIE-LOOKING THING! DO WE HAVE ANY EERIE-LOOKING CHARACTERS ABOARD?
NOT THAT I'VE SEEN!
BUT THERE'S ONE SAILOR WHO SEEMS AWFULLY GABBY!
YES! THAT BEARDED ONE! HE DOES MORE TALKING THAN EVEN DONALD!
LET'S GO HEAR WHAT HE SAYS!
AND I'M TELLING YOU AGAIN, MATEYS—
THE GLOOMGURGLE STRAITS ARE HAUNTED! I'VE SEEN THE SPOOK, MYSELF! I'VE FELT THE WIND OF HIS SWORD AS HE TRIED TO GIVE ME A SHORT SHAVE!
HE'S OLD RAIDER NICK, AND THE ONLY WAY TO ESCAPE HIM IS TO JUMP OVER-BOARD AND LET HIM HAVE THE SHIP!
!
!
SOUNDS AS IF HE IS PRIMING THE CREW WITH THAT GHOST NONSENSE!
HE'LL HAVE THEM SCARED HALF OVER THE SIDE BEFORE WE EVEN GET INTO THE STRAITS!
UNCA DONALD, WE'VE FOUND A SUSPICIOUS CHARACTER!
COME TAKE THIS GUY'S FINGER-PRINTS!
HE WAS GRIPPING THE RAIL RIGHT THERE!
YEEEK! THOSE UNHUMAN PRINTS AGAIN! THAT SEAMAN IS A GHOST!

MALARKEY! HE'S JUST A *LEGPULLER* WHO WEARS SOME KIND OF *PLASTIC GLOVES!*

AND I'M TELLING YOU AGAIN, MATEYS—

*S*O—

SEE, UNCA DONALD?

I SURE DO! THIS CASE IS SOLVED! ALL I HAVE TO DO NOW IS *WATCH* THAT GUY!

*B*ACK AT THE LIGHT-HOUSE!

I'M GOING TO TAKE *MY* SHARE OF TONIGHT'S HAUL AND BUILD *GOLD KENNELS* FOR MY WOLF PACKS!

I'M GOING TO BUILD A *GOLD HENHOUSE* WITH MINE—WHERE MY FOXES CAN PRACTICE CHICKEN STEALING!

176-176

BEAGLE BOYS

176-617

176-671

I'M GOING TO BUILD A *GOLD CHAIR* WITH MINE! ONE I CAN FINISH MY DAYS IN— *WARM* AND COMFY!

YOU'LL FINISH YOUR DAYS IN A *WARM* CHAIR, ALL RIGHT— WITH A BUILT-IN *HEATING* SYSTEM!

176-671

BEAGLE BOYS INC.

176-167

BEAGLE BOYS INC.

I'M GOING TO BUILD—

AND *I'M* GOING TO BUILD THE BIGGEST *HEADACHE* IN THE NORTH PACIFIC IF I HAVE TO LISTEN TO THIS HOGWASH TILL TEN O'CLOCK!

176-716

BEAGLE BOYS INC.

*T*EN O'CLOCK FINALLY COMES!

RAIDER NICK'S REEF LIGHT OFF THE STARBOARD BOW, CAP'N!

FINE! PROCEED SLOWLY THROUGH THE STRAIT, WATCH-ING CLOSELY FOR ANY—AH-*UNUSUAL* OBSTACLES!

SOMETHING'S *WRONG!* LOUIE WAS SUPPOSED TO SIGNAL US WITH HIS FLASHLIGHT FROM THE ROCKS!

BUT NOT A BLINK!

DO YOU THINK WE HAD BETTER *ROW ASHORE* AND SEE WHAT'S UP?

I *KNOW* WE HAD BETTER! I CAN FEEL *TROUBLE* IN MY BONES!

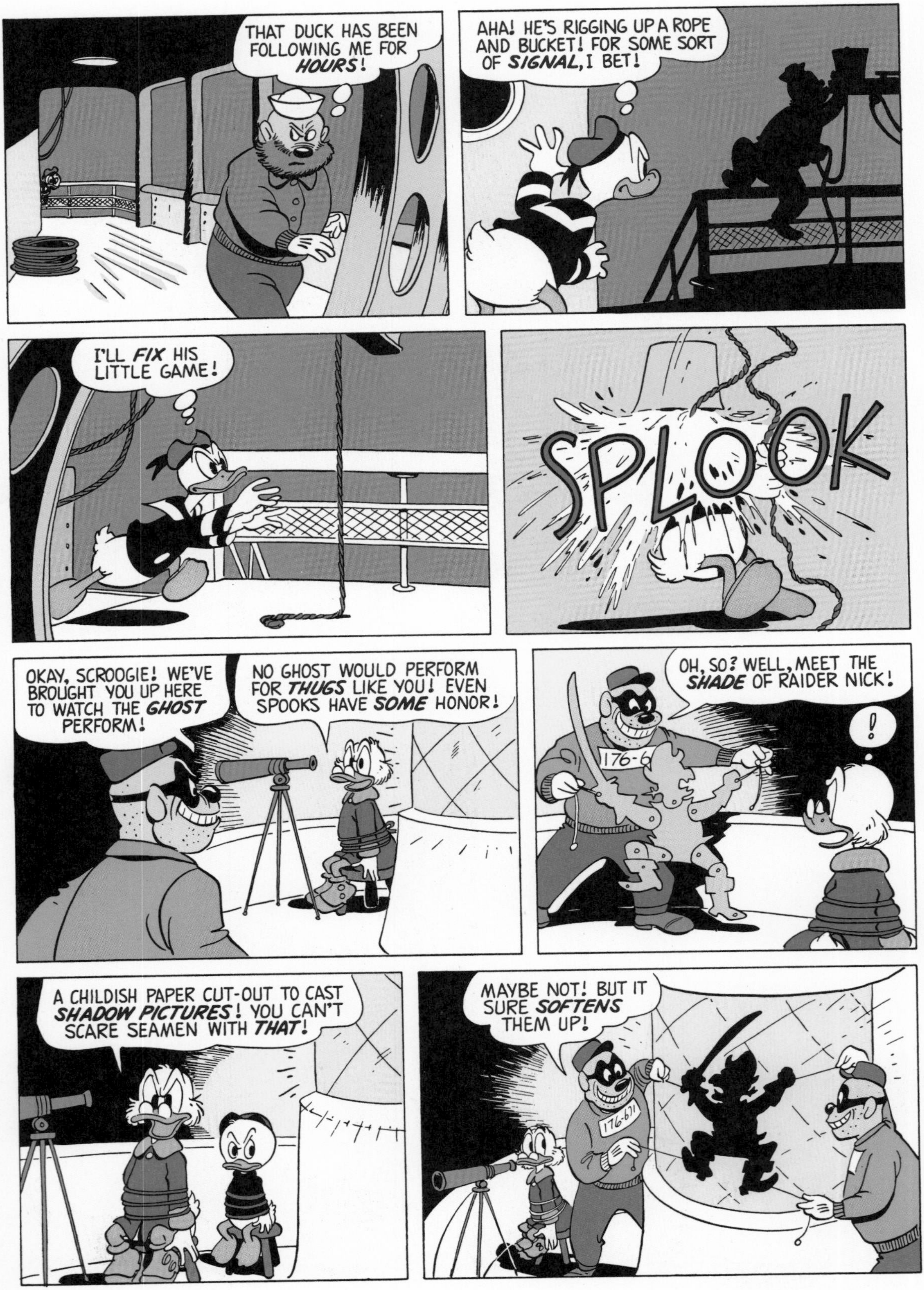
THAT DUCK HAS BEEN FOLLOWING ME FOR HOURS!
AHA! HE'S RIGGING UP A ROPE AND BUCKET! FOR SOME SORT OF SIGNAL, I BET!
I'LL FIX HIS LITTLE GAME!
SPLOOK
OKAY, SCROOGIE! WE'VE BROUGHT YOU UP HERE TO WATCH THE GHOST PERFORM!
NO GHOST WOULD PERFORM FOR THUGS LIKE YOU! EVEN SPOOKS HAVE SOME HONOR!
OH, SO? WELL, MEET THE SHADE OF RAIDER NICK!
176-6
!
A CHILDISH PAPER CUT-OUT TO CAST SHADOW PICTURES! YOU CAN'T SCARE SEAMEN WITH THAT!
MAYBE NOT! BUT IT SURE SOFTENS THEM UP!
176-671

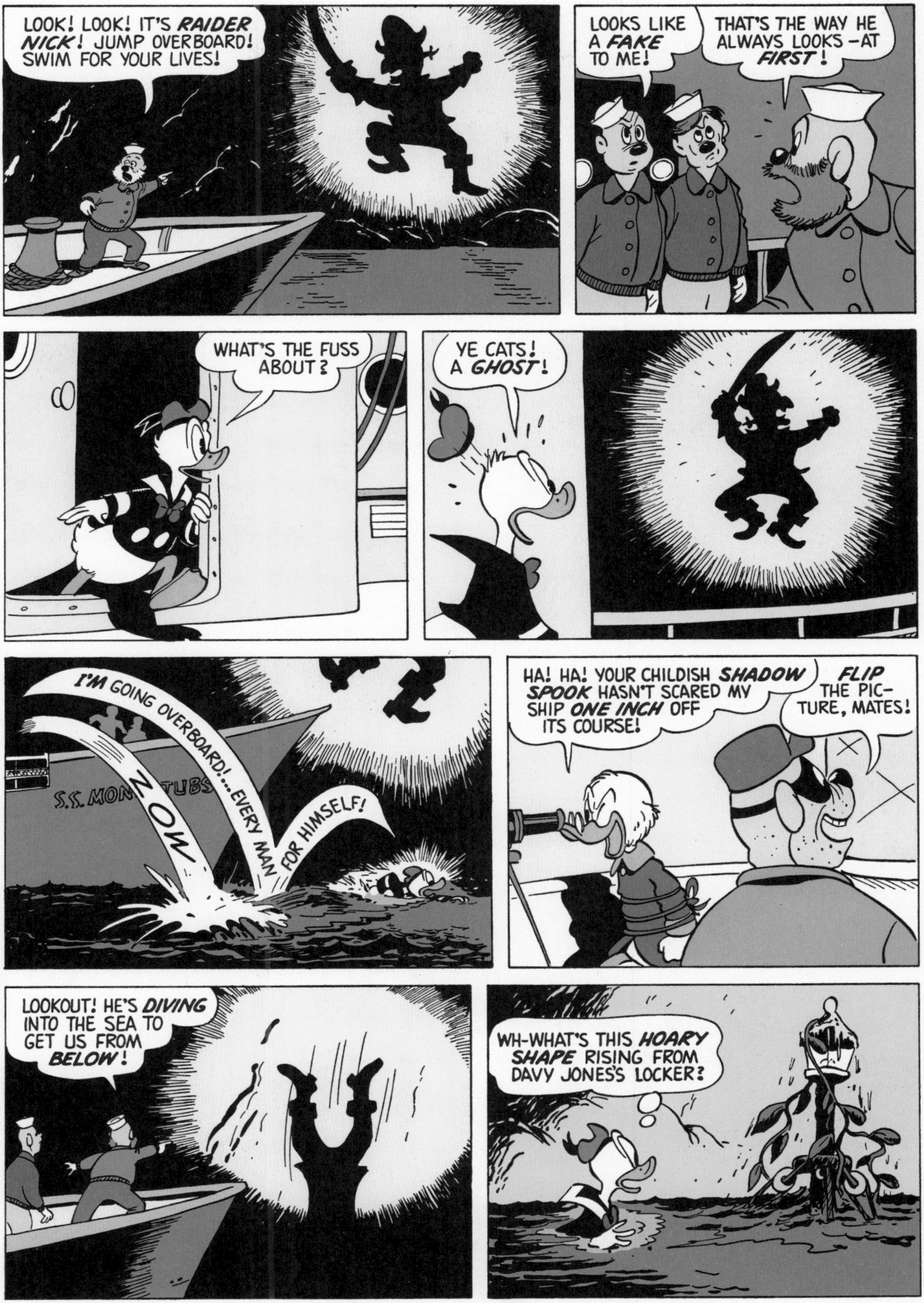
LOOK! LOOK! IT'S RAIDER NICK! JUMP OVERBOARD! SWIM FOR YOUR LIVES!
LOOKS LIKE A FAKE TO ME!
THAT'S THE WAY HE ALWAYS LOOKS —AT FIRST!
WHAT'S THE FUSS ABOUT?
YE CATS! A GHOST!
I'M GOING OVERBOARD!... EVERY MAN FOR HIMSELF!
ZOW
HA! HA! YOUR CHILDISH SHADOW SPOOK HASN'T SCARED MY SHIP ONE INCH OFF ITS COURSE!
FLIP THE PIC-TURE, MATES!
LOOKOUT! HE'S DIVING INTO THE SEA TO GET US FROM BELOW!
WH-WHAT'S THIS HOARY SHAPE RISING FROM DAVY JONES'S LOCKER?

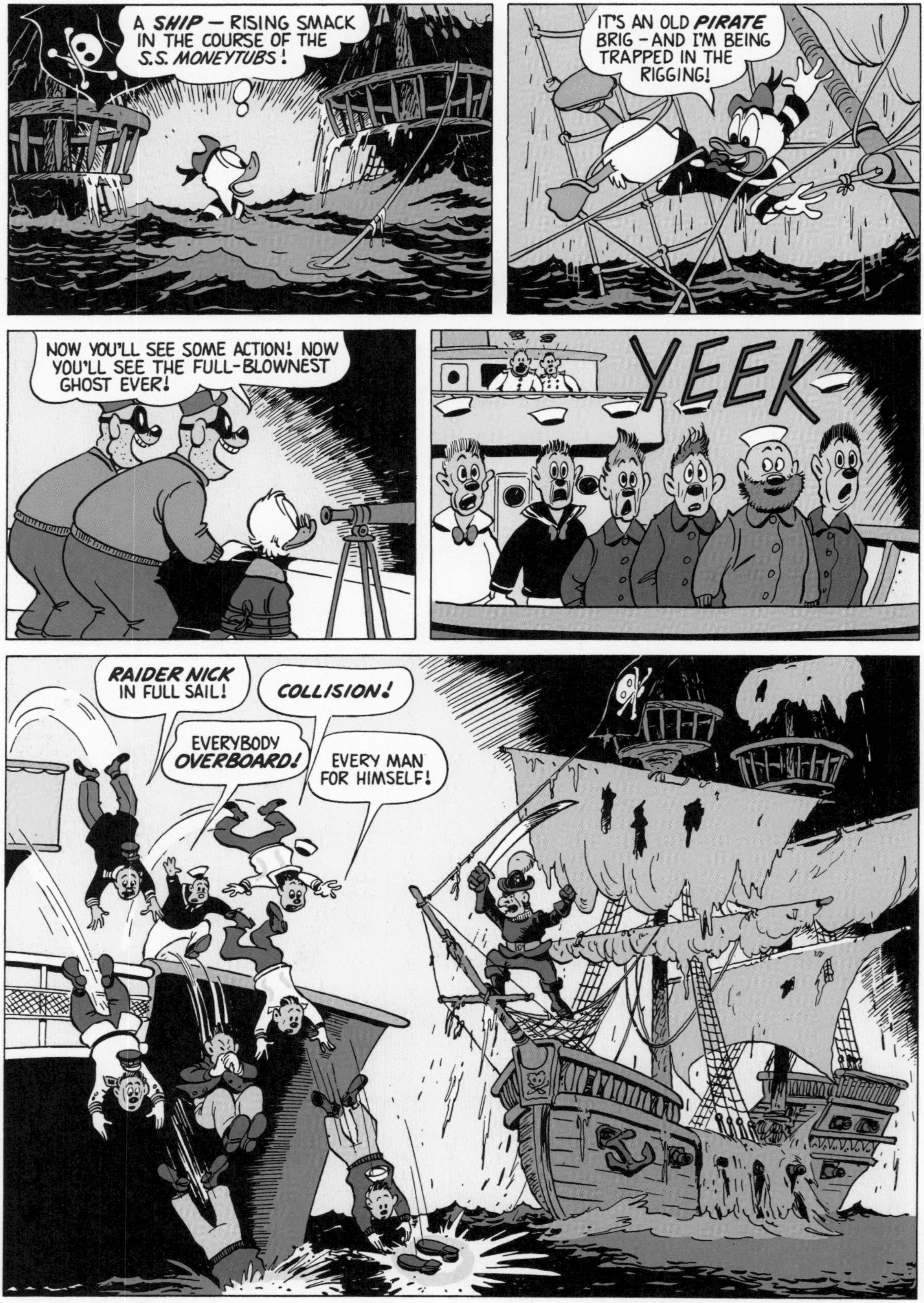
A SHIP — RISING SMACK IN THE COURSE OF THE S.S. MONEYTUBS!
IT'S AN OLD PIRATE BRIG – AND I'M BEING TRAPPED IN THE RIGGING!
NOW YOU'LL SEE SOME ACTION! NOW YOU'LL SEE THE FULL-BLOWNEST GHOST EVER!
YEEK
RAIDER NICK IN FULL SAIL!
COLLISION!
EVERYBODY OVERBOARD!
EVERY MAN FOR HIMSELF!

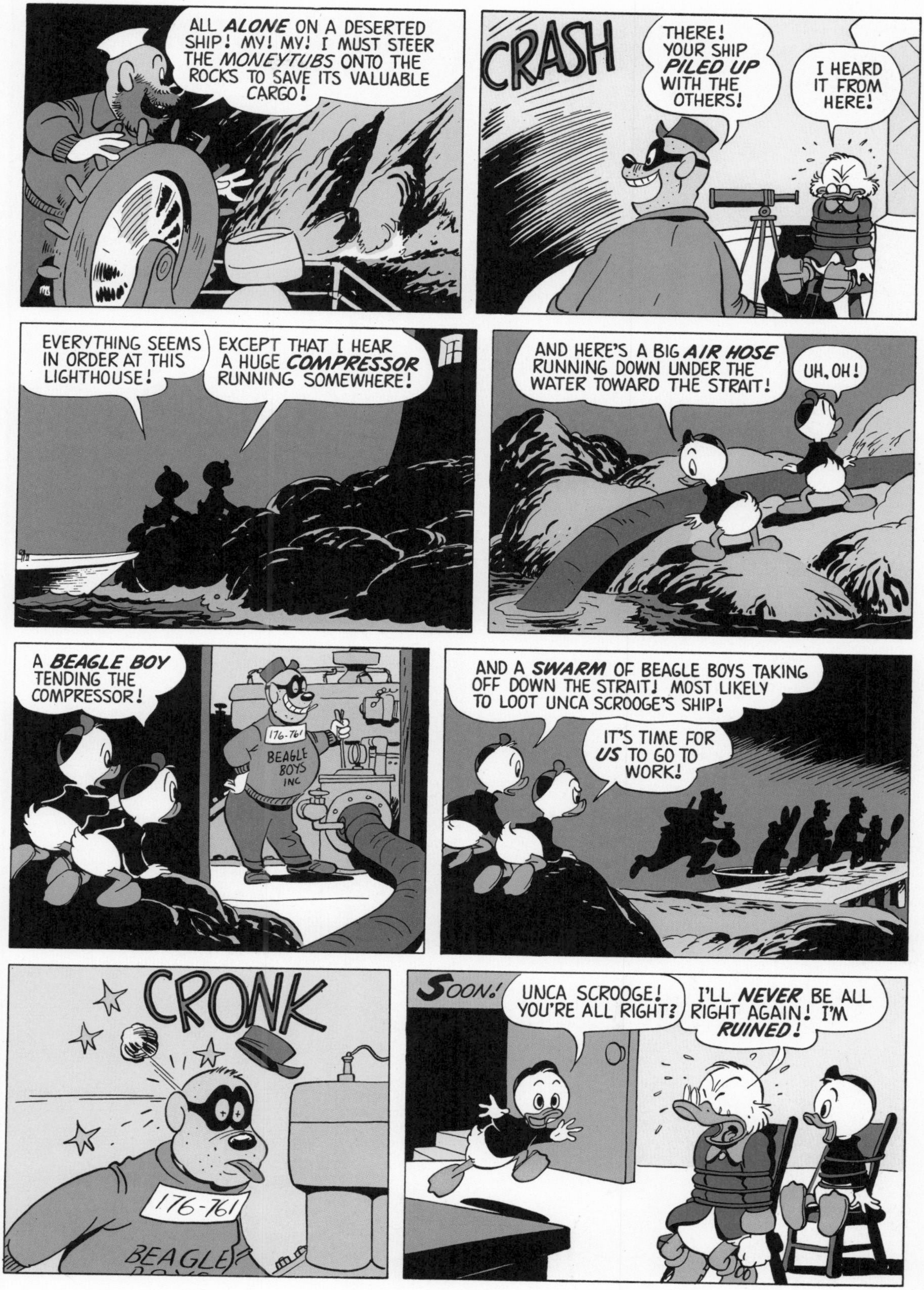
ALL ALONE ON A DESERTED SHIP! MY! MY! I MUST STEER THE MONEYTUBS ONTO THE ROCKS TO SAVE ITS VALUABLE CARGO!
CRASH
THERE! YOUR SHIP PILED UP WITH THE OTHERS!
I HEARD IT FROM HERE!
EVERYTHING SEEMS IN ORDER AT THIS LIGHTHOUSE!
EXCEPT THAT I HEAR A HUGE COMPRESSOR RUNNING SOMEWHERE!
AND HERE'S A BIG AIR HOSE RUNNING DOWN UNDER THE WATER TOWARD THE STRAIT!
UH, OH!
A BEAGLE BOY TENDING THE COMPRESSOR!
176-761
BEAGLE BOYS INC
AND A SWARM OF BEAGLE BOYS TAKING OFF DOWN THE STRAIT! MOST LIKELY TO LOOT UNCA SCROOGE'S SHIP!
IT'S TIME FOR US TO GO TO WORK!
CRONK
176-761
BEAGLE
SOON!
UNCA SCROOGE! YOU'RE ALL RIGHT?
I'LL NEVER BE ALL RIGHT AGAIN! I'M RUINED!

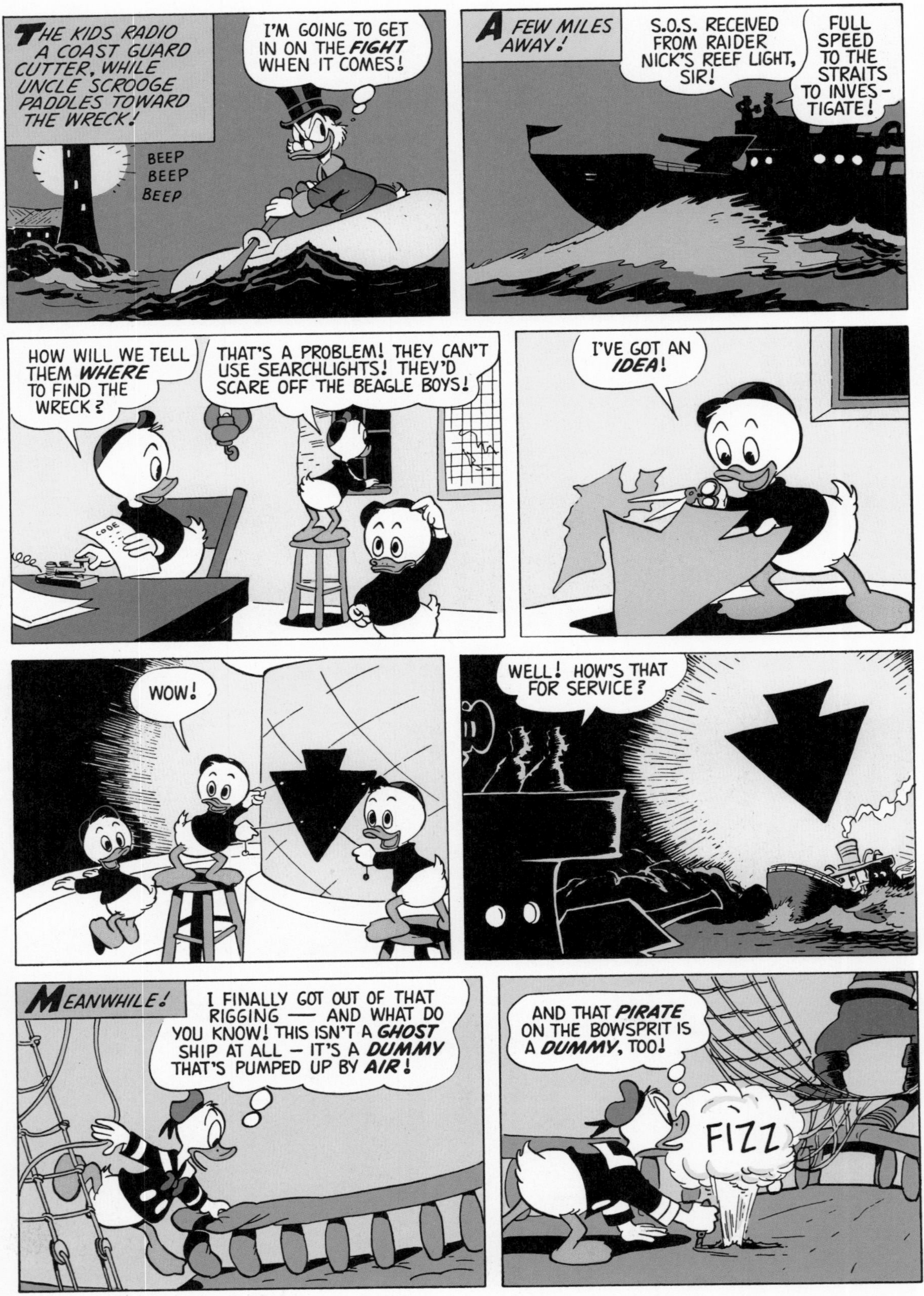
THE KIDS RADIO A COAST GUARD CUTTER, WHILE UNCLE SCROOGE PADDLES TOWARD THE WRECK!
I'M GOING TO GET IN ON THE FIGHT WHEN IT COMES!
BEEP BEEP BEEP
A FEW MILES AWAY!
S.O.S. RECEIVED FROM RAIDER NICK'S REEF LIGHT, SIR!
FULL SPEED TO THE STRAITS TO INVES-TIGATE!
HOW WILL WE TELL THEM WHERE TO FIND THE WRECK?
THAT'S A PROBLEM! THEY CAN'T USE SEARCHLIGHTS! THEY'D SCARE OFF THE BEAGLE BOYS!
CODE
I'VE GOT AN IDEA!
WOW!
WELL! HOW'S THAT FOR SERVICE?
MEANWHILE!
I FINALLY GOT OUT OF THAT RIGGING — AND WHAT DO YOU KNOW! THIS ISN'T A GHOST SHIP AT ALL – IT'S A DUMMY THAT'S PUMPED UP BY AIR!
AND THAT PIRATE ON THE BOWSPRIT IS A DUMMY, TOO!
FIZZ

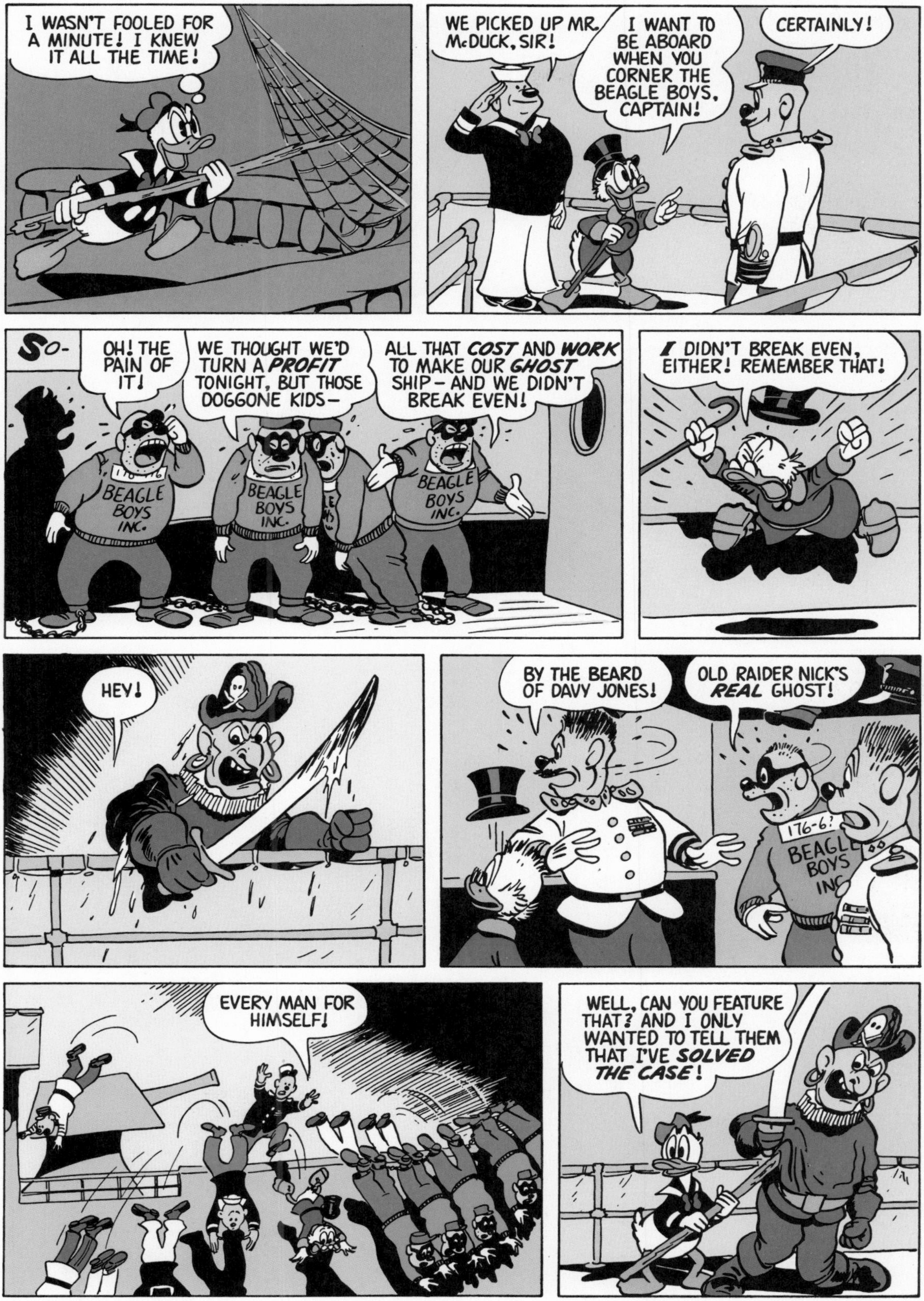
I WASN'T FOOLED FOR A MINUTE! I KNEW IT ALL THE TIME!
WE PICKED UP MR. McDUCK, SIR!
I WANT TO BE ABOARD WHEN YOU CORNER THE BEAGLE BOYS, CAPTAIN!
CERTAINLY!
SO-
OH! THE PAIN OF IT!
WE THOUGHT WE'D TURN A PROFIT TONIGHT, BUT THOSE DOGGONE KIDS—
ALL THAT COST AND WORK TO MAKE OUR GHOST SHIP — AND WE DIDN'T BREAK EVEN!
BEAGLE BOYS INC.
I DIDN'T BREAK EVEN, EITHER! REMEMBER THAT!
HEY!
BY THE BEARD OF DAVY JONES!
OLD RAIDER NICK'S REAL GHOST!
176-67
BEAGLE BOYS INC
EVERY MAN FOR HIMSELF!
WELL, CAN YOU FEATURE THAT? AND I ONLY WANTED TO TELL THEM THAT I'VE SOLVED THE CASE!

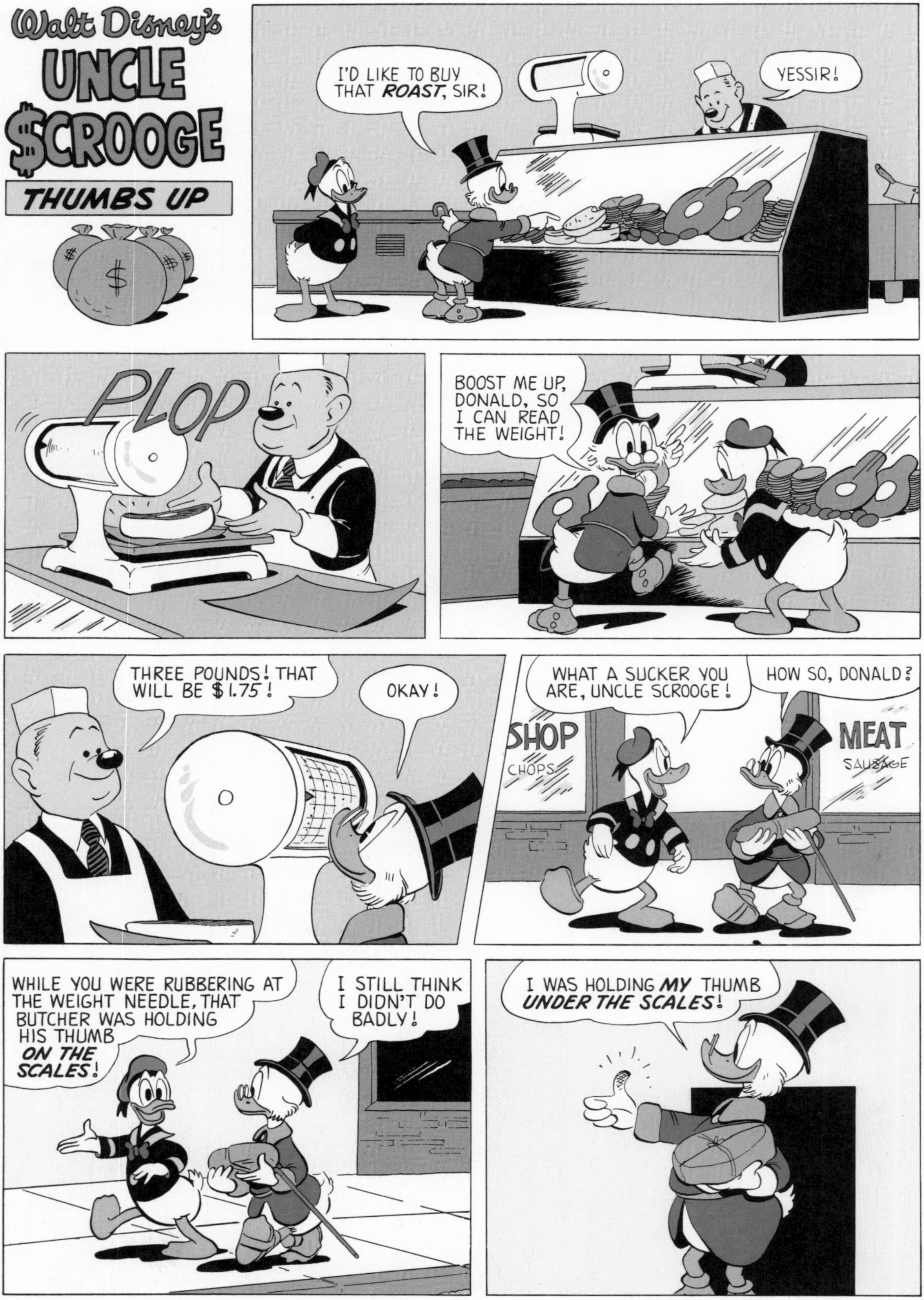
Walt Disney's
UNCLE $CROOGE
THUMBS UP
I'D LIKE TO BUY THAT ROAST, SIR!
YESSIR!
PLOP
BOOST ME UP, DONALD, SO I CAN READ THE WEIGHT!
THREE POUNDS! THAT WILL BE $1.75!
OKAY!
WHAT A SUCKER YOU ARE, UNCLE SCROOGE!
HOW SO, DONALD?
SHOP
CHOPS
MEAT
SAUSAGE
WHILE YOU WERE RUBBERING AT THE WEIGHT NEEDLE, THAT BUTCHER WAS HOLDING HIS THUMB ON THE SCALES!
I STILL THINK I DIDN'T DO BADLY!
I WAS HOLDING MY THUMB UNDER THE SCALES!

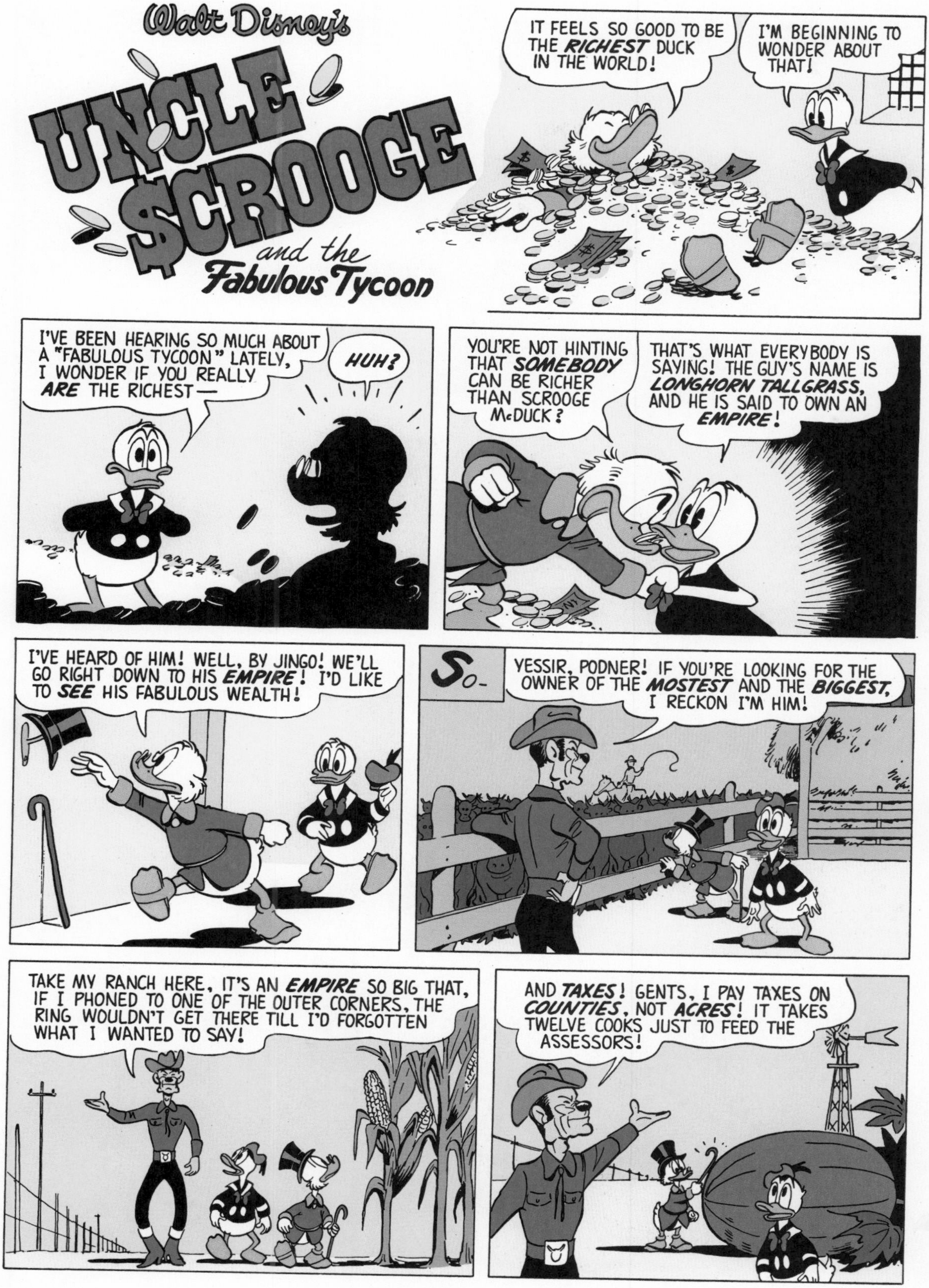
Walt Disney's
UNCLE $CROOGE
and the Fabulous Tycoon
IT FEELS SO GOOD TO BE THE RICHEST DUCK IN THE WORLD!
I'M BEGINNING TO WONDER ABOUT THAT!
I'VE BEEN HEARING SO MUCH ABOUT A "FABULOUS TYCOON" LATELY, I WONDER IF YOU REALLY ARE THE RICHEST—
HUH?
YOU'RE NOT HINTING THAT SOMEBODY CAN BE RICHER THAN SCROOGE McDUCK?
THAT'S WHAT EVERYBODY IS SAYING! THE GUY'S NAME IS LONGHORN TALLGRASS, AND HE IS SAID TO OWN AN EMPIRE!
I'VE HEARD OF HIM! WELL, BY JINGO! WE'LL GO RIGHT DOWN TO HIS EMPIRE! I'D LIKE TO SEE HIS FABULOUS WEALTH!
SO-
YESSIR, PODNER! IF YOU'RE LOOKING FOR THE OWNER OF THE MOSTEST AND THE BIGGEST, I RECKON I'M HIM!
TAKE MY RANCH HERE, IT'S AN EMPIRE SO BIG THAT, IF I PHONED TO ONE OF THE OUTER CORNERS, THE RING WOULDN'T GET THERE TILL I'D FORGOTTEN WHAT I WANTED TO SAY!
AND TAXES! GENTS, I PAY TAXES ON COUNTIES, NOT ACRES! IT TAKES TWELVE COOKS JUST TO FEED THE ASSESSORS!

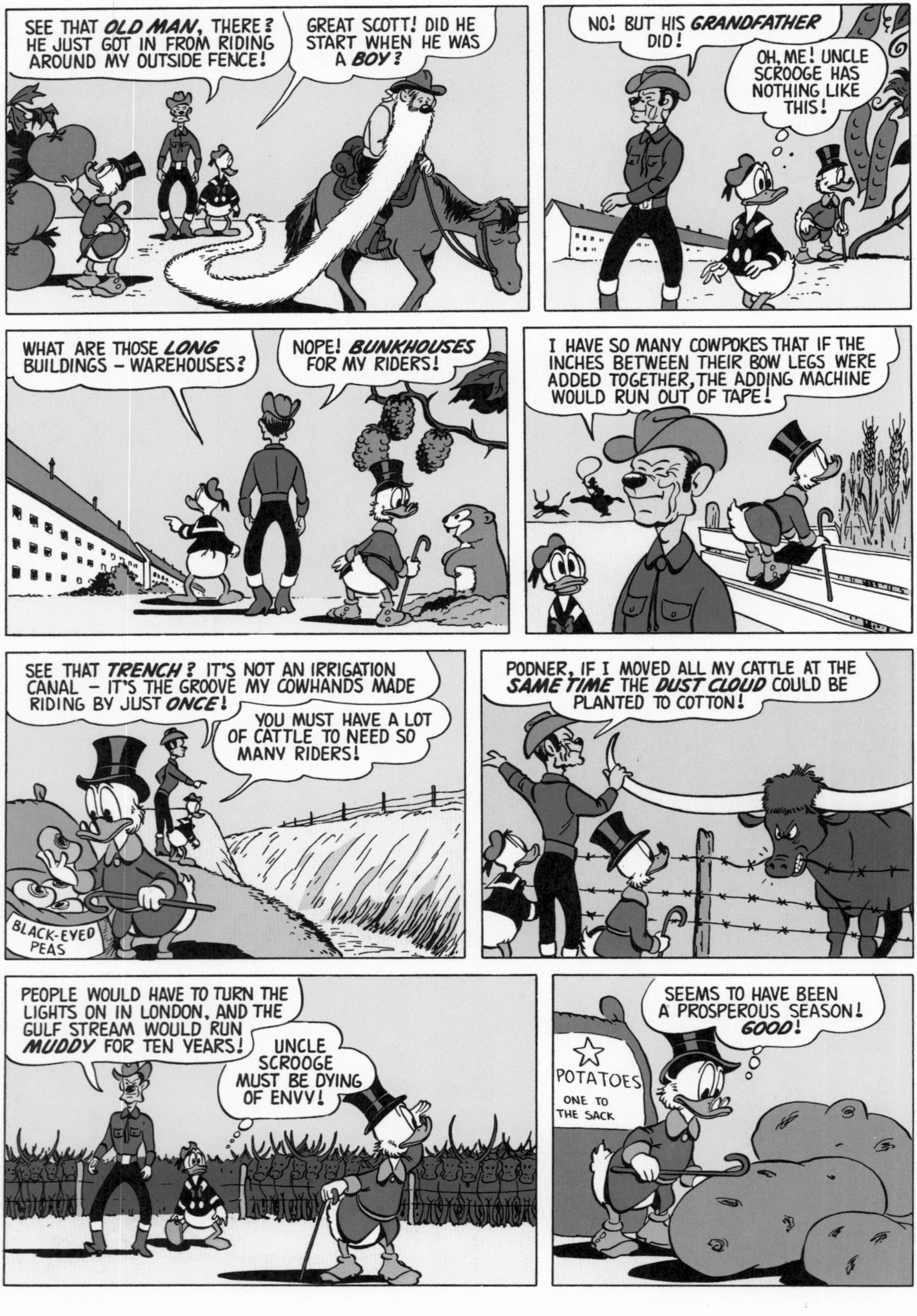

SEE THAT OLD MAN, THERE? HE JUST GOT IN FROM RIDING AROUND MY OUTSIDE FENCE!
GREAT SCOTT! DID HE START WHEN HE WAS A BOY?
NO! BUT HIS GRANDFATHER DID!
OH, ME! UNCLE SCROOGE HAS NOTHING LIKE THIS!
WHAT ARE THOSE LONG BUILDINGS – WAREHOUSES?
NOPE! BUNKHOUSES FOR MY RIDERS!
I HAVE SO MANY COWPOKES THAT IF THE INCHES BETWEEN THEIR BOW LEGS WERE ADDED TOGETHER, THE ADDING MACHINE WOULD RUN OUT OF TAPE!
SEE THAT TRENCH? IT'S NOT AN IRRIGATION CANAL – IT'S THE GROOVE MY COWHANDS MADE RIDING BY JUST ONCE!
YOU MUST HAVE A LOT OF CATTLE TO NEED SO MANY RIDERS!
BLACK-EYED PEAS
PODNER, IF I MOVED ALL MY CATTLE AT THE SAME TIME THE DUST CLOUD COULD BE PLANTED TO COTTON!
PEOPLE WOULD HAVE TO TURN THE LIGHTS ON IN LONDON, AND THE GULF STREAM WOULD RUN MUDDY FOR TEN YEARS!
UNCLE SCROOGE MUST BE DYING OF ENVY!
SEEMS TO HAVE BEEN A PROSPEROUS SEASON! GOOD!
POTATOES
ONE TO THE SACK

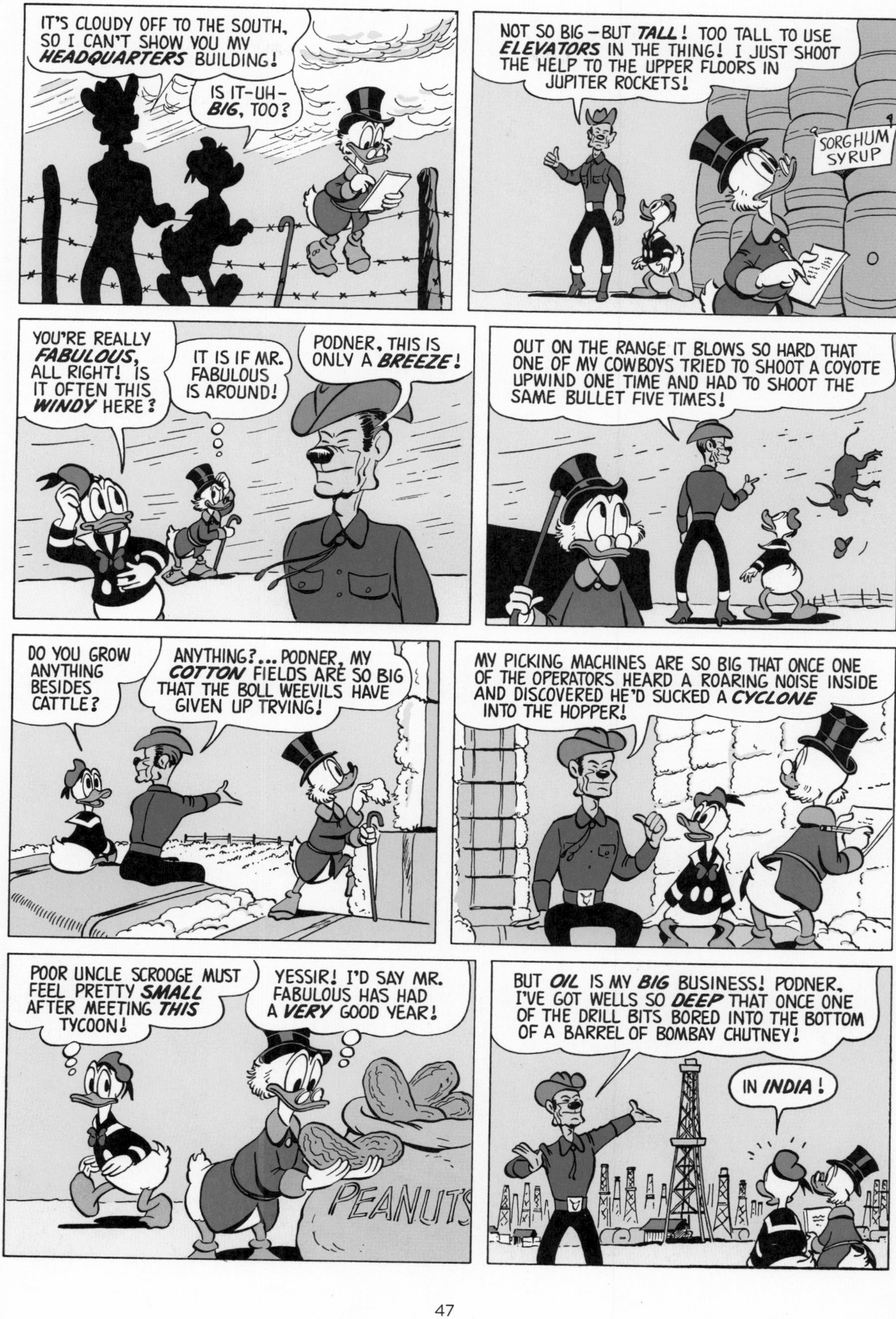

IT'S CLOUDY OFF TO THE SOUTH, SO I CAN'T SHOW YOU MY HEADQUARTERS BUILDING!
IS IT-UH-BIG, TOO?
NOT SO BIG—BUT TALL! TOO TALL TO USE ELEVATORS IN THE THING! I JUST SHOOT THE HELP TO THE UPPER FLOORS IN JUPITER ROCKETS!
SORGHUM SYRUP
YOU'RE REALLY FABULOUS, ALL RIGHT! IS IT OFTEN THIS WINDY HERE?
IT IS IF MR. FABULOUS IS AROUND!
PODNER, THIS IS ONLY A BREEZE!
OUT ON THE RANGE IT BLOWS SO HARD THAT ONE OF MY COWBOYS TRIED TO SHOOT A COYOTE UPWIND ONE TIME AND HAD TO SHOOT THE SAME BULLET FIVE TIMES!
DO YOU GROW ANYTHING BESIDES CATTLE?
ANYTHING?... PODNER, MY COTTON FIELDS ARE SO BIG THAT THE BOLL WEEVILS HAVE GIVEN UP TRYING!
MY PICKING MACHINES ARE SO BIG THAT ONCE ONE OF THE OPERATORS HEARD A ROARING NOISE INSIDE AND DISCOVERED HE'D SUCKED A CYCLONE INTO THE HOPPER!
POOR UNCLE SCROOGE MUST FEEL PRETTY SMALL AFTER MEETING THIS TYCOON!
YESSIR! I'D SAY MR. FABULOUS HAS HAD A VERY GOOD YEAR!
PEANUTS
BUT OIL IS MY BIG BUSINESS! PODNER, I'VE GOT WELLS SO DEEP THAT ONCE ONE OF THE DRILL BITS BORED INTO THE BOTTOM OF A BARREL OF BOMBAY CHUTNEY!
IN INDIA!

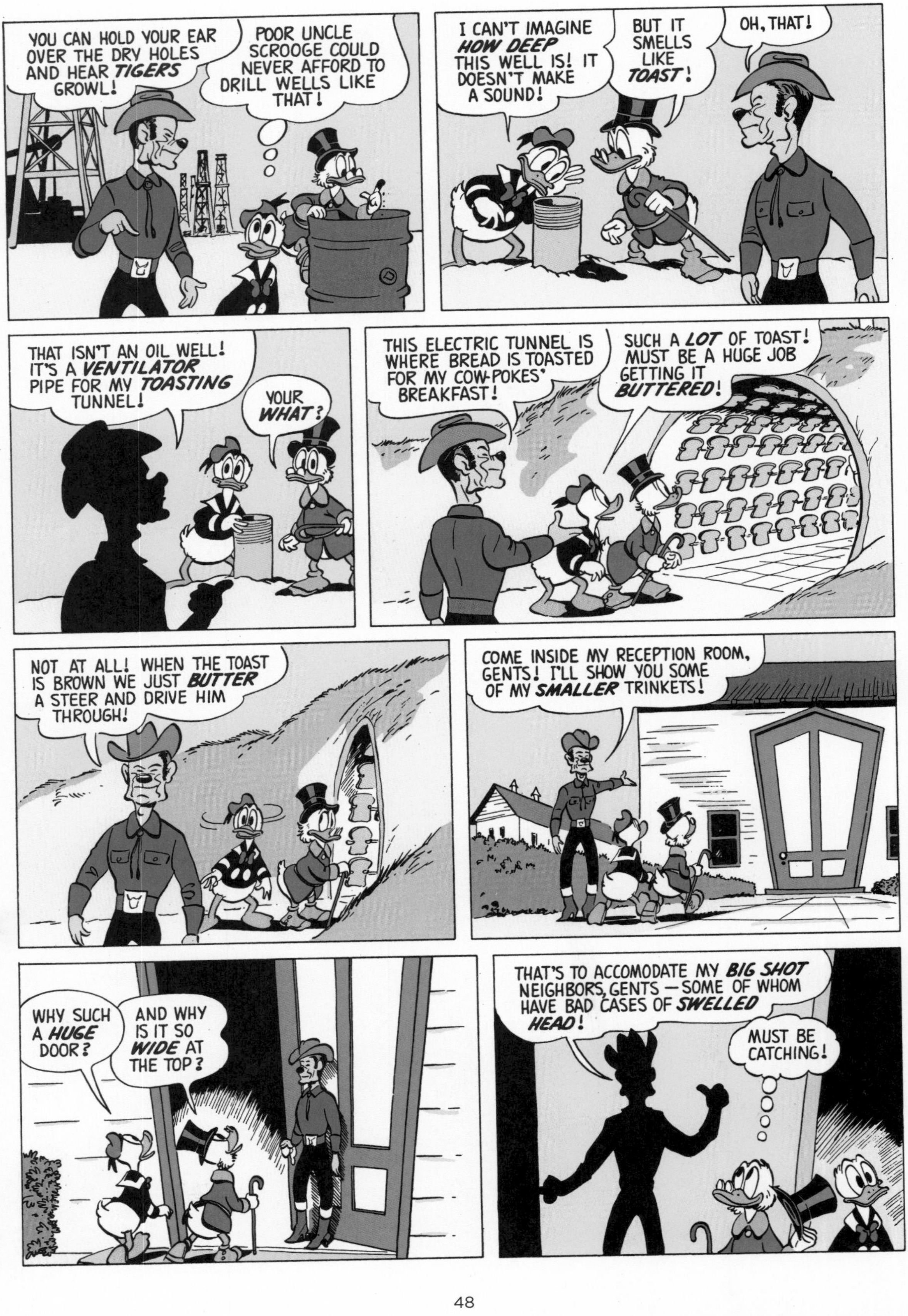

YOU CAN HOLD YOUR EAR OVER THE DRY HOLES AND HEAR TIGERS GROWL!
POOR UNCLE SCROOGE COULD NEVER AFFORD TO DRILL WELLS LIKE THAT!
I CAN'T IMAGINE HOW DEEP THIS WELL IS! IT DOESN'T MAKE A SOUND!
BUT IT SMELLS LIKE TOAST!
OH, THAT!
THAT ISN'T AN OIL WELL! IT'S A VENTILATOR PIPE FOR MY TOASTING TUNNEL!
YOUR WHAT?
THIS ELECTRIC TUNNEL IS WHERE BREAD IS TOASTED FOR MY COW-POKES' BREAKFAST!
SUCH A LOT OF TOAST! MUST BE A HUGE JOB GETTING IT BUTTERED!
NOT AT ALL! WHEN THE TOAST IS BROWN WE JUST BUTTER A STEER AND DRIVE HIM THROUGH!
COME INSIDE MY RECEPTION ROOM, GENTS! I'LL SHOW YOU SOME OF MY SMALLER TRINKETS!
WHY SUCH A HUGE DOOR?
AND WHY IS IT SO WIDE AT THE TOP?
THAT'S TO ACCOMODATE MY BIG SHOT NEIGHBORS, GENTS — SOME OF WHOM HAVE BAD CASES OF SWELLED HEAD!
MUST BE CATCHING!

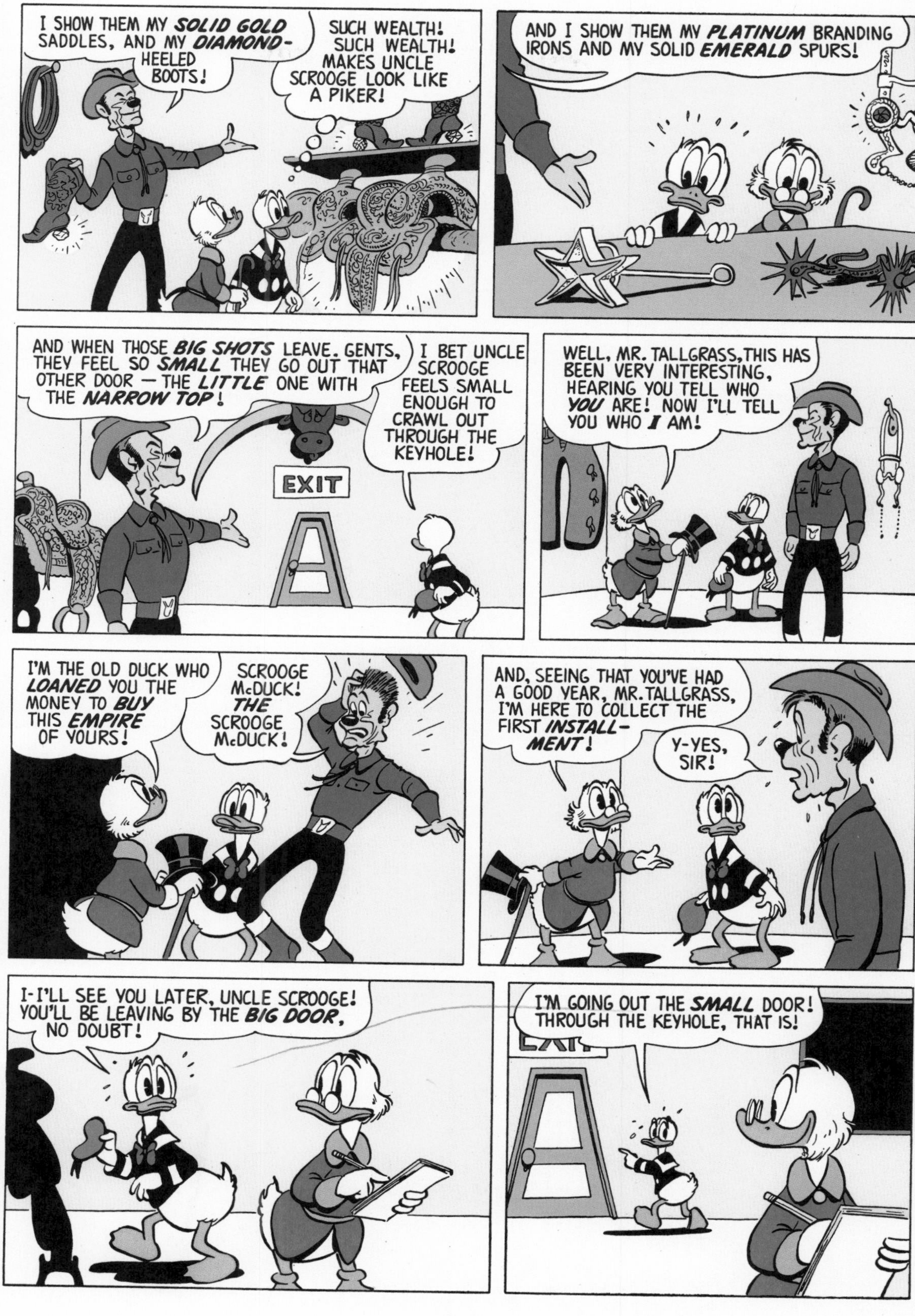
I SHOW THEM MY SOLID GOLD SADDLES, AND MY DIAMOND-HEELED BOOTS!
SUCH WEALTH! SUCH WEALTH! MAKES UNCLE SCROOGE LOOK LIKE A PIKER!
AND I SHOW THEM MY PLATINUM BRANDING IRONS AND MY SOLID EMERALD SPURS!
AND WHEN THOSE BIG SHOTS LEAVE. GENTS, THEY FEEL SO SMALL THEY GO OUT THAT OTHER DOOR — THE LITTLE ONE WITH THE NARROW TOP!
I BET UNCLE SCROOGE FEELS SMALL ENOUGH TO CRAWL OUT THROUGH THE KEYHOLE!
EXIT
WELL, MR. TALLGRASS, THIS HAS BEEN VERY INTERESTING, HEARING YOU TELL WHO YOU ARE! NOW I'LL TELL YOU WHO I AM!
I'M THE OLD DUCK WHO LOANED YOU THE MONEY TO BUY THIS EMPIRE OF YOURS!
SCROOGE McDUCK! THE SCROOGE McDUCK!
AND, SEEING THAT YOU'VE HAD A GOOD YEAR, MR. TALLGRASS, I'M HERE TO COLLECT THE FIRST INSTALL-MENT!
Y-YES, SIR!
I-I'LL SEE YOU LATER, UNCLE SCROOGE! YOU'LL BE LEAVING BY THE BIG DOOR, NO DOUBT!
I'M GOING OUT THE SMALL DOOR! THROUGH THE KEYHOLE, THAT IS!

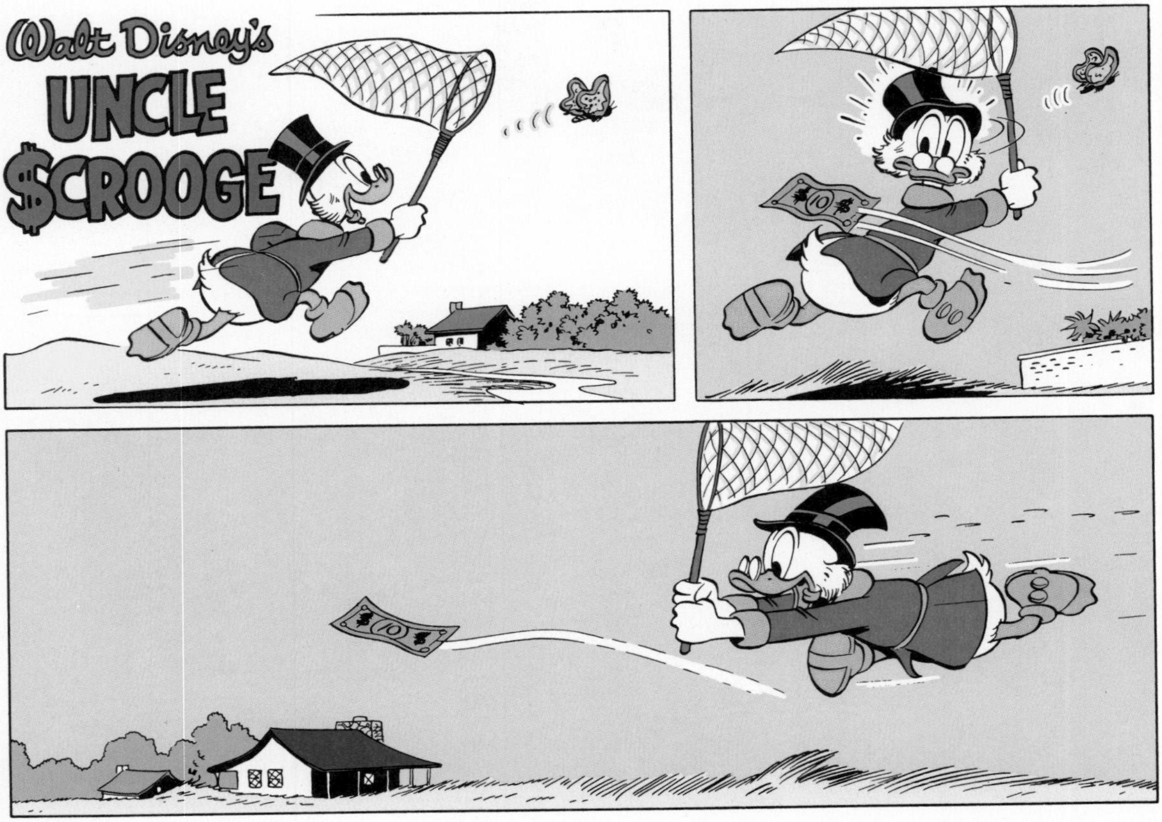
Walt Disney's
UNCLE
$CROOGE

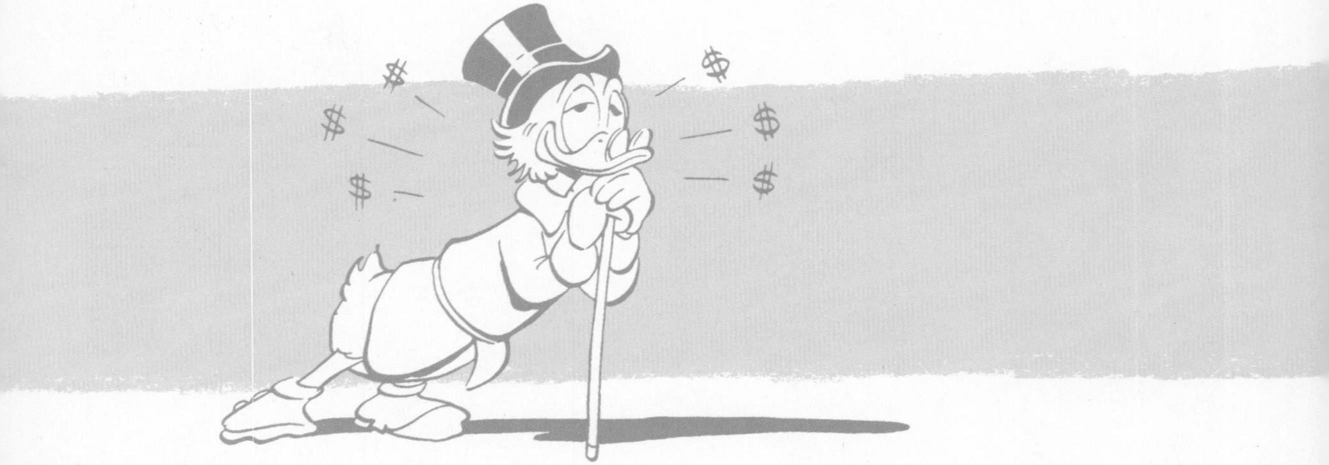

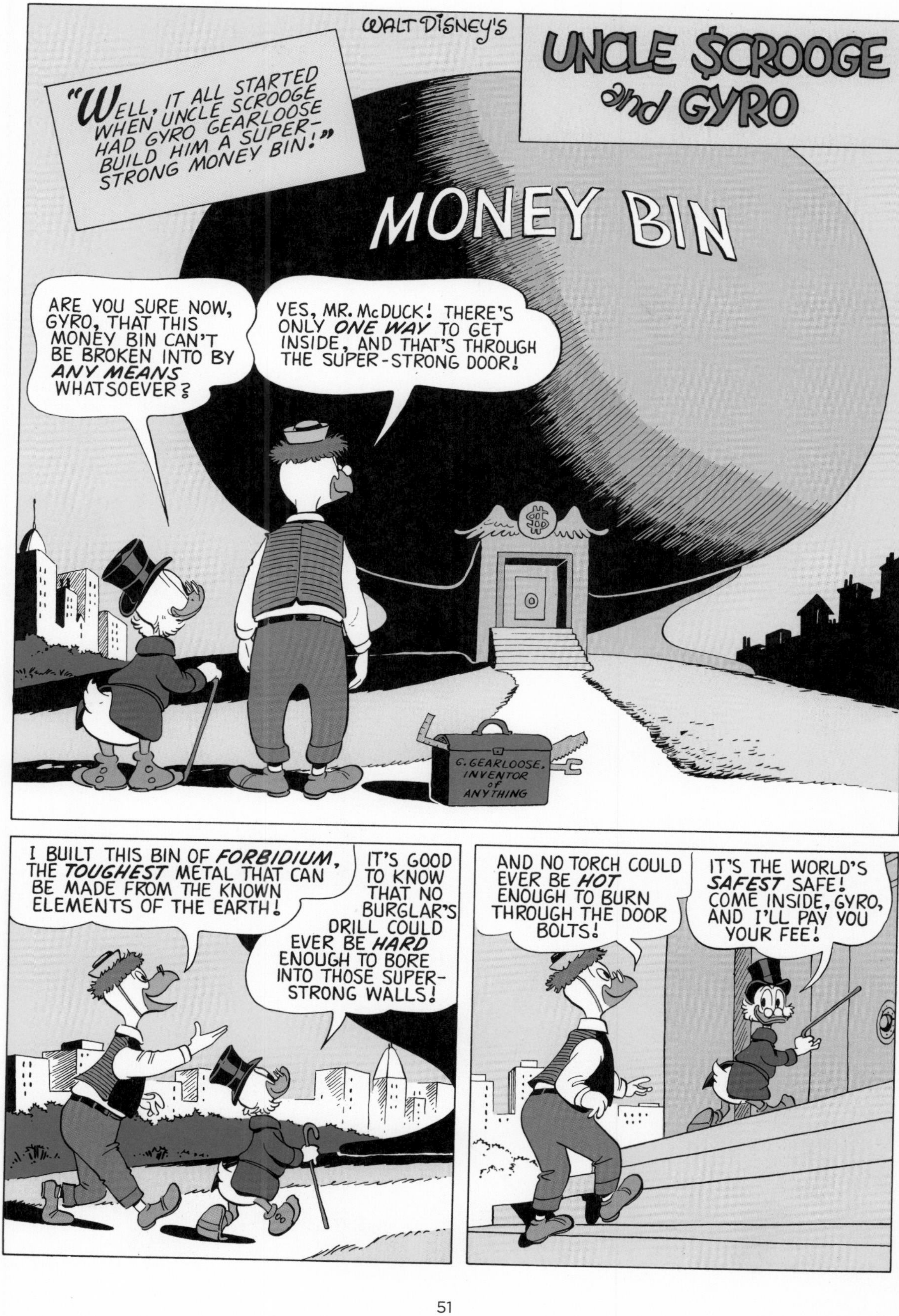

WALT DISNEY'S
UNCLE $CROOGE and GYRO
"WELL, IT ALL STARTED WHEN UNCLE SCROOGE HAD GYRO GEARLOOSE BUILD HIM A SUPER-STRONG MONEY BIN!"
MONEY BIN
ARE YOU SURE NOW, GYRO, THAT THIS MONEY BIN CAN'T BE BROKEN INTO BY ANY MEANS WHATSOEVER?
YES, MR. McDUCK! THERE'S ONLY ONE WAY TO GET INSIDE, AND THAT'S THROUGH THE SUPER-STRONG DOOR!
G. GEARLOOSE, INVENTOR of ANYTHING
I BUILT THIS BIN OF FORBIDIUM, THE TOUGHEST METAL THAT CAN BE MADE FROM THE KNOWN ELEMENTS OF THE EARTH!
IT'S GOOD TO KNOW THAT NO BURGLAR'S DRILL COULD EVER BE HARD ENOUGH TO BORE INTO THOSE SUPER-STRONG WALLS!
AND NO TORCH COULD EVER BE HOT ENOUGH TO BURN THROUGH THE DOOR BOLTS!
IT'S THE WORLD'S SAFEST SAFE! COME INSIDE, GYRO, AND I'LL PAY YOU YOUR FEE!

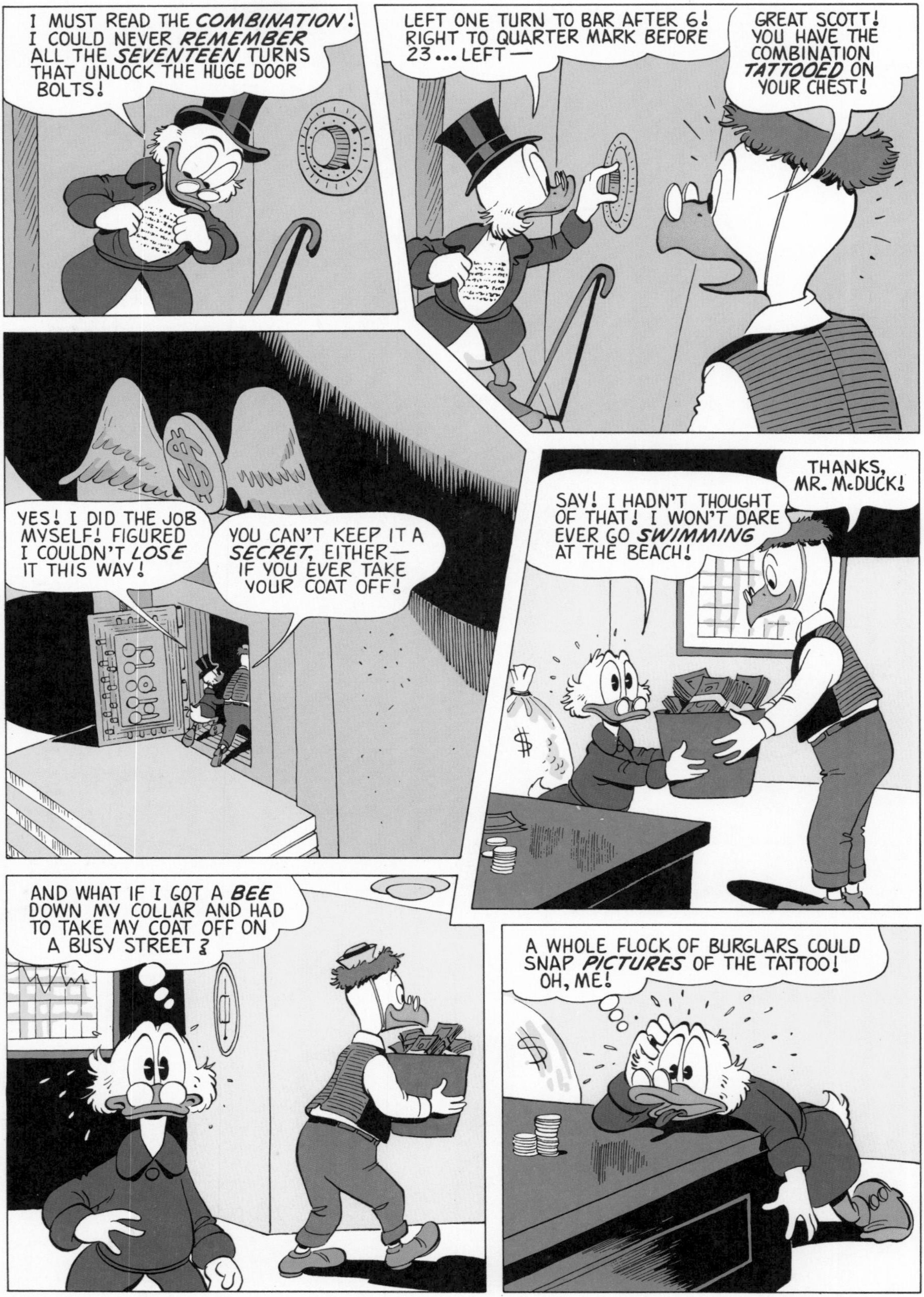
I MUST READ THE COMBINATION! I COULD NEVER REMEMBER ALL THE SEVENTEEN TURNS THAT UNLOCK THE HUGE DOOR BOLTS!
LEFT ONE TURN TO BAR AFTER 6! RIGHT TO QUARTER MARK BEFORE 23... LEFT—
GREAT SCOTT! YOU HAVE THE COMBINATION TATTOOED ON YOUR CHEST!
YES! I DID THE JOB MYSELF! FIGURED I COULDN'T LOSE IT THIS WAY!
YOU CAN'T KEEP IT A SECRET, EITHER— IF YOU EVER TAKE YOUR COAT OFF!
SAY! I HADN'T THOUGHT OF THAT! I WON'T DARE EVER GO SWIMMING AT THE BEACH!
THANKS, MR. McDUCK!
AND WHAT IF I GOT A BEE DOWN MY COLLAR AND HAD TO TAKE MY COAT OFF ON A BUSY STREET?
A WHOLE FLOCK OF BURGLARS COULD SNAP PICTURES OF THE TATTOO! OH, ME!

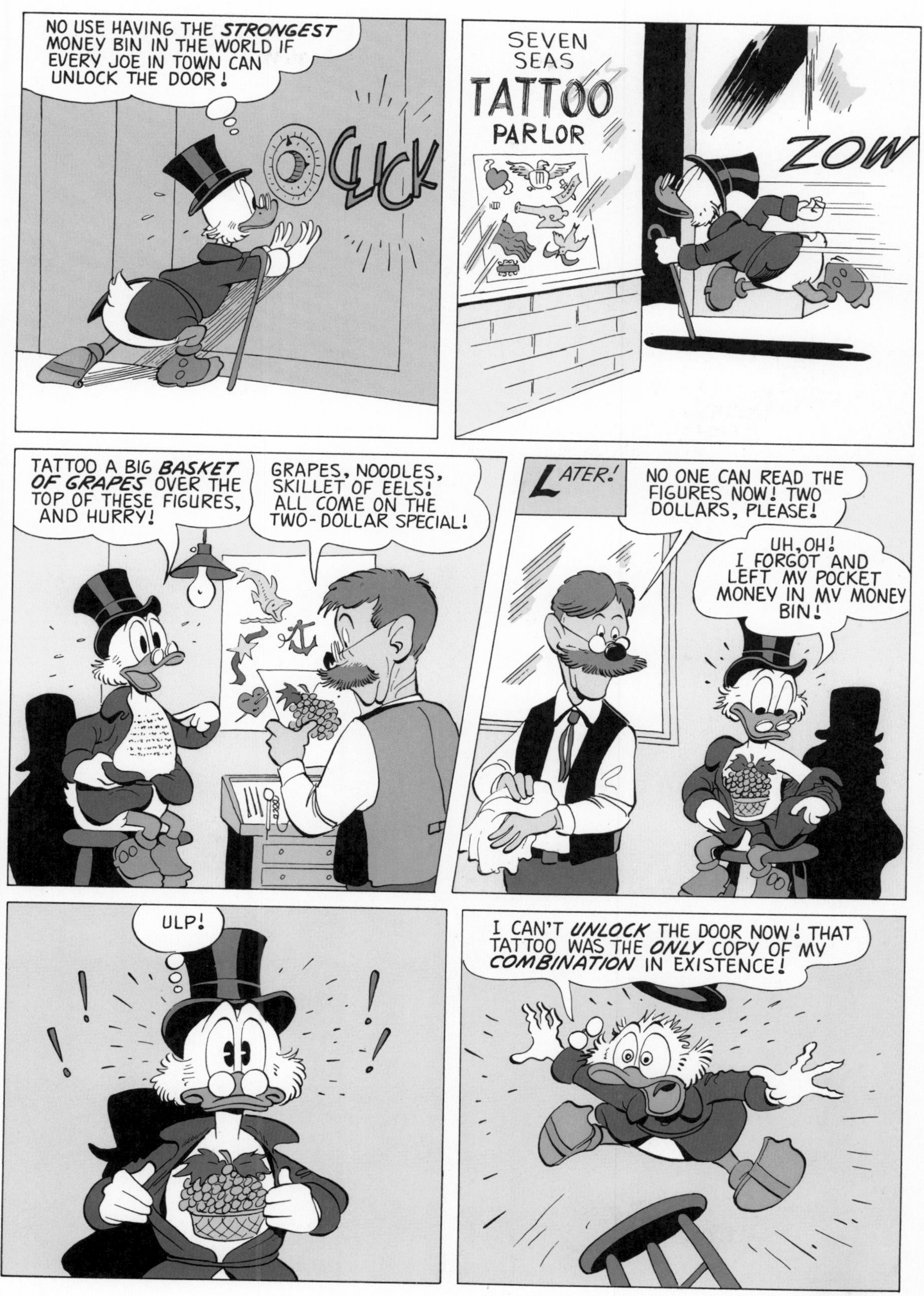
NO USE HAVING THE STRONGEST MONEY BIN IN THE WORLD IF EVERY JOE IN TOWN CAN UNLOCK THE DOOR!
CLICK
SEVEN SEAS TATTOO PARLOR
ZOW
TATTOO A BIG BASKET OF GRAPES OVER THE TOP OF THESE FIGURES, AND HURRY!
GRAPES, NOODLES, SKILLET OF EELS! ALL COME ON THE TWO-DOLLAR SPECIAL!
LATER!
NO ONE CAN READ THE FIGURES NOW! TWO DOLLARS, PLEASE!
UH, OH! I FORGOT AND LEFT MY POCKET MONEY IN MY MONEY BIN!
ULP!
I CAN'T UNLOCK THE DOOR NOW! THAT TATTOO WAS THE ONLY COPY OF MY COMBINATION IN EXISTENCE!

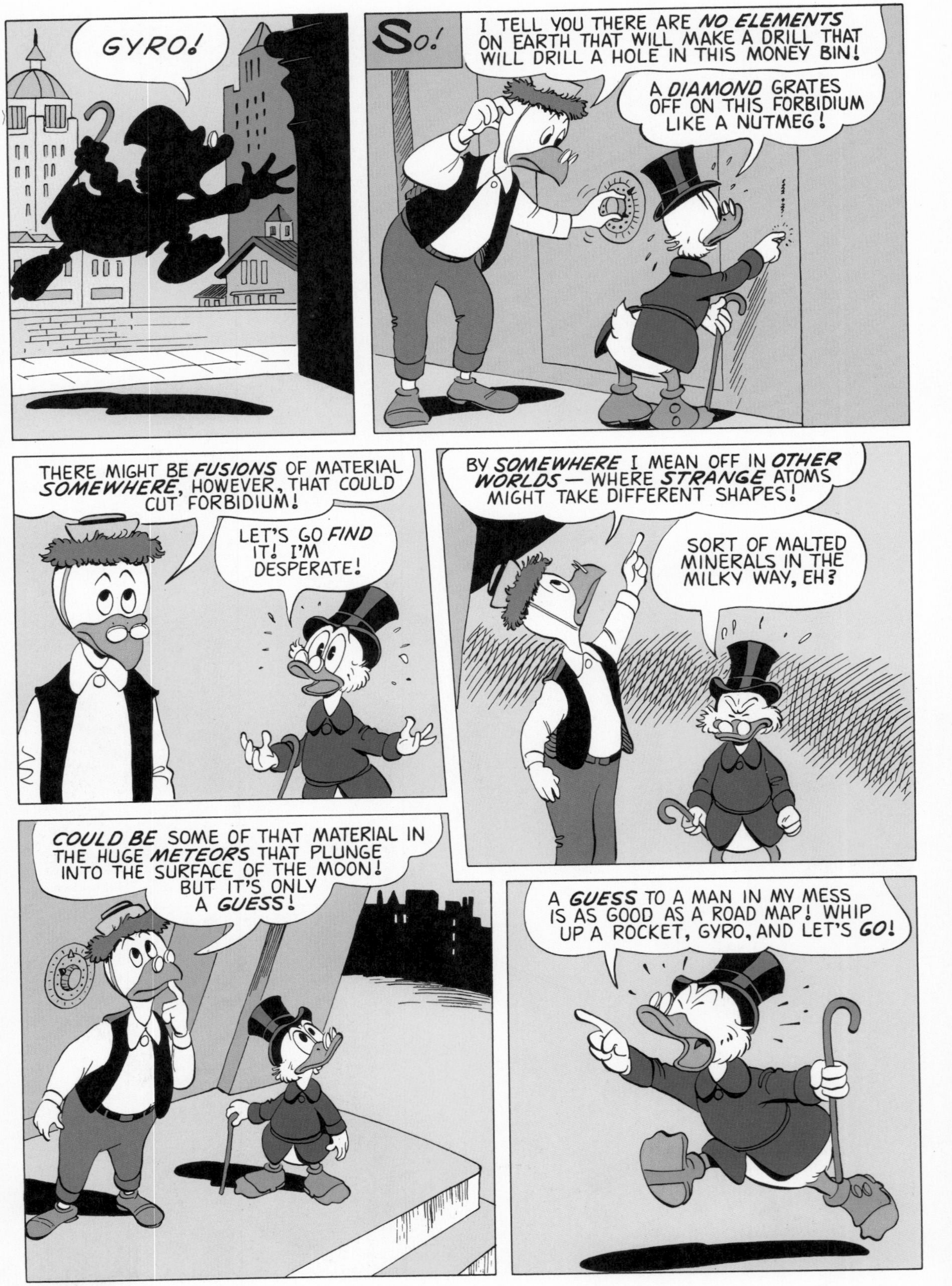
GYRO!
So!
I TELL YOU THERE ARE NO ELEMENTS ON EARTH THAT WILL MAKE A DRILL THAT WILL DRILL A HOLE IN THIS MONEY BIN!
A DIAMOND GRATES OFF ON THIS FORBIDIUM LIKE A NUTMEG!
THERE MIGHT BE FUSIONS OF MATERIAL SOMEWHERE, HOWEVER, THAT COULD CUT FORBIDIUM!
LET'S GO FIND IT! I'M DESPERATE!
BY SOMEWHERE I MEAN OFF IN OTHER WORLDS — WHERE STRANGE ATOMS MIGHT TAKE DIFFERENT SHAPES!
SORT OF MALTED MINERALS IN THE MILKY WAY, EH?
COULD BE SOME OF THAT MATERIAL IN THE HUGE METEORS THAT PLUNGE INTO THE SURFACE OF THE MOON! BUT IT'S ONLY A GUESS!
A GUESS TO A MAN IN MY MESS IS AS GOOD AS A ROAD MAP! WHIP UP A ROCKET, GYRO, AND LET'S GO!

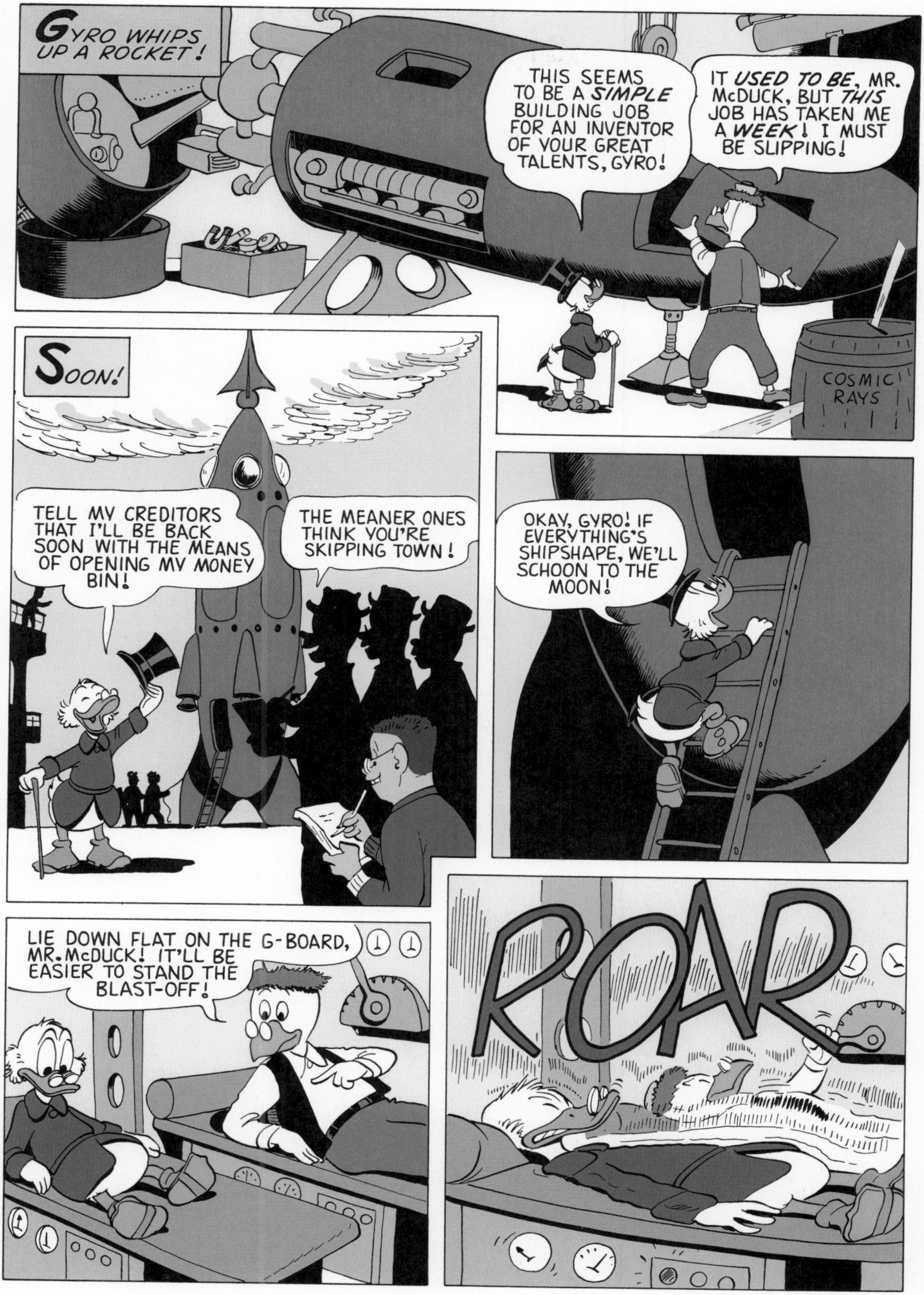
GYRO WHIPS UP A ROCKET!
THIS SEEMS TO BE A SIMPLE BUILDING JOB FOR AN INVENTOR OF YOUR GREAT TALENTS, GYRO!
IT USED TO BE, MR. McDUCK, BUT THIS JOB HAS TAKEN ME A WEEK! I MUST BE SLIPPING!
COSMIC RAYS
SOON!
TELL MY CREDITORS THAT I'LL BE BACK SOON WITH THE MEANS OF OPENING MY MONEY BIN!
THE MEANER ONES THINK YOU'RE SKIPPING TOWN!
OKAY, GYRO! IF EVERYTHING'S SHIPSHAPE, WE'LL SCHOON TO THE MOON!
LIE DOWN FLAT ON THE G-BOARD, MR. McDUCK! IT'LL BE EASIER TO STAND THE BLAST-OFF!
ROAR

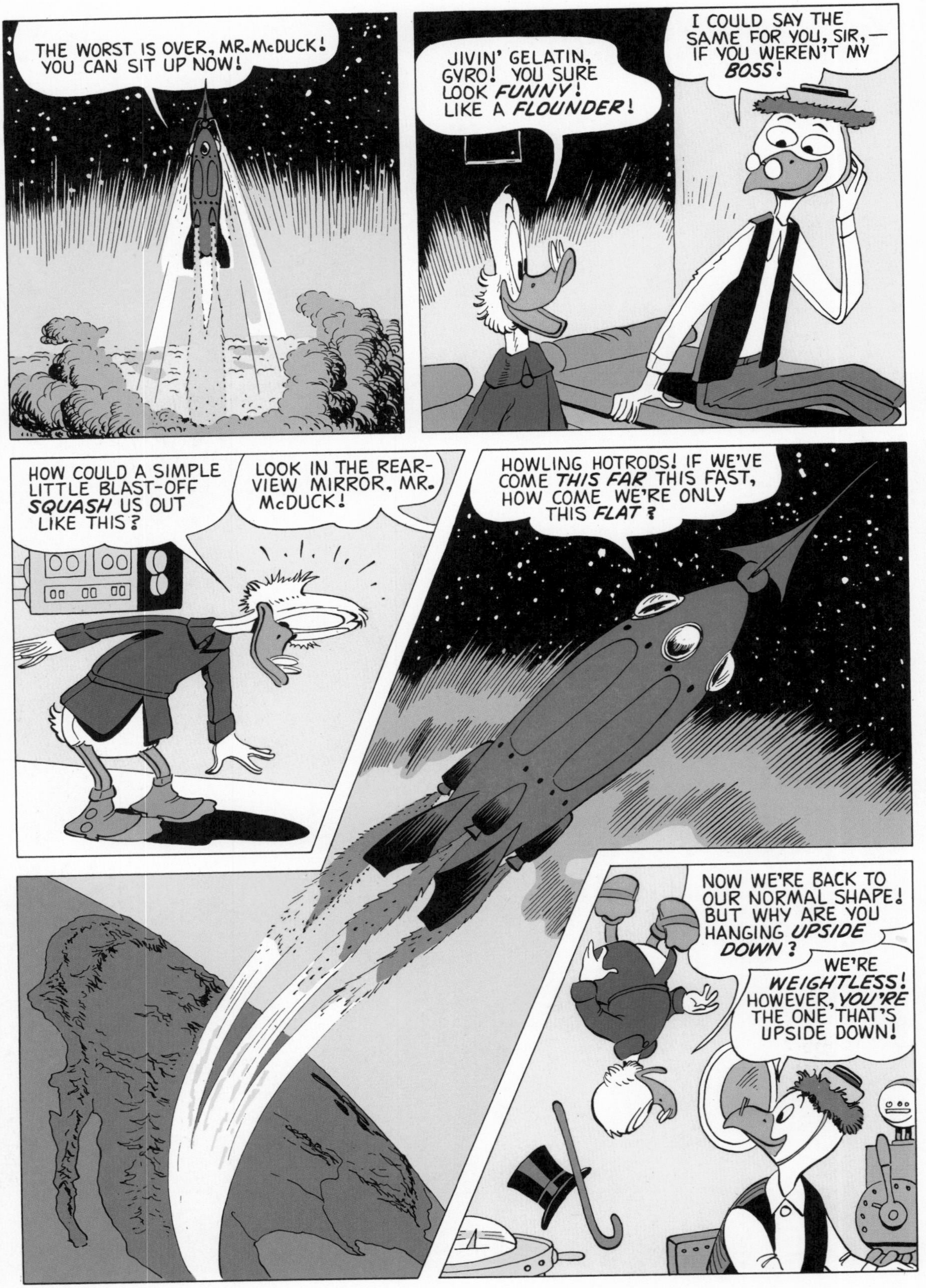
THE WORST IS OVER, MR. McDUCK! YOU CAN SIT UP NOW!
JIVIN' GELATIN, GYRO! YOU SURE LOOK FUNNY! LIKE A FLOUNDER!
I COULD SAY THE SAME FOR YOU, SIR,— IF YOU WEREN'T MY BOSS!
HOW COULD A SIMPLE LITTLE BLAST-OFF SQUASH US OUT LIKE THIS?
LOOK IN THE REAR-VIEW MIRROR, MR. McDUCK!
HOWLING HOTRODS! IF WE'VE COME THIS FAR THIS FAST, HOW COME WE'RE ONLY THIS FLAT?
NOW WE'RE BACK TO OUR NORMAL SHAPE! BUT WHY ARE YOU HANGING UPSIDE DOWN?
WE'RE WEIGHTLESS! HOWEVER, YOU'RE THE ONE THAT'S UPSIDE DOWN!

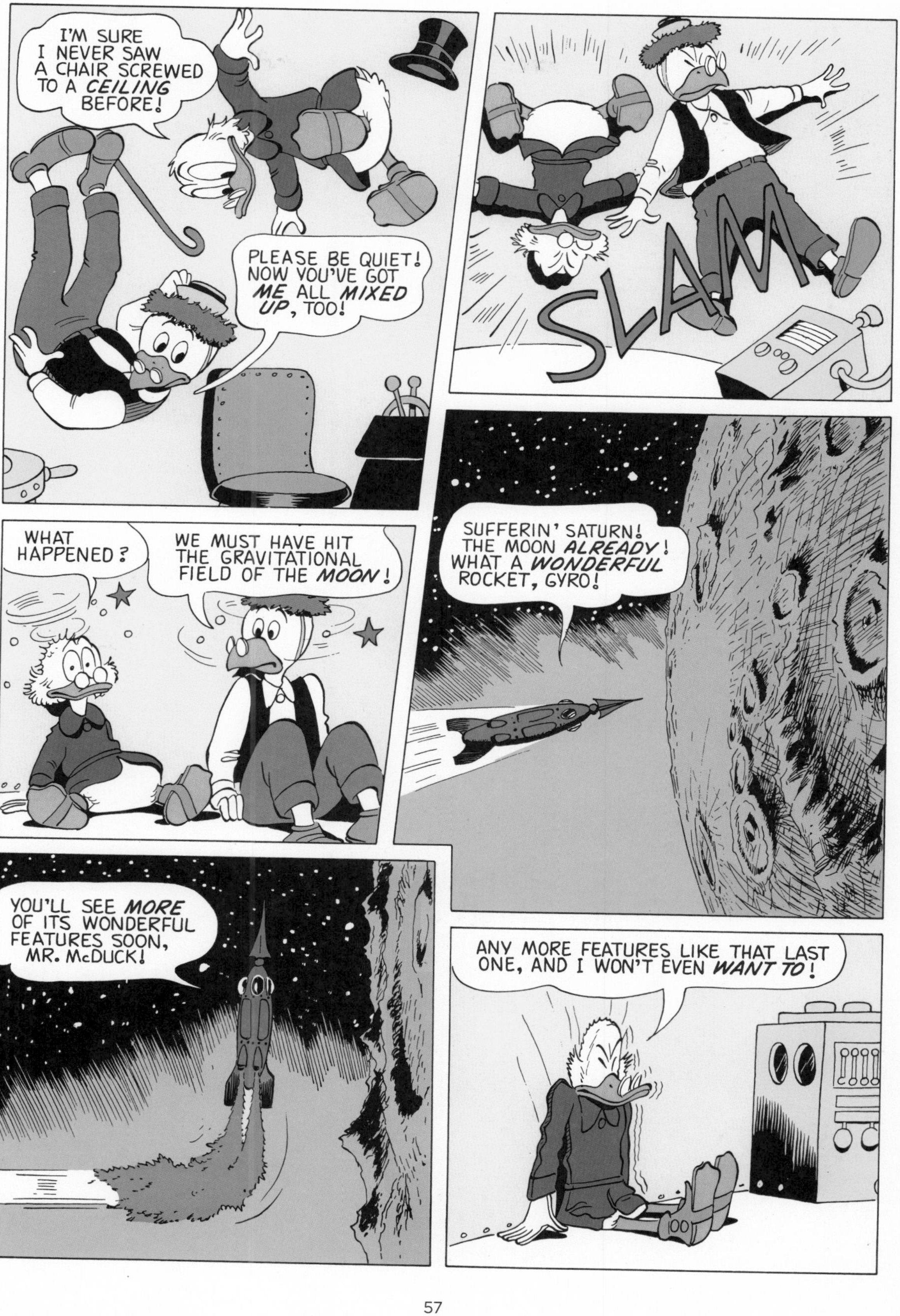
I'M SURE I NEVER SAW A CHAIR SCREWED TO A CEILING BEFORE!
PLEASE BE QUIET! NOW YOU'VE GOT ME ALL MIXED UP, TOO!
SLAM
WHAT HAPPENED?
WE MUST HAVE HIT THE GRAVITATIONAL FIELD OF THE MOON!
SUFFERIN' SATURN! THE MOON ALREADY! WHAT A WONDERFUL ROCKET, GYRO!
YOU'LL SEE MORE OF ITS WONDERFUL FEATURES SOON, MR. McDUCK!
ANY MORE FEATURES LIKE THAT LAST ONE, AND I WON'T EVEN WANT TO!

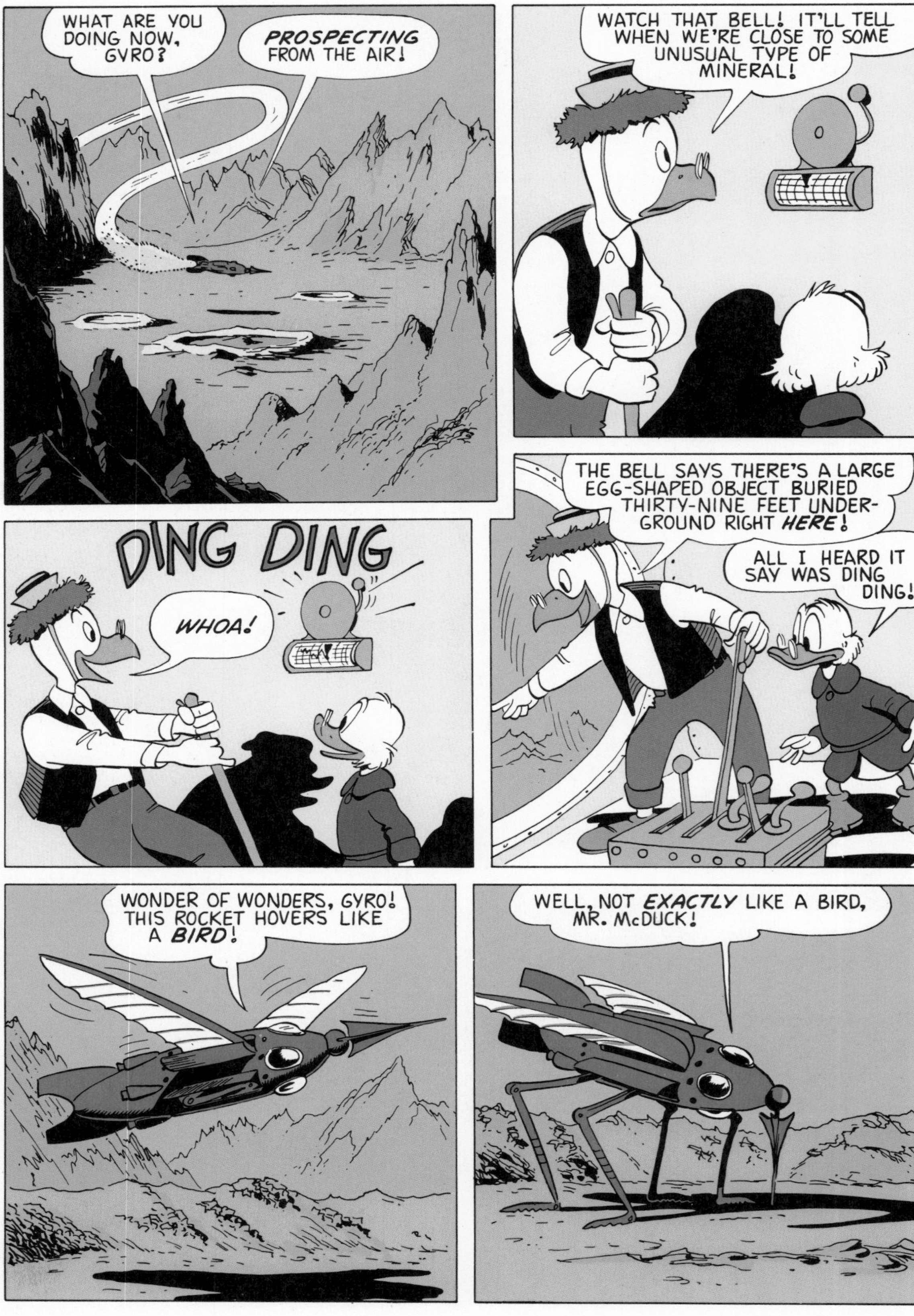
WHAT ARE YOU DOING NOW, GYRO?
PROSPECTING FROM THE AIR!
WATCH THAT BELL! IT'LL TELL WHEN WE'RE CLOSE TO SOME UNUSUAL TYPE OF MINERAL!
DING DING
WHOA!
THE BELL SAYS THERE'S A LARGE EGG-SHAPED OBJECT BURIED THIRTY-NINE FEET UNDER-GROUND RIGHT HERE!
ALL I HEARD IT SAY WAS DING DING!
WONDER OF WONDERS, GYRO! THIS ROCKET HOVERS LIKE A BIRD!
WELL, NOT EXACTLY LIKE A BIRD, MR. McDUCK!

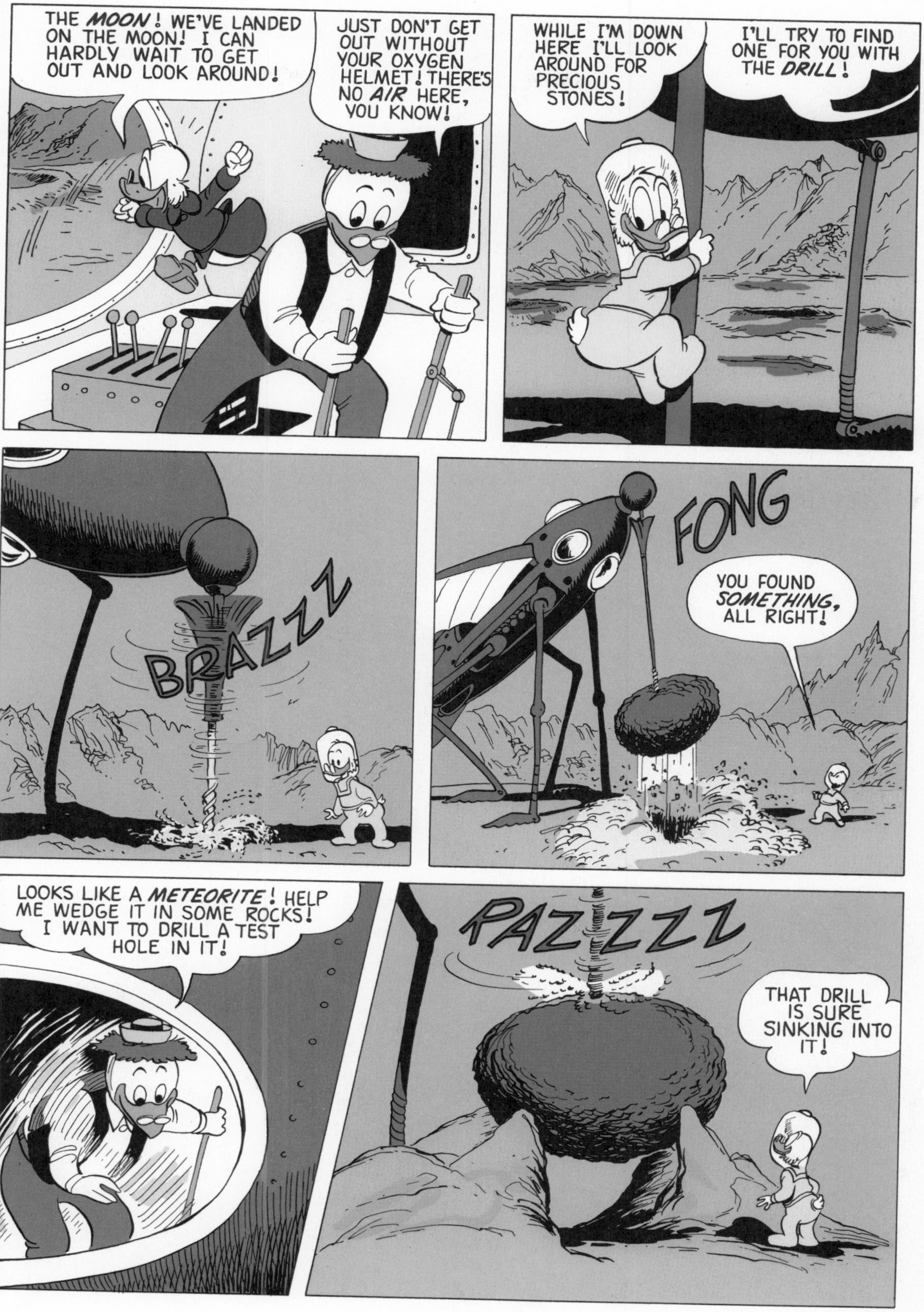
THE MOON! WE'VE LANDED ON THE MOON! I CAN HARDLY WAIT TO GET OUT AND LOOK AROUND!
JUST DON'T GET OUT WITHOUT YOUR OXYGEN HELMET! THERE'S NO AIR HERE, YOU KNOW!
WHILE I'M DOWN HERE I'LL LOOK AROUND FOR PRECIOUS STONES!
I'LL TRY TO FIND ONE FOR YOU WITH THE DRILL!
BRAZZZ
FONG
YOU FOUND SOMETHING, ALL RIGHT!
LOOKS LIKE A METEORITE! HELP ME WEDGE IT IN SOME ROCKS! I WANT TO DRILL A TEST HOLE IN IT!
PAZZZZ
THAT DRILL IS SURE SINKING INTO IT!

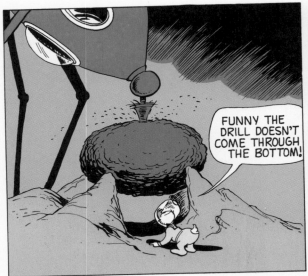

FUNNY THE DRILL DOESN'T COME THROUGH THE BOTTOM!

UH, OH! IT'S *WORN OFF* LIKE A PIECE OF *CHALK!*

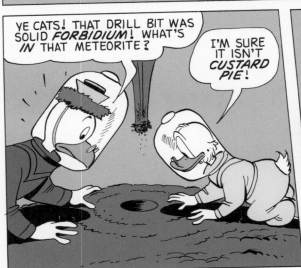

YE CATS! THAT DRILL BIT WAS SOLID *FORBIDIUM!* WHAT'S *IN* THAT METEORITE?

I'M SURE IT ISN'T *CUSTARD PIE!*

WE'LL BLAST THE *CRUST* OFF WITH DYNAMITE AND HAVE A LOOK!

BLAM

A *JEWEL* OF SOME SORT! BUT *BIG!*

STRANGE-LOOKING MATERIAL! LIKE A CROSS BETWEEN A *DIAMOND* AND A *GRINDSTONE!*

I NEVER SAW SUCH MINERAL ANYWHERE ON *EARTH!*

I THINK IT'S THE SOLIDIFIED HEAD OF AN ANCIENT *COMET!*

LET'S TEST IT, GYRO! SEE IF IT'LL *MELT* UNDER HEAT!

THE *HOTTEST* FLAME I CAN PRODUCE DOESN'T SOFTEN IT A DEGREE!

AND FORBIDIUM COULDN'T DENT IT!

IT'S THE MATERIAL WE CAME HERE TO FIND! IT'S THE STUFF THAT'S GOING TO OPEN MY MONEY BIN!

IT SURE IS! I'LL LOAD IT ABOARD THE ROCKET!

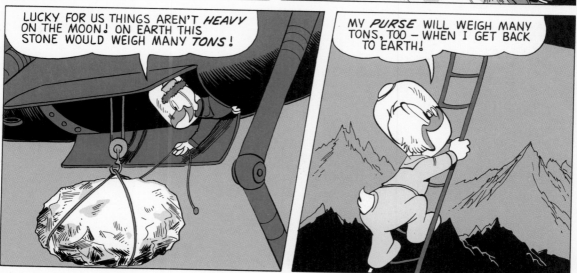

LUCKY FOR US THINGS AREN'T *HEAVY* ON THE MOON! ON EARTH THIS STONE WOULD WEIGH MANY *TONS!*

MY *PURSE* WILL WEIGH MANY TONS, TOO — WHEN I GET BACK TO EARTH!

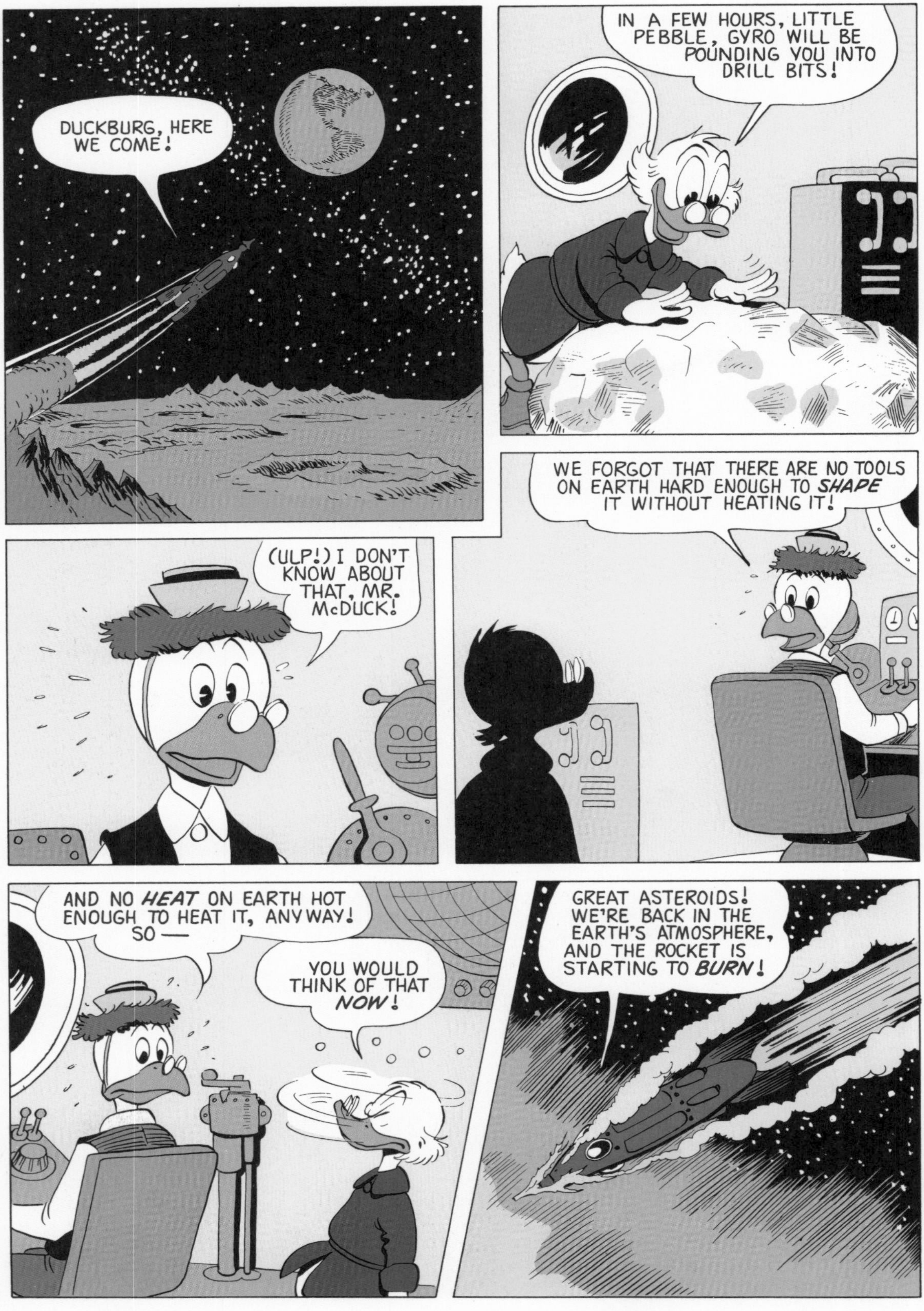
DUCKBURG, HERE WE COME!
IN A FEW HOURS, LITTLE PEBBLE, GYRO WILL BE POUNDING YOU INTO DRILL BITS!
WE FORGOT THAT THERE ARE NO TOOLS ON EARTH HARD ENOUGH TO SHAPE IT WITHOUT HEATING IT!
(ULP!) I DON'T KNOW ABOUT THAT, MR. McDUCK!
AND NO HEAT ON EARTH HOT ENOUGH TO HEAT IT, ANYWAY! SO —
YOU WOULD THINK OF THAT NOW!
GREAT ASTEROIDS! WE'RE BACK IN THE EARTH'S ATMOSPHERE, AND THE ROCKET IS STARTING TO BURN!

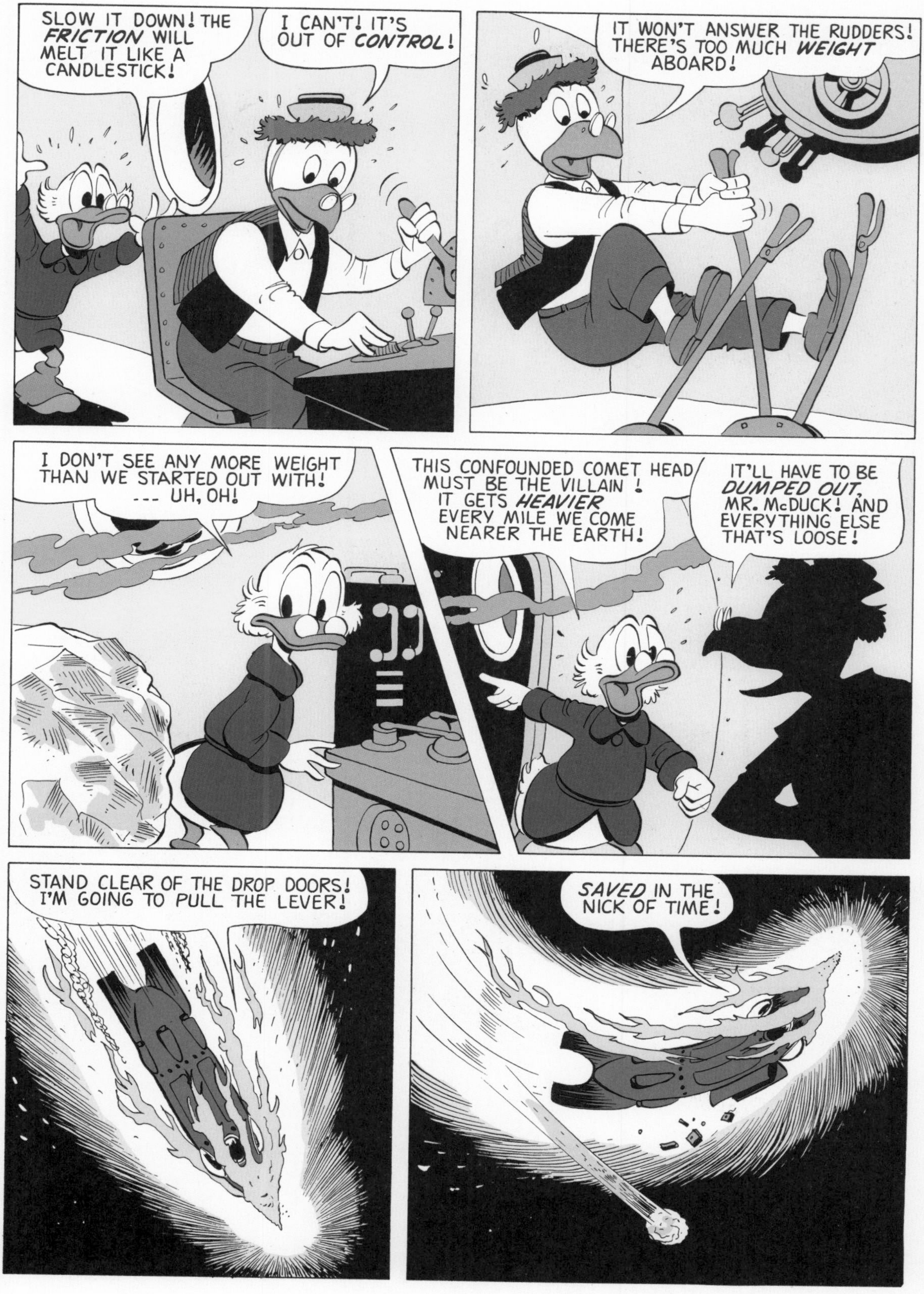
SLOW IT DOWN! THE FRICTION WILL MELT IT LIKE A CANDLESTICK!
I CAN'T! IT'S OUT OF CONTROL!
IT WON'T ANSWER THE RUDDERS! THERE'S TOO MUCH WEIGHT ABOARD!
I DON'T SEE ANY MORE WEIGHT THAN WE STARTED OUT WITH! --- UH, OH!
THIS CONFOUNDED COMET HEAD MUST BE THE VILLAIN! IT GETS HEAVIER EVERY MILE WE COME NEARER THE EARTH!
IT'LL HAVE TO BE DUMPED OUT, MR. McDUCK! AND EVERYTHING ELSE THAT'S LOOSE!
STAND CLEAR OF THE DROP DOORS! I'M GOING TO PULL THE LEVER!
SAVED IN THE NICK OF TIME!

THAT WAS THE CLOSEST SHAVE WE'LL *EVER* HAVE, MR. McDUCK!

I WONDER WHAT WILL BECOME OF THE THINGS WE DUMPED OUT?

WOW! THEY'RE BURNING UP LIKE FLASH POWDER! THE RADIO, THE TOOL BOX — EVERYTHING!

WHAT ABOUT THE COMET HEAD? IS FRICTION BURNING *IT*, TOO?

I DON'T SEE THE DOGGONED THING! IT MUST HAVE FALLEN CLEAR OUT OF SIGHT!

IT *BETTER* BURN UP! IT COULD CAUSE AN AWFUL LOT OF *DAMAGE* WHEN IT HITS!

OH, ME! ALL I NEED NOW IS A SUIT FOR DAMAGES!

*F*AR BELOW, THE ONCE MOLTEN COMET HEAD ROARS TOWARD EARTH AT THOUSANDS OF MILES A MINUTE! IT IS NOT EVEN HEATED TO A DULL GLOW!

A FAMILIAR CITY COMES INTO VIEW — *DUCKBURG!*

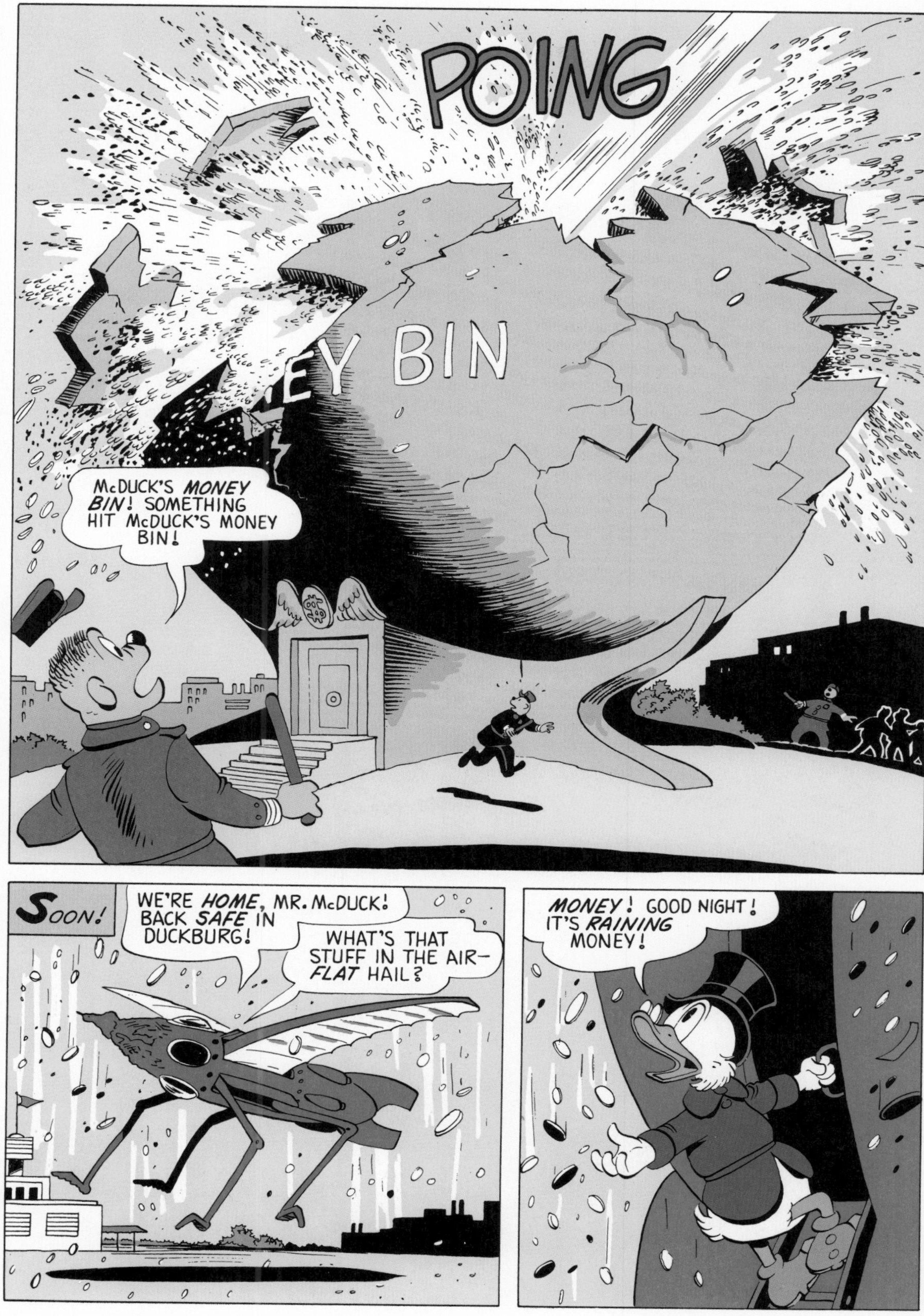
POING
EY BIN
McDUCK'S MONEY BIN! SOMETHING HIT McDUCK'S MONEY BIN!
SOON!
WE'RE HOME, MR. McDUCK! BACK SAFE IN DUCKBURG!
WHAT'S THAT STUFF IN THE AIR— FLAT HAIL?
MONEY! GOOD NIGHT! IT'S RAINING MONEY!

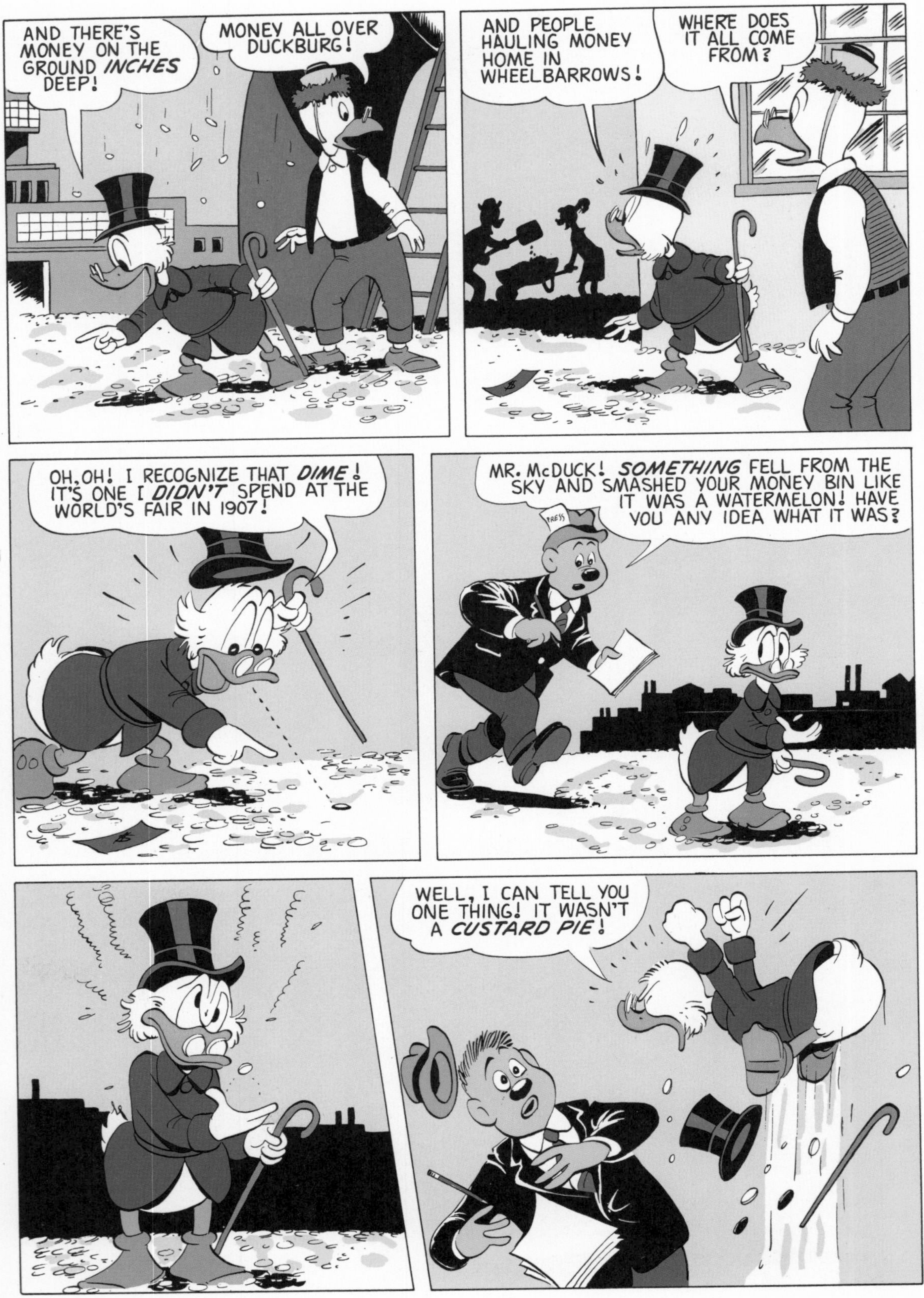
AND THERE'S MONEY ON THE GROUND *INCHES* DEEP!
MONEY ALL OVER DUCKBURG!
AND PEOPLE HAULING MONEY HOME IN WHEELBARROWS!
WHERE DOES IT ALL COME FROM?
OH, OH! I RECOGNIZE THAT *DIME*! IT'S ONE I *DIDN'T* SPEND AT THE WORLD'S FAIR IN 1907!
MR. McDUCK! *SOMETHING* FELL FROM THE SKY AND SMASHED YOUR MONEY BIN LIKE IT WAS A WATERMELON! HAVE YOU ANY IDEA WHAT IT WAS?
PRESS
WELL, I CAN TELL YOU ONE THING! IT WASN'T A *CUSTARD PIE*!

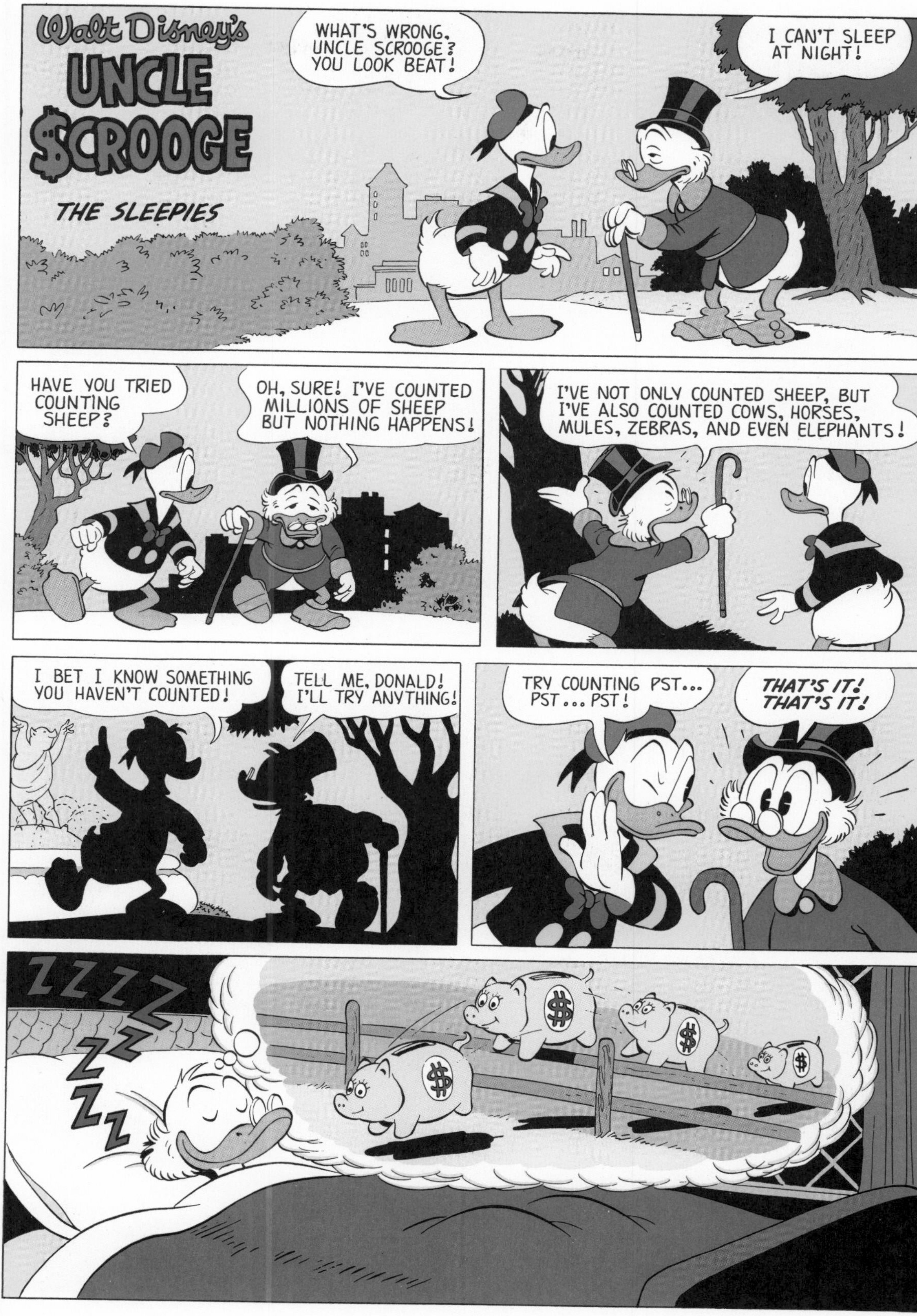
Walt Disney's
UNCLE $CROOGE
THE SLEEPIES
WHAT'S WRONG, UNCLE SCROOGE? YOU LOOK BEAT!
I CAN'T SLEEP AT NIGHT!
HAVE YOU TRIED COUNTING SHEEP?
OH, SURE! I'VE COUNTED MILLIONS OF SHEEP BUT NOTHING HAPPENS!
I'VE NOT ONLY COUNTED SHEEP, BUT I'VE ALSO COUNTED COWS, HORSES, MULES, ZEBRAS, AND EVEN ELEPHANTS!
I BET I KNOW SOMETHING YOU HAVEN'T COUNTED!
TELL ME, DONALD! I'LL TRY ANYTHING!
TRY COUNTING PST... PST... PST!
THAT'S IT! THAT'S IT!
ZZZZZ
ZZZZ

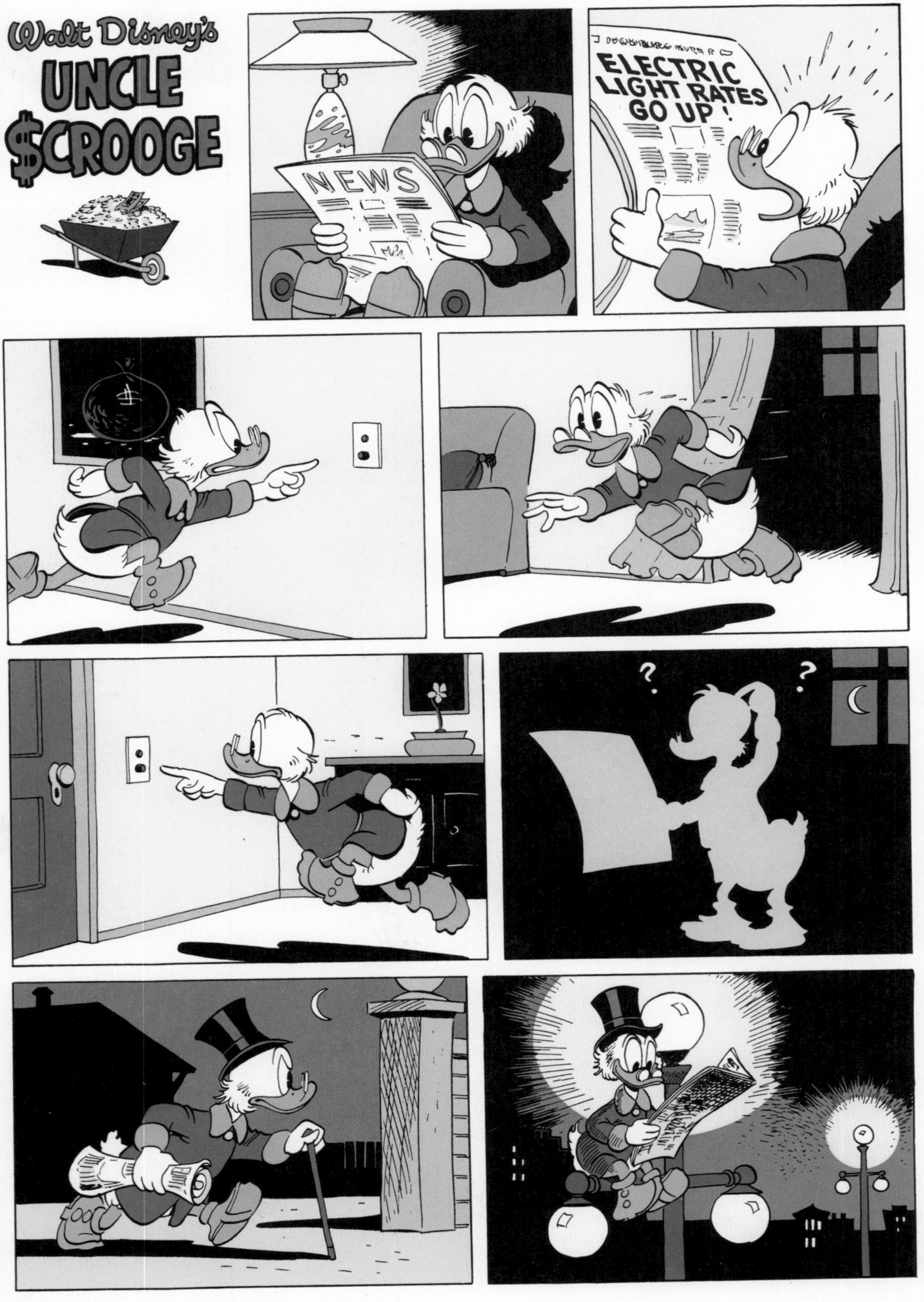
Walt Disney's
UNCLE $CROOGE
NEWS
ELECTRIC LIGHT RATES GO UP!
?
?

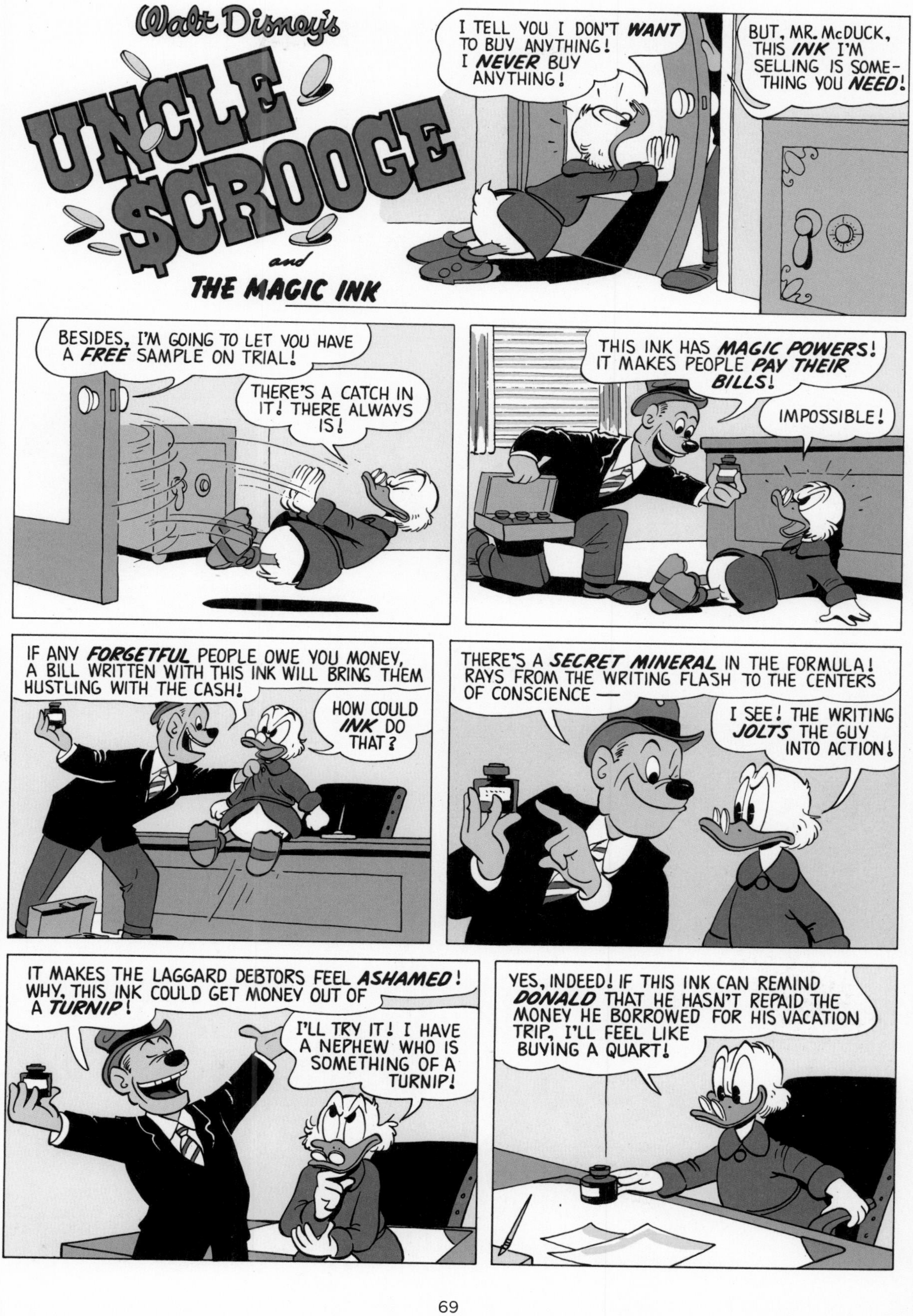

Walt Disney's
UNCLE $CROOGE
and
THE MAGIC INK
I TELL YOU I DON'T WANT TO BUY ANYTHING! I NEVER BUY ANYTHING!
BUT, MR. McDUCK, THIS INK I'M SELLING IS SOMETHING YOU NEED!
BESIDES, I'M GOING TO LET YOU HAVE A FREE SAMPLE ON TRIAL!
THERE'S A CATCH IN IT! THERE ALWAYS IS!
THIS INK HAS MAGIC POWERS! IT MAKES PEOPLE PAY THEIR BILLS!
IMPOSSIBLE!
IF ANY FORGETFUL PEOPLE OWE YOU MONEY, A BILL WRITTEN WITH THIS INK WILL BRING THEM HUSTLING WITH THE CASH!
HOW COULD INK DO THAT?
THERE'S A SECRET MINERAL IN THE FORMULA! RAYS FROM THE WRITING FLASH TO THE CENTERS OF CONSCIENCE —
I SEE! THE WRITING JOLTS THE GUY INTO ACTION!
IT MAKES THE LAGGARD DEBTORS FEEL ASHAMED! WHY, THIS INK COULD GET MONEY OUT OF A TURNIP!
I'LL TRY IT! I HAVE A NEPHEW WHO IS SOMETHING OF A TURNIP!
YES, INDEED! IF THIS INK CAN REMIND DONALD THAT HE HASN'T REPAID THE MONEY HE BORROWED FOR HIS VACATION TRIP, I'LL FEEL LIKE BUYING A QUART!

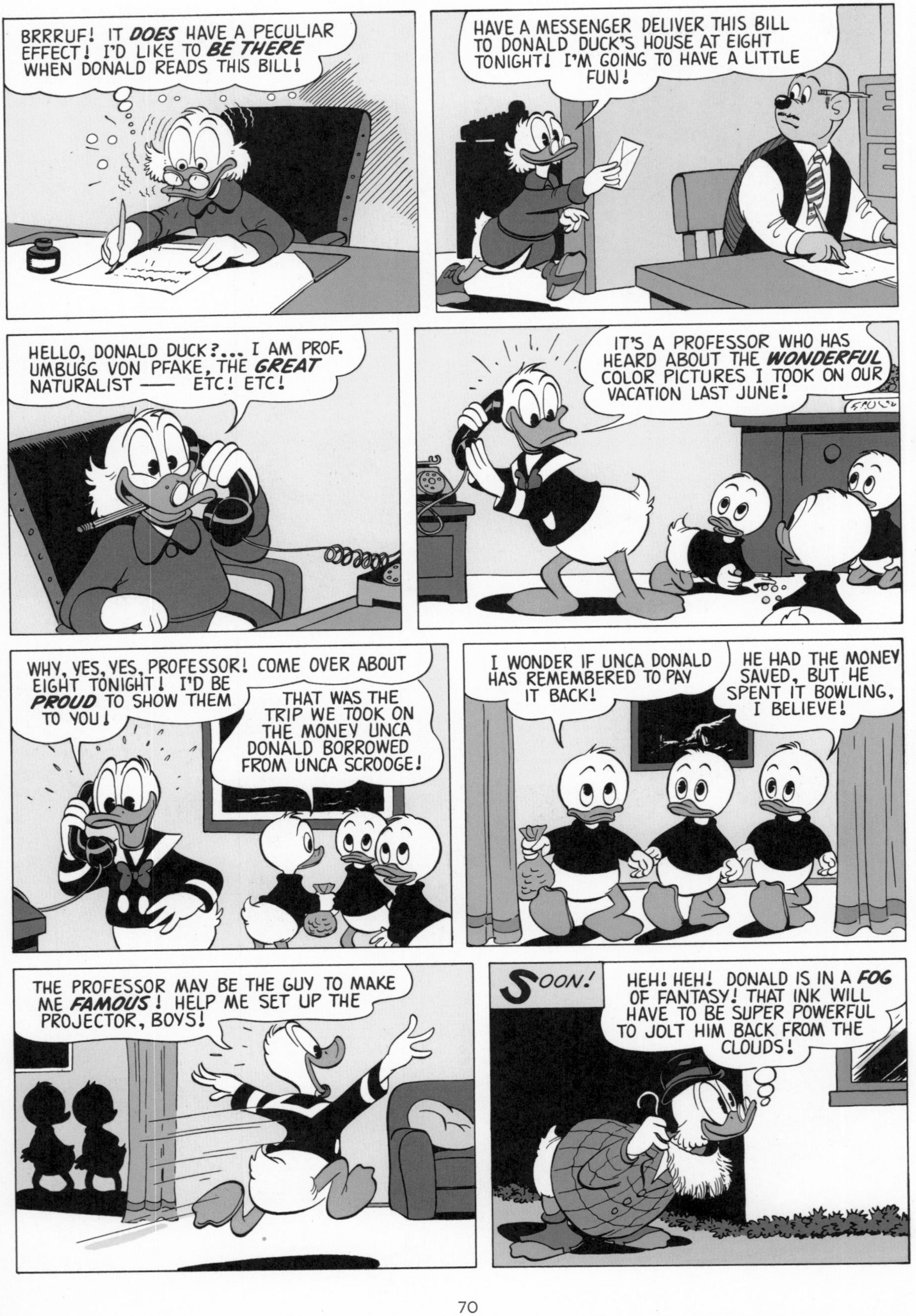
BRRRUF! IT DOES HAVE A PECULIAR EFFECT! I'D LIKE TO BE THERE WHEN DONALD READS THIS BILL!
HAVE A MESSENGER DELIVER THIS BILL TO DONALD DUCK'S HOUSE AT EIGHT TONIGHT! I'M GOING TO HAVE A LITTLE FUN!
HELLO, DONALD DUCK?... I AM PROF. UMBUGG VON PFAKE, THE GREAT NATURALIST — ETC! ETC!
IT'S A PROFESSOR WHO HAS HEARD ABOUT THE WONDERFUL COLOR PICTURES I TOOK ON OUR VACATION LAST JUNE!
WHY, YES, YES, PROFESSOR! COME OVER ABOUT EIGHT TONIGHT! I'D BE PROUD TO SHOW THEM TO YOU!
THAT WAS THE TRIP WE TOOK ON THE MONEY UNCA DONALD BORROWED FROM UNCA SCROOGE!
I WONDER IF UNCA DONALD HAS REMEMBERED TO PAY IT BACK!
HE HAD THE MONEY SAVED, BUT HE SPENT IT BOWLING, I BELIEVE!
THE PROFESSOR MAY BE THE GUY TO MAKE ME FAMOUS! HELP ME SET UP THE PROJECTOR, BOYS!
SOON!
HEH! HEH! DONALD IS IN A FOG OF FANTASY! THAT INK WILL HAVE TO BE SUPER POWERFUL TO JOLT HIM BACK FROM THE CLOUDS!

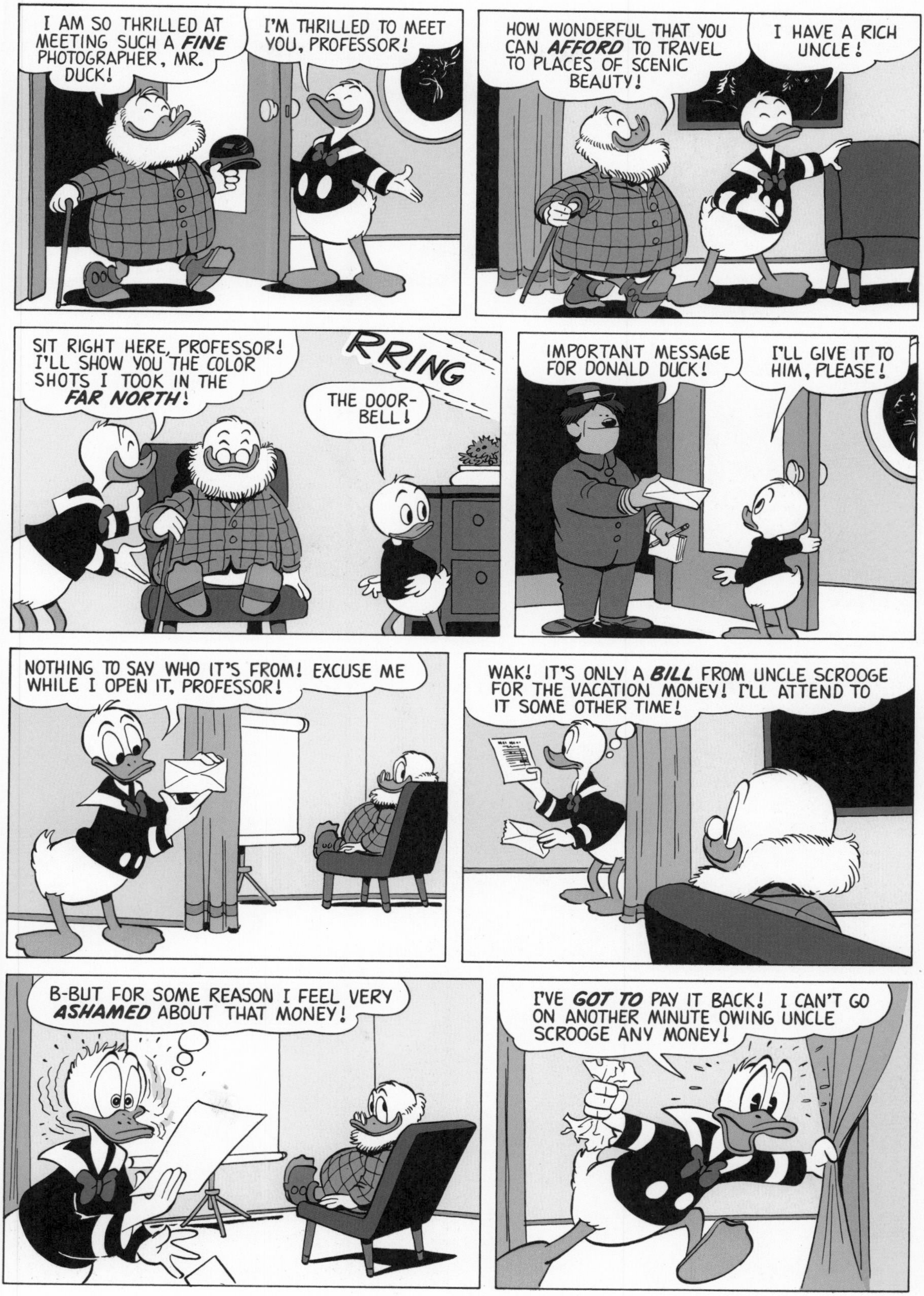
I AM SO THRILLED AT MEETING SUCH A FINE PHOTOGRAPHER, MR. DUCK!
I'M THRILLED TO MEET YOU, PROFESSOR!
HOW WONDERFUL THAT YOU CAN AFFORD TO TRAVEL TO PLACES OF SCENIC BEAUTY!
I HAVE A RICH UNCLE!
SIT RIGHT HERE, PROFESSOR! I'LL SHOW YOU THE COLOR SHOTS I TOOK IN THE FAR NORTH!
RRING
THE DOOR-BELL!
IMPORTANT MESSAGE FOR DONALD DUCK!
I'LL GIVE IT TO HIM, PLEASE!
NOTHING TO SAY WHO IT'S FROM! EXCUSE ME WHILE I OPEN IT, PROFESSOR!
WAK! IT'S ONLY A BILL FROM UNCLE SCROOGE FOR THE VACATION MONEY! I'LL ATTEND TO IT SOME OTHER TIME!
B-BUT FOR SOME REASON I FEEL VERY ASHAMED ABOUT THAT MONEY!
I'VE GOT TO PAY IT BACK! I CAN'T GO ON ANOTHER MINUTE OWING UNCLE SCROOGE ANY MONEY!

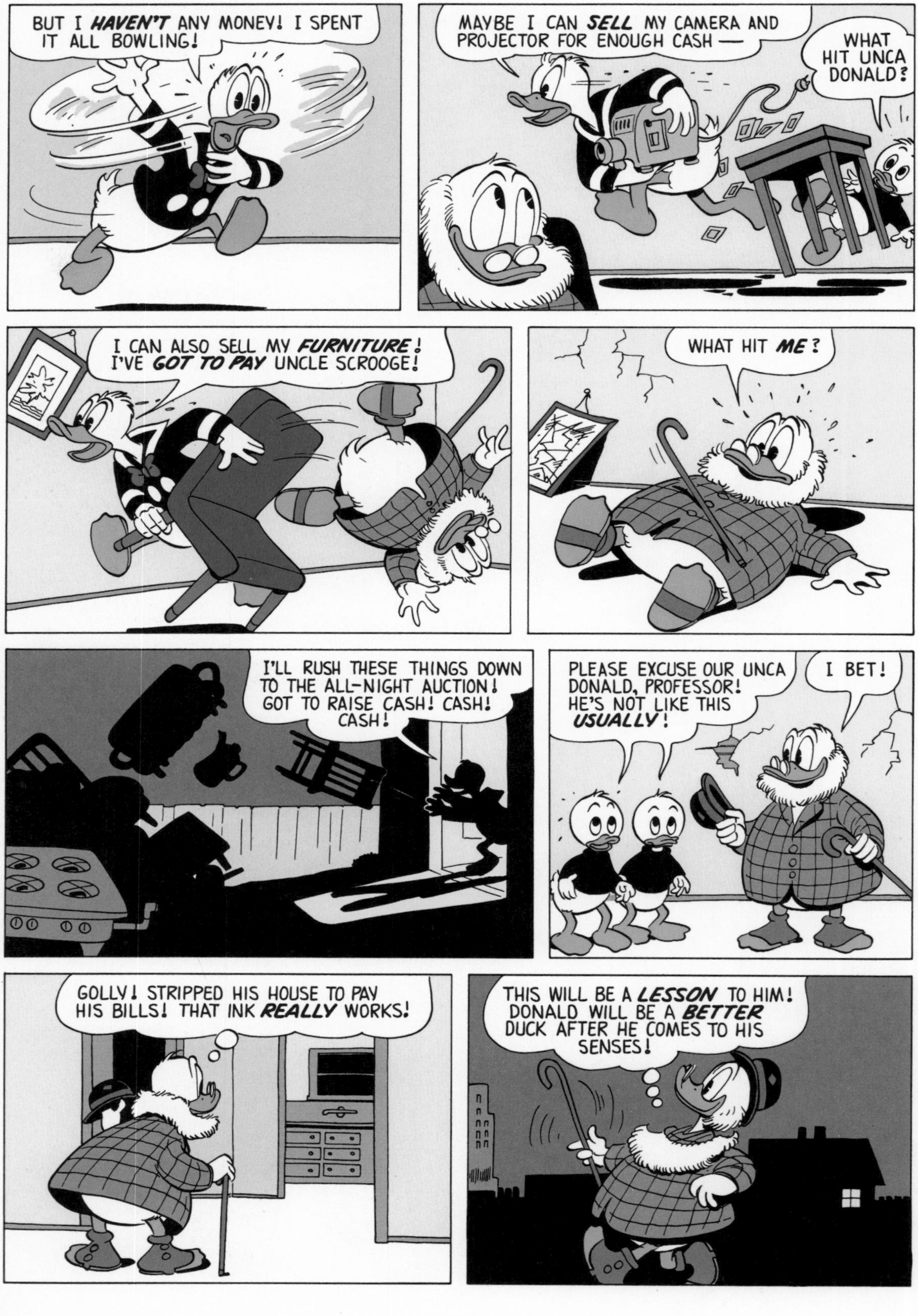
BUT I HAVEN'T ANY MONEY! I SPENT IT ALL BOWLING!
MAYBE I CAN SELL MY CAMERA AND PROJECTOR FOR ENOUGH CASH —
WHAT HIT UNCA DONALD?
I CAN ALSO SELL MY FURNITURE! I'VE GOT TO PAY UNCLE SCROOGE!
WHAT HIT ME?
I'LL RUSH THESE THINGS DOWN TO THE ALL-NIGHT AUCTION! GOT TO RAISE CASH! CASH! CASH!
PLEASE EXCUSE OUR UNCA DONALD, PROFESSOR! HE'S NOT LIKE THIS USUALLY!
I BET!
GOLLY! STRIPPED HIS HOUSE TO PAY HIS BILLS! THAT INK REALLY WORKS!
THIS WILL BE A LESSON TO HIM! DONALD WILL BE A BETTER DUCK AFTER HE COMES TO HIS SENSES!

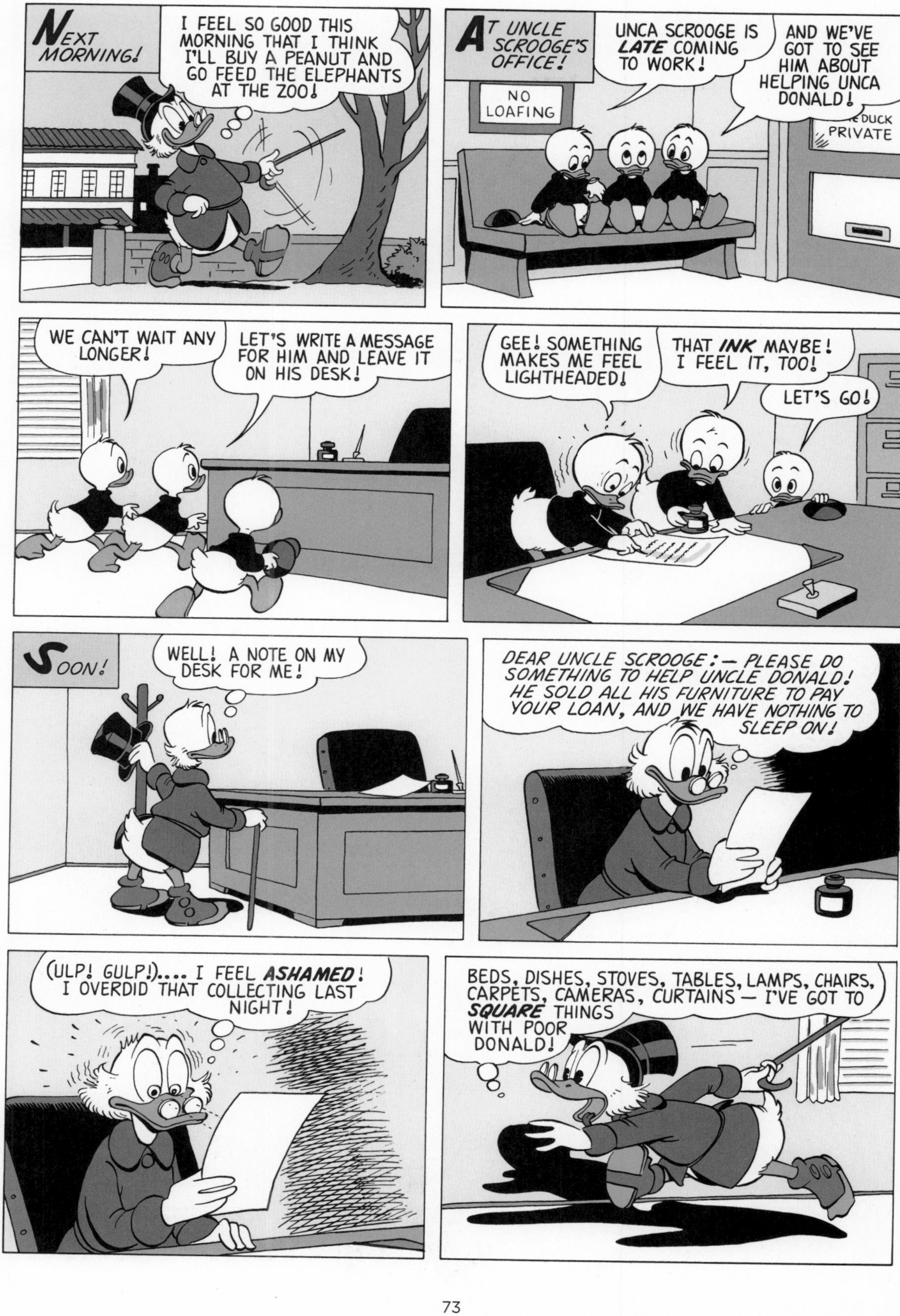
NEXT MORNING!
I FEEL SO GOOD THIS MORNING THAT I THINK I'LL BUY A PEANUT AND GO FEED THE ELEPHANTS AT THE ZOO!
AT UNCLE SCROOGE'S OFFICE!
NO LOAFING
UNCA SCROOGE IS LATE COMING TO WORK!
AND WE'VE GOT TO SEE HIM ABOUT HELPING UNCA DONALD!
PRIVATE
WE CAN'T WAIT ANY LONGER!
LET'S WRITE A MESSAGE FOR HIM AND LEAVE IT ON HIS DESK!
GEE! SOMETHING MAKES ME FEEL LIGHTHEADED!
THAT INK MAYBE! I FEEL IT, TOO!
LET'S GO!
SOON!
WELL! A NOTE ON MY DESK FOR ME!
DEAR UNCLE SCROOGE:— PLEASE DO SOMETHING TO HELP UNCLE DONALD! HE SOLD ALL HIS FURNITURE TO PAY YOUR LOAN, AND WE HAVE NOTHING TO SLEEP ON!
(ULP! GULP!).... I FEEL ASHAMED! I OVERDID THAT COLLECTING LAST NIGHT!
BEDS, DISHES, STOVES, TABLES, LAMPS, CHAIRS, CARPETS, CAMERAS, CURTAINS — I'VE GOT TO SQUARE THINGS WITH POOR DONALD!

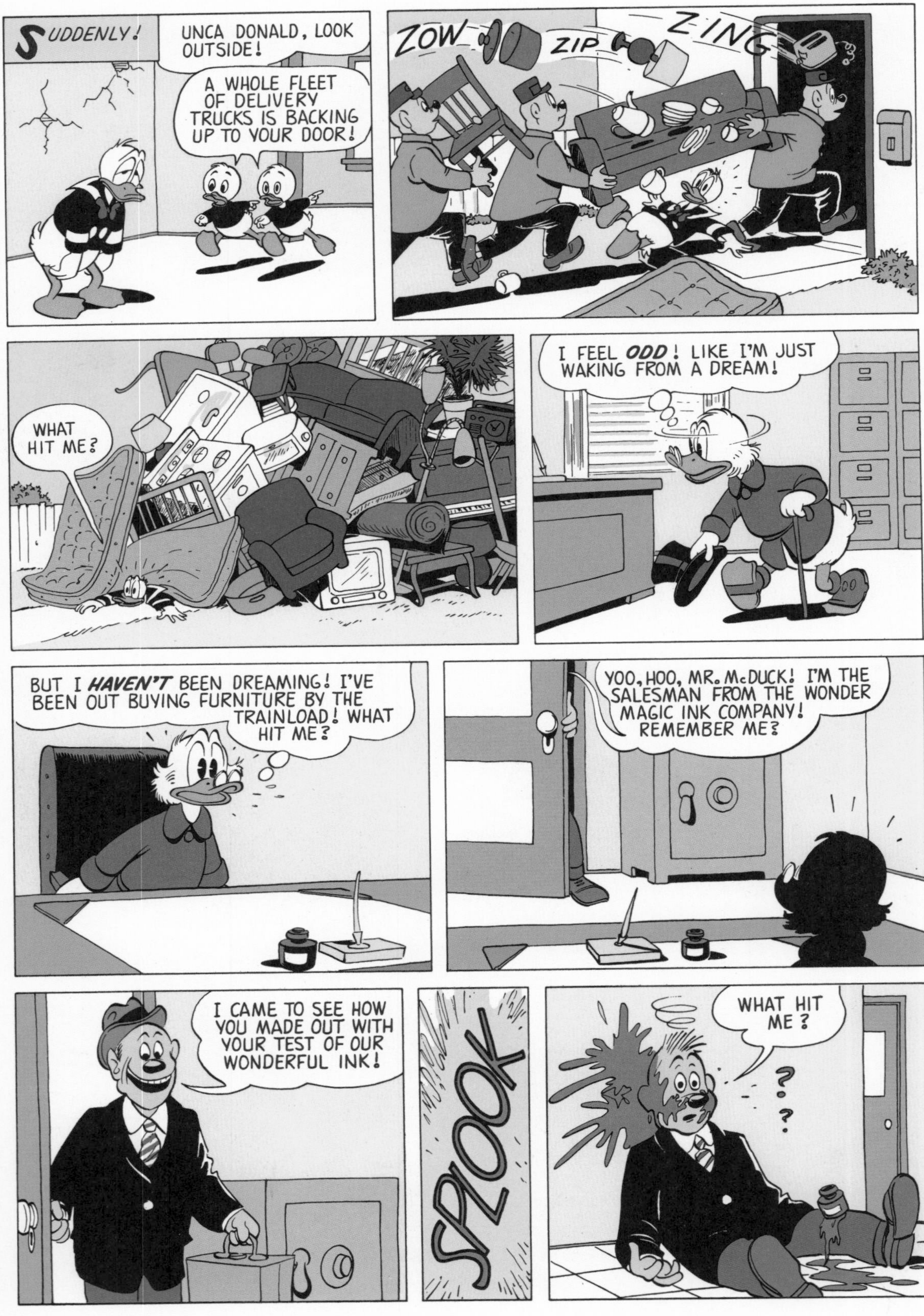
SUDDENLY!
UNCA DONALD, LOOK OUTSIDE!
A WHOLE FLEET OF DELIVERY TRUCKS IS BACKING UP TO YOUR DOOR!
ZOW
ZIP
ZING
WHAT HIT ME?
I FEEL ODD! LIKE I'M JUST WAKING FROM A DREAM!
BUT I HAVEN'T BEEN DREAMING! I'VE BEEN OUT BUYING FURNITURE BY THE TRAINLOAD! WHAT HIT ME?
YOO, HOO, MR. McDUCK! I'M THE SALESMAN FROM THE WONDER MAGIC INK COMPANY! REMEMBER ME?
I CAME TO SEE HOW YOU MADE OUT WITH YOUR TEST OF OUR WONDERFUL INK!
SPLOOK
WHAT HIT ME?

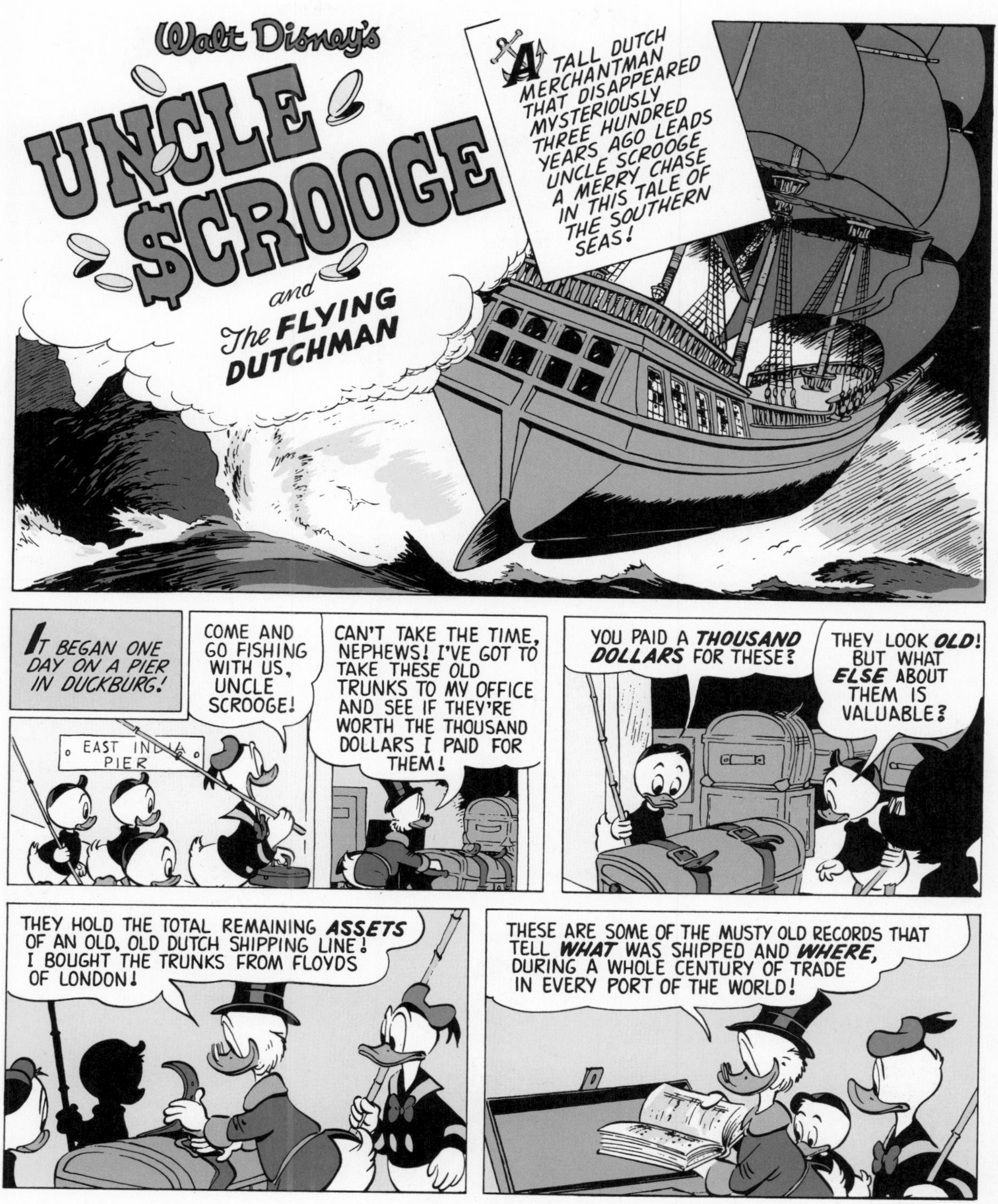
Walt Disney's
UNCLE $CROOGE
and The FLYING DUTCHMAN
A TALL DUTCH MERCHANTMAN THAT DISAPPEARED MYSTERIOUSLY THREE HUNDRED YEARS AGO LEADS UNCLE SCROOGE A MERRY CHASE IN THIS TALE OF THE SOUTHERN SEAS!
IT BEGAN ONE DAY ON A PIER IN DUCKBURG!
EAST INDIA PIER
COME AND GO FISHING WITH US, UNCLE SCROOGE!
CAN'T TAKE THE TIME, NEPHEWS! I'VE GOT TO TAKE THESE OLD TRUNKS TO MY OFFICE AND SEE IF THEY'RE WORTH THE THOUSAND DOLLARS I PAID FOR THEM!
YOU PAID A THOUSAND DOLLARS FOR THESE?
THEY LOOK OLD! BUT WHAT ELSE ABOUT THEM IS VALUABLE?
THEY HOLD THE TOTAL REMAINING ASSETS OF AN OLD, OLD DUTCH SHIPPING LINE! I BOUGHT THE TRUNKS FROM FLOYDS OF LONDON!
THESE ARE SOME OF THE MUSTY OLD RECORDS THAT TELL WHAT WAS SHIPPED AND WHERE, DURING A WHOLE CENTURY OF TRADE IN EVERY PORT OF THE WORLD!

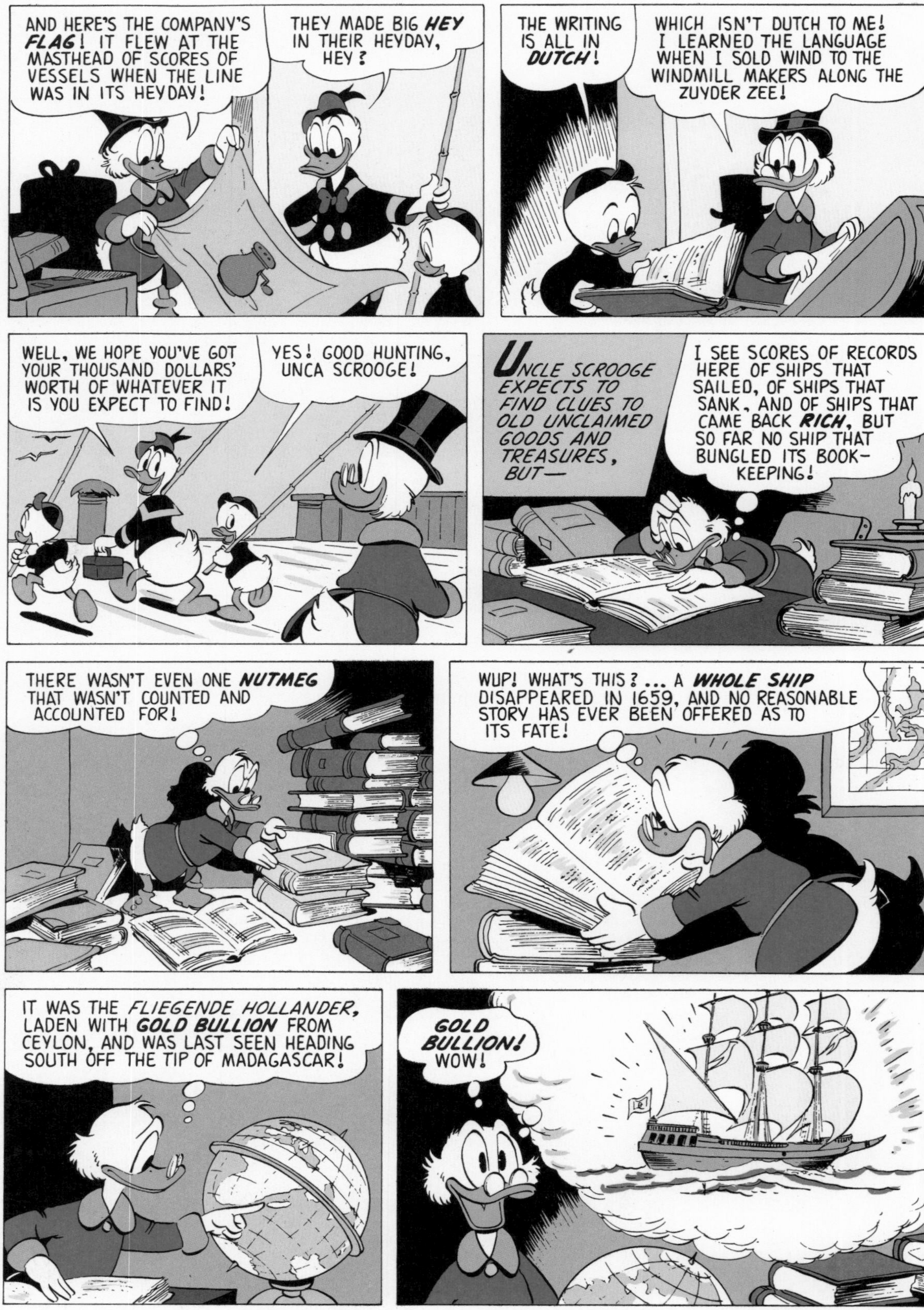
AND HERE'S THE COMPANY'S FLAG! IT FLEW AT THE MASTHEAD OF SCORES OF VESSELS WHEN THE LINE WAS IN ITS HEYDAY!
THEY MADE BIG HEY IN THEIR HEYDAY, HEY?
THE WRITING IS ALL IN DUTCH!
WHICH ISN'T DUTCH TO ME! I LEARNED THE LANGUAGE WHEN I SOLD WIND TO THE WINDMILL MAKERS ALONG THE ZUYDER ZEE!
WELL, WE HOPE YOU'VE GOT YOUR THOUSAND DOLLARS' WORTH OF WHATEVER IT IS YOU EXPECT TO FIND!
YES! GOOD HUNTING, UNCA SCROOGE!
UNCLE SCROOGE EXPECTS TO FIND CLUES TO OLD UNCLAIMED GOODS AND TREASURES, BUT—
I SEE SCORES OF RECORDS HERE OF SHIPS THAT SAILED, OF SHIPS THAT SANK, AND OF SHIPS THAT CAME BACK RICH, BUT SO FAR NO SHIP THAT BUNGLED ITS BOOK-KEEPING!
THERE WASN'T EVEN ONE NUTMEG THAT WASN'T COUNTED AND ACCOUNTED FOR!
WUP! WHAT'S THIS? ... A WHOLE SHIP DISAPPEARED IN 1659, AND NO REASONABLE STORY HAS EVER BEEN OFFERED AS TO ITS FATE!
IT WAS THE FLIEGENDE HOLLANDER, LADEN WITH GOLD BULLION FROM CEYLON, AND WAS LAST SEEN HEADING SOUTH OFF THE TIP OF MADAGASCAR!
GOLD BULLION! WOW!

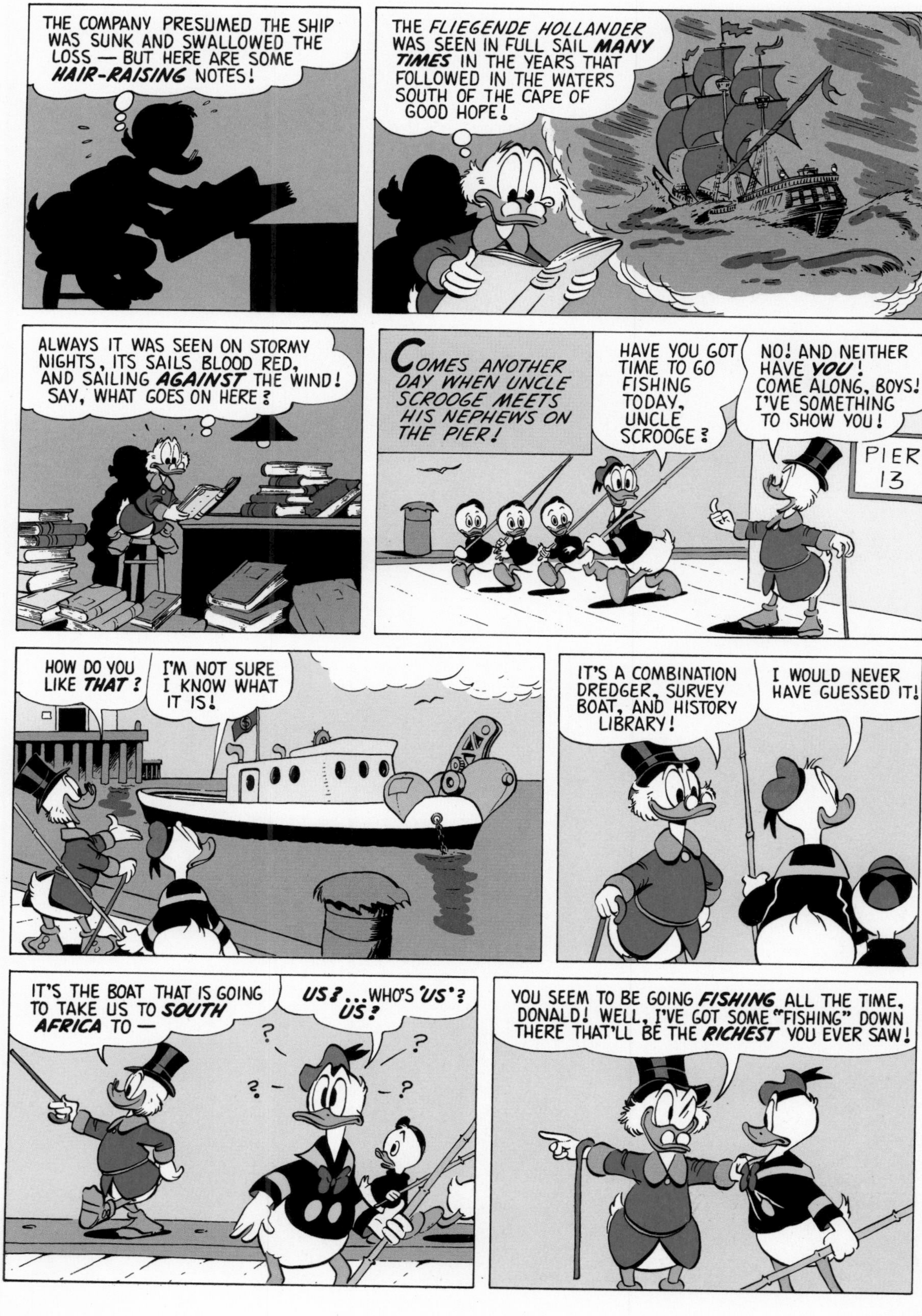
THE COMPANY PRESUMED THE SHIP WAS SUNK AND SWALLOWED THE LOSS — BUT HERE ARE SOME HAIR-RAISING NOTES!
THE FLIEGENDE HOLLANDER WAS SEEN IN FULL SAIL MANY TIMES IN THE YEARS THAT FOLLOWED IN THE WATERS SOUTH OF THE CAPE OF GOOD HOPE!
ALWAYS IT WAS SEEN ON STORMY NIGHTS, ITS SAILS BLOOD RED, AND SAILING AGAINST THE WIND! SAY, WHAT GOES ON HERE?
COMES ANOTHER DAY WHEN UNCLE SCROOGE MEETS HIS NEPHEWS ON THE PIER!
HAVE YOU GOT TIME TO GO FISHING TODAY, UNCLE SCROOGE?
NO! AND NEITHER HAVE YOU! COME ALONG, BOYS! I'VE SOMETHING TO SHOW YOU!
PIER 13
HOW DO YOU LIKE THAT?
I'M NOT SURE I KNOW WHAT IT IS!
IT'S A COMBINATION DREDGER, SURVEY BOAT, AND HISTORY LIBRARY!
I WOULD NEVER HAVE GUESSED IT!
IT'S THE BOAT THAT IS GOING TO TAKE US TO SOUTH AFRICA TO —
US?...WHO'S "US"? US?
YOU SEEM TO BE GOING FISHING ALL THE TIME, DONALD! WELL, I'VE GOT SOME "FISHING" DOWN THERE THAT'LL BE THE RICHEST YOU EVER SAW!

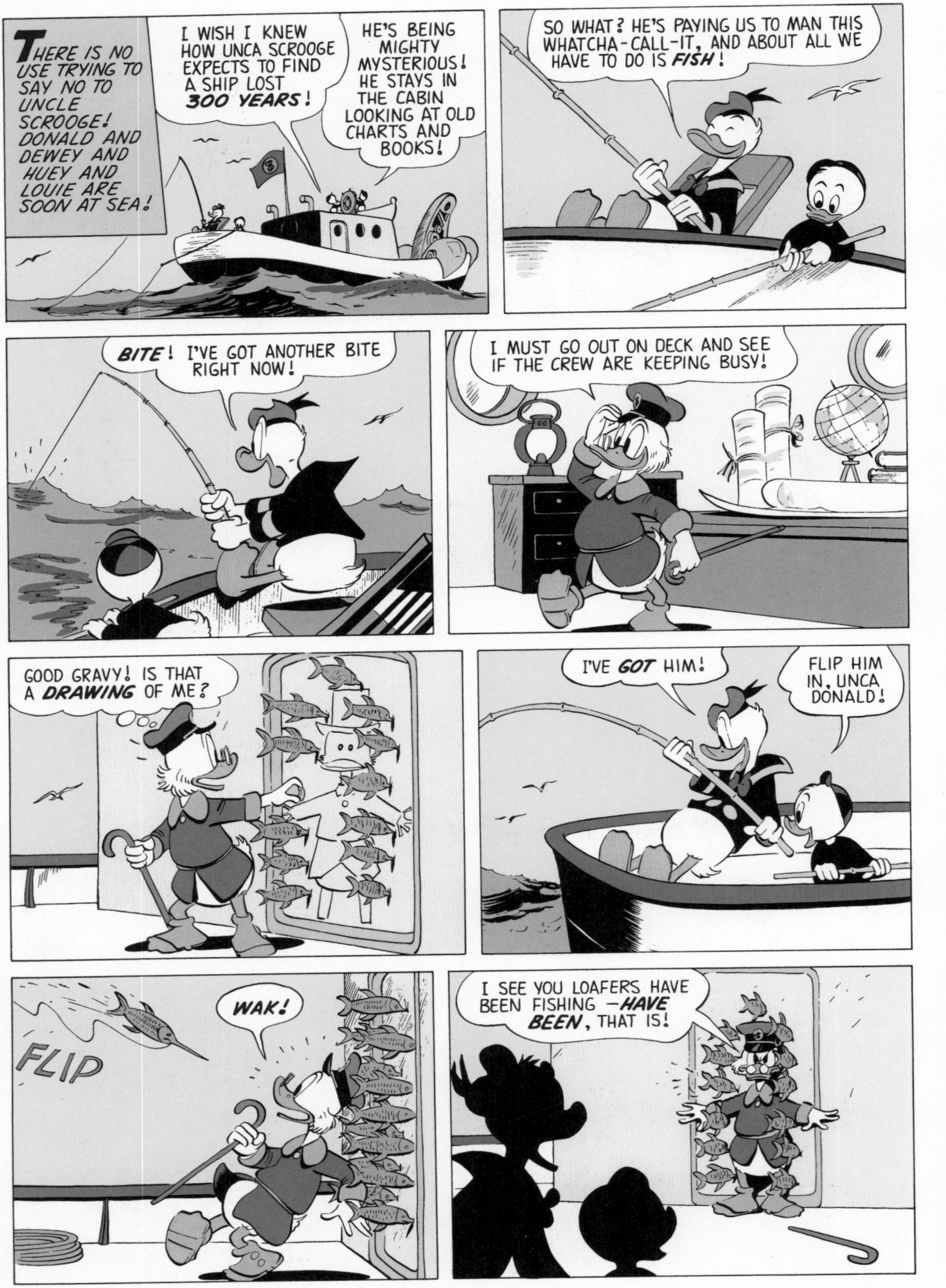
THERE IS NO USE TRYING TO SAY NO TO UNCLE SCROOGE! DONALD AND DEWEY AND HUEY AND LOUIE ARE SOON AT SEA!
I WISH I KNEW HOW UNCA SCROOGE EXPECTS TO FIND A SHIP LOST 300 YEARS!
HE'S BEING MIGHTY MYSTERIOUS! HE STAYS IN THE CABIN LOOKING AT OLD CHARTS AND BOOKS!
SO WHAT? HE'S PAYING US TO MAN THIS WHATCHA-CALL-IT, AND ABOUT ALL WE HAVE TO DO IS FISH!
BITE! I'VE GOT ANOTHER BITE RIGHT NOW!
I MUST GO OUT ON DECK AND SEE IF THE CREW ARE KEEPING BUSY!
GOOD GRAVY! IS THAT A DRAWING OF ME?
I'VE GOT HIM!
FLIP HIM IN, UNCA DONALD!
FLIP
WAK!
I SEE YOU LOAFERS HAVE BEEN FISHING —HAVE BEEN, THAT IS!

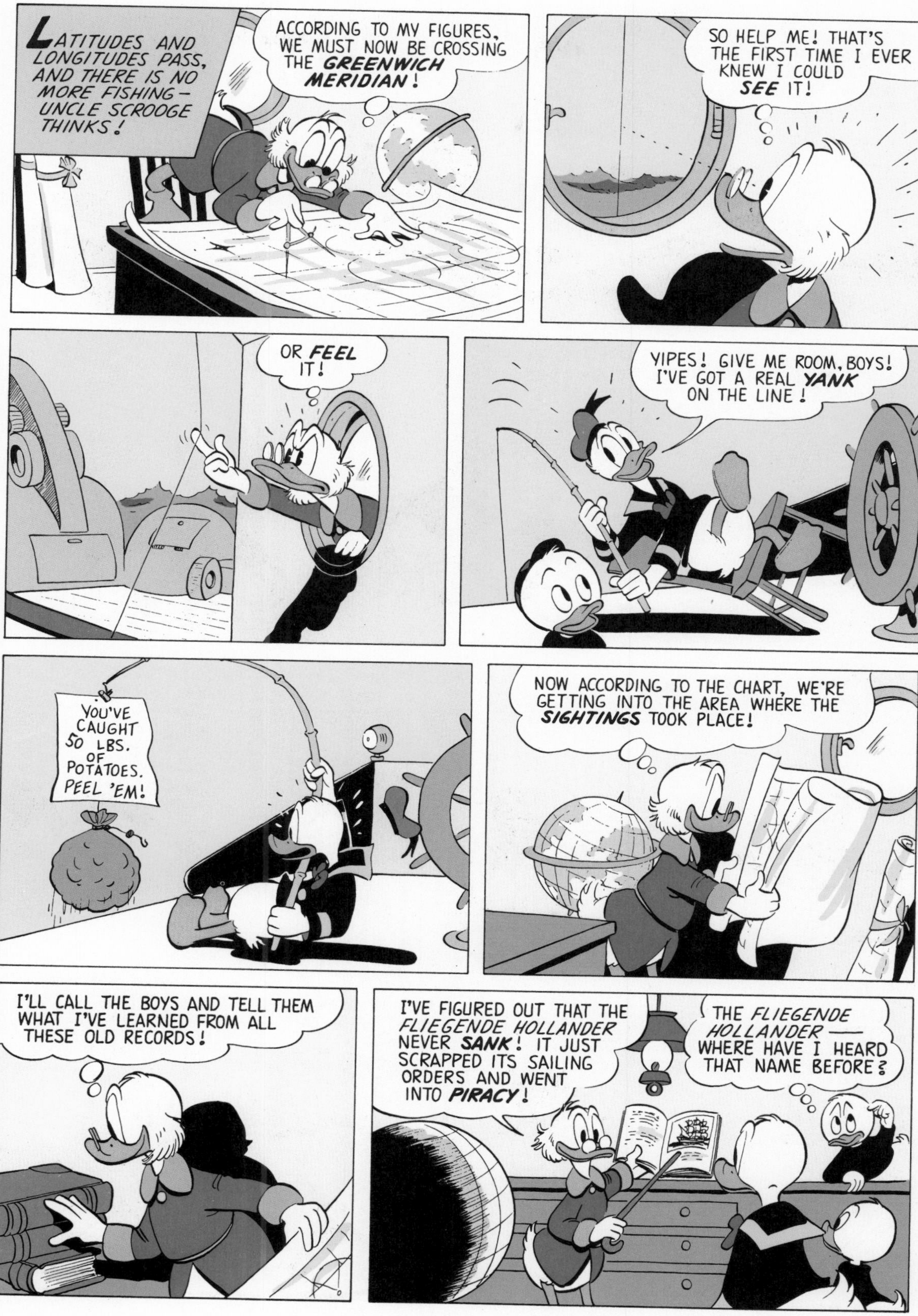
LATITUDES AND LONGITUDES PASS, AND THERE IS NO MORE FISHING— UNCLE SCROOGE THINKS!
ACCORDING TO MY FIGURES, WE MUST NOW BE CROSSING THE GREENWICH MERIDIAN!
SO HELP ME! THAT'S THE FIRST TIME I EVER KNEW I COULD SEE IT!
OR FEEL IT!
YIPES! GIVE ME ROOM, BOYS! I'VE GOT A REAL YANK ON THE LINE!
YOU'VE CAUGHT 50 LBS. OF POTATOES. PEEL 'EM!
NOW ACCORDING TO THE CHART, WE'RE GETTING INTO THE AREA WHERE THE SIGHTINGS TOOK PLACE!
I'LL CALL THE BOYS AND TELL THEM WHAT I'VE LEARNED FROM ALL THESE OLD RECORDS!
I'VE FIGURED OUT THAT THE FLIEGENDE HOLLANDER NEVER SANK! IT JUST SCRAPPED ITS SAILING ORDERS AND WENT INTO PIRACY!
THE FLIEGENDE HOLLANDER — WHERE HAVE I HEARD THAT NAME BEFORE?

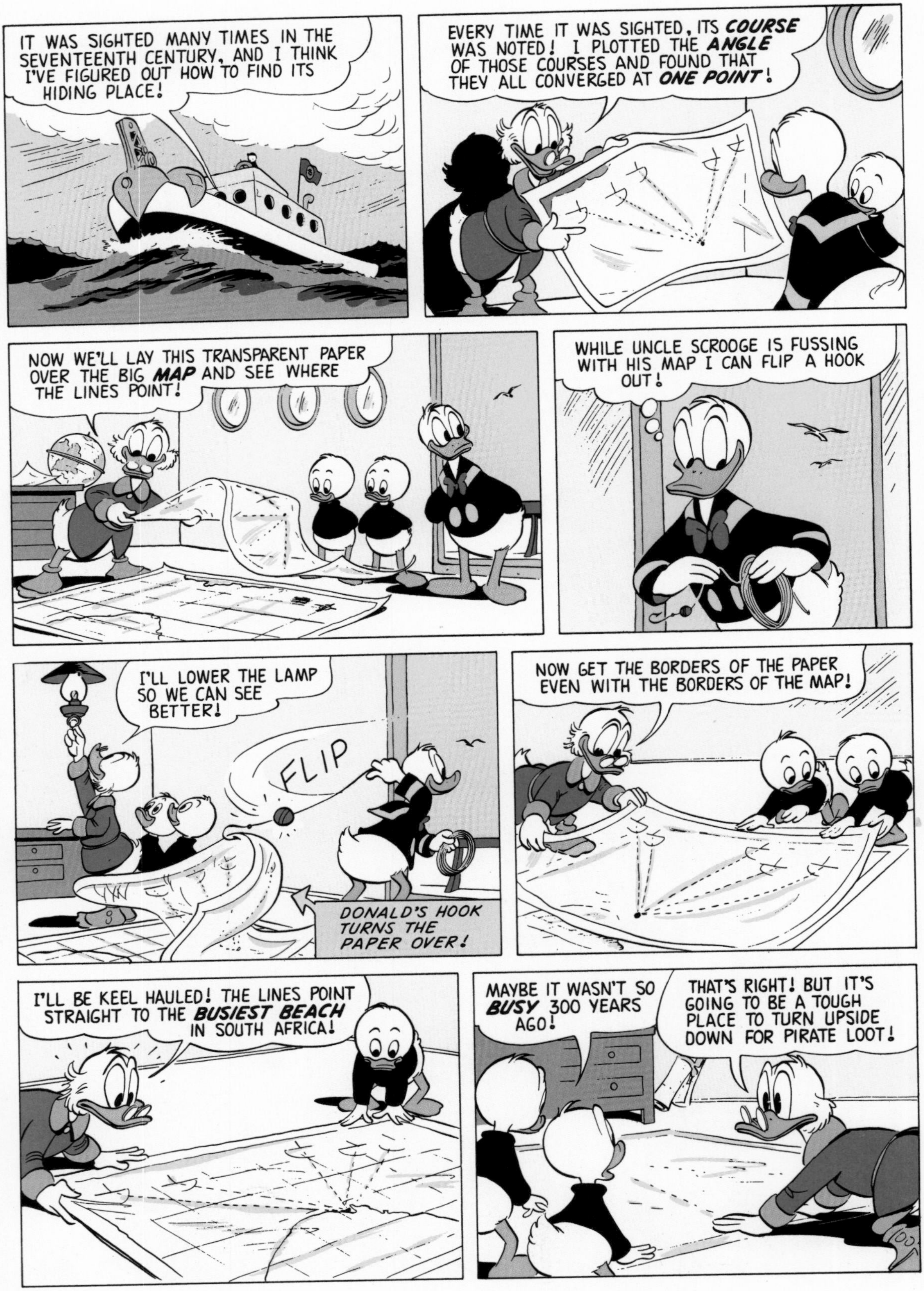
IT WAS SIGHTED MANY TIMES IN THE SEVENTEENTH CENTURY, AND I THINK I'VE FIGURED OUT HOW TO FIND ITS HIDING PLACE!
EVERY TIME IT WAS SIGHTED, ITS COURSE WAS NOTED! I PLOTTED THE ANGLE OF THOSE COURSES AND FOUND THAT THEY ALL CONVERGED AT ONE POINT!
NOW WE'LL LAY THIS TRANSPARENT PAPER OVER THE BIG MAP AND SEE WHERE THE LINES POINT!
WHILE UNCLE SCROOGE IS FUSSING WITH HIS MAP I CAN FLIP A HOOK OUT!
I'LL LOWER THE LAMP SO WE CAN SEE BETTER!
FLIP
DONALD'S HOOK TURNS THE PAPER OVER!
NOW GET THE BORDERS OF THE PAPER EVEN WITH THE BORDERS OF THE MAP!
I'LL BE KEEL HAULED! THE LINES POINT STRAIGHT TO THE BUSIEST BEACH IN SOUTH AFRICA!
MAYBE IT WASN'T SO BUSY 300 YEARS AGO!
THAT'S RIGHT! BUT IT'S GOING TO BE A TOUGH PLACE TO TURN UPSIDE DOWN FOR PIRATE LOOT!

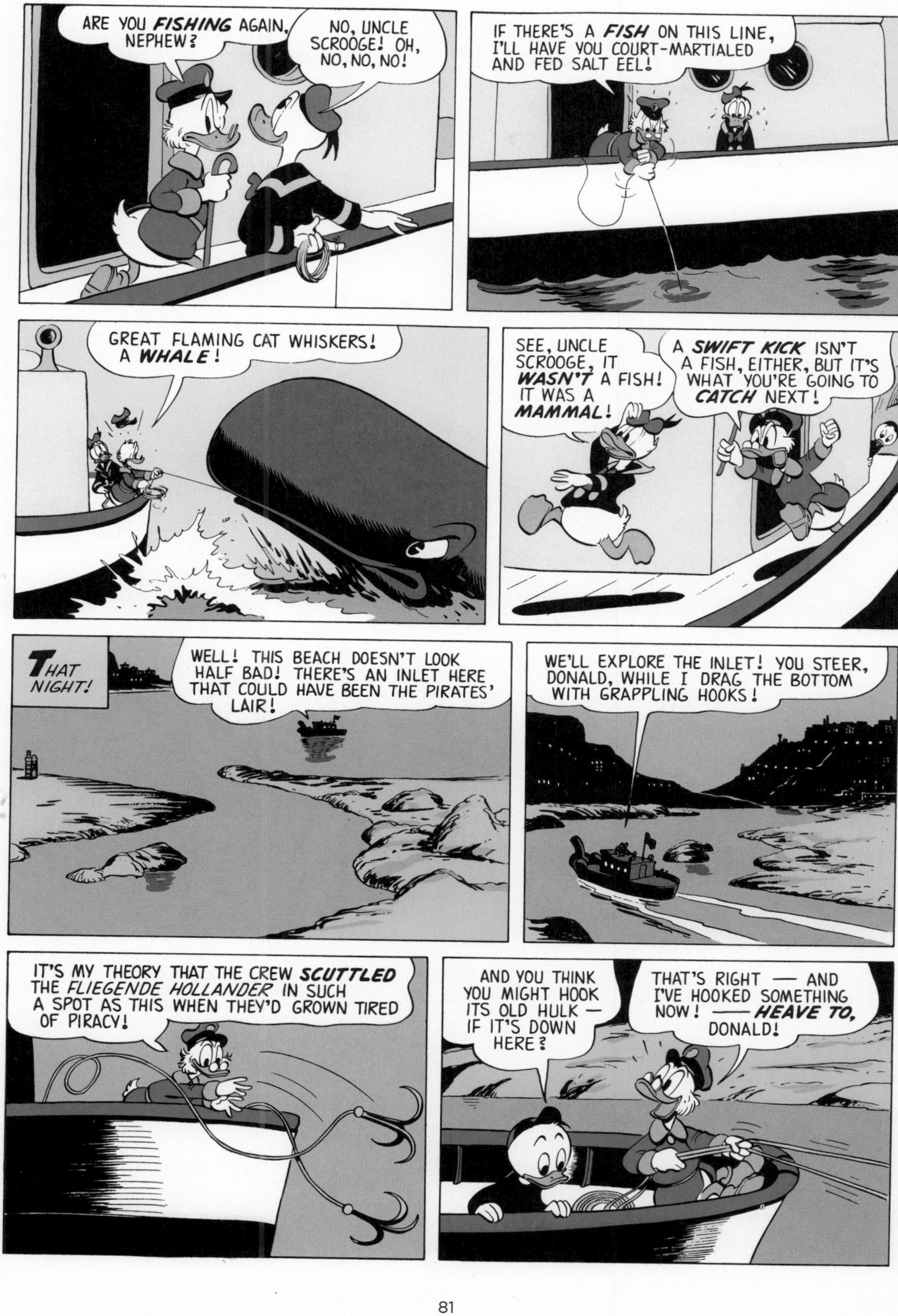
ARE YOU *FISHING* AGAIN, NEPHEW?
NO, UNCLE SCROOGE! OH, NO, NO, NO!
IF THERE'S A *FISH* ON THIS LINE, I'LL HAVE YOU COURT-MARTIALED AND FED SALT EEL!
GREAT FLAMING CAT WHISKERS! A *WHALE*!
SEE, UNCLE SCROOGE, IT *WASN'T* A FISH! IT WAS A *MAMMAL*!
A *SWIFT KICK* ISN'T A FISH, EITHER, BUT IT'S WHAT YOU'RE GOING TO *CATCH* NEXT!
THAT NIGHT!
WELL! THIS BEACH DOESN'T LOOK HALF BAD! THERE'S AN INLET HERE THAT COULD HAVE BEEN THE PIRATES' LAIR!
WE'LL EXPLORE THE INLET! YOU STEER, DONALD, WHILE I DRAG THE BOTTOM WITH GRAPPLING HOOKS!
IT'S MY THEORY THAT THE CREW *SCUTTLED* THE *FLIEGENDE HOLLANDER* IN SUCH A SPOT AS THIS WHEN THEY'D GROWN TIRED OF PIRACY!
AND YOU THINK YOU MIGHT HOOK ITS OLD HULK — IF IT'S DOWN HERE?
THAT'S RIGHT — AND I'VE HOOKED SOMETHING NOW! — *HEAVE TO,* DONALD!

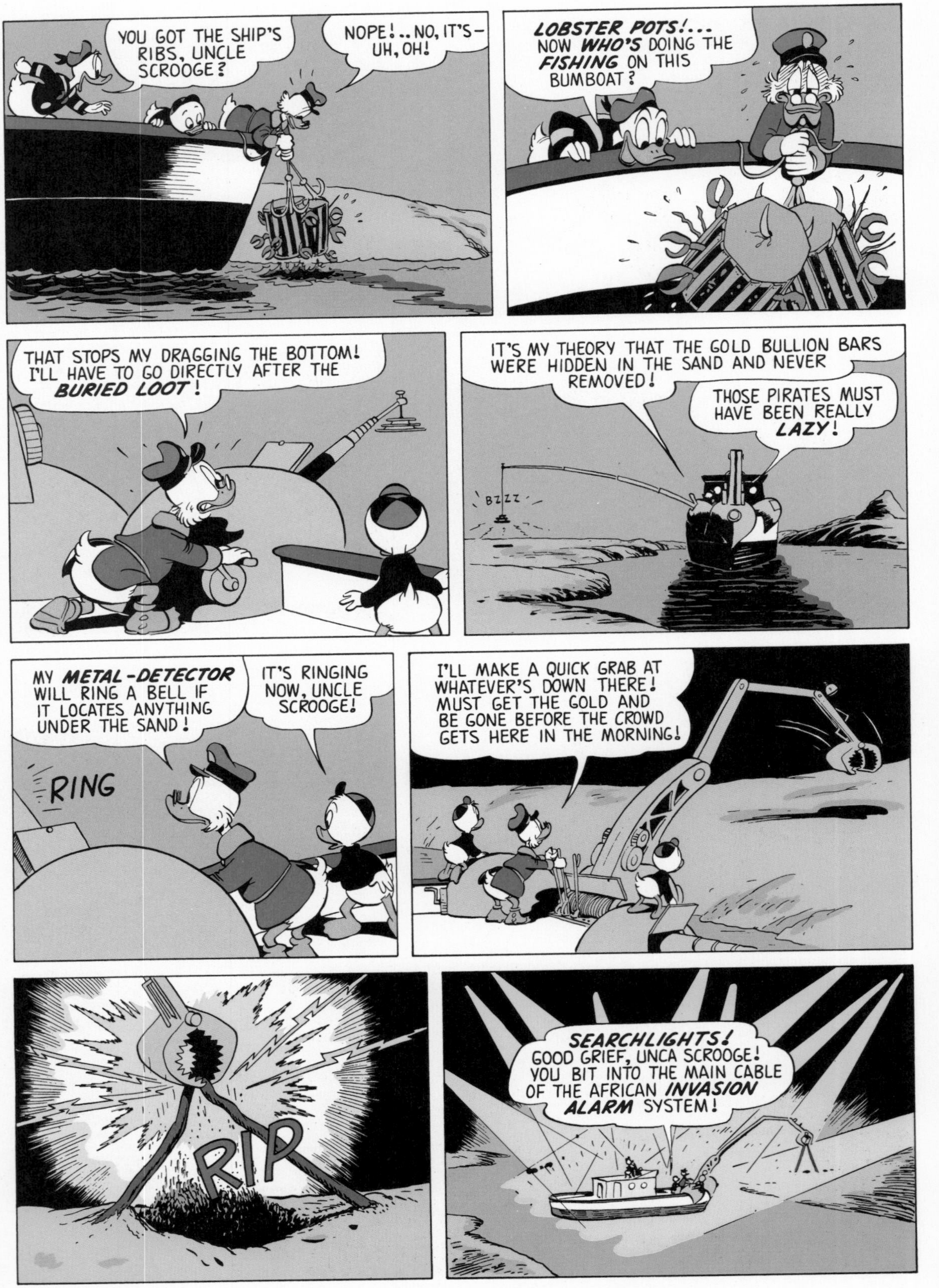
YOU GOT THE SHIP'S RIBS, UNCLE SCROOGE?
NOPE! .. NO, IT'S— UH, OH!
LOBSTER POTS!... NOW WHO'S DOING THE FISHING ON THIS BUMBOAT?
THAT STOPS MY DRAGGING THE BOTTOM! I'LL HAVE TO GO DIRECTLY AFTER THE BURIED LOOT!
IT'S MY THEORY THAT THE GOLD BULLION BARS WERE HIDDEN IN THE SAND AND NEVER REMOVED!
THOSE PIRATES MUST HAVE BEEN REALLY LAZY!
BZZZ
MY METAL-DETECTOR WILL RING A BELL IF IT LOCATES ANYTHING UNDER THE SAND!
IT'S RINGING NOW, UNCLE SCROOGE!
RING
I'LL MAKE A QUICK GRAB AT WHATEVER'S DOWN THERE! MUST GET THE GOLD AND BE GONE BEFORE THE CROWD GETS HERE IN THE MORNING!
RIP
SEARCHLIGHTS! GOOD GRIEF, UNCA SCROOGE! YOU BIT INTO THE MAIN CABLE OF THE AFRICAN INVASION ALARM SYSTEM!

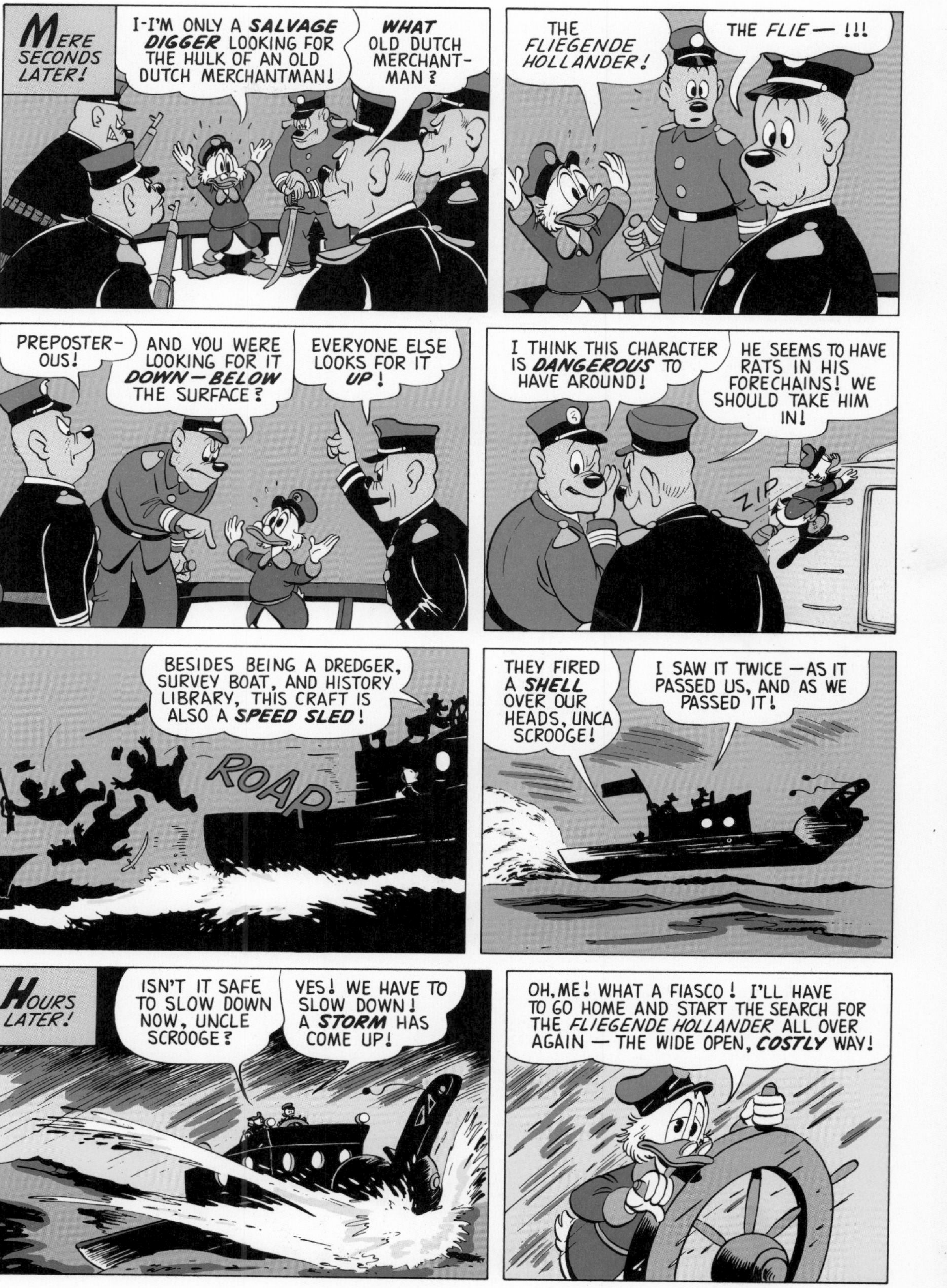

MERE SECONDS LATER!
I-I'M ONLY A SALVAGE DIGGER LOOKING FOR THE HULK OF AN OLD DUTCH MERCHANTMAN!
WHAT OLD DUTCH MERCHANT-MAN?
THE FLIEGENDE HOLLANDER!
THE FLIE— !!!
PREPOSTER-OUS!
AND YOU WERE LOOKING FOR IT DOWN—BELOW THE SURFACE?
EVERYONE ELSE LOOKS FOR IT UP!
I THINK THIS CHARACTER IS DANGEROUS TO HAVE AROUND!
HE SEEMS TO HAVE RATS IN HIS FORECHAINS! WE SHOULD TAKE HIM IN!
ZIP
BESIDES BEING A DREDGER, SURVEY BOAT, AND HISTORY LIBRARY, THIS CRAFT IS ALSO A SPEED SLED!
ROAR
THEY FIRED A SHELL OVER OUR HEADS, UNCA SCROOGE!
I SAW IT TWICE—AS IT PASSED US, AND AS WE PASSED IT!
HOURS LATER!
ISN'T IT SAFE TO SLOW DOWN NOW, UNCLE SCROOGE?
YES! WE HAVE TO SLOW DOWN! A STORM HAS COME UP!
OH, ME! WHAT A FIASCO! I'LL HAVE TO GO HOME AND START THE SEARCH FOR THE FLIEGENDE HOLLANDER ALL OVER AGAIN—THE WIDE OPEN, COSTLY WAY!

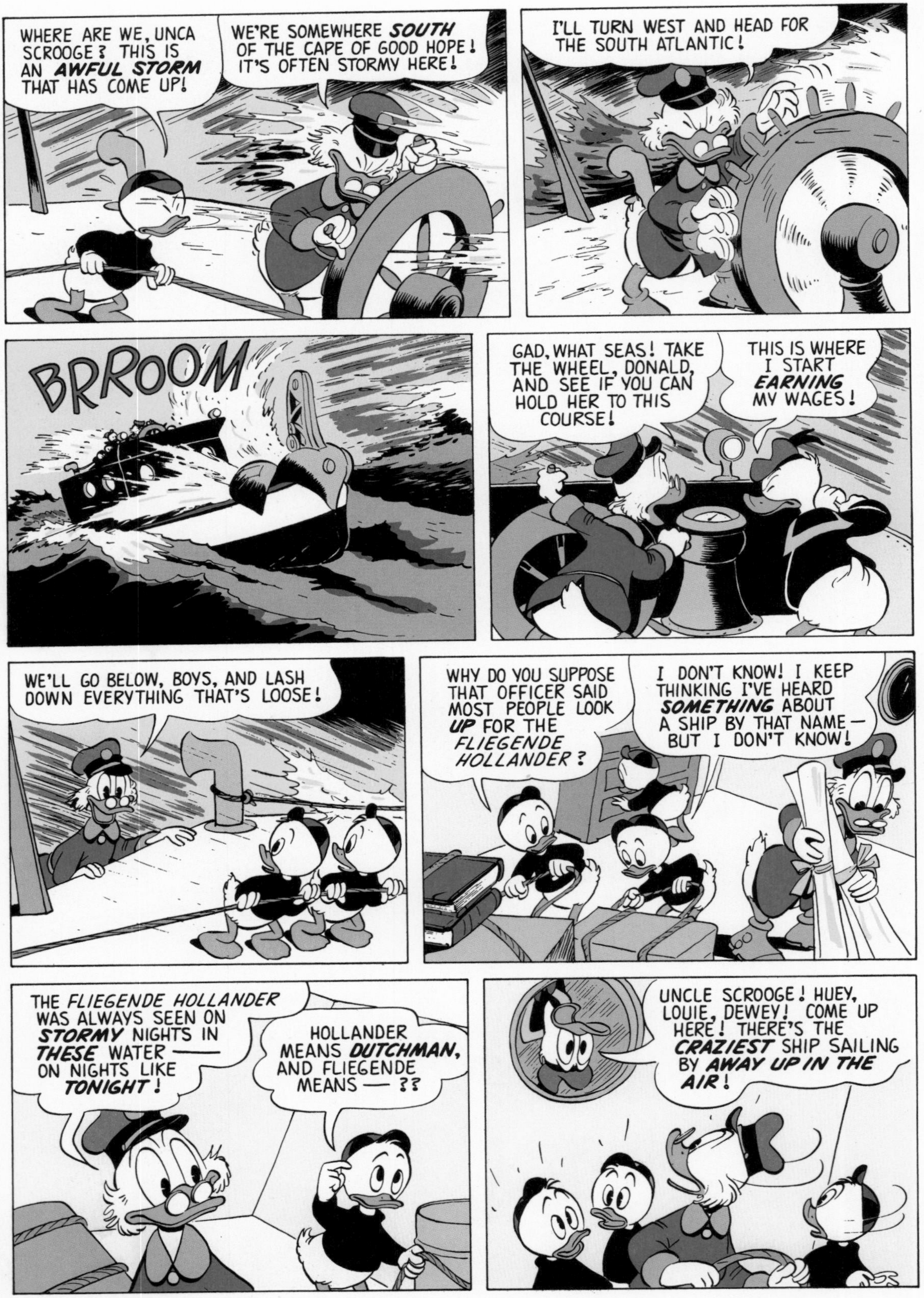
WHERE ARE WE, UNCA SCROOGE? THIS IS AN AWFUL STORM THAT HAS COME UP!
WE'RE SOMEWHERE SOUTH OF THE CAPE OF GOOD HOPE! IT'S OFTEN STORMY HERE!
I'LL TURN WEST AND HEAD FOR THE SOUTH ATLANTIC!
BRROOM
GAD, WHAT SEAS! TAKE THE WHEEL, DONALD, AND SEE IF YOU CAN HOLD HER TO THIS COURSE!
THIS IS WHERE I START EARNING MY WAGES!
WE'LL GO BELOW, BOYS, AND LASH DOWN EVERYTHING THAT'S LOOSE!
WHY DO YOU SUPPOSE THAT OFFICER SAID MOST PEOPLE LOOK UP FOR THE FLIEGENDE HOLLANDER?
I DON'T KNOW! I KEEP THINKING I'VE HEARD SOMETHING ABOUT A SHIP BY THAT NAME— BUT I DON'T KNOW!
THE FLIEGENDE HOLLANDER WAS ALWAYS SEEN ON STORMY NIGHTS IN THESE WATER—— ON NIGHTS LIKE TONIGHT!
HOLLANDER MEANS DUTCHMAN, AND FLIEGENDE MEANS — ??
UNCLE SCROOGE! HUEY, LOUIE, DEWEY! COME UP HERE! THERE'S THE CRAZIEST SHIP SAILING BY AWAY UP IN THE AIR!

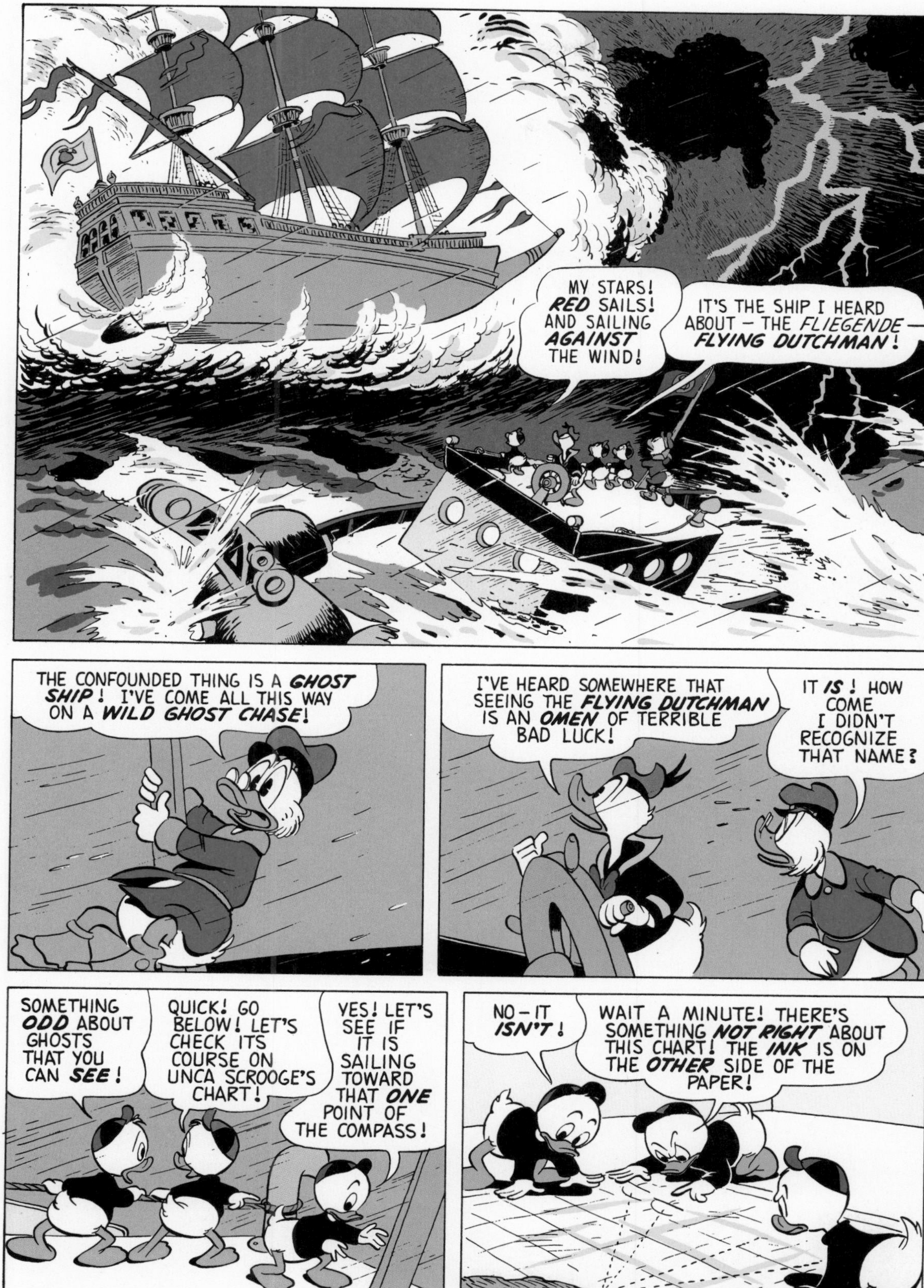
MY STARS! RED SAILS! AND SAILING AGAINST THE WIND!
IT'S THE SHIP I HEARD ABOUT — THE FLIEGENDE — FLYING DUTCHMAN!
THE CONFOUNDED THING IS A GHOST SHIP! I'VE COME ALL THIS WAY ON A WILD GHOST CHASE!
I'VE HEARD SOMEWHERE THAT SEEING THE FLYING DUTCHMAN IS AN OMEN OF TERRIBLE BAD LUCK!
IT IS! HOW COME I DIDN'T RECOGNIZE THAT NAME?
SOMETHING ODD ABOUT GHOSTS THAT YOU CAN SEE!
QUICK! GO BELOW! LET'S CHECK ITS COURSE ON UNCA SCROOGE'S CHART!
YES! LET'S SEE IF IT IS SAILING TOWARD THAT ONE POINT OF THE COMPASS!
NO — IT ISN'T!
WAIT A MINUTE! THERE'S SOMETHING NOT RIGHT ABOUT THIS CHART! THE INK IS ON THE OTHER SIDE OF THE PAPER!

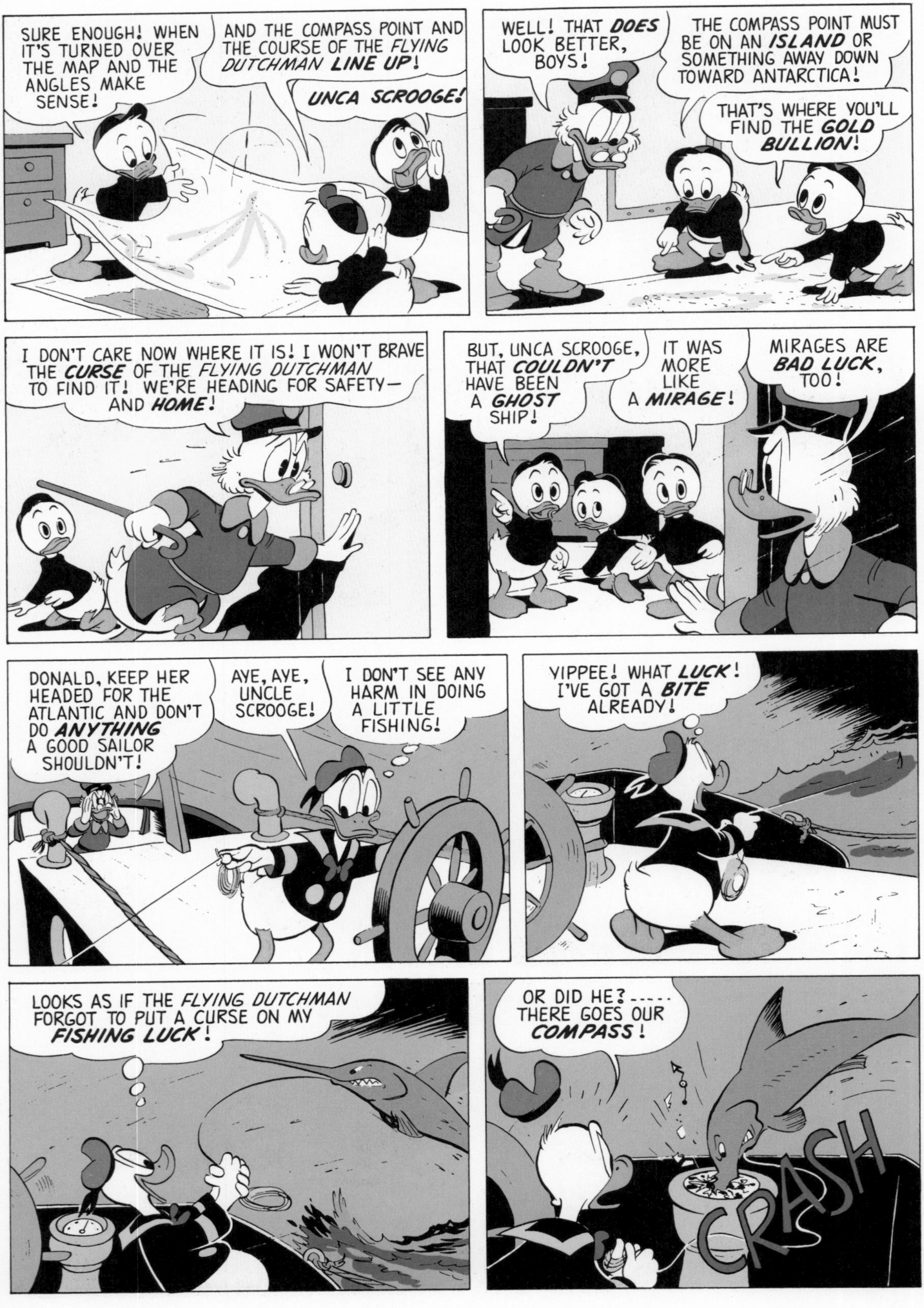
SURE ENOUGH! WHEN IT'S TURNED OVER THE MAP AND THE ANGLES MAKE SENSE!
AND THE COMPASS POINT AND THE COURSE OF THE FLYING DUTCHMAN LINE UP!
UNCA SCROOGE!
WELL! THAT DOES LOOK BETTER, BOYS!
THE COMPASS POINT MUST BE ON AN ISLAND OR SOMETHING AWAY DOWN TOWARD ANTARCTICA!
THAT'S WHERE YOU'LL FIND THE GOLD BULLION!
I DON'T CARE NOW WHERE IT IS! I WON'T BRAVE THE CURSE OF THE FLYING DUTCHMAN TO FIND IT! WE'RE HEADING FOR SAFETY— AND HOME!
BUT, UNCA SCROOGE, THAT COULDN'T HAVE BEEN A GHOST SHIP!
IT WAS MORE LIKE A MIRAGE!
MIRAGES ARE BAD LUCK, TOO!
DONALD, KEEP HER HEADED FOR THE ATLANTIC AND DON'T DO ANYTHING A GOOD SAILOR SHOULDN'T!
AYE, AYE, UNCLE SCROOGE!
I DON'T SEE ANY HARM IN DOING A LITTLE FISHING!
YIPPEE! WHAT LUCK! I'VE GOT A BITE ALREADY!
LOOKS AS IF THE FLYING DUTCHMAN FORGOT TO PUT A CURSE ON MY FISHING LUCK!
OR DID HE? ----- THERE GOES OUR COMPASS!
CRASH

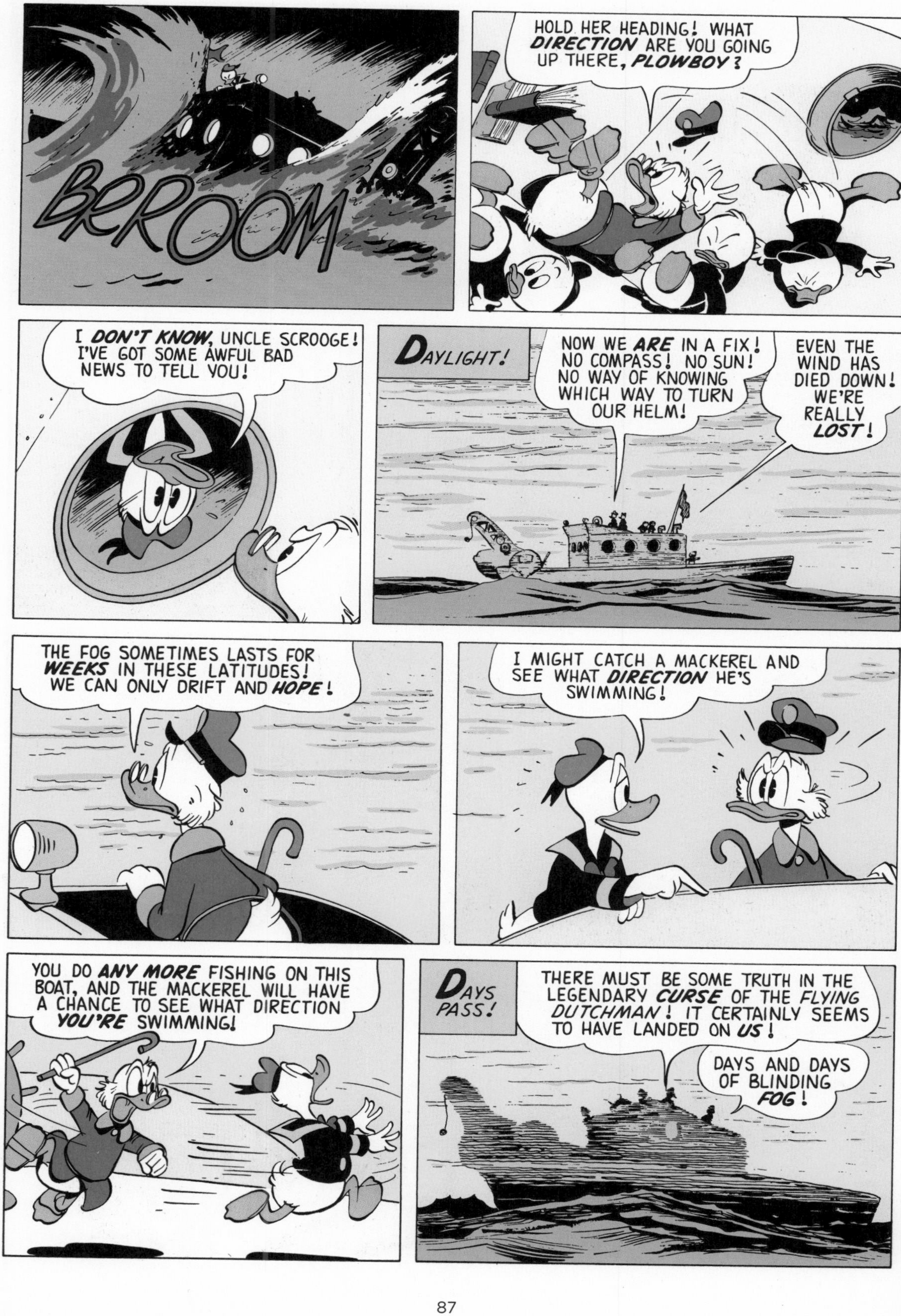
BRROOM
HOLD HER HEADING! WHAT DIRECTION ARE YOU GOING UP THERE, PLOWBOY?
I DON'T KNOW, UNCLE SCROOGE! I'VE GOT SOME AWFUL BAD NEWS TO TELL YOU!
DAYLIGHT!
NOW WE ARE IN A FIX! NO COMPASS! NO SUN! NO WAY OF KNOWING WHICH WAY TO TURN OUR HELM!
EVEN THE WIND HAS DIED DOWN! WE'RE REALLY LOST!
THE FOG SOMETIMES LASTS FOR WEEKS IN THESE LATITUDES! WE CAN ONLY DRIFT AND HOPE!
I MIGHT CATCH A MACKEREL AND SEE WHAT DIRECTION HE'S SWIMMING!
YOU DO ANY MORE FISHING ON THIS BOAT, AND THE MACKEREL WILL HAVE A CHANCE TO SEE WHAT DIRECTION YOU'RE SWIMMING!
DAYS PASS!
THERE MUST BE SOME TRUTH IN THE LEGENDARY CURSE OF THE FLYING DUTCHMAN! IT CERTAINLY SEEMS TO HAVE LANDED ON US!
DAYS AND DAYS OF BLINDING FOG!

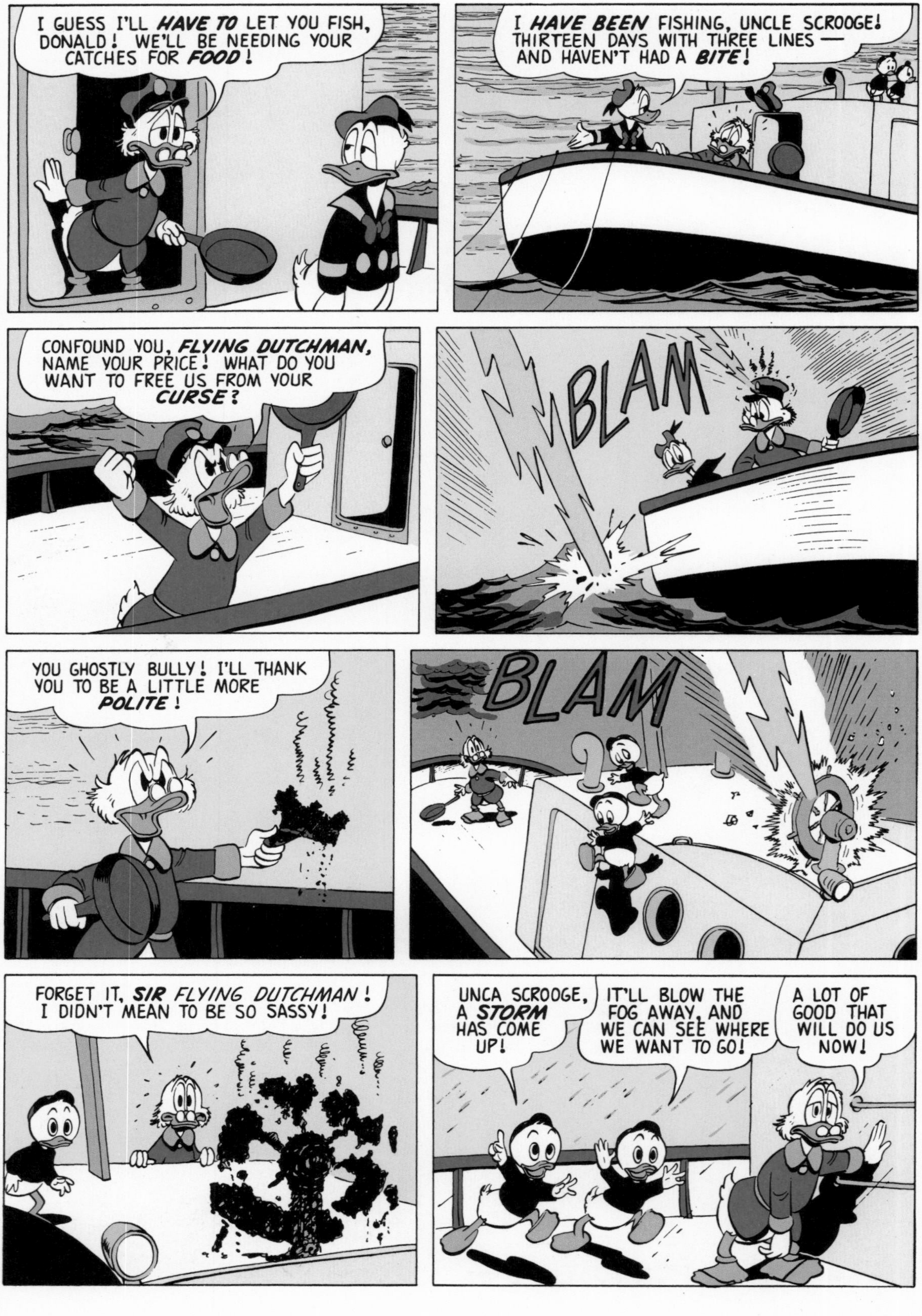
I GUESS I'LL HAVE TO LET YOU FISH, DONALD! WE'LL BE NEEDING YOUR CATCHES FOR FOOD!
I HAVE BEEN FISHING, UNCLE SCROOGE! THIRTEEN DAYS WITH THREE LINES — AND HAVEN'T HAD A BITE!
CONFOUND YOU, FLYING DUTCHMAN, NAME YOUR PRICE! WHAT DO YOU WANT TO FREE US FROM YOUR CURSE?
BLAM
YOU GHOSTLY BULLY! I'LL THANK YOU TO BE A LITTLE MORE POLITE!
BLAM
FORGET IT, SIR FLYING DUTCHMAN! I DIDN'T MEAN TO BE SO SASSY!
UNCA SCROOGE, A STORM HAS COME UP!
IT'LL BLOW THE FOG AWAY, AND WE CAN SEE WHERE WE WANT TO GO!
A LOT OF GOOD THAT WILL DO US NOW!

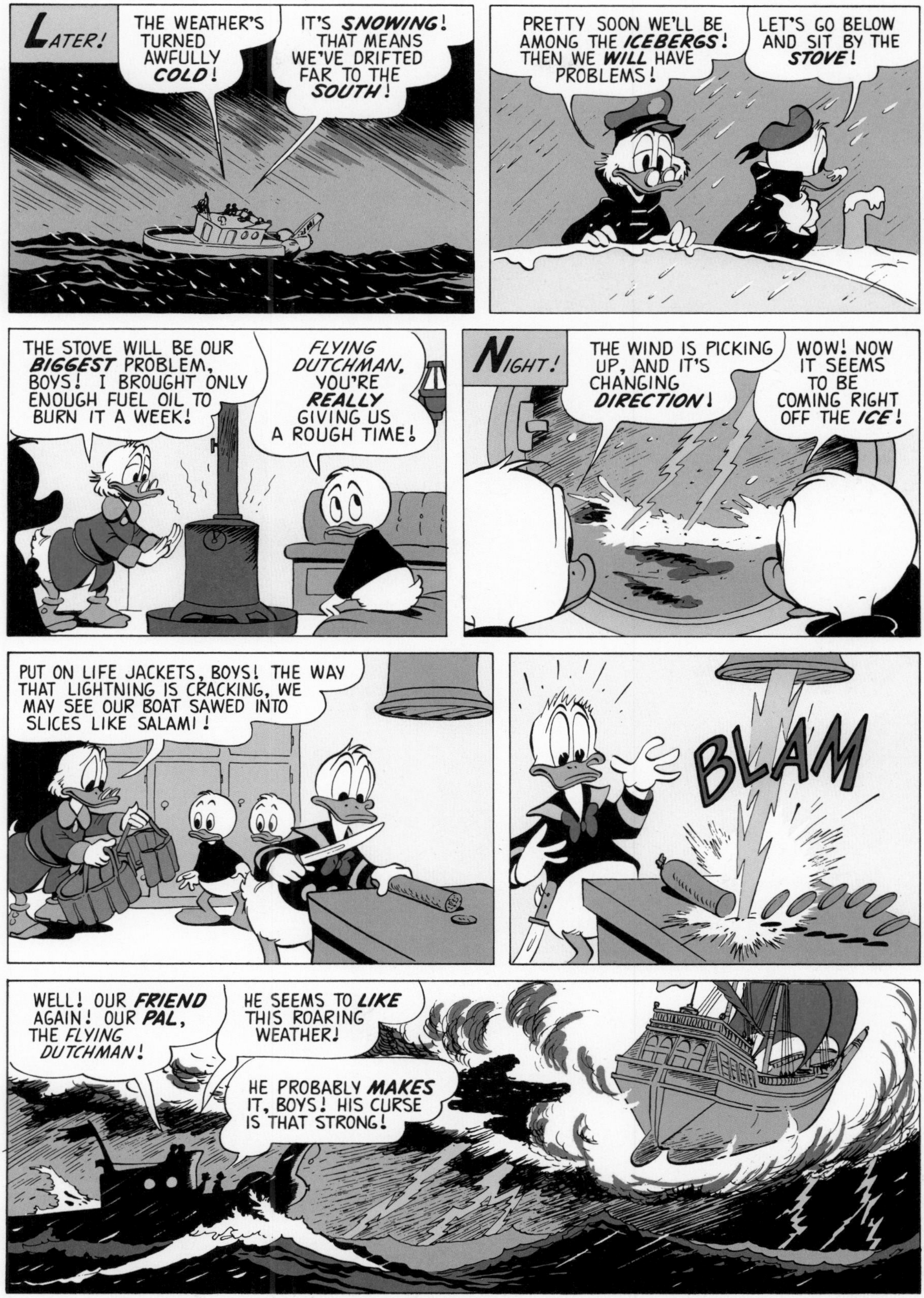
LATER!
THE WEATHER'S TURNED AWFULLY COLD!
IT'S SNOWING! THAT MEANS WE'VE DRIFTED FAR TO THE SOUTH!
PRETTY SOON WE'LL BE AMONG THE ICEBERGS! THEN WE WILL HAVE PROBLEMS!
LET'S GO BELOW AND SIT BY THE STOVE!
THE STOVE WILL BE OUR BIGGEST PROBLEM, BOYS! I BROUGHT ONLY ENOUGH FUEL OIL TO BURN IT A WEEK!
FLYING DUTCHMAN, YOU'RE REALLY GIVING US A ROUGH TIME!
NIGHT!
THE WIND IS PICKING UP, AND IT'S CHANGING DIRECTION!
WOW! NOW IT SEEMS TO BE COMING RIGHT OFF THE ICE!
PUT ON LIFE JACKETS, BOYS! THE WAY THAT LIGHTNING IS CRACKING, WE MAY SEE OUR BOAT SAWED INTO SLICES LIKE SALAMI!
BLAM
WELL! OUR FRIEND AGAIN! OUR PAL, THE FLYING DUTCHMAN!
HE SEEMS TO LIKE THIS ROARING WEATHER!
HE PROBABLY MAKES IT, BOYS! HIS CURSE IS THAT STRONG!

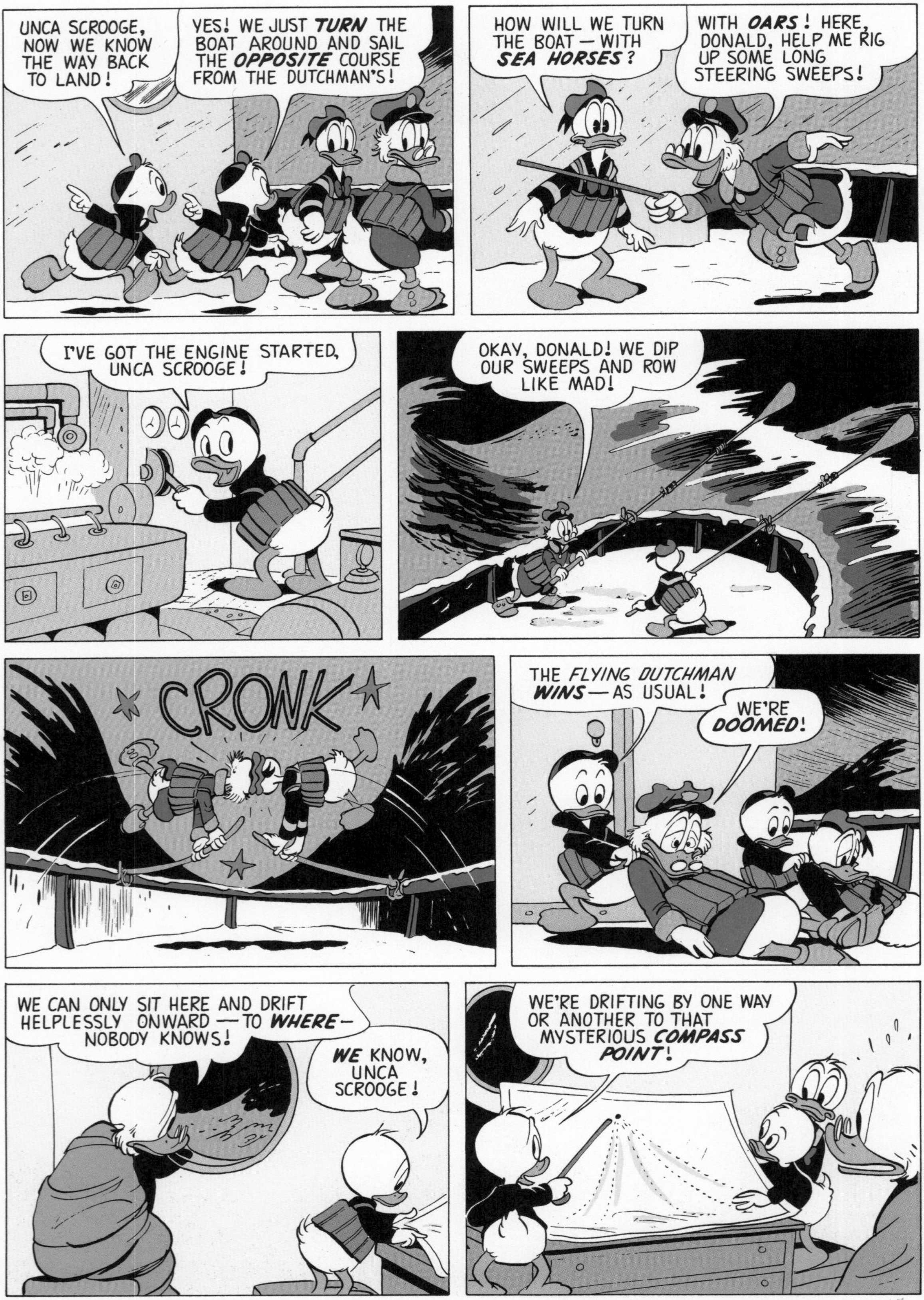
UNCA SCROOGE, NOW WE KNOW THE WAY BACK TO LAND!
YES! WE JUST TURN THE BOAT AROUND AND SAIL THE OPPOSITE COURSE FROM THE DUTCHMAN'S!
HOW WILL WE TURN THE BOAT — WITH SEA HORSES?
WITH OARS! HERE, DONALD, HELP ME RIG UP SOME LONG STEERING SWEEPS!
I'VE GOT THE ENGINE STARTED, UNCA SCROOGE!
OKAY, DONALD! WE DIP OUR SWEEPS AND ROW LIKE MAD!
CRONK
THE FLYING DUTCHMAN WINS — AS USUAL!
WE'RE DOOMED!
WE CAN ONLY SIT HERE AND DRIFT HELPLESSLY ONWARD — TO WHERE — NOBODY KNOWS!
WE KNOW, UNCA SCROOGE!
WE'RE DRIFTING BY ONE WAY OR ANOTHER TO THAT MYSTERIOUS COMPASS POINT!

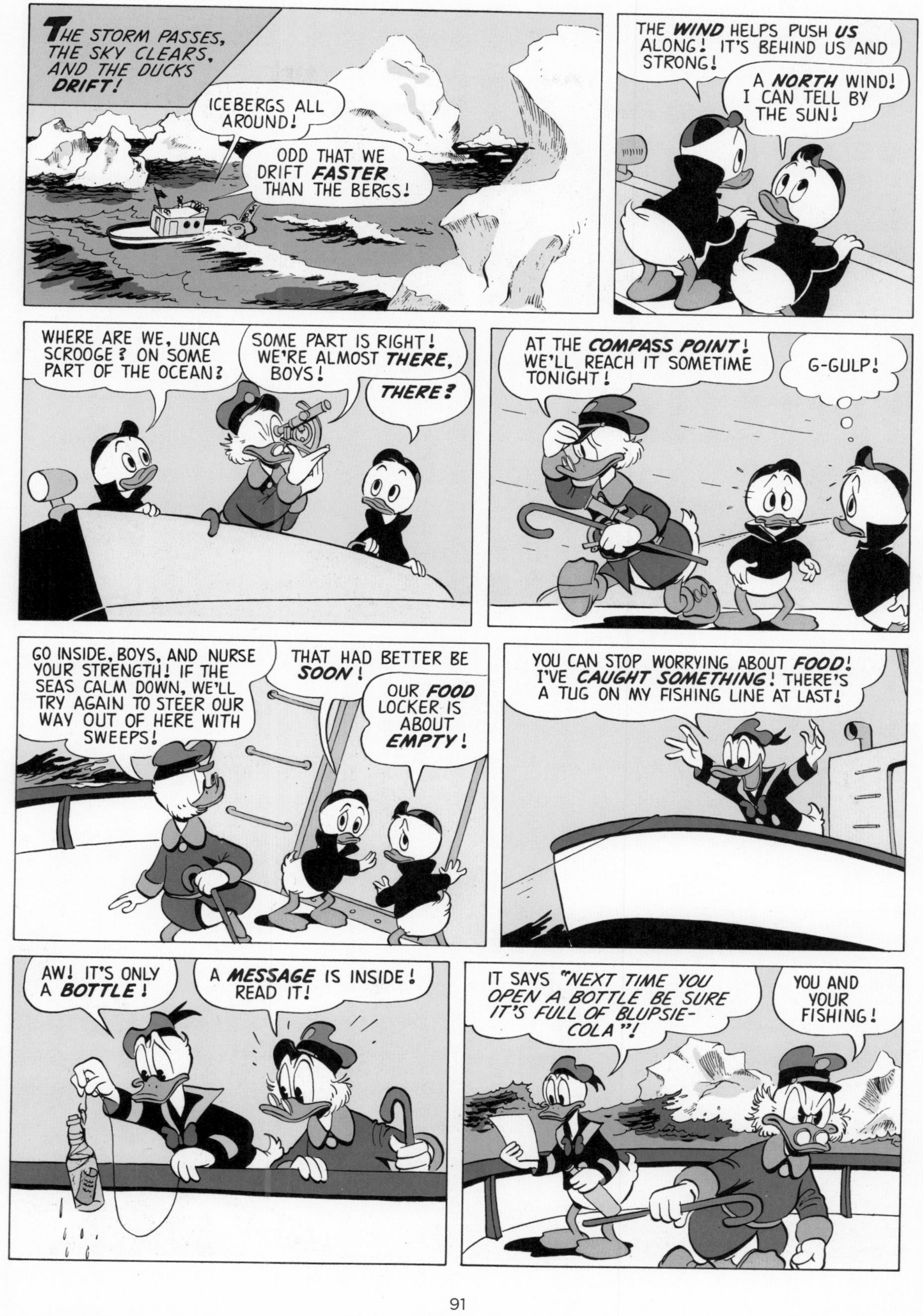
THE STORM PASSES, THE SKY CLEARS, AND THE DUCKS DRIFT!
ICEBERGS ALL AROUND!
ODD THAT WE DRIFT FASTER THAN THE BERGS!
THE WIND HELPS PUSH US ALONG! IT'S BEHIND US AND STRONG!
A NORTH WIND! I CAN TELL BY THE SUN!
WHERE ARE WE, UNCA SCROOGE? ON SOME PART OF THE OCEAN?
SOME PART IS RIGHT! WE'RE ALMOST THERE, BOYS!
THERE?
AT THE COMPASS POINT! WE'LL REACH IT SOMETIME TONIGHT!
G-GULP!
GO INSIDE, BOYS, AND NURSE YOUR STRENGTH! IF THE SEAS CALM DOWN, WE'LL TRY AGAIN TO STEER OUR WAY OUT OF HERE WITH SWEEPS!
THAT HAD BETTER BE SOON!
OUR FOOD LOCKER IS ABOUT EMPTY!
YOU CAN STOP WORRYING ABOUT FOOD! I'VE CAUGHT SOMETHING! THERE'S A TUG ON MY FISHING LINE AT LAST!
AW! IT'S ONLY A BOTTLE!
A MESSAGE IS INSIDE! READ IT!
IT SAYS "NEXT TIME YOU OPEN A BOTTLE BE SURE IT'S FULL OF BLUPSIE-COLA"!
YOU AND YOUR FISHING!

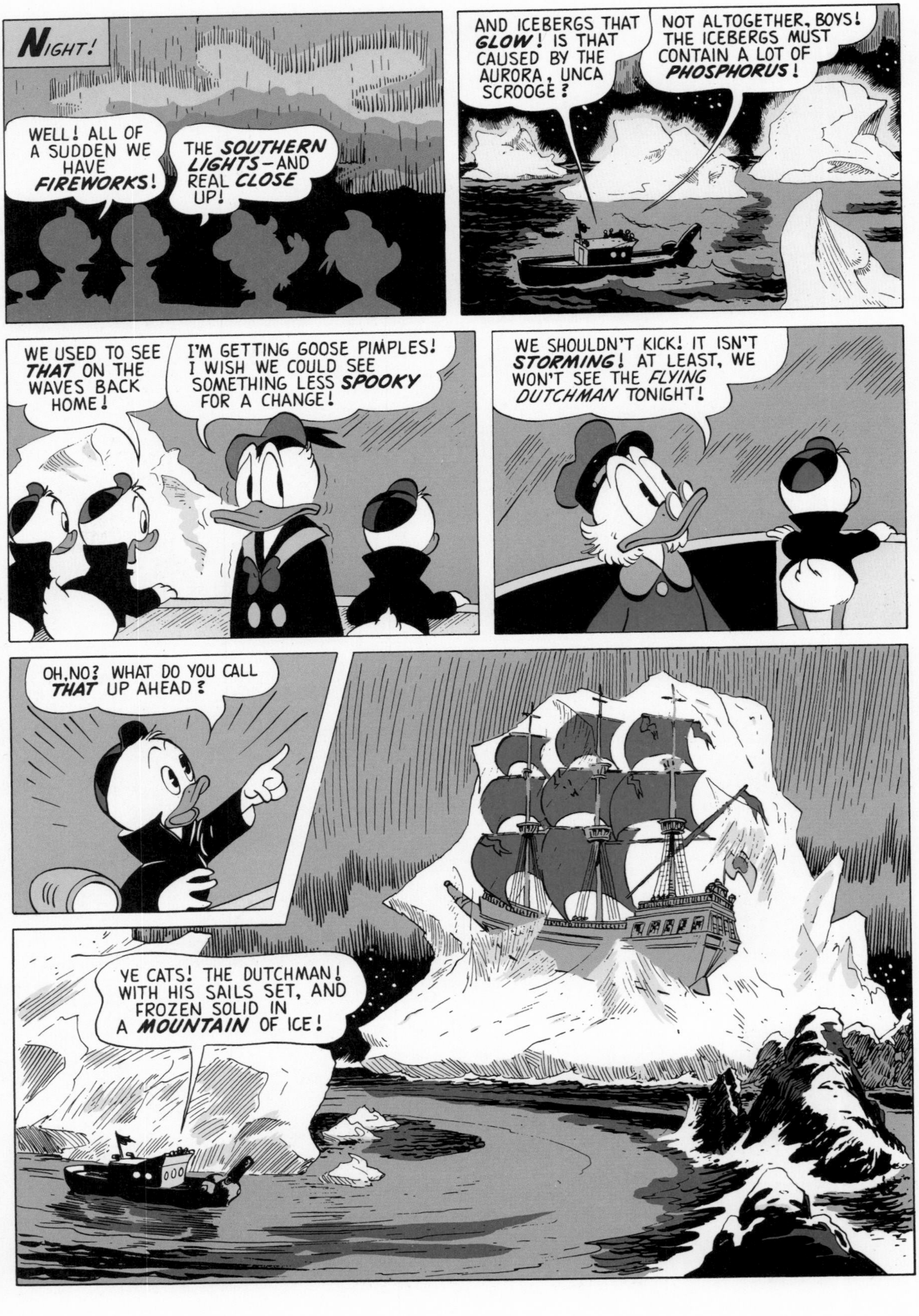
NIGHT!
WELL! ALL OF A SUDDEN WE HAVE FIREWORKS!
THE SOUTHERN LIGHTS—AND REAL CLOSE UP!
AND ICEBERGS THAT GLOW! IS THAT CAUSED BY THE AURORA, UNCA SCROOGE?
NOT ALTOGETHER, BOYS! THE ICEBERGS MUST CONTAIN A LOT OF PHOSPHORUS!
WE USED TO SEE THAT ON THE WAVES BACK HOME!
I'M GETTING GOOSE PIMPLES! I WISH WE COULD SEE SOMETHING LESS SPOOKY FOR A CHANGE!
WE SHOULDN'T KICK! IT ISN'T STORMING! AT LEAST, WE WON'T SEE THE FLYING DUTCHMAN TONIGHT!
OH, NO? WHAT DO YOU CALL THAT UP AHEAD?
YE CATS! THE DUTCHMAN! WITH HIS SAILS SET, AND FROZEN SOLID IN A MOUNTAIN OF ICE!

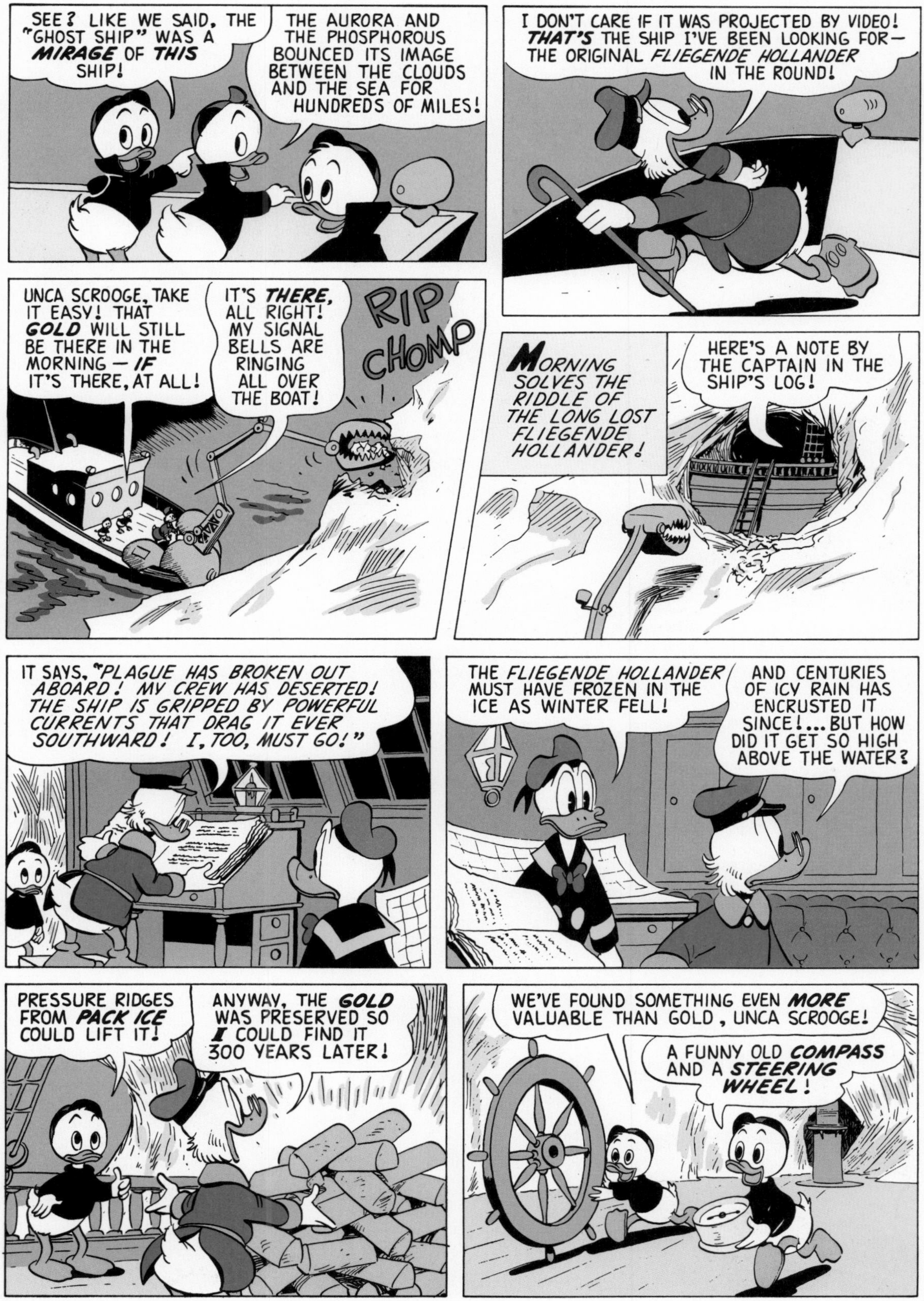
SEE? LIKE WE SAID, THE "GHOST SHIP" WAS A MIRAGE OF THIS SHIP!
THE AURORA AND THE PHOSPHOROUS BOUNCED ITS IMAGE BETWEEN THE CLOUDS AND THE SEA FOR HUNDREDS OF MILES!
I DON'T CARE IF IT WAS PROJECTED BY VIDEO! THAT'S THE SHIP I'VE BEEN LOOKING FOR— THE ORIGINAL FLIEGENDE HOLLANDER IN THE ROUND!
UNCA SCROOGE, TAKE IT EASY! THAT GOLD WILL STILL BE THERE IN THE MORNING — IF IT'S THERE, AT ALL!
IT'S THERE, ALL RIGHT! MY SIGNAL BELLS ARE RINGING ALL OVER THE BOAT!
RIP
CHOMP
MORNING SOLVES THE RIDDLE OF THE LONG LOST FLIEGENDE HOLLANDER!
HERE'S A NOTE BY THE CAPTAIN IN THE SHIP'S LOG!
IT SAYS, "PLAGUE HAS BROKEN OUT ABOARD! MY CREW HAS DESERTED! THE SHIP IS GRIPPED BY POWERFUL CURRENTS THAT DRAG IT EVER SOUTHWARD! I, TOO, MUST GO!"
THE FLIEGENDE HOLLANDER MUST HAVE FROZEN IN THE ICE AS WINTER FELL!
AND CENTURIES OF ICY RAIN HAS ENCRUSTED IT SINCE!... BUT HOW DID IT GET SO HIGH ABOVE THE WATER?
PRESSURE RIDGES FROM PACK ICE COULD LIFT IT!
ANYWAY, THE GOLD WAS PRESERVED SO I COULD FIND IT 300 YEARS LATER!
WE'VE FOUND SOMETHING EVEN MORE VALUABLE THAN GOLD, UNCA SCROOGE!
A FUNNY OLD COMPASS AND A STEERING WHEEL!

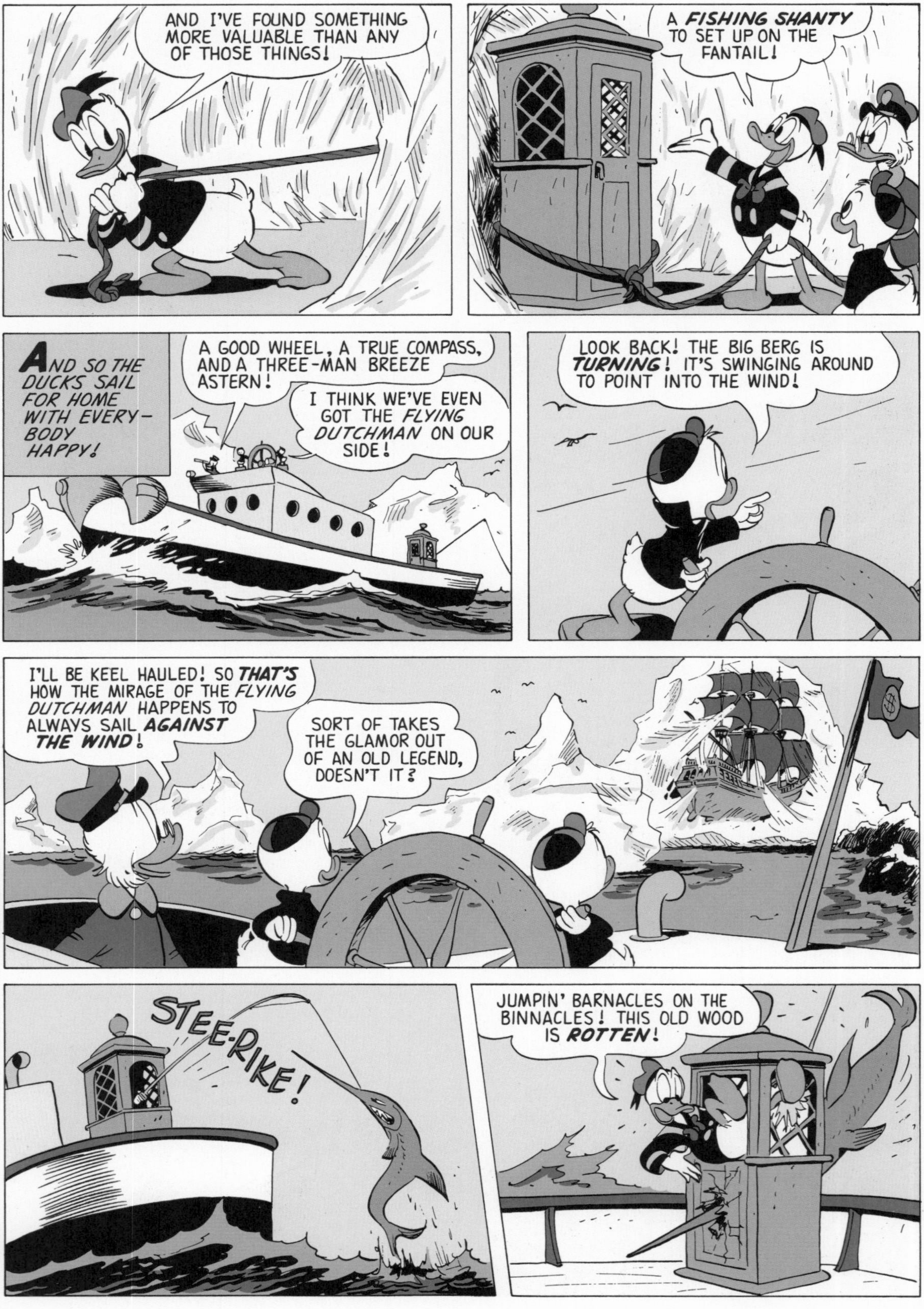
AND I'VE FOUND SOMETHING MORE VALUABLE THAN ANY OF THOSE THINGS!
A *FISHING SHANTY* TO SET UP ON THE FANTAIL!
AND SO THE DUCKS SAIL FOR HOME WITH EVERY-BODY HAPPY!
A GOOD WHEEL, A TRUE COMPASS, AND A THREE-MAN BREEZE ASTERN!
I THINK WE'VE EVEN GOT THE *FLYING DUTCHMAN* ON OUR SIDE!
LOOK BACK! THE BIG BERG IS *TURNING*! IT'S SWINGING AROUND TO POINT INTO THE WIND!
I'LL BE KEEL HAULED! SO *THAT'S* HOW THE MIRAGE OF THE *FLYING DUTCHMAN* HAPPENS TO ALWAYS SAIL *AGAINST THE WIND*!
SORT OF TAKES THE GLAMOR OUT OF AN OLD LEGEND, DOESN'T IT?
STEE-RIKE!
JUMPIN' BARNACLES ON THE BINNACLES! THIS OLD WOOD IS *ROTTEN*!

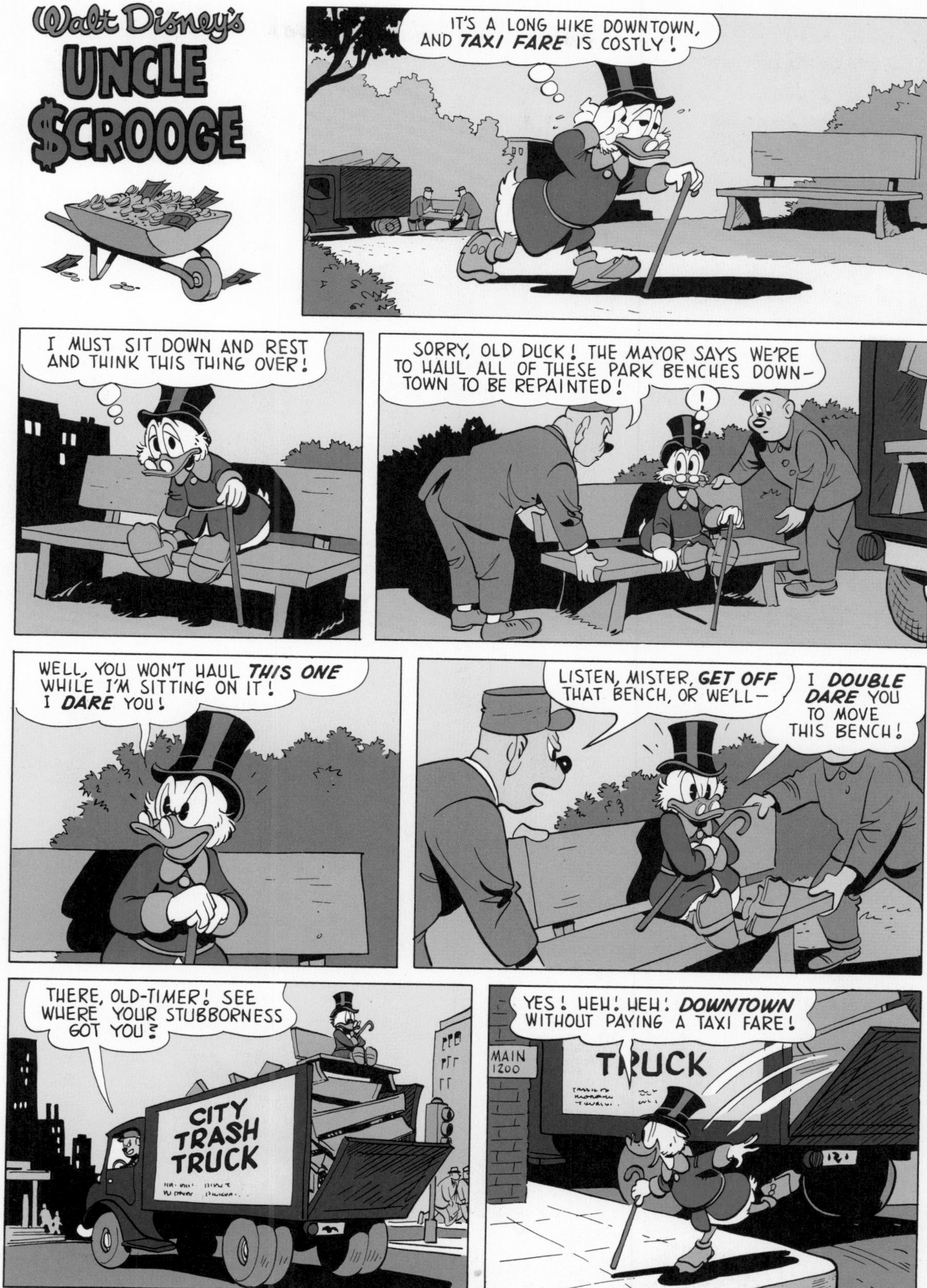
Walt Disney's
UNCLE $CROOGE
IT'S A LONG HIKE DOWNTOWN, AND TAXI FARE IS COSTLY!
I MUST SIT DOWN AND REST AND THINK THIS THING OVER!
SORRY, OLD DUCK! THE MAYOR SAYS WE'RE TO HAUL ALL OF THESE PARK BENCHES DOWN-TOWN TO BE REPAINTED!
!
WELL, YOU WON'T HAUL THIS ONE WHILE I'M SITTING ON IT! I DARE YOU!
LISTEN, MISTER, GET OFF THAT BENCH, OR WE'LL—
I DOUBLE DARE YOU TO MOVE THIS BENCH!
THERE, OLD-TIMER! SEE WHERE YOUR STUBBORNESS GOT YOU?
CITY TRASH TRUCK
YES! HEH! HEH! DOWNTOWN WITHOUT PAYING A TAXI FARE!
MAIN 1200
TRUCK

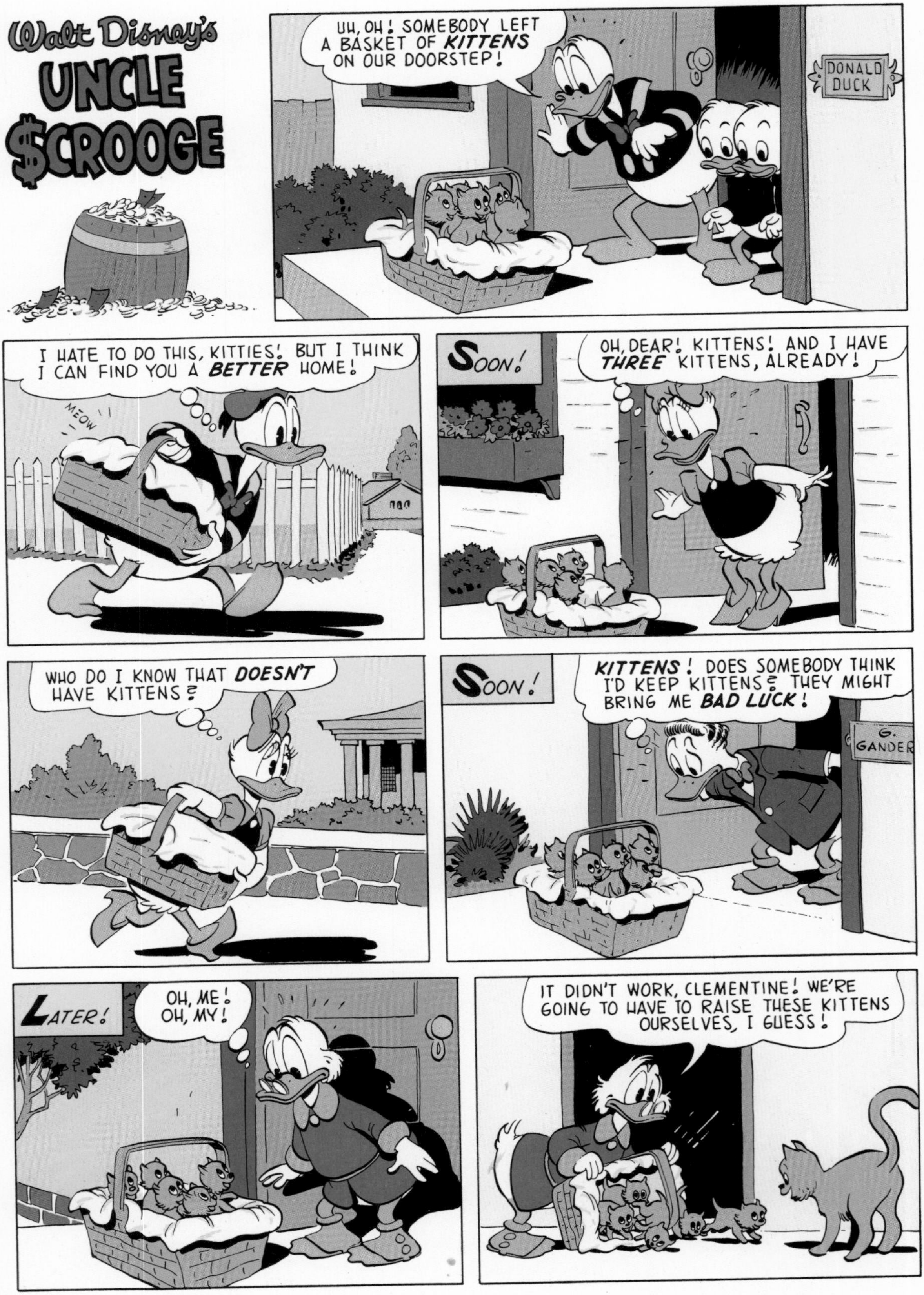
Walt Disney's
UNCLE $CROOGE
UH, OH! SOMEBODY LEFT A BASKET OF KITTENS ON OUR DOORSTEP!
DONALD DUCK
I HATE TO DO THIS, KITTIES! BUT I THINK I CAN FIND YOU A BETTER HOME!
MEOW
SOON!
OH, DEAR! KITTENS! AND I HAVE THREE KITTENS, ALREADY!
WHO DO I KNOW THAT DOESN'T HAVE KITTENS?
SOON!
KITTENS! DOES SOMEBODY THINK I'D KEEP KITTENS? THEY MIGHT BRING ME BAD LUCK!
G. GANDER
LATER!
OH, ME! OH, MY!
IT DIDN'T WORK, CLEMENTINE! WE'RE GOING TO HAVE TO RAISE THESE KITTENS OURSELVES, I GUESS!

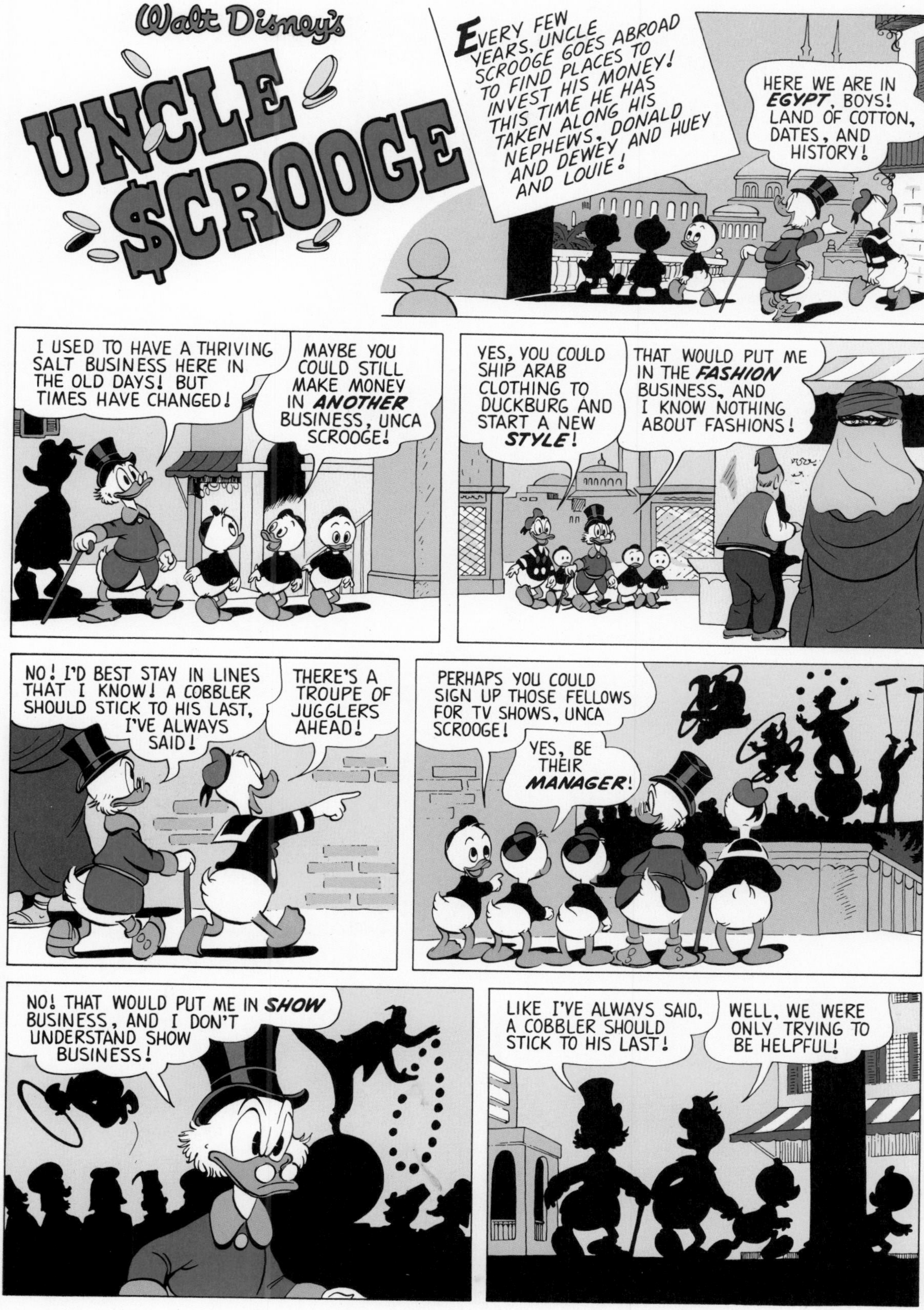
Walt Disney's
UNCLE $CROOGE
EVERY FEW YEARS, UNCLE SCROOGE GOES ABROAD TO FIND PLACES TO INVEST HIS MONEY! THIS TIME HE HAS TAKEN ALONG HIS NEPHEWS, DONALD AND DEWEY AND HUEY AND LOUIE!
HERE WE ARE IN EGYPT, BOYS! LAND OF COTTON, DATES, AND HISTORY!
I USED TO HAVE A THRIVING SALT BUSINESS HERE IN THE OLD DAYS! BUT TIMES HAVE CHANGED!
MAYBE YOU COULD STILL MAKE MONEY IN ANOTHER BUSINESS, UNCA SCROOGE!
YES, YOU COULD SHIP ARAB CLOTHING TO DUCKBURG AND START A NEW STYLE!
THAT WOULD PUT ME IN THE FASHION BUSINESS, AND I KNOW NOTHING ABOUT FASHIONS!
NO! I'D BEST STAY IN LINES THAT I KNOW! A COBBLER SHOULD STICK TO HIS LAST, I'VE ALWAYS SAID!
THERE'S A TROUPE OF JUGGLERS AHEAD!
PERHAPS YOU COULD SIGN UP THOSE FELLOWS FOR TV SHOWS, UNCA SCROOGE!
YES, BE THEIR MANAGER!
NO! THAT WOULD PUT ME IN SHOW BUSINESS, AND I DON'T UNDERSTAND SHOW BUSINESS!
LIKE I'VE ALWAYS SAID, A COBBLER SHOULD STICK TO HIS LAST!
WELL, WE WERE ONLY TRYING TO BE HELPFUL!

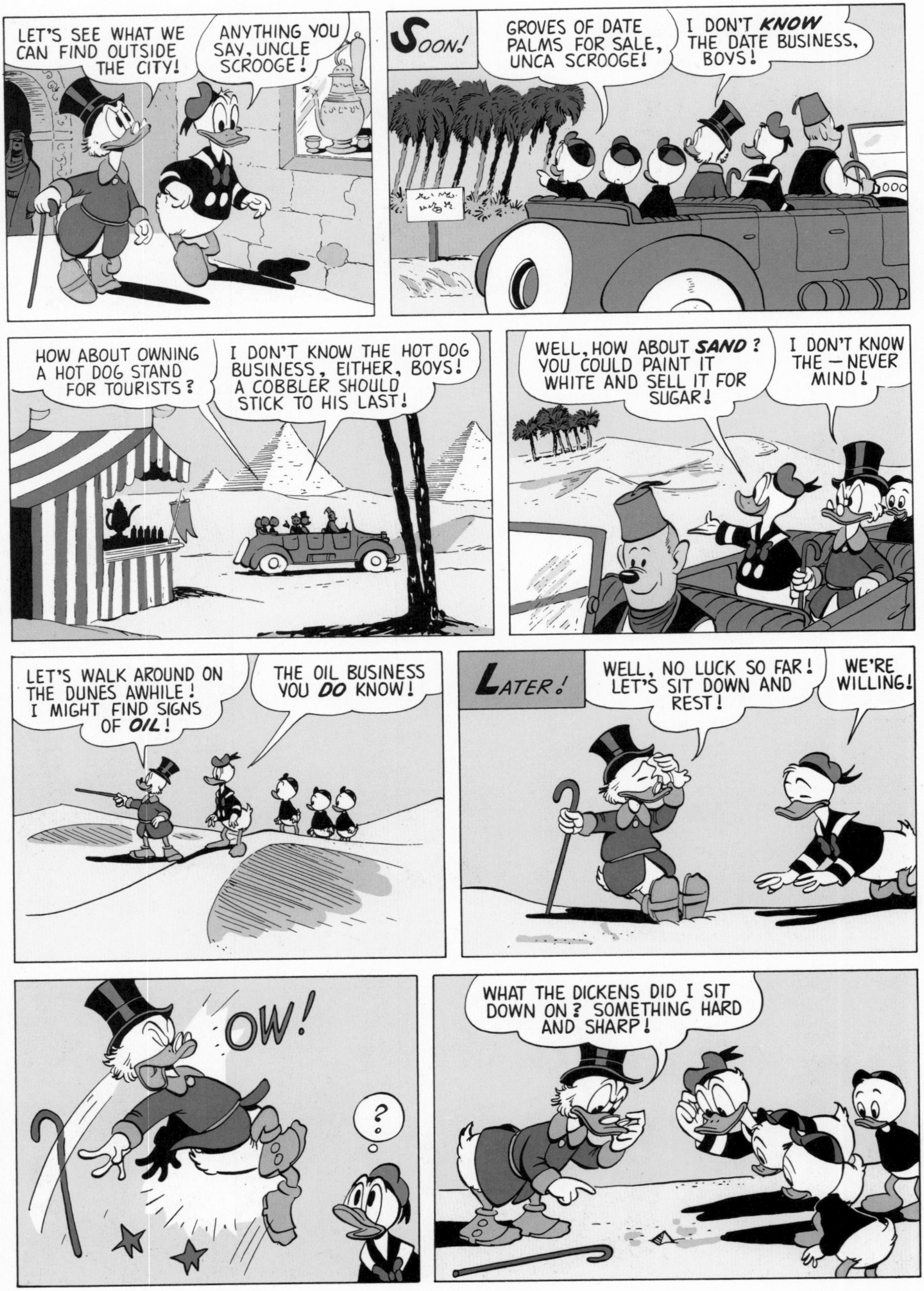

LET'S SEE WHAT WE CAN FIND OUTSIDE THE CITY!
ANYTHING YOU SAY, UNCLE SCROOGE!
SOON!
GROVES OF DATE PALMS FOR SALE, UNCA SCROOGE!
I DON'T KNOW THE DATE BUSINESS, BOYS!
HOW ABOUT OWNING A HOT DOG STAND FOR TOURISTS?
I DON'T KNOW THE HOT DOG BUSINESS, EITHER, BOYS! A COBBLER SHOULD STICK TO HIS LAST!
WELL, HOW ABOUT SAND? YOU COULD PAINT IT WHITE AND SELL IT FOR SUGAR!
I DON'T KNOW THE — NEVER MIND!
LET'S WALK AROUND ON THE DUNES AWHILE! I MIGHT FIND SIGNS OF OIL!
THE OIL BUSINESS YOU DO KNOW!
LATER!
WELL, NO LUCK SO FAR! LET'S SIT DOWN AND REST!
WE'RE WILLING!
OW!
?
WHAT THE DICKENS DID I SIT DOWN ON? SOMETHING HARD AND SHARP!

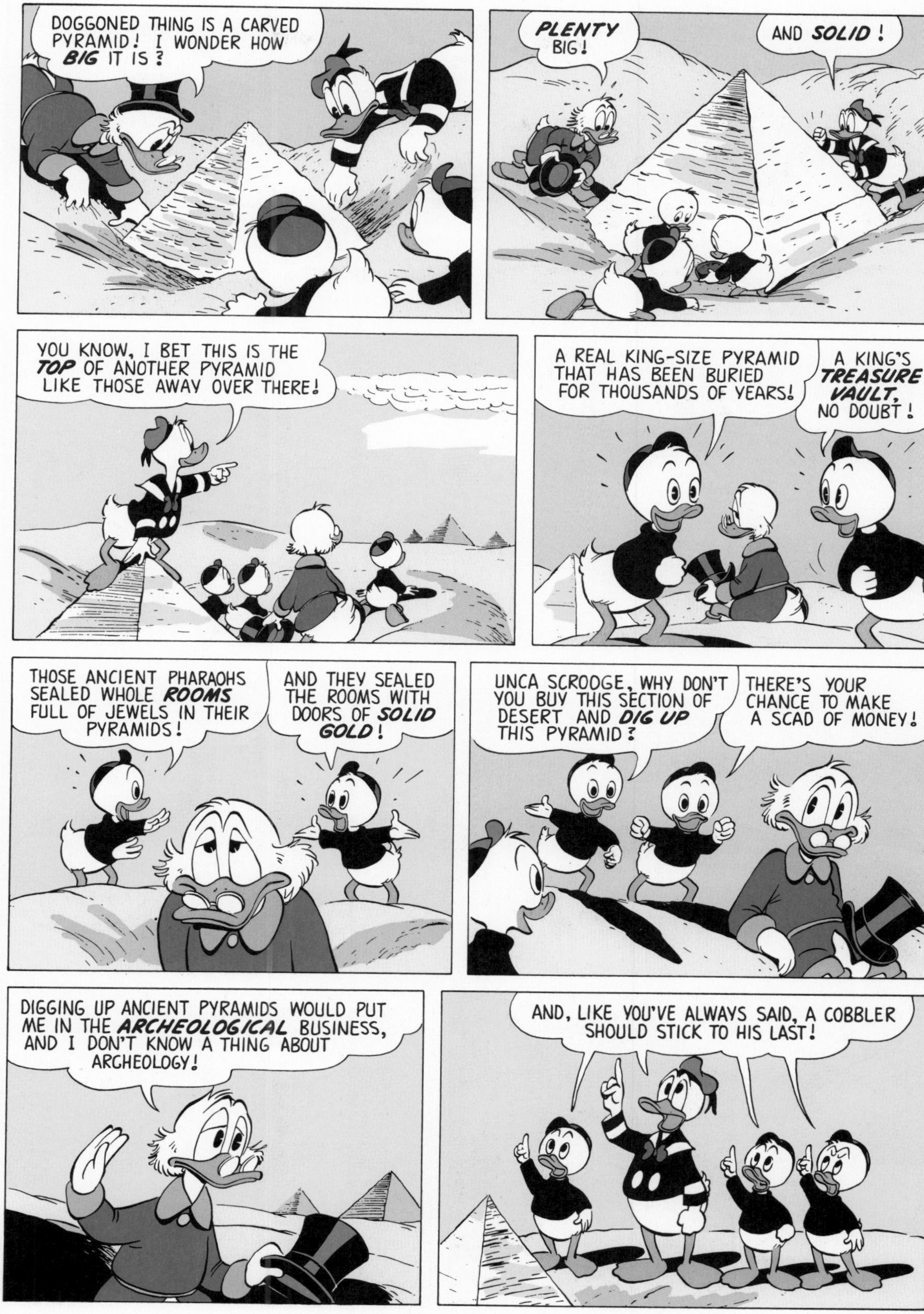
DOGGONED THING IS A CARVED PYRAMID! I WONDER HOW BIG IT IS?
PLENTY BIG!
AND SOLID!
YOU KNOW, I BET THIS IS THE TOP OF ANOTHER PYRAMID LIKE THOSE AWAY OVER THERE!
A REAL KING-SIZE PYRAMID THAT HAS BEEN BURIED FOR THOUSANDS OF YEARS!
A KING'S TREASURE VAULT, NO DOUBT!
THOSE ANCIENT PHARAOHS SEALED WHOLE ROOMS FULL OF JEWELS IN THEIR PYRAMIDS!
AND THEY SEALED THE ROOMS WITH DOORS OF SOLID GOLD!
UNCA SCROOGE, WHY DON'T YOU BUY THIS SECTION OF DESERT AND DIG UP THIS PYRAMID?
THERE'S YOUR CHANCE TO MAKE A SCAD OF MONEY!
DIGGING UP ANCIENT PYRAMIDS WOULD PUT ME IN THE ARCHEOLOGICAL BUSINESS, AND I DON'T KNOW A THING ABOUT ARCHEOLOGY!
AND, LIKE YOU'VE ALWAYS SAID, A COBBLER SHOULD STICK TO HIS LAST!

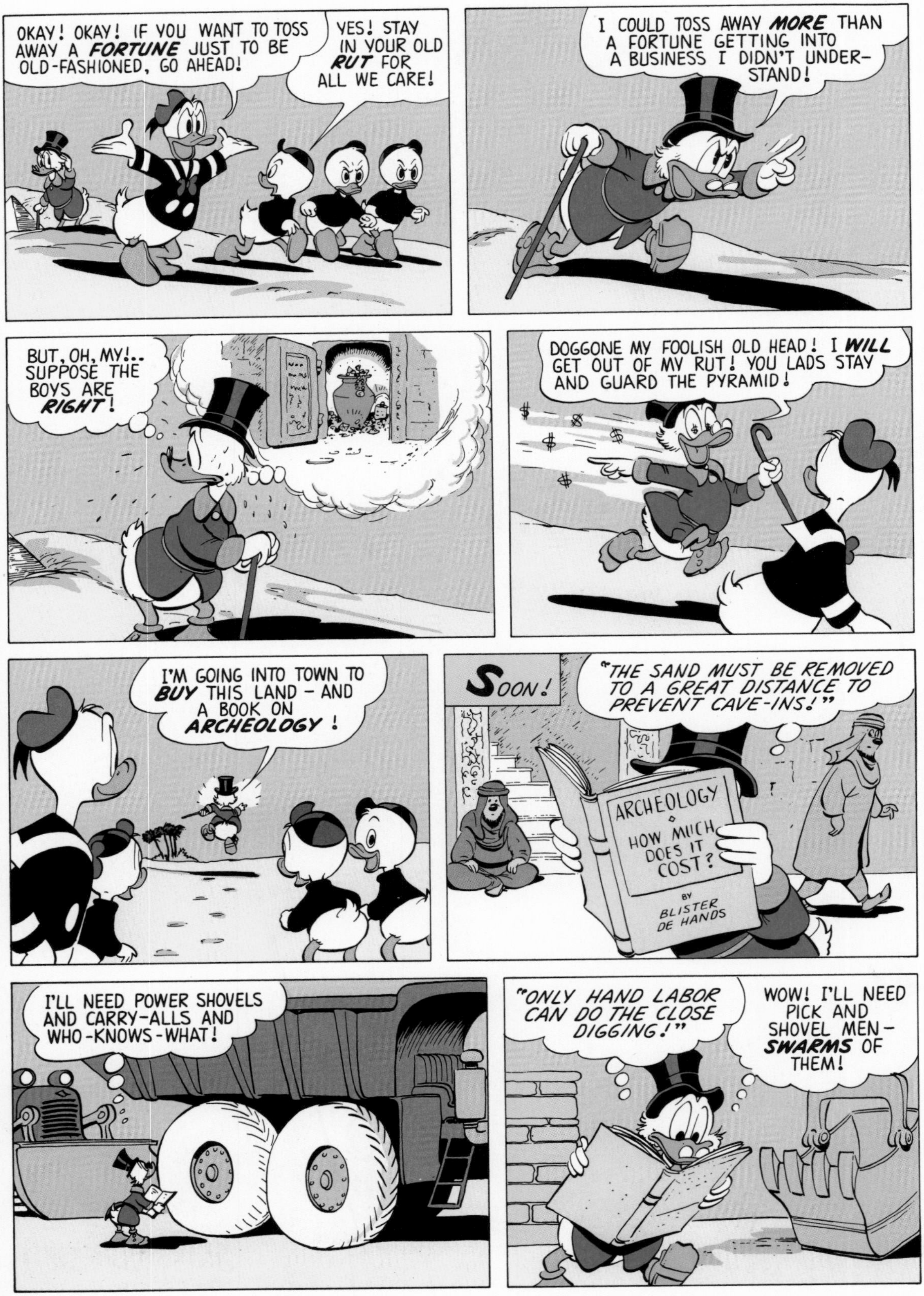
OKAY! OKAY! IF YOU WANT TO TOSS AWAY A **FORTUNE** JUST TO BE OLD-FASHIONED, GO AHEAD!
YES! STAY IN YOUR OLD **RUT** FOR ALL WE CARE!
I COULD TOSS AWAY **MORE** THAN A FORTUNE GETTING INTO A BUSINESS I DIDN'T UNDER-STAND!
BUT, OH, MY!.. SUPPOSE THE BOYS ARE **RIGHT**!
DOGGONE MY FOOLISH OLD HEAD! I **WILL** GET OUT OF MY RUT! YOU LADS STAY AND GUARD THE PYRAMID!
I'M GOING INTO TOWN TO **BUY** THIS LAND – AND A BOOK ON **ARCHEOLOGY**!
SOON!
"THE SAND MUST BE REMOVED TO A GREAT DISTANCE TO PREVENT CAVE-INS!"
ARCHEOLOGY
HOW MUCH DOES IT COST?
BY BLISTER DE HANDS
I'LL NEED POWER SHOVELS AND CARRY-ALLS AND WHO-KNOWS-WHAT!
"ONLY HAND LABOR CAN DO THE CLOSE DIGGING!"
WOW! I'LL NEED PICK AND SHOVEL MEN– **SWARMS** OF THEM!

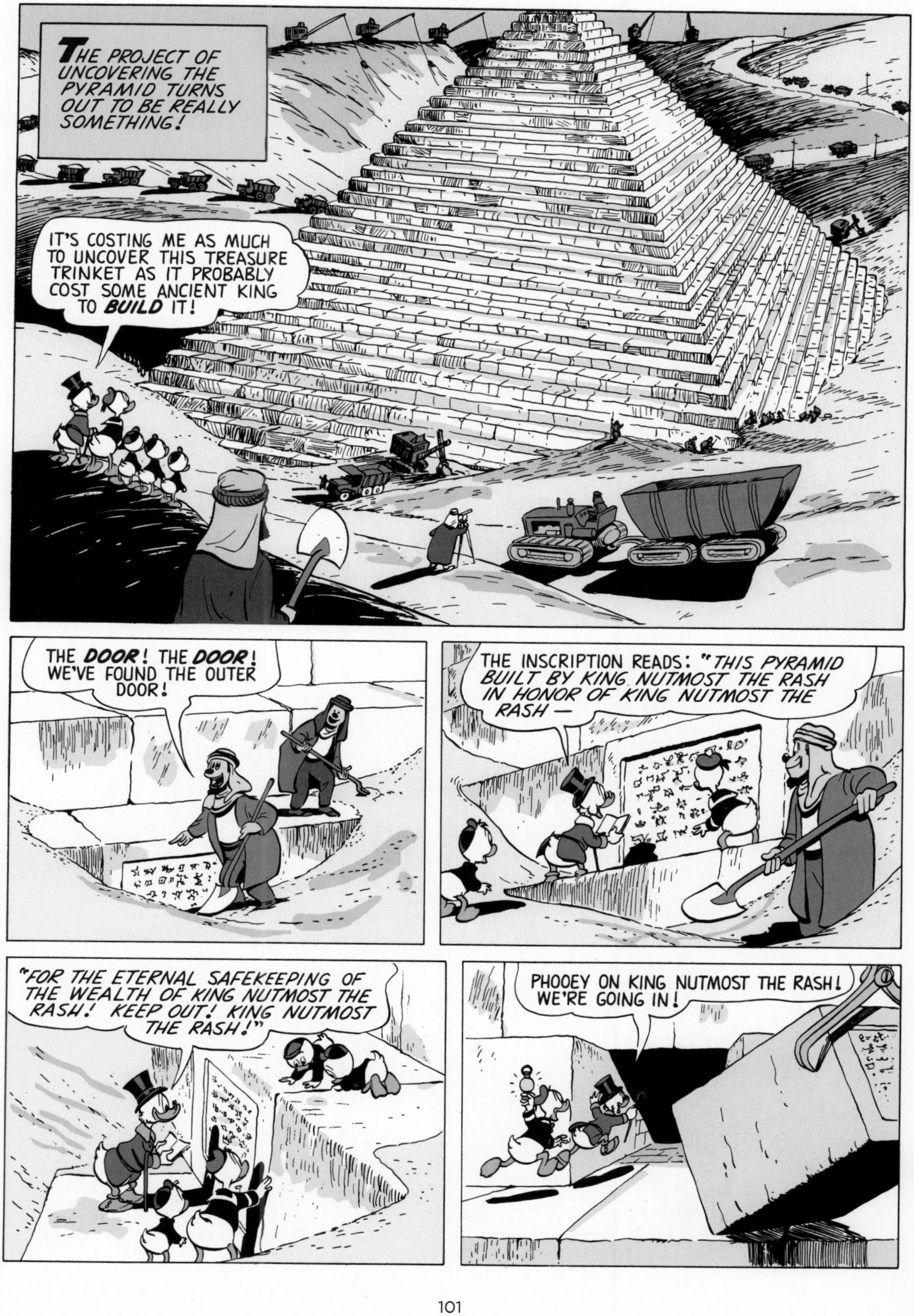
THE PROJECT OF UNCOVERING THE PYRAMID TURNS OUT TO BE REALLY SOMETHING!
IT'S COSTING ME AS MUCH TO UNCOVER THIS TREASURE TRINKET AS IT PROBABLY COST SOME ANCIENT KING TO BUILD IT!
THE DOOR! THE DOOR! WE'VE FOUND THE OUTER DOOR!
THE INSCRIPTION READS: "THIS PYRAMID BUILT BY KING NUTMOST THE RASH IN HONOR OF KING NUTMOST THE RASH —
"FOR THE ETERNAL SAFEKEEPING OF THE WEALTH OF KING NUTMOST THE RASH! KEEP OUT! KING NUTMOST THE RASH!"
PHOOEY ON KING NUTMOST THE RASH! WE'RE GOING IN!

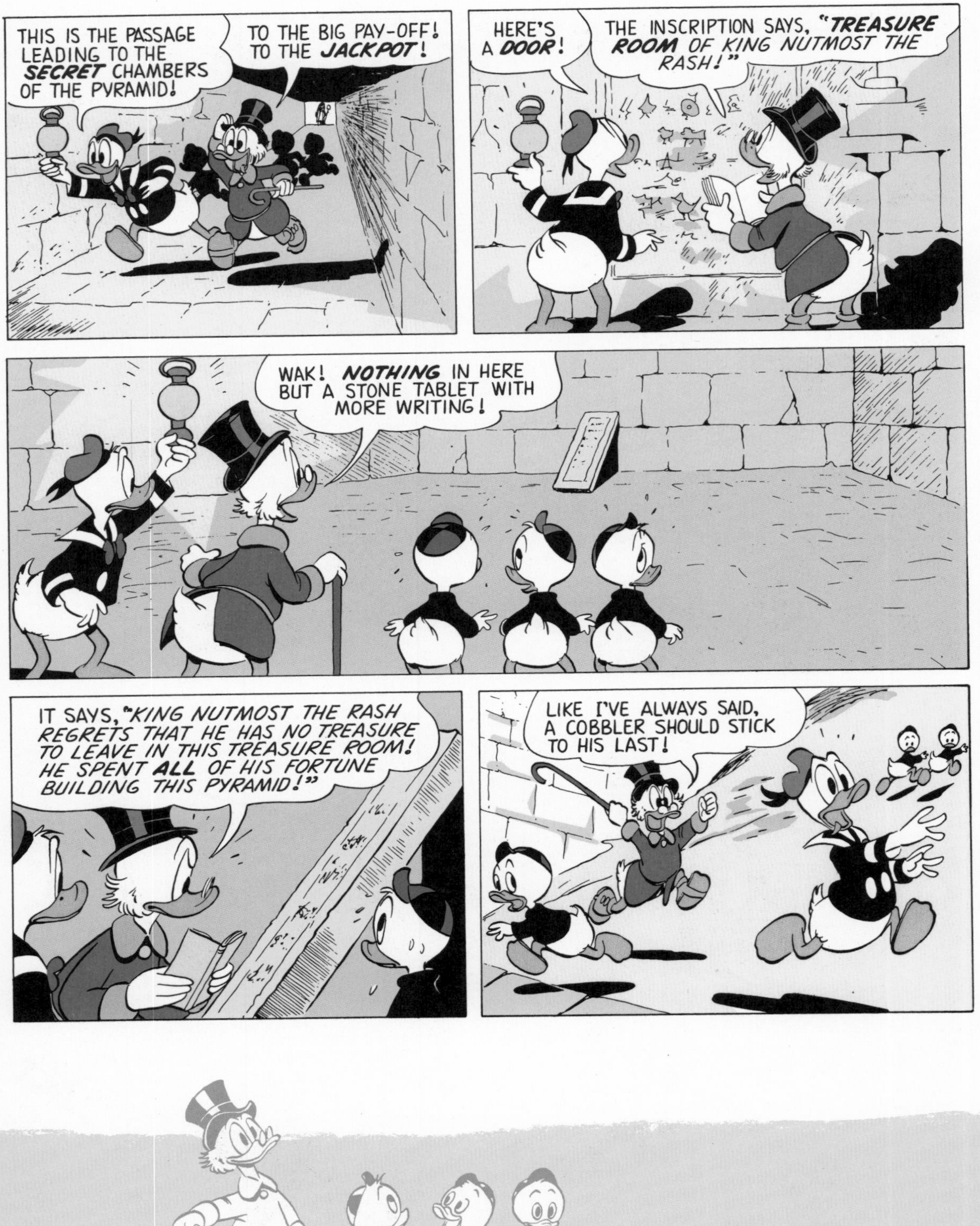
THIS IS THE PASSAGE LEADING TO THE SECRET CHAMBERS OF THE PYRAMID!
TO THE BIG PAY-OFF! TO THE JACKPOT!
HERE'S A DOOR!
THE INSCRIPTION SAYS, "TREASURE ROOM OF KING NUTMOST THE RASH!"
WAK! NOTHING IN HERE BUT A STONE TABLET WITH MORE WRITING!
IT SAYS, "KING NUTMOST THE RASH REGRETS THAT HE HAS NO TREASURE TO LEAVE IN THIS TREASURE ROOM! HE SPENT ALL OF HIS FORTUNE BUILDING THIS PYRAMID!"
LIKE I'VE ALWAYS SAID, A COBBLER SHOULD STICK TO HIS LAST!

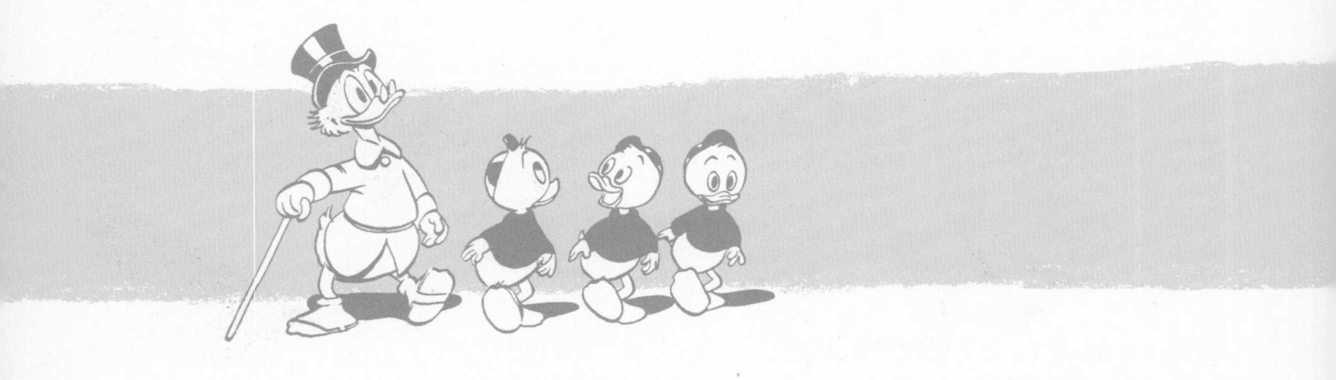

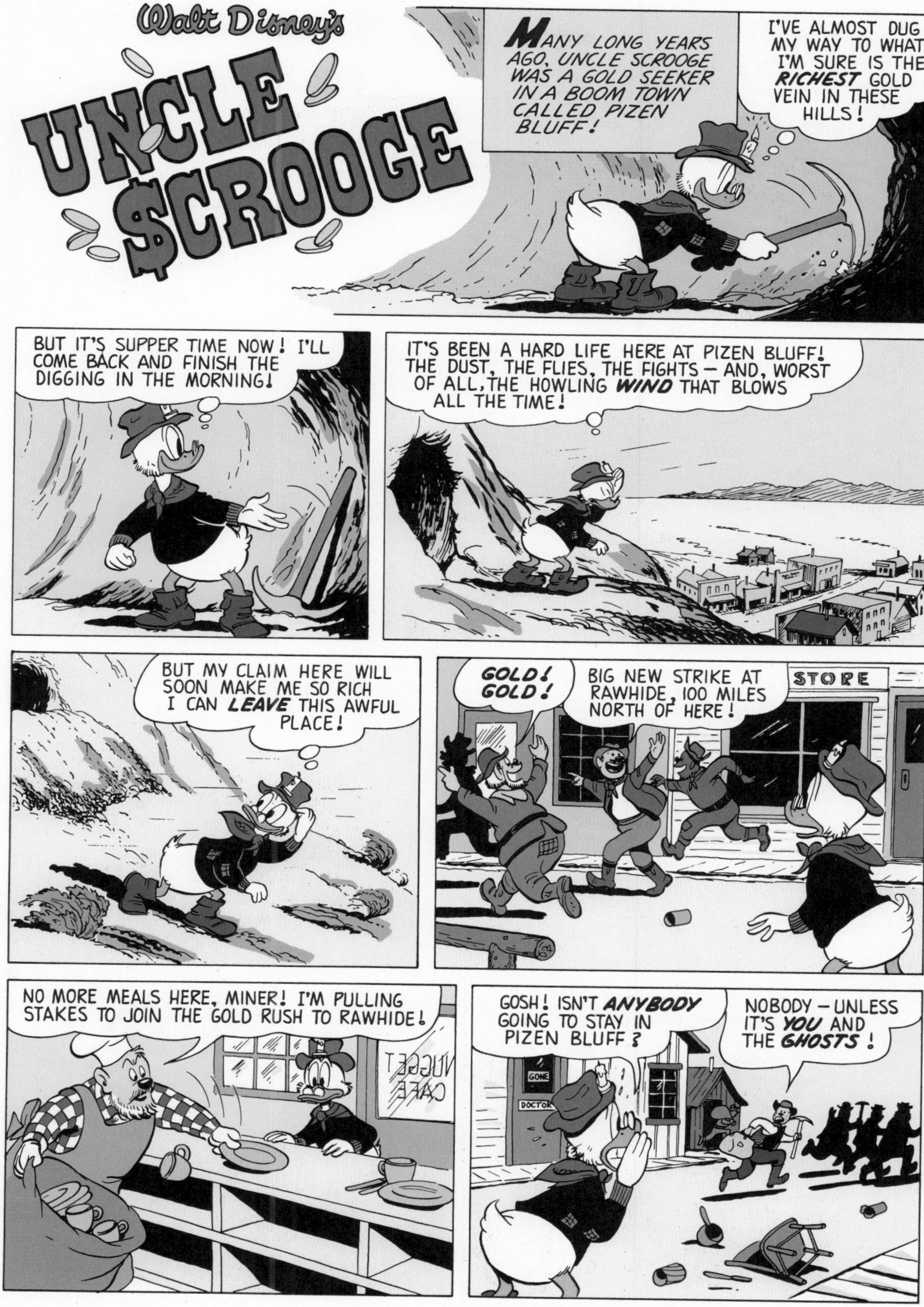
Walt Disney's
UNCLE $CROOGE
MANY LONG YEARS AGO, UNCLE SCROOGE WAS A GOLD SEEKER IN A BOOM TOWN CALLED PIZEN BLUFF!
I'VE ALMOST DUG MY WAY TO WHAT I'M SURE IS THE RICHEST GOLD VEIN IN THESE HILLS!
BUT IT'S SUPPER TIME NOW! I'LL COME BACK AND FINISH THE DIGGING IN THE MORNING!
IT'S BEEN A HARD LIFE HERE AT PIZEN BLUFF! THE DUST, THE FLIES, THE FIGHTS — AND, WORST OF ALL, THE HOWLING WIND THAT BLOWS ALL THE TIME!
BUT MY CLAIM HERE WILL SOON MAKE ME SO RICH I CAN LEAVE THIS AWFUL PLACE!
GOLD! GOLD!
BIG NEW STRIKE AT RAWHIDE, 100 MILES NORTH OF HERE!
STORE
NO MORE MEALS HERE, MINER! I'M PULLING STAKES TO JOIN THE GOLD RUSH TO RAWHIDE!
NUGGET CAFE
GOSH! ISN'T ANYBODY GOING TO STAY IN PIZEN BLUFF?
NOBODY — UNLESS IT'S YOU AND THE GHOSTS!
GONE
DOCTOR

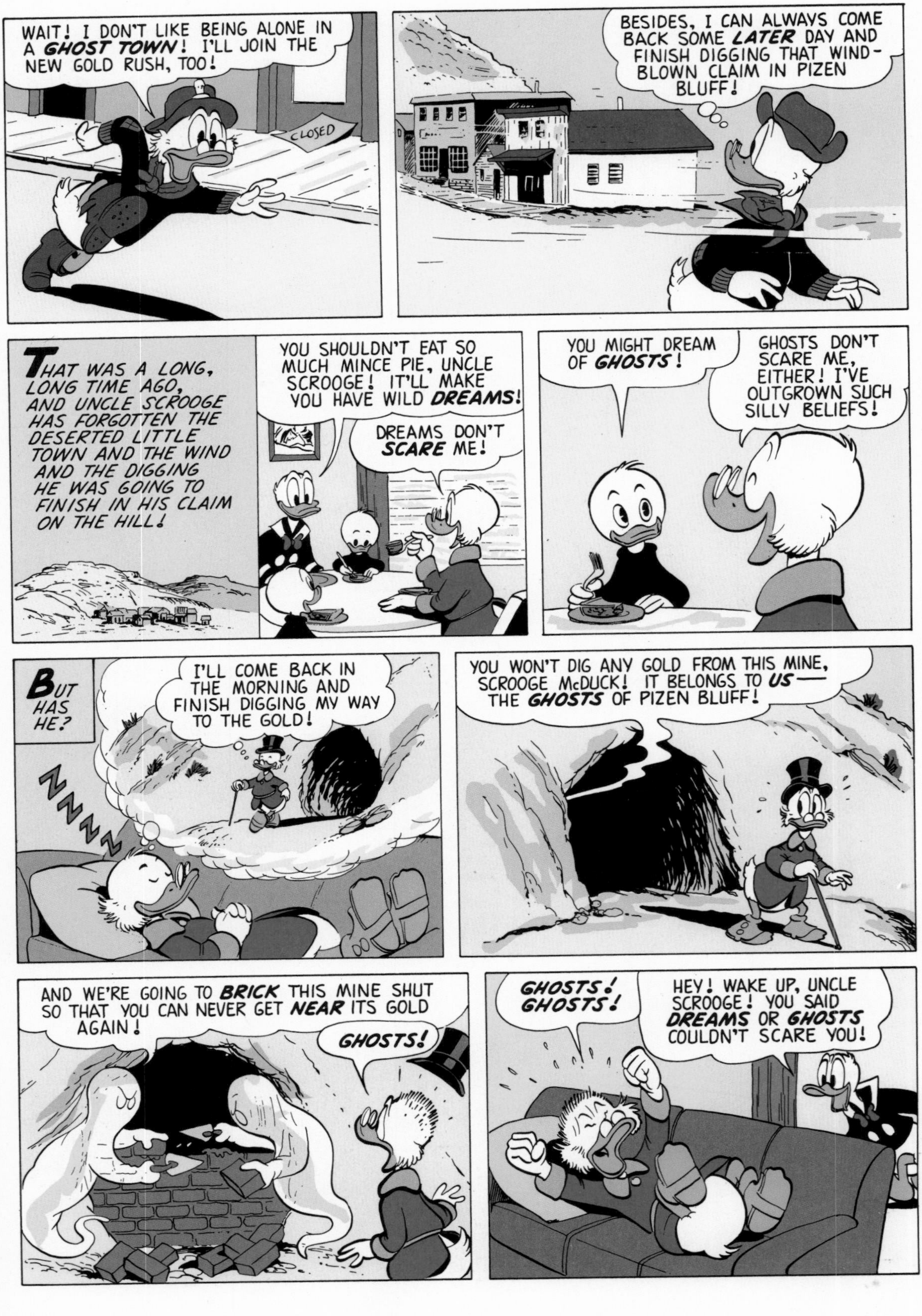
WAIT! I DON'T LIKE BEING ALONE IN A GHOST TOWN! I'LL JOIN THE NEW GOLD RUSH, TOO!
CLOSED
BESIDES, I CAN ALWAYS COME BACK SOME LATER DAY AND FINISH DIGGING THAT WIND-BLOWN CLAIM IN PIZEN BLUFF!
THAT WAS A LONG, LONG TIME AGO, AND UNCLE SCROOGE HAS FORGOTTEN THE DESERTED LITTLE TOWN AND THE WIND AND THE DIGGING HE WAS GOING TO FINISH IN HIS CLAIM ON THE HILL!
YOU SHOULDN'T EAT SO MUCH MINCE PIE, UNCLE SCROOGE! IT'LL MAKE YOU HAVE WILD DREAMS!
DREAMS DON'T SCARE ME!
YOU MIGHT DREAM OF GHOSTS!
GHOSTS DON'T SCARE ME, EITHER! I'VE OUTGROWN SUCH SILLY BELIEFS!
BUT HAS HE?
I'LL COME BACK IN THE MORNING AND FINISH DIGGING MY WAY TO THE GOLD!
ZZZZ
YOU WON'T DIG ANY GOLD FROM THIS MINE, SCROOGE McDUCK! IT BELONGS TO US— THE GHOSTS OF PIZEN BLUFF!
AND WE'RE GOING TO BRICK THIS MINE SHUT SO THAT YOU CAN NEVER GET NEAR ITS GOLD AGAIN!
GHOSTS!
GHOSTS! GHOSTS!
HEY! WAKE UP, UNCLE SCROOGE! YOU SAID DREAMS OR GHOSTS COULDN'T SCARE YOU!

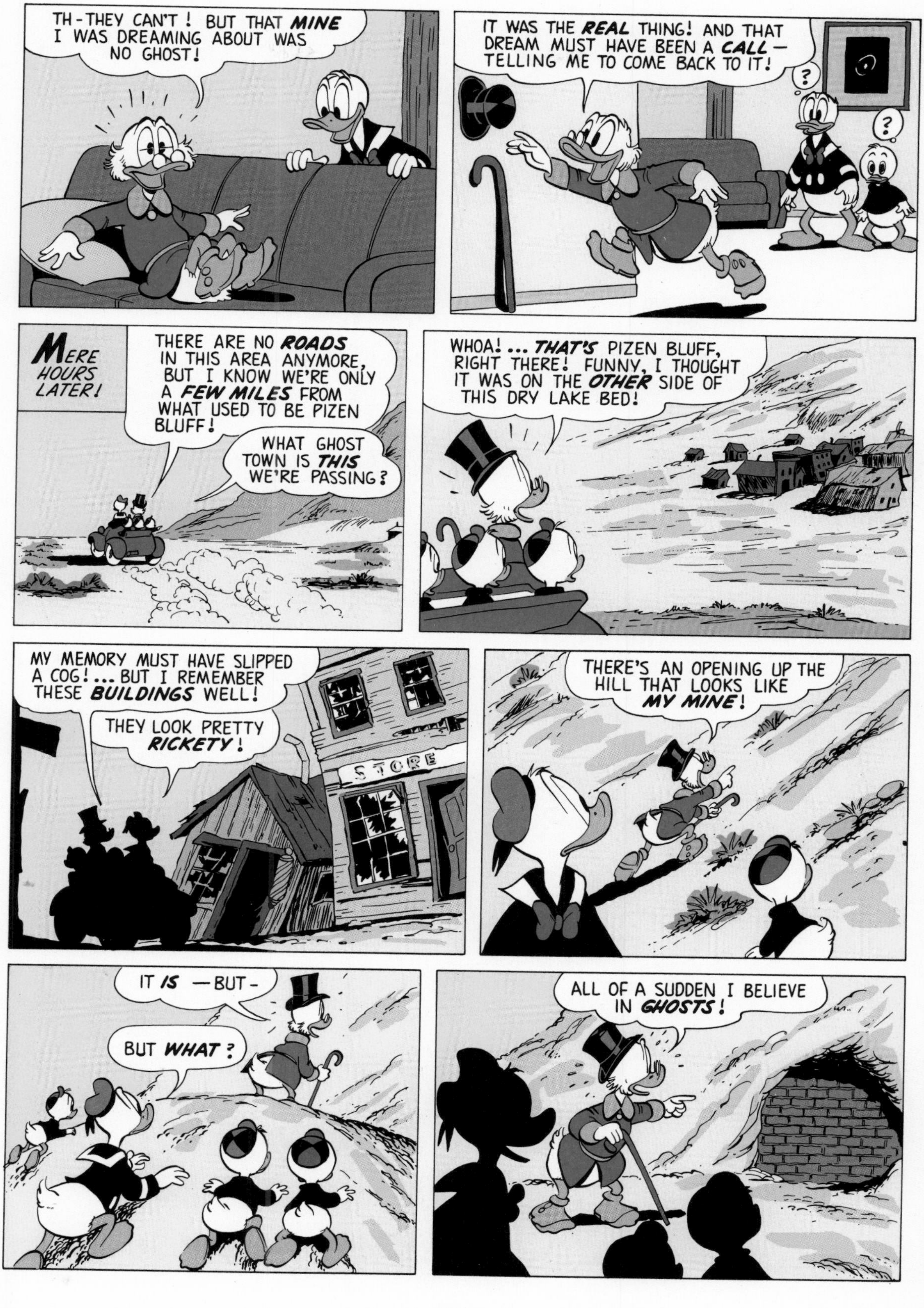
TH-THEY CAN'T! BUT THAT MINE I WAS DREAMING ABOUT WAS NO GHOST!
IT WAS THE REAL THING! AND THAT DREAM MUST HAVE BEEN A CALL — TELLING ME TO COME BACK TO IT!
?
?
MERE HOURS LATER!
THERE ARE NO ROADS IN THIS AREA ANYMORE, BUT I KNOW WE'RE ONLY A FEW MILES FROM WHAT USED TO BE PIZEN BLUFF!
WHAT GHOST TOWN IS THIS WE'RE PASSING?
WHOA! ... THAT'S PIZEN BLUFF, RIGHT THERE! FUNNY, I THOUGHT IT WAS ON THE OTHER SIDE OF THIS DRY LAKE BED!
MY MEMORY MUST HAVE SLIPPED A COG! ... BUT I REMEMBER THESE BUILDINGS WELL!
THEY LOOK PRETTY RICKETY!
STORE
THERE'S AN OPENING UP THE HILL THAT LOOKS LIKE MY MINE!
IT IS —BUT-
BUT WHAT?
ALL OF A SUDDEN I BELIEVE IN GHOSTS!

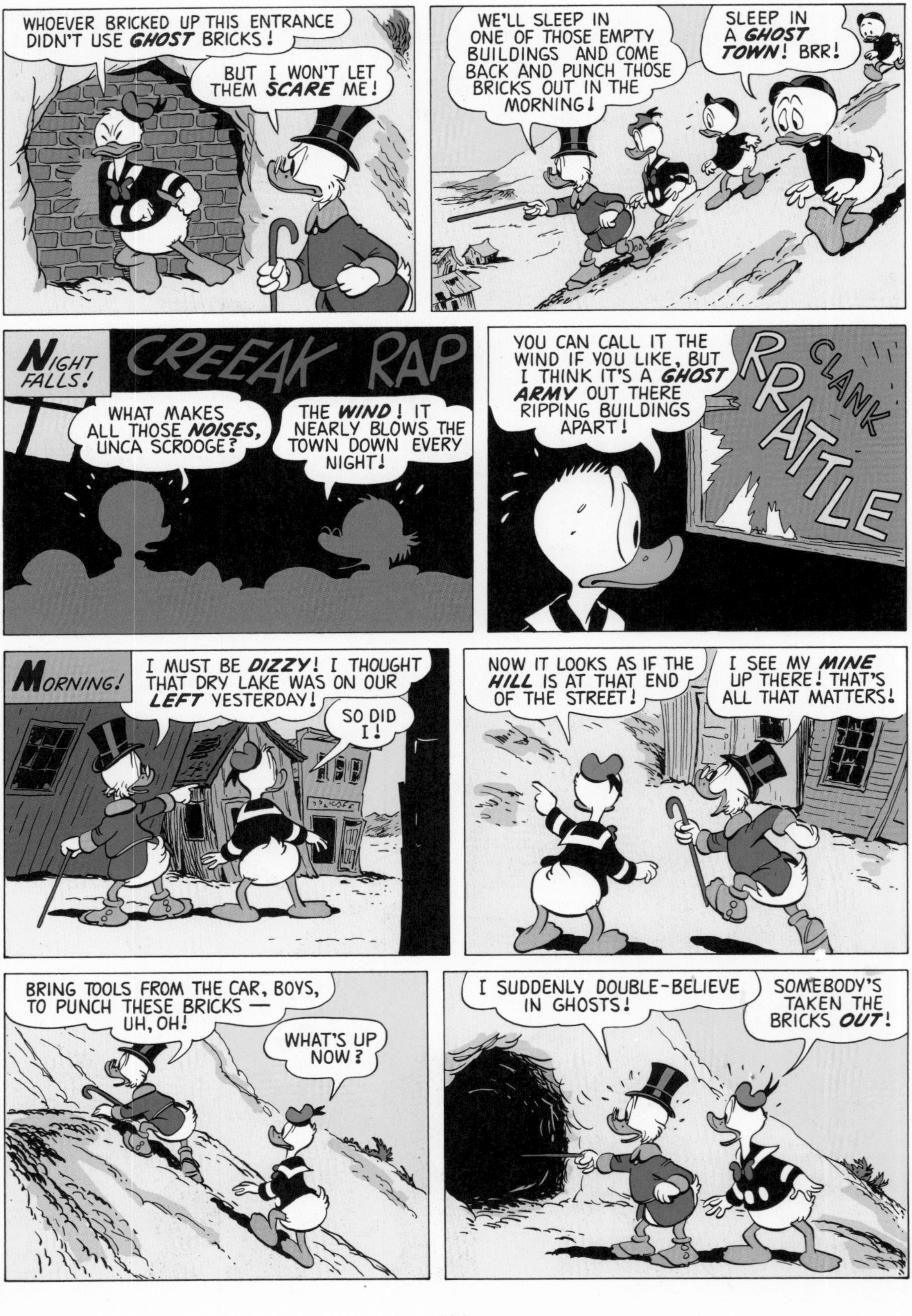
WHOEVER BRICKED UP THIS ENTRANCE DIDN'T USE GHOST BRICKS!
BUT I WON'T LET THEM SCARE ME!
WE'LL SLEEP IN ONE OF THOSE EMPTY BUILDINGS AND COME BACK AND PUNCH THOSE BRICKS OUT IN THE MORNING!
SLEEP IN A GHOST TOWN! BRR!
NIGHT FALLS!
CREEAK RAP
WHAT MAKES ALL THOSE NOISES, UNCA SCROOGE?
THE WIND! IT NEARLY BLOWS THE TOWN DOWN EVERY NIGHT!
YOU CAN CALL IT THE WIND IF YOU LIKE, BUT I THINK IT'S A GHOST ARMY OUT THERE RIPPING BUILDINGS APART!
RRATTLE
CLANK
MORNING!
I MUST BE DIZZY! I THOUGHT THAT DRY LAKE WAS ON OUR LEFT YESTERDAY!
SO DID I!
NOW IT LOOKS AS IF THE HILL IS AT THAT END OF THE STREET!
I SEE MY MINE UP THERE! THAT'S ALL THAT MATTERS!
BRING TOOLS FROM THE CAR, BOYS, TO PUNCH THESE BRICKS — UH, OH!
WHAT'S UP NOW?
I SUDDENLY DOUBLE-BELIEVE IN GHOSTS!
SOMEBODY'S TAKEN THE BRICKS OUT!

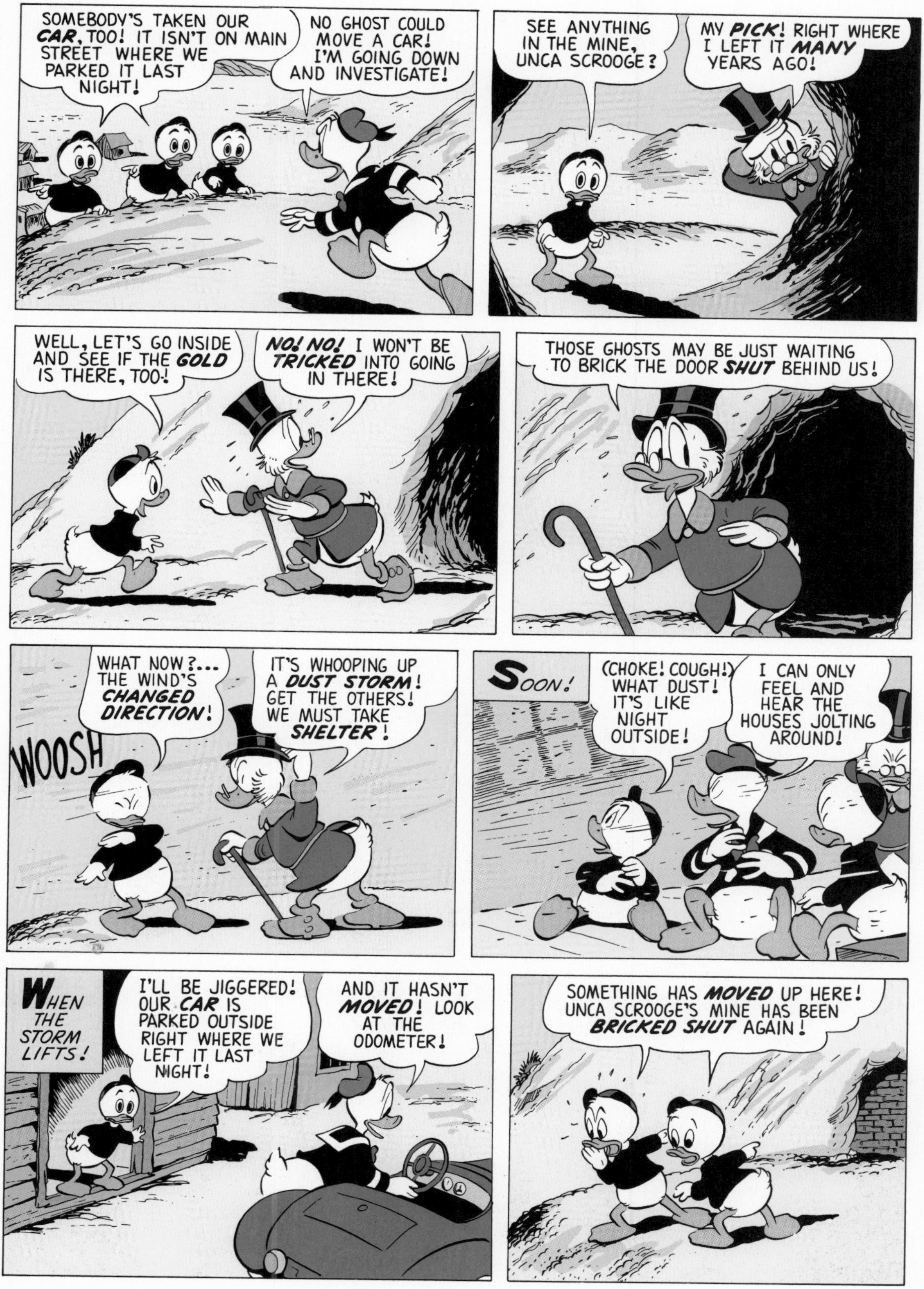
SOMEBODY'S TAKEN OUR CAR, TOO! IT ISN'T ON MAIN STREET WHERE WE PARKED IT LAST NIGHT!
NO GHOST COULD MOVE A CAR! I'M GOING DOWN AND INVESTIGATE!
SEE ANYTHING IN THE MINE, UNCA SCROOGE?
MY PICK! RIGHT WHERE I LEFT IT MANY YEARS AGO!
WELL, LET'S GO INSIDE AND SEE IF THE GOLD IS THERE, TOO!
NO! NO! I WON'T BE TRICKED INTO GOING IN THERE!
THOSE GHOSTS MAY BE JUST WAITING TO BRICK THE DOOR SHUT BEHIND US!
WOOSH
WHAT NOW?... THE WIND'S CHANGED DIRECTION!
IT'S WHOOPING UP A DUST STORM! GET THE OTHERS! WE MUST TAKE SHELTER!
SOON!
(CHOKE! COUGH!) WHAT DUST! IT'S LIKE NIGHT OUTSIDE!
I CAN ONLY FEEL AND HEAR THE HOUSES JOLTING AROUND!
WHEN THE STORM LIFTS!
I'LL BE JIGGERED! OUR CAR IS PARKED OUTSIDE RIGHT WHERE WE LEFT IT LAST NIGHT!
AND IT HASN'T MOVED! LOOK AT THE ODOMETER!
SOMETHING HAS MOVED UP HERE! UNCA SCROOGE'S MINE HAS BEEN BRICKED SHUT AGAIN!

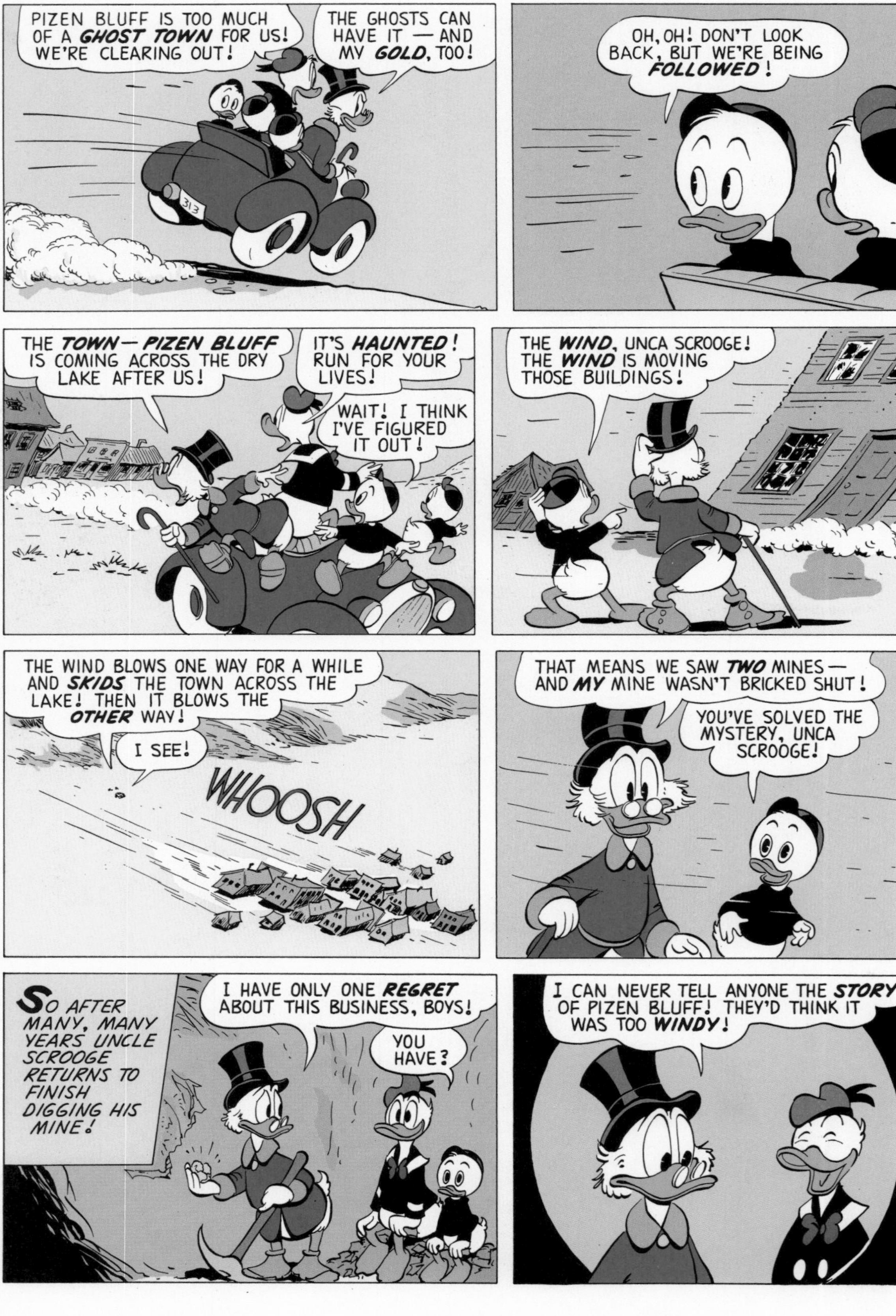
PIZEN BLUFF IS TOO MUCH OF A GHOST TOWN FOR US! WE'RE CLEARING OUT!
THE GHOSTS CAN HAVE IT — AND MY GOLD, TOO!
313
OH, OH! DON'T LOOK BACK, BUT WE'RE BEING FOLLOWED!
THE TOWN— PIZEN BLUFF IS COMING ACROSS THE DRY LAKE AFTER US!
IT'S HAUNTED! RUN FOR YOUR LIVES!
WAIT! I THINK I'VE FIGURED IT OUT!
THE WIND, UNCA SCROOGE! THE WIND IS MOVING THOSE BUILDINGS!
THE WIND BLOWS ONE WAY FOR A WHILE AND SKIDS THE TOWN ACROSS THE LAKE! THEN IT BLOWS THE OTHER WAY!
I SEE!
WHOOSH
THAT MEANS WE SAW TWO MINES— AND MY MINE WASN'T BRICKED SHUT!
YOU'VE SOLVED THE MYSTERY, UNCA SCROOGE!
SO AFTER MANY, MANY YEARS UNCLE SCROOGE RETURNS TO FINISH DIGGING HIS MINE!
I HAVE ONLY ONE REGRET ABOUT THIS BUSINESS, BOYS!
YOU HAVE?
I CAN NEVER TELL ANYONE THE STORY OF PIZEN BLUFF! THEY'D THINK IT WAS TOO WINDY!

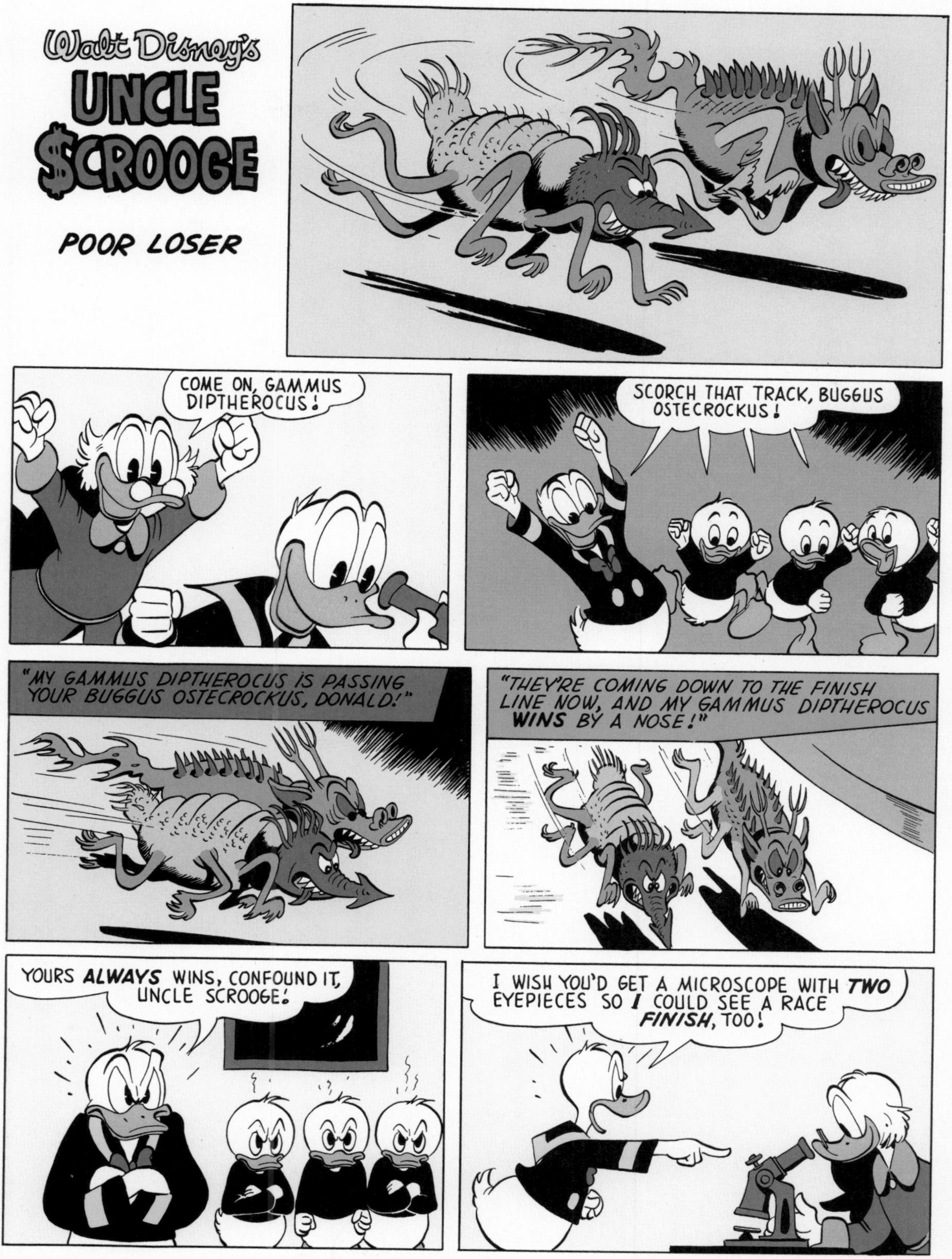
Walt Disney's
UNCLE $CROOGE
POOR LOSER
COME ON, GAMMUS DIPTHEROCUS!
SCORCH THAT TRACK, BUGGUS OSTECROCKUS!
"MY GAMMUS DIPTHEROCUS IS PASSING YOUR BUGGUS OSTECROCKUS, DONALD!"
"THEY'RE COMING DOWN TO THE FINISH LINE NOW, AND MY GAMMUS DIPTHEROCUS WINS BY A NOSE!"
YOURS ALWAYS WINS, CONFOUND IT, UNCLE SCROOGE!
I WISH YOU'D GET A MICROSCOPE WITH TWO EYEPIECES SO I COULD SEE A RACE FINISH, TOO!

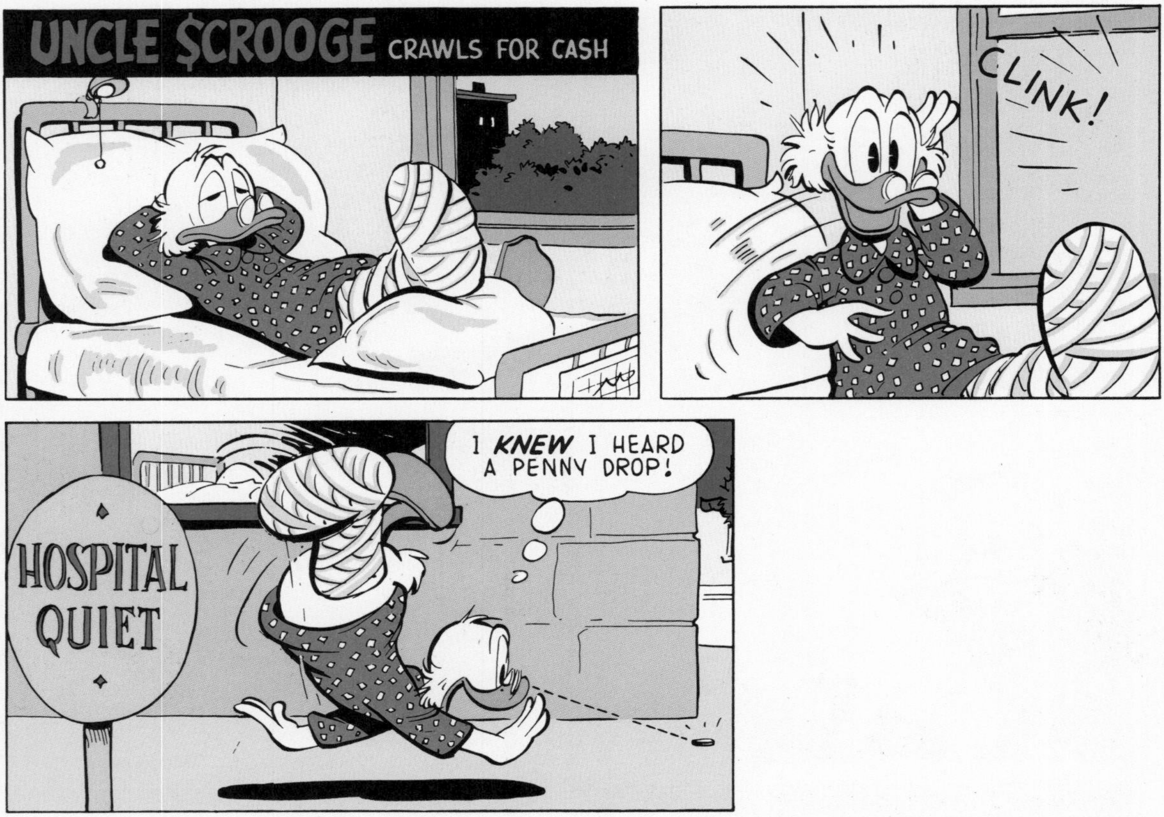
UNCLE $CROOGE CRAWLS FOR CASH
CLINK!
I KNEW I HEARD A PENNY DROP!
HOSPITAL QUIET

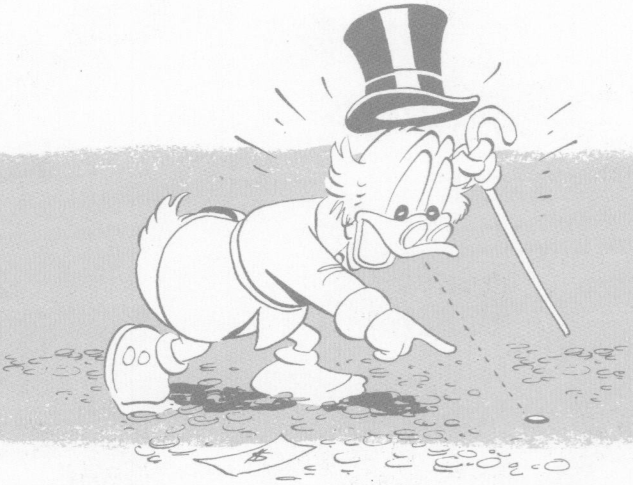

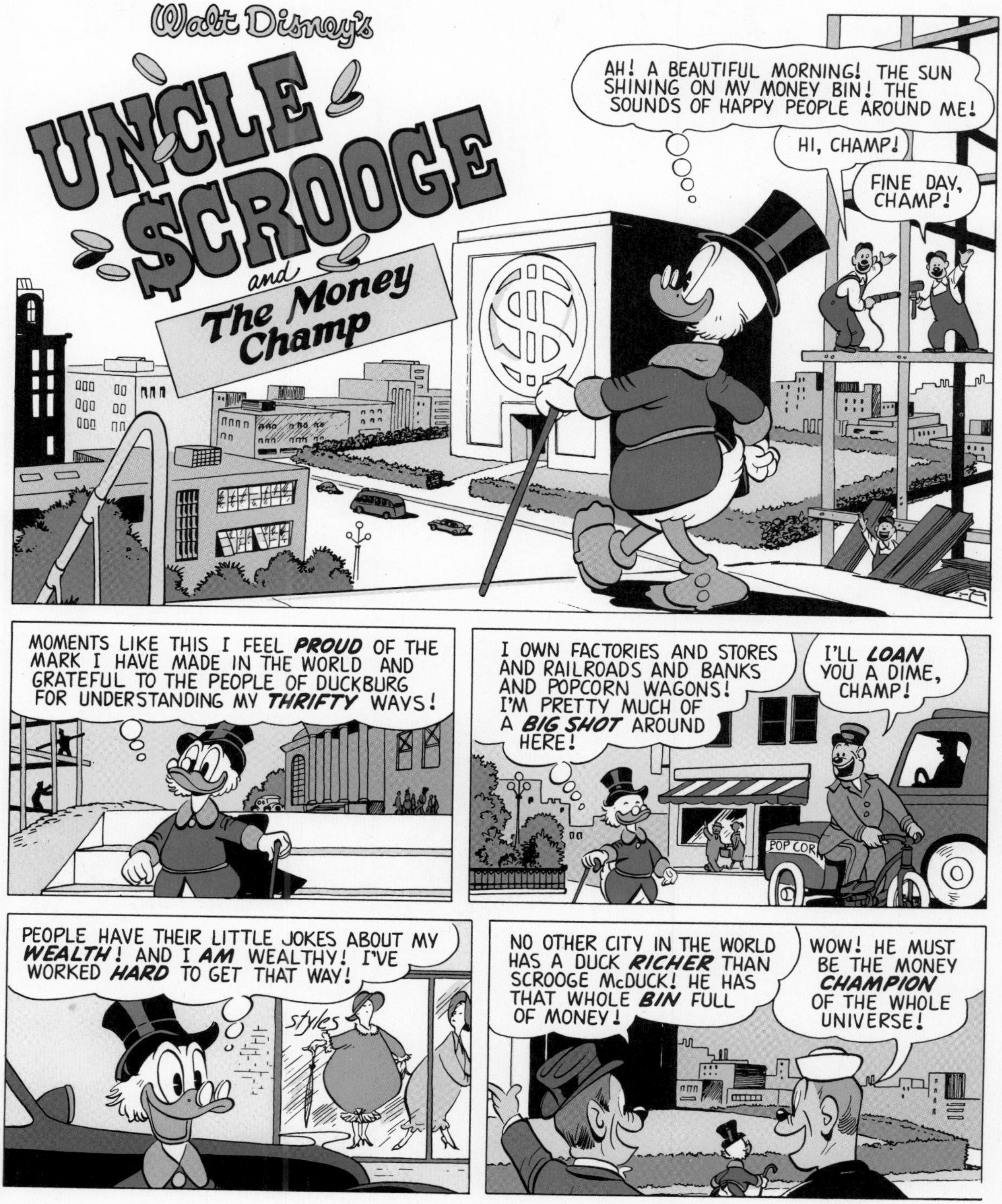
Walt Disney's
UNCLE $CROOGE
and
The Money Champ
AH! A BEAUTIFUL MORNING! THE SUN SHINING ON MY MONEY BIN! THE SOUNDS OF HAPPY PEOPLE AROUND ME!
HI, CHAMP!
FINE DAY, CHAMP!
MOMENTS LIKE THIS I FEEL **PROUD** OF THE MARK I HAVE MADE IN THE WORLD AND GRATEFUL TO THE PEOPLE OF DUCKBURG FOR UNDERSTANDING MY **THRIFTY** WAYS!
I OWN FACTORIES AND STORES AND RAILROADS AND BANKS AND POPCORN WAGONS! I'M PRETTY MUCH OF A **BIG SHOT** AROUND HERE!
I'LL **LOAN** YOU A DIME, CHAMP!
POP COR
PEOPLE HAVE THEIR LITTLE JOKES ABOUT MY **WEALTH**! AND I **AM** WEALTHY! I'VE WORKED **HARD** TO GET THAT WAY!
styles
NO OTHER CITY IN THE WORLD HAS A DUCK **RICHER** THAN SCROOGE McDUCK! HE HAS THAT WHOLE **BIN** FULL OF MONEY!
WOW! HE MUST BE THE MONEY **CHAMPION** OF THE WHOLE UNIVERSE!

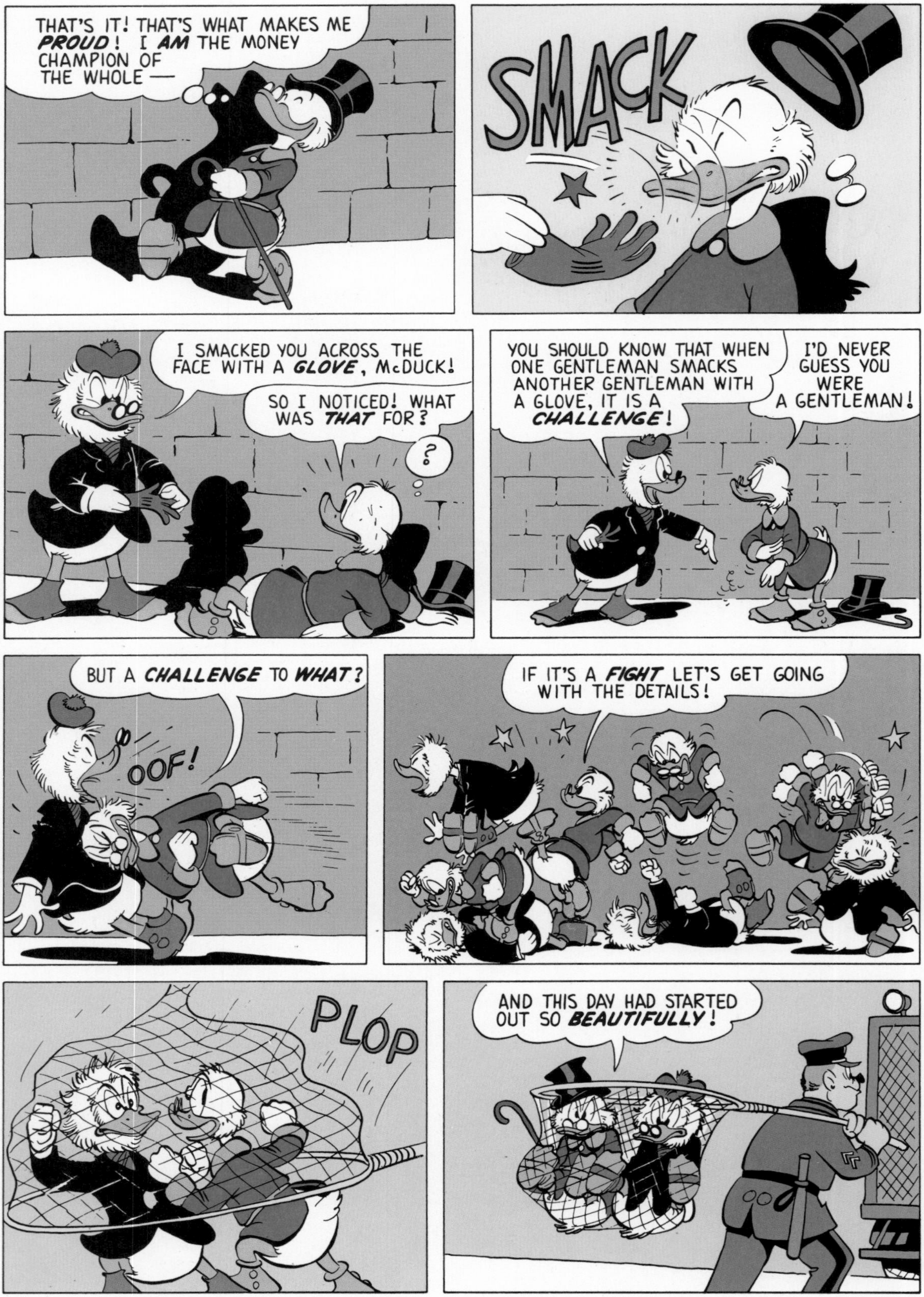
THAT'S IT! THAT'S WHAT MAKES ME PROUD! I AM THE MONEY CHAMPION OF THE WHOLE —
SMACK
I SMACKED YOU ACROSS THE FACE WITH A GLOVE, McDUCK!
SO I NOTICED! WHAT WAS THAT FOR?
?
YOU SHOULD KNOW THAT WHEN ONE GENTLEMAN SMACKS ANOTHER GENTLEMAN WITH A GLOVE, IT IS A CHALLENGE!
I'D NEVER GUESS YOU WERE A GENTLEMAN!
BUT A CHALLENGE TO WHAT?
OOF!
IF IT'S A FIGHT LET'S GET GOING WITH THE DETAILS!
PLOP
AND THIS DAY HAD STARTED OUT SO BEAUTIFULLY!

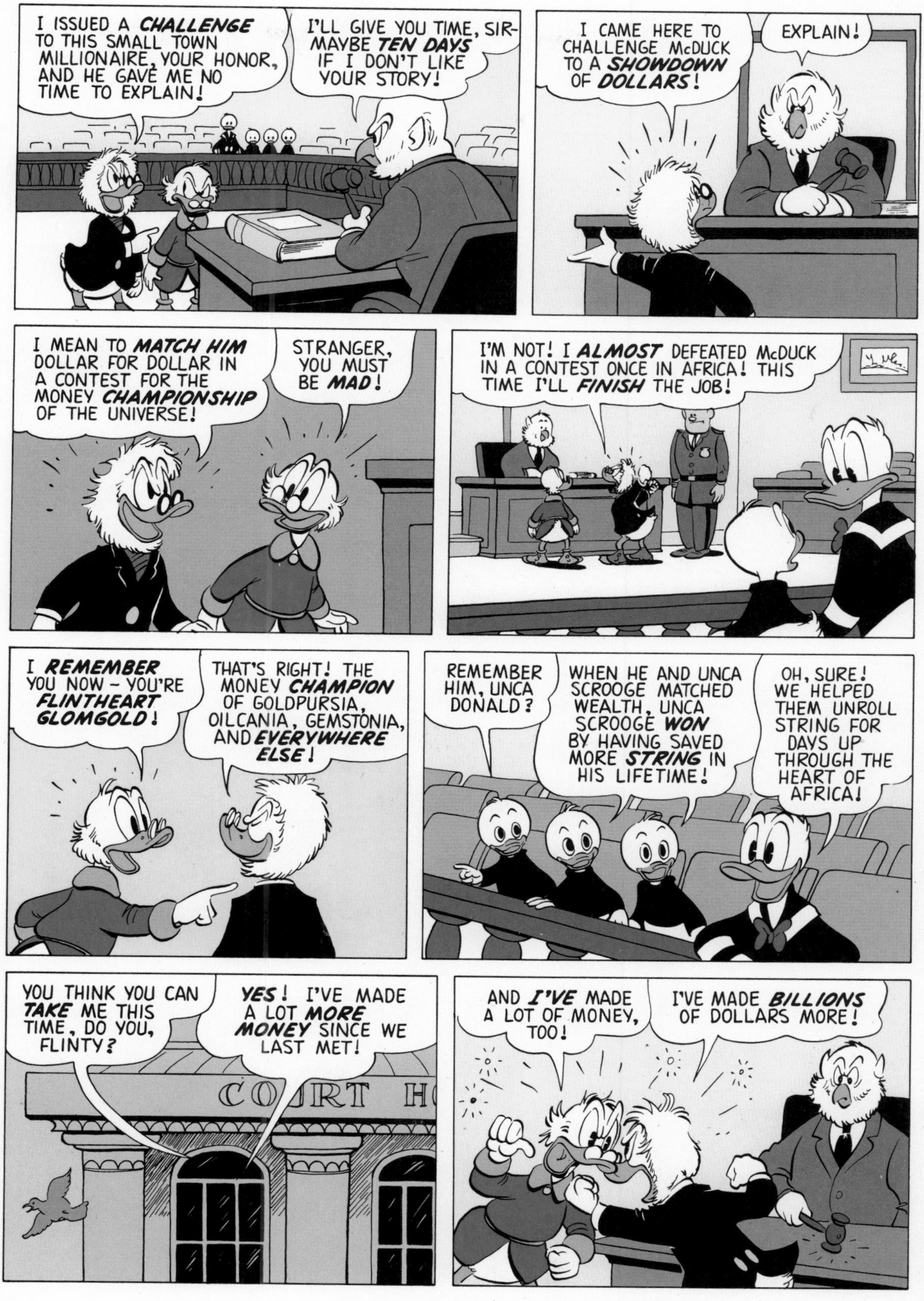

I ISSUED A CHALLENGE TO THIS SMALL TOWN MILLIONAIRE, YOUR HONOR, AND HE GAVE ME NO TIME TO EXPLAIN!
I'LL GIVE YOU TIME, SIR—MAYBE TEN DAYS IF I DON'T LIKE YOUR STORY!
I CAME HERE TO CHALLENGE McDUCK TO A SHOWDOWN OF DOLLARS!
EXPLAIN!
I MEAN TO MATCH HIM DOLLAR FOR DOLLAR IN A CONTEST FOR THE MONEY CHAMPIONSHIP OF THE UNIVERSE!
STRANGER, YOU MUST BE MAD!
I'M NOT! I ALMOST DEFEATED McDUCK IN A CONTEST ONCE IN AFRICA! THIS TIME I'LL FINISH THE JOB!
I REMEMBER YOU NOW – YOU'RE FLINTHEART GLOMGOLD!
THAT'S RIGHT! THE MONEY CHAMPION OF GOLDPURSIA, OILCANIA, GEMSTONIA, AND EVERYWHERE ELSE!
REMEMBER HIM, UNCA DONALD?
WHEN HE AND UNCA SCROOGE MATCHED WEALTH, UNCA SCROOGE WON BY HAVING SAVED MORE STRING IN HIS LIFETIME!
OH, SURE! WE HELPED THEM UNROLL STRING FOR DAYS UP THROUGH THE HEART OF AFRICA!
YOU THINK YOU CAN TAKE ME THIS TIME, DO YOU, FLINTY?
YES! I'VE MADE A LOT MORE MONEY SINCE WE LAST MET!
COURT H
AND I'VE MADE A LOT OF MONEY, TOO!
I'VE MADE BILLIONS OF DOLLARS MORE!

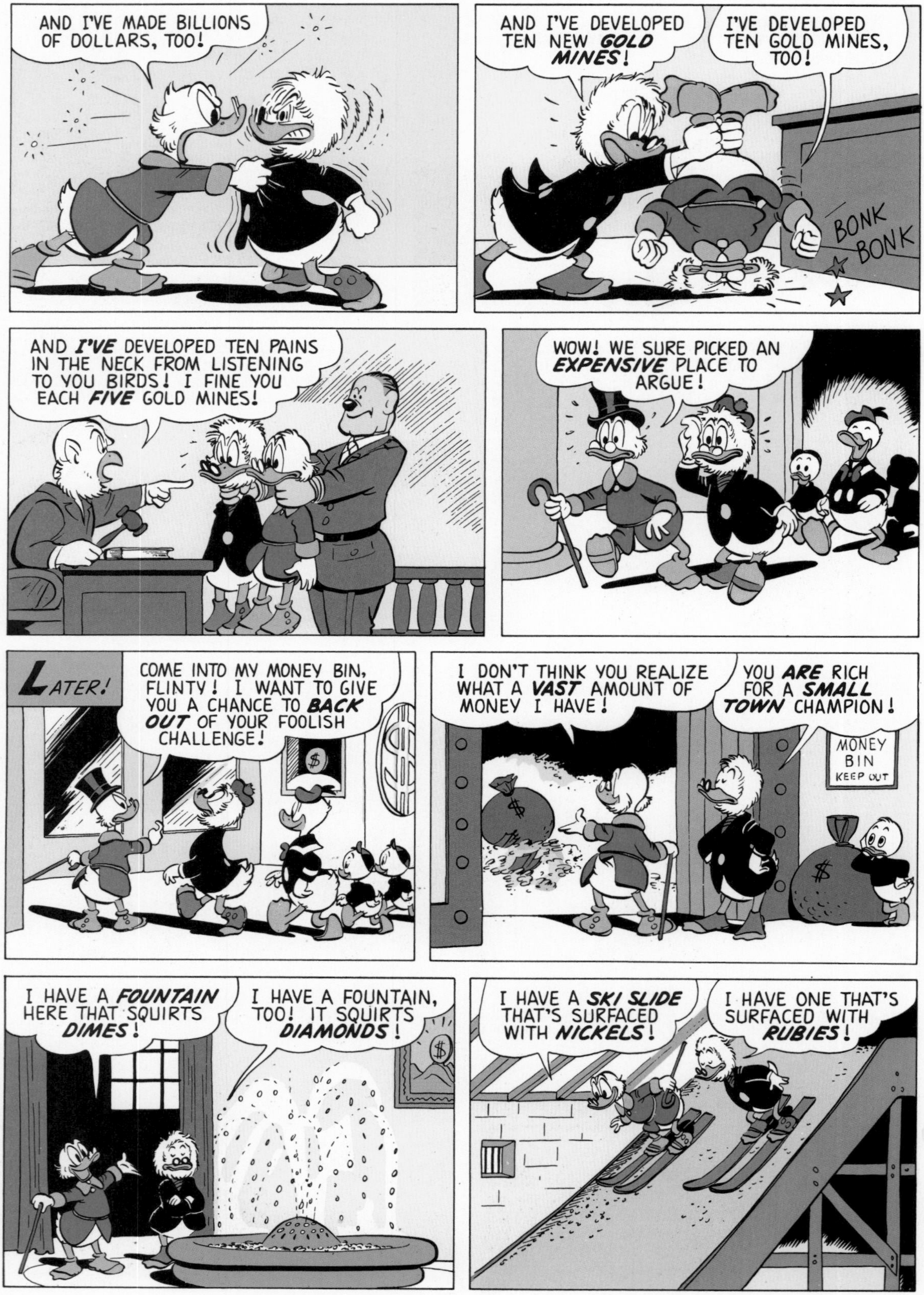
AND I'VE MADE BILLIONS OF DOLLARS, TOO!
AND I'VE DEVELOPED TEN NEW GOLD MINES!
I'VE DEVELOPED TEN GOLD MINES, TOO!
BONK
BONK
AND I'VE DEVELOPED TEN PAINS IN THE NECK FROM LISTENING TO YOU BIRDS! I FINE YOU EACH FIVE GOLD MINES!
WOW! WE SURE PICKED AN EXPENSIVE PLACE TO ARGUE!
LATER!
COME INTO MY MONEY BIN, FLINTY! I WANT TO GIVE YOU A CHANCE TO BACK OUT OF YOUR FOOLISH CHALLENGE!
I DON'T THINK YOU REALIZE WHAT A VAST AMOUNT OF MONEY I HAVE!
YOU ARE RICH FOR A SMALL TOWN CHAMPION!
MONEY BIN KEEP OUT
I HAVE A FOUNTAIN HERE THAT SQUIRTS DIMES!
I HAVE A FOUNTAIN, TOO! IT SQUIRTS DIAMONDS!
I HAVE A SKI SLIDE THAT'S SURFACED WITH NICKELS!
I HAVE ONE THAT'S SURFACED WITH RUBIES!

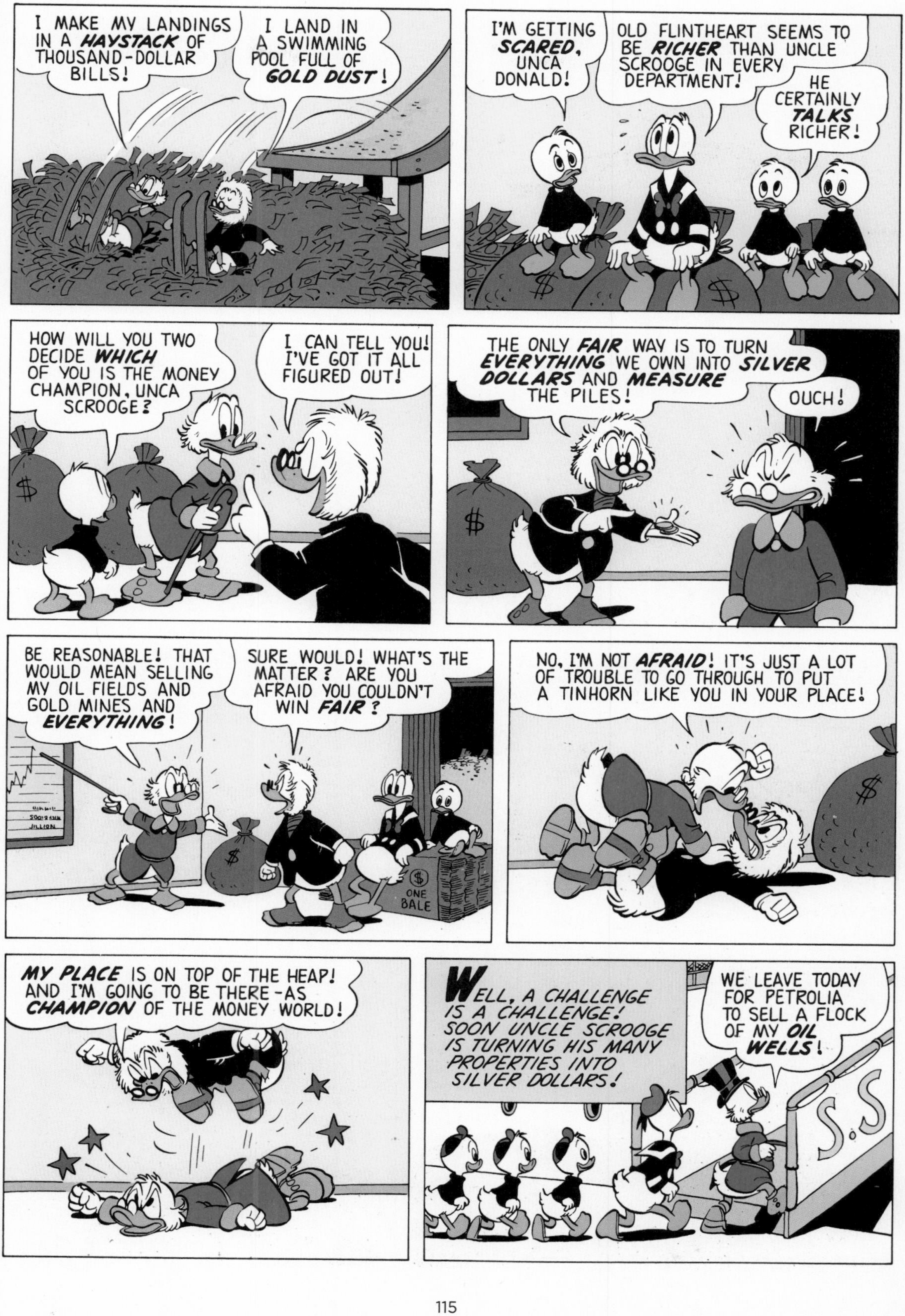
I MAKE MY LANDINGS IN A HAYSTACK OF THOUSAND-DOLLAR BILLS!
I LAND IN A SWIMMING POOL FULL OF GOLD DUST!
I'M GETTING SCARED, UNCA DONALD!
OLD FLINTHEART SEEMS TO BE RICHER THAN UNCLE SCROOGE IN EVERY DEPARTMENT!
HE CERTAINLY TALKS RICHER!
HOW WILL YOU TWO DECIDE WHICH OF YOU IS THE MONEY CHAMPION, UNCA SCROOGE?
I CAN TELL YOU! I'VE GOT IT ALL FIGURED OUT!
THE ONLY FAIR WAY IS TO TURN EVERYTHING WE OWN INTO SILVER DOLLARS AND MEASURE THE PILES!
OUCH!
BE REASONABLE! THAT WOULD MEAN SELLING MY OIL FIELDS AND GOLD MINES AND EVERYTHING!
SURE WOULD! WHAT'S THE MATTER? ARE YOU AFRAID YOU COULDN'T WIN FAIR?
ONE BALE
NO, I'M NOT AFRAID! IT'S JUST A LOT OF TROUBLE TO GO THROUGH TO PUT A TINHORN LIKE YOU IN YOUR PLACE!
MY PLACE IS ON TOP OF THE HEAP! AND I'M GOING TO BE THERE-AS CHAMPION OF THE MONEY WORLD!
WELL, A CHALLENGE IS A CHALLENGE! SOON UNCLE SCROOGE IS TURNING HIS MANY PROPERTIES INTO SILVER DOLLARS!
WE LEAVE TODAY FOR PETROLIA TO SELL A FLOCK OF MY OIL WELLS!
S.S

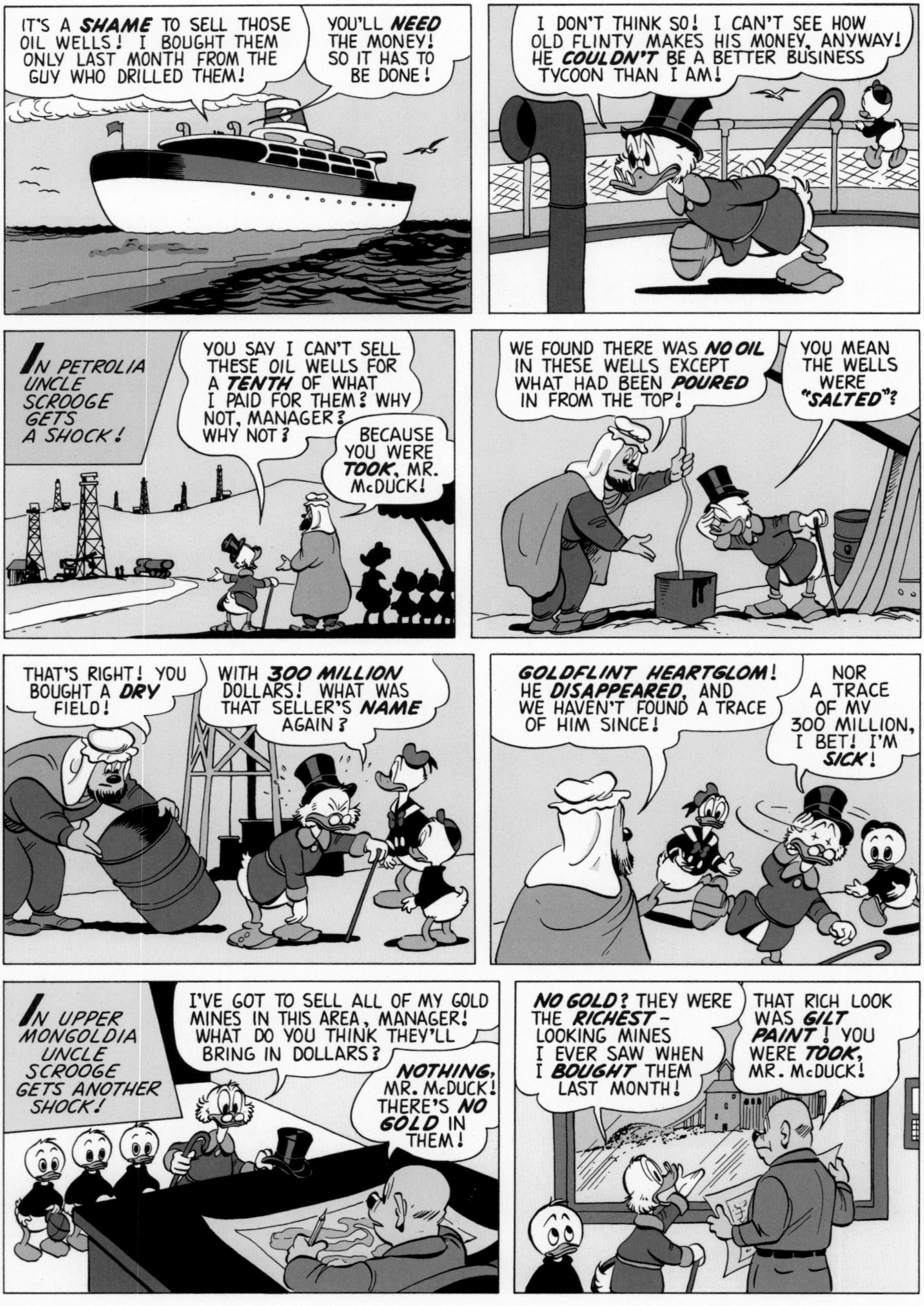
IT'S A SHAME TO SELL THOSE OIL WELLS! I BOUGHT THEM ONLY LAST MONTH FROM THE GUY WHO DRILLED THEM!
YOU'LL NEED THE MONEY! SO IT HAS TO BE DONE!
I DON'T THINK SO! I CAN'T SEE HOW OLD FLINTY MAKES HIS MONEY, ANYWAY! HE COULDN'T BE A BETTER BUSINESS TYCOON THAN I AM!
IN PETROLIA UNCLE SCROOGE GETS A SHOCK!
YOU SAY I CAN'T SELL THESE OIL WELLS FOR A TENTH OF WHAT I PAID FOR THEM? WHY NOT, MANAGER? WHY NOT?
BECAUSE YOU WERE TOOK, MR. McDUCK!
WE FOUND THERE WAS NO OIL IN THESE WELLS EXCEPT WHAT HAD BEEN POURED IN FROM THE TOP!
YOU MEAN THE WELLS WERE "SALTED"?
THAT'S RIGHT! YOU BOUGHT A DRY FIELD!
WITH 300 MILLION DOLLARS! WHAT WAS THAT SELLER'S NAME AGAIN?
GOLDFLINT HEARTGLOM! HE DISAPPEARED, AND WE HAVEN'T FOUND A TRACE OF HIM SINCE!
NOR A TRACE OF MY 300 MILLION, I BET! I'M SICK!
IN UPPER MONGOLDIA UNCLE SCROOGE GETS ANOTHER SHOCK!
I'VE GOT TO SELL ALL OF MY GOLD MINES IN THIS AREA, MANAGER! WHAT DO YOU THINK THEY'LL BRING IN DOLLARS?
NOTHING, MR. McDUCK! THERE'S NO GOLD IN THEM!
NO GOLD? THEY WERE THE RICHEST-LOOKING MINES I EVER SAW WHEN I BOUGHT THEM LAST MONTH!
THAT RICH LOOK WAS GILT PAINT! YOU WERE TOOK, MR. McDUCK!

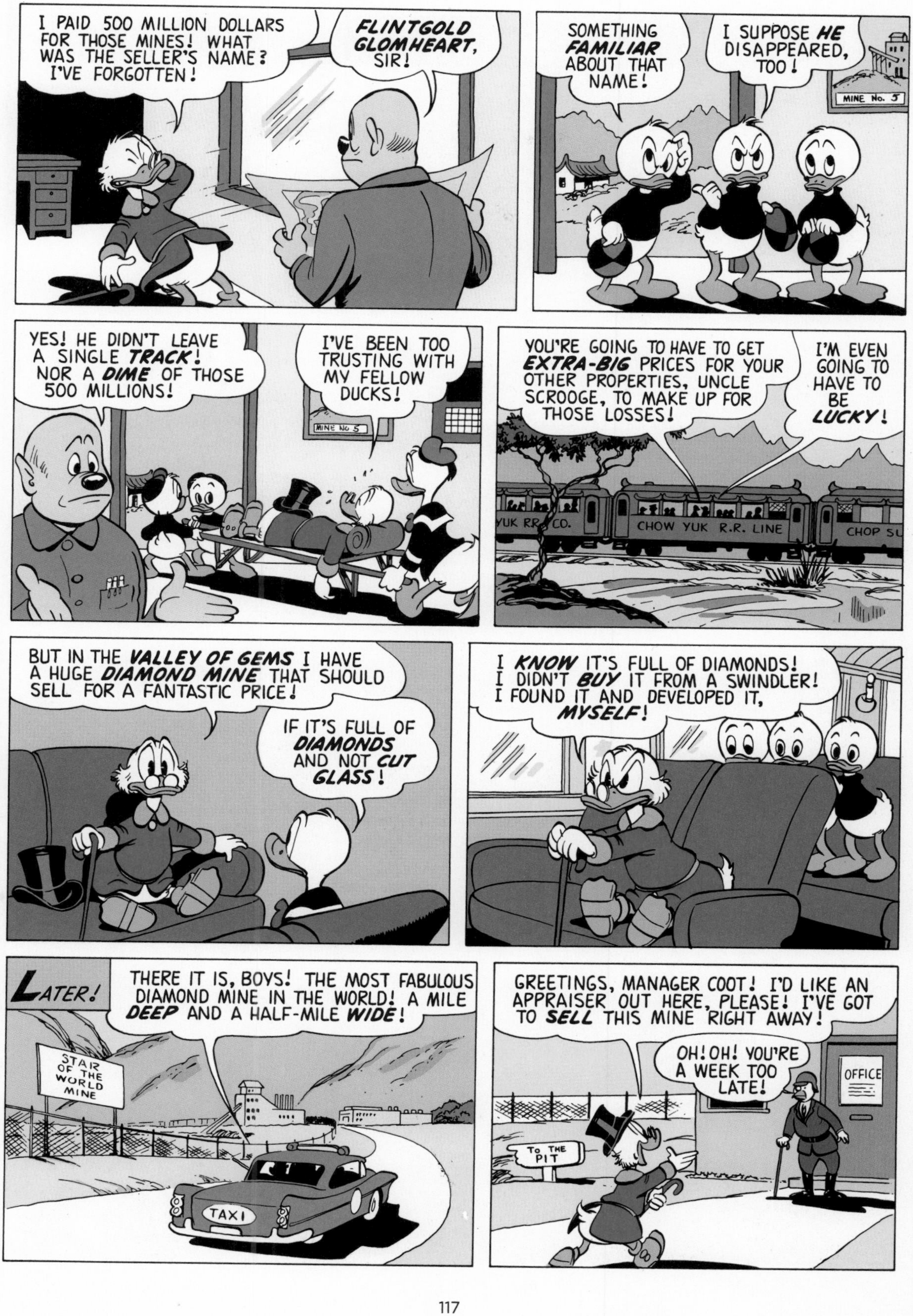
I PAID 500 MILLION DOLLARS FOR THOSE MINES! WHAT WAS THE SELLER'S NAME? I'VE FORGOTTEN!
FLINTGOLD GLOMHEART, SIR!
SOMETHING FAMILIAR ABOUT THAT NAME!
I SUPPOSE HE DISAPPEARED, TOO!
MINE No. 5
YES! HE DIDN'T LEAVE A SINGLE TRACK! NOR A DIME OF THOSE 500 MILLIONS!
I'VE BEEN TOO TRUSTING WITH MY FELLOW DUCKS!
MINE No. 5
YOU'RE GOING TO HAVE TO GET EXTRA-BIG PRICES FOR YOUR OTHER PROPERTIES, UNCLE SCROOGE, TO MAKE UP FOR THOSE LOSSES!
I'M EVEN GOING TO HAVE TO BE LUCKY!
YUK RR CO.
CHOW YUK R.R. LINE
CHOP SU
BUT IN THE VALLEY OF GEMS I HAVE A HUGE DIAMOND MINE THAT SHOULD SELL FOR A FANTASTIC PRICE!
IF IT'S FULL OF DIAMONDS AND NOT CUT GLASS!
I KNOW IT'S FULL OF DIAMONDS! I DIDN'T BUY IT FROM A SWINDLER! I FOUND IT AND DEVELOPED IT, MYSELF!
LATER!
THERE IT IS, BOYS! THE MOST FABULOUS DIAMOND MINE IN THE WORLD! A MILE DEEP AND A HALF-MILE WIDE!
STAR OF THE WORLD MINE
TAXI
GREETINGS, MANAGER COOT! I'D LIKE AN APPRAISER OUT HERE, PLEASE! I'VE GOT TO SELL THIS MINE RIGHT AWAY!
OH! OH! YOU'RE A WEEK TOO LATE!
OFFICE
TO THE PIT

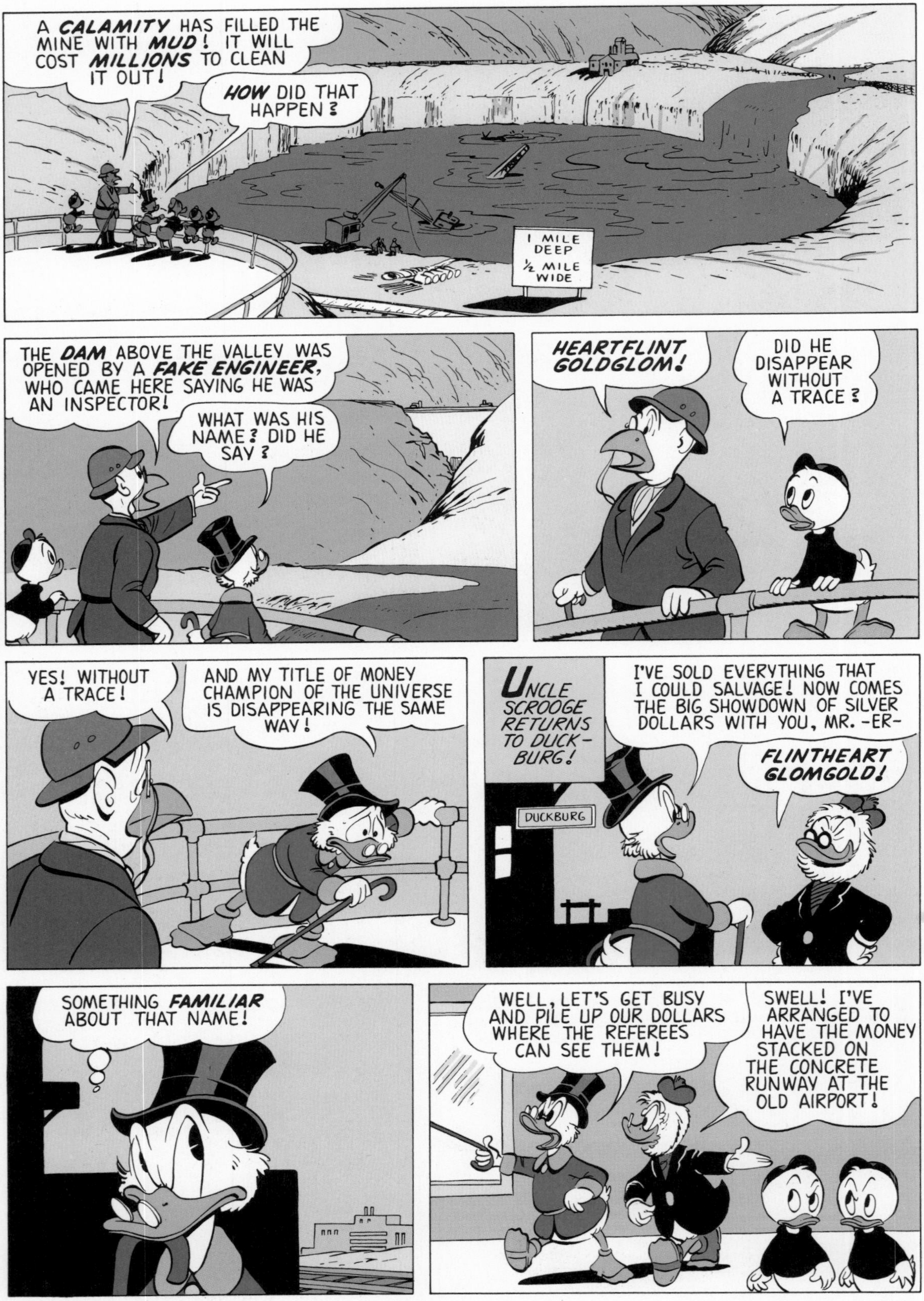
A CALAMITY HAS FILLED THE MINE WITH MUD! IT WILL COST MILLIONS TO CLEAN IT OUT!
HOW DID THAT HAPPEN?
I MILE DEEP
1/2 MILE WIDE
THE DAM ABOVE THE VALLEY WAS OPENED BY A FAKE ENGINEER, WHO CAME HERE SAYING HE WAS AN INSPECTOR!
WHAT WAS HIS NAME? DID HE SAY?
HEARTFLINT GOLDGLOM!
DID HE DISAPPEAR WITHOUT A TRACE?
YES! WITHOUT A TRACE!
AND MY TITLE OF MONEY CHAMPION OF THE UNIVERSE IS DISAPPEARING THE SAME WAY!
UNCLE SCROOGE RETURNS TO DUCKBURG!
I'VE SOLD EVERYTHING THAT I COULD SALVAGE! NOW COMES THE BIG SHOWDOWN OF SILVER DOLLARS WITH YOU, MR. -ER-
FLINTHEART GLOMGOLD!
DUCKBURG
SOMETHING FAMILIAR ABOUT THAT NAME!
WELL, LET'S GET BUSY AND PILE UP OUR DOLLARS WHERE THE REFEREES CAN SEE THEM!
SWELL! I'VE ARRANGED TO HAVE THE MONEY STACKED ON THE CONCRETE RUNWAY AT THE OLD AIRPORT!

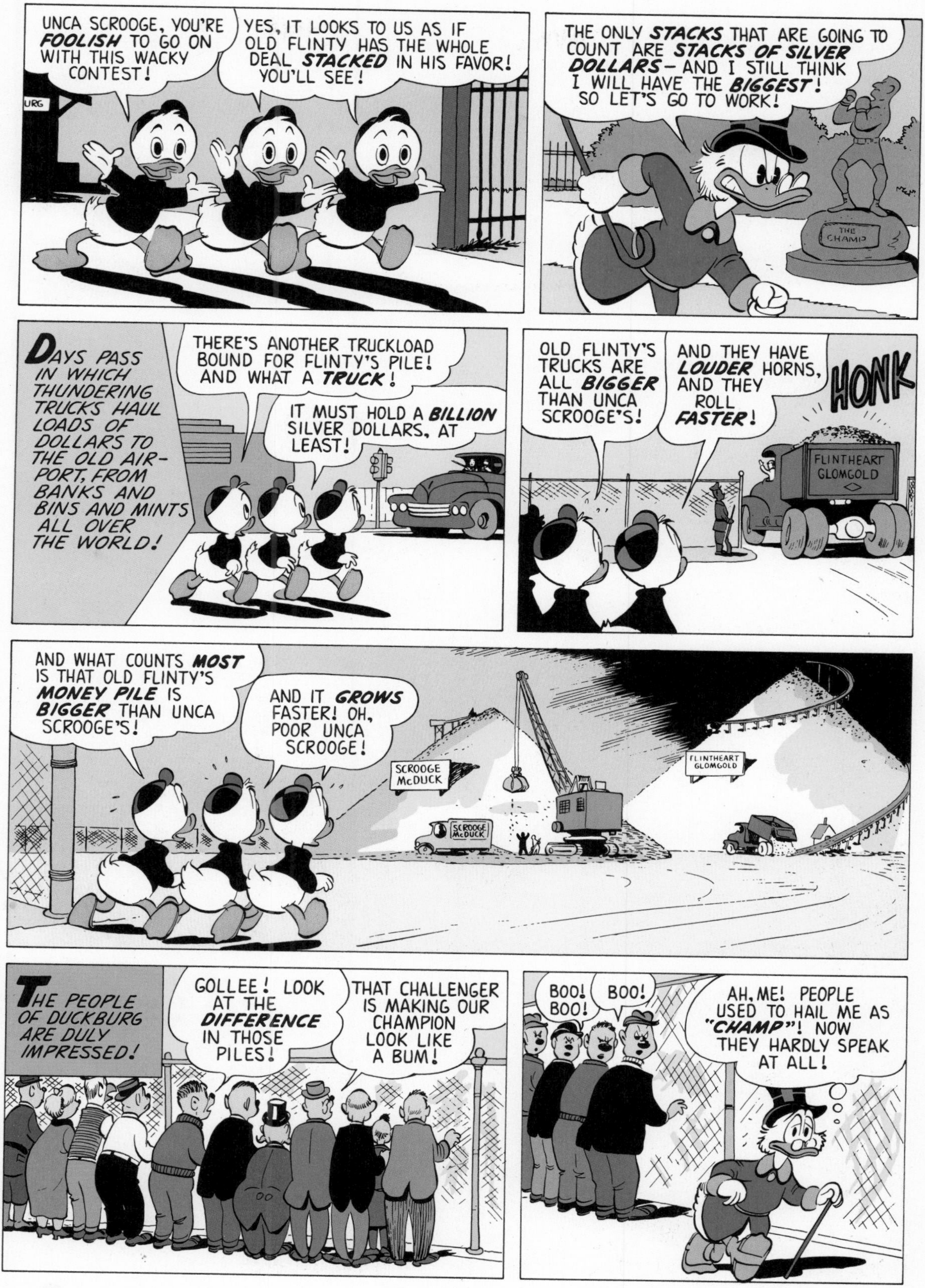
UNCA SCROOGE, YOU'RE FOOLISH TO GO ON WITH THIS WACKY CONTEST!
YES, IT LOOKS TO US AS IF OLD FLINTY HAS THE WHOLE DEAL STACKED IN HIS FAVOR! YOU'LL SEE!
THE ONLY STACKS THAT ARE GOING TO COUNT ARE STACKS OF SILVER DOLLARS – AND I STILL THINK I WILL HAVE THE BIGGEST! SO LET'S GO TO WORK!
THE CHAMP
DAYS PASS IN WHICH THUNDERING TRUCKS HAUL LOADS OF DOLLARS TO THE OLD AIR-PORT, FROM BANKS AND BINS AND MINTS ALL OVER THE WORLD!
THERE'S ANOTHER TRUCKLOAD BOUND FOR FLINTY'S PILE! AND WHAT A TRUCK!
IT MUST HOLD A BILLION SILVER DOLLARS, AT LEAST!
OLD FLINTY'S TRUCKS ARE ALL BIGGER THAN UNCA SCROOGE'S!
AND THEY HAVE LOUDER HORNS, AND THEY ROLL FASTER!
HONK
FLINTHEART GLOMGOLD
AND WHAT COUNTS MOST IS THAT OLD FLINTY'S MONEY PILE IS BIGGER THAN UNCA SCROOGE'S!
AND IT GROWS FASTER! OH, POOR UNCA SCROOGE!
SCROOGE McDUCK
FLINTHEART GLOMGOLD
SCROOGE McDUCK
THE PEOPLE OF DUCKBURG ARE DULY IMPRESSED!
GOLLEE! LOOK AT THE DIFFERENCE IN THOSE PILES!
THAT CHALLENGER IS MAKING OUR CHAMPION LOOK LIKE A BUM!
BOO! BOO!
BOO!
AH, ME! PEOPLE USED TO HAIL ME AS "CHAMP"! NOW THEY HARDLY SPEAK AT ALL!

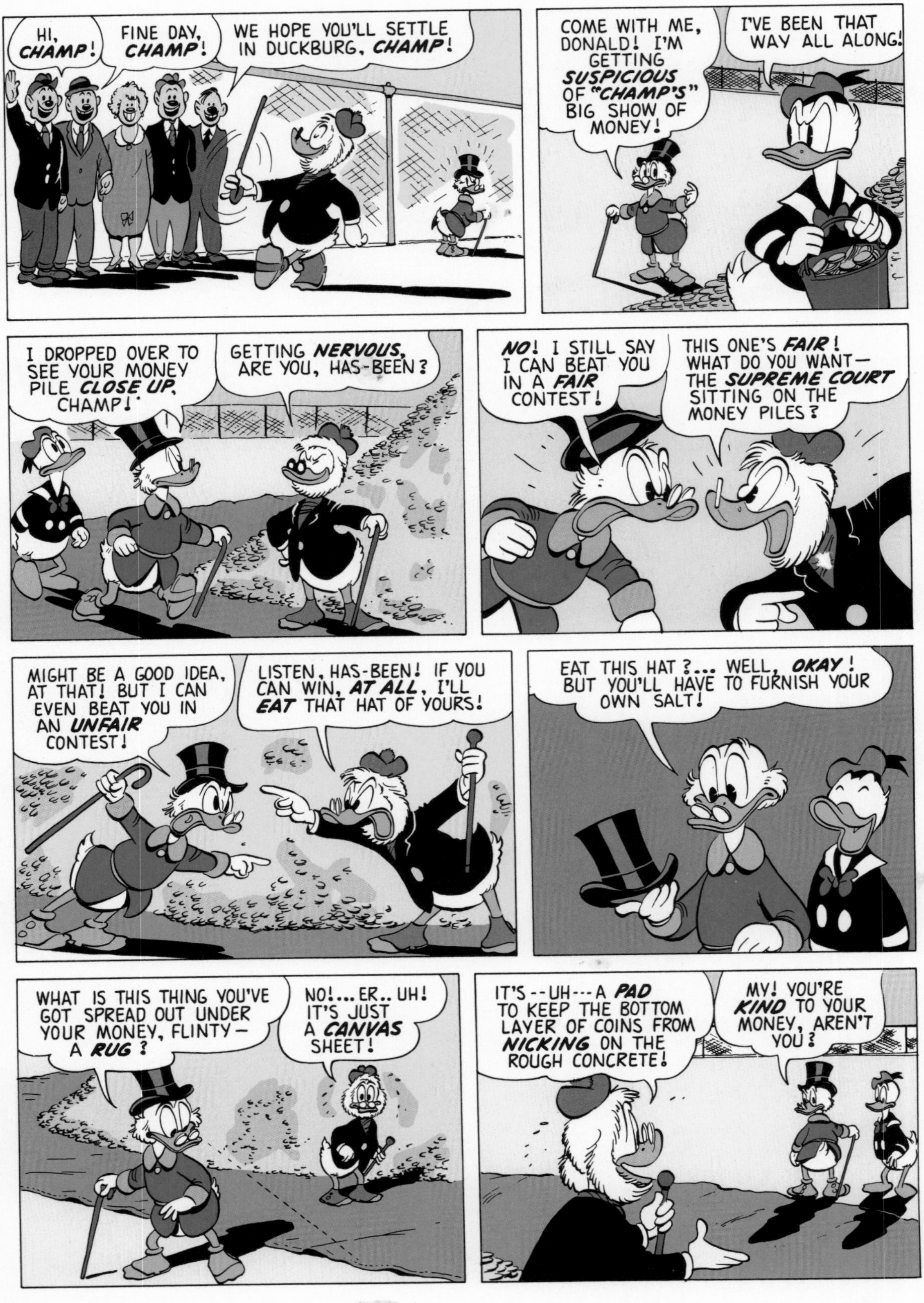

HI, CHAMP!
FINE DAY, CHAMP!
WE HOPE YOU'LL SETTLE IN DUCKBURG, CHAMP!
COME WITH ME, DONALD! I'M GETTING SUSPICIOUS OF "CHAMP'S" BIG SHOW OF MONEY!
I'VE BEEN THAT WAY ALL ALONG!
I DROPPED OVER TO SEE YOUR MONEY PILE CLOSE UP, CHAMP!
GETTING NERVOUS, ARE YOU, HAS-BEEN?
NO! I STILL SAY I CAN BEAT YOU IN A FAIR CONTEST!
THIS ONE'S FAIR! WHAT DO YOU WANT— THE SUPREME COURT SITTING ON THE MONEY PILES?
MIGHT BE A GOOD IDEA, AT THAT! BUT I CAN EVEN BEAT YOU IN AN UNFAIR CONTEST!
LISTEN, HAS-BEEN! IF YOU CAN WIN, AT ALL, I'LL EAT THAT HAT OF YOURS!
EAT THIS HAT?... WELL, OKAY! BUT YOU'LL HAVE TO FURNISH YOUR OWN SALT!
WHAT IS THIS THING YOU'VE GOT SPREAD OUT UNDER YOUR MONEY, FLINTY— A RUG?
NO!... ER.. UH! IT'S JUST A CANVAS SHEET!
IT'S --UH--- A PAD TO KEEP THE BOTTOM LAYER OF COINS FROM NICKING ON THE ROUGH CONCRETE!
MY! YOU'RE KIND TO YOUR MONEY, AREN'T YOU?

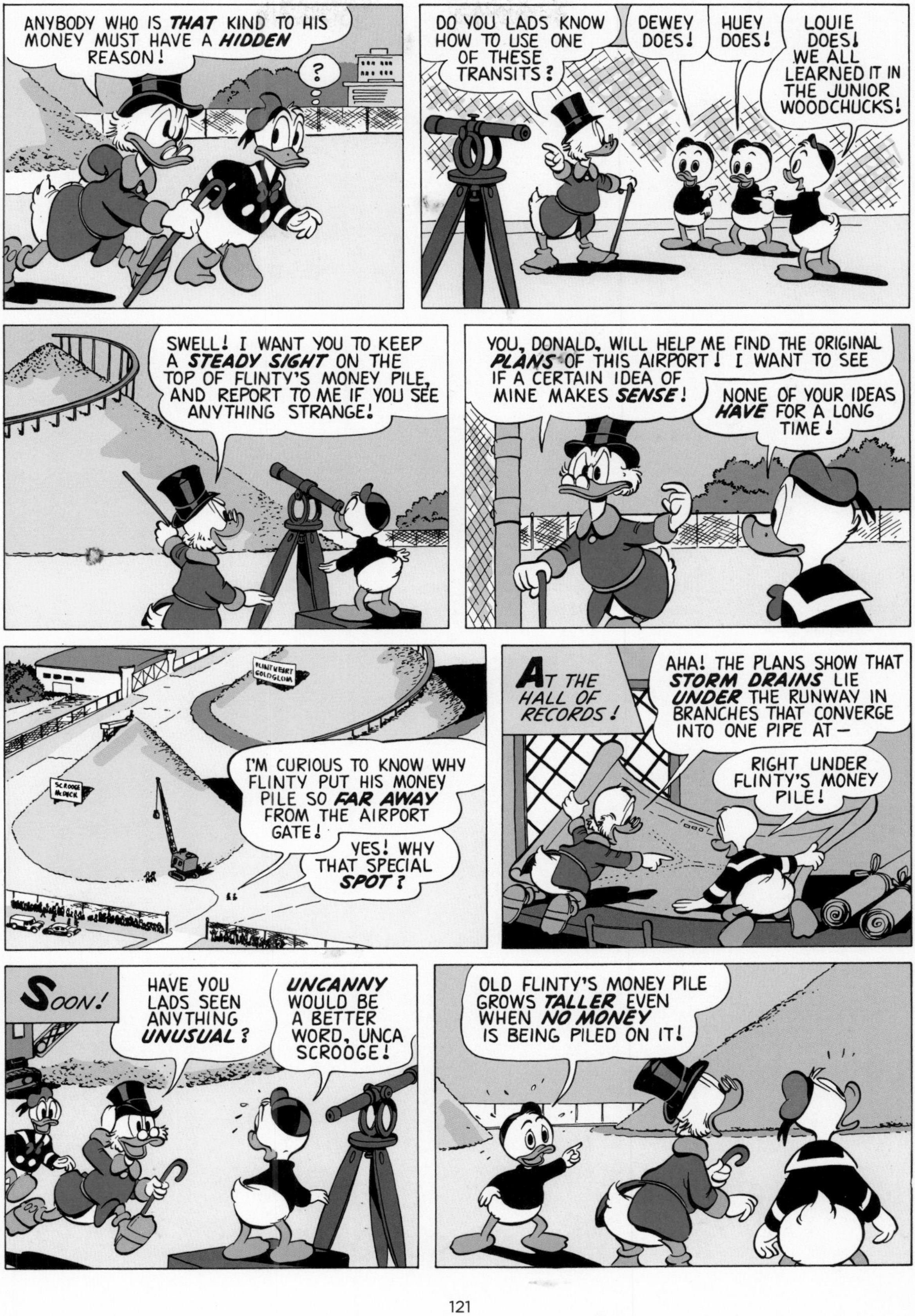

ANYBODY WHO IS THAT KIND TO HIS MONEY MUST HAVE A HIDDEN REASON!
?
DO YOU LADS KNOW HOW TO USE ONE OF THESE TRANSITS?
DEWEY DOES!
HUEY DOES!
LOUIE DOES! WE ALL LEARNED IT IN THE JUNIOR WOODCHUCKS!
SWELL! I WANT YOU TO KEEP A STEADY SIGHT ON THE TOP OF FLINTY'S MONEY PILE, AND REPORT TO ME IF YOU SEE ANYTHING STRANGE!
YOU, DONALD, WILL HELP ME FIND THE ORIGINAL PLANS OF THIS AIRPORT! I WANT TO SEE IF A CERTAIN IDEA OF MINE MAKES SENSE!
NONE OF YOUR IDEAS HAVE FOR A LONG TIME!
I'M CURIOUS TO KNOW WHY FLINTY PUT HIS MONEY PILE SO FAR AWAY FROM THE AIRPORT GATE!
YES! WHY THAT SPECIAL SPOT?
AT THE HALL OF RECORDS!
AHA! THE PLANS SHOW THAT STORM DRAINS LIE UNDER THE RUNWAY IN BRANCHES THAT CONVERGE INTO ONE PIPE AT—
RIGHT UNDER FLINTY'S MONEY PILE!
SOON!
HAVE YOU LADS SEEN ANYTHING UNUSUAL?
UNCANNY WOULD BE A BETTER WORD, UNCA SCROOGE!
OLD FLINTY'S MONEY PILE GROWS TALLER EVEN WHEN NO MONEY IS BEING PILED ON IT!

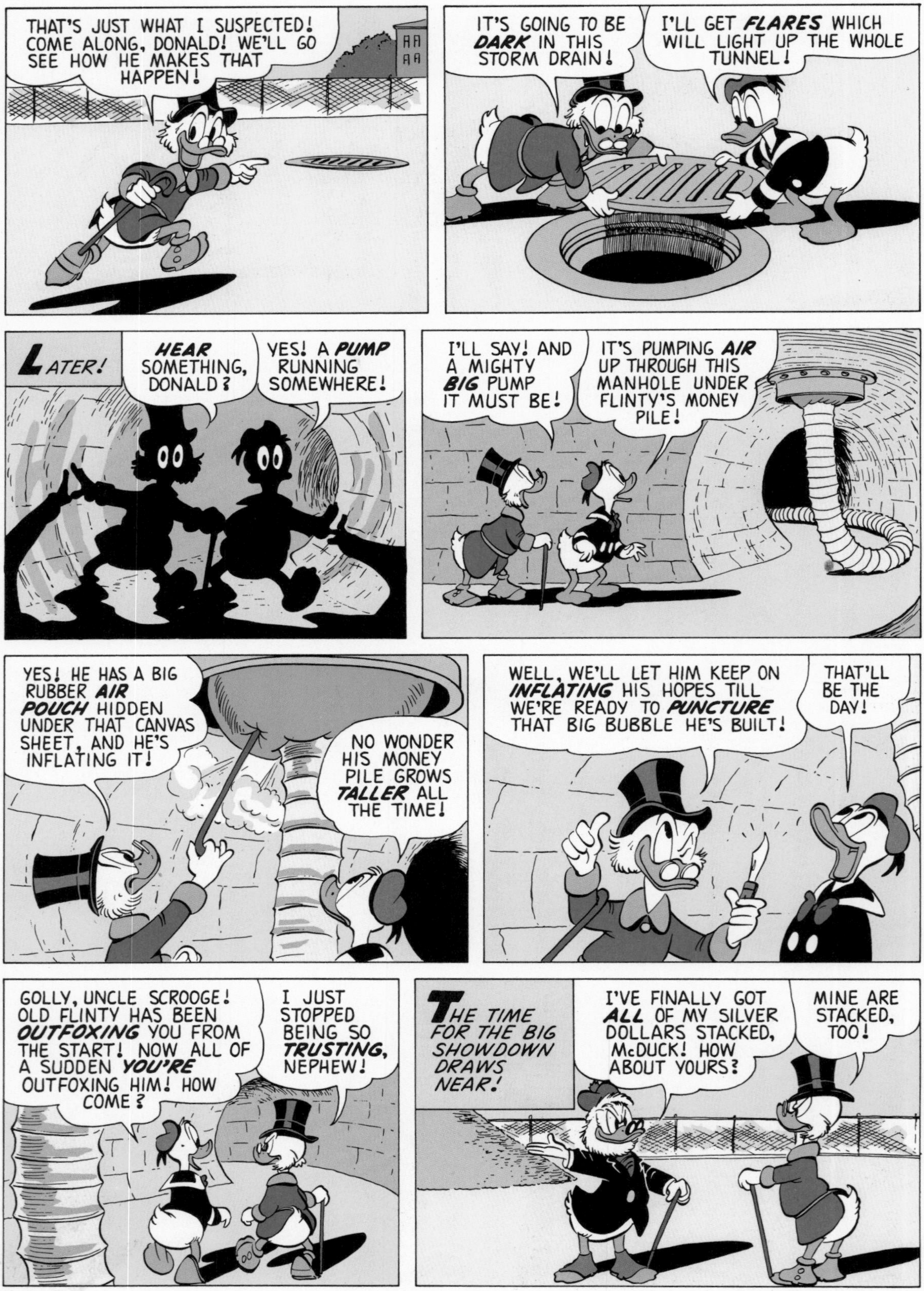
THAT'S JUST WHAT I SUSPECTED! COME ALONG, DONALD! WE'LL GO SEE HOW HE MAKES THAT HAPPEN!
IT'S GOING TO BE DARK IN THIS STORM DRAIN!
I'LL GET FLARES WHICH WILL LIGHT UP THE WHOLE TUNNEL!
LATER!
HEAR SOMETHING, DONALD?
YES! A PUMP RUNNING SOMEWHERE!
I'LL SAY! AND A MIGHTY BIG PUMP IT MUST BE!
IT'S PUMPING AIR UP THROUGH THIS MANHOLE UNDER FLINTY'S MONEY PILE!
YES! HE HAS A BIG RUBBER AIR POUCH HIDDEN UNDER THAT CANVAS SHEET, AND HE'S INFLATING IT!
NO WONDER HIS MONEY PILE GROWS TALLER ALL THE TIME!
WELL, WE'LL LET HIM KEEP ON INFLATING HIS HOPES TILL WE'RE READY TO PUNCTURE THAT BIG BUBBLE HE'S BUILT!
THAT'LL BE THE DAY!
GOLLY, UNCLE SCROOGE! OLD FLINTY HAS BEEN OUTFOXING YOU FROM THE START! NOW ALL OF A SUDDEN YOU'RE OUTFOXING HIM! HOW COME?
I JUST STOPPED BEING SO TRUSTING, NEPHEW!
THE TIME FOR THE BIG SHOWDOWN DRAWS NEAR!
I'VE FINALLY GOT ALL OF MY SILVER DOLLARS STACKED, McDUCK! HOW ABOUT YOURS?
MINE ARE STACKED, TOO!

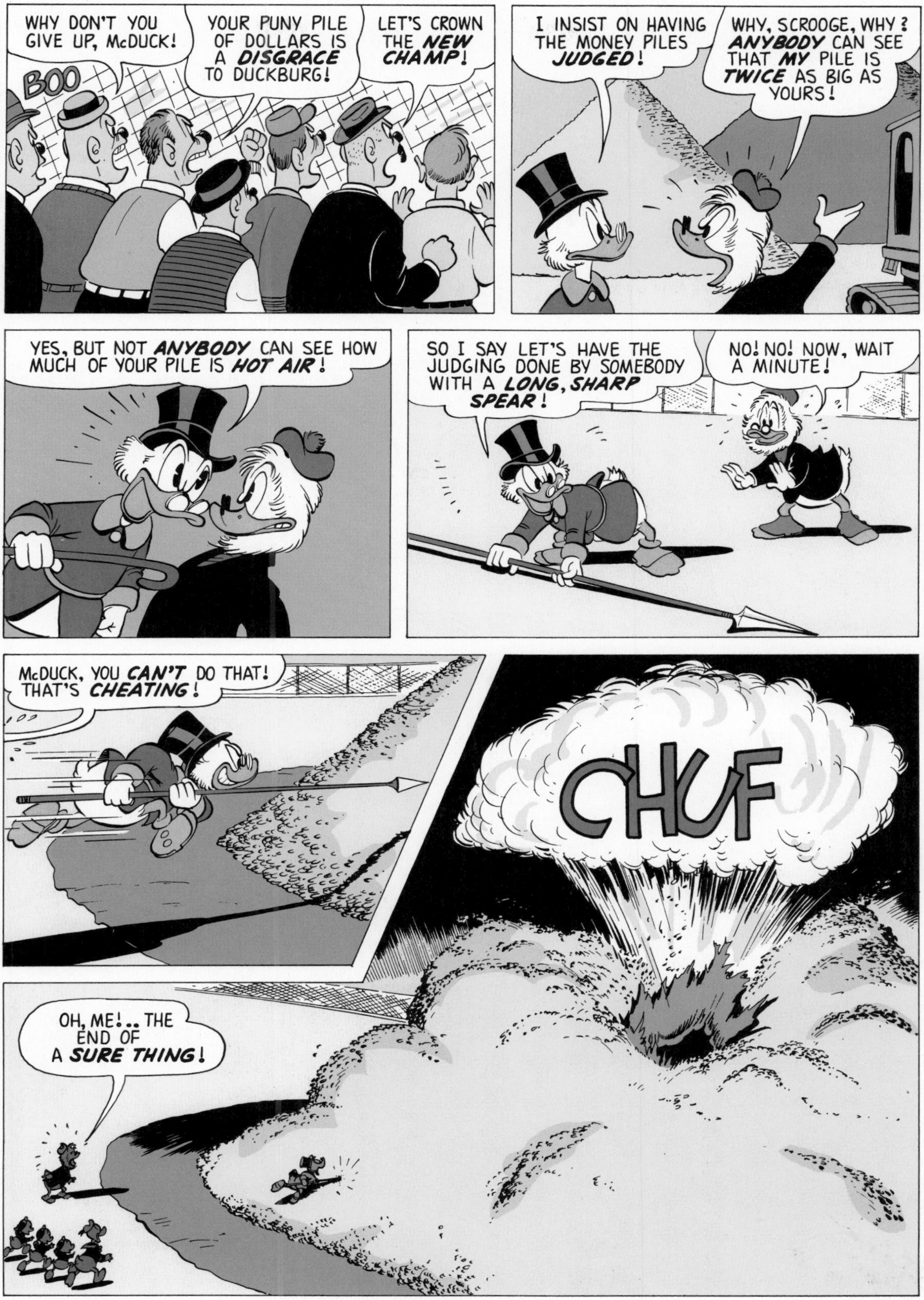
WHY DON'T YOU GIVE UP, McDUCK!
BOO
YOUR PUNY PILE OF DOLLARS IS A DISGRACE TO DUCKBURG!
LET'S CROWN THE NEW CHAMP!
I INSIST ON HAVING THE MONEY PILES JUDGED!
WHY, SCROOGE, WHY? ANYBODY CAN SEE THAT MY PILE IS TWICE AS BIG AS YOURS!
YES, BUT NOT ANYBODY CAN SEE HOW MUCH OF YOUR PILE IS HOT AIR!
SO I SAY LET'S HAVE THE JUDGING DONE BY SOMEBODY WITH A LONG, SHARP SPEAR!
NO! NO! NOW, WAIT A MINUTE!
McDUCK, YOU CAN'T DO THAT! THAT'S CHEATING!
CHUF
OH, ME!.. THE END OF A SURE THING!

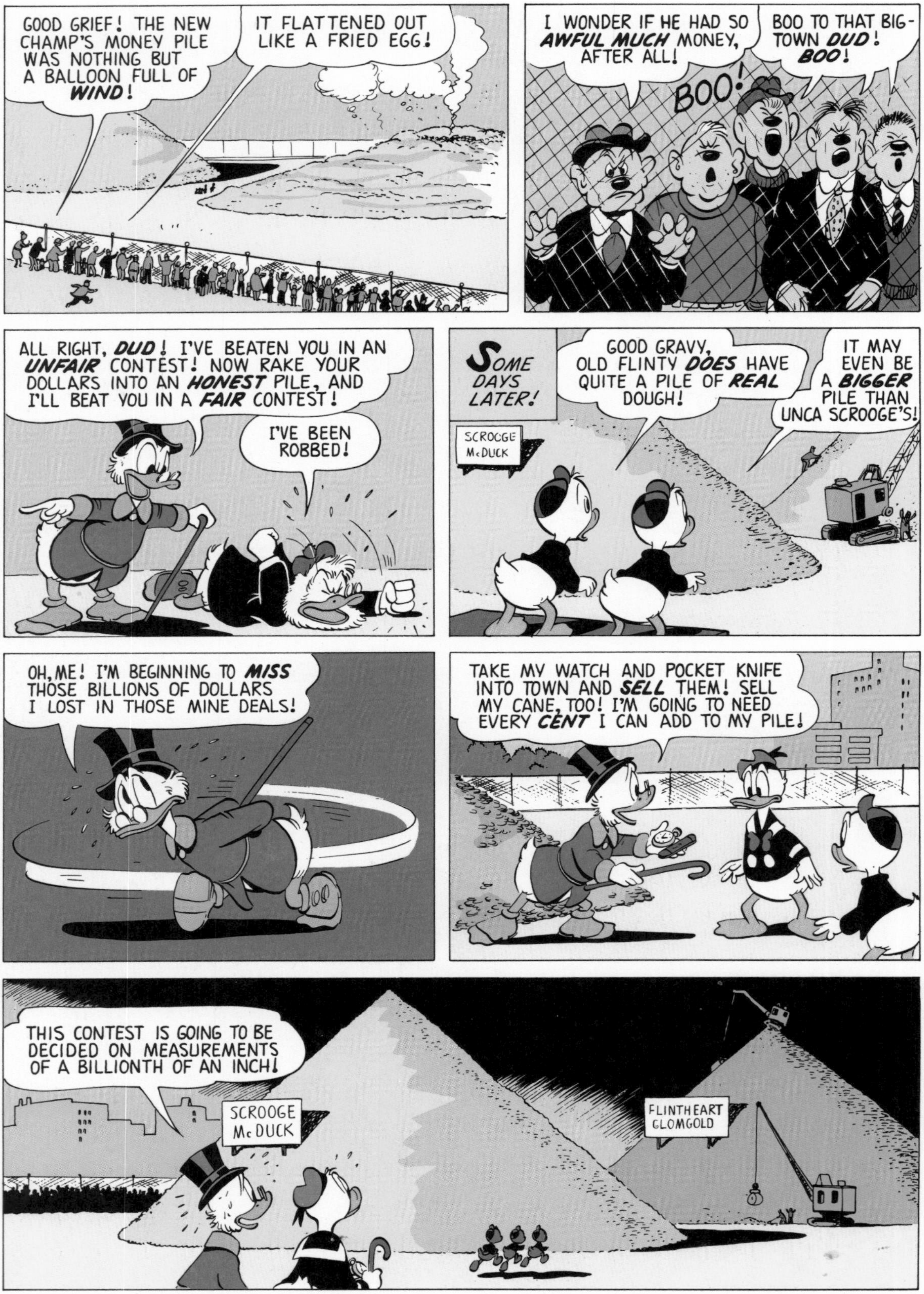
GOOD GRIEF! THE NEW CHAMP'S MONEY PILE WAS NOTHING BUT A BALLOON FULL OF WIND!
IT FLATTENED OUT LIKE A FRIED EGG!
I WONDER IF HE HAD SO AWFUL MUCH MONEY, AFTER ALL!
BOO TO THAT BIG-TOWN DUD! BOO!
BOO!
ALL RIGHT, DUD! I'VE BEATEN YOU IN AN UNFAIR CONTEST! NOW RAKE YOUR DOLLARS INTO AN HONEST PILE, AND I'LL BEAT YOU IN A FAIR CONTEST!
I'VE BEEN ROBBED!
SOME DAYS LATER!
GOOD GRAVY, OLD FLINTY DOES HAVE QUITE A PILE OF REAL DOUGH!
IT MAY EVEN BE A BIGGER PILE THAN UNCA SCROOGE'S!
SCROOGE McDUCK
OH, ME! I'M BEGINNING TO MISS THOSE BILLIONS OF DOLLARS I LOST IN THOSE MINE DEALS!
TAKE MY WATCH AND POCKET KNIFE INTO TOWN AND SELL THEM! SELL MY CANE, TOO! I'M GOING TO NEED EVERY CENT I CAN ADD TO MY PILE!
THIS CONTEST IS GOING TO BE DECIDED ON MEASUREMENTS OF A BILLIONTH OF AN INCH!
SCROOGE McDUCK
FLINTHEART GLOMGOLD

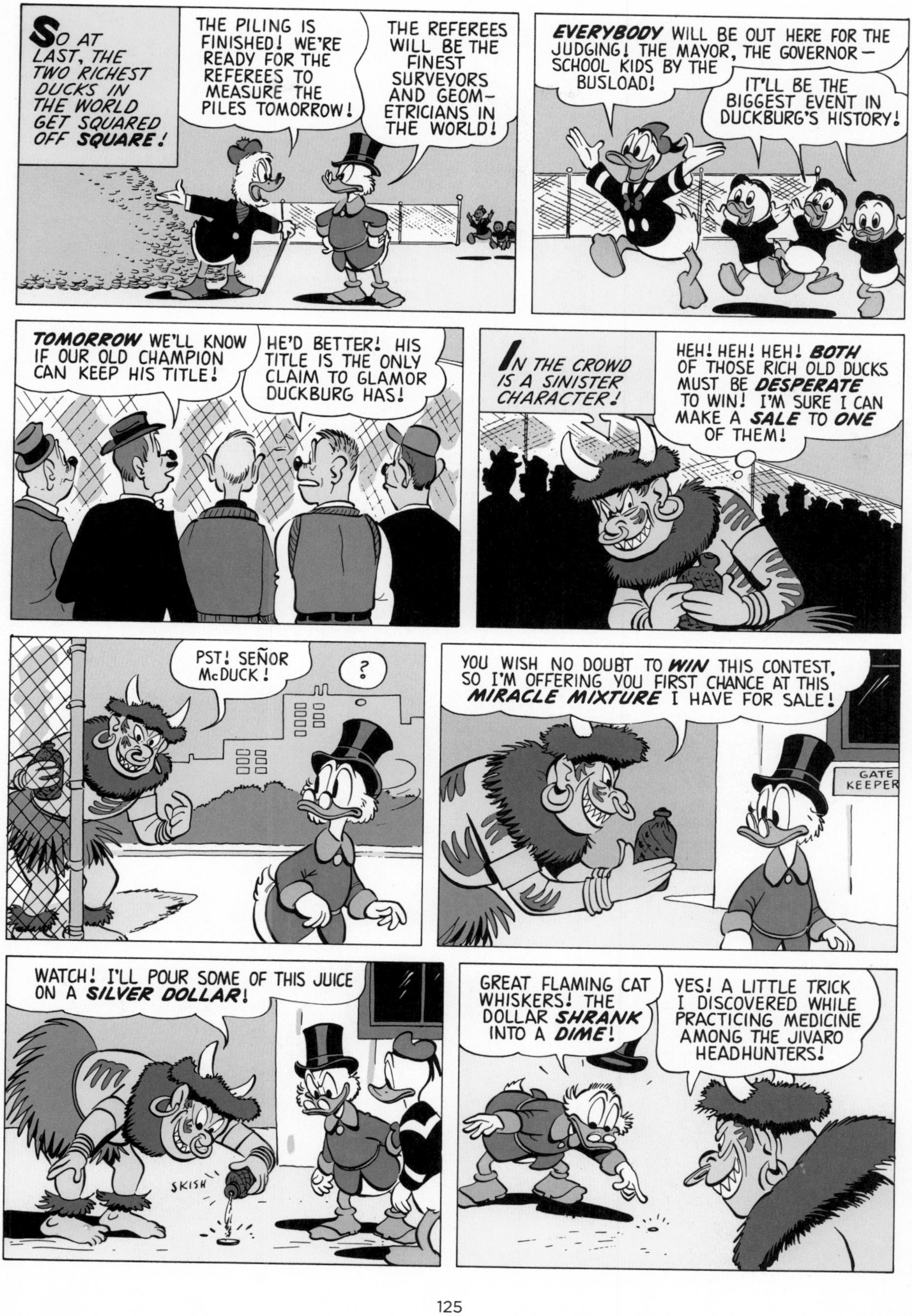
SO AT LAST, THE TWO RICHEST DUCKS IN THE WORLD GET SQUARED OFF SQUARE!
THE PILING IS FINISHED! WE'RE READY FOR THE REFEREES TO MEASURE THE PILES TOMORROW!
THE REFEREES WILL BE THE FINEST SURVEYORS AND GEOMETRICIANS IN THE WORLD!
EVERYBODY WILL BE OUT HERE FOR THE JUDGING! THE MAYOR, THE GOVERNOR— SCHOOL KIDS BY THE BUSLOAD!
IT'LL BE THE BIGGEST EVENT IN DUCKBURG'S HISTORY!
TOMORROW WE'LL KNOW IF OUR OLD CHAMPION CAN KEEP HIS TITLE!
HE'D BETTER! HIS TITLE IS THE ONLY CLAIM TO GLAMOR DUCKBURG HAS!
IN THE CROWD IS A SINISTER CHARACTER!
HEH! HEH! HEH! BOTH OF THOSE RICH OLD DUCKS MUST BE DESPERATE TO WIN! I'M SURE I CAN MAKE A SALE TO ONE OF THEM!
PST! SEÑOR McDUCK!
?
YOU WISH NO DOUBT TO WIN THIS CONTEST, SO I'M OFFERING YOU FIRST CHANCE AT THIS MIRACLE MIXTURE I HAVE FOR SALE!
GATE KEEPER
WATCH! I'LL POUR SOME OF THIS JUICE ON A SILVER DOLLAR!
SKISH
GREAT FLAMING CAT WHISKERS! THE DOLLAR SHRANK INTO A DIME!
YES! A LITTLE TRICK I DISCOVERED WHILE PRACTICING MEDICINE AMONG THE JIVARO HEADHUNTERS!

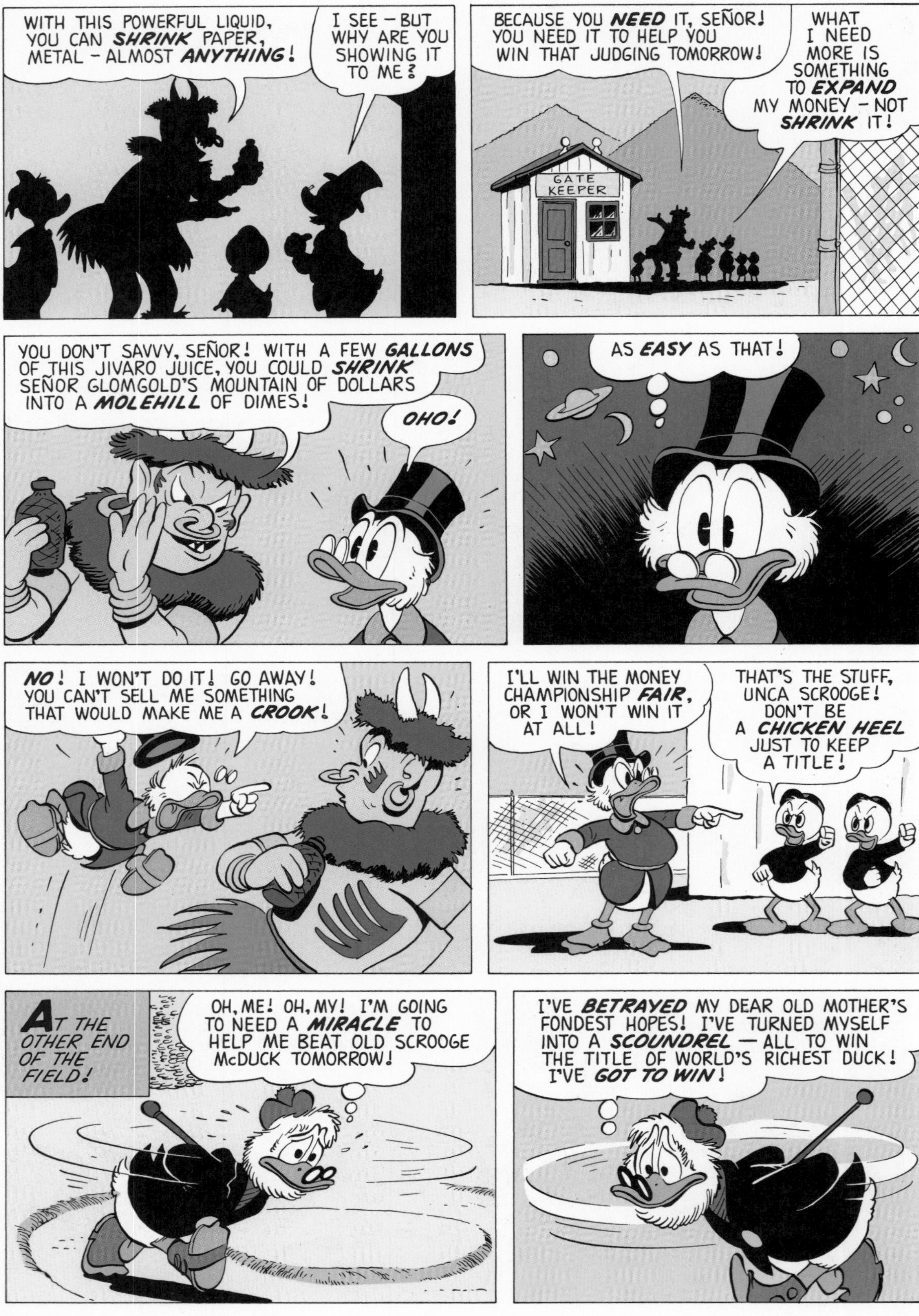

WITH THIS POWERFUL LIQUID, YOU CAN SHRINK PAPER, METAL – ALMOST ANYTHING!
I SEE – BUT WHY ARE YOU SHOWING IT TO ME?
BECAUSE YOU NEED IT, SEÑOR! YOU NEED IT TO HELP YOU WIN THAT JUDGING TOMORROW!
WHAT I NEED MORE IS SOMETHING TO EXPAND MY MONEY – NOT SHRINK IT!
GATE KEEPER
YOU DON'T SAVVY, SEÑOR! WITH A FEW GALLONS OF THIS JIVARO JUICE, YOU COULD SHRINK SEÑOR GLOMGOLD'S MOUNTAIN OF DOLLARS INTO A MOLEHILL OF DIMES!
OHO!
AS EASY AS THAT!
NO! I WON'T DO IT! GO AWAY! YOU CAN'T SELL ME SOMETHING THAT WOULD MAKE ME A CROOK!
I'LL WIN THE MONEY CHAMPIONSHIP FAIR, OR I WON'T WIN IT AT ALL!
THAT'S THE STUFF, UNCA SCROOGE! DON'T BE A CHICKEN HEEL JUST TO KEEP A TITLE!
AT THE OTHER END OF THE FIELD!
OH, ME! OH, MY! I'M GOING TO NEED A MIRACLE TO HELP ME BEAT OLD SCROOGE McDUCK TOMORROW!
I'VE BETRAYED MY DEAR OLD MOTHER'S FONDEST HOPES! I'VE TURNED MYSELF INTO A SCOUNDREL — ALL TO WIN THE TITLE OF WORLD'S RICHEST DUCK! I'VE GOT TO WIN!

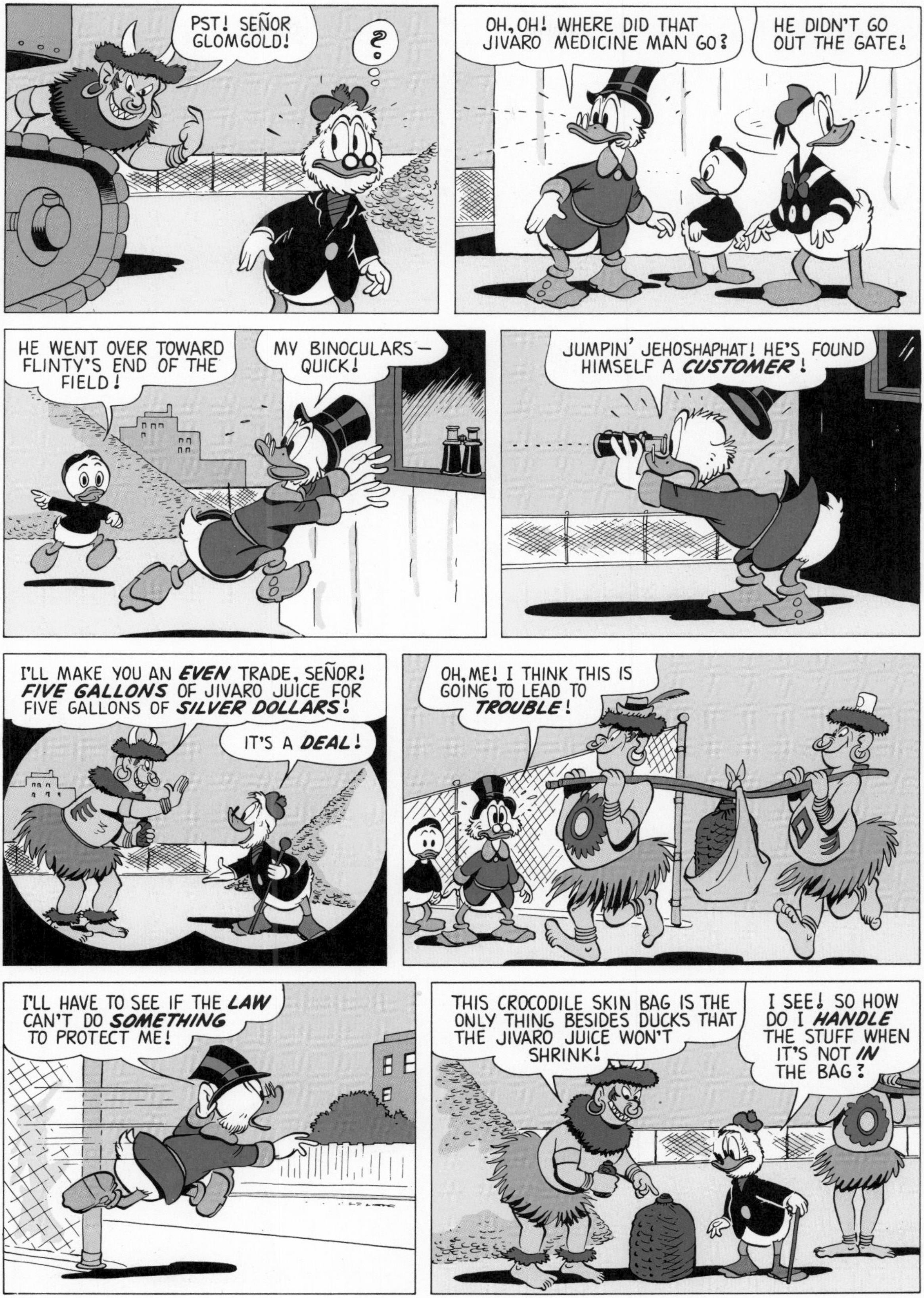
PST! SEÑOR GLOMGOLD!
?
OH, OH! WHERE DID THAT JIVARO MEDICINE MAN GO?
HE DIDN'T GO OUT THE GATE!
HE WENT OVER TOWARD FLINTY'S END OF THE FIELD!
MY BINOCULARS— QUICK!
JUMPIN' JEHOSHAPHAT! HE'S FOUND HIMSELF A CUSTOMER!
I'LL MAKE YOU AN EVEN TRADE, SEÑOR! FIVE GALLONS OF JIVARO JUICE FOR FIVE GALLONS OF SILVER DOLLARS!
IT'S A DEAL!
OH, ME! I THINK THIS IS GOING TO LEAD TO TROUBLE!
I'LL HAVE TO SEE IF THE LAW CAN'T DO SOMETHING TO PROTECT ME!
THIS CROCODILE SKIN BAG IS THE ONLY THING BESIDES DUCKS THAT THE JIVARO JUICE WON'T SHRINK!
I SEE! SO HOW DO I HANDLE THE STUFF WHEN IT'S NOT IN THE BAG?

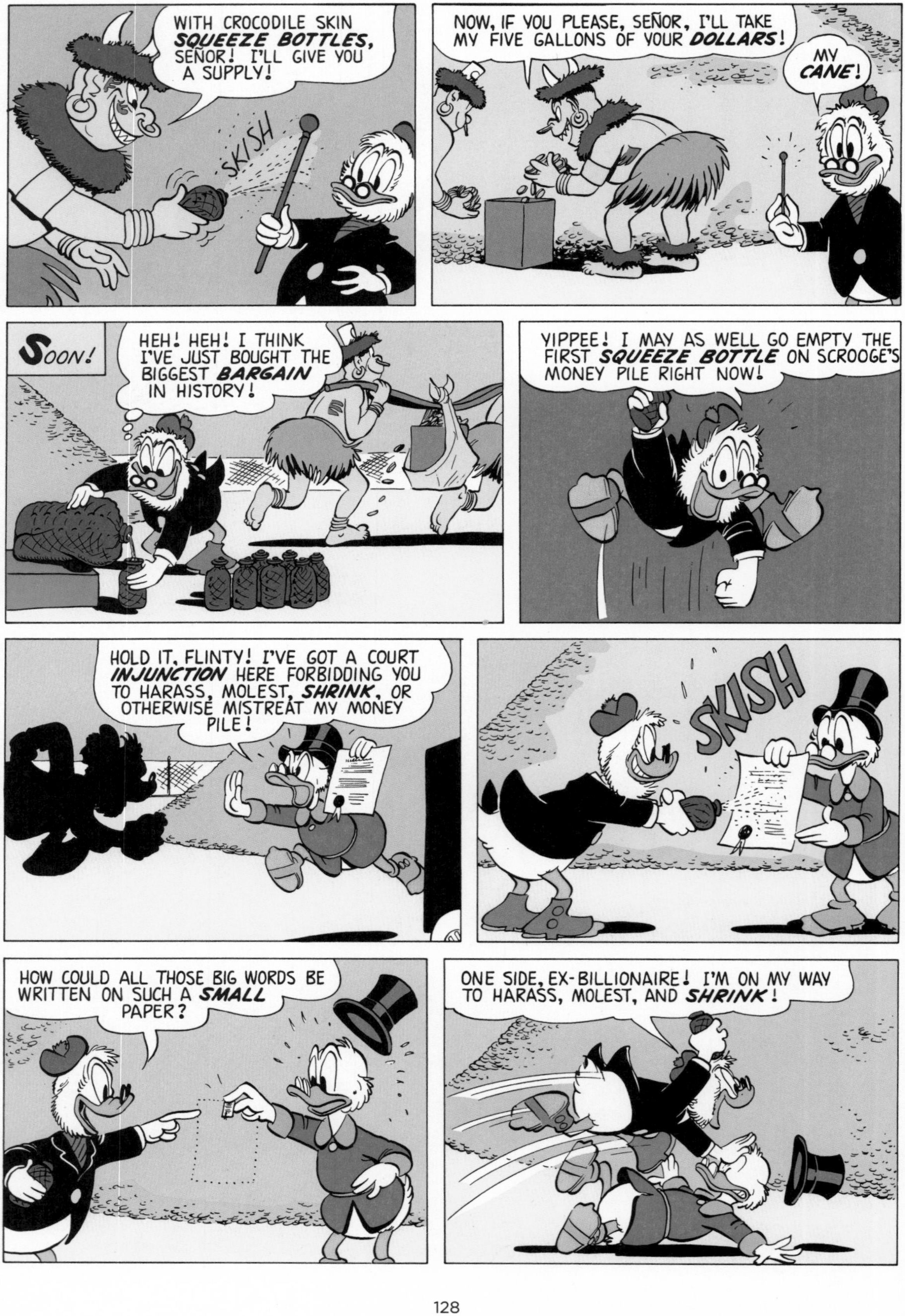
WITH CROCODILE SKIN SQUEEZE BOTTLES, SEÑOR! I'LL GIVE YOU A SUPPLY!
SKISH
NOW, IF YOU PLEASE, SEÑOR, I'LL TAKE MY FIVE GALLONS OF YOUR DOLLARS!
MY CANE!
SOON!
HEH! HEH! I THINK I'VE JUST BOUGHT THE BIGGEST BARGAIN IN HISTORY!
YIPPEE! I MAY AS WELL GO EMPTY THE FIRST SQUEEZE BOTTLE ON SCROOGE'S MONEY PILE RIGHT NOW!
HOLD IT, FLINTY! I'VE GOT A COURT INJUNCTION HERE FORBIDDING YOU TO HARASS, MOLEST, SHRINK, OR OTHERWISE MISTREAT MY MONEY PILE!
SKISH
HOW COULD ALL THOSE BIG WORDS BE WRITTEN ON SUCH A SMALL PAPER?
ONE SIDE, EX-BILLIONAIRE! I'M ON MY WAY TO HARASS, MOLEST, AND SHRINK!

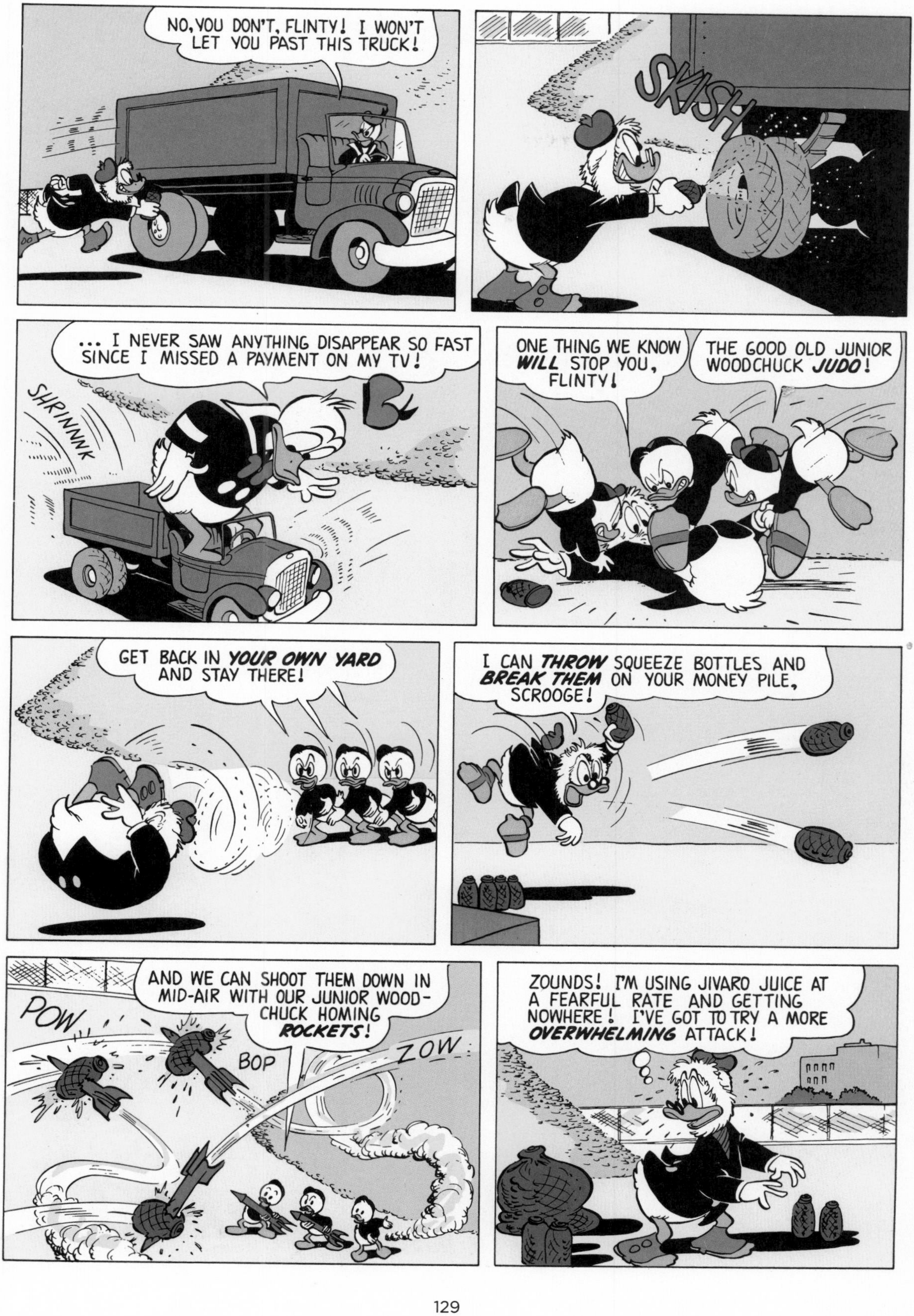

NO, YOU DON'T, FLINTY! I WON'T LET YOU PAST THIS TRUCK!
SKISH
... I NEVER SAW ANYTHING DISAPPEAR SO FAST SINCE I MISSED A PAYMENT ON MY TV!
SHRINNNK
ONE THING WE KNOW WILL STOP YOU, FLINTY!
THE GOOD OLD JUNIOR WOODCHUCK JUDO!
GET BACK IN YOUR OWN YARD AND STAY THERE!
I CAN THROW SQUEEZE BOTTLES AND BREAK THEM ON YOUR MONEY PILE, SCROOGE!
AND WE CAN SHOOT THEM DOWN IN MID-AIR WITH OUR JUNIOR WOOD-CHUCK HOMING ROCKETS!
POW
BOP
ZOW
ZOUNDS! I'M USING JIVARO JUICE AT A FEARFUL RATE AND GETTING NOWHERE! I'VE GOT TO TRY A MORE OVERWHELMING ATTACK!

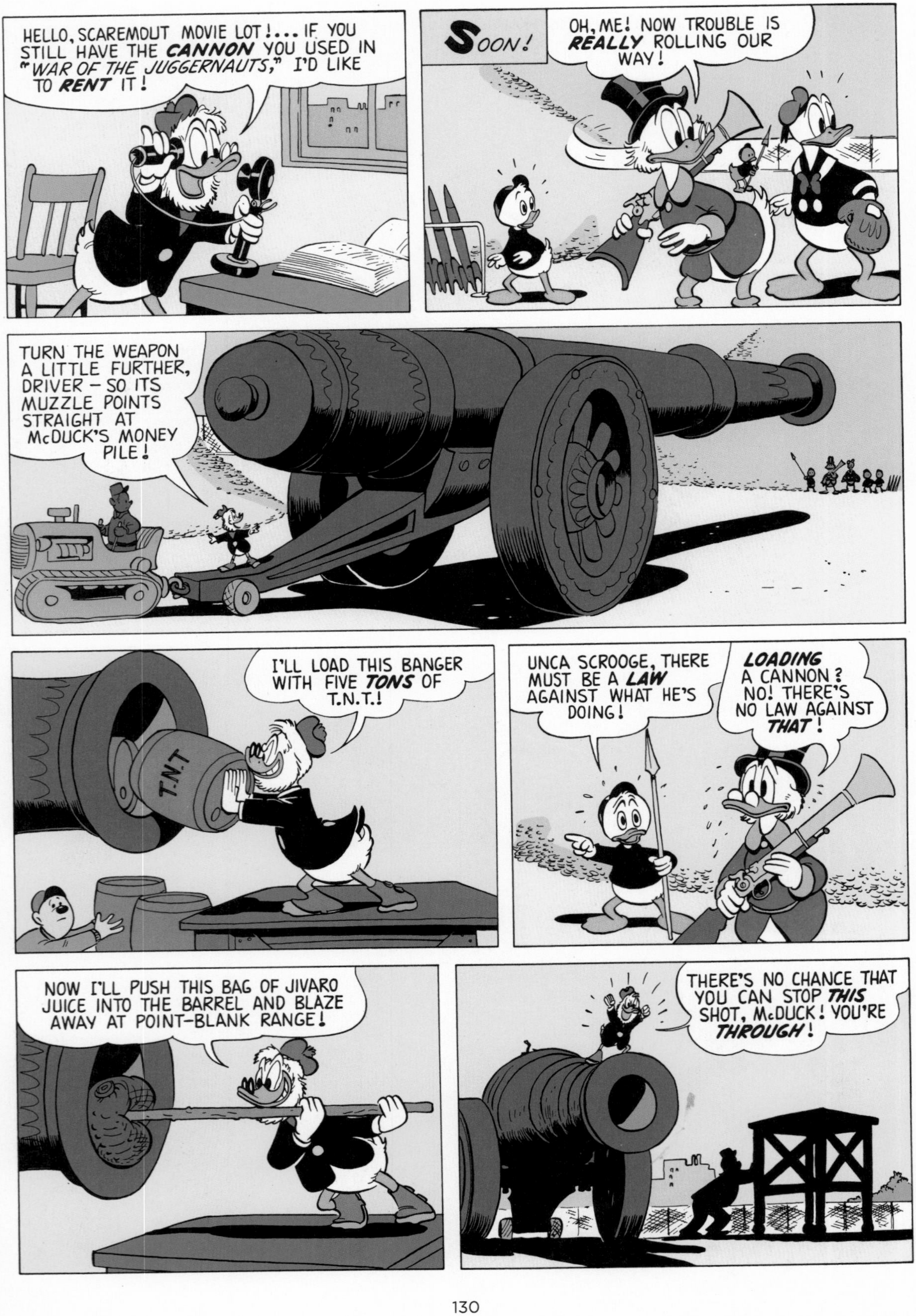
HELLO, SCAREMOUT MOVIE LOT!... IF YOU STILL HAVE THE CANNON YOU USED IN "WAR OF THE JUGGERNAUTS," I'D LIKE TO RENT IT!
SOON!
OH, ME! NOW TROUBLE IS REALLY ROLLING OUR WAY!
TURN THE WEAPON A LITTLE FURTHER, DRIVER — SO ITS MUZZLE POINTS STRAIGHT AT McDUCK'S MONEY PILE!
I'LL LOAD THIS BANGER WITH FIVE TONS OF T.N.T.!
T.N.T
UNCA SCROOGE, THERE MUST BE A LAW AGAINST WHAT HE'S DOING!
LOADING A CANNON? NO! THERE'S NO LAW AGAINST THAT!
NOW I'LL PUSH THIS BAG OF JIVARO JUICE INTO THE BARREL AND BLAZE AWAY AT POINT-BLANK RANGE!
THERE'S NO CHANCE THAT YOU CAN STOP THIS SHOT, McDUCK! YOU'RE THROUGH!

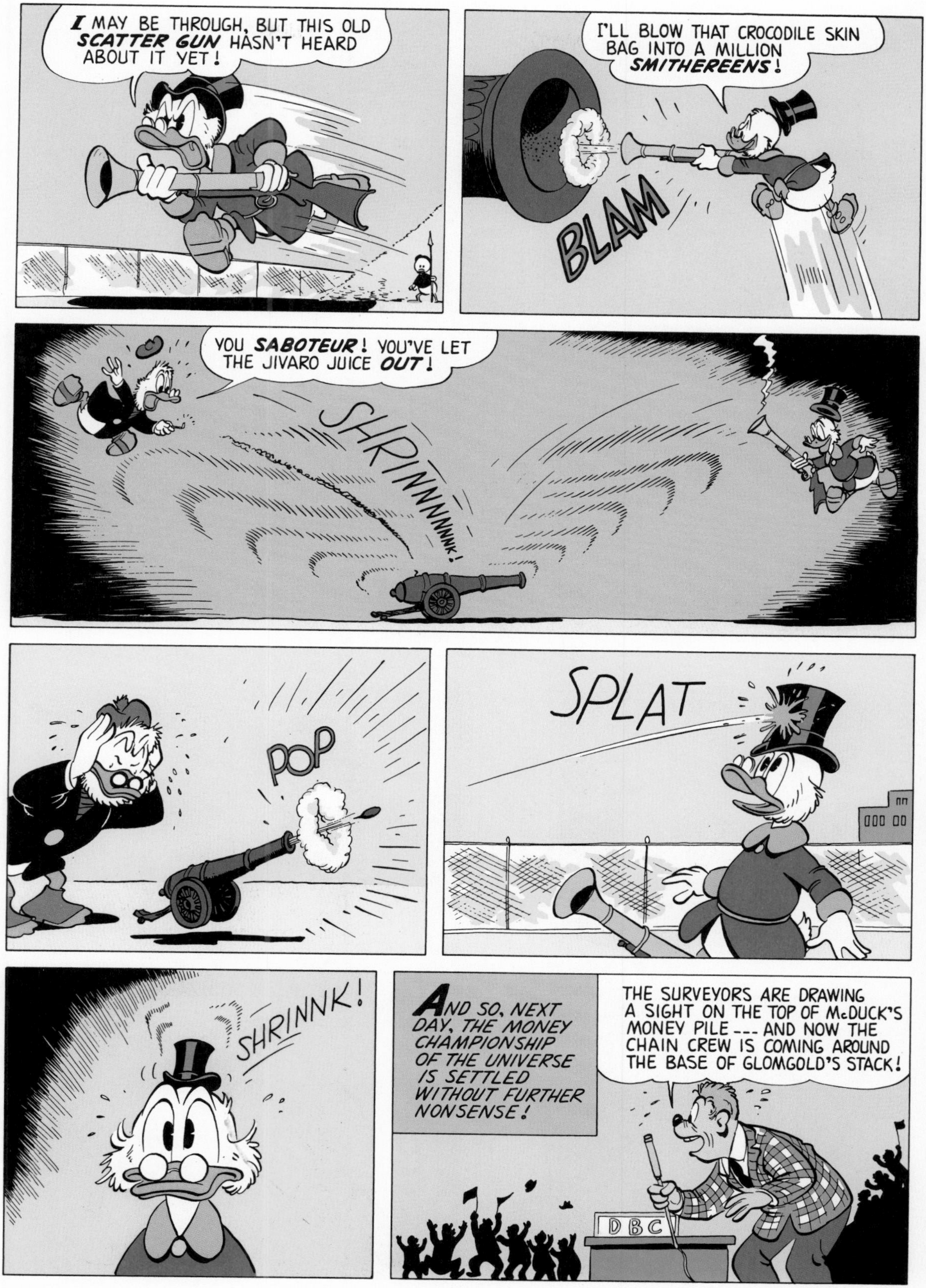

I MAY BE THROUGH, BUT THIS OLD SCATTER GUN HASN'T HEARD ABOUT IT YET!
I'LL BLOW THAT CROCODILE SKIN BAG INTO A MILLION SMITHEREENS!
BLAM
YOU SABOTEUR! YOU'VE LET THE JIVARO JUICE OUT!
SHRINNNNNNK!
POP
SPLAT
SHRINNK!
AND SO, NEXT DAY, THE MONEY CHAMPIONSHIP OF THE UNIVERSE IS SETTLED WITHOUT FURTHER NONSENSE!
THE SURVEYORS ARE DRAWING A SIGHT ON THE TOP OF McDUCK'S MONEY PILE --- AND NOW THE CHAIN CREW IS COMING AROUND THE BASE OF GLOMGOLD'S STACK!
DBC

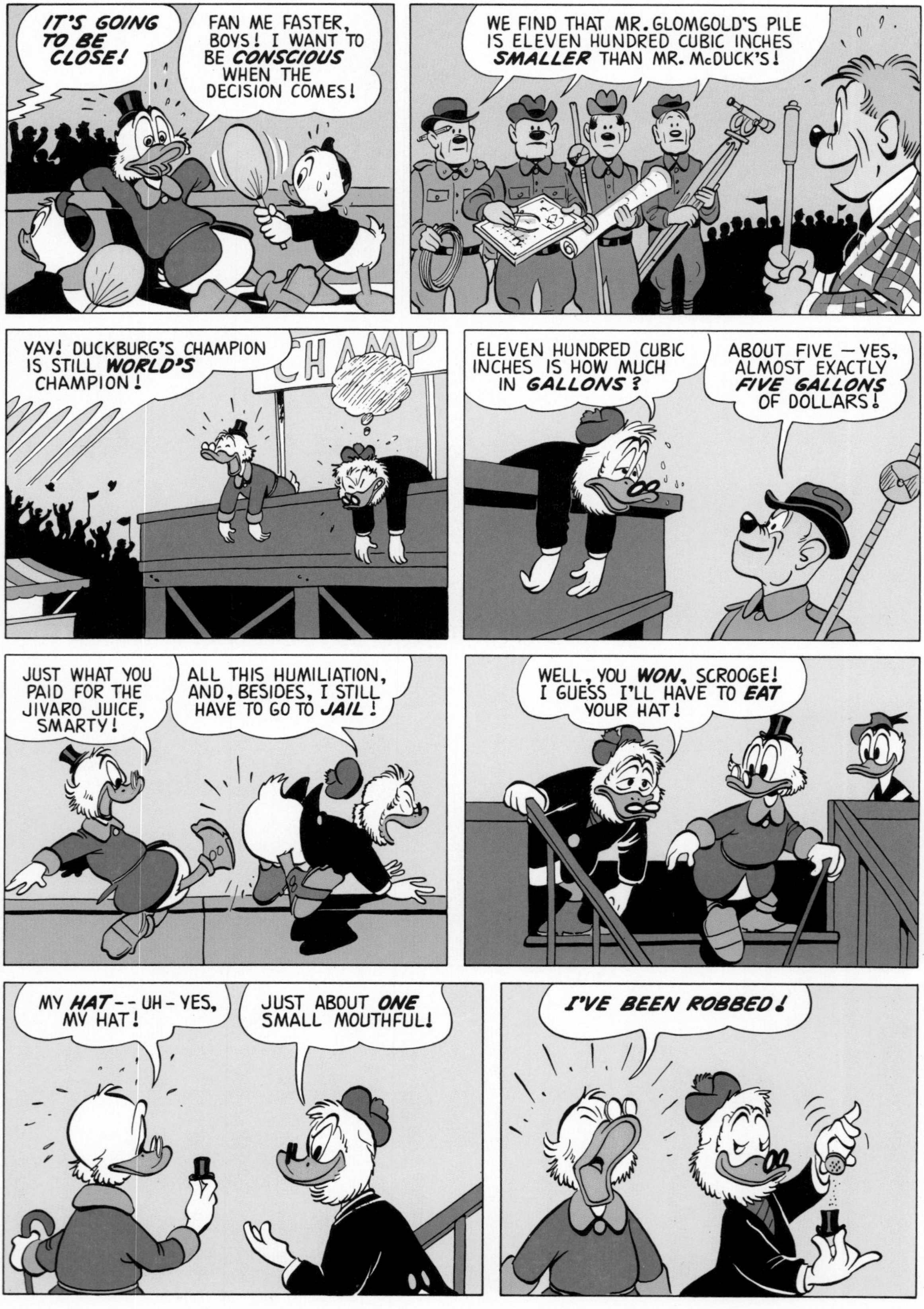
IT'S GOING TO BE CLOSE!
FAN ME FASTER, BOYS! I WANT TO BE CONSCIOUS WHEN THE DECISION COMES!
WE FIND THAT MR. GLOMGOLD'S PILE IS ELEVEN HUNDRED CUBIC INCHES SMALLER THAN MR. McDUCK'S!
YAY! DUCKBURG'S CHAMPION IS STILL WORLD'S CHAMPION!
CHAMP
ELEVEN HUNDRED CUBIC INCHES IS HOW MUCH IN GALLONS?
ABOUT FIVE — YES, ALMOST EXACTLY FIVE GALLONS OF DOLLARS!
JUST WHAT YOU PAID FOR THE JIVARO JUICE, SMARTY!
ALL THIS HUMILIATION, AND, BESIDES, I STILL HAVE TO GO TO JAIL!
WELL, YOU WON, SCROOGE! I GUESS I'LL HAVE TO EAT YOUR HAT!
MY HAT-- UH - YES, MY HAT!
JUST ABOUT ONE SMALL MOUTHFUL!
I'VE BEEN ROBBED!

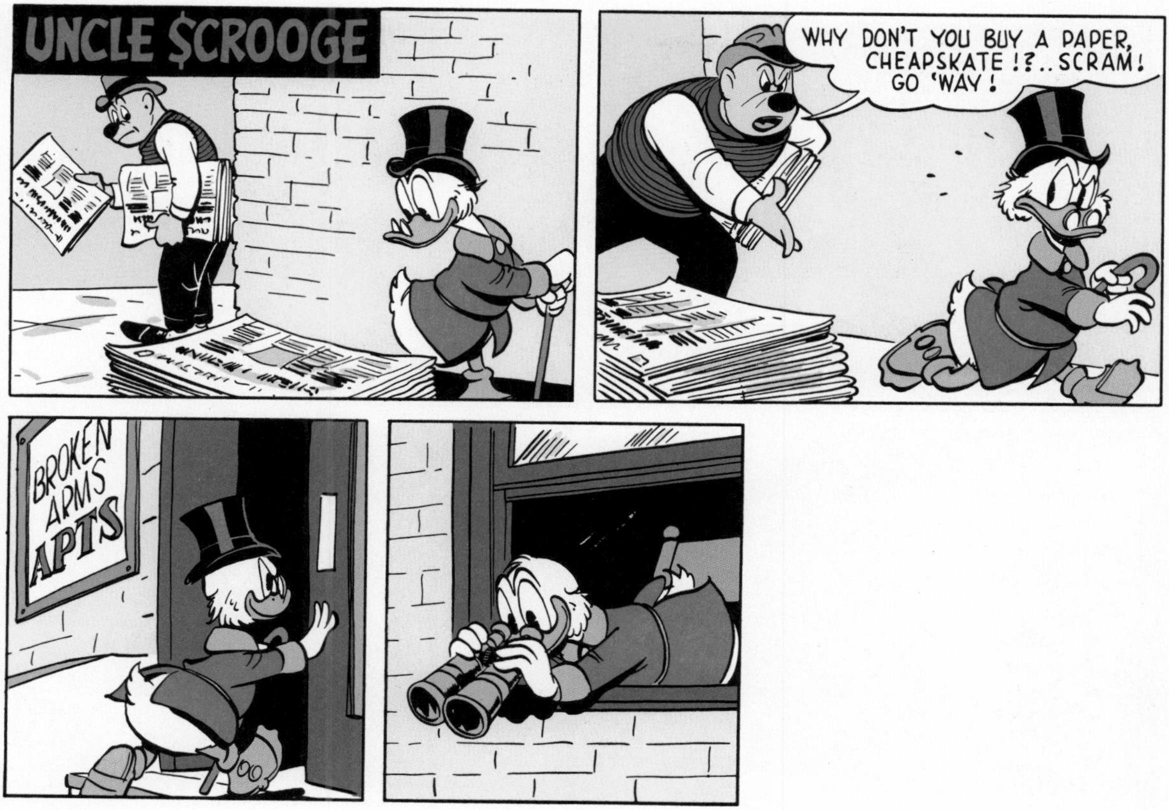
UNCLE $CROOGE
WHY DON'T YOU BUY A PAPER, CHEAPSKATE !?.. SCRAM! GO 'WAY!
BROKEN ARMS APTS

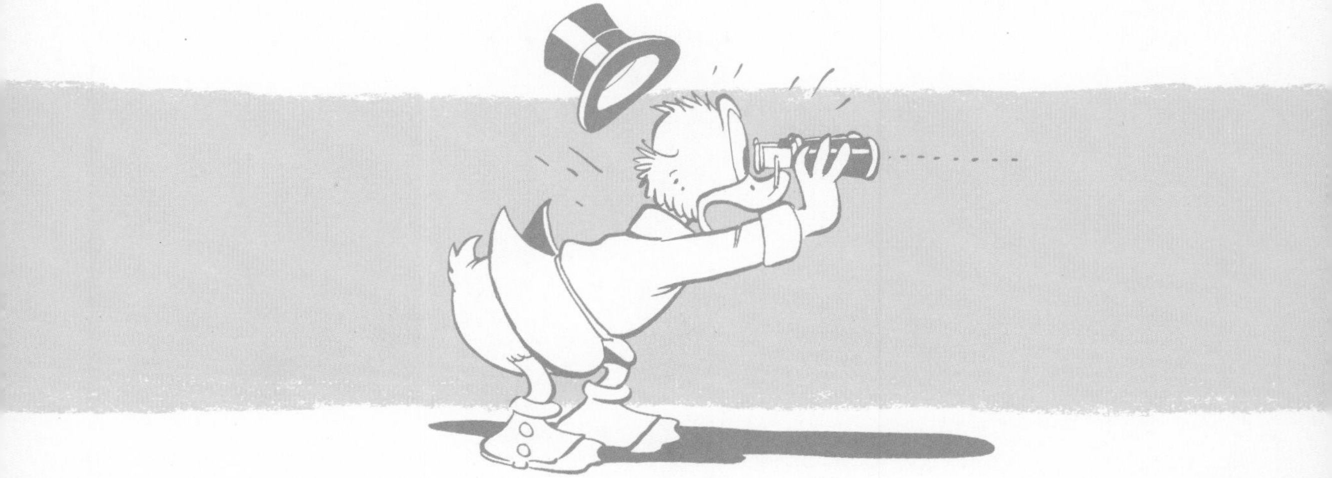

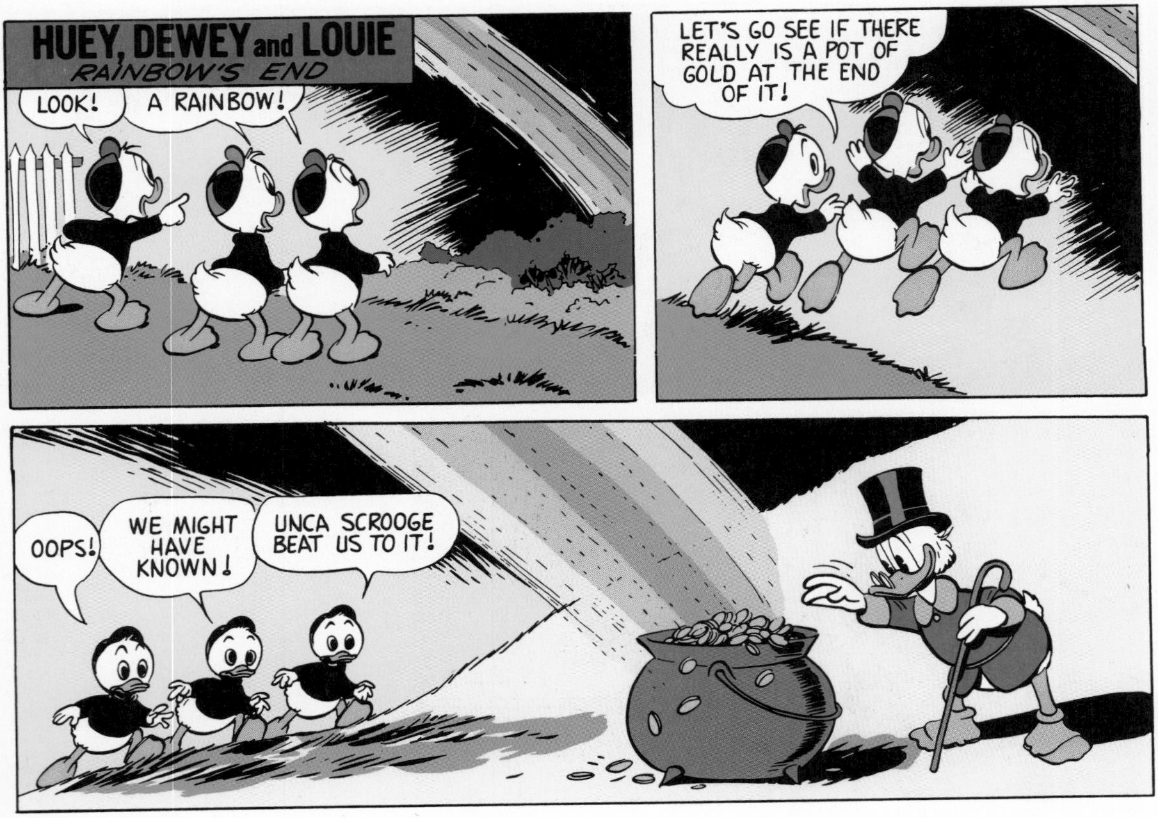
HUEY, DEWEY and LOUIE
RAINBOW'S END
LOOK!
A RAINBOW!
LET'S GO SEE IF THERE REALLY IS A POT OF GOLD AT THE END OF IT!
OOPS!
WE MIGHT HAVE KNOWN!
UNCA SCROOGE BEAT US TO IT!

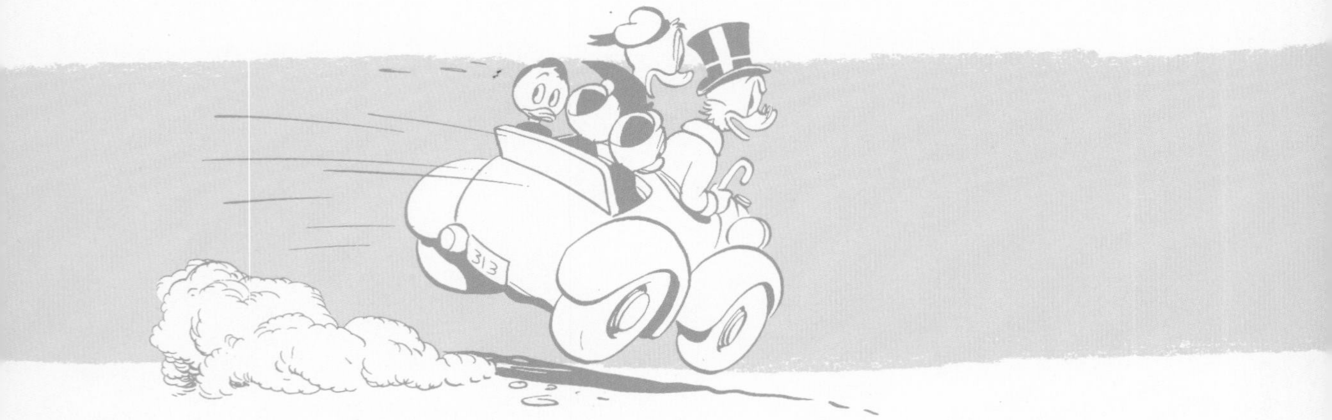
313

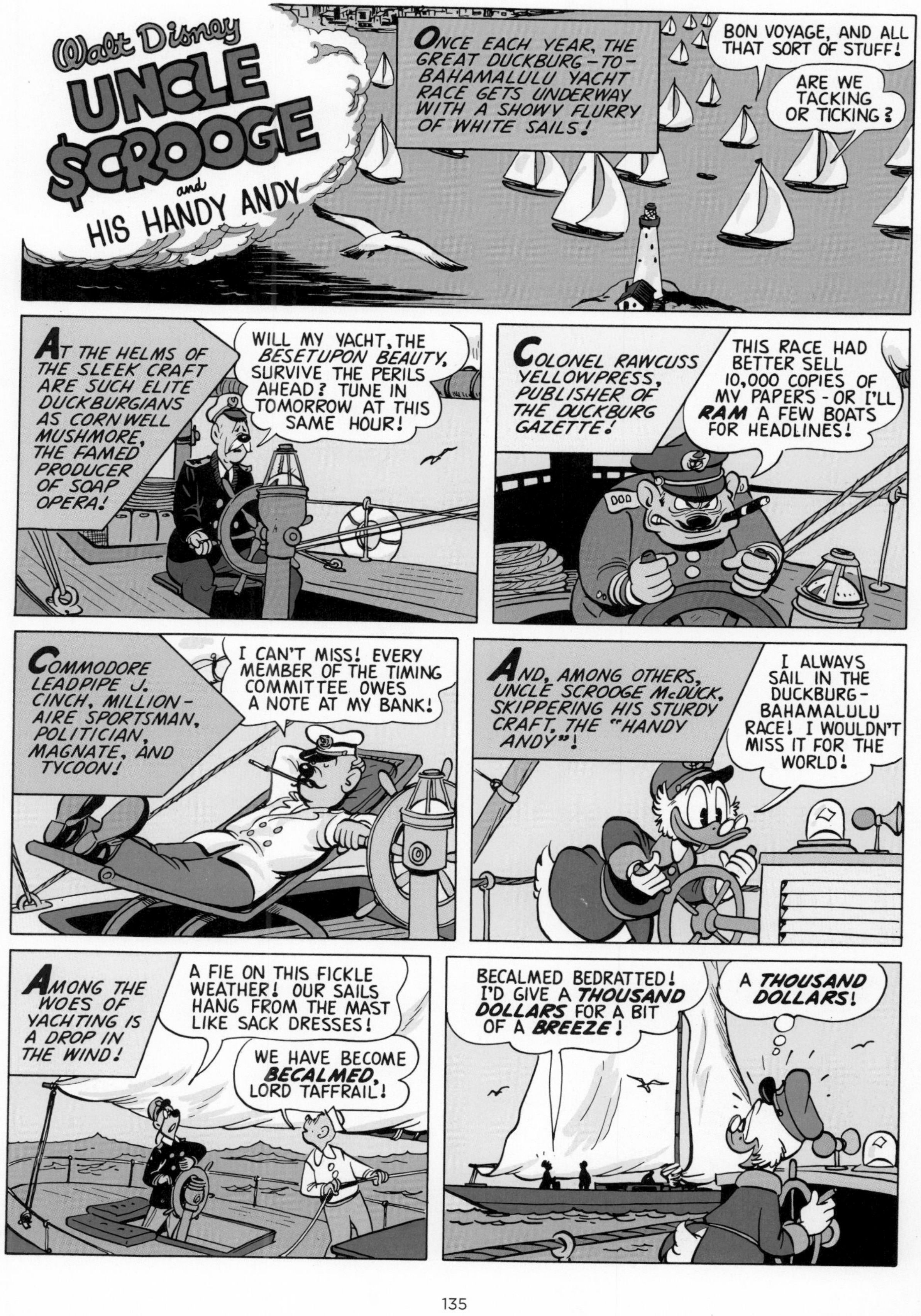
Walt Disney
UNCLE $CROOGE
and
HIS HANDY ANDY
ONCE EACH YEAR, THE GREAT DUCKBURG-TO-BAHAMALULU YACHT RACE GETS UNDERWAY WITH A SHOWY FLURRY OF WHITE SAILS!
BON VOYAGE, AND ALL THAT SORT OF STUFF!
ARE WE TACKING OR TICKING?
AT THE HELMS OF THE SLEEK CRAFT ARE SUCH ELITE DUCKBURGIANS AS CORNWELL MUSHMORE, THE FAMED PRODUCER OF SOAP OPERA!
WILL MY YACHT, THE *BESETUPON BEAUTY*, SURVIVE THE PERILS AHEAD? TUNE IN TOMORROW AT THIS SAME HOUR!
COLONEL RAWCUSS YELLOWPRESS, PUBLISHER OF THE DUCKBURG GAZETTE!
THIS RACE HAD BETTER SELL 10,000 COPIES OF MY PAPERS - OR I'LL **RAM** A FEW BOATS FOR HEADLINES!
DOD
COMMODORE LEADPIPE J. CINCH, MILLION-AIRE SPORTSMAN, POLITICIAN, MAGNATE, AND TYCOON!
I CAN'T MISS! EVERY MEMBER OF THE TIMING COMMITTEE OWES A NOTE AT MY BANK!
AND, AMONG OTHERS, UNCLE SCROOGE McDUCK, SKIPPERING HIS STURDY CRAFT, THE "HANDY ANDY"!
I ALWAYS SAIL IN THE DUCKBURG-BAHAMALULU RACE! I WOULDN'T MISS IT FOR THE WORLD!
AMONG THE WOES OF YACHTING IS A DROP IN THE WIND!
A FIE ON THIS FICKLE WEATHER! OUR SAILS HANG FROM THE MAST LIKE SACK DRESSES!
WE HAVE BECOME **BECALMED**, LORD TAFFRAIL!
BECALMED BEDRATTED! I'D GIVE A **THOUSAND DOLLARS** FOR A BIT OF A **BREEZE**!
A **THOUSAND DOLLARS**!

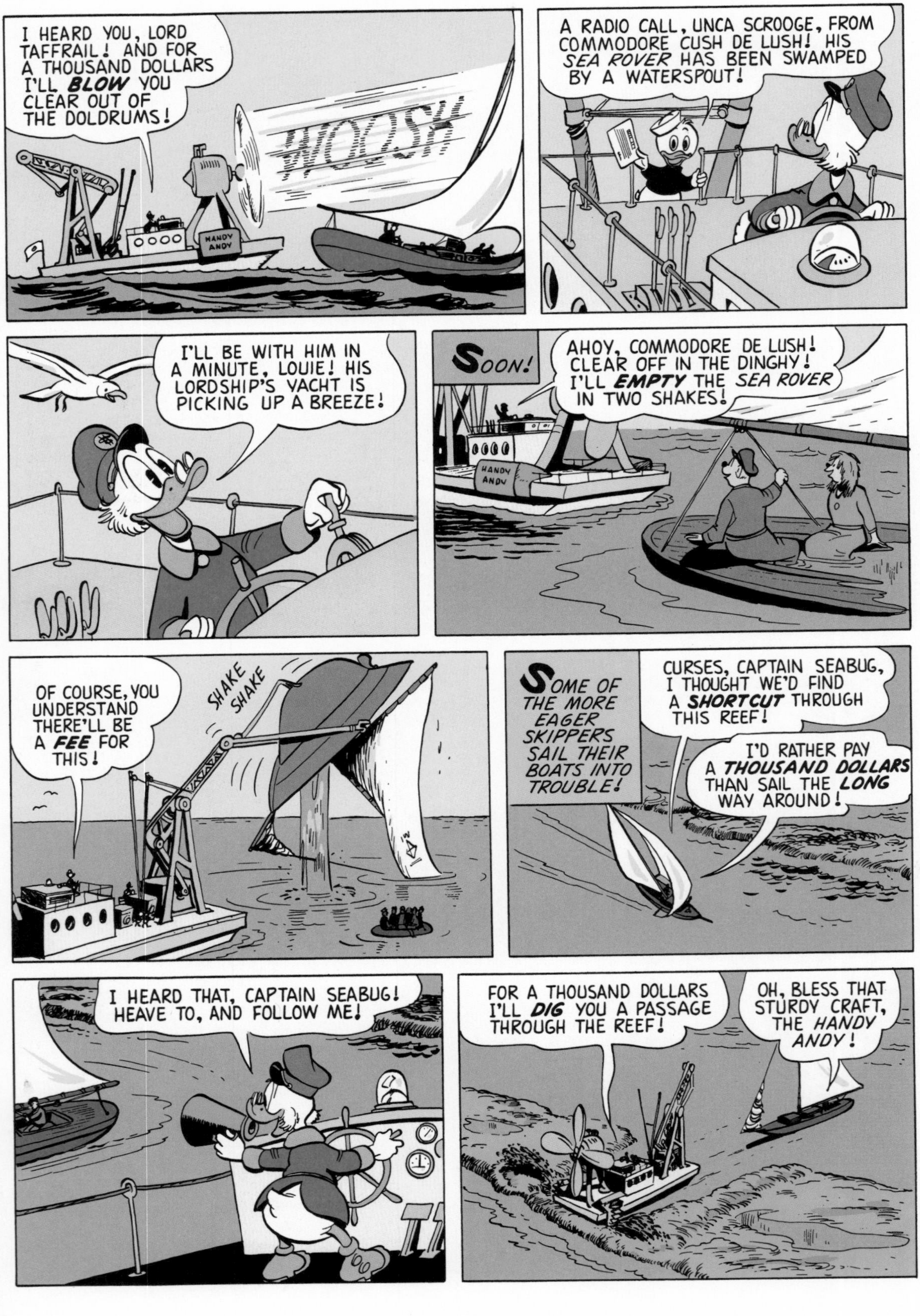
I HEARD YOU, LORD TAFFRAIL! AND FOR A THOUSAND DOLLARS I'LL BLOW YOU CLEAR OUT OF THE DOLDRUMS!
WOOSH
HANDY ANDY
A RADIO CALL, UNCA SCROOGE, FROM COMMODORE CUSH DE LUSH! HIS SEA ROVER HAS BEEN SWAMPED BY A WATERSPOUT!
I'LL BE WITH HIM IN A MINUTE, LOUIE! HIS LORDSHIP'S YACHT IS PICKING UP A BREEZE!
SOON!
AHOY, COMMODORE DE LUSH! CLEAR OFF IN THE DINGHY! I'LL EMPTY THE SEA ROVER IN TWO SHAKES!
HANDY ANDY
OF COURSE, YOU UNDERSTAND THERE'LL BE A FEE FOR THIS!
SHAKE SHAKE
SOME OF THE MORE EAGER SKIPPERS SAIL THEIR BOATS INTO TROUBLE!
CURSES, CAPTAIN SEABUG, I THOUGHT WE'D FIND A SHORTCUT THROUGH THIS REEF!
I'D RATHER PAY A THOUSAND DOLLARS THAN SAIL THE LONG WAY AROUND!
I HEARD THAT, CAPTAIN SEABUG! HEAVE TO, AND FOLLOW ME!
FOR A THOUSAND DOLLARS I'LL DIG YOU A PASSAGE THROUGH THE REEF!
OH, BLESS THAT STURDY CRAFT, THE HANDY ANDY!

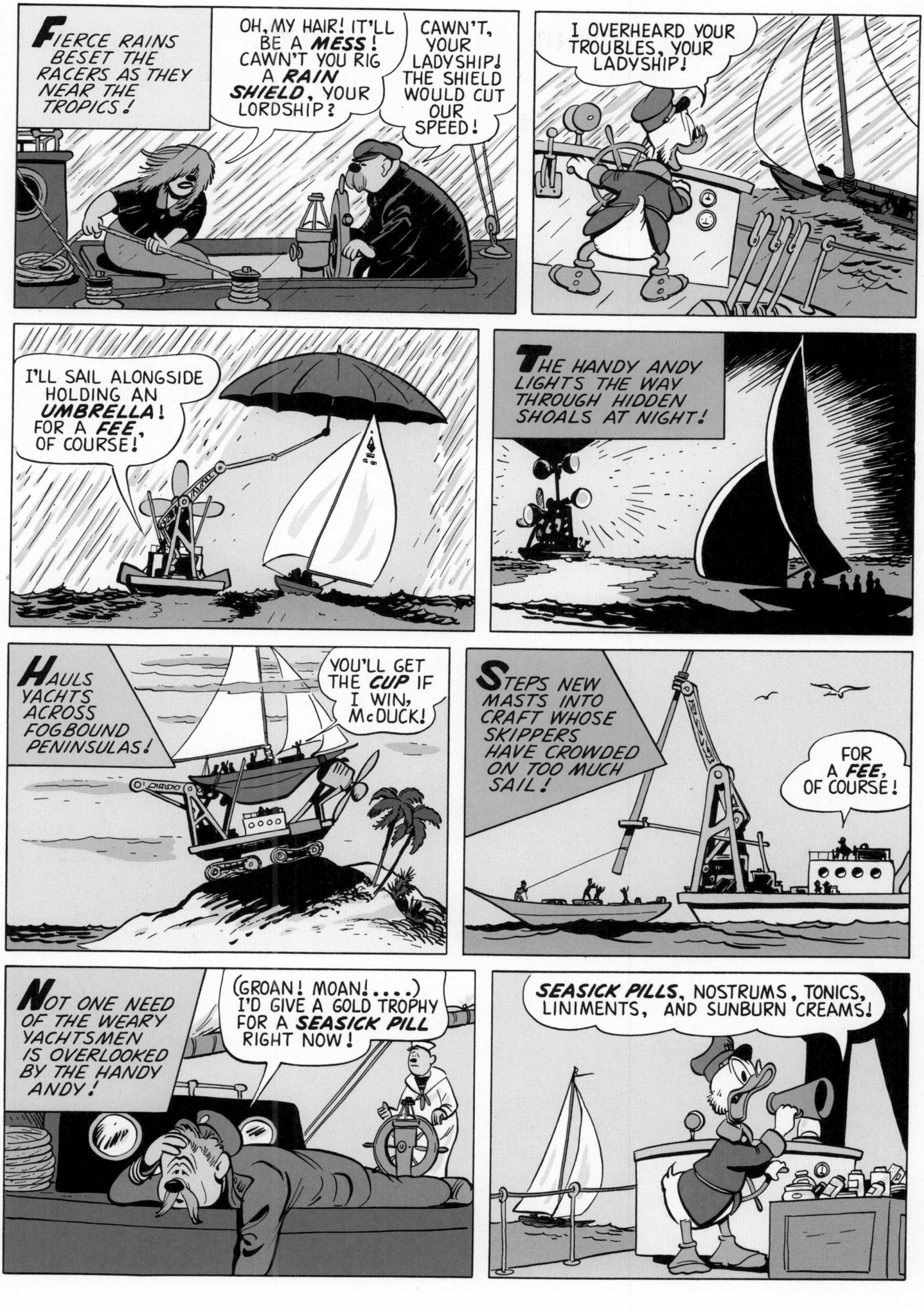

FIERCE RAINS BESET THE RACERS AS THEY NEAR THE TROPICS!
OH, MY HAIR! IT'LL BE A MESS! CAWN'T YOU RIG A RAIN SHIELD, YOUR LORDSHIP?
CAWN'T, YOUR LADYSHIP! THE SHIELD WOULD CUT OUR SPEED!
I OVERHEARD YOUR TROUBLES, YOUR LADYSHIP!
I'LL SAIL ALONGSIDE HOLDING AN UMBRELLA! FOR A FEE, OF COURSE!
THE HANDY ANDY LIGHTS THE WAY THROUGH HIDDEN SHOALS AT NIGHT!
HAULS YACHTS ACROSS FOGBOUND PENINSULAS!
YOU'LL GET THE CUP IF I WIN, McDUCK!
STEPS NEW MASTS INTO CRAFT WHOSE SKIPPERS HAVE CROWDED ON TOO MUCH SAIL!
FOR A FEE, OF COURSE!
NOT ONE NEED OF THE WEARY YACHTSMEN IS OVERLOOKED BY THE HANDY ANDY!
(GROAN! MOAN!....) I'D GIVE A GOLD TROPHY FOR A SEASICK PILL RIGHT NOW!
SEASICK PILLS, NOSTRUMS, TONICS, LINIMENTS, AND SUNBURN CREAMS!

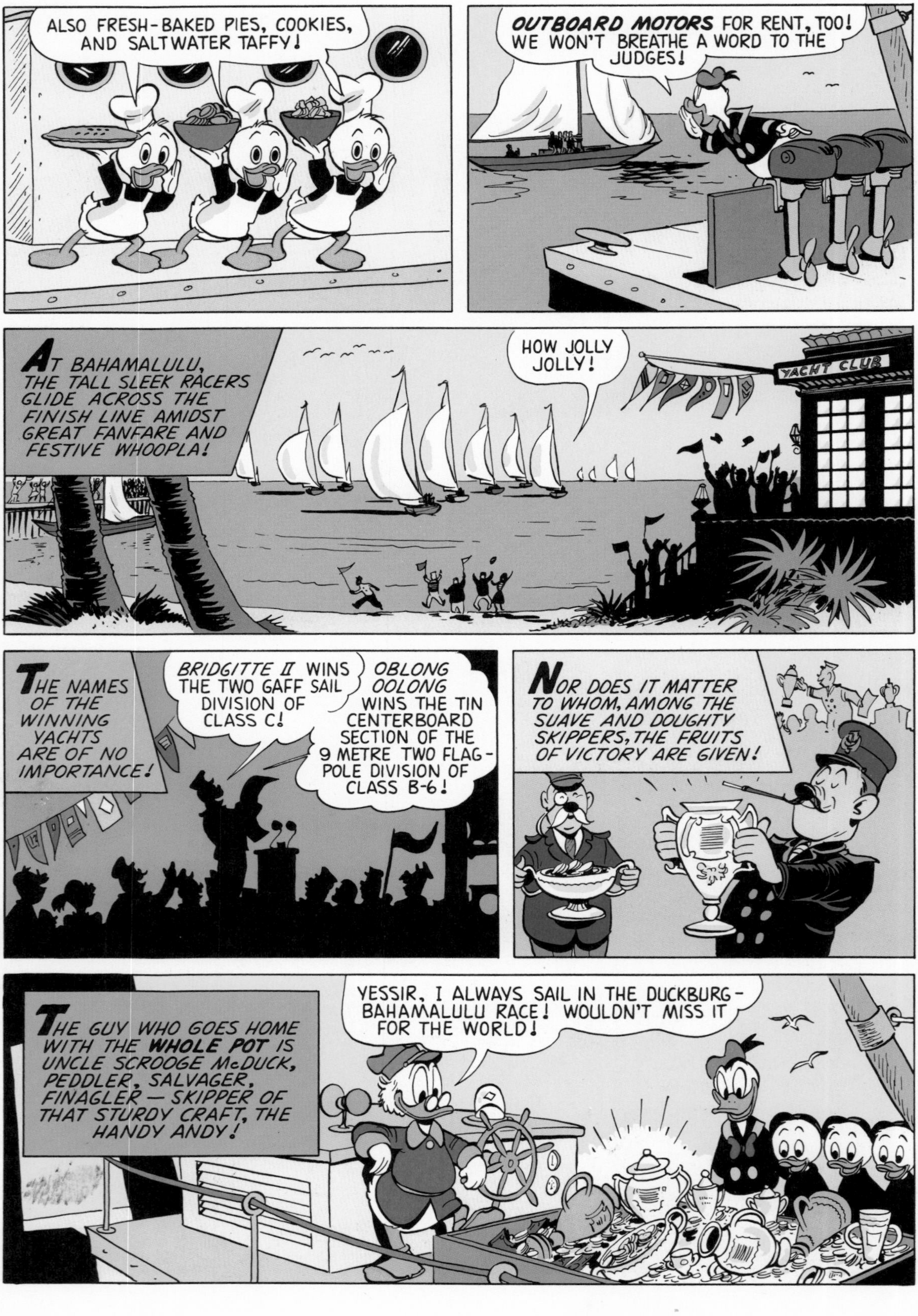
ALSO FRESH-BAKED PIES, COOKIES, AND SALTWATER TAFFY!
OUTBOARD MOTORS FOR RENT, TOO! WE WON'T BREATHE A WORD TO THE JUDGES!
AT BAHAMALULU, THE TALL SLEEK RACERS GLIDE ACROSS THE FINISH LINE AMIDST GREAT FANFARE AND FESTIVE WHOOPLA!
HOW JOLLY JOLLY!
YACHT CLUB
THE NAMES OF THE WINNING YACHTS ARE OF NO IMPORTANCE!
BRIDGITTE II WINS THE TWO GAFF SAIL DIVISION OF CLASS C!
OBLONG OOLONG WINS THE TIN CENTERBOARD SECTION OF THE 9 METRE TWO FLAG-POLE DIVISION OF CLASS B-6!
NOR DOES IT MATTER TO WHOM, AMONG THE SUAVE AND DOUGHTY SKIPPERS, THE FRUITS OF VICTORY ARE GIVEN!
THE GUY WHO GOES HOME WITH THE WHOLE POT IS UNCLE SCROOGE McDUCK, PEDDLER, SALVAGER, FINAGLER — SKIPPER OF THAT STURDY CRAFT, THE HANDY ANDY!
YESSIR, I ALWAYS SAIL IN THE DUCKBURG-BAHAMALULU RACE! WOULDN'T MISS IT FOR THE WORLD!

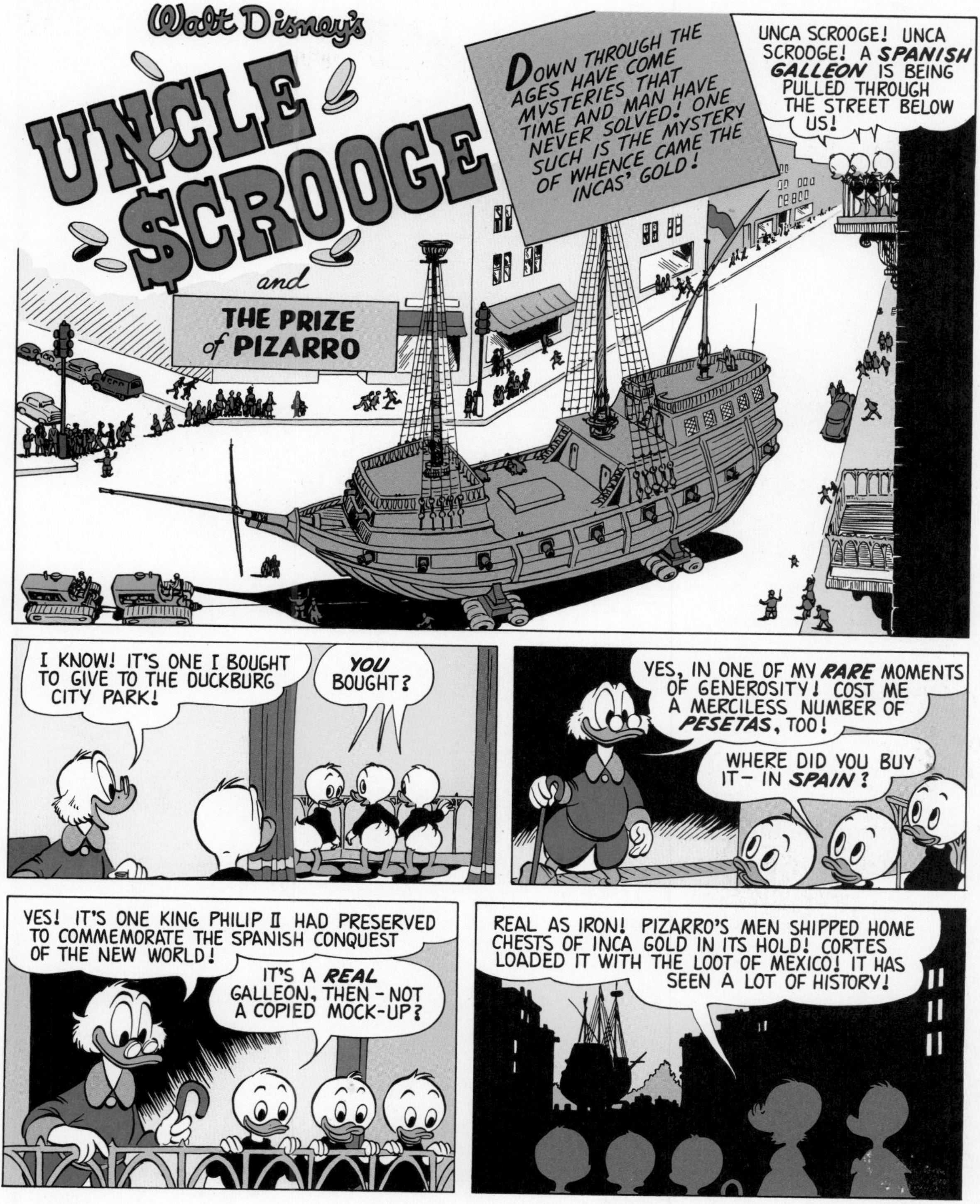
Walt Disney's
UNCLE $CROOGE
and
THE PRIZE of PIZARRO
DOWN THROUGH THE AGES HAVE COME MYSTERIES THAT TIME AND MAN HAVE NEVER SOLVED! ONE SUCH IS THE MYSTERY OF WHENCE CAME THE INCAS' GOLD!
UNCA SCROOGE! UNCA SCROOGE! A SPANISH GALLEON IS BEING PULLED THROUGH THE STREET BELOW US!
I KNOW! IT'S ONE I BOUGHT TO GIVE TO THE DUCKBURG CITY PARK!
YOU BOUGHT?
YES, IN ONE OF MY RARE MOMENTS OF GENEROSITY! COST ME A MERCILESS NUMBER OF PESETAS, TOO!
WHERE DID YOU BUY IT— IN SPAIN?
YES! IT'S ONE KING PHILIP II HAD PRESERVED TO COMMEMORATE THE SPANISH CONQUEST OF THE NEW WORLD!
IT'S A REAL GALLEON, THEN - NOT A COPIED MOCK-UP?
REAL AS IRON! PIZARRO'S MEN SHIPPED HOME CHESTS OF INCA GOLD IN ITS HOLD! CORTES LOADED IT WITH THE LOOT OF MEXICO! IT HAS SEEN A LOT OF HISTORY!

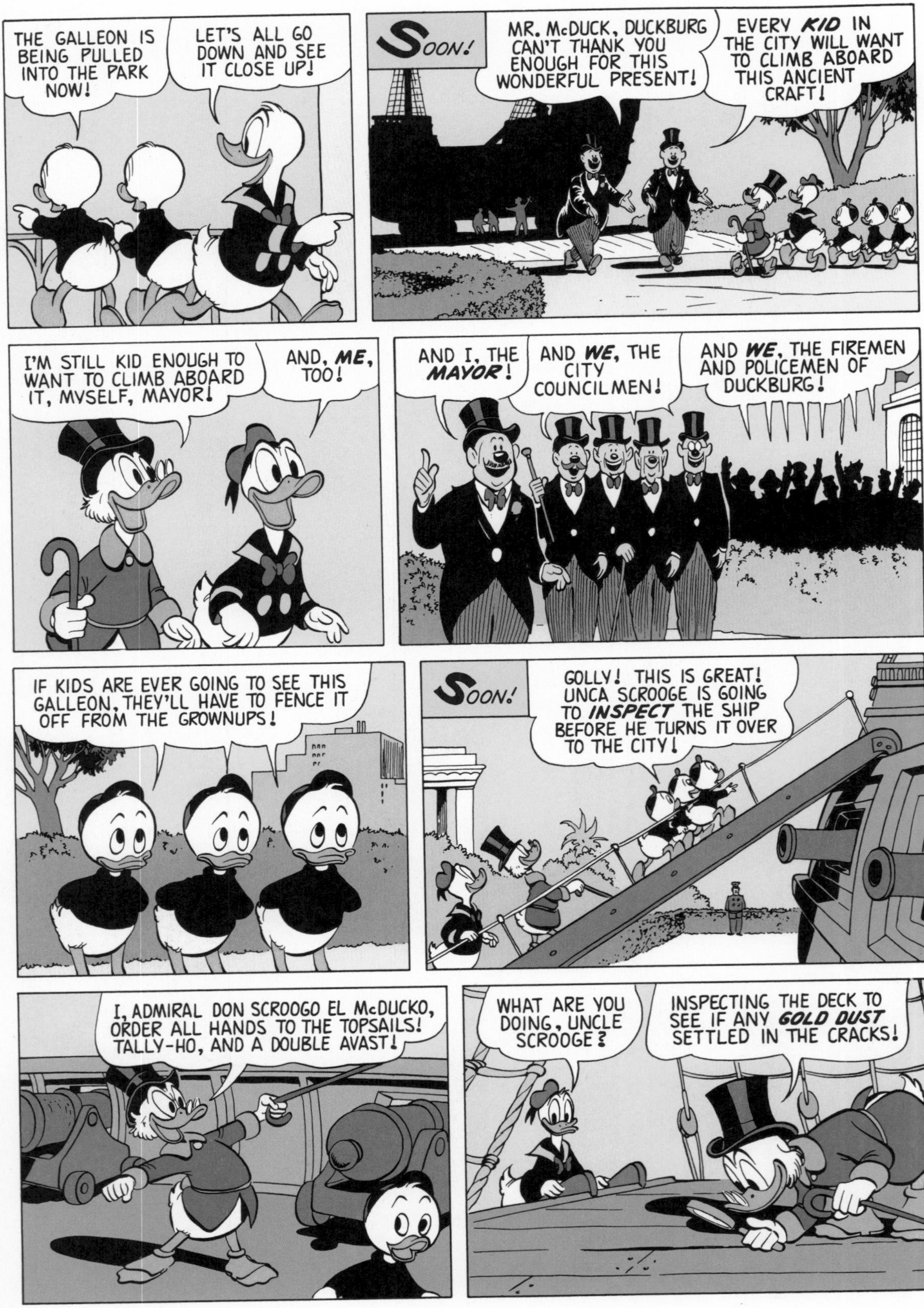
THE GALLEON IS BEING PULLED INTO THE PARK NOW!
LET'S ALL GO DOWN AND SEE IT CLOSE UP!
SOON!
MR. McDUCK, DUCKBURG CAN'T THANK YOU ENOUGH FOR THIS WONDERFUL PRESENT!
EVERY KID IN THE CITY WILL WANT TO CLIMB ABOARD THIS ANCIENT CRAFT!
I'M STILL KID ENOUGH TO WANT TO CLIMB ABOARD IT, MYSELF, MAYOR!
AND, ME, TOO!
AND I, THE MAYOR!
AND WE, THE CITY COUNCILMEN!
AND WE, THE FIREMEN AND POLICEMEN OF DUCKBURG!
IF KIDS ARE EVER GOING TO SEE THIS GALLEON, THEY'LL HAVE TO FENCE IT OFF FROM THE GROWNUPS!
SOON!
GOLLY! THIS IS GREAT! UNCA SCROOGE IS GOING TO INSPECT THE SHIP BEFORE HE TURNS IT OVER TO THE CITY!
I, ADMIRAL DON SCROOGO EL McDUCKO, ORDER ALL HANDS TO THE TOPSAILS! TALLY-HO, AND A DOUBLE AVAST!
WHAT ARE YOU DOING, UNCLE SCROOGE?
INSPECTING THE DECK TO SEE IF ANY GOLD DUST SETTLED IN THE CRACKS!

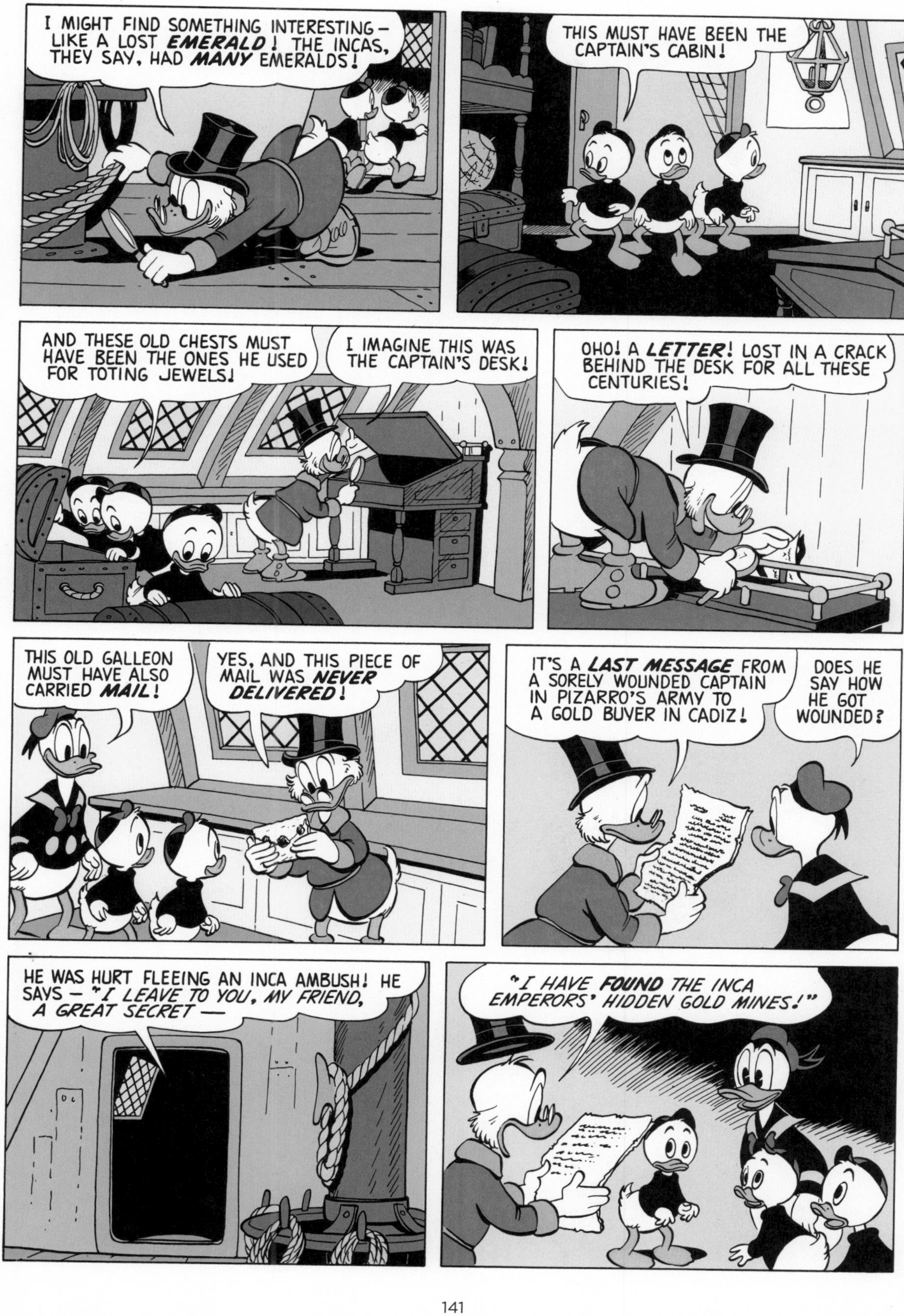
I MIGHT FIND SOMETHING INTERESTING– LIKE A LOST EMERALD! THE INCAS, THEY SAY, HAD MANY EMERALDS!
THIS MUST HAVE BEEN THE CAPTAIN'S CABIN!
AND THESE OLD CHESTS MUST HAVE BEEN THE ONES HE USED FOR TOTING JEWELS!
I IMAGINE THIS WAS THE CAPTAIN'S DESK!
OHO! A LETTER! LOST IN A CRACK BEHIND THE DESK FOR ALL THESE CENTURIES!
THIS OLD GALLEON MUST HAVE ALSO CARRIED MAIL!
YES, AND THIS PIECE OF MAIL WAS NEVER DELIVERED!
IT'S A LAST MESSAGE FROM A SORELY WOUNDED CAPTAIN IN PIZARRO'S ARMY TO A GOLD BUYER IN CADIZ!
DOES HE SAY HOW HE GOT WOUNDED?
HE WAS HURT FLEEING AN INCA AMBUSH! HE SAYS – "I LEAVE TO YOU, MY FRIEND, A GREAT SECRET —
"I HAVE FOUND THE INCA EMPERORS' HIDDEN GOLD MINES!"

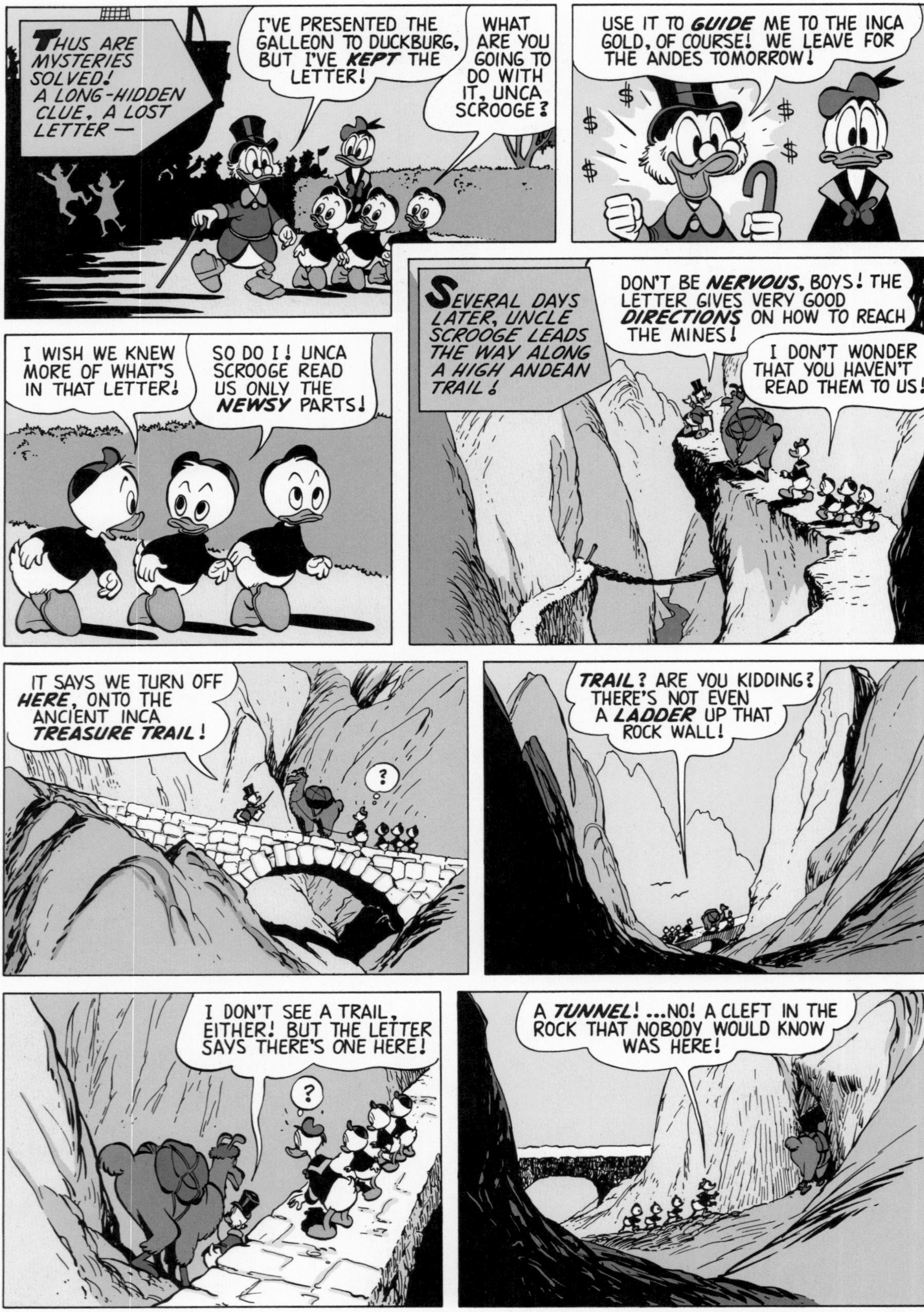
THUS ARE MYSTERIES SOLVED! A LONG-HIDDEN CLUE, A LOST LETTER—
I'VE PRESENTED THE GALLEON TO DUCKBURG, BUT I'VE KEPT THE LETTER!
WHAT ARE YOU GOING TO DO WITH IT, UNCA SCROOGE?
USE IT TO GUIDE ME TO THE INCA GOLD, OF COURSE! WE LEAVE FOR THE ANDES TOMORROW!
I WISH WE KNEW MORE OF WHAT'S IN THAT LETTER!
SO DO I! UNCA SCROOGE READ US ONLY THE NEWSY PARTS!
SEVERAL DAYS LATER, UNCLE SCROOGE LEADS THE WAY ALONG A HIGH ANDEAN TRAIL!
DON'T BE NERVOUS, BOYS! THE LETTER GIVES VERY GOOD DIRECTIONS ON HOW TO REACH THE MINES!
I DON'T WONDER THAT YOU HAVEN'T READ THEM TO US!
IT SAYS WE TURN OFF HERE, ONTO THE ANCIENT INCA TREASURE TRAIL!
?
TRAIL? ARE YOU KIDDING? THERE'S NOT EVEN A LADDER UP THAT ROCK WALL!
I DON'T SEE A TRAIL, EITHER! BUT THE LETTER SAYS THERE'S ONE HERE!
?
A TUNNEL! ...NO! A CLEFT IN THE ROCK THAT NOBODY WOULD KNOW WAS HERE!

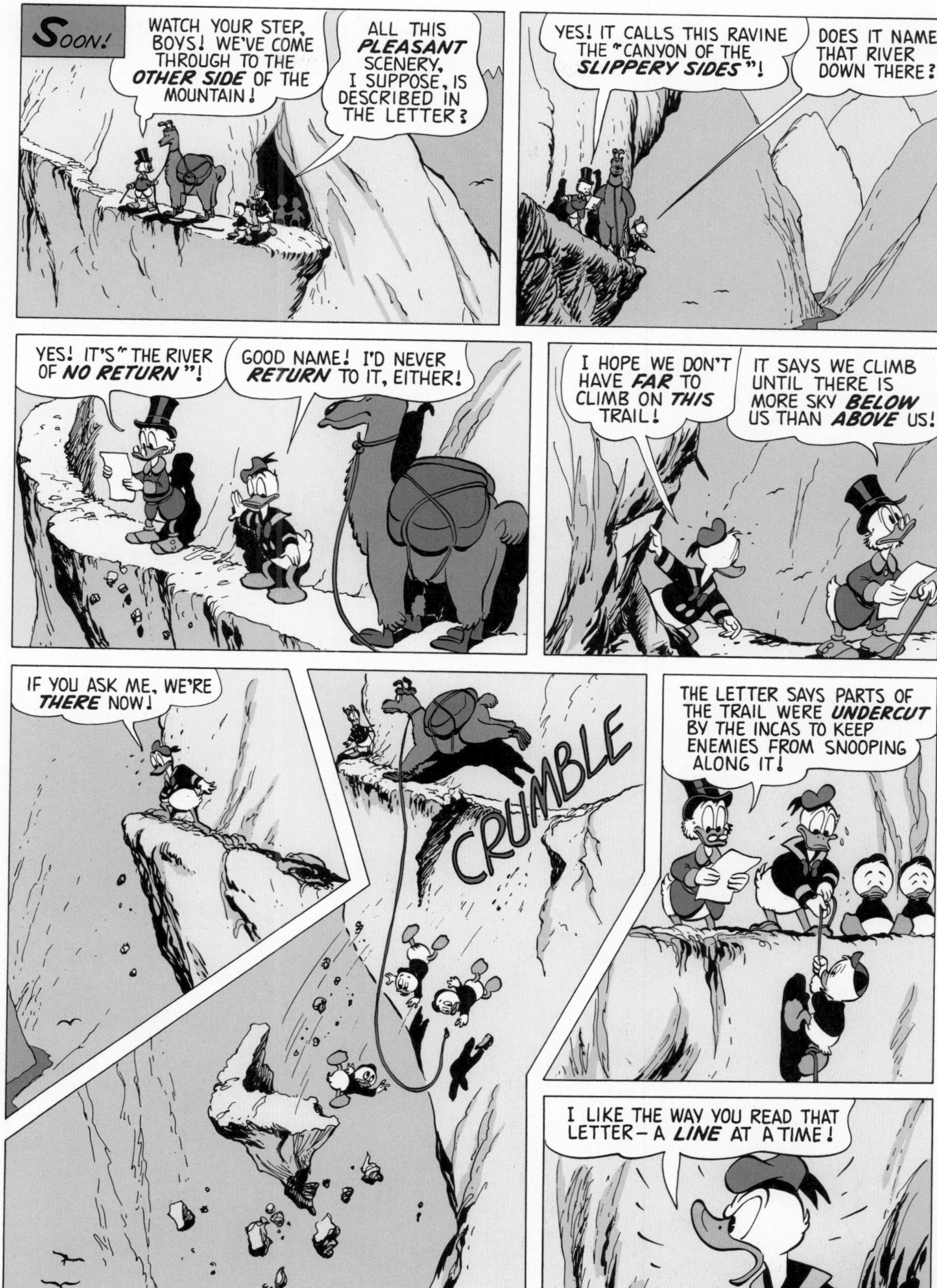
SOON!
WATCH YOUR STEP, BOYS! WE'VE COME THROUGH TO THE OTHER SIDE OF THE MOUNTAIN!
ALL THIS PLEASANT SCENERY, I SUPPOSE, IS DESCRIBED IN THE LETTER?
YES! IT CALLS THIS RAVINE THE "CANYON OF THE SLIPPERY SIDES"!
DOES IT NAME THAT RIVER DOWN THERE?
YES! IT'S "THE RIVER OF NO RETURN"!
GOOD NAME! I'D NEVER RETURN TO IT, EITHER!
I HOPE WE DON'T HAVE FAR TO CLIMB ON THIS TRAIL!
IT SAYS WE CLIMB UNTIL THERE IS MORE SKY BELOW US THAN ABOVE US!
IF YOU ASK ME, WE'RE THERE NOW!
CRUMBLE
THE LETTER SAYS PARTS OF THE TRAIL WERE UNDERCUT BY THE INCAS TO KEEP ENEMIES FROM SNOOPING ALONG IT!
I LIKE THE WAY YOU READ THAT LETTER — A LINE AT A TIME!

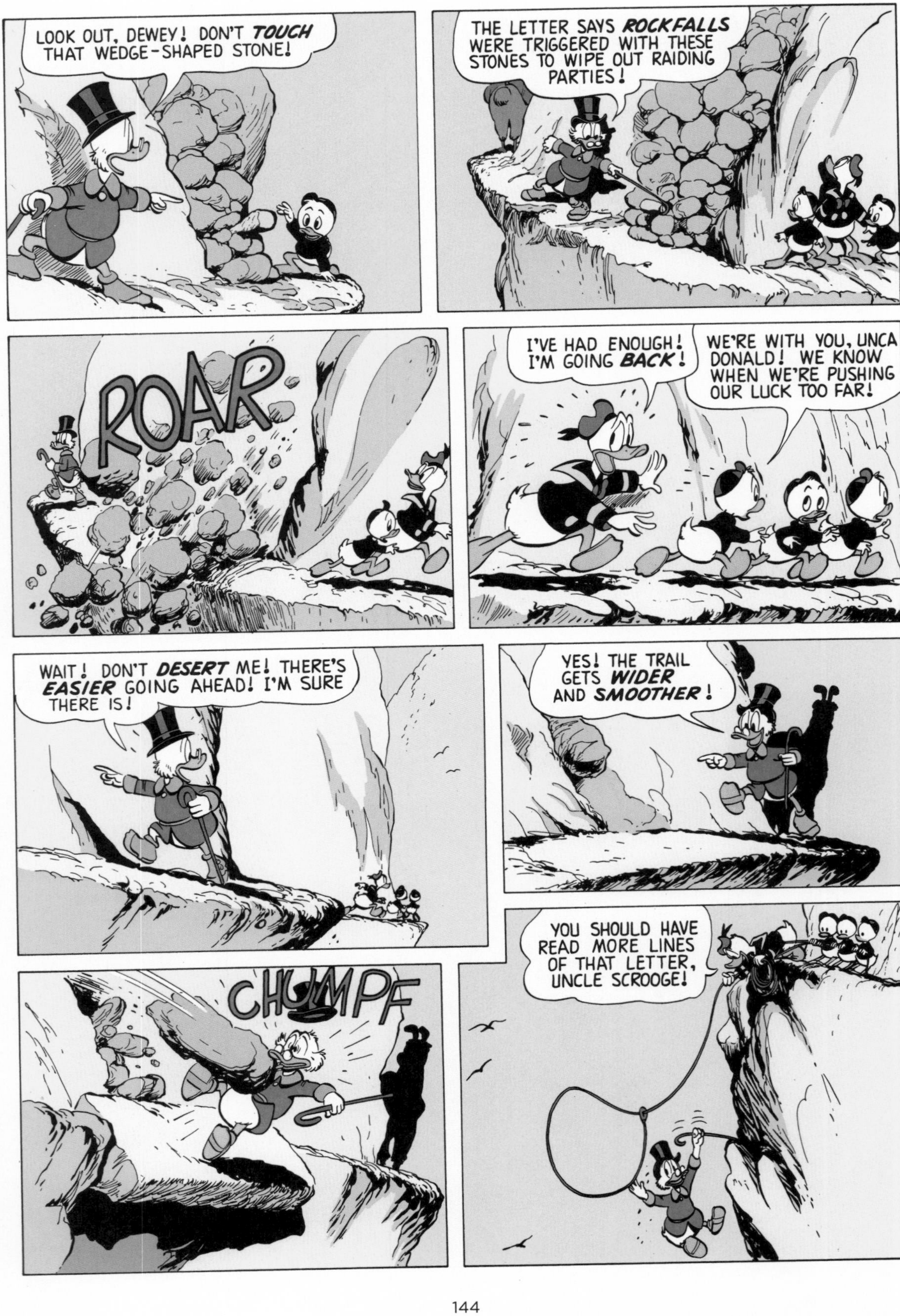
LOOK OUT, DEWEY! DON'T TOUCH THAT WEDGE-SHAPED STONE!
THE LETTER SAYS ROCKFALLS WERE TRIGGERED WITH THESE STONES TO WIPE OUT RAIDING PARTIES!
ROAR
I'VE HAD ENOUGH! I'M GOING BACK!
WE'RE WITH YOU, UNCA DONALD! WE KNOW WHEN WE'RE PUSHING OUR LUCK TOO FAR!
WAIT! DON'T DESERT ME! THERE'S EASIER GOING AHEAD! I'M SURE THERE IS!
YES! THE TRAIL GETS WIDER AND SMOOTHER!
CHUMPF
YOU SHOULD HAVE READ MORE LINES OF THAT LETTER, UNCLE SCROOGE!

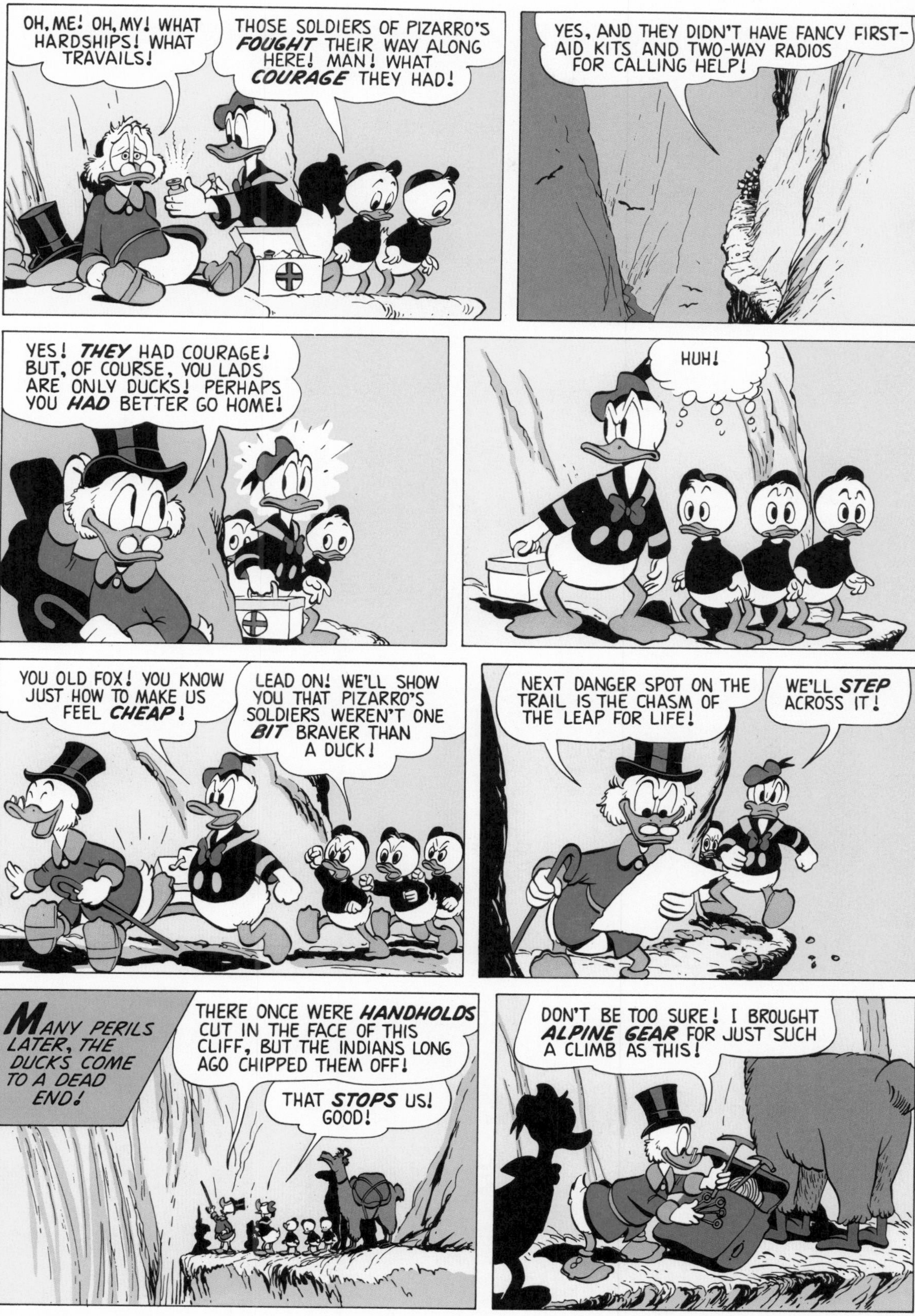
OH, ME! OH, MY! WHAT HARDSHIPS! WHAT TRAVAILS!
THOSE SOLDIERS OF PIZARRO'S FOUGHT THEIR WAY ALONG HERE! MAN! WHAT COURAGE THEY HAD!
YES, AND THEY DIDN'T HAVE FANCY FIRST-AID KITS AND TWO-WAY RADIOS FOR CALLING HELP!
YES! THEY HAD COURAGE! BUT, OF COURSE, YOU LADS ARE ONLY DUCKS! PERHAPS YOU HAD BETTER GO HOME!
HUH!
YOU OLD FOX! YOU KNOW JUST HOW TO MAKE US FEEL CHEAP!
LEAD ON! WE'LL SHOW YOU THAT PIZARRO'S SOLDIERS WEREN'T ONE BIT BRAVER THAN A DUCK!
NEXT DANGER SPOT ON THE TRAIL IS THE CHASM OF THE LEAP FOR LIFE!
WE'LL STEP ACROSS IT!
MANY PERILS LATER, THE DUCKS COME TO A DEAD END!
THERE ONCE WERE HANDHOLDS CUT IN THE FACE OF THIS CLIFF, BUT THE INDIANS LONG AGO CHIPPED THEM OFF!
THAT STOPS US! GOOD!
DON'T BE TOO SURE! I BROUGHT ALPINE GEAR FOR JUST SUCH A CLIMB AS THIS!

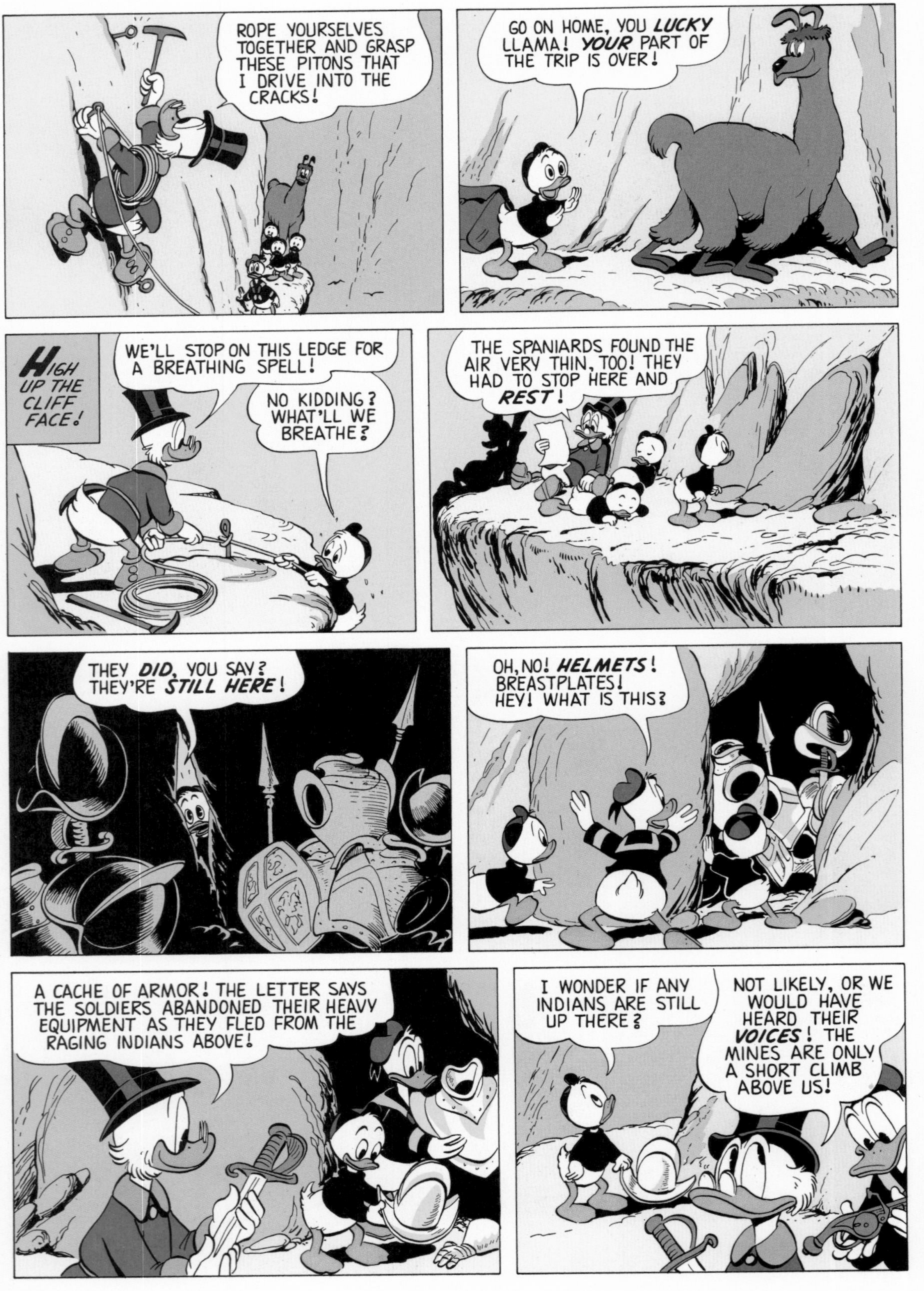

ROPE YOURSELVES TOGETHER AND GRASP THESE PITONS THAT I DRIVE INTO THE CRACKS!
GO ON HOME, YOU *LUCKY* LLAMA! *YOUR* PART OF THE TRIP IS OVER!
HIGH UP THE CLIFF FACE!
WE'LL STOP ON THIS LEDGE FOR A BREATHING SPELL!
NO KIDDING? WHAT'LL WE BREATHE?
THE SPANIARDS FOUND THE AIR VERY THIN, TOO! THEY HAD TO STOP HERE AND *REST*!
THEY *DID*, YOU SAY? THEY'RE *STILL HERE*!
OH, NO! *HELMETS*! BREASTPLATES! HEY! WHAT IS THIS?
A CACHE OF ARMOR! THE LETTER SAYS THE SOLDIERS ABANDONED THEIR HEAVY EQUIPMENT AS THEY FLED FROM THE RAGING INDIANS ABOVE!
I WONDER IF ANY INDIANS ARE STILL UP THERE?
NOT LIKELY, OR WE WOULD HAVE HEARD THEIR *VOICES*! THE MINES ARE ONLY A SHORT CLIMB ABOVE US!

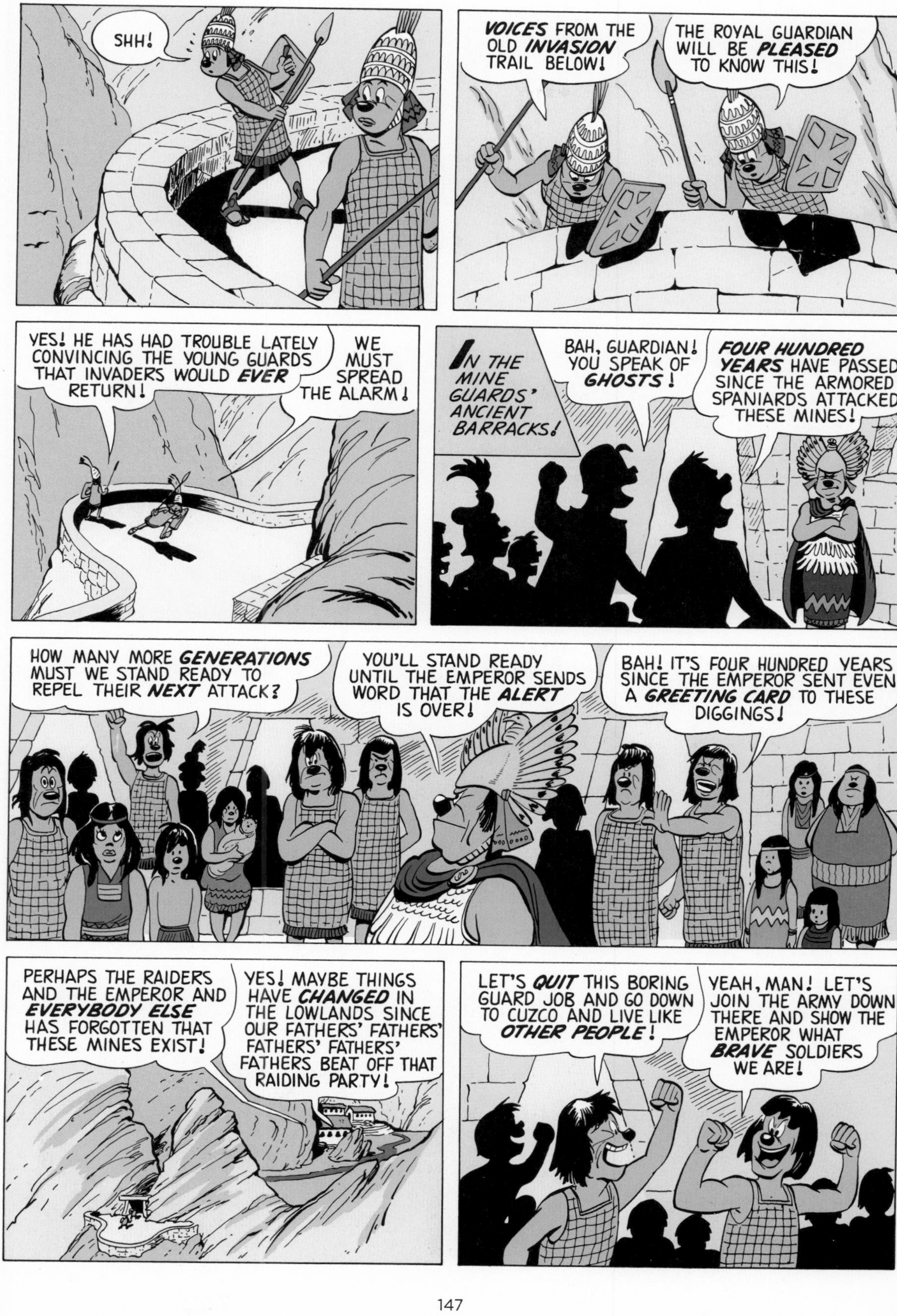
SHH!
VOICES FROM THE OLD INVASION TRAIL BELOW!
THE ROYAL GUARDIAN WILL BE PLEASED TO KNOW THIS!
YES! HE HAS HAD TROUBLE LATELY CONVINCING THE YOUNG GUARDS THAT INVADERS WOULD EVER RETURN!
WE MUST SPREAD THE ALARM!
IN THE MINE GUARDS' ANCIENT BARRACKS!
BAH, GUARDIAN! YOU SPEAK OF GHOSTS!
FOUR HUNDRED YEARS HAVE PASSED SINCE THE ARMORED SPANIARDS ATTACKED THESE MINES!
HOW MANY MORE GENERATIONS MUST WE STAND READY TO REPEL THEIR NEXT ATTACK?
YOU'LL STAND READY UNTIL THE EMPEROR SENDS WORD THAT THE ALERT IS OVER!
BAH! IT'S FOUR HUNDRED YEARS SINCE THE EMPEROR SENT EVEN A GREETING CARD TO THESE DIGGINGS!
PERHAPS THE RAIDERS AND THE EMPEROR AND EVERYBODY ELSE HAS FORGOTTEN THAT THESE MINES EXIST!
YES! MAYBE THINGS HAVE CHANGED IN THE LOWLANDS SINCE OUR FATHERS' FATHERS' FATHERS' FATHERS' FATHERS BEAT OFF THAT RAIDING PARTY!
LET'S QUIT THIS BORING GUARD JOB AND GO DOWN TO CUZCO AND LIVE LIKE OTHER PEOPLE!
YEAH, MAN! LET'S JOIN THE ARMY DOWN THERE AND SHOW THE EMPEROR WHAT BRAVE SOLDIERS WE ARE!

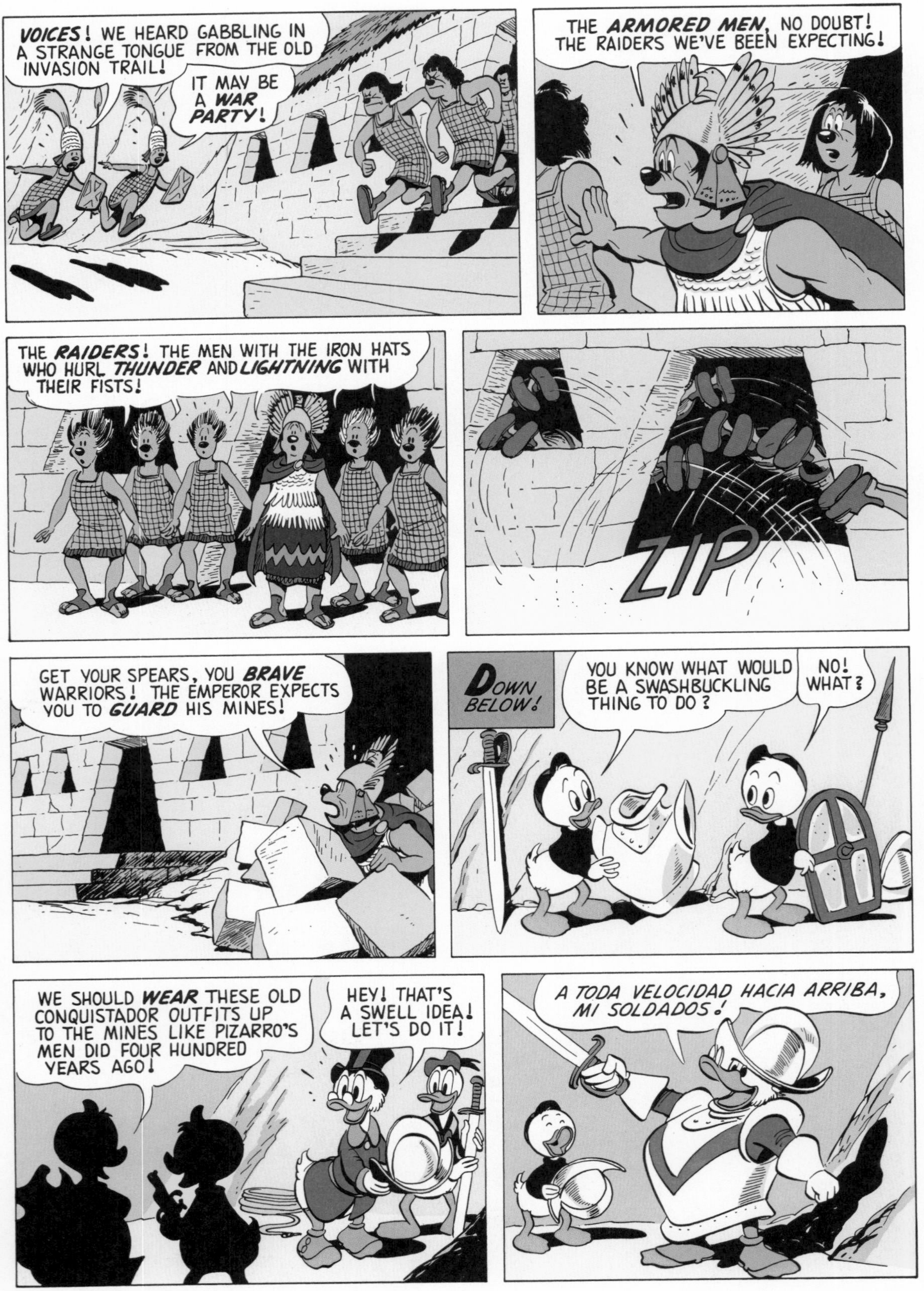
VOICES! WE HEARD GABBLING IN A STRANGE TONGUE FROM THE OLD INVASION TRAIL!
IT MAY BE A WAR PARTY!
THE ARMORED MEN, NO DOUBT! THE RAIDERS WE'VE BEEN EXPECTING!
THE RAIDERS! THE MEN WITH THE IRON HATS WHO HURL THUNDER AND LIGHTNING WITH THEIR FISTS!
ZIP
GET YOUR SPEARS, YOU BRAVE WARRIORS! THE EMPEROR EXPECTS YOU TO GUARD HIS MINES!
DOWN BELOW!
YOU KNOW WHAT WOULD BE A SWASHBUCKLING THING TO DO?
NO! WHAT?
WE SHOULD WEAR THESE OLD CONQUISTADOR OUTFITS UP TO THE MINES LIKE PIZARRO'S MEN DID FOUR HUNDRED YEARS AGO!
HEY! THAT'S A SWELL IDEA! LET'S DO IT!
A TODA VELOCIDAD HACIA ARRIBA, MI SOLDADOS!

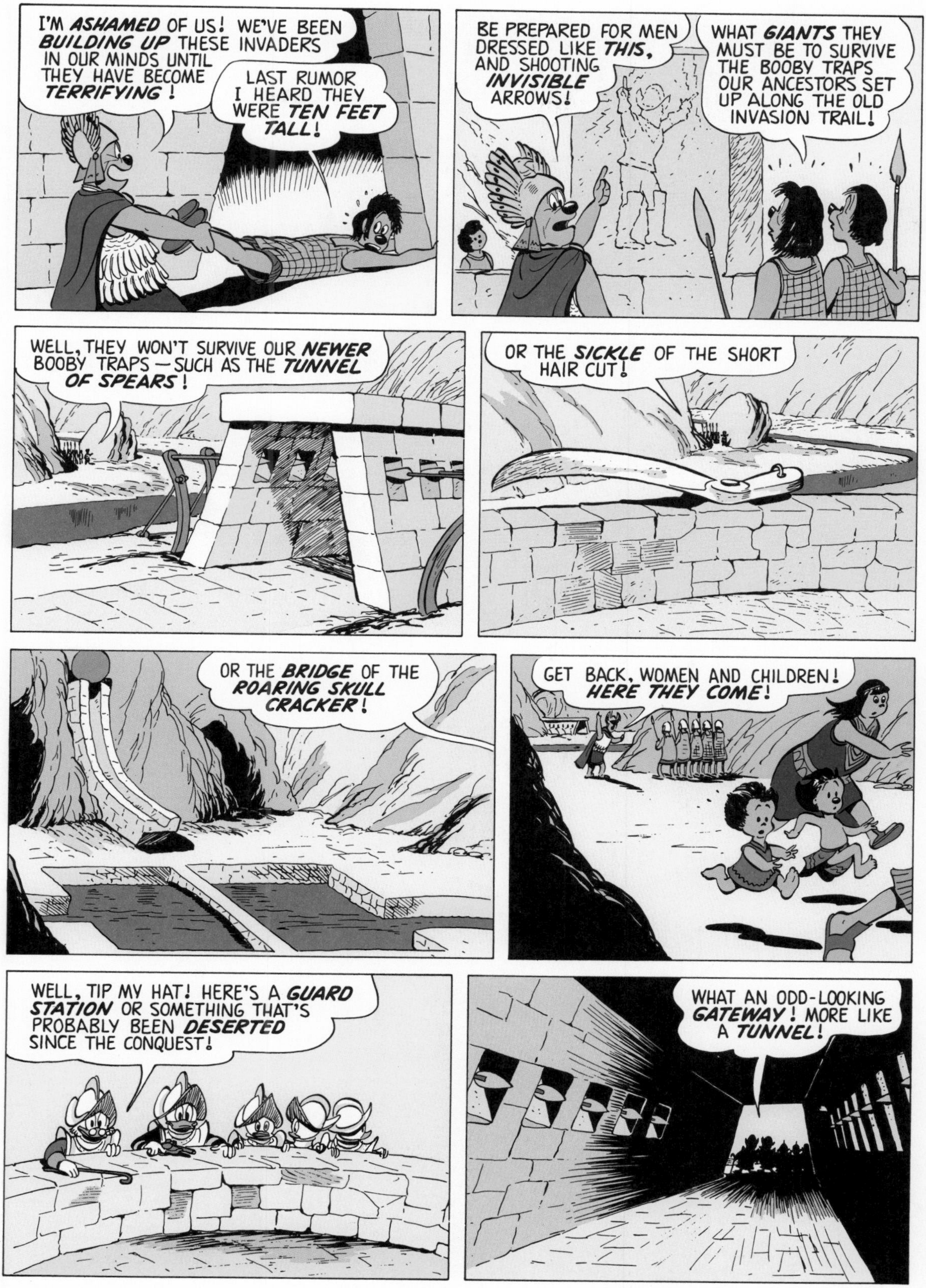
I'M ASHAMED OF US! WE'VE BEEN BUILDING UP THESE INVADERS IN OUR MINDS UNTIL THEY HAVE BECOME TERRIFYING!
LAST RUMOR I HEARD THEY WERE TEN FEET TALL!
BE PREPARED FOR MEN DRESSED LIKE THIS, AND SHOOTING INVISIBLE ARROWS!
WHAT GIANTS THEY MUST BE TO SURVIVE THE BOOBY TRAPS OUR ANCESTORS SET UP ALONG THE OLD INVASION TRAIL!
WELL, THEY WON'T SURVIVE OUR NEWER BOOBY TRAPS — SUCH AS THE TUNNEL OF SPEARS!
OR THE SICKLE OF THE SHORT HAIR CUT!
OR THE BRIDGE OF THE ROARING SKULL CRACKER!
GET BACK, WOMEN AND CHILDREN! HERE THEY COME!
WELL, TIP MY HAT! HERE'S A GUARD STATION OR SOMETHING THAT'S PROBABLY BEEN DESERTED SINCE THE CONQUEST!
WHAT AN ODD-LOOKING GATEWAY! MORE LIKE A TUNNEL!

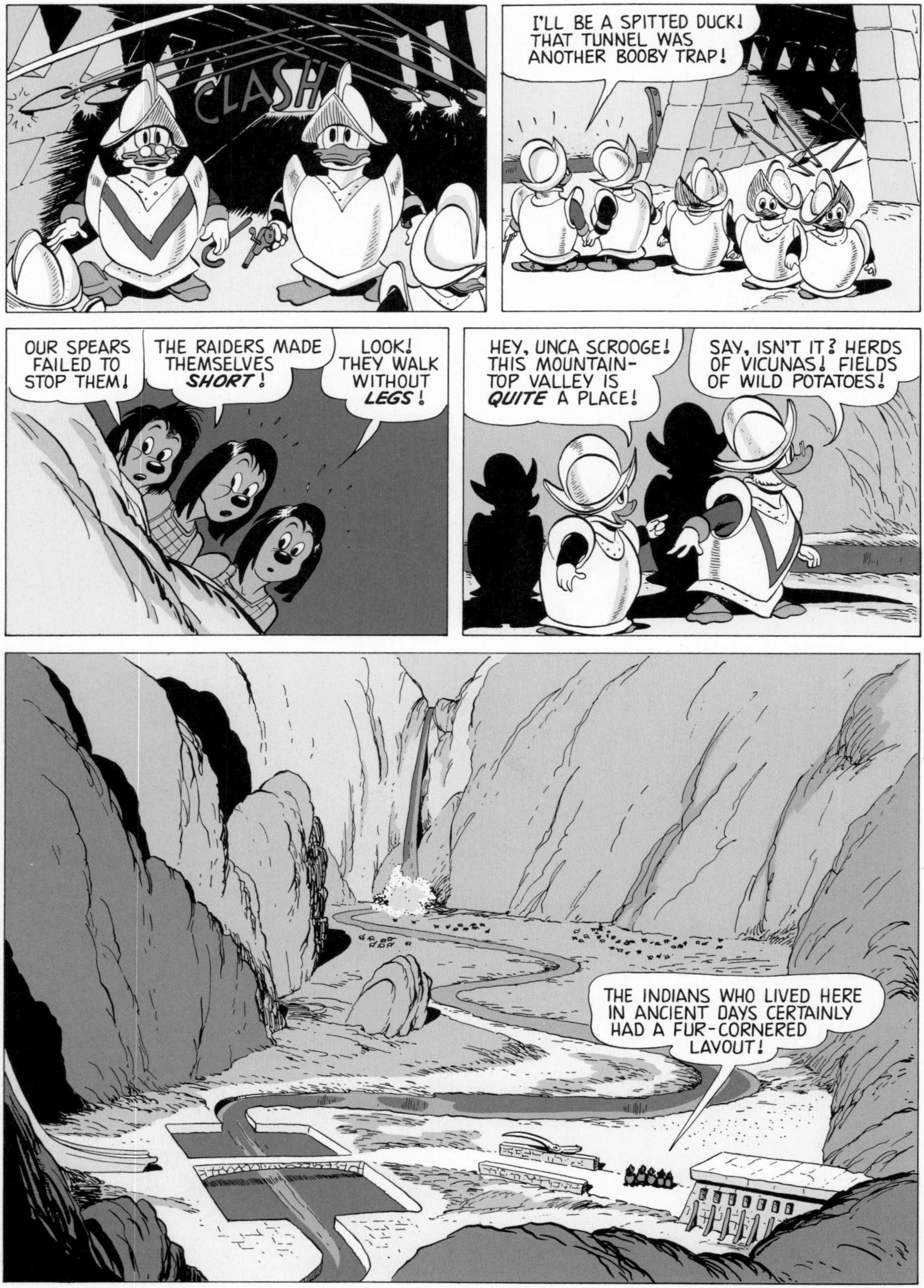
CLASH
I'LL BE A SPITTED DUCK! THAT TUNNEL WAS ANOTHER BOOBY TRAP!
OUR SPEARS FAILED TO STOP THEM!
THE RAIDERS MADE THEMSELVES SHORT!
LOOK! THEY WALK WITHOUT LEGS!
HEY, UNCA SCROOGE! THIS MOUNTAIN-TOP VALLEY IS QUITE A PLACE!
SAY, ISN'T IT? HERDS OF VICUNAS! FIELDS OF WILD POTATOES!
THE INDIANS WHO LIVED HERE IN ANCIENT DAYS CERTAINLY HAD A FUR-CORNERED LAYOUT!

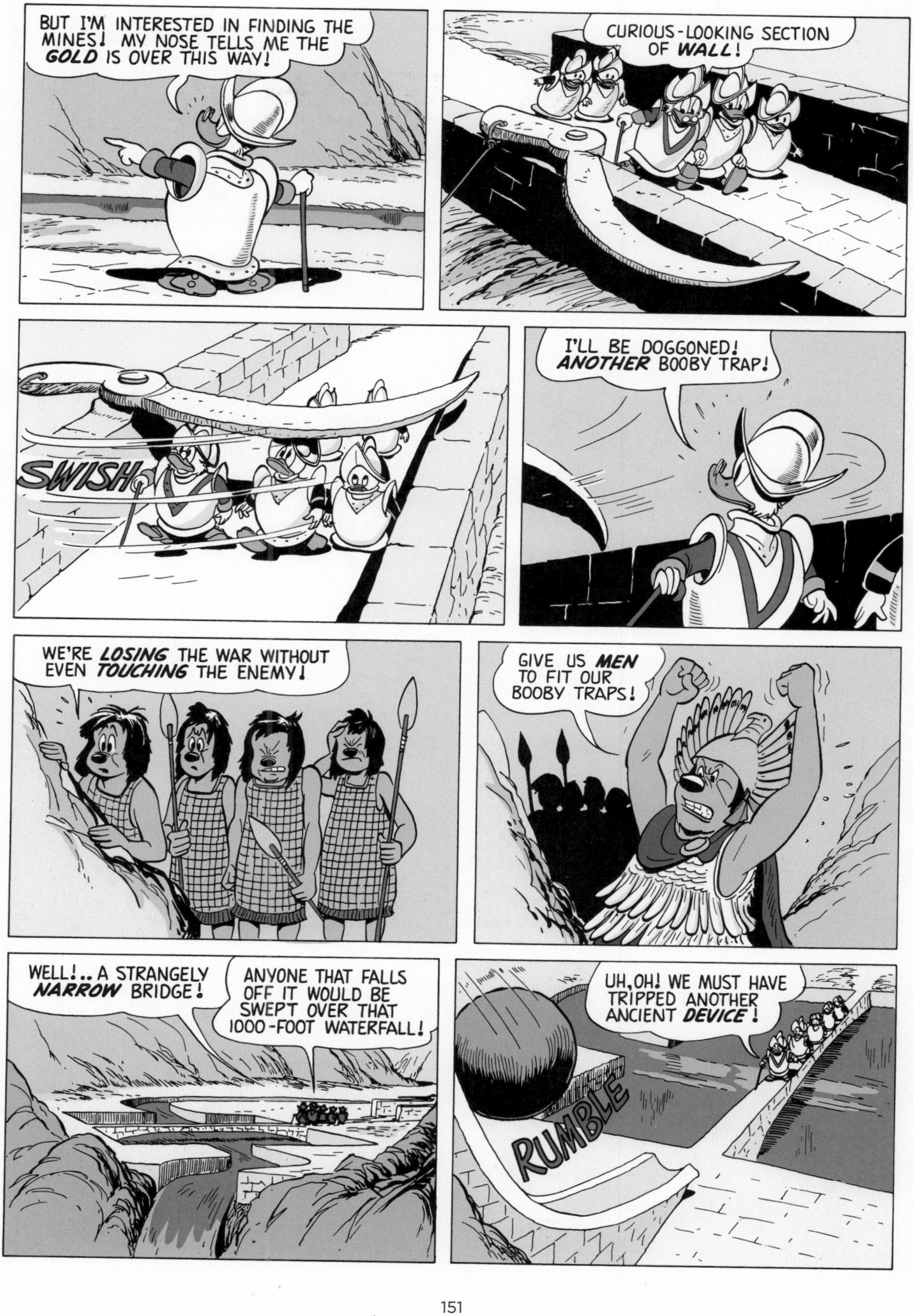

BUT I'M INTERESTED IN FINDING THE MINES! MY NOSE TELLS ME THE GOLD IS OVER THIS WAY!
CURIOUS-LOOKING SECTION OF WALL!
SWISH
I'LL BE DOGGONED! ANOTHER BOOBY TRAP!
WE'RE LOSING THE WAR WITHOUT EVEN TOUCHING THE ENEMY!
GIVE US MEN TO FIT OUR BOOBY TRAPS!
WELL!.. A STRANGELY NARROW BRIDGE!
ANYONE THAT FALLS OFF IT WOULD BE SWEPT OVER THAT 1000-FOOT WATERFALL!
UH, OH! WE MUST HAVE TRIPPED ANOTHER ANCIENT DEVICE!
RUMBLE

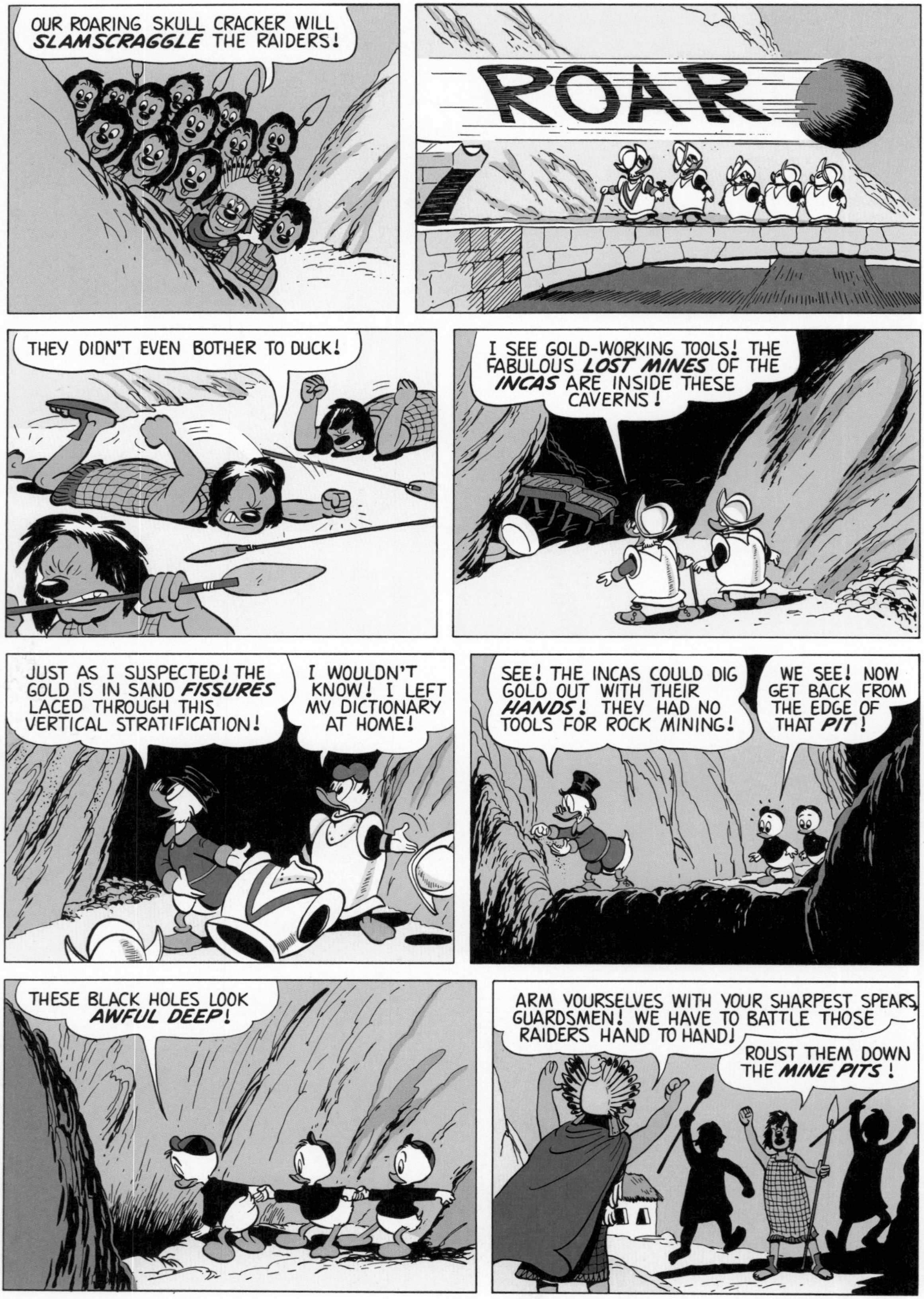
OUR ROARING SKULL CRACKER WILL SLAMSCRAGGLE THE RAIDERS!
ROAR
THEY DIDN'T EVEN BOTHER TO DUCK!
I SEE GOLD-WORKING TOOLS! THE FABULOUS LOST MINES OF THE INCAS ARE INSIDE THESE CAVERNS!
JUST AS I SUSPECTED! THE GOLD IS IN SAND FISSURES LACED THROUGH THIS VERTICAL STRATIFICATION!
I WOULDN'T KNOW! I LEFT MY DICTIONARY AT HOME!
SEE! THE INCAS COULD DIG GOLD OUT WITH THEIR HANDS! THEY HAD NO TOOLS FOR ROCK MINING!
WE SEE! NOW GET BACK FROM THE EDGE OF THAT PIT!
THESE BLACK HOLES LOOK AWFUL DEEP!
ARM YOURSELVES WITH YOUR SHARPEST SPEARS, GUARDSMEN! WE HAVE TO BATTLE THOSE RAIDERS HAND TO HAND!
ROUST THEM DOWN THE MINE PITS!

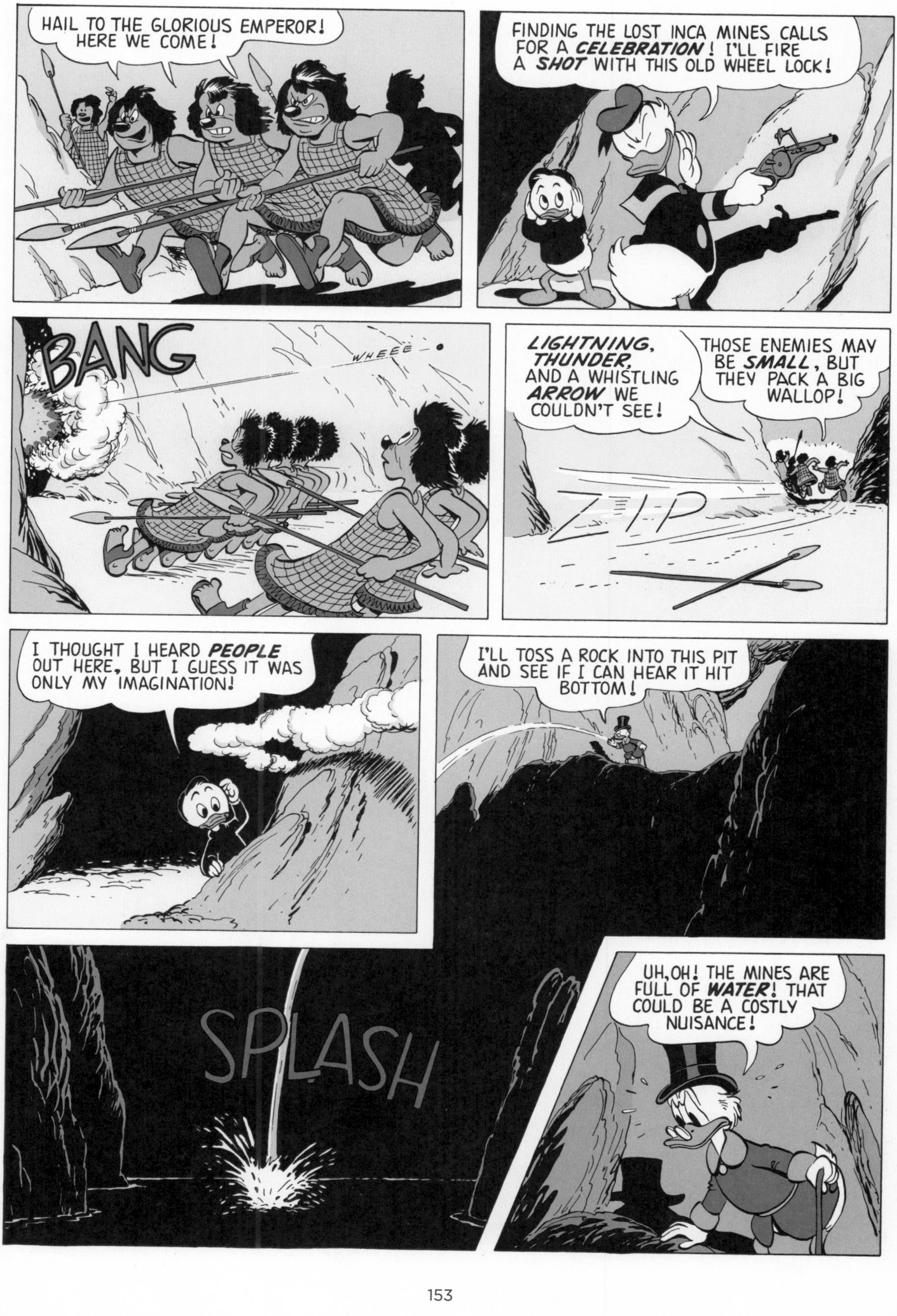

HAIL TO THE GLORIOUS EMPEROR! HERE WE COME!
FINDING THE LOST INCA MINES CALLS FOR A **CELEBRATION**! I'LL FIRE A **SHOT** WITH THIS OLD WHEEL LOCK!
BANG
WHEEE
LIGHTNING, THUNDER, AND A WHISTLING **ARROW** WE COULDN'T SEE!
THOSE ENEMIES MAY BE **SMALL**, BUT THEY PACK A BIG WALLOP!
ZIP
I THOUGHT I HEARD **PEOPLE** OUT HERE, BUT I GUESS IT WAS ONLY MY IMAGINATION!
I'LL TOSS A ROCK INTO THIS PIT AND SEE IF I CAN HEAR IT HIT BOTTOM!
SPLASH
UH,OH! THE MINES ARE FULL OF **WATER**! THAT COULD BE A COSTLY NUISANCE!

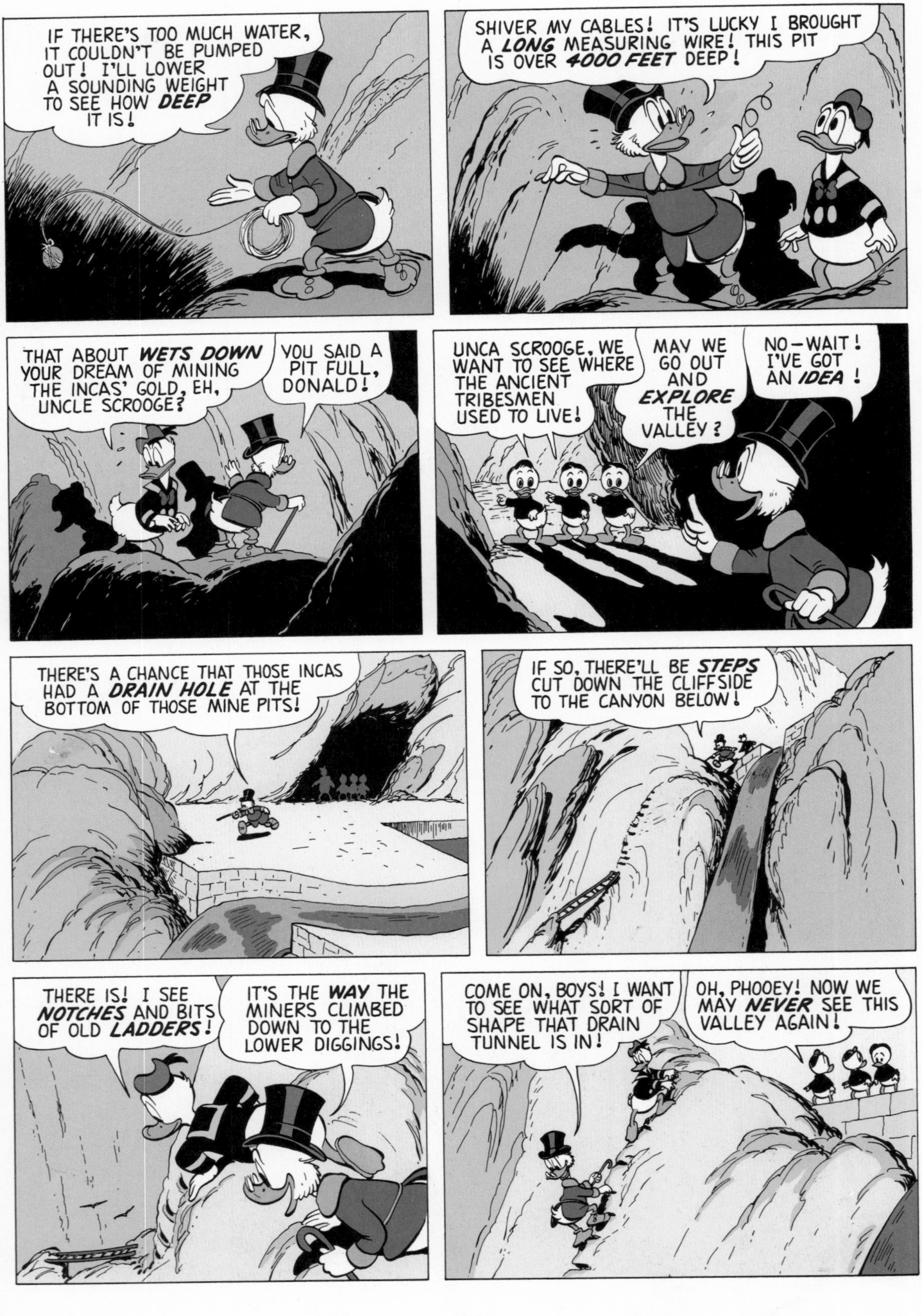
IF THERE'S TOO MUCH WATER, IT COULDN'T BE PUMPED OUT! I'LL LOWER A SOUNDING WEIGHT TO SEE HOW DEEP IT IS!
SHIVER MY CABLES! IT'S LUCKY I BROUGHT A LONG MEASURING WIRE! THIS PIT IS OVER 4000 FEET DEEP!
THAT ABOUT WETS DOWN YOUR DREAM OF MINING THE INCAS' GOLD, EH, UNCLE SCROOGE?
YOU SAID A PIT FULL, DONALD!
UNCA SCROOGE, WE WANT TO SEE WHERE THE ANCIENT TRIBESMEN USED TO LIVE!
MAY WE GO OUT AND EXPLORE THE VALLEY?
NO—WAIT! I'VE GOT AN IDEA!
THERE'S A CHANCE THAT THOSE INCAS HAD A DRAIN HOLE AT THE BOTTOM OF THOSE MINE PITS!
IF SO, THERE'LL BE STEPS CUT DOWN THE CLIFFSIDE TO THE CANYON BELOW!
THERE IS! I SEE NOTCHES AND BITS OF OLD LADDERS!
IT'S THE WAY THE MINERS CLIMBED DOWN TO THE LOWER DIGGINGS!
COME ON, BOYS! I WANT TO SEE WHAT SORT OF SHAPE THAT DRAIN TUNNEL IS IN!
OH, PHOOEY! NOW WE MAY NEVER SEE THIS VALLEY AGAIN!

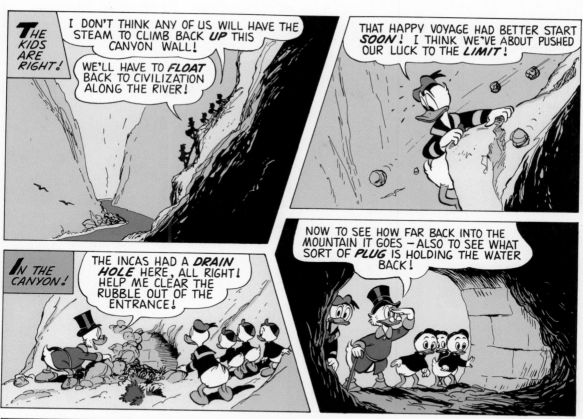

THE KIDS ARE RIGHT! I DON'T THINK ANY OF US WILL HAVE THE STEAM TO CLIMB BACK *UP* THIS CANYON WALL!

WE'LL HAVE TO *FLOAT* BACK TO CIVILIZATION ALONG THE RIVER!

THAT HAPPY VOYAGE HAD BETTER START *SOON*! I THINK WE'VE ABOUT PUSHED OUR LUCK TO THE *LIMIT*!

IN THE CANYON! THE INCAS HAD A *DRAIN HOLE* HERE, ALL RIGHT! HELP ME CLEAR THE RUBBLE OUT OF THE ENTRANCE!

NOW TO SEE HOW FAR BACK INTO THE MOUNTAIN IT GOES — ALSO TO SEE WHAT SORT OF *PLUG* IS HOLDING THE WATER BACK!

THE RAIDERS HAVE FOUND OUR ANCESTORS' *TUNNEL*!

THEY ARE POKING THEIR NOSY BEAKS *INSIDE*!

WE MUST SIGNAL THE GUARDS THAT THE *ZERO HOUR* IS HERE!

YES! THERE'S ONLY *ONE WAY* LEFT TO SAVE THE EMPEROR'S GOLD!

WHAT GOES, ROYAL GUARDSMAN? IS IT *SERIOUS*?

YES! TO THE PIT HEAD, WARRIORS! WE MUST SPRING OUR *LAST BOOBY TRAP*!

LET'S HOPE THESE FEEBLE TORCHES LAST LONG ENOUGH TO GET US BACK OUT OF THIS CREEPY TUNNEL!

UNCA SCROOGE, YOU LEAD US INTO THE *SCARIEST* PLACES!

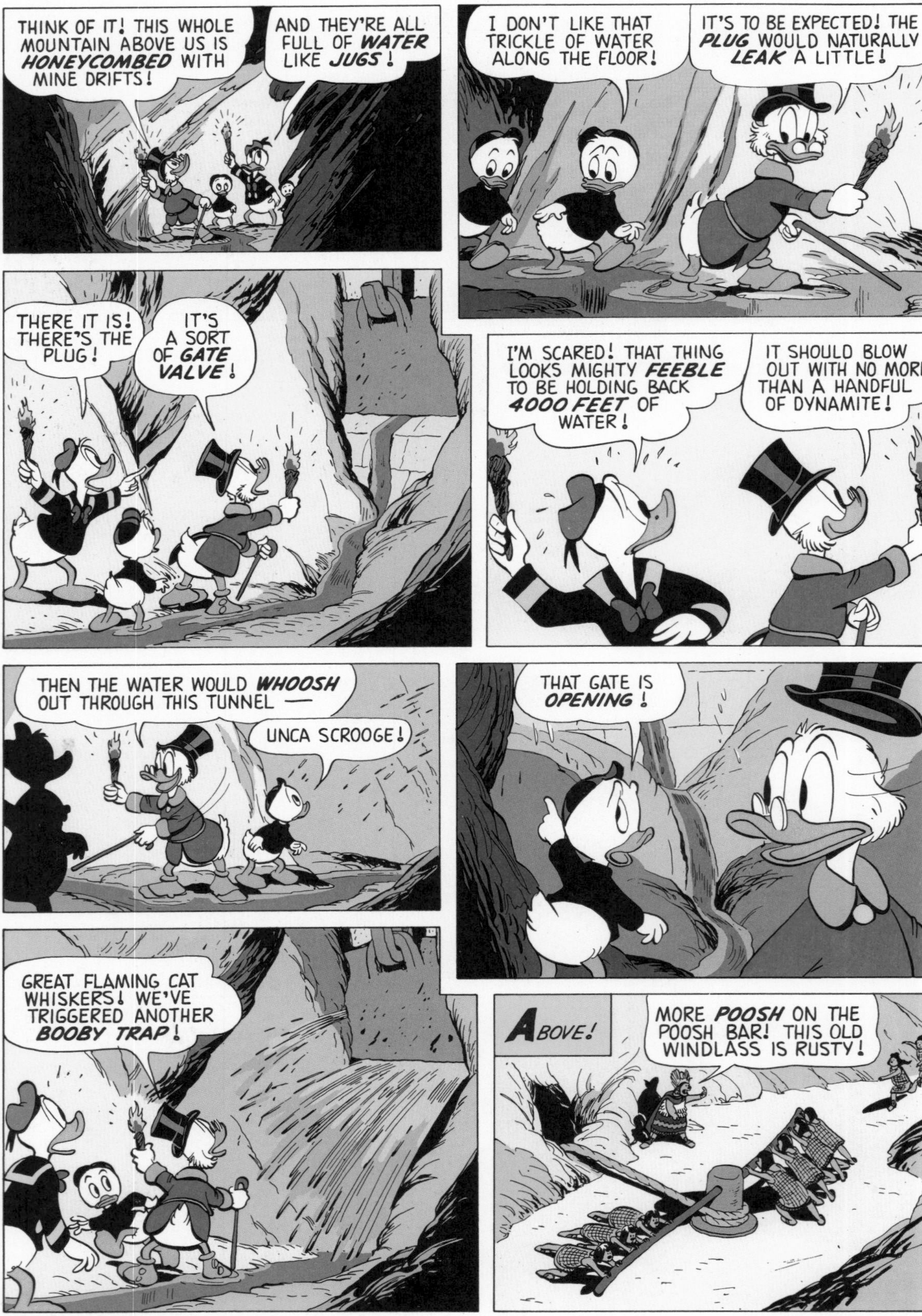

THINK OF IT! THIS WHOLE MOUNTAIN ABOVE US IS HONEYCOMBED WITH MINE DRIFTS!
AND THEY'RE ALL FULL OF WATER LIKE JUGS!
I DON'T LIKE THAT TRICKLE OF WATER ALONG THE FLOOR!
IT'S TO BE EXPECTED! THE PLUG WOULD NATURALLY LEAK A LITTLE!
THERE IT IS! THERE'S THE PLUG!
IT'S A SORT OF GATE VALVE!
I'M SCARED! THAT THING LOOKS MIGHTY FEEBLE TO BE HOLDING BACK 4000 FEET OF WATER!
IT SHOULD BLOW OUT WITH NO MORE THAN A HANDFUL OF DYNAMITE!
THEN THE WATER WOULD WHOOSH OUT THROUGH THIS TUNNEL —
UNCA SCROOGE!
THAT GATE IS OPENING!
GREAT FLAMING CAT WHISKERS! WE'VE TRIGGERED ANOTHER BOOBY TRAP!
ABOVE!
MORE POOSH ON THE POOSH BAR! THIS OLD WINDLASS IS RUSTY!

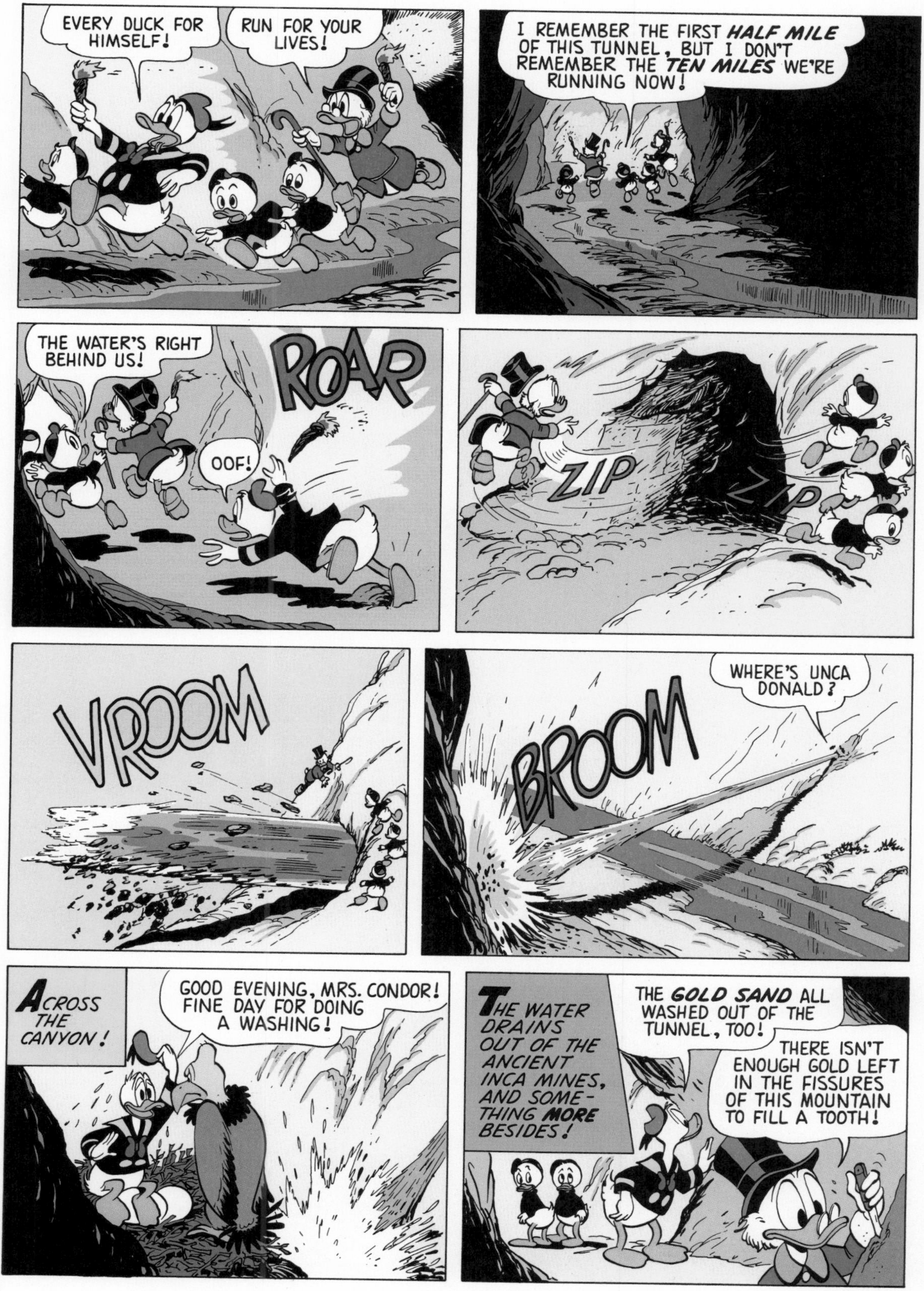
EVERY DUCK FOR HIMSELF!
RUN FOR YOUR LIVES!
I REMEMBER THE FIRST HALF MILE OF THIS TUNNEL, BUT I DON'T REMEMBER THE TEN MILES WE'RE RUNNING NOW!
THE WATER'S RIGHT BEHIND US!
ROAR
OOF!
ZIP
ZIP
VROOM
BROOM
WHERE'S UNCA DONALD?
ACROSS THE CANYON!
GOOD EVENING, MRS. CONDOR! FINE DAY FOR DOING A WASHING!
THE WATER DRAINS OUT OF THE ANCIENT INCA MINES, AND SOMETHING MORE BESIDES!
THE GOLD SAND ALL WASHED OUT OF THE TUNNEL, TOO!
THERE ISN'T ENOUGH GOLD LEFT IN THE FISSURES OF THIS MOUNTAIN TO FILL A TOOTH!

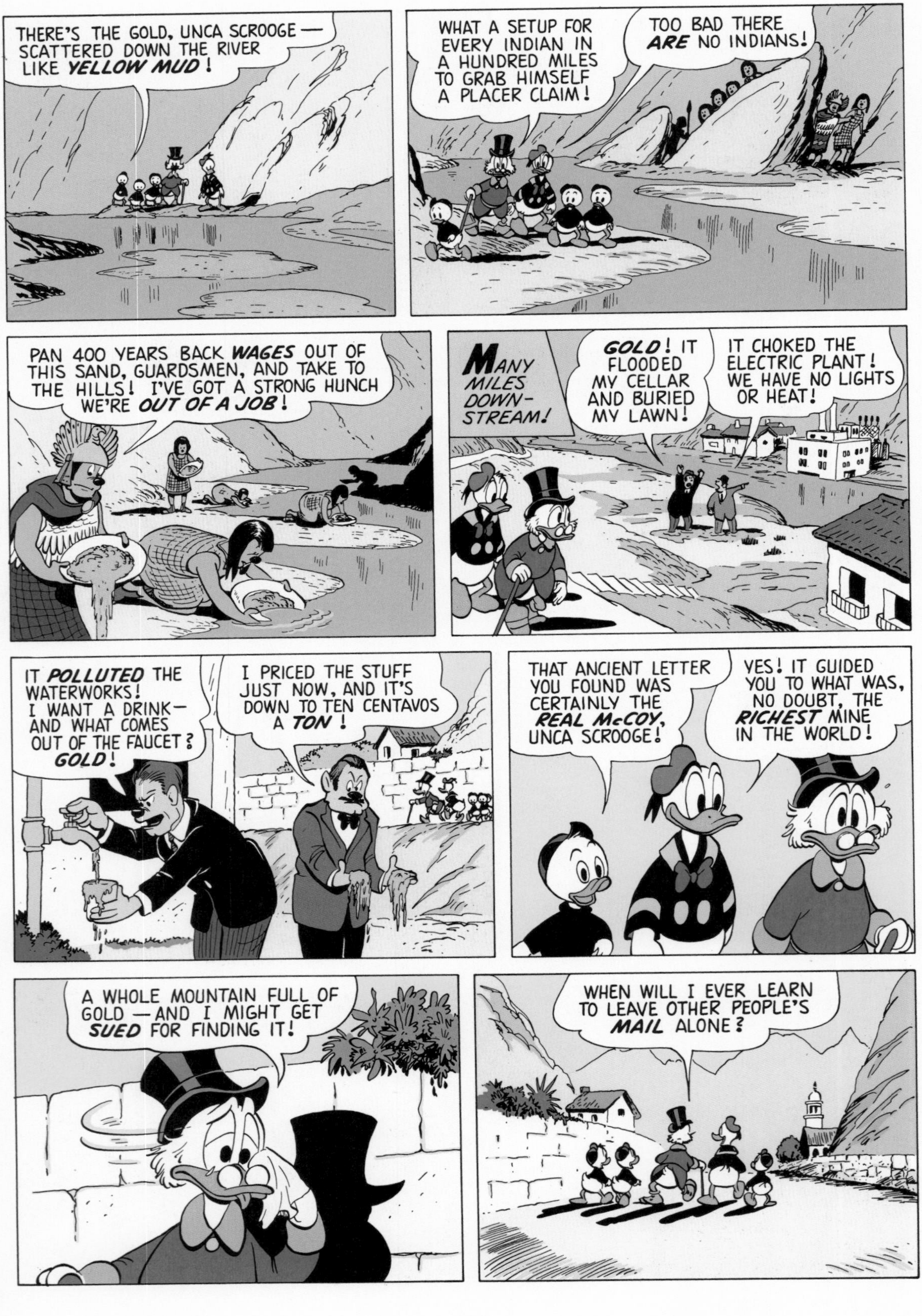
THERE'S THE GOLD, UNCA SCROOGE — SCATTERED DOWN THE RIVER LIKE YELLOW MUD!
WHAT A SETUP FOR EVERY INDIAN IN A HUNDRED MILES TO GRAB HIMSELF A PLACER CLAIM!
TOO BAD THERE ARE NO INDIANS!
PAN 400 YEARS BACK WAGES OUT OF THIS SAND, GUARDSMEN, AND TAKE TO THE HILLS! I'VE GOT A STRONG HUNCH WE'RE OUT OF A JOB!
MANY MILES DOWN-STREAM!
GOLD! IT FLOODED MY CELLAR AND BURIED MY LAWN!
IT CHOKED THE ELECTRIC PLANT! WE HAVE NO LIGHTS OR HEAT!
IT POLLUTED THE WATERWORKS! I WANT A DRINK— AND WHAT COMES OUT OF THE FAUCET? GOLD!
I PRICED THE STUFF JUST NOW, AND IT'S DOWN TO TEN CENTAVOS A TON!
THAT ANCIENT LETTER YOU FOUND WAS CERTAINLY THE REAL McCOY, UNCA SCROOGE!
YES! IT GUIDED YOU TO WHAT WAS, NO DOUBT, THE RICHEST MINE IN THE WORLD!
A WHOLE MOUNTAIN FULL OF GOLD — AND I MIGHT GET SUED FOR FINDING IT!
WHEN WILL I EVER LEARN TO LEAVE OTHER PEOPLE'S MAIL ALONE?

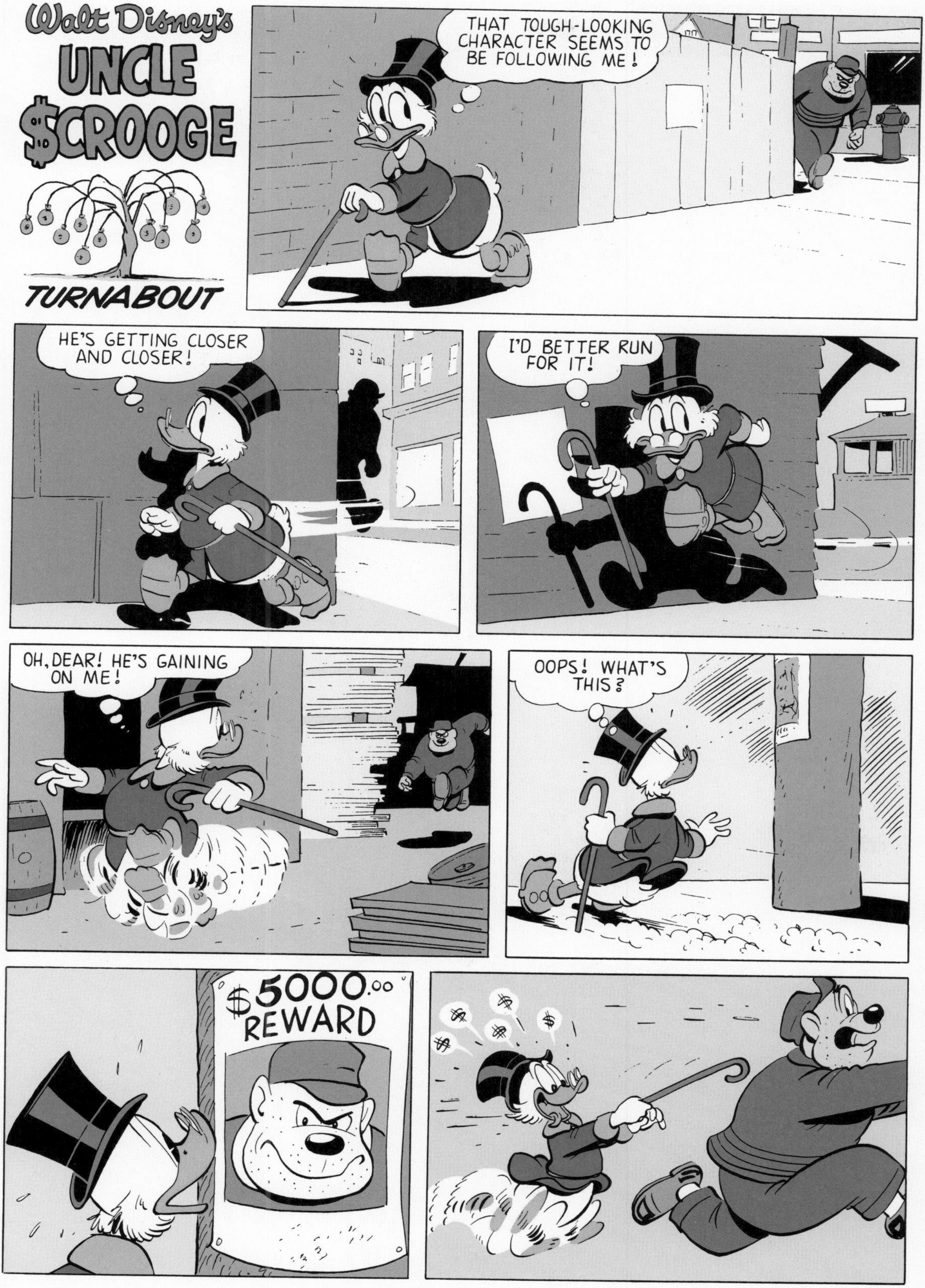

Walt Disney's
UNCLE $CROOGE
TURNABOUT
THAT TOUGH-LOOKING CHARACTER SEEMS TO BE FOLLOWING ME!
HE'S GETTING CLOSER AND CLOSER!
I'D BETTER RUN FOR IT!
OH, DEAR! HE'S GAINING ON ME!
OOPS! WHAT'S THIS?
$5000.00 REWARD

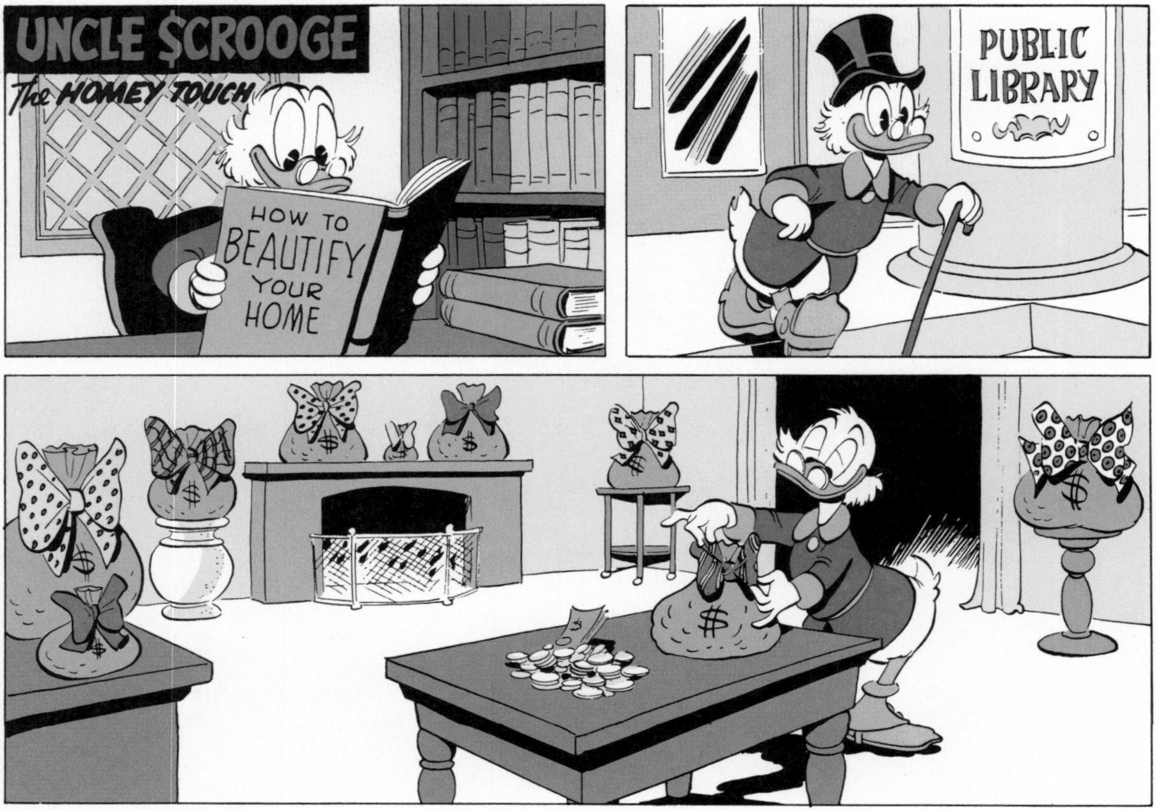
UNCLE $CROOGE
The HOMEY TOUCH
HOW TO BEAUTIFY YOUR HOME
PUBLIC LIBRARY

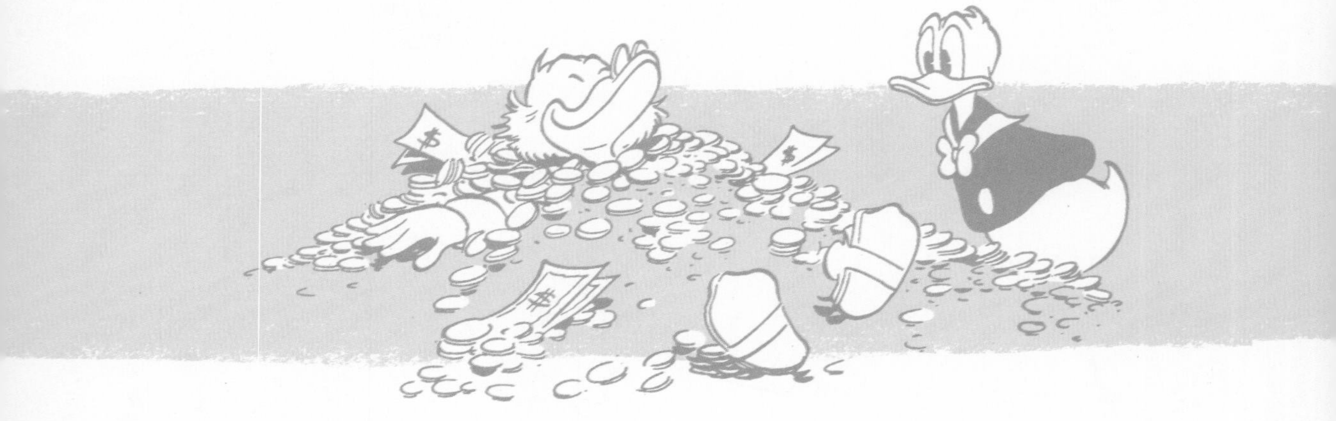

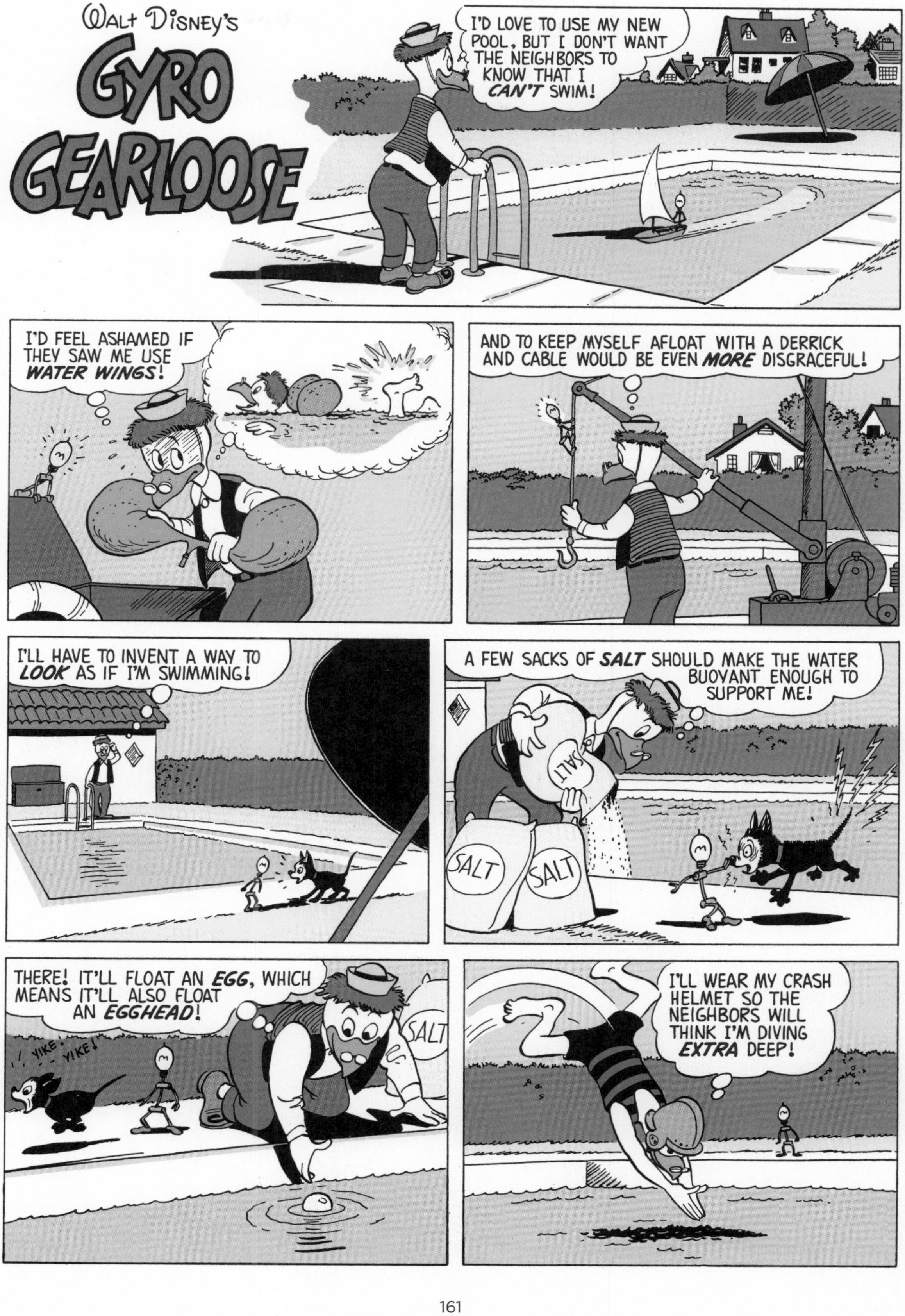
WALT DISNEY'S
GYRO GEARLOOSE
I'D LOVE TO USE MY NEW POOL, BUT I DON'T WANT THE NEIGHBORS TO KNOW THAT I CAN'T SWIM!
I'D FEEL ASHAMED IF THEY SAW ME USE WATER WINGS!
AND TO KEEP MYSELF AFLOAT WITH A DERRICK AND CABLE WOULD BE EVEN MORE DISGRACEFUL!
I'LL HAVE TO INVENT A WAY TO LOOK AS IF I'M SWIMMING!
A FEW SACKS OF SALT SHOULD MAKE THE WATER BUOYANT ENOUGH TO SUPPORT ME!
SALT
SALT
SALT
THERE! IT'LL FLOAT AN EGG, WHICH MEANS IT'LL ALSO FLOAT AN EGGHEAD!
YIKE! YIKE!
SALT
I'LL WEAR MY CRASH HELMET SO THE NEIGHBORS WILL THINK I'M DIVING EXTRA DEEP!

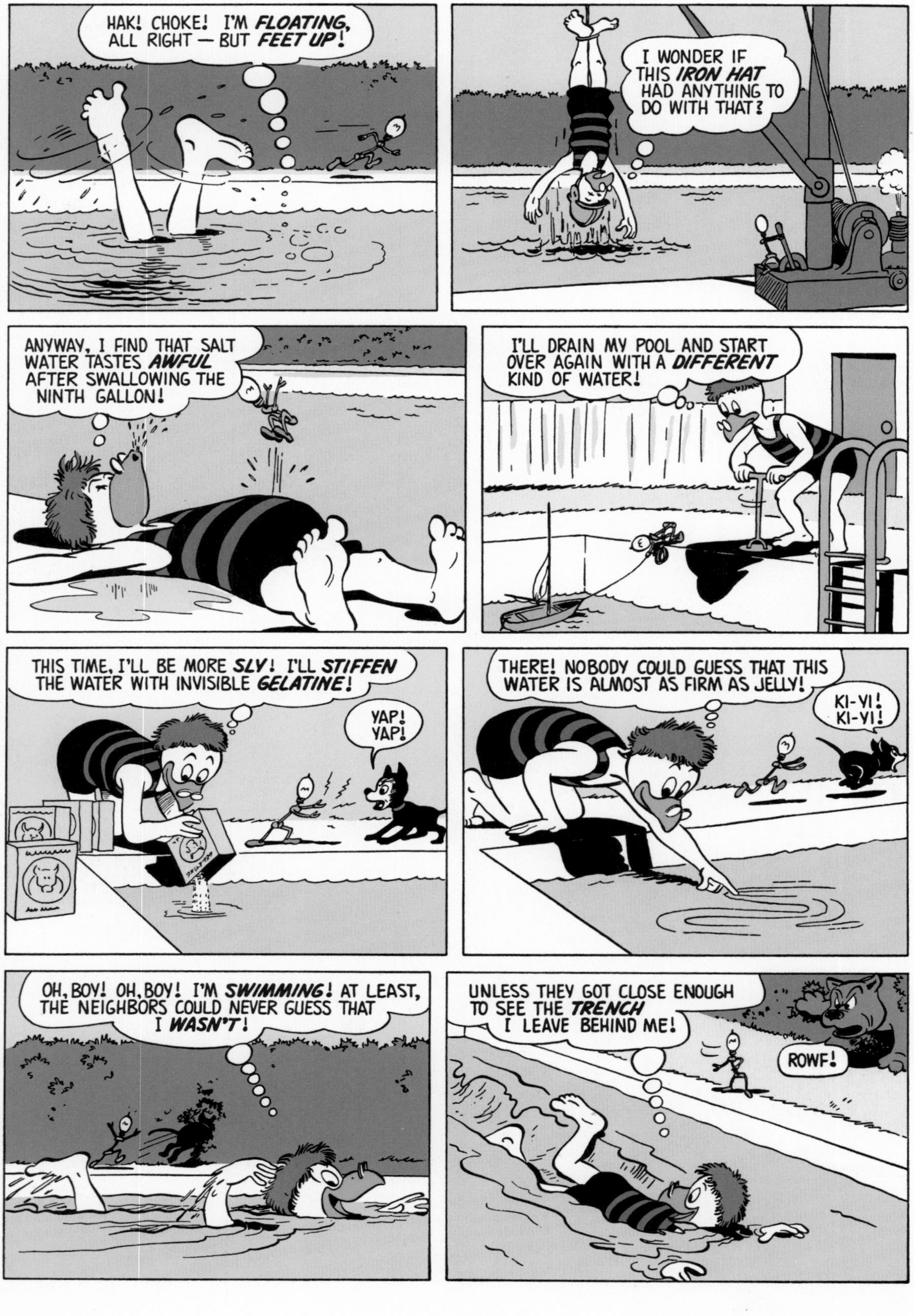
HAK! CHOKE! I'M FLOATING, ALL RIGHT — BUT FEET UP!
I WONDER IF THIS IRON HAT HAD ANYTHING TO DO WITH THAT?
ANYWAY, I FIND THAT SALT WATER TASTES AWFUL AFTER SWALLOWING THE NINTH GALLON!
I'LL DRAIN MY POOL AND START OVER AGAIN WITH A DIFFERENT KIND OF WATER!
THIS TIME, I'LL BE MORE SLY! I'LL STIFFEN THE WATER WITH INVISIBLE GELATINE!
YAP! YAP!
THERE! NOBODY COULD GUESS THAT THIS WATER IS ALMOST AS FIRM AS JELLY!
KI-YI! KI-YI!
OH, BOY! OH, BOY! I'M SWIMMING! AT LEAST, THE NEIGHBORS COULD NEVER GUESS THAT I WASN'T!
UNLESS THEY GOT CLOSE ENOUGH TO SEE THE TRENCH I LEAVE BEHIND ME!
ROWF!

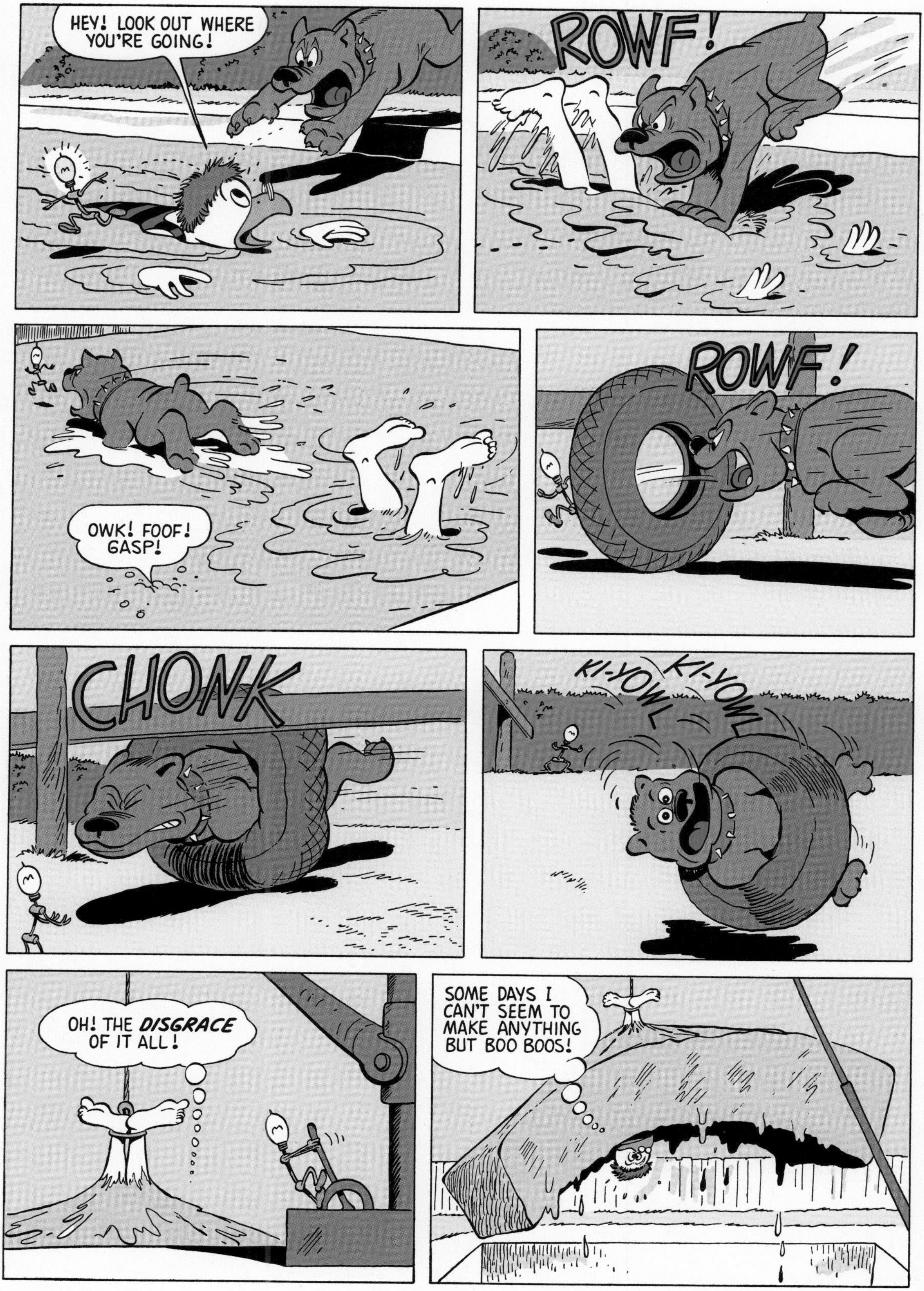
HEY! LOOK OUT WHERE YOU'RE GOING!
ROWF!
OWK! FOOF! GASP!
ROWF!
CHONK
KI-YOWL
KI-YOWL
OH! THE *DISGRACE* OF IT ALL!
SOME DAYS I CAN'T SEEM TO MAKE ANYTHING BUT BOO BOOS!

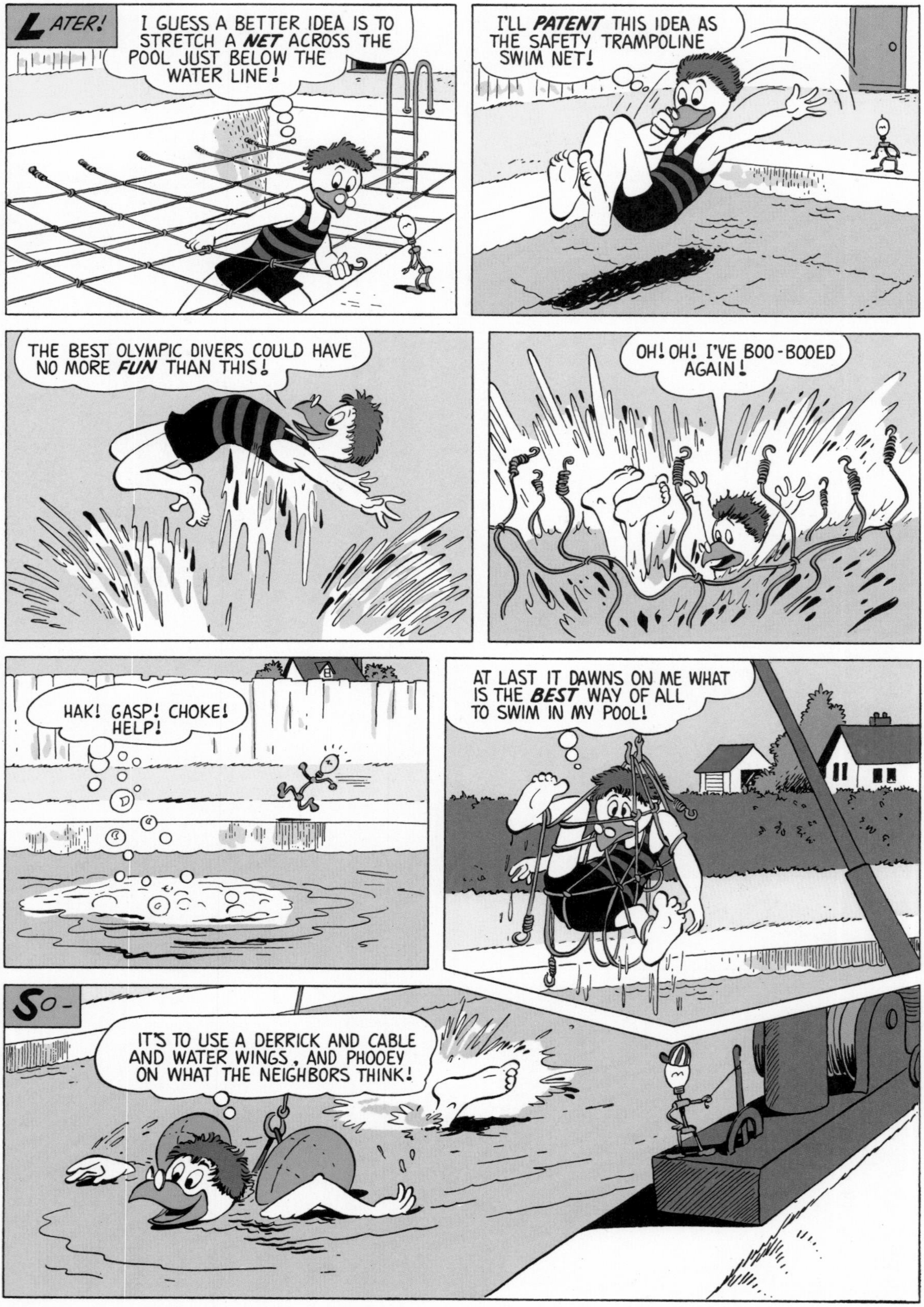
LATER!
I GUESS A BETTER IDEA IS TO STRETCH A NET ACROSS THE POOL JUST BELOW THE WATER LINE!
I'LL PATENT THIS IDEA AS THE SAFETY TRAMPOLINE SWIM NET!
THE BEST OLYMPIC DIVERS COULD HAVE NO MORE FUN THAN THIS!
OH! OH! I'VE BOO-BOOED AGAIN!
HAK! GASP! CHOKE! HELP!
AT LAST IT DAWNS ON ME WHAT IS THE BEST WAY OF ALL TO SWIM IN MY POOL!
SO-
IT'S TO USE A DERRICK AND CABLE AND WATER WINGS, AND PHOOEY ON WHAT THE NEIGHBORS THINK!

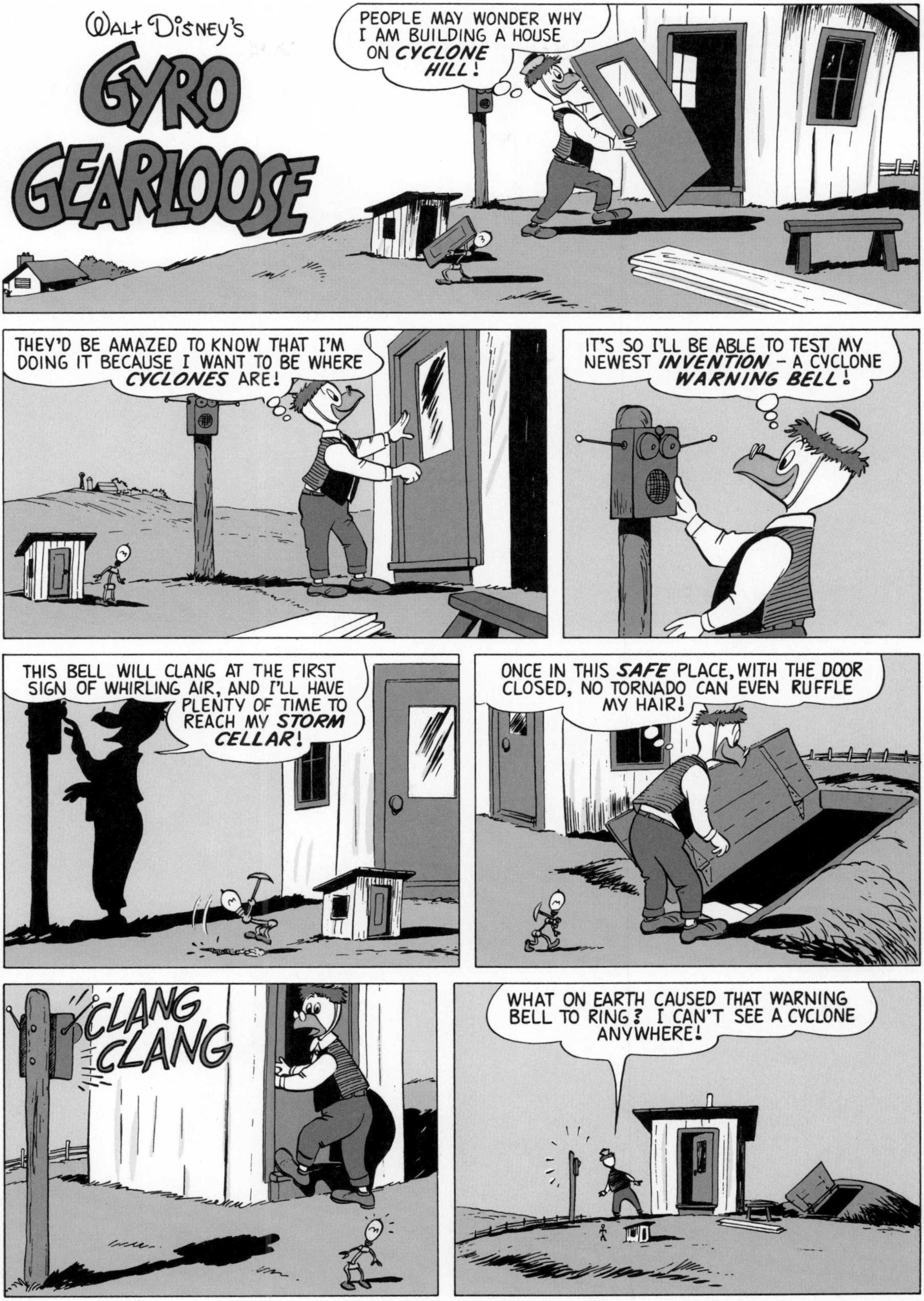
WALT DISNEY'S
GYRO GEARLOOSE
PEOPLE MAY WONDER WHY I AM BUILDING A HOUSE ON CYCLONE HILL!
THEY'D BE AMAZED TO KNOW THAT I'M DOING IT BECAUSE I WANT TO BE WHERE CYCLONES ARE!
IT'S SO I'LL BE ABLE TO TEST MY NEWEST INVENTION – A CYCLONE WARNING BELL!
THIS BELL WILL CLANG AT THE FIRST SIGN OF WHIRLING AIR, AND I'LL HAVE PLENTY OF TIME TO REACH MY STORM CELLAR!
ONCE IN THIS SAFE PLACE, WITH THE DOOR CLOSED, NO TORNADO CAN EVEN RUFFLE MY HAIR!
CLANG CLANG
WHAT ON EARTH CAUSED THAT WARNING BELL TO RING? I CAN'T SEE A CYCLONE ANYWHERE!

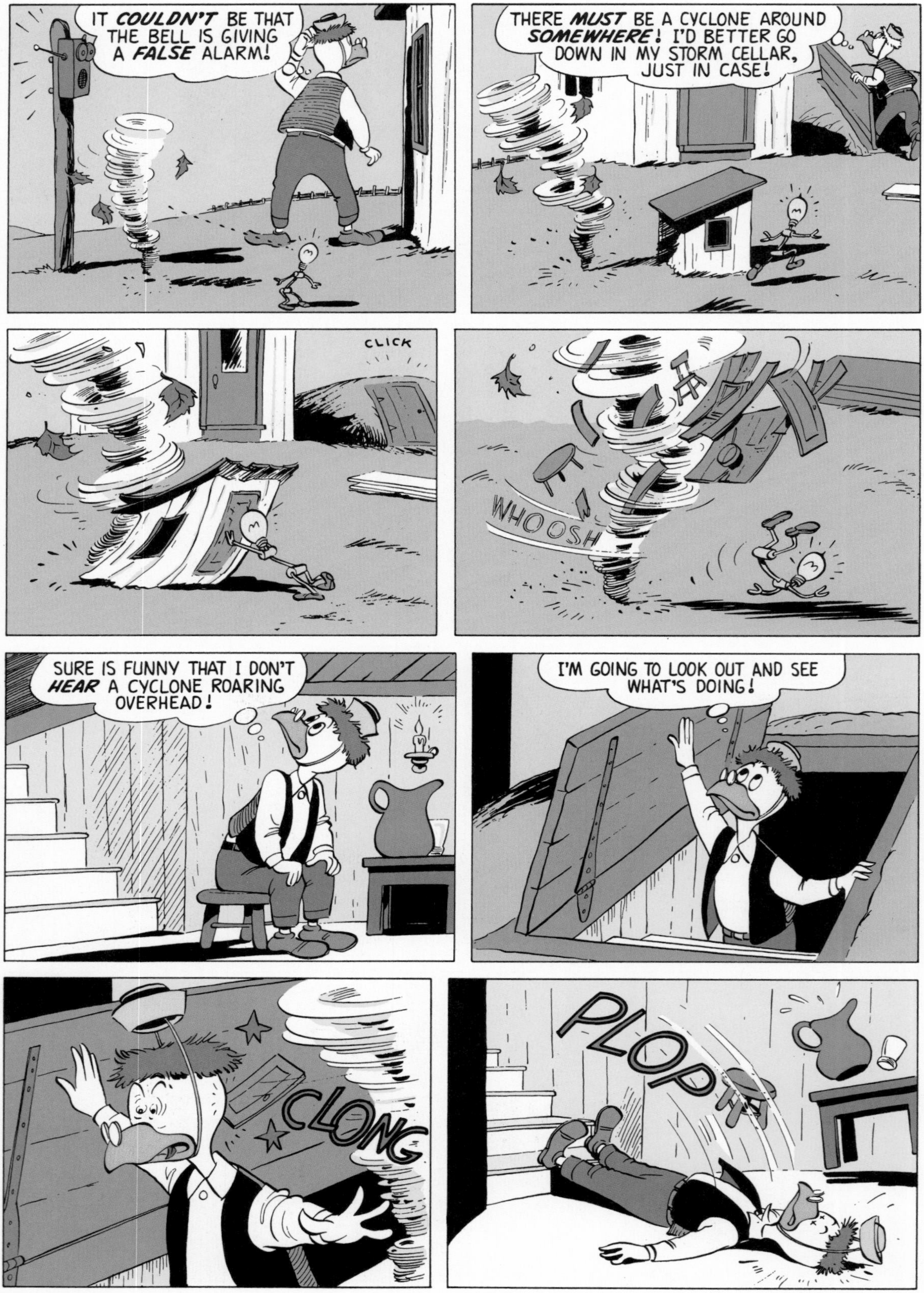
IT COULDN'T BE THAT THE BELL IS GIVING A FALSE ALARM!
THERE MUST BE A CYCLONE AROUND SOMEWHERE! I'D BETTER GO DOWN IN MY STORM CELLAR, JUST IN CASE!
CLICK
WHOOSH
SURE IS FUNNY THAT I DON'T HEAR A CYCLONE ROARING OVERHEAD!
I'M GOING TO LOOK OUT AND SEE WHAT'S DOING!
CLONG
PLOP

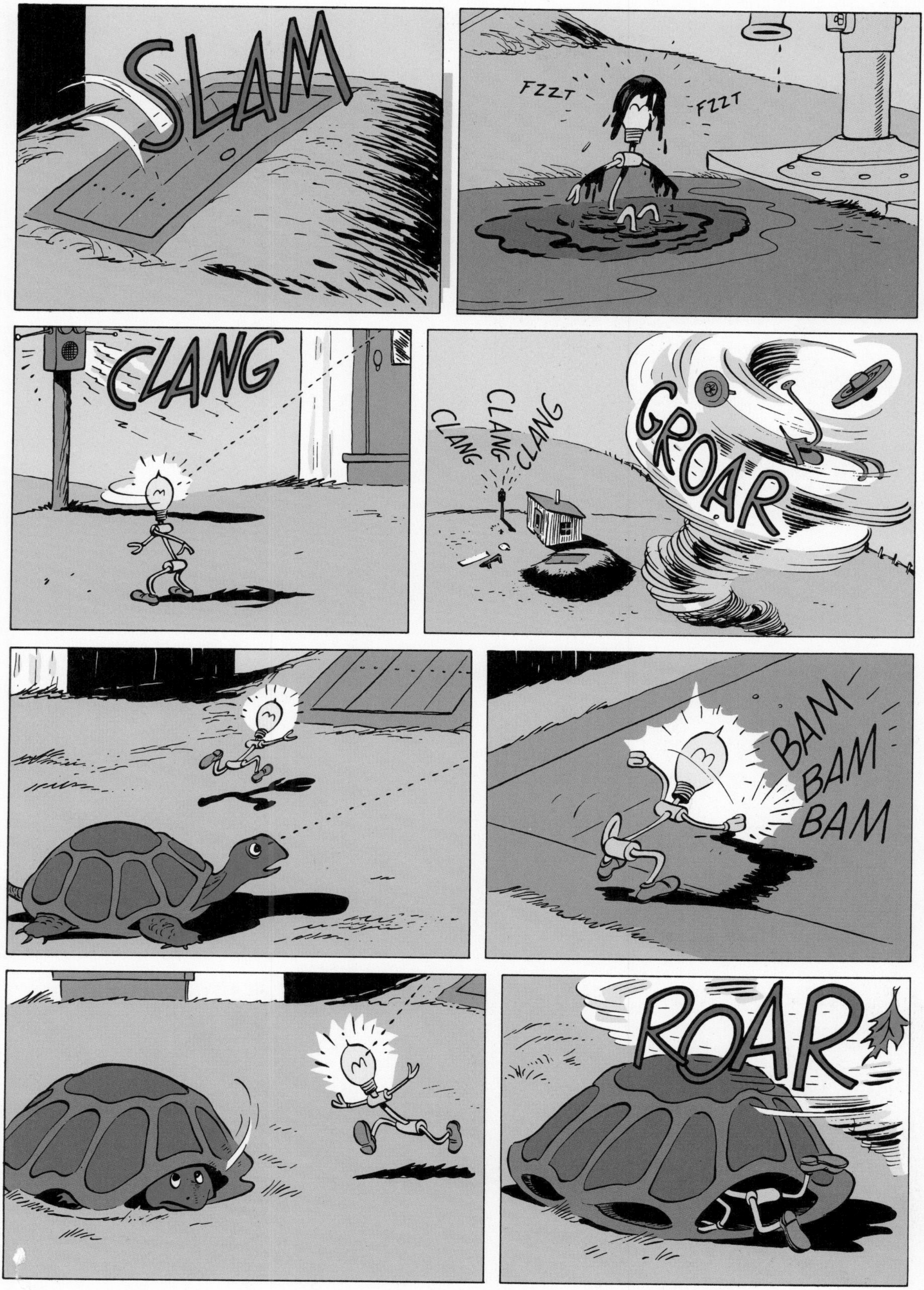
SLAM
FZZT
FZZT
CLANG
CLANG
CLANG
CLANG
GROAR
BAM
BAM
BAM
ROAR

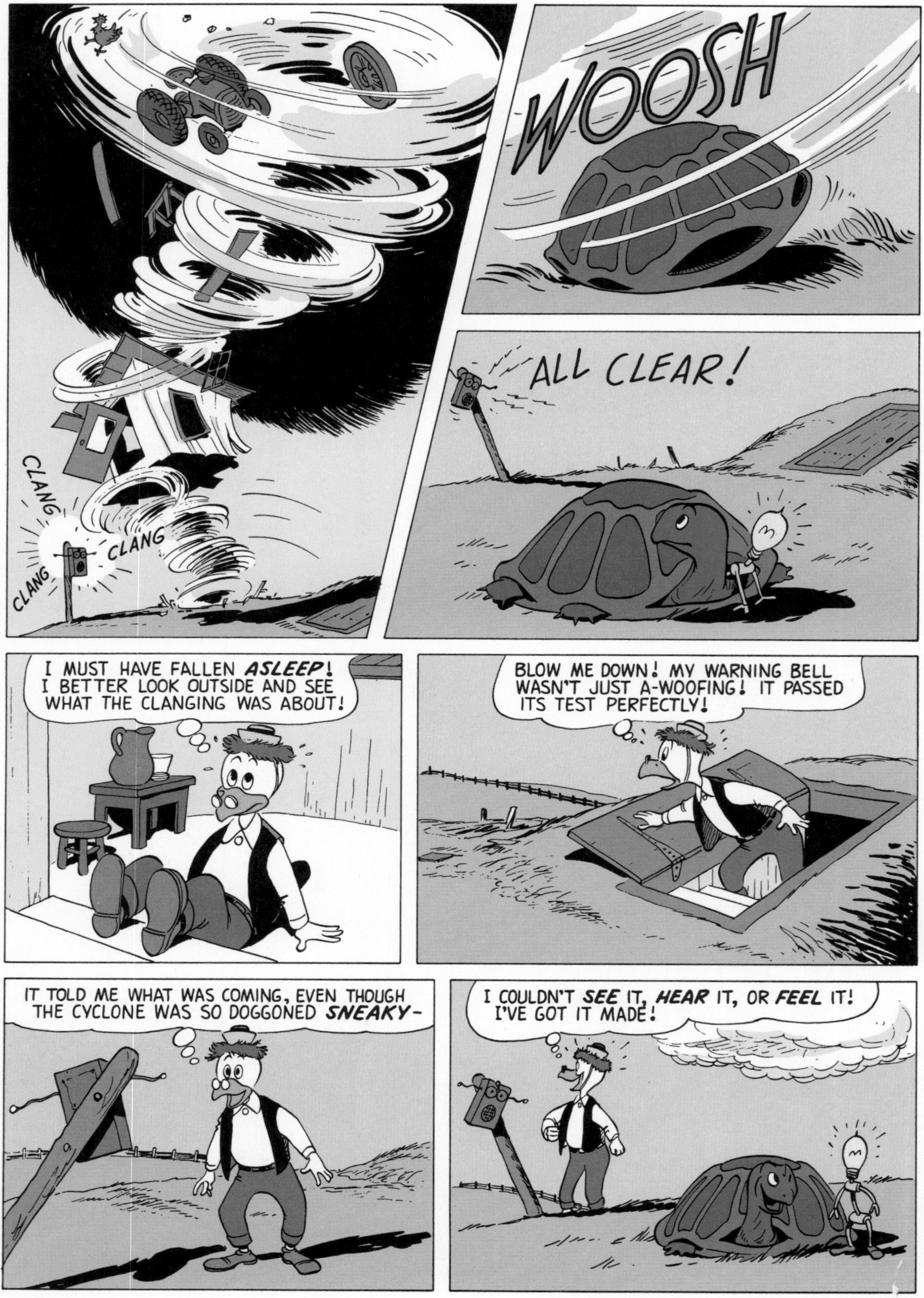
CLANG
CLANG
CLANG
WOOSH
ALL CLEAR!
I MUST HAVE FALLEN ASLEEP! I BETTER LOOK OUTSIDE AND SEE WHAT THE CLANGING WAS ABOUT!
BLOW ME DOWN! MY WARNING BELL WASN'T JUST A-WOOFING! IT PASSED ITS TEST PERFECTLY!
IT TOLD ME WHAT WAS COMING, EVEN THOUGH THE CYCLONE WAS SO DOGGONED SNEAKY-
I COULDN'T SEE IT, HEAR IT, OR FEEL IT! I'VE GOT IT MADE!

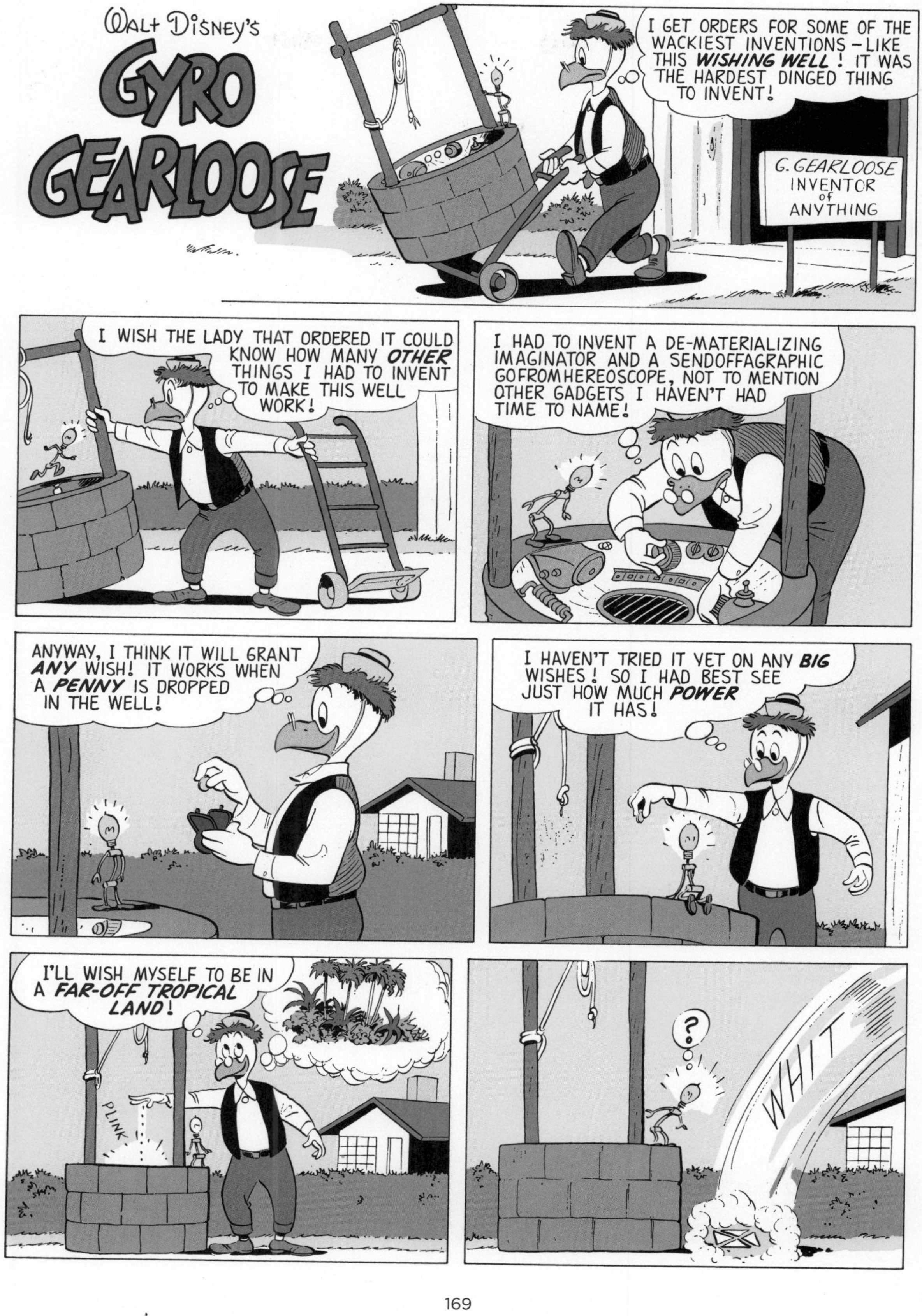

WALT DISNEY'S
GYRO GEARLOOSE
I GET ORDERS FOR SOME OF THE WACKIEST INVENTIONS – LIKE THIS WISHING WELL! IT WAS THE HARDEST DINGED THING TO INVENT!
G. GEARLOOSE INVENTOR of ANYTHING
I WISH THE LADY THAT ORDERED IT COULD KNOW HOW MANY OTHER THINGS I HAD TO INVENT TO MAKE THIS WELL WORK!
I HAD TO INVENT A DE-MATERIALIZING IMAGINATOR AND A SENDOFFAGRAPHIC GOFROMHEREOSCOPE, NOT TO MENTION OTHER GADGETS I HAVEN'T HAD TIME TO NAME!
ANYWAY, I THINK IT WILL GRANT ANY WISH! IT WORKS WHEN A PENNY IS DROPPED IN THE WELL!
I HAVEN'T TRIED IT YET ON ANY BIG WISHES! SO I HAD BEST SEE JUST HOW MUCH POWER IT HAS!
I'LL WISH MYSELF TO BE IN A FAR-OFF TROPICAL LAND!
PLINK
?
WHIT

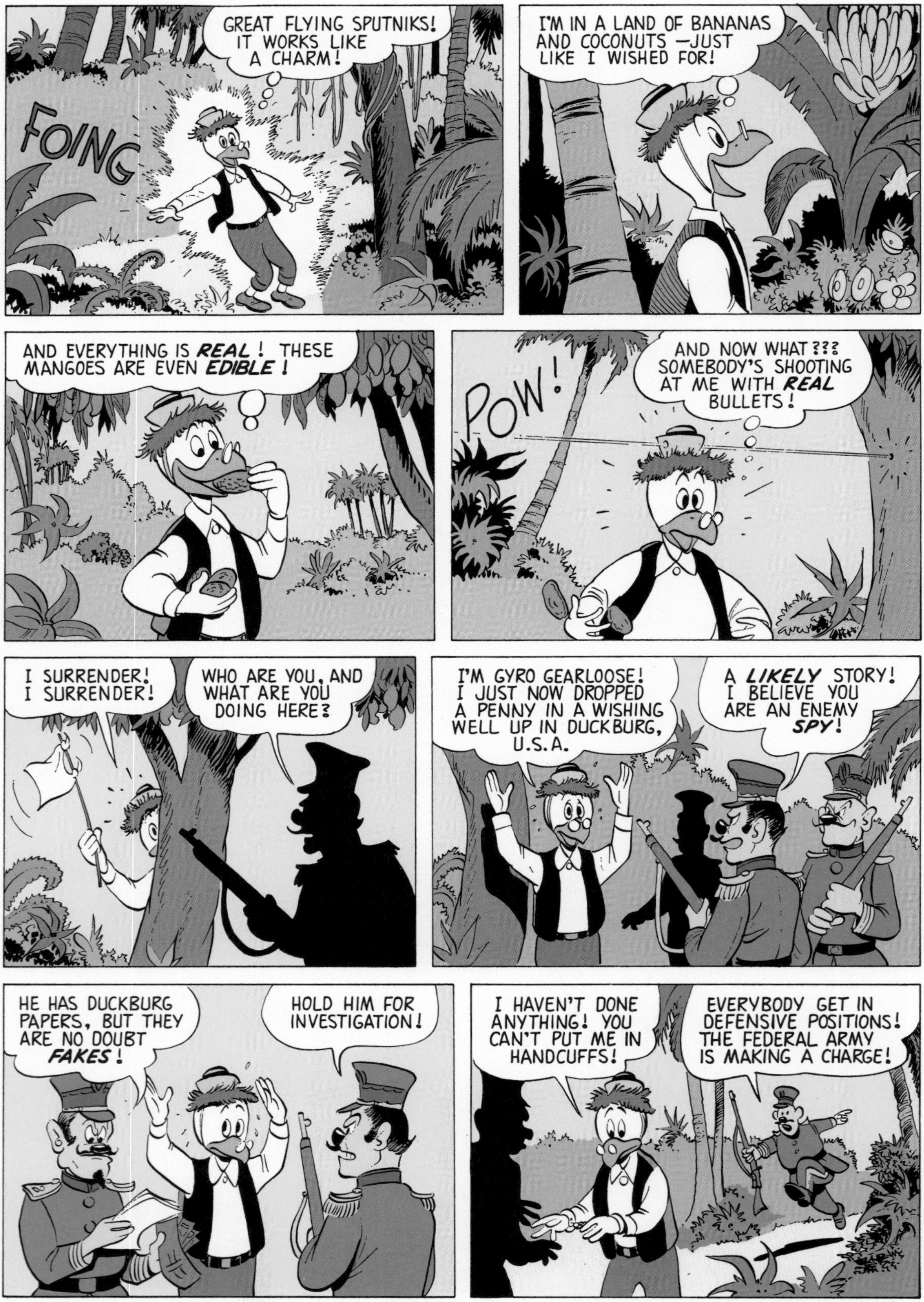
FOING
GREAT FLYING SPUTNIKS! IT WORKS LIKE A CHARM!
I'M IN A LAND OF BANANAS AND COCONUTS —JUST LIKE I WISHED FOR!
AND EVERYTHING IS ***REAL*** ! THESE MANGOES ARE EVEN ***EDIBLE*** !
POW!
AND NOW WHAT??? SOMEBODY'S SHOOTING AT ME WITH ***REAL*** BULLETS!
I SURRENDER! I SURRENDER!
WHO ARE YOU, AND WHAT ARE YOU DOING HERE?
I'M GYRO GEARLOOSE! I JUST NOW DROPPED A PENNY IN A WISHING WELL UP IN DUCKBURG, U.S.A.
A ***LIKELY*** STORY! I BELIEVE YOU ARE AN ENEMY ***SPY***!
HE HAS DUCKBURG PAPERS, BUT THEY ARE NO DOUBT ***FAKES*** !
HOLD HIM FOR INVESTIGATION!
I HAVEN'T DONE ANYTHING! YOU CAN'T PUT ME IN HANDCUFFS!
EVERYBODY GET IN DEFENSIVE POSITIONS! THE FEDERAL ARMY IS MAKING A CHARGE!

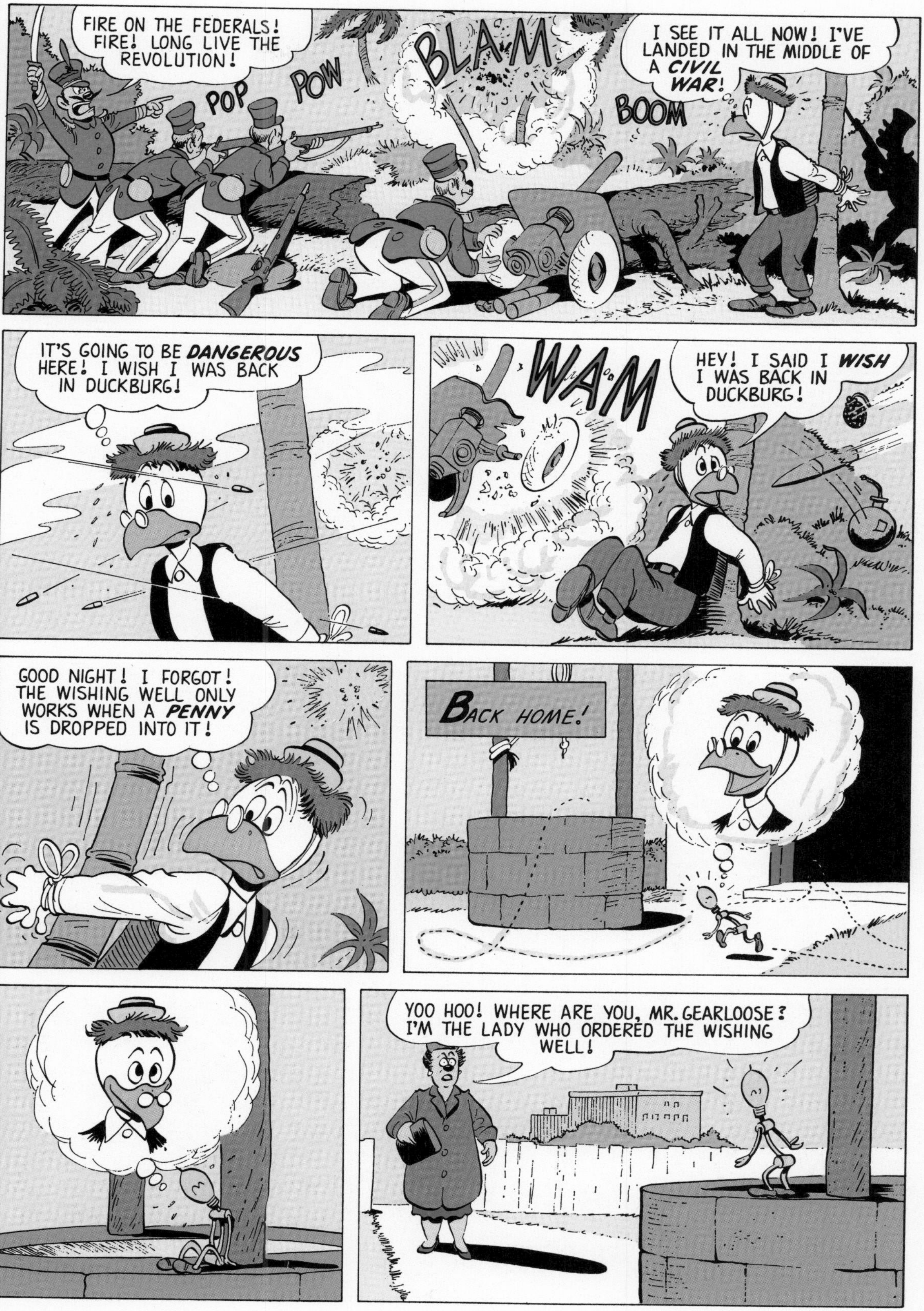
FIRE ON THE FEDERALS! FIRE! LONG LIVE THE REVOLUTION!
POP
POW
BLAM
BOOM
I SEE IT ALL NOW! I'VE LANDED IN THE MIDDLE OF A CIVIL WAR!
IT'S GOING TO BE DANGEROUS HERE! I WISH I WAS BACK IN DUCKBURG!
WAM
HEY! I SAID I WISH I WAS BACK IN DUCKBURG!
GOOD NIGHT! I FORGOT! THE WISHING WELL ONLY WORKS WHEN A PENNY IS DROPPED INTO IT!
BACK HOME!
YOO HOO! WHERE ARE YOU, MR. GEARLOOSE? I'M THE LADY WHO ORDERED THE WISHING WELL!

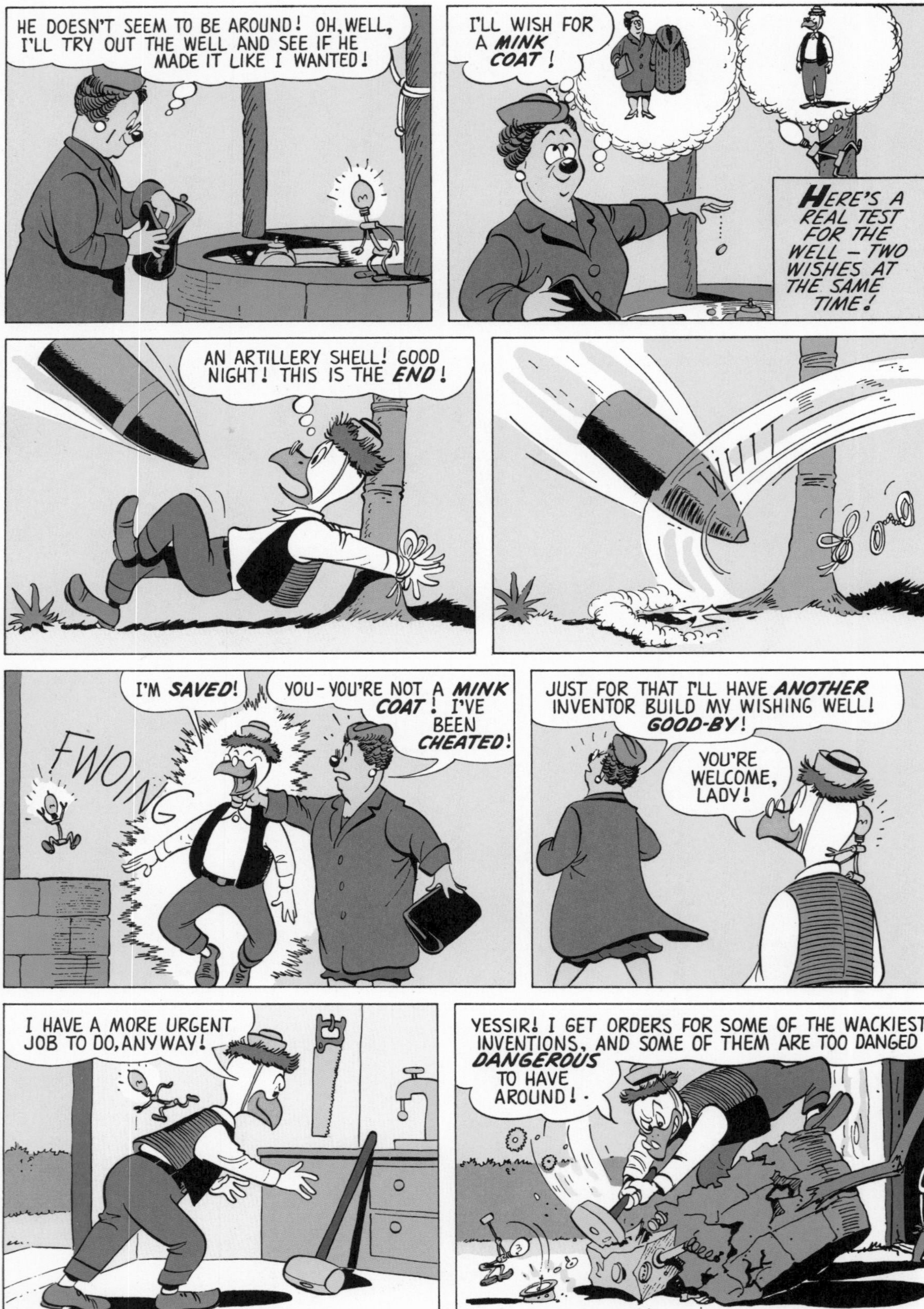
HE DOESN'T SEEM TO BE AROUND! OH, WELL, I'LL TRY OUT THE WELL AND SEE IF HE MADE IT LIKE I WANTED!
I'LL WISH FOR A MINK COAT!
HERE'S A REAL TEST FOR THE WELL — TWO WISHES AT THE SAME TIME!
AN ARTILLERY SHELL! GOOD NIGHT! THIS IS THE END!
WHIT
I'M SAVED!
FWOING
YOU-YOU'RE NOT A MINK COAT! I'VE BEEN CHEATED!
JUST FOR THAT I'LL HAVE ANOTHER INVENTOR BUILD MY WISHING WELL! GOOD-BY!
YOU'RE WELCOME, LADY!
I HAVE A MORE URGENT JOB TO DO, ANYWAY!
YESSIR! I GET ORDERS FOR SOME OF THE WACKIEST INVENTIONS, AND SOME OF THEM ARE TOO DANGED DANGEROUS TO HAVE AROUND!

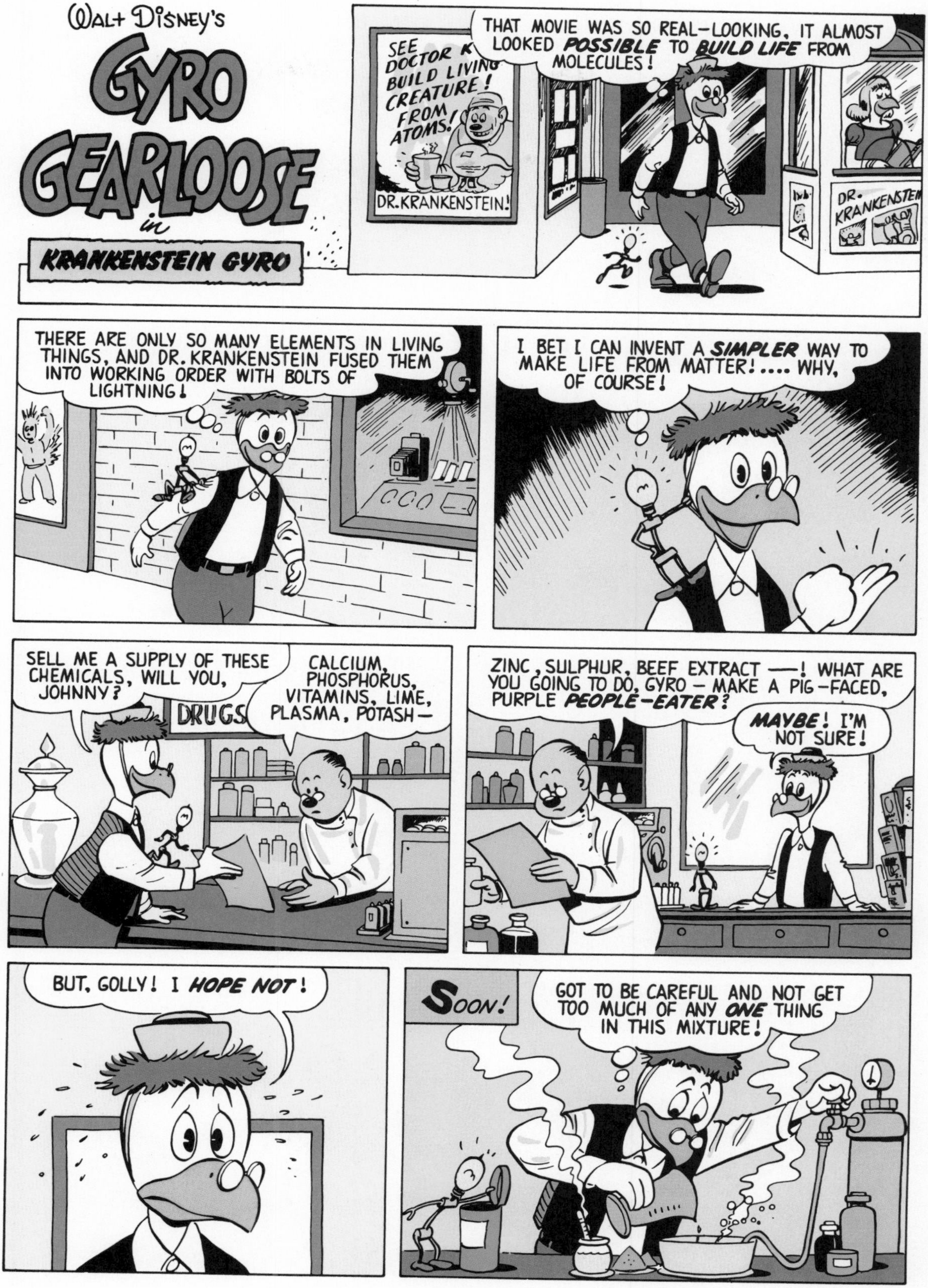
WALT DISNEY'S
GYRO GEARLOOSE
in
KRANKENSTEIN GYRO
SEE DOCTOR K BUILD LIVING CREATURE! FROM ATOMS!
DR. KRANKENSTEIN!
THAT MOVIE WAS SO REAL-LOOKING, IT ALMOST LOOKED POSSIBLE TO BUILD LIFE FROM MOLECULES!
DR. KRANKENSTEIN
THERE ARE ONLY SO MANY ELEMENTS IN LIVING THINGS, AND DR. KRANKENSTEIN FUSED THEM INTO WORKING ORDER WITH BOLTS OF LIGHTNING!
I BET I CAN INVENT A SIMPLER WAY TO MAKE LIFE FROM MATTER! .... WHY, OF COURSE!
SELL ME A SUPPLY OF THESE CHEMICALS, WILL YOU, JOHNNY?
CALCIUM, PHOSPHORUS, VITAMINS, LIME, PLASMA, POTASH—
DRUGS
ZINC, SULPHUR, BEEF EXTRACT —! WHAT ARE YOU GOING TO DO, GYRO – MAKE A PIG-FACED, PURPLE PEOPLE-EATER?
MAYBE! I'M NOT SURE!
BUT, GOLLY! I HOPE NOT!
SOON!
GOT TO BE CAREFUL AND NOT GET TOO MUCH OF ANY ONE THING IN THIS MIXTURE!

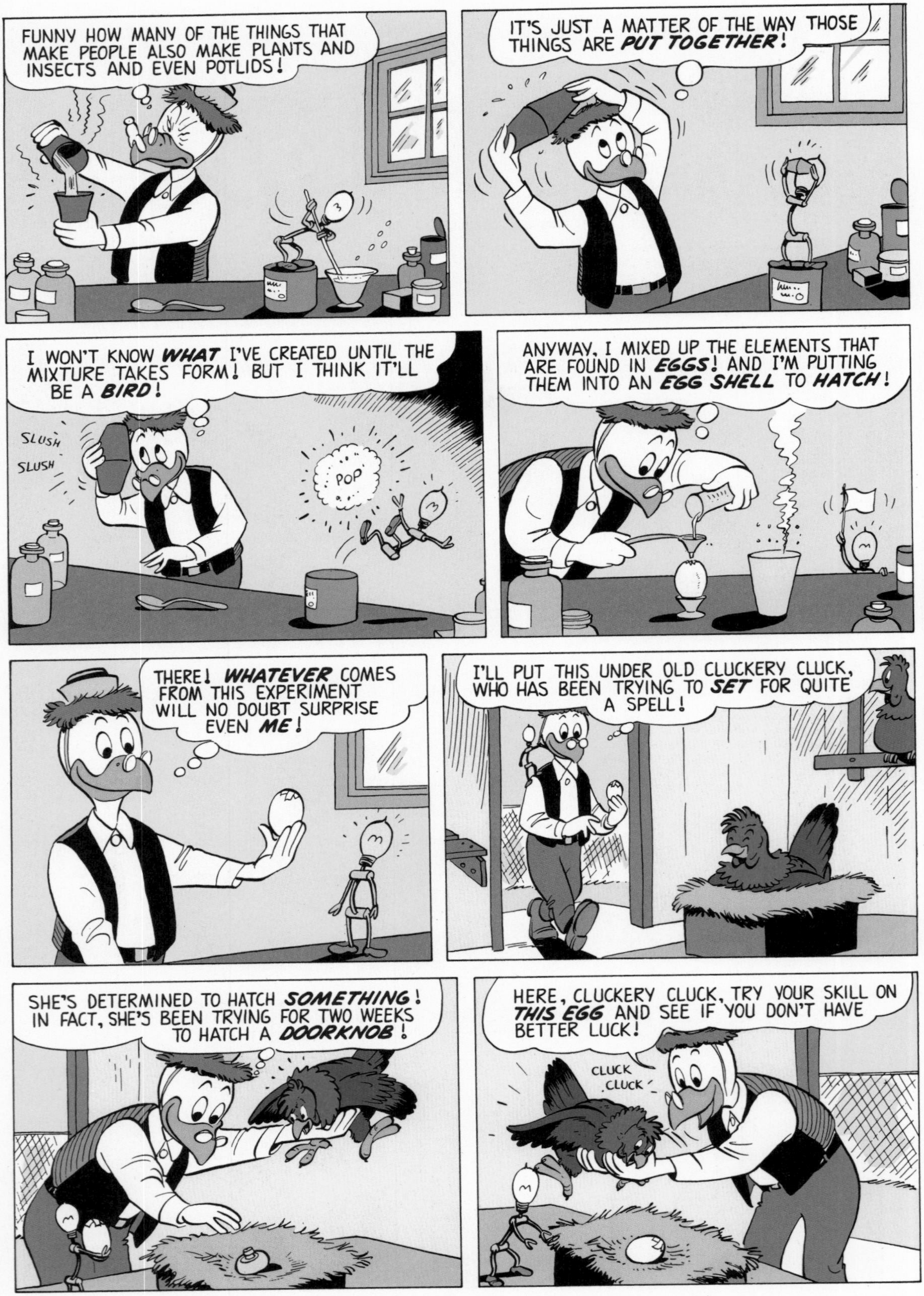
FUNNY HOW MANY OF THE THINGS THAT MAKE PEOPLE ALSO MAKE PLANTS AND INSECTS AND EVEN POTLIDS!
IT'S JUST A MATTER OF THE WAY THOSE THINGS ARE PUT TOGETHER!
I WON'T KNOW WHAT I'VE CREATED UNTIL THE MIXTURE TAKES FORM! BUT I THINK IT'LL BE A BIRD!
SLUSH
SLUSH
POP
ANYWAY, I MIXED UP THE ELEMENTS THAT ARE FOUND IN EGGS! AND I'M PUTTING THEM INTO AN EGG SHELL TO HATCH!
THERE! WHATEVER COMES FROM THIS EXPERIMENT WILL NO DOUBT SURPRISE EVEN ME!
I'LL PUT THIS UNDER OLD CLUCKERY CLUCK, WHO HAS BEEN TRYING TO SET FOR QUITE A SPELL!
SHE'S DETERMINED TO HATCH SOMETHING! IN FACT, SHE'S BEEN TRYING FOR TWO WEEKS TO HATCH A DOORKNOB!
HERE, CLUCKERY CLUCK, TRY YOUR SKILL ON THIS EGG AND SEE IF YOU DON'T HAVE BETTER LUCK!
CLUCK
CLUCK

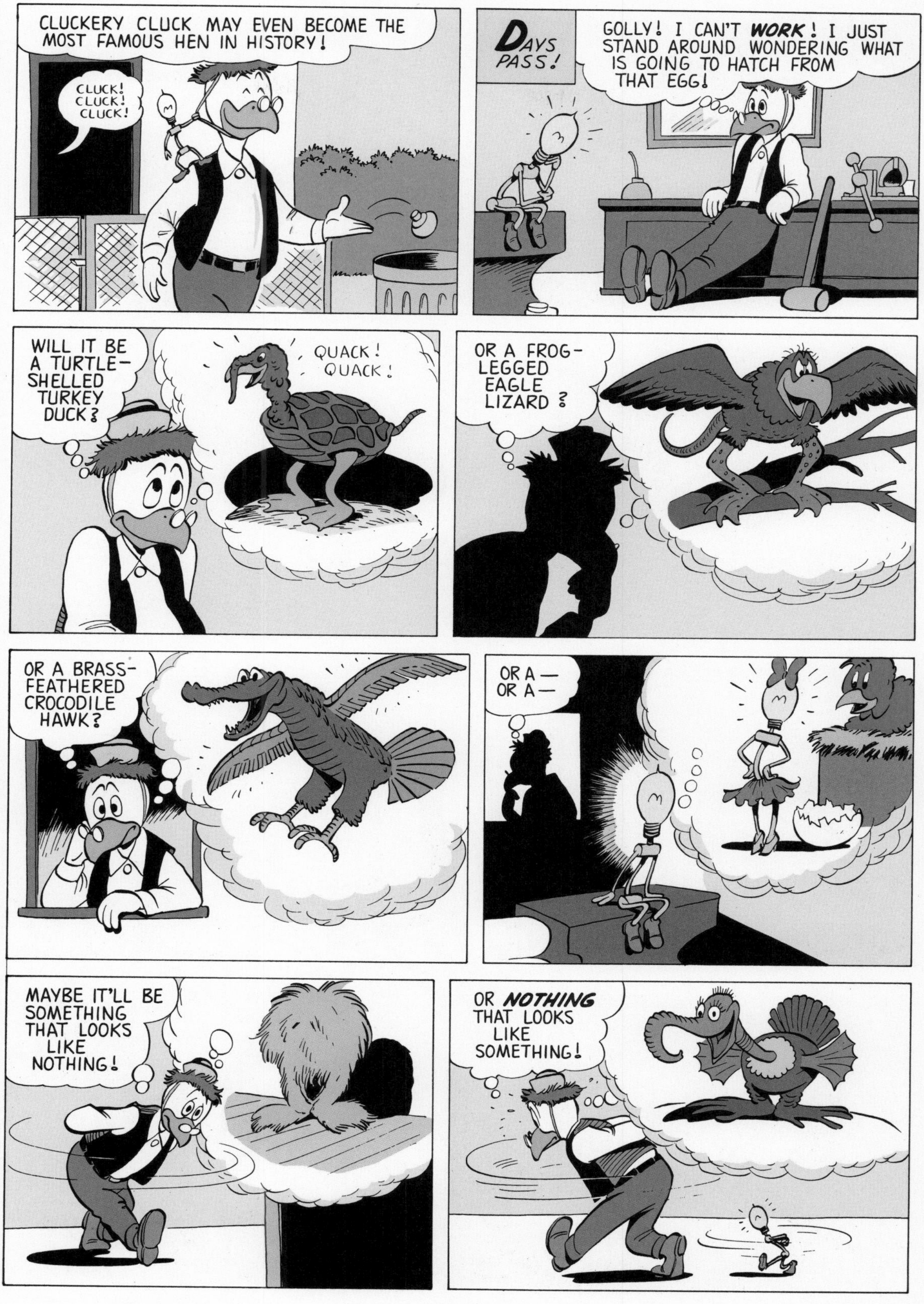
CLUCKERY CLUCK MAY EVEN BECOME THE MOST FAMOUS HEN IN HISTORY!
CLUCK! CLUCK! CLUCK!
DAYS PASS!
GOLLY! I CAN'T WORK! I JUST STAND AROUND WONDERING WHAT IS GOING TO HATCH FROM THAT EGG!
WILL IT BE A TURTLE-SHELLED TURKEY DUCK?
QUACK! QUACK!
OR A FROG-LEGGED EAGLE LIZARD?
OR A BRASS-FEATHERED CROCODILE HAWK?
OR A— OR A—
MAYBE IT'LL BE SOMETHING THAT LOOKS LIKE NOTHING!
OR NOTHING THAT LOOKS LIKE SOMETHING!

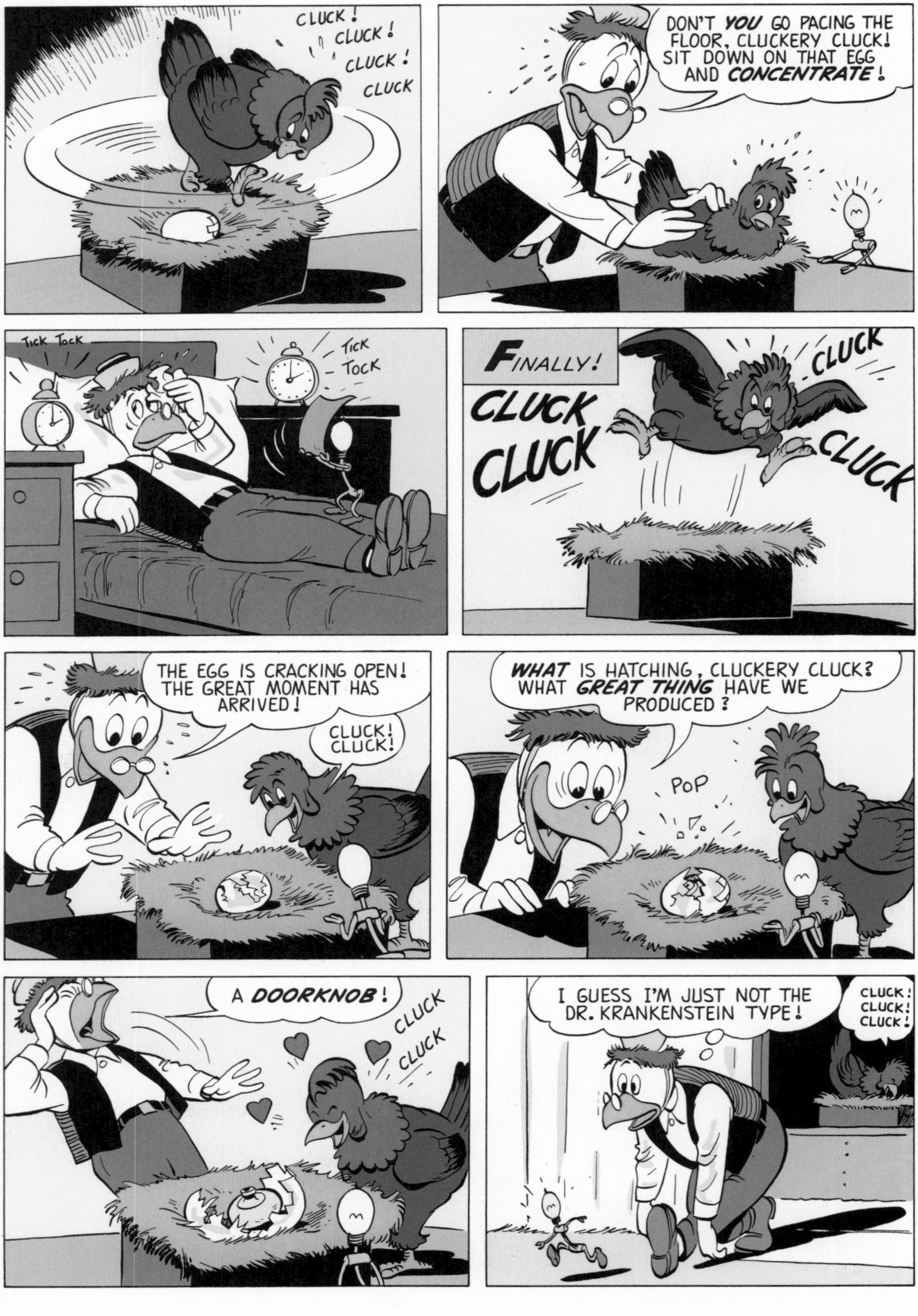
CLUCK!
CLUCK!
CLUCK!
CLUCK
DON'T YOU GO PACING THE FLOOR, CLUCKERY CLUCK! SIT DOWN ON THAT EGG AND CONCENTRATE!
TICK TOCK
TICK
TOCK
FINALLY!
CLUCK
CLUCK
CLUCK
CLUCK
THE EGG IS CRACKING OPEN! THE GREAT MOMENT HAS ARRIVED!
CLUCK! CLUCK!
WHAT IS HATCHING, CLUCKERY CLUCK? WHAT GREAT THING HAVE WE PRODUCED?
POP
A DOORKNOB!
CLUCK
CLUCK
I GUESS I'M JUST NOT THE DR. KRANKENSTEIN TYPE!
CLUCK!
CLUCK!
CLUCK!

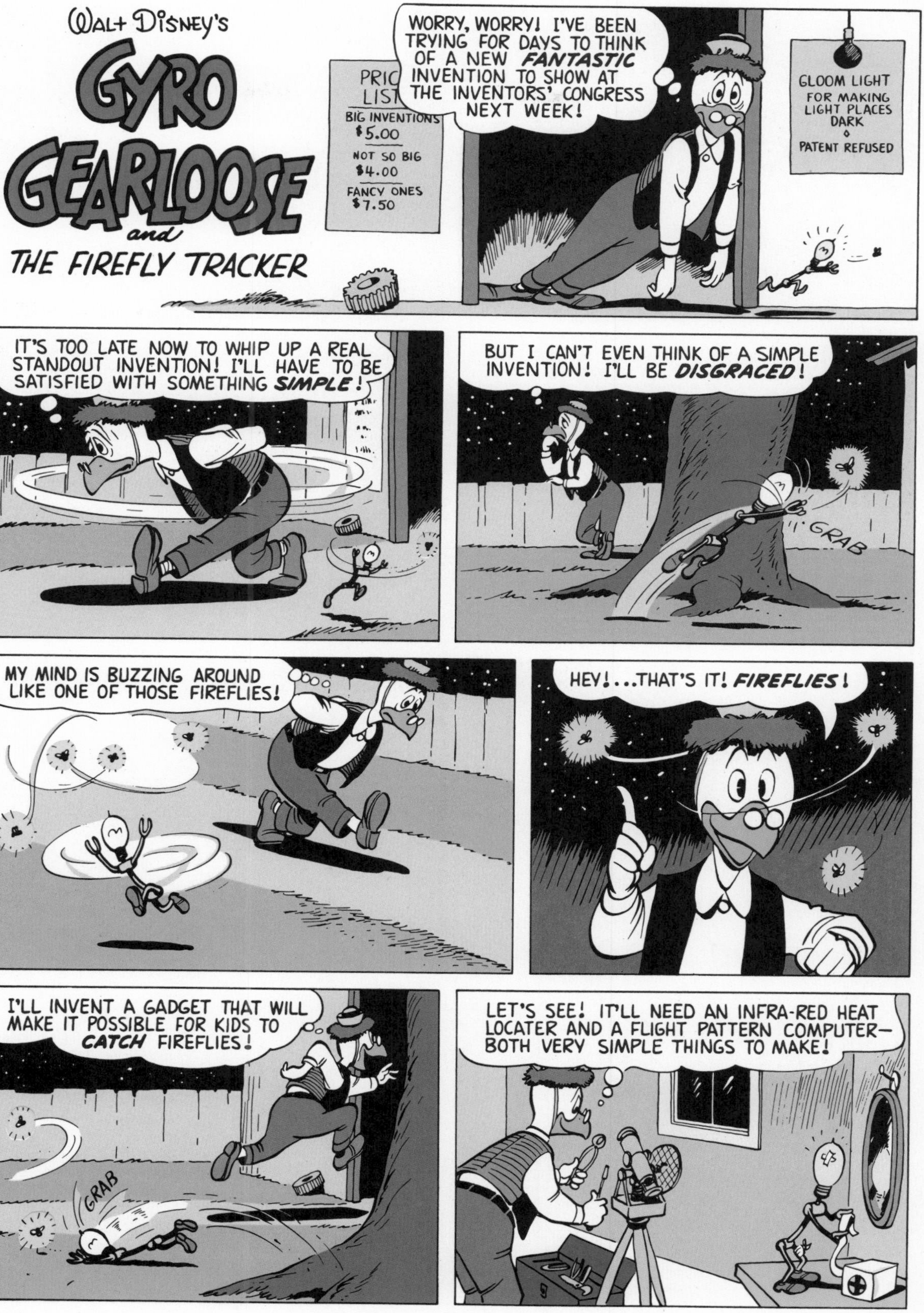
WALT DISNEY'S
GYRO GEARLOOSE
and
THE FIREFLY TRACKER
PRIC
LIST
BIG INVENTIONS $5.00
NOT SO BIG $4.00
FANCY ONES $7.50
WORRY, WORRY! I'VE BEEN TRYING FOR DAYS TO THINK OF A NEW FANTASTIC INVENTION TO SHOW AT THE INVENTORS' CONGRESS NEXT WEEK!
GLOOM LIGHT FOR MAKING LIGHT PLACES DARK
PATENT REFUSED
IT'S TOO LATE NOW TO WHIP UP A REAL STANDOUT INVENTION! I'LL HAVE TO BE SATISFIED WITH SOMETHING SIMPLE!
BUT I CAN'T EVEN THINK OF A SIMPLE INVENTION! I'LL BE DISGRACED!
GRAB
MY MIND IS BUZZING AROUND LIKE ONE OF THOSE FIREFLIES!
HEY!...THAT'S IT! FIREFLIES!
I'LL INVENT A GADGET THAT WILL MAKE IT POSSIBLE FOR KIDS TO CATCH FIREFLIES!
GRAB
LET'S SEE! IT'LL NEED AN INFRA-RED HEAT LOCATER AND A FLIGHT PATTERN COMPUTER— BOTH VERY SIMPLE THINGS TO MAKE!

NOW BATTERIES TO RUN THE *TRACKER* AND *CHART MARKER*!

I'LL TRY IT OUT ON THESE PESKY FIREFLIES OUTSIDE!

GADGET, DRAW A SIGHT ON THAT GLOWING LITTLE DODGER AND TELL ME *WHERE* HE'LL BE IN *SEVEN SECONDS*!

THE INDICATOR SAYS ONE FOOT BEHIND AND TWO INCHES TO THE LEFT OF POINT ZERO!

CLICK CLICK

HEY! THAT'S RIGHT WHERE *I* AM!

SWAT

I DID IT! I INVENTED SOMETHING THAT NOBODY CAN SAY ISN'T FANTASTIC!

CLICK CLICK

CLICK CLICK CLICK

GADGET SAYS FIREFLY WILL BE *HERE*!

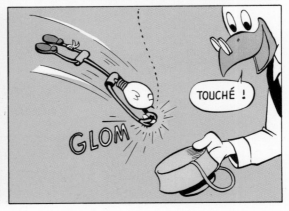

TOUCHÉ!

GLOM

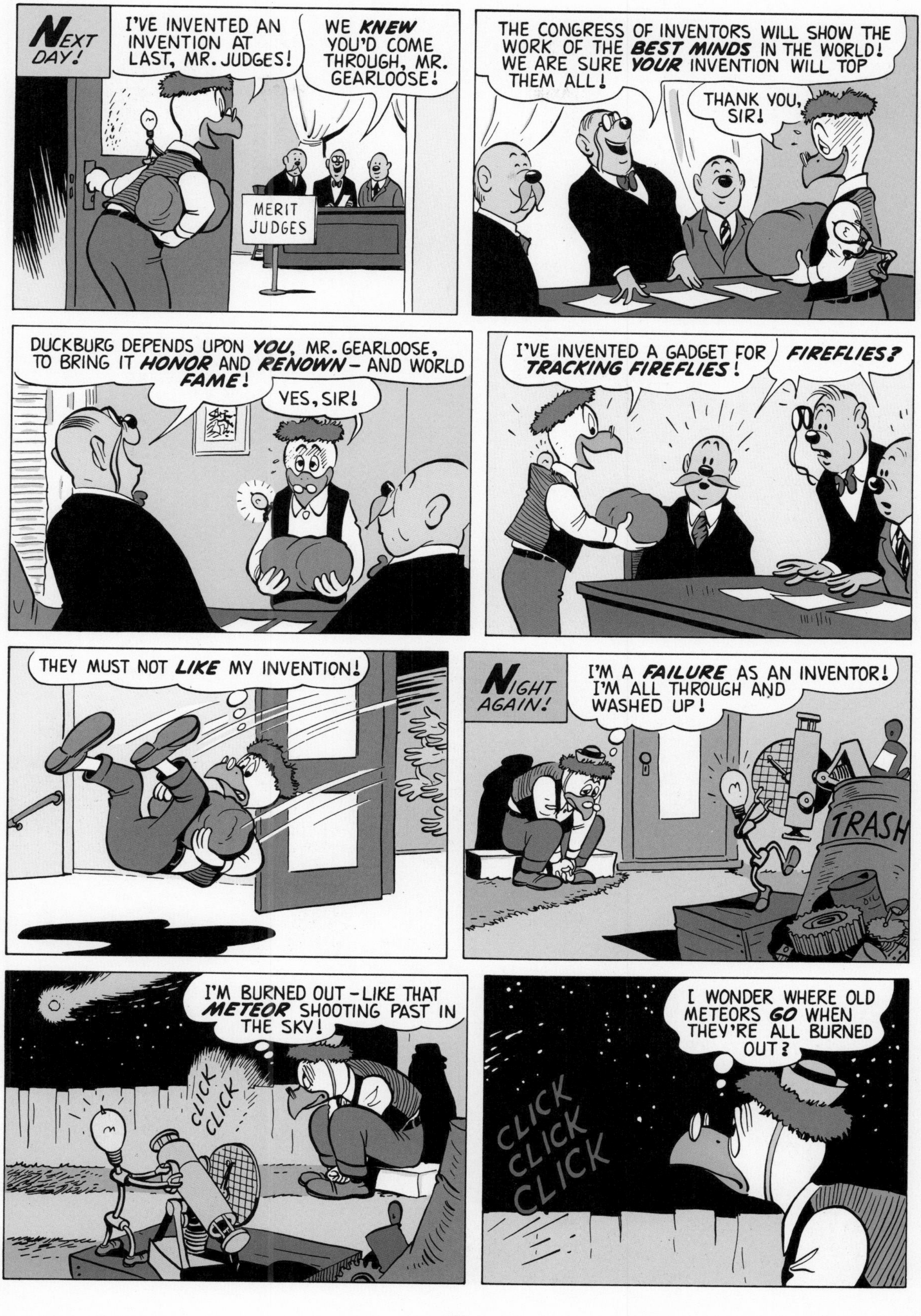
NEXT DAY!
I'VE INVENTED AN INVENTION AT LAST, MR. JUDGES!
WE KNEW YOU'D COME THROUGH, MR. GEARLOOSE!
MERIT JUDGES
THE CONGRESS OF INVENTORS WILL SHOW THE WORK OF THE BEST MINDS IN THE WORLD! WE ARE SURE YOUR INVENTION WILL TOP THEM ALL!
THANK YOU, SIR!
DUCKBURG DEPENDS UPON YOU, MR. GEARLOOSE, TO BRING IT HONOR AND RENOWN – AND WORLD FAME!
YES, SIR!
I'VE INVENTED A GADGET FOR TRACKING FIREFLIES!
FIREFLIES?
THEY MUST NOT LIKE MY INVENTION!
NIGHT AGAIN!
I'M A FAILURE AS AN INVENTOR! I'M ALL THROUGH AND WASHED UP!
TRASH
I'M BURNED OUT – LIKE THAT METEOR SHOOTING PAST IN THE SKY!
CLICK CLICK
I WONDER WHERE OLD METEORS GO WHEN THEY'RE ALL BURNED OUT?
CLICK CLICK CLICK

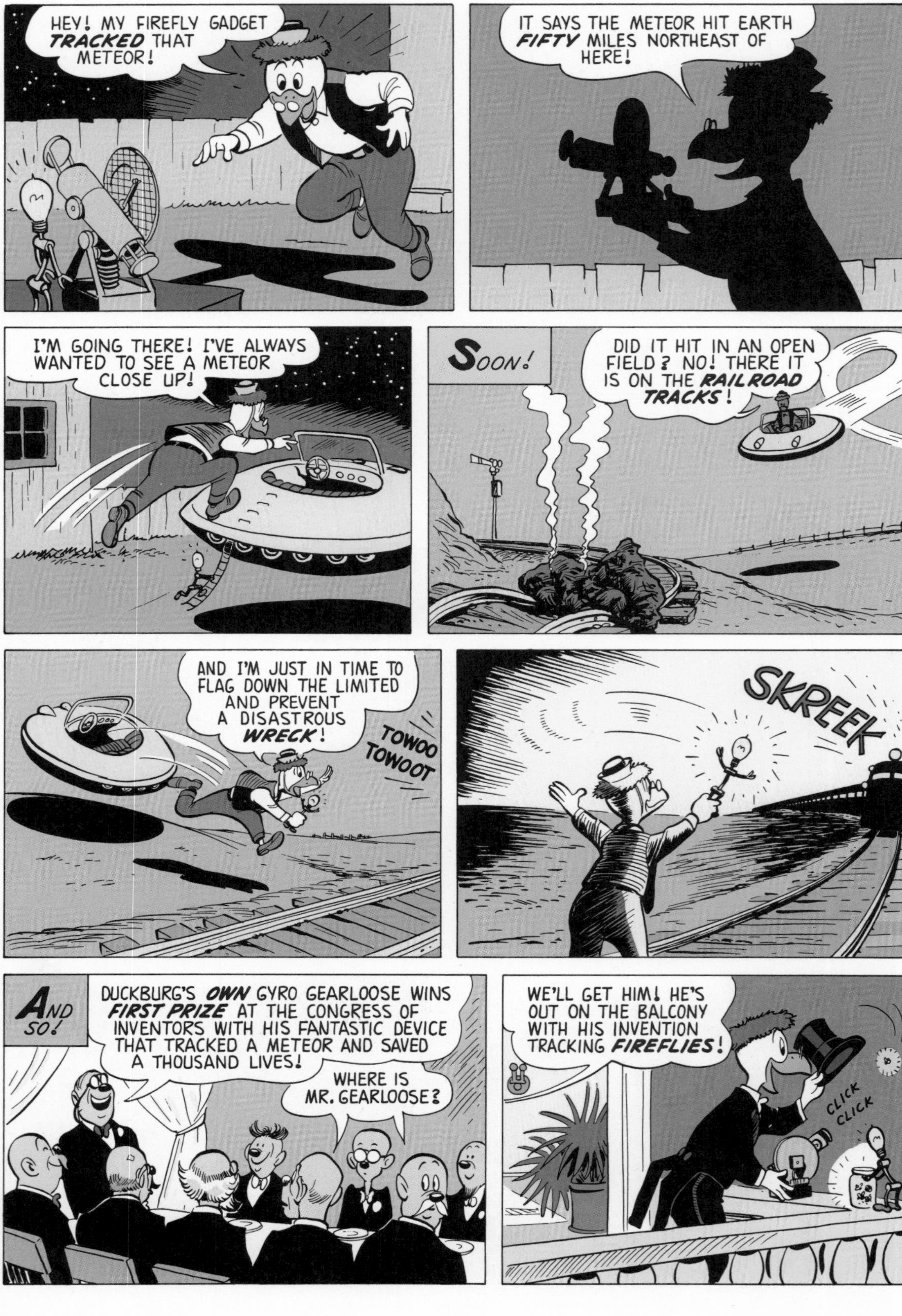
HEY! MY FIREFLY GADGET TRACKED THAT METEOR!
IT SAYS THE METEOR HIT EARTH FIFTY MILES NORTHEAST OF HERE!
I'M GOING THERE! I'VE ALWAYS WANTED TO SEE A METEOR CLOSE UP!
SOON!
DID IT HIT IN AN OPEN FIELD? NO! THERE IT IS ON THE RAILROAD TRACKS!
AND I'M JUST IN TIME TO FLAG DOWN THE LIMITED AND PREVENT A DISASTROUS WRECK!
TOWOO TOWOOT
SKREEK
AND SO!
DUCKBURG'S OWN GYRO GEARLOOSE WINS FIRST PRIZE AT THE CONGRESS OF INVENTORS WITH HIS FANTASTIC DEVICE THAT TRACKED A METEOR AND SAVED A THOUSAND LIVES!
WHERE IS MR. GEARLOOSE?
WE'LL GET HIM! HE'S OUT ON THE BALCONY WITH HIS INVENTION TRACKING FIREFLIES!
CLICK CLICK

SEPT.-NOV.

Walt Disney's UNCLE $CROOGE

10¢

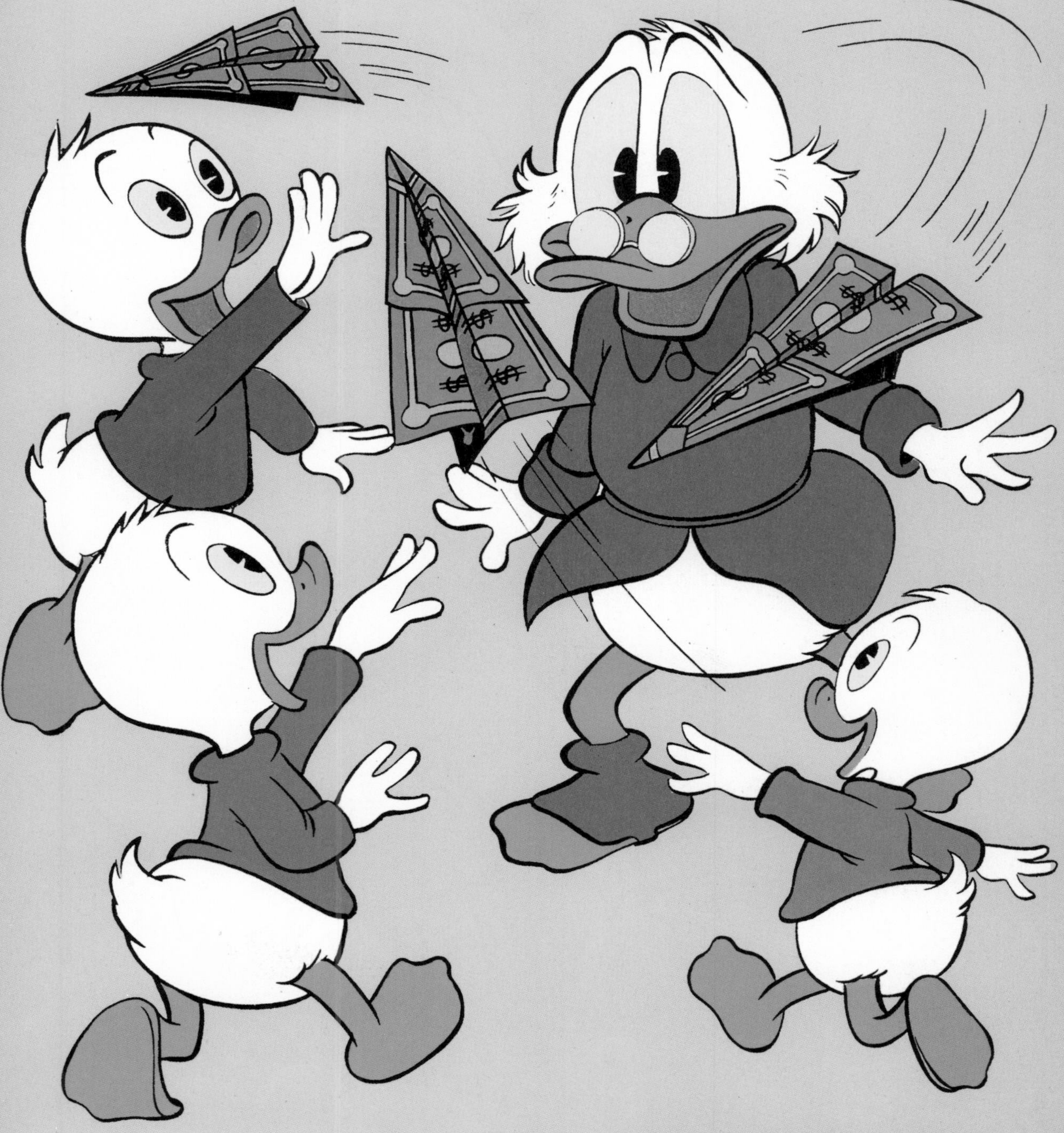

Walt Disney's

Still 10¢

UNCLE $CROOGE

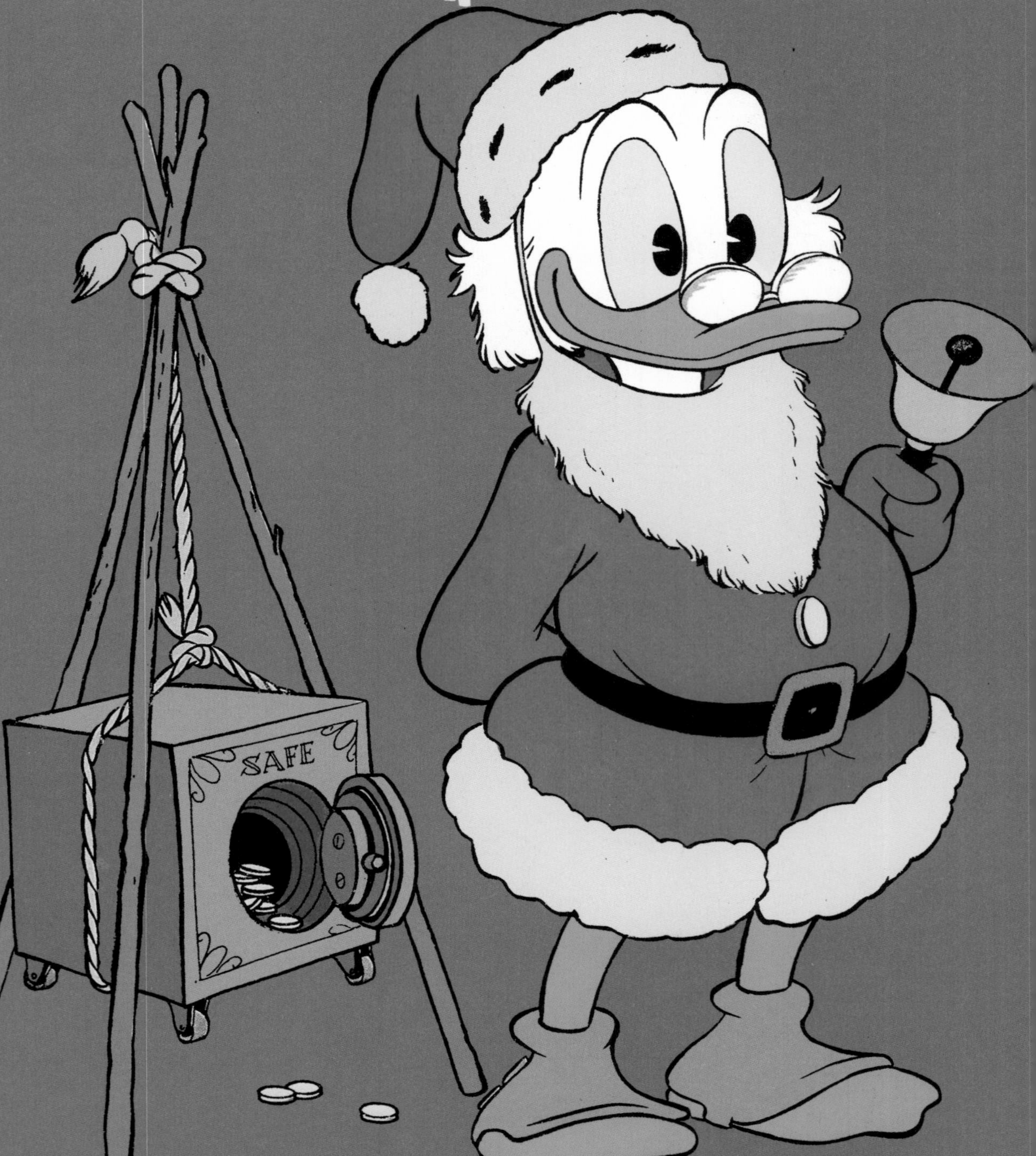
SAFE

Story Notes

UNCLE SCROOGE AND THE TWENTY-FOUR CARAT MOON *p. 1*

The premise behind Carl Barks's "Uncle Scrooge and the Twenty-four Carat Moon" (p. 1) is as ludicrous as it is delightful — that hiding behind our familiar moon is a smaller moon made not of green cheese, but of solid gold. Naturally, Uncle Scrooge is lured to it like a moth to a flame, but so are other tycoons from around the world — as well as some very familiar crooks — all of whom build custom rockets to fly there so that they can be the first to stake a claim. It's the California Gold Rush in space! (Note that Barks's story was written eleven years before the first moon landing, and as such, it is pure science fiction.)

The rocket race between the Ducks and their adversaries is brimming with delightful gags, from the fat rocket of the greedy Scrooge who wants to bring back as much gold as possible to the threatening shark-shaped rocket of the Beagle Boys. In all the skirmishes, Scrooge emerges victorious, but only due to the creativity and resourcefulness of his nephews. When they finally do land to claim the golden moon, they discover that someone else has already beaten them to it — a settler from the planet Venus!

It's a classic Barks parable, in which we discover that wealth isn't all it's cracked up to be. This King Midas lesson is a recurring theme in Barks's work — see, for example, the classic "The Magic Hourglass" (Volume 9 in this series, *Walt Disney's Donald Duck: "The Pixilated Parrot"*), another memorable masterpiece in which the Ducks discover how worthless a lake full of diamonds can be when all you really need is a sip of water.

But in "The Twenty-four Carat Moon," Barks goes one step farther. Besides showing us that gold, per se, isn't worth much when it's

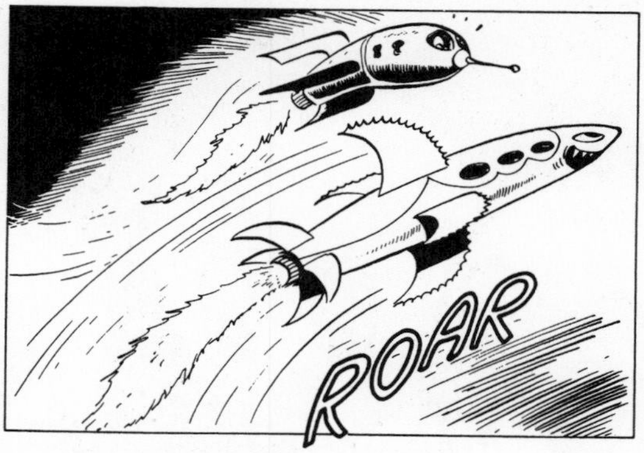
ROAR

all you have, he also shows us the true value of something we ordinarily take for granted — a fistful of dirt. Because the dirt contains practically every element in the periodic table, the Venusian can create an entire world from it using his "magnetic attracter."

That miraculous machine, by the way, shows Barks's genius as a storyteller. It's just a small throwaway detail in the economy of this story, but it opens up so many narrative possibilities that the imagination of the reader wanders off, conjuring alternative developments and endings suggested by this single creative spark.

Barks's wise message is that true wealth is to be found in everyday life — we must discover it in the simple things that surround us (dirt), rather than chasing implausible treasures (a moon made of gold).

— LEONARDO GORI AND FRANCESCO STAJANO

UNCLE SCROOGE AND THE STRANGE SHIPWRECKS *p. 23*

Carl Barks bends the genres of slapstick, mystery, horror, and high-seas adventure to distinctly surreal effect in this overtly

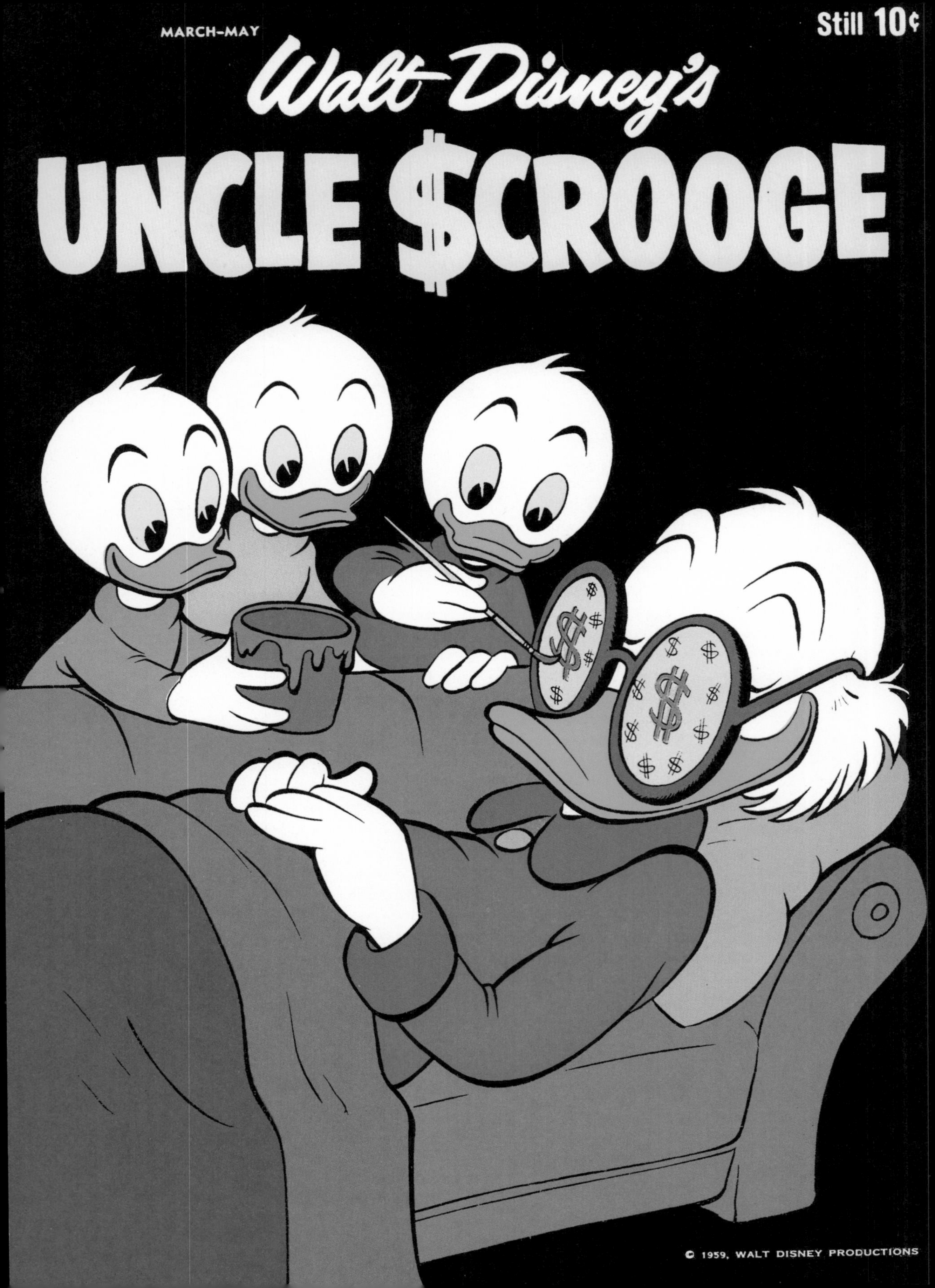
MARCH–MAY
Still 10¢
Walt Disney's
UNCLE $CROOGE
© 1959, WALT DISNEY PRODUCTIONS

self-reflexive story. Fundamentally about deception and delusion, it is emblematic of a period in which he was subverting both the naturalistic splendor and the mythic grandeur of his previous Scrooge stories with what seems like deliberately preposterous flights of fancy that dare you to take him at face value.

Motifs and devices are untethered from logic to further this exercise in self-parody. In an echo of that earlier nightmarish tale about mysterious shipwrecks, "No Such Varmint" (see *Volume 10, Walt Disney's Donald Duck: "Terror of the Beagle Boys"*), Donald has convinced himself that he is a great detective, but he is unable to make sense of the greasy rubber marks he finds everywhere.

And, as if aware of their usual shortcomings in the disguise department, the Beagle Boys have taken extra care to hide their domino masks and to shave their stubble. But they have forgotten about their white gloves, they still dress identically, and they fail to suppress their tendency to double up with each other, even for simple tasks. Their spectacularly weird, pepper-induced unmasking comes during a food fight that recalls the first-act set piece of "The Secret of Atlantis" (see Volume 12, *Walt Disney's Uncle Scrooge: "Only a Poor Old Man"*).

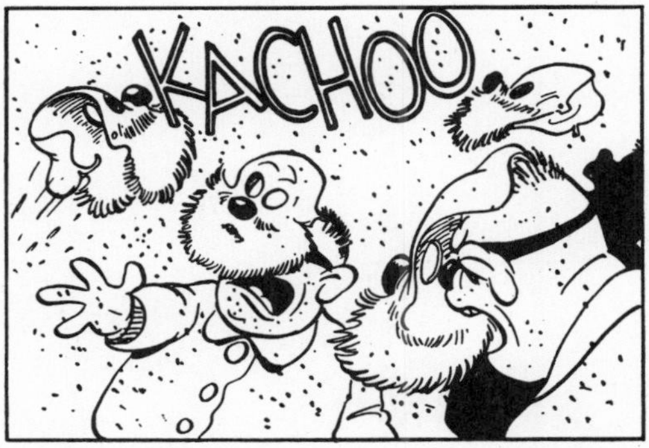
KACHOO

On the list of his works for Western Publishing that Barks compiled in 1969, he noted that this story "... was stretched from a short one by Nick George." Nick George (1910–1977) was a colleague from Barks's animation days at Disney Studios in the early 1940s, and one imagines a film synopsis of his being the source material here. It's hard to say, but it

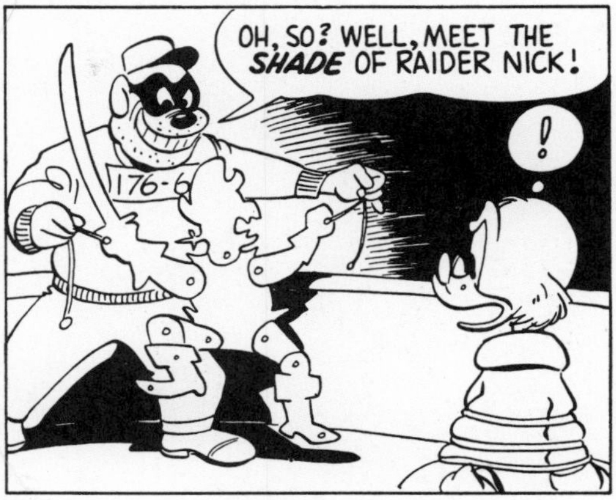
OH, SO? WELL, MEET THE *SHADE* OF RAIDER NICK!
!
176-6

seems likely that George provided Barks with the premise of a fake ghost ship — the design of the Raider Nick dummy, for one, seems uncharacteristically corny for Barks, as if it were a visitor from a neighboring storyworld. That the Beagles' expensive lure essentially consists of an inflatable dummy and a cardboard jumping jack, however, is surely a Barksian touch, and provides an ironic contrast to the more genuinely "horriferocius" *Flying Dutchman* that Barks would introduce six months later (see p. 75).

Barks obviously improvised much of the rest, to incoherent if often delightful effect — the patiently built, rhythmically paced setup to Scrooge literally hitting the ceiling is masterful slapstick. Scrooge chasing Donald on a high wire for two panels is a strange non-sequitur. And then there is the surprising fatalism of the Beagles morbidly joking with each other about warm chairs with built-in heating systems. As they red-facedly and endearingly acknowledge elsewhere in the story, crime clearly does not pay.

Indeed, the Beagles are ultimately foiled — as they so often are — by the nephews, who appropriate the beacon used to create the illusion of a supernatural threat and expose the hollow rubber hoax. The giant black arrow the kids insert stands out on the page almost like a glyph of illuminated rationality, warding off the ghosts of past ideas that have haunted the story.

— MATTHIAS WIVEL

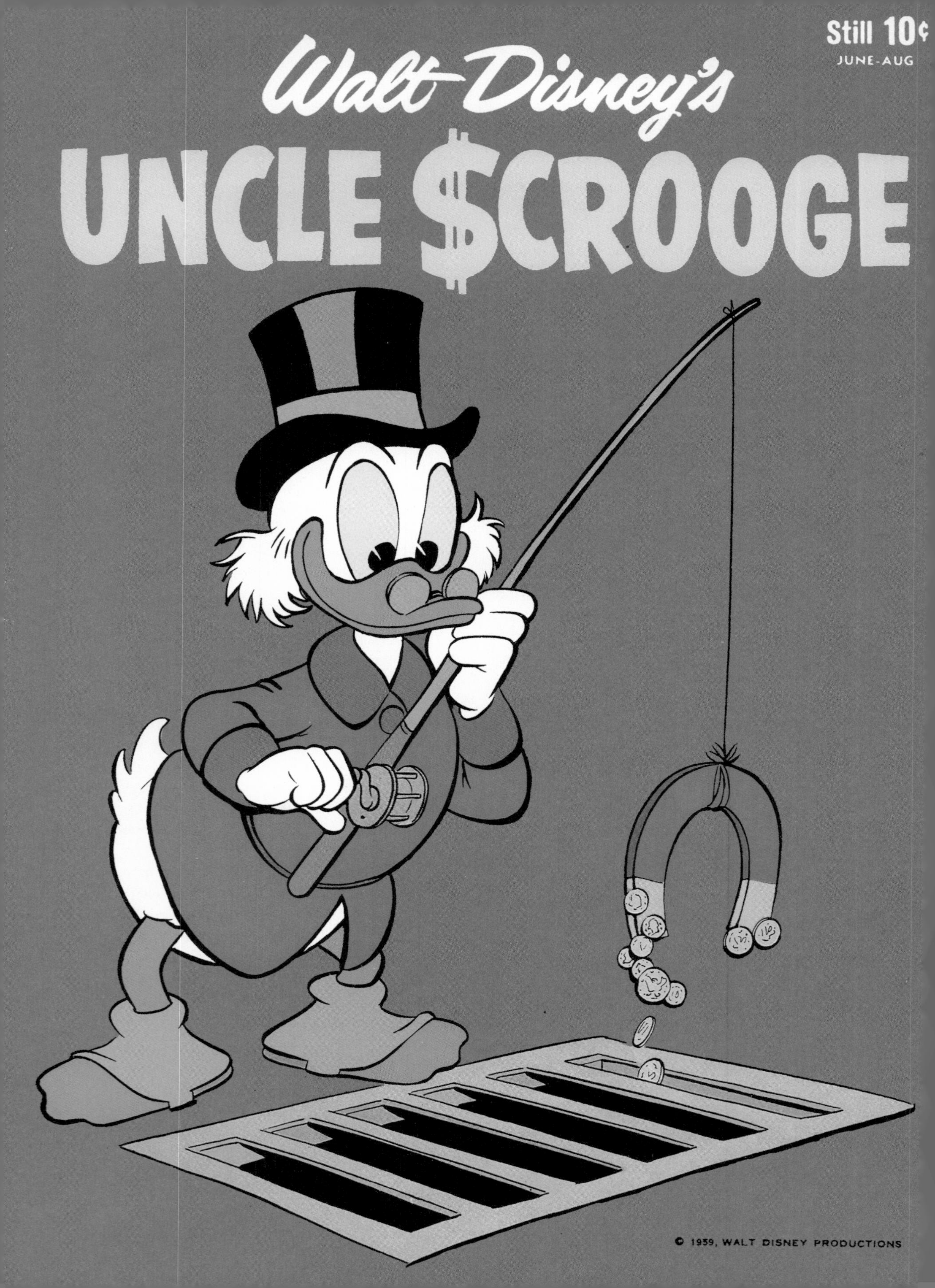
Still 10¢
JUNE-AUG
Walt Disney's
UNCLE $CROOGE
© 1959, WALT DISNEY PRODUCTIONS

UNCLE SCROOGE AND THE FABULOUS TYCOON *p. 45*

At five pages, "Uncle Scrooge and the Fabulous Tycoon" is an odd length for a Carl Barks story. Like the even shorter Gyro Gearloose entries in this volume, it demands more than a simple joke, but it doesn't support an involved story. Nonetheless, working with that constraint, Barks admirably fits narrative content to frame.

Structure is streamlined — a quick set-up and swift resolution are sandwiched around a string of linked gags (which themselves call back to antique novelty postcards that depict harvesting gigantic fruits and vegetables or catching impossibly large fish). What evolves is a portrait of each of the characters.

Gullible Donald grows increasingly wowed before being decisively enlightened. Longhorn Tallgrass (who bears more than a passing resemblance to the Cattle King in "Twenty-four Carat Moon") revels in his braggadocio, only to be effectively deflated. Apart from a preliminary outburst, Scrooge bides his time, scrutinizing it all, unflappable. After all, how often has he prevailed in grander contests of amassed wealth? (You can find at least one such story in this very volume.)

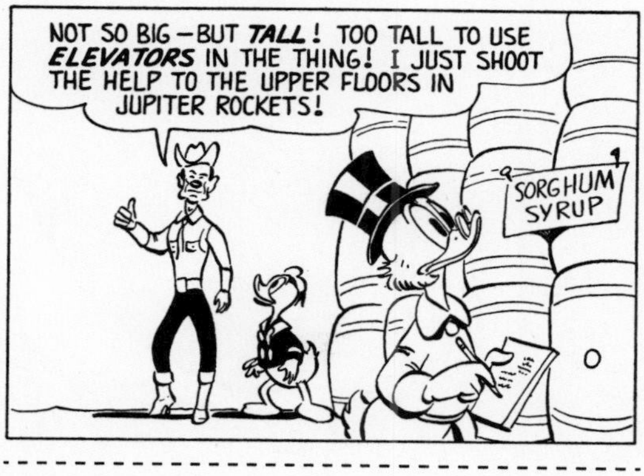
NOT SO BIG—BUT *TALL*! TOO TALL TO USE *ELEVATORS* IN THE THING! I JUST SHOOT THE HELP TO THE UPPER FLOORS IN JUPITER ROCKETS!
SORGHUM SYRUP

In simplified structure, character development, extended middle, and authoritative ending, "The Fabulous Tycoon" harkens back to the Book of Job. As in the biblical text, Longhorn struts his success before Scrooge (far less thunderously than the Whirlwind) sets him straight. Scrooge's just-the-facts revelation of Longhorn's origin echoes the biblical Voice's question, "Where were you when I set the foundations of the world?" — without, of course, any of the original's theological and philosophical significance.

— RICH KREINER

THE FORBIDIUM MONEY BIN *p. 51*

From the bloated money bin in the opening panel to Scrooge's closing "custard pie" conniption, this story is a Barksian gem. Scrooge and Gyro are Carl Barks's most celebrated and successful creations, but they rarely team up, and their interactions throughout this (literally) shoot-for-the-moon tale are genuinely hilarious from panel one.

Gearloose's easy genius and unflappable manners provide an intriguing shift away from the manic panics that drive most of Scrooge's adventures with Donald and the nephews. Instead, there is a slow-burn, deadpan, Laurel-and-Hardy quality to the way that Gyro graciously accepts his payment when Scrooge nonchalantly hands over a pail full of cash.

What's more, it's a pretty darned fun adventure, free of the added shenanigans and ethnic grotesques that sometimes clog or compromise Barks's satiric drive. Published in 1958, post–Sputnik 1 (which was launched October 4, 1957), Barks gets in several digs about delays in the American space program, the extremes of space travel, and the ridiculous notions of wildcat drilling on the moon for new riches and resources.

The very name of Gyro's newest mega-metal alloy, forbidium, provides a subtle hint of menace, but Scrooge and Gyro's discovery of the super-dense comet head on the moon leads to the very disaster that Gyro had developed forbidium to prevent.

Meanwhile, readers are treated to a number of original gags and gaffs, including a prospecting mosquito-like rocket ship, a cadre of snarky wisecracking reporters, and most deliciously of all, the bizarre sequence wherein Scrooge decides to blot out his original tattoo with a concealing new image. There may not

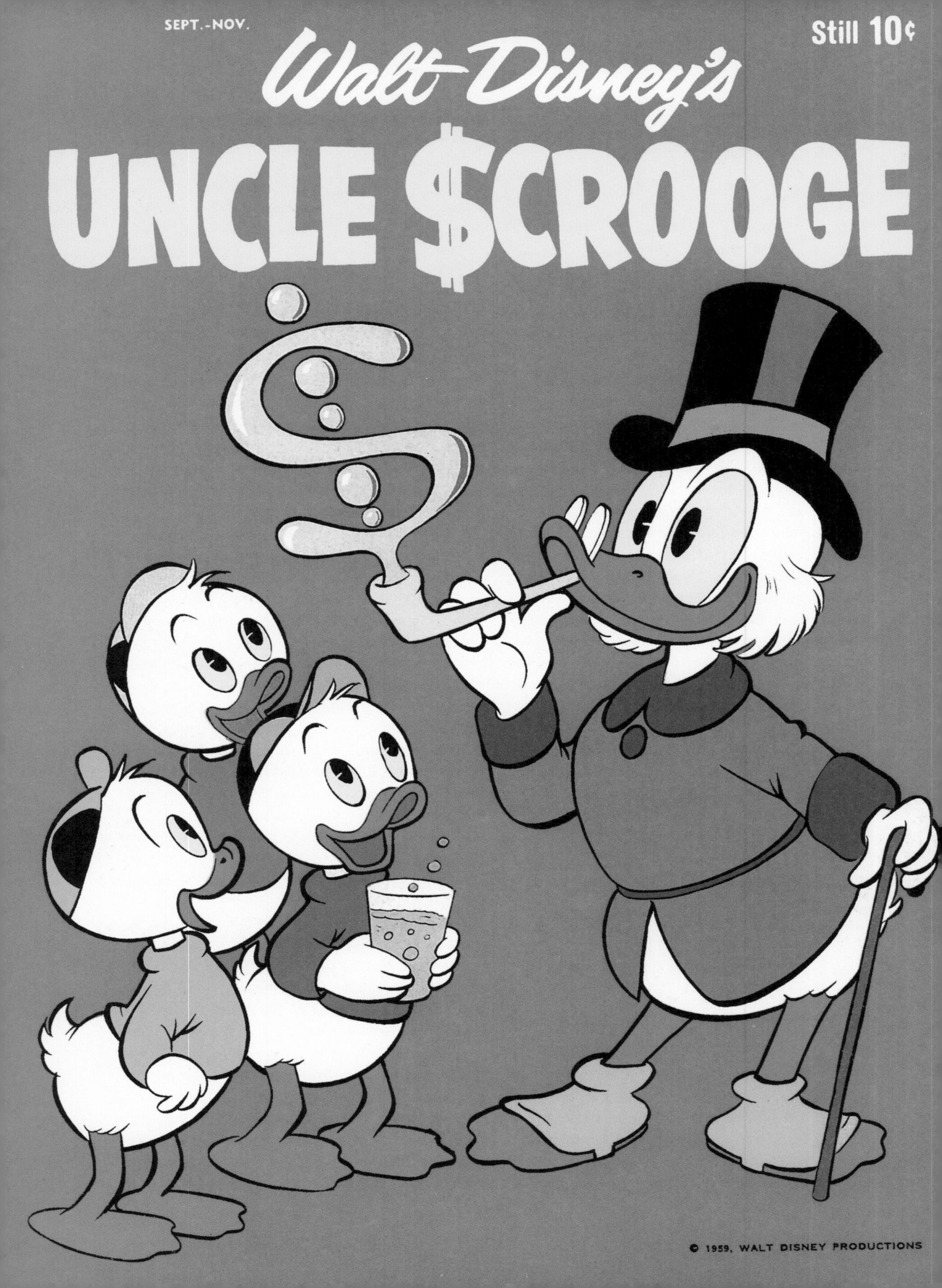
SEPT.-NOV.
Still 10¢
Walt Disney's
UNCLE $CROOGE
© 1959, WALT DISNEY PRODUCTIONS

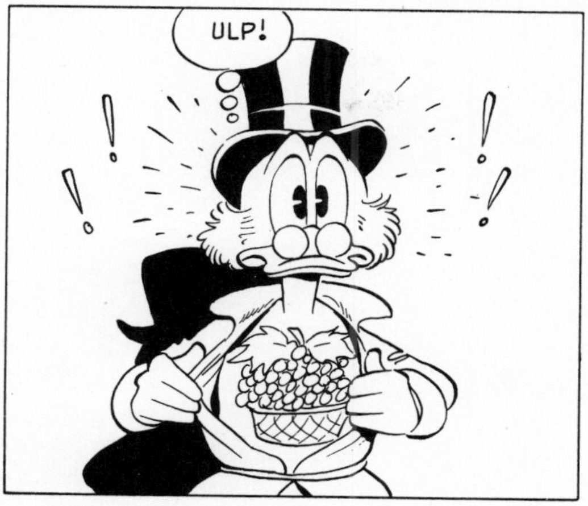
ULP!

be a single panel in Barks's work as hilariously outré as the one revealing Scrooge's basket of plump, purple grapes rampant across his bared chest. It's certainly one of Barks's most outlandish and inscrutable images, and perhaps in some ways, an accurate metaphor for his use of incongruous pairings throughout many of his farces, satires, and misadventures.

Finally, there are this story's formal innovations. The oversized panel that depicts the destruction of the forbidium money bin is a hilariously rendered debacle, but even that can't compete with the frantic diagonals Barks deploys to emphasize the comedic synergy between Scrooge and Gyro and the punishing physics of space travel. With so many slanted verticals, it feels as though the story's narrative framework has been predicting the coming of its super-dense bin-smasher all along.

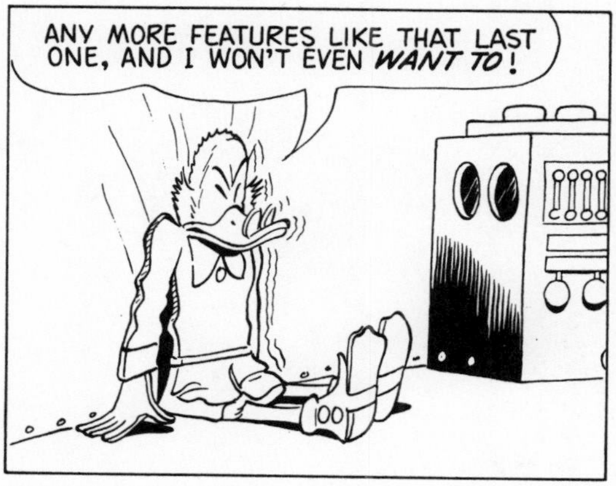
ANY MORE FEATURES LIKE THAT LAST ONE, AND I WON'T EVEN *WANT TO*!
100

Within these incongruous borders, Barks inserts flounder-flat parodies of his ducktagonists' conventional character design. Toying with the comedic potential of G-forces, torque, and weightlessness, his goofy exaggerations also lampoon space exploration, interstellar prospecting, and Cold War competition for aerospace dominance and forbidium-fortified security. With its rocket-ship mosquitos, grape tattoos, petrified meteors, and "skillets of eels," this wild rock chase includes some of Barks's most amusing comedic contradictions.

— DANIEL F. YEZBICK

UNCLE SCROOGE AND THE MAGIC INK

p. 69

As this volume shows, Gyro Gearloose was a very active cast member for Carl Barks during this period. Curious, then, that when it came to the invention of "magic ink," that phenomenal product was introduced by a pushy if otherwise generic huckster. Perhaps Gyro was overlooked in order to spare him the rough treatment the salesman receives from Scrooge at the end. In truth, the actual originator of the remarkable fluid was probably Barks's daughter, Peggy, who came up with the story idea.

The plot is a variation of turnabout being fair play, however inadvertent that turnabout was. Apart from the "What hit me?" refrain, the most emphatic humor lies in the visual bits — Donald's frenzied activity as he succumbs to the ink's influence; *everybody's* wobbly reaction whenever they employ it; Scrooge's preposterous disguise; Donald's new household furnishings stuffed into his house beyond its limits and spilling chaotically out the front entrance — these are calculated crowd pleasers, drawn large.

Far more understated is Scrooge on the phone on page 2, panel 3 (p. 70). A pencil in his beak disguises his voice. His lower eyes are devilishly swelled, as if to foreshadow that the devious plan he's hatching is all but destined to be turned against him.

— RICH KREINER

UNCLE SCROOGE AND THE FLYING DUTCHMAN *p. 75*

Among the most fascinating sea legends, the one about the *Flying Dutchman* stands out. At the helm of this phantom ship is a blasphemous captain, condemned to sail eternally against the wind. The legend was reportedly inspired by a 17th century Dutchman, Bernard Fokke, who, because of the incredible speed at which he sailed between his homeland and the island of Java, was said to have made a pact with the devil. The legend has inspired several authors, including German composer Richard Wagner (*Der fliegende Holländer*, 1843), American writer Washington Irving (*The Flying Dutchman on Tappan Sea*, 1855) — and, of course, Carl Barks ("Uncle Scrooge and the Flying Dutchman," 1959).

Barks adapted the legend according to his own needs, actually debunking it and turning it instead into a treasure hunt that eventually brings the Ducks to Antarctica. Yet he kept the impressive image of the *Fliegende Holländer* sailing against the wind, up in the sky above the sea — an image that he would later reproduce in no less than four of his oil paintings between 1972 and 1991. There also seems to be a reference to Samuel Taylor Coleridge's poem, "The Rime of the Ancient Mariner" (1798) in the final part of the sequence that depicts the Ducks' search as their boat is being pushed southward by the storm, as was the Ancient Mariner's sailing ship. (Barks would later go back to the "Rime" theme in his 1966 Donald and Daisy story, "The Not-So-Ancient Mariner.")

It is interesting that several gags in the story, as well as the changes in Scrooge's boat's route, are generated by Donald's obsession with fishing, which is a recurring theme throughout the story. Also note that Barks teaches the readers a lesson when a whale bites Donald's line — as Donald points out, "it *wasn't* a fish! It was a *mammal*!"

"Uncle Scrooge and the Flying Dutchman" also provides one of the many facts about

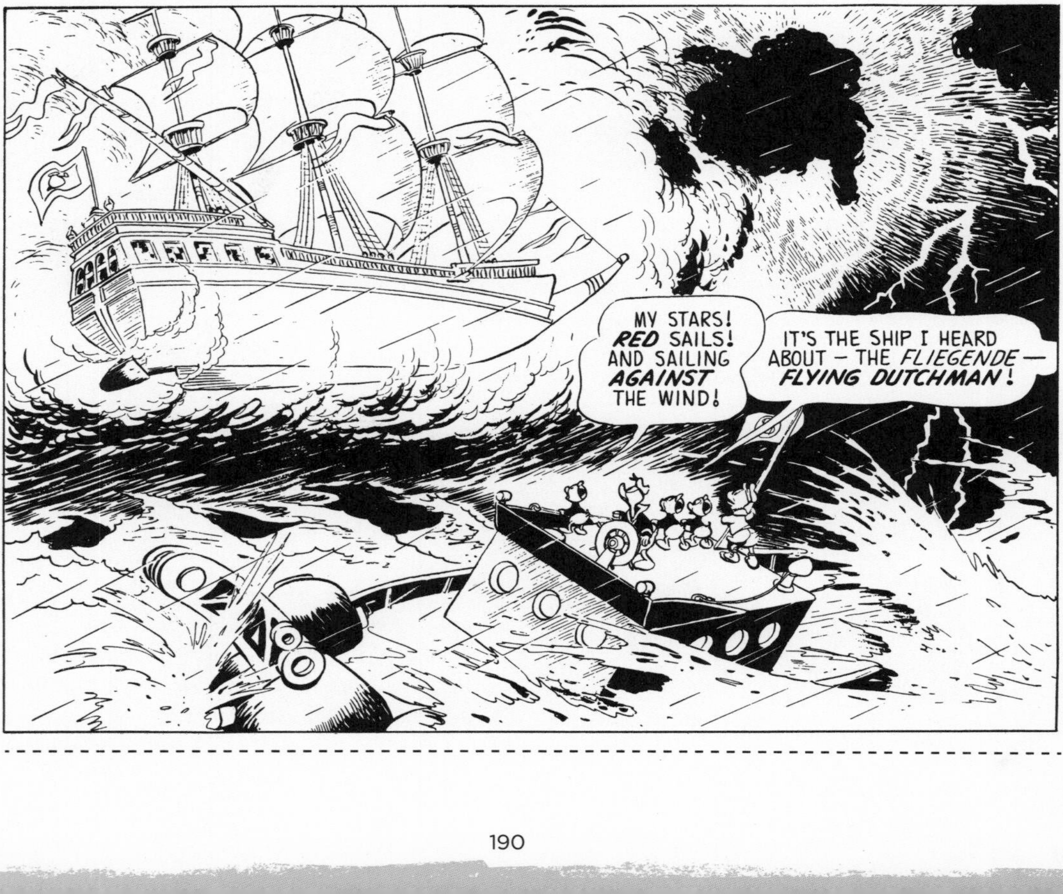
MY STARS! RED SAILS! AND SAILING AGAINST THE WIND!
IT'S THE SHIP I HEARD ABOUT – THE FLIEGENDE – FLYING DUTCHMAN!

Scrooge's youth that Barks occasionally sprinkled into his stories. On page 2 (p. 76), Scrooge declares, "I learned [Dutch] when I sold wind to the windmill makers along the Zuyder Zee" — a fact that Don Rosa later referenced in his monumental series, The Life and Times of Scrooge McDuck (*The Complete Life and Times of Scrooge McDuck*, Volume 1, Fantagraphics Books, 2019) in Chapter 11, "The Empire-Builder From Calisota."

Unbeknownst to Barks when he developed his story, another Disney artist had already written and drawn a comics version of the very same legend. Romano Scarpa's "Donald Duck and the Legend of the Flying Scotsman" was published in Italy in November 1957. (Its U.S. version, "Uncle Scrooge — The Flying Scot," appeared in late 1998.) As the title suggests, Scarpa turned the Flying Dutchman into a Scotsman — an ancestor of Scrooge's named Danblane McDuck who had been sailing the skies over Honduras for 292 years.

— ALBERTO BECATTINI

PYRAMID SCHEME *p. 97*

"Pyramid Scheme" follows a familiar Carl Barks plot — after initially refusing to invest in a risky business opportunity, Uncle Scrooge succumbs to temptation and pours riches into the project, only to lose all his money because he was right to be cautious in the first place.

Barks's sense of symmetry is comically exquisite. In building the pyramid to house his treasures, King Nutmost the Rash spends everything he owns — and thus no longer needs the space to store what he no longer has. Millennia later, hungry for gold and jewels, Scrooge excavates the pyramid and gets nothing for his trouble but Nutmost's pathetic note about wasting "*all* of his fortune building this pyramid." The same white elephant tramples Nutmost and Scrooge.

The usual Barks virtues are present in "Pyramid Scheme" — the silhouettes that represent the jugglers and ducks on the opening page are masterful, the half-page vista shot

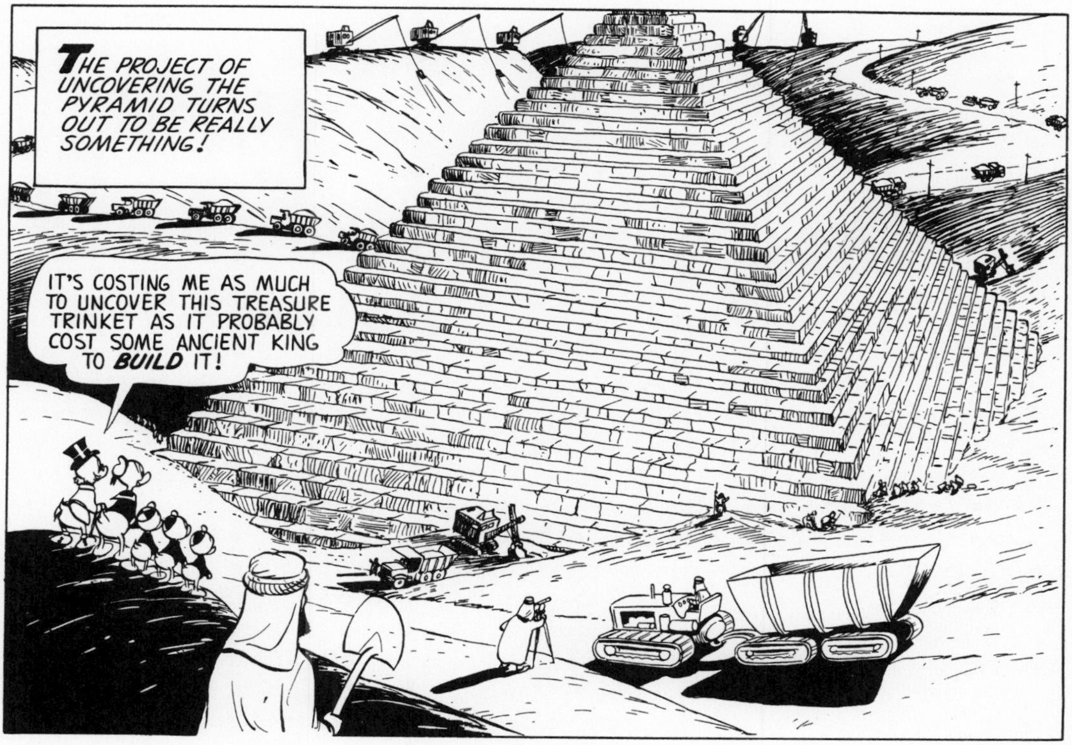
THE PROJECT OF UNCOVERING THE PYRAMID TURNS OUT TO BE REALLY SOMETHING!
IT'S COSTING ME AS MUCH TO UNCOVER THIS TREASURE TRINKET AS IT PROBABLY COST SOME ANCIENT KING TO BUILD IT!

of the unearthed pyramid on page 5 (p. 101) is magnificent, and the title of the book Scrooge reads on page 4 (p. 100) (*Archeology: How Much Does It Cost?* by Blister de Hands) should be required reading for all graduate students in archeology.

Ironically, however, the moral of the story — the old saw "A cobbler should stick to his last" — has been debunked by the rise of world-wide disposable consumption — any cobbler who stuck to their last is now out of business, because nobody buys shoes worth repairing anymore. So what's an impossibly rich investor like Uncle Scrooge to believe in our era of mega-capitalism?

— CRAIG FISCHER

RETURN TO PIZEN BLUFF *p. 103*

Carl Barks's Ducks live in more of a mortal, not mystical, world. Even Magica De Spell is more of an alchemist than a sorceress in his stories (while for other creators she is clearly a witch). And ghosts are always fake — sometimes it is a fraud, sometimes just a natural phenomenon.

In this story, Pizen Bluff had become a ghost town years earlier because all of its inhabitants left in search of a bigger gold mine. Even Scrooge abandoned his claim. When he comes back with his nephews, they are scared by ghosts moving Pizen Bluff houses, but it is really just the wind, and so Scrooge can finish digging up his gold.

The story is just a six-pager, but it will become very important for Don Rosa. He uses it in "The Vigilante of Pizen Bluff," Chapter 6B of his Life and Times of Scrooge McDuck saga (*The Complete Life and Times of Scrooge McDuck*, Volume 2, Fantagraphics Books, 2019). Barks's "Return to Pizen Bluff," set in Arizona in 1890, features Scrooge with historical Western legends Buffalo Bill, Geronimo, Annie Oakley, the Dalton Boys, and showman Phineas T. Barnum.

Barks may only have scratched the surface with this story, but after he left it behind, another creator would mine even more gold from it.

— STEFANO PRIARONE

UNCLE SCROOGE AND THE MONEY CHAMP *p. 111*

Flintheart Glomgold — what's that guy's deal?

Carl Barks's answer for the anti-Scrooge is such a richly nuanced nuisance that one could easily forget that the character only appeared in three of the master's stories. The direct reference to the events of "The Second-Richest Duck" (*Walt Disney's Uncle Scrooge: "The Lost Crown of Genghis Khan,"* Volume 16) in "Uncle Scrooge and the Money Champ" is one of the few times Barks ever used traditional comic book continuity in his work. Barks's comics can always stand on their own without backstory, so it's unusual to see Barks feel that Glomgold must be reestablished as Scrooge's rival in a such an expositional fashion and that his challenge for the title of "money champ" must be a rematch.

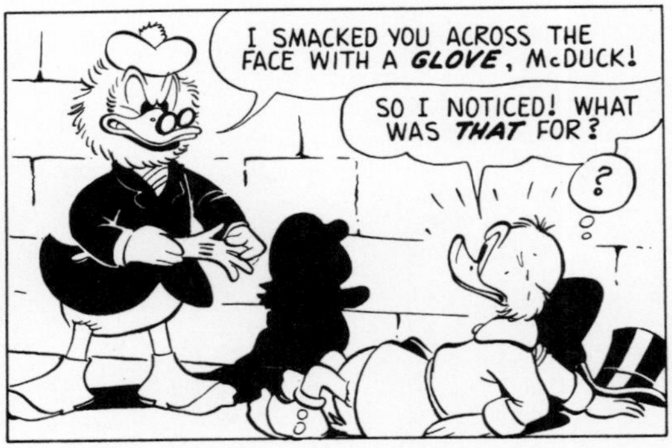
I SMACKED YOU ACROSS THE FACE WITH A GLOVE, McDUCK!
SO I NOTICED! WHAT WAS THAT FOR?
?

And what a rematch it is, too — one in which Scrooge must convert his fortune to silver dollars so that he and Glomgold can see whose is bigger. While the original challenge in "Second-Richest Duck" was less about skullduggery and more about two old coots facing the elements, Glomgold has now developed a truly vindictive streak. He *hates* Scrooge and wants to see him defeated, suffering, humiliated, and outclassed. Even if Scrooge refused to participate in this ruse, Glomgold still has the satisfaction of scamming Scrooge out of a couple of fortunes by posing as three different aliases weeks prior to this money champ challenge. Brother, that's action!

At the story's climax, an opportunistic medicine man arrives to offer Scrooge a "miracle mixture" that will shrink any metal. Some of Barks's finest staging ensues by way of strikingly hilarious contrast. We watch Scrooge struggle with this moral dilemma for a whole page, but ultimately send the con artist on his way.

Immediately, at the rival silver dollar pile: "Pst! Señor Glomgold!" And that's really all we need to see. Via telescope, Scrooge sees Glomgold seal the deal. No need to know how Glomgold came to his decision — it's so much funnier without it.

Ultimately, Scrooge doesn't use his wits to defeat Glomgold in "Money Champ," just brute force. What else can you do when your enemy shouts, "I'm on my way to harass, molest, and *shrink*"? The conclusion is abrupt, Scrooge's victory inevitable and ironic, and, almost as an aside, Glomgold commiserates, "All this humiliation, and, besides, I still have to go to *jail!*" A very clever quip, too, because Barks's editors would've never let Glomgold get off with just eating Scrooge's hat as punishment. But even jail time isn't satisfaction, as Scrooge sees it. Wouldn't you, too, feel robbed if given that final snarky grin by Flintheart Glomgold?

— THAD KOMOROWSKI

UNCLE SCROOGE AND HIS HANDY ANDY *p. 135*

"Uncle Scrooge and His Handy Andy" is a brief story, but Carl Barks was a master at both long and short yarns. In this short one, we are told that among the annual events taking place in the Ducks' city there is the "great Duckburg-to-Bahamalulu yacht race" — Bahamalulu being an obvious portmanteau of the "Bahamas" and "Honolulu" — which is strictly reserved for "elite Duckburgians."

Barks might have taken his inspiration for the name of Scrooge's ship from *Handy Andy*, probably the most popular novel by 19th-century Irish writer Samuel Lover. The "sturdy craft" is extremely versatile and is equipped with an array of devices worthy of Gyro Gearloose.

The story is interesting not on account of its plot, which is indeed very thin, but for Barks's ability to visualize the characters according to their different yearnings and moods. Among them stands out the aggressive-looking *Duckburg Gazette* publisher, Colonel Rawcuss Yellowpress, who might refer to former U.S. Cavalry officer and comic book pioneer Major Malcolm Wheeler-Nicholson.

Scrooge's facial expression and dialogue as he first appears in the story are misleading, as Barks makes us think that Scrooge is all-in for the yacht race, but the final panel reveals that, for Scrooge, winning the race is not an end in itself, but, rather, just a means to achieve his own prizes.

— ALBERTO BECATTINI

UNCLE SCROOGE AND THE PRIZE OF PIZARRO *p. 139*

In "Uncle Scrooge and the Prize of Pizarro," Carl Barks employs many of the characteristics that typically make his Ducks' encounters with bygone civilizations so engaging and entertaining. There's travel to a dramatic environment, exposure to an exotic culture, derring-do aplenty, distinctive perils, and nonstop spectacle. Yet what also makes this specific tale so memorable is Barks's absolute mastery of (for lack of a better term) the formal elements of storytelling that are unique to comics.

Composition of picture and page — the way a reader's eyes are guided — is crucial with a shifting yarn of complicated parts such

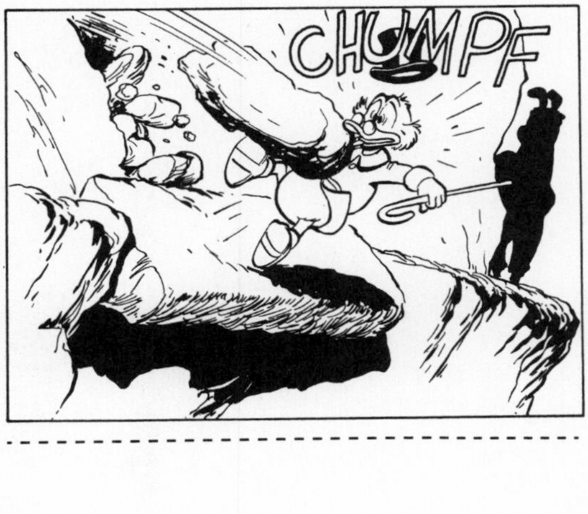
CHUMPF

as this one. Take a look at the opening panel. The Uncle Scrooge logo in the upper left quadrant swings upward toward a tilted caption whose text sets the stage for the story to come. Following along that diagonal, our gaze moves to a dialogue balloon, then drops to its speakers, the nephews, who are standing below. Continuing downward, our eyes sweep along the arc of the precisely positioned galleon (Barks even enlists the handsome ship's bowsprit to helpfully point the way) to the lower left quadrant of the panel — and on to the continuation of the story in the second tier.

More subtly, note how our vantage point throughout the story moves back and forth between medium-range images and panoramic vistas to keep us apprised of the characters' emotional states and the relevant aspects of the larger environment. We know where we, and where things, stand.

Pacing is also critical, especially before the momentum of the quest pushes us along. Strong beats at the end of early pages propel us forward.

Barks routinely supplied a factual patina of historical insight in order to more plausibly ground his talking-duck fantasies. On page 1 (p. 139), after a flurry of real-world names and particulars, Scrooge concludes by collapsing "a lot of history" with a casual encapsulation, assuring readers that details won't impede adventure. Ending page 3 (p. 141), we read the hat-popping revelation that the missing Incan gold has been found! Page 4 (p. 142) closes with the pivotal moment when the scenic, established route is abandoned for a hidden, mysterious one.

Usually when the Ducks discover thriving "lost" civilizations and meet their hosts, the animated interplay between their contrasting sensibilities is a fertile source of humor. But in this story, observational comedy is largely supplied by the remarks and misconceptions of the inhabitants regarding the interlopers. Their physical separation requires an extra juggling of parties and perspectives by Barks, but it rewards with a persistent narrative tension — will they or won't they ever connect?

Certainly some of the most memorable facets of this tale are the inventive dangers of the booby traps. In fact, it's easy to imagine an impressionable young Steven Spielberg taking note of their thrilling effect for later use in his Indiana Jones movies — the pointed projectiles shooting from the walls and the boulder rolling down an incline at the beginning of *Raiders of the Lost Ark*, as well as the water explosively gushing from cave's mouth late in *Indiana Jones and the Temple of Doom*.
— RICH KREINER

THE GYRO GEARLOOSE STORIES

When I realized that I'd be writing about five Gyro Gearloose stories in this essay, I decided to pretend that all occur back-to-back, one immediately after the other, a cascade of adventures that demonstrate Gyro's brilliance and indefatigable work ethic.

The events of "Gyro Goes for a Dip!" (p. 161) could conceivably happen in a single summer day, assuming Gyro has immediate access to the supplies he needs to salinate

HOW MANY MORE **GENERATIONS** MUST WE STAND READY TO REPEL THEIR **NEXT** ATTACK?

YOU'LL STAND READY UNTIL THE EMPEROR SENDS WORD THAT THE **ALERT** IS OVER!

BAH! IT'S FOUR HUNDRED YEARS SINCE THE EMPEROR SENT EVEN A **GREETING CARD** TO THESE DIGGINGS!

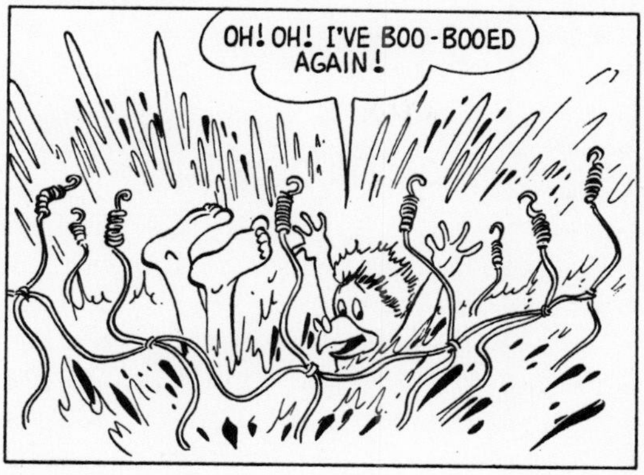
OH! OH! I'VE BOO-BOOED AGAIN!

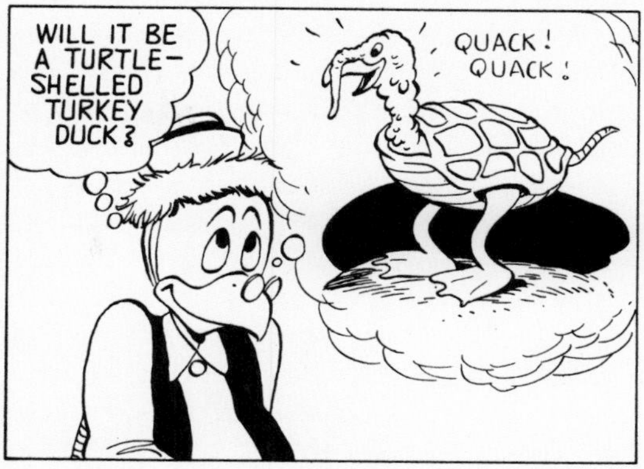
WILL IT BE A TURTLE-SHELLED TURKEY DUCK?
QUACK! QUACK!

and gelatinize water, while "Gyro Gearloose and the Firefly Tracker" (p. 177) spans approximately three days — Barks uses the captions "Next day!" "Night again!" and "Soon!" to skip over uneventful portions of the narrative.

Arranging and reading these stories consecutively, however, gives Gyro a research program that any scientist, mad or sane, would envy and emphasizes for us that Gyro is Barks's most sustained contribution to the genre of science fiction. Occasionally Uncle Scrooge will sell corn to Micro-Ducks from outer space, but every single day Gyro Gearloose strives to achieve *miracles*.

As a genre, science fiction has been ambivalent toward humanity's search for knowledge. In many science fiction novels and films, the scientist is a hero, a savior who invents a device that repels an alien invasion or saves the Earth from ecological catastrophe, but there remains a persistent counter-tradition that warns us of scientific overreach — of Dr. Frankenstein recklessly violating natural law by resurrecting the dead.

There's a similar ambivalence toward knowledge in this batch of Gyro stories. In several, Gyro plays the heroic inventor, as when he uses his firefly tracker's unexpected capacity to chart meteors to save the lives of a train full of travelers and when he risks his own safety to test a cyclone warning bell.

In "The House on Cyclone Hill" (p. 165), however, Gyro's heroism is undermined by his quick retreat to his underground storm cellar at the top of page 2 (p. 166), since he leaves Little Helper in danger out in the open. Gyro's relentless pursuit of the working invention leads him to abandon his vulnerable friend.

In other stories, Barks's comedic tone ominously clashes with Gyro's excessive ambitions. "Krankenstein Gyro" (p. 173) begins with Gyro strolling out of a matinee screening of a pseudonymous Frankenstein movie, mulling over how he might create life like the doctor did. Gyro is oblivious to any of the ethical dangers of playing God. The rest of the story is itself a farce-in-the-retelling version of *Frankenstein*, where Gyro indiscriminately mixes ingredients such as plasma and beef extract ("*Whatever* comes from this experiment will no doubt surprise even *me!*") and only succeeds in restoring to the chicken her beloved doorknob. The plot is a nonsensical pretext for Barks's joyous drawings of odd creatures (including "a brass-feathered crocodile hawk" and a female companion for lonely Little Helper) on page 3 (p. 175).

Gyro plays God again in "The Wishing Well" (p. 169) where he assembles an array of devices ("a de-materializing imaginator, and a sendoffagraphic gofromhereoscope") to create a wishing well that really works, i.e., that will grant any wish, instantaneously. Further, Gyro has been commissioned to build the God Well by a bourgeois matron whose aspirations luckily don't go beyond owning a fur coat.

At least the dangers Gyro faces in the civil war battle convince him that some technologies are too dangerous to exist. As he destroys the God Well, Gyro finally gets the cautionary message at the center of *Frankenstein*, but there's still an odd clash between this delayed realization and Barks's blithe refusal to take seriously any of the moral implications of breeding life and building omnipotent machines. The dangers of overreaching technology suffused much of Cold War culture, but not these Gyro Gearloose stories — each unfolds in its own four-page fantasy world, untroubled by ideology and ethics.

Another flourish I'll mention is specific to Barks's Gyro stories — the small presence of Little Helper underfoot or in the background of the image, taking actions that mirror or compliment Gyro's activities. This parallelism reminds me of the comic-strip convention of having two panel sequences — one larger and one smaller — drawn by the same cartoonist and linked as a visual whole, even if the two sets of panels tell different narratives.

(George Herriman introduced Krazy Kat and Ignatz in a tiny strip below the main show of *The Dingbat Family* [1910–1916]. Chris Ware, in the opening of *Rusty Brown* (2019), chronicles Rusty and Chalky White waking up for school. Chalky's morning routine runs as a small counterpoint beneath larger panels of Rusty shoveling snow and daydreaming.)

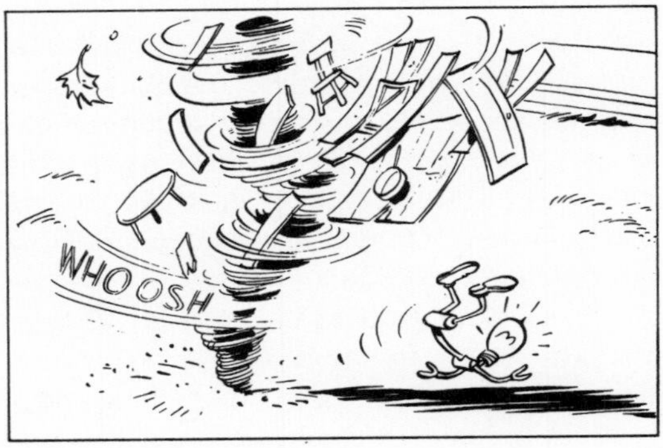
WHOOSH

I complained about how Gyro's uncharacteristic behavior in "The House on Cyclone Hill" put Little Helper in the path of a dangerous whirlwind, but this threat brings Helper to the foreground of both the panels and our attention on page 3 (p. 167), as Helper improvises using a turtle's shell as a tornado shelter. Even though Gyro's wild inventions — and his responses to the consequences that result from these inventions — are the focus of these stories, Barks also gives his bulb-headed sidekick a chance to shine.

— CRAIG FISCHER

UNCLE SCROOGE ONE-PAGERS

This bouquet of full- and half-page yarns reveals how little room Barks really needs to carry off a good joke. The shortest vignettes like "Bill Wind" (p. 50), "News from Afar" (p. 133), and "Uncle Scrooge Crawls for Cash" (p. 110), are particularly nuanced in their three-panel comedic recoding of familiar scenarios like butterfly collecting, scanning headlines, or hospital convalescence. In each case, the humor turns on the strip's emphasis of Scrooge's enthusiasm for successfully squeezing bargains and benefits out of thin air.

Likewise, "Rainbow's End" (p. 134) is quite elegant in its use of cheery rainbow tones to illuminate Scrooge's affection for wealth, not to mention his preternatural knack for getting to lost treasures, cash bonanzas, and pots of gold before anybody else. The nephews are as charmed to find him inevitably staking his claim as they are to discover the rainbow in the first place. Scrooge's almost paternal expression, and the gentle arc of his open hand reaching out to the glimmering goodies seem warm with love and appreciation — the close compassionate posture of a confidante, parent, or (ahem) *uncle* gently acknowledging a fond acquaintance.

Equally pleasing and joyous expressions close out the other three-panel gags, revealing Barks's gift for making Scrooge's money lust more about the fun of profiting than the folly of greed. Another half-pager, "The Homey Touch" (p. 160), hilariously exploits this distinction. As Barks parodies the decorating guides that define tasteful domestic trends (not unlike today's Martha Stewart or Marie Kondo), Scrooge beautifies his home by accessorizing his heaping bags of that which he loves most with accent ribbons and goofy bows. The gag confirms that he cares less about the value of their contents than the physical beauty of their fullness. It is the objective presence of money that he adores

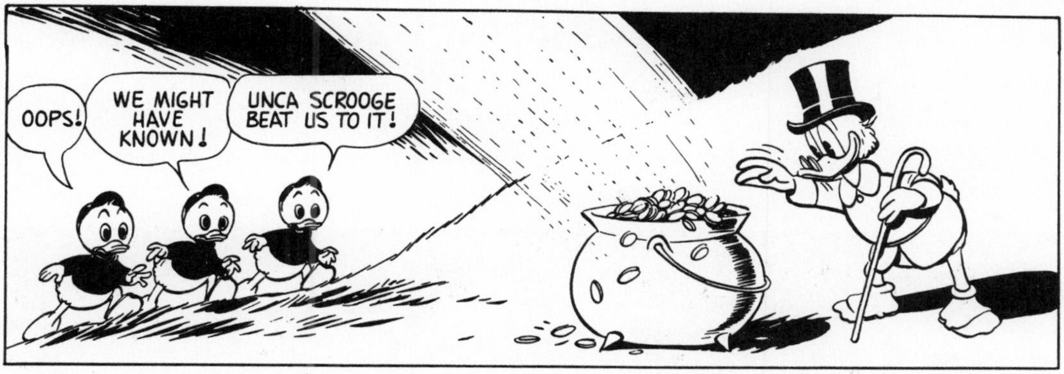
OOPS!
WE MIGHT HAVE KNOWN!
UNCA SCROOGE BEAT US TO IT!

and adorns, not its fiscal power or economic worth.

Barks's full-page micro-stories are also surprisingly succinct, tightly constructed little bonus bombs of compact comedy crammed inside the spare corners and extra edges of comic-book layouts. Examples like "Lights Out" (p. 68), "Immovable Miser" (p. 95), "Thumbs Up" (p. 44), and "Turnabout" (p. 159) work along the same principles as their shorter cousins, showcasing Scrooge's canny talents at exploiting outside schemes, threats, and interests. Even in the bizarre bacterial races of "Poor Loser" (p. 109), where Barks indulges in a kooky fusion of the scientific and the monstrous, Scrooge ends up victorious at a microscopic level.

In some cases, like "The Sleepies" (p. 67), he requires the advice of others, and in both "All Choked Up" (p. 21) and "Kitty Go Round" (p. 96), he is briefly foiled in his efforts. Yet he fails graciously in both situations, and the true comedic closure carries over to other, unsuspecting characters. Consider the grateful mother kitten's obvious delight in the return of her litter or the horse's outrageous disappointment when he chokes up Scrooge's roll of greenbacks instead of the tasty apple he expected.

My favorite of these mini-comedies is "Moolah on the Move" (p. 22), where Scrooge playfully compares his hay wagon of cash to a delightfully chummy rajah with his own gravel truck full of jewels. Both men gladly appreciate the other's ridiculous use of working-class vehicles to contain and convey their overwhelming wealth. The rajah and the plutoduck also share the same absurdly personal love for the beauty and bounty of their endless treasures. Much like "All Choked Up," the humor turns on a ridiculous literalization of familiar metaphors for wealth and privilege, but instead of the usual rivalry filled with quests, duels, and schemes, this brief encounter leaves both players rich in friendship as well as wherewithal.

Finally, these ultra-short stories attest to Barks's unflinching work ethic as he builds so much extra value into his brief but fully rendered scenes and settings. A hilarious toga-clad pig fountain lingers in the background of "The Sleepies," while the meticulously detailed lumberyards and back alleys of "Turnabout" and "Moolah on the Move" are cluttered with accurately urban sights and sundries.

Even the manicured parks and elegant silhouettes of "All Choked Up" and "Immovable Miser" involve picturesque public spaces loaded with pleasing scenery. The doorstep drama of "Kitty Go Round" also includes an exquisitely composed moment where Daisy hurries past a neoclassical bandstand, complete with a distant but dramatic American flag hung proudly between its columns.

All told, these tiny tales provide enormous evidence that Barks rarely cut corners, even when it came to filling them.

— DANIEL F. YEZBICK

Carl Barks

LIFE AMONG THE DUCKS

by DONALD AULT

ABOVE: *Carl Barks at the 1982 San Diego Comic-Con. Photo by Alan Light.*

"I was a real misfit," Carl Barks said, thinking back over an early life of hard labor — as a farmer, a logger, a mule-skinner, a rivet heater, and a printing press feeder — before he was hired as a full-time cartoonist for an obscure risqué magazine in 1931.

Barks was born in 1901 and (mostly) raised in Merrill, Oregon. He had always wanted to be a cartoonist, but everything that happened to him in his early years seemed to stand in his way. He suffered a significant hearing loss after a bout with the measles. His mother died. He had to leave school after the eighth grade. His father suffered a mental breakdown. His older brother was whisked off to World War I.

His first marriage, in 1921, was to a woman who was unsympathetic to his dreams and who ultimately bore two children "by accident," as Barks phrased it. The two divorced in 1930.

In 1931, he pulled up stakes from Merrill and headed to Minnesota, leaving his mother-in-law, whom he trusted more than his wife, in charge of his children.

Arriving in Minneapolis, he went to work for the *Calgary EyeOpener*, that risqué magazine. He thought he would finally be drawing cartoons full time, but the editor and most of the staff were alcoholics, so Barks ended up running the whole show.

In 1935 he took "a great gamble" and, on the strength of some cartoons he'd submitted in response to an advertisement from the Disney Studio, he moved to California and entered an animation trial period. He was soon promoted to "story man" in Disney's Donald Duck animation unit, where he made significant contributions to 36 Donald cartoon shorts between 1936 and 1942, including helping to create Huey, Dewey, and Louie for "Donald's Nephews" in 1938. Ultimately, though, he grew dissatisfied. The production of animated cartoons "by committee," as he described it, stifled his imagination.

For that and other reasons, in 1942 he left Disney to run a chicken farm. But when he was offered a chance by Western Publishing to write and illustrate a new series of Donald Duck comic book stories, he jumped at it. The comic book format suited him, and the quality of his work persuaded the editors to grant him a freedom and autonomy he'd never known and that few others were ever granted. He would go on to write and draw more than 6,000 pages in over 500 stories and uncounted hundreds of covers between 1942 and 1966 for Western's Dell and Gold Key imprints.

Barks had almost no formal art training. He had taught himself how to draw by imitating his early favorite artists — Winsor McCay (*Little Nemo*), Frederick Opper (*Happy Hooligan*), Elzie Segar (*Popeye*), and Floyd Gottfredson (*Mickey Mouse*).

He taught himself how to write well by going back to the grammar books he had shunned in school, making up jingles and rhymes, and inventing other linguistic exercises to get a natural feel for the rhythm and dialogue of sequential narrative.

Barks married again in 1938, but that union ended disastrously in divorce in 1951. In 1954, Barks married Margaret Wynnfred Williams, known as Garé, who soon began assisting him by lettering and inking backgrounds on his comic book work. They remained happily together until her death in 1993.

He did his work in the California desert and often mailed his stories in to the office. He worked his stories over and over "backward and forward." Barks was not a vain man, but he had confidence in his talent. He knew what hard work was, and he knew that he'd put his best efforts into every story he produced.

On those occasions when he did go into Western's offices, he would "just dare anybody to see if they could improve on it." His confidence was justified. His work was largely responsible for some of the best-selling comic books in the world — *Walt Disney's Comics and Stories* and *Uncle Scrooge*.

Because Western's policy was to keep their writers and artists anonymous, readers never knew the name of the "good duck artist" — but they could spot the superiority of his work. When fans, determined to solve the mystery of his anonymity, finally tracked him down (not unlike an adventure Huey, Dewey, and Louie might embark upon), Barks was quite happy to correspond and otherwise communicate with his legion of aficionados.

Given all the obstacles of his early years and the dark days that haunted him off and on for the rest of his life, it's remarkable that he laughed so easily and loved to make others laugh.

In the process of expanding Donald Duck's character far beyond the hot-tempered Donald of animation, Barks created a moveable locale (Duckburg) and a cast of dynamic characters: Scrooge McDuck, the Beagle Boys, Gladstone Gander, Gyro Gearloose, the Junior Woodchucks. And there were hundreds of others who made only one memorable appearance in the engaging, imaginative, and unpredictable comedy-adventures that he wrote and drew from scratch for nearly a quarter of a century.

Among many other honors, Carl Barks was one of the three initial inductees into the Will Eisner Comic Book Hall of Fame for comic book creators in 1987. (The other two were Jack Kirby and Will Eisner.) In 1991, Barks became the only Disney comic book artist to be recognized as a "Disney Legend," a special award created by Disney "to acknowledge and honor the many individuals whose imagination, talents, and dreams have created the Disney magic."

As Roy Disney said on Barks's passing in 2000 at age 99, "He challenged our imaginations and took us on some of the greatest adventures we have ever known. His prolific comic book creations entertained many generations of devoted fans and influenced countless artists over the years…. His timeless tales will stand as a legacy to his originality and brilliant artistic vision."

Contributors

Donald Ault (October 5, 1942–April 13, 2019) was Professor of English at the University of Florida, founder and editor of *ImageTexT: Interdisciplinary Comics Studies*, author of two books on William Blake (*Visionary Physics* and *Narrative Unbound*), editor of *Carl Barks: Conversations*, and executive producer of the video *The Duck Man: An Interview with Carl Barks*. We are grateful for his pioneering work in comics studies and for his generosity in sharing his extensive insight and knowledge of the life and artistry of Carl Barks.

Alberto Becattini was born in Florence, Italy. He has taught high school English since 1983. Since 1978, he has written essays for Italian and U.S. publications about comics, specializing in Disney characters and American comics generally. Since 1992, he has been a freelance writer and consultant for The Walt Disney Company-Italy, contributing to such series as *Zio Paperone*, *Maestri Disney*, *Tesori Disney*, *Disney Anni d'Oro*, *La Grande Dinastia dei Paperi*, and *Gli Anni d'Oro di Topolino*.

Craig Fischer is Associate Professor of English at Appalachian State University. His Monsters Eat Critics column, about comics' multifarious genres, runs at *The Comics Journal* website (tcj.com).

Leonardo Gori is a comics scholar and collector, especially of syndicated newspaper strips of the 1930s and Italian Disney authors. He has written, with Frank Stajano and others, many books on Italian "fumetti" and American comics in Italy. He has also written thrillers, which have been translated into Spanish, Portuguese, and Korean.

Thad Komorowski is an animation historian and digital restoration artist with a long-standing professional relationship with Disney comics. He is a regular contributor to Fantagraphics's Walt Disney archival collections and translates stories for IDW's Disney comic books and Fantagraphics's *Disney Masters* series. He is the author of *Sick Little Monkeys: The Unauthorized Ren & Stimpy Story* and co-author of a forthcoming history of New York studio animation.

Rich Kreiner is a longtime writer for *The Comics Journal* and a longertime reader of Carl Barks. He lives with wife and cat in Maine.

Stefano Priarone was born in Northwestern Italy about the time when a retired Carl Barks was storyboarding his last Junior Woodchucks stories. He writes about popular culture in many Italian newspapers and magazines, was a contributor to the Italian complete Carl Barks collection, and wrote his thesis in economics about Uncle Scrooge as an entrepreneur (for which he blames his aunt, who read him Barks's Scrooge stories when he was 3 years old).

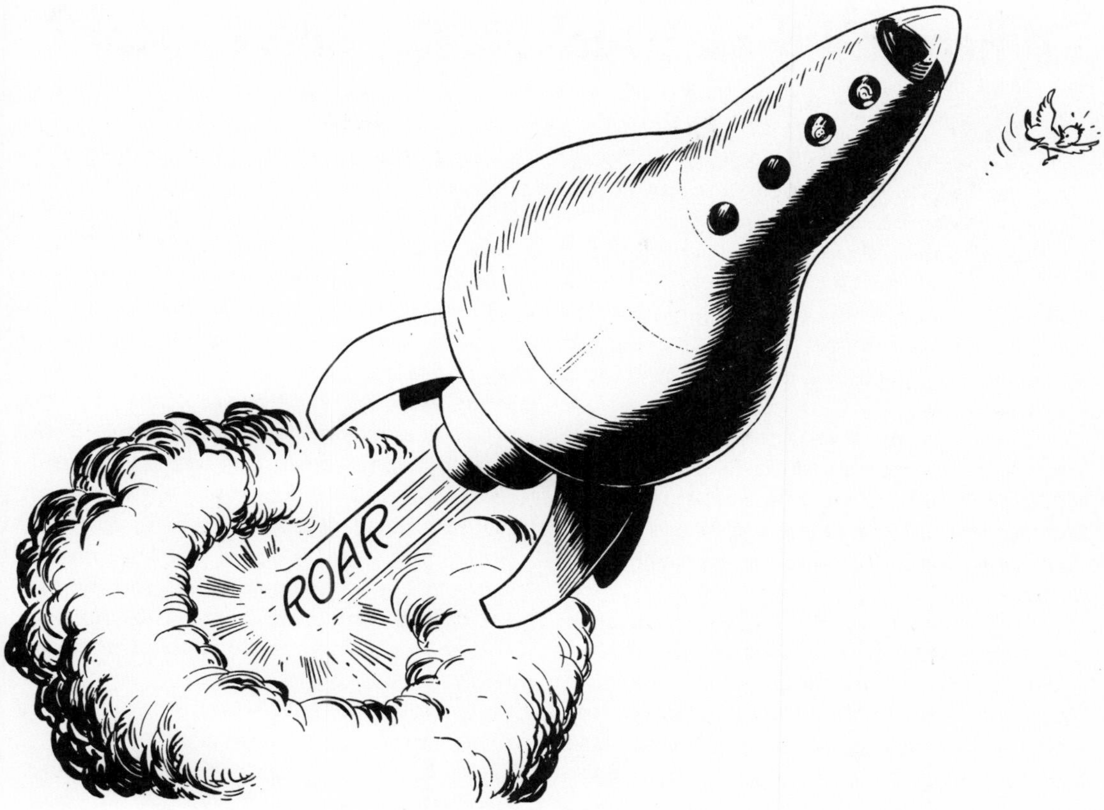
ROAR

Francesco (Frank) Stajano is a full professor at the 800-year-old University of Cambridge, a Fellow of Trinity College, a founding director of two hi-tech start-up companies, and a licensed teacher in the Japanese "Way of the Sword." As a comics scholar, he has co-authored books on Don Rosa and Floyd Gottfredson and written essays on many others. Over the decades, he became a correspondent and personal friend of many of his favorite Disney creators and was occasionally hosted as overnight guest by Barks, Rosa, Cimino, Cavazzano, and Ziche.

Matthias Wivel is Curator of Sixteenth-Century Italian Painting at the National Gallery, London. He has written widely about comics for a decade and a half.

Daniel F. Yezbick grew up in Detroit, Michigan, reading Carl Barks's comics in Gold Key and Whitman reprints. Since then, he has wandered the nation in Barksian fashion, pursuing a variety of odd jobs including bartender, sheep wrangler, technical writer, and college professor. He now teaches comics, film studies, and writing courses at Forest Park College. His essays on Barks and Disney comics have appeared in a variety of anthologies including *Icons of the American Comic Book*, *Comics Through Time*, and *Critical Survey of Graphic Novels: History, Theme, and Technique*. He is the author of *Perfect Nonsense: The Chaotic Comics and Goofy Games of George Carlson* (Fantagraphics, 2014). He currently lives in South St. Louis with his wife, Rosalie, their two children, and one wise, old hound.

Where did these Duck stories first appear?

The Complete Carl Barks Disney Library collects Donald Duck and Uncle Scrooge stories by Carl Barks that were originally published in the traditional American four-color comic book format. Barks's first Duck story appeared in October 1942. The volumes in this project are numbered chronologically but are being released in a different order. This is Volume 22.

Stories within a volume may or may not follow the publication sequence of the original comic books. We may take the liberty of rearranging the sequence of the stories within a volume for editorial or presentation purposes.

The original comic books were published under the Dell logo and some appeared in the so-called *Four Color* series — a name that appeared nowhere inside the comic book itself, but is generally agreed upon by historians to refer to the series of "one-shot" comic books published by Dell that have sequential numbering. The *Four Color* issues are also sometimes referred to as "One Shots."

Some of the stories in this volume were originally published without a title. Some stories were retroactively assigned a title when they were reprinted in later years. Some stories were given titles by Barks in correspondence or interviews. (Sometimes Barks referred to the same story with different titles.) Some stories were never given an official title but have been informally assigned one by fans and indexers. For the untitled stories in this volume, we have used the title that seems most appropriate. The unofficial titles appear below with an asterisk enclosed in parentheses (*).

The following is the order in which these stories were originally published.

***Uncle Scrooge* #23 (September-November 1958)**
- Cover
- Moola on the Move (*)
- Uncle Scrooge and the Strange Shipwrecks
- Gyro Goes for a Dip (*)
- Uncle Scrooge and the Fabulous Tycoon
- All Choked Up (*)
- Lights Out (*)

***Disneyland Birthday Party* #1 (October 1958)**
- The Forbidium Money Bin (*)

***Uncle Scrooge* #24 (December 1958-February 1959)**
- Cover
- Uncle Scrooge and the Twenty-four Carat Moon
- The House on Cyclone Hill (*)
- Uncle Scrooge and the Magic Ink

***Uncle Scrooge* #25 (March-May 1959)**
- Cover
- Immovable Miser (*)
- Uncle Scrooge and the Flying Dutchman
- The Wishing Well (*)
- Pyramid Scheme (*)
- Bill Wind (*)
- News From Afar (*)
- Kitty-Go-Round (*)

***Uncle Scrooge* #26 (June-August 1959)**
- Cover
- Uncle Scrooge and the Prize of Pizarro
- Krankenstein Gyro
- Return to Pizen Bluff (*)

***Uncle Scrooge* #27 (September-November 1959)**
- Cover
- Uncle Scrooge and the Money Champ
- Gyro Gearloose and the Firefly Tracker
- Uncle Scrooge and His Handy Andy
- Uncle Scrooge Crawls for Cash

***Donald Duck* #71 (May-June 1960)**
- Rainbow's End

***Uncle Scrooge* #32 (December 1960-February 1961)**
- The Homey Touch
- Turnabout

***Uncle Scrooge* #33 (March-May 1961)**
- Thumbs Up

***Donald Duck* #79 (September-October 1961)**
- Poor Loser

***Donald Duck* #81 (January-February 1962)**
- The Sleepies